Shadows
in the
Shining City

A NOVEL

Book Two of the Anthems of al-Andalus Series

JOHN D. CRESSLER

Mechanicsburg, Pennsylvania   USA

Published by Sunbury Press, Inc.
50 West Main Street, Suite A
Mechanicsburg, Pennsylvania 17055

www.sunburypress.com

For information about special discounts for bulk purchases, please contact Sunbury Press Orders Dept. at (855) 338-8359 or orders@sunburypress.com.

To request one of our authors for speaking engagements or book signings, please contact Sunbury Press Publicity Dept. at publicity@sunburypress.com.

ISBN: 978-1-62006-345-3 (Trade Paperback)
ISBN: 978-1-62006-346-2 (Mobipocket)
ISBN: 978-1-62006-347-9 (ePub)

FIRST SUNBURY PRESS EDITION: June 2014

Product of the United States of America
0 1 1 2 3 5 8 13 21 34 55

Set in Bookman Old Style
Designed by Lawrence Knorr
Cover by Lawrence Knorr
Edited by Jennifer Melendrez

Continue the Enlightenment!

Books by John D. Cressler

Historical Fiction

Anthems of al-Andalus Series
Emeralds of the Alhambra
Shadows in the Shining City

Non-fiction: General Audience

Reinventing Teenagers:
The Gentle Art of Instilling Character in Our Young People
Silicon Earth:
Introduction to the Microelectronics and Nanotechnology Revolution

Non-fiction: Technical

Silicon-Germanium Heterojunction
Bipolar Transistors
Silicon Heterostructure Handbook:
Materials, Fabrication, Devices, Circuits and Applications of SiGe and
Si Strained-Layer Epitaxy
Extreme Environment Electronics

For more information on any of these books, please visit:
http://johndcressler.com

Praise for John D. Cressler's
Shadows of the Shining City

"An inspiring and deeply moving novel on both the nature of love and the many beautiful possibilities brought to life when religions learn to coexist."

—*Shirin Ebadi, Nobel Peace Prize Laureate*

"A mesmerizing love story ... filled with vivid historical descriptions of treachery and strategies in politics, religion, power, and love during the Golden Age of Moorish Spain."

—*Valerie Jackson, In Conversation (Between the Lines),*
National Public Radio

"This is the second novel in Cressler's *Anthems of al-Andalus Series*, where the legacy of the Arab/Islamic civilization in medieval Spain, with its refinements, its enduring tolerance, and its esthetic dynamism is celebrated. A novel about love, political strife, and cultural conflicts, it is written in a rich and shimmering style carrying an implicit message on the value of recognizing the achievements of the "other," and asserting the fact that there is no fixed center for human creativity and progress."

—*Salma Khadra Jayyusi, poet, writer, and literary historian.*
Founder and Director of EAST-WEST NEXUS/ PROTA for the
Dissemination in English of Arabic cultural achievements

"An enthralling narrative to a shocking history. In this novel of 10th century Spain during the critical transition in the Muslim world from a progressive leader to a cruel megalomaniac, the author brings the reader straight into the landscape, the majesty and the struggles for power which cast the shadows upon al-Zahra, the Shining City. Cressler brilliantly weaves together fact and fiction, passion and intrigue, the throes of love, and the violence of war. With great attention to detail, he artfully unfolds the drama of a young and forbidden love, exquisitely keeping us rapt in the story, wondering in each moment, what will happen next?"

—*Rabbi Rachael M. Bregman, Temple Beth Tefilloh*

"Another tour de force! Cressler submerges us in a luxurious narrative evoking the loves, lives, intrigue, and history of 10th century Córdoba, a time of religious and political amity among Muslims, Jews, and Christians. Our master storyteller provides a

cautionary tale of how human desire can corrupt the power of love through the love of power. We cheer for Rayhana and Zafir while we witness the horror of books burning on the pyre of one man's insane desire to stem the love of knowledge. We rejoice in the many triumphs of al-Andalus, yet despair at lessons not yet learned about how human beings may live and love together. *Shadows in the Shining City* is a lovely, moving, and inspiring story of how it might have been. We believe!"
—*Professor Susan Abraham, Loyola Marymount University*

"Cressler is a master of meticulously researched detail. His intricately woven characters plumb the depths of love and fear, cunning treachery and wisdom, immersing the reader into the heart of 10th century al-Andalus as it balances on the edge of a cosmic shift, with repercussions that continue to reverberate today. What better way to learn history than through the eyes of lovers both young and seasoned: lovers of books and scientific discovery, of beauty and of harmony among diverse peoples, and ultimately, human love that defies all obstacles to proclaim, 'I believe'!"
—*Cathy Devlin Crosby, Cofounder of Neshama Interfaith Center*

"Cressler is a master of rich description, pulling the reader into each scene. An incredible love story supported and sustained by the remarkable coexistence of religions that characterized that magical era. (We) are left yearning for a return to *convivencia*."
—*Father Bruce Maivelett, S.J., Jesuit Superior,*
Ignatius House Retreat Center

"Cressler's suspenseful novel, set at a decisive moment in Spain's pre-modern history, challenges our all too comfortable prejudices about medieval culture as the eternal dark "other," an allegedly primitive and less cultured period we have long left behind. Under the deceptive garment of an engaging love story, Cressler reveals the human continuities between the medieval past and the modern present, confronts twenty-first century religious intolerance with the decline of a relatively peaceful *convivencia* among tenth-century Spanish Muslims, Christians, and Jews, and celebrates the powerful role of learning and intellectual curiosity for interfaith dialogue."
—*Professor Richard Utz, Chair, School of Literature, Media and*
Communication, Georgia Tech, and President,
International Society for the Study of Medievalism

Reader Reviews

"Cressler has done it again! Against a tapestry of historical grandeur and religious conflict in 10th century Spain, he has woven a compelling tale of political intrigue, cultural turmoil, and forbidden love. Page turning was never so easy, or so unstoppable! Can't wait for the third installment of this memorable trilogy!"
—Roger A. Meyer, M.D.

"A medieval masterpiece filled with love, intrigue, betrayal, and passion ... (that) leaves the reader thirsting for more!"
—Dennis Day

"A superbly written novel (that allows readers) to glimpse the complex events that shaped Spain ... (and) become living witnesses to a slice of the history of al-Andalus, which Cressler brings to life with such love and care."
—Acar Nazli

"Takes you into the intrigue of a sophisticated civilization in medieval Córdoba. Full of ambitious plots, secrets, and true love. It kept me on the edge of my seat!"
—Trish Byers

"A love story inspiring to those lucky enough to have been loved unconditionally, and to those who hope for such a blessing someday. This riveting story kept me on edge throughout."
—Preston Bennett

"A fast-paced, fun read that makes medieval Spain come alive. Characters of differing cultures and faiths come to life in a way that shows the goodness that is *possible* when we are tolerant."
—Patty Smith

"A love story (that) will make you see that times change but mankind remains the same; capable of *great* love and *awful* treachery. Take a trip back to 10th century Spain and see people of faith—Muslim, Christian, and Jew—live with and love one another. There is hope for us all and it begins with *love*."
—Bud Treanor

"I have undergone an education about a period of time of which I knew little, and best of all is that in becoming educated, I was thoroughly entertained!"
—Bob Wilhelm

"You will be awestruck (and) your breath will be taken away over and over again as you read the beautiful love story of two young people ... whose unwavering love outshines the powerful, intriguing political forces set against their union."

—*Denise Black*

"(Cressler is) a first-rate storyteller. Wonderful three-dimensional characters, dramatic situations, and fascinating historical and cultural details."

—*Tom Nadar, Ph.D.*

"Exhilarating! A beautifully told story of love that finds a way to triumph. Historically compelling, with characters that make the time come alive."

—*Tom Jablonski*

"Weaves fiction and fact into a suspenseful, intriguing, passionate saga. A compelling story exploring themes of love, religion, and the thirst for power. A must read!"

—*Barbara Nalbone*

For my Maria:

My lover.
My best friend.
My beloved.
You are the center of my universe,
the origin of my happiness.

I believe.

My Beloved Comes

You came to me just before
The Christians rang their bells.
The half-moon was rising
Looking like an old man's eyebrow
Or a delicate instep.

And although it was still night,
When you came, a rainbow
Gleamed on the horizon,
Showing as many colors
As a peacock's tail.

Ibn Hazm
(994-1063 C.E. – Córdoba)

Contents

Map 1. The Iberian peninsula in the spring of 975 C.E., with the borders of the Caliphate of Córdoba and the Christian kingdoms in the north indicated. Battles are marked by stars.

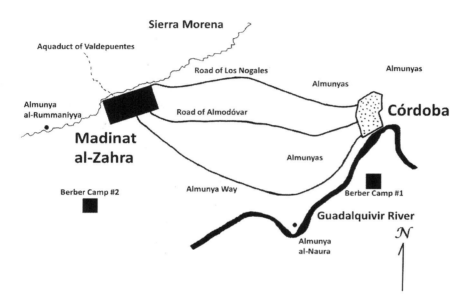

Map 2. The location of Madinat al-Zahra with respect to Córdoba proper. They are separated by about four and one-half miles along the Almunya Way. Almunyas (lavish retreats for the Córdoban elite) fill the land between the two. Note the two Berber camps.

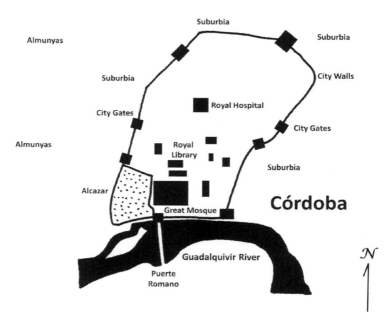

Map 3. Cordoba in 975 C.E., showing the city walls, the Great Mosque, the Alcazar (Royal Palace), the seven buildings of the Royal Library, and the Royal Hospital. Extensive suburbs surround the city walls, with the almunyas stretching beyond those.

Madinat al-Zahra

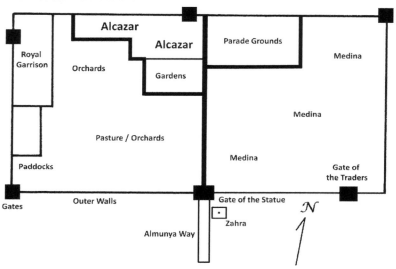

Map 4. *The layout of Madinat al-Zahra. The outer walls bounded 112 hectares of land (4,900 feet east-to-west, by 2,460 feet north-to-south). Most of the action takes place in the Alcazar (Royal Palace).*

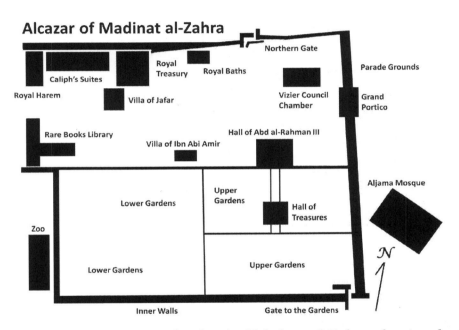

Alcazar of Madinat al-Zahra

Northern Gate

Caliph's Suites

Royal Treasury

Royal Baths

Parade Grounds

Royal Harem

Villa of Jafar

Vizier Council Chamber

Grand Portico

Rare Books Library

Villa of Ibn Abi Amir

Hall of Abd al-Rahman III

Aljama Mosque

Lower Gardens

Upper Gardens

Hall of Treasures

Zoo

Lower Gardens

Upper Gardens

𝒩

Inner Walls

Gate to the Gardens

Map 5. The Alcazar (Royal Palace) of Madinat al-Zahra, showing the locations which figure in the story.

Characters

Aaron - Book purveyor working for Levi al-Attar
Abd al-Kabir - Leader of the confederation of rich merchant families of Córdoba
Abu al-Qasim (Abulcasis) - Royal Physician and Vizier of Medicine
Ahmed al-Qadir - General Ghalib's second-in-command
Al-Mughira ibn al-Nasir - Brother of Caliph al-Hakam II
Alonso al-Rahib - Mozarab, Christian Monsignor, Vicar General and assistant to Reccimund
Arib ibn Said - Polymath and Vizier to Constantinople
Aslam - Henchman of Ibn Abi Amir
Bashir al-Najib - Commander of the Slavic Guard
Bishop Dietrich of Metz - Trusted advisor to Emperor Otto II
Brother Cleo - Benedictine monk, scholar and physician from the Benedictine Abbey at Cluny, in Burgundy
Bundar - Henchman of Subh and Jibril al-Azhar
Caliph Abd al-Rahman III - Father (now dead) of Caliph al-Hakam II and builder of Madinat al-Zahra
Caliph al-Hakam II - Umayyad Caliph of al-Andalus
Caliph al-Muti - Caliph of the Abbasid Empire, whose capital is in Baghdad
Don Diego Alavar - White Hands' second-in-command
Durr - Rayhana's lady in waiting
Durri the Small - Vizier of the Royal Treasury
Emperor Otto II - Emperor of the Holy Roman Empire
Emperor Tzimisces - Emperor of the Byzantine Empire
Faiq al-Nizami - Master of the Tiraz (Textile Factory of the Royal Court) and Royal Courier Service
Father Maiolus - Abbot of the Benedictine Abbey at Cluny
Fatik - Male concubine in the Royal Harem
Garcia Fernandez - Christian Count of Castile; also known as White Hands
Ghalib al-Nasiri - General and Military Vizier to the Caliph
Hamid al-Tariq - Sheikh of the Banu Birzal, a Berber clan of the Rif Mountains
Hayal - Female slave of Ibn Abi Amir
Hisham II - Caliph al-Hakam II's son and heir
Imam Abd al-Gafur - Imam of a mosque in Algeciras and friend of the Ibn Abi Amir family
Iuliana al-Nasrani - Wife of Zaheid al-Nasrani
Jafar al-Mushafi - Grand Vizier to the Caliph
Jafar al-Tariq (al-Andalusi) - Brother of Hamid al-Tariq and Commander of the Cavalry of the Banu Birzal
Jawdhar - Master of the Royal Jewels and Master of the Caliph's Falcons
Jibril al-Azhar - Head Eunuch of the Royal Harem
Khalil Abi Amir - Ibn Abi Amir's younger son
Levi al-Attar - Royal Purveyor of Books and close friend of Samuel al-Tayyib
Mamun al-Numan - Head of one of Córdoba's powerful merchant families
Maryam - Elder daughter of Durri the Small
Miriam al-Tayyib - Elder daughter of Samuel and Rebekah

Muhammad ibn Abi Amir - Vizier to Africa and Qadi of the Maghreb

Muhja - Male concubine in the Royal Harem

Nuh - Male servant of the Caliph

Omar - Henchman of Sultan ibn Guennoun of the Idrisid Kingdom

Peter Strobel - Diplomat from the Holy Roman Empire

Rayhana Abi Amir - Ibn Abi Amir's daughter

Rayya Abi Amir - Ibn Abi Amir's dead wife

Rebekah al-Tayyib - Wife of Samuel al-Tayyib

Reccimund (Rabi ibn Zyad) - Mozarab, Christian Bishop of Elmira, and Vizier of Dhimmi

Salma Abi Amir - Ibn Abi Amir's mother

Salim Abi Amir - Ibn Abi Amir's elder son

Samuel al-Tayyib - Jewish polymath, Royal Librarian and Vizier of Books

Sara al-Tayyib - Younger daughter of Samuel and Rebekah

Subh - Concubine, then wife, of Caliph al-Hakam II, and mother of Hisham II, his only heir; originally a Christian Basque princess, now Sultana

Suktan - Ibn Abi Amir's Banu Birzal bodyguard

Sultan al-Muizz - Sultan of the Fatimid Empire in the Maghreb, North Africa

Sultan ibn Guennoun - Sultan of the Berber Idrisid Kingdom in the Maghreb, North Africa

Tahir - Ibn Abi Amir's Banu Birzal bodyguard

Ulla al-Tariq - Youngest daughter of Sheikh Hamid al-Tariq of the Banu Birzal and Ibn Abi Amir's wife

Zafir Saffar - Royal Translator, protégé of Samuel al-Tayyib

Zaheid al-Nasrani - Mozarab (Christian) scholar and close friend of Samuel al-Tayyib

A Note to Readers:

Substantive back matter is contained in this book, including: personal reflections, an historical primer, a language and pronunciation guide, copious photographs, a bibliography, and short introductions to the ancient Greeks, the camera obscura, and the Great Mosque of Córdoba.

Muslim, Arabic, Jewish and Christian terms which may be unfamiliar are included in a glossary. Such words are italicized when they first appear, but not afterwards.

Bindings

Madinat al-Zahra, one and a half *leagues* west of Córdoba, **8 April 975**.

The breathy, warbled whisper of ancient Greek drifts ethereally from the vellum pages of the thick, dusty volume set high above the cool, white marble floor. The words are muted, almost imperceptible, but gilded with a playful edge, as if the poet is eager to game, excited by the belated arrival of some long-anticipated turn of events.

The young man reluctantly retreats from the splayed, leather-bound book laid before him, uncertain of the precise source of the interruption. He sets his reed pen down, rubs the fatigue from his eyes, then searches the crammed floor-to-ceiling bookshelves for some hint of the disturbance. Nothing. He holds his breath and cups his ears, sensing that he is missing something obvious. The faint, wistful cry of a cuckoo, but no more. He exhales loudly. Abhorring unsolved puzzles, he frowns his disapproval then returns to his work with a shrug.

A moment later his head snaps up, his grin spontaneous as the recognition dawns. The white star blossoms of the bitter oranges have opened at last. The young man sits up straight, then closes his eyes to invite the otherworldly scent into sharper focus, inhaling a full breath. The tangy floral citrus melody shyly bends its seductive curves from the recesses of the shadows and stands close now at playful attention.

A satisfied smile settles on the young man's handsome face as he slowly exhales. Sated with his favorite punctuation mark of spring, he opens his eyes and looks up and over his left shoulder to the open window high above, the entry point of his unexpected guest. A lanky beam of white-laced yellow angles into the room, chalked into the floor by the fine downy dust released after centuries by cracking open the sleeping volumes.

The morning sun tightens the young man's pupils, revealing remarkable, brilliant emerald irises. These are not the eyes of an Arab; they trace to the rugged mountain lands of Caratania, three hundred leagues to the northeast of Córdoba.

Delighted with spring's gamesome stealth, the young man begins to hum a favorite childhood melody as he settles back into the tedious but pleasant business of translation to Arabic of the thousand-year-old Greek play set before him.

1

The volume nestled high above the floor shoulders its way out of the neat vertical stack to the edge of the shelf, where it smiles down upon the young man. The poet flexes his leather binding just enough to nudge his neighbor awake, eager to while away the morning hours with a hushed reckoning of the latest gossip among the dusty pages of the *caliph's* Rare Books Library.

———— ◙ ————

The room is unusual in its layout, but impressive by any measure; vault-like though cozy, formal but inviting, comfortable as a finely worked calfskin glove. The dark-stained, ornately carved, floor-to-ceiling bookshelves line the walls of the entire room and are stuffed with thick, leather-bound volumes. Skylights puncture the ceiling at the four corners allowing modest natural light to enter, but otherwise there are no windows. There is an oversized heavy wooden door with multiple metal locks that opens to the alley beyond. On the other side of the room there is a matching interior door that leads to the adjoining unexplored caverns. The walls are much taller than might be expected for a room this size, evidently to accommodate more books. On each of the four sides of the room a wheeled wooden stepladder rests at a sharp angle between a metal track set in the white marble floor and a runner attached to the top of the bookcases, allowing easy access to the upper reaches.

At the focal point of the room rests a priceless, six-foot tall, exquisitely carved wooden cabinet. The cherry wood has been stained dark and polished to a lavish red-copper sheen, inlaid with a delicate looping spider-web of ivory and lapis lazuli. Fragile creamy alabaster panels have been polished translucent thin and set inside the four doors of the cabinet, masking its contents. Locked within are forty numbered, leather-bound volumes, arranged sequentially, top right to lower left. A small gold plaque is affixed to the front of the cabinet, the engraved feminine cursive swirls and dots and curves of the Arabic calligraphy proclaiming its owner: "Master Catalog of Rare Books in the Royal Library of Caliph al-Hakam II of Córdoba. May Allah Bless the Written Word."

In the far corner of the room sits a massive, low-slung desk large enough for four scribes. Ornate solid silver oil lamps lord over the desk, their dozens of tight golden flames casting a warm, welcoming glow onto the workspace. Several tapered candles on the desk lend additional illumination, to be slid where needed.

On a plush silk floor pillow behind the desk sits a bearded, middle-aged man in a flowing turmeric-yellow robe with royal blue piping and sash. A royal blue *yarmulke* rests atop his gray-tinged tussock.

A dozen volumes lie open on the desk, one pulled forward commanding attention, the others haphazardly shoved back at odd angles, patiently waiting their turn. With his left hand he dips his reed pen into the inkwell and proceeds to hurriedly scratch on the paper beside him. He looks back to the text, reads for a moment, then scratches again on the paper. Without looking, his right hand paws the edge of the desk for his tea. Milky steam meanders skyward in thin, undulating tendrils, the scent of mint and honey, precise, penetrating. He locates the cup and lifts it to his mouth without taking his eyes from the words on the page. He slurps to dull the burn then sets the cup back down, his lips moving silently as he wrestles with the meaning of the text. He furls his eyebrows then crosses out his last line and begins anew, furiously scratching the paper now as his reed struggles to keep pace with his thoughts.

He looks up from the *codex* at the sharp, metallic snap of the exterior door latch. Reed suspended a half-inch above the paper, he casually tracks the visitor's approach, his head tilted, chin lifted ever so slightly, his expression one of anxious anticipation overlaid by a thin veneer of detached amusement. The visitor pads silently across the room, arriving finally at the desk. The visitor locks eyes with the seated man, folds his arms to make his point, then freezes into a statue, prepared to wait all day.

This is a game these two have played many times. The turmeric man has not blinked once, but the mounting anticipation easily has its way with his will, peeling the amused veneer back in wide strips. Straight-faced, he raises his right eyebrow into a silent question mark, unsuccessfully fighting his widening grin. He blurts out, "Well, Levi, speak up, speak up. The suspense is killing me!"

The visitor's face fans into a beaming smile as he chuckles, the outcome of their amusement never in question. Patience has never been his friend's best virtue. "You will not believe it, Samuel. A treasure trove. Aaron spent a month chasing down that tall tale from the Syrian merchant."

"The Jewish papermaker? With connections to Egypt?"

"Yes. Aaron found him in the Old Quarter in Constantinople." Levi smiles. "It turns out the cache does exist after all, just as the Syrian said. The papermaker claims they were removed from the Great Library at Alexandria just before it was accidentally burned by Emperor Aurelian when his troops sacked the city. They were supposedly hidden in amphorae in a cave on the coast, then forgotten."

"Curious. That was seven hundred years ago, Levi. Removed how? By whom? Why?"

"Unknown. A friend of a friend of a friend brought them to the papermaker's attention two years back. On his next visit to Egypt he snapped them up, likely for a pittance. He claims there are more to be had."

"I see. Have you seen them?"

Levi's eyes sparkle as his bright smile returns. "Aaron arrived this morning."

"How much did he have to pay?"

"Three hundred gold dinars. The papermaker demanded five, but Aaron is a shrewd one. Not a hint that he was an agent of the caliph's royal book purveyor. Simply an avid collector ... with modestly deep pockets. He appealed to their shared Jewish appreciation for the preservation of rare books." Both men smile. "As you will soon see, it was a bargain by any measure."

Samuel nods his approval. "Good, good. The caliph will be pleased."

"Should I send word of their arrival?"

Samuel considers. "Have you examined the cache's contents?"

"Only a quick look. They are Greek, but I cannot say more with certainty. I was surprised to see that the pages are on vellum, not papyrus, and have been assembled as codices using Coptic binding, with tooled leather covers. There are twenty-seven in all. They do bear catalog stamps from Alexandria's Great Library, which would fit the papermaker's claims."

"Their condition?"

"Fair, for the most part. Faded, but readable. Several show some water damage. The bindings have failed on one, and pieces are missing from it. But these codices are clearly ancient."

"Interesting ..."

"The broken volume has detailed annotations with elaborate sketches in the margins, but my Greek is not good enough to decipher it. It is obvious that it was heavily used by its original owner. My guess would be a scientific or engineering treatise from the Greek Golden Age. Originals from that period would have been on vellum, as you know." He pauses, then continues, "I did happen to notice two spines bearing the name Aristotle." He beams.

Samuel opens his eyes wide. "Indeed ..." His head joins his chest as he strokes his beard and weighs his friend's words. "My beloved Aristotle ... perhaps this time there will be something new." He falls into silent thought. Levi knows from experience to allow the royal librarian sufficient time for the wheels to cease their spinning.

Samuel looks up and says, "Before we inform the caliph of the acquisition I would like to examine the cache myself ... to ensure a complete inventory. You know how he hates to be teased by promised delicacies that do not deliver." Samuel offers a wry smile.

Levi laughs. "I assumed as much. The crate is being brought here as we speak."

Samuel unkinks his body, stands, moves around his desk, then clasps Levi's shoulders affectionately as he smiles broadly, shaking the smaller man. "You have done well, my friend, very well, indeed. Let us share a meal this evening and I will give you my thoughts on the contents. Rebekah and the girls would love to see you. Join us for the beginning of Shabbat."

"I would enjoy that."

"Good, good. Compliment Aaron for me. His commission will be doubled. Oh, and send for Zafir. I will need his Greek."

Levi smiles warmly, then dips his head with a single angled nod, turns and slips from the room, pleased with himself.

Samuel eases into his contemplative posture, his arms pinned behind his back, middle-finger and thumb locked around his wrist. He chews his cheek as he begins to pace the length of the room, calculating the intriguing possibilities.

As the young man reads the dense black squiggles set upon the papyrus, he stops. "Lysistrata, you are quite the woman." He laughs. "Quite the woman." He reads the line once more, chasing it with an amused chuckle followed by a soft whistle. He lifts his head and settles into his standard translation posture as he considers the best choice of words; left thumb hooked under his chin, index finger stretched vertical across his lips to the tip of his nose, other fingers curled.

After a moment the truest of many possibilities suggests itself. He dips his reed into the inkwell and without hesitation hurriedly scratches on the paper beside him. Preserving the nuances of humor during translation is never an easy task, but he welcomes the challenge. He stops, looks back to the book, and traces his finger along the text left to right as he reads the next line. Then he lifts his finger to his lips once more as he weighs the best fit, scratches again, right to left now, a Greek-Arabic tug-of-war that will mark his day until the sun settles low.

5

He looks up as he registers the distinctive pattern of the knock. *Knock,* pause, *knock-knock-knock,* pause, *knock.* Levi opens the door and slips into the cozy room. The two exchange a smile.

"Good morning, Zafir."

"You are up early, Levi. I thought you never rose before noon on a workday."

The older man chuckles. "Only on special occasions, my boy."

"Ahhh ... Aaron has arrived?"

"Indeed he has, indeed he has. Wait until you see what he has brought us this time."

Zafir lifts his right eyebrow into a silent question mark, a trademark borrowed from his master.

Levi smiles and continues. "Greek. Supposedly rescued from the Great Library of Alexandria before it was burned." He pauses. "And two volumes of Aristotle."

Zafir's eyes widen. "Excellent. Master Samuel will be delighted."

"Yes. He sent for you. As we both know, your Greek is better than his. Though do not tell him I said as much."

Zafir grins. "Your secret is safe."

"Tell me about your latest project."

Zafir looks first to the open codex, then to his half-filled paper pad, then back to Levi. The young man's bright smile is contagious. "An unknown play by Aristophanes. A most unusual comedy. Ribald. Hilarious."

Levi grins as he nods his approval. "Do tell."

"The play is set during the great war of the Peloponnese between the Athenians and the Spartans. The Greeks have endured twenty-seven years of slaughter, settling into a tense stalemate, no end in sight. Lysistrata, a woman of the Athenian court, dreams up an ingenious plan to quickly end the hostilities once and for all." Zafir stops to heighten the suspense.

Levi lifts both his palms skyward then beckons with his fingers. "And?"

Zafir grins. "She persuades the women of Athens and Sparta to withhold all sexual privileges from their husbands and lovers until the men on both sides sue for peace."

Levi laughs loudly. "Indeed. And did it work?"

Zafir beams. "What do you think?"

Levi laughs again. "I am guessing the war was over in a week."

Zafir acknowledges with a grin and an affirmative tick of his head.

"I look forward to reading it. When will it be complete?"

6

"Within a few weeks if all goes well, though the arrival of this new cache may delay things. Rest assured, you will be the first to see it, Levi, as always. The caliph will be amused, and the grand imam will be offended. As usual."

Levi chuckles. "Excellent. Keep up the good work, my boy." He turns to leave, then stops and looks back at the younger man. "By the way, the details of the cache are to remain between the three of us. For now."

Zafir nods. The great mysteries of the ancient pagans are always a delicate matter.

A smooth, flat stone well thrown to the east from the entrance door of the Rare Books Library could strike the villa of the family of Muhammad ibn Abi Amir. The dwelling is nestled on the lower level of the *Alcazar*, the royal palace complex, and given his modest station on the *Vizier* Council, the Ibn Abi Amir home is comfortable but not lavish, at least by the standards of Madinat al-Zahra.

The villa is two-storied and surrounds an intimate peristyle bricked courtyard with a scalloped marble-floor fountain set at the very center. Head-high orange trees in large ceramic planters mark the four corners of the courtyard, their deep green waxy leaves bathed in a sea of delicate five-starred white blossoms that have just begun to crack open and spill their riches into the soft breeze.

She lies on her back adjacent the gurgling fountain, her mass of unruly dark brown curls scattered over the pillow. The morning sun has just broken over the roof edge, the sharp line of the shadow on the serpentine brickwork creeping back from the columns at a minute but measured pace. Her left hand suspends the thin leather-bound volume midair a foot from her face. She is deathly still, the only hint of life the rapid tandem flick of her eyes, from right to left, right to left, as she skims down the page. The double-tone hue of her irises is arresting, unusually textured amber starbursts set within honey brown.

The finely-robed man enters the courtyard from a side room on his way to the front gate and abruptly stops to stare. His hands find his hips as he frowns and says, "What are you doing lying in the courtyard, Rayhana?" When she does not acknowledge his presence, he sighs and raises his voice. "Rayhana?"

Her eyes reluctantly retreat from the page as she lowers the book then struggles to focus on her father. Her expression is one of mild confusion dabbed here and there with resentment over the interruption. "Yes, *Baba*?"

"And?"

"And what, Baba?"

"And what are you doing?"

"Reading, Baba."

His frown is deepening with each exchange. "What are you reading, Rayhana?"

Without moving her head she closes the thin volume on her thumb and rotates it to show him the cover as she says, "Reccimund's *Calendar of Córdoba*, Baba. Fascinating."

The man frowns. "Reccimund is his Christian name, Rayhana. You should refer to him properly. Rabi ibn Zyad."

She responds with a not-so-subtle dose of sarcasm, "Rabi ibn Zyad's *Calendar of Córdoba*, Baba. Fascinating."

The frown remains. "Where did you get it?"

"Salim brought it home from the *madrasa*."

"I do not approve of you reading Christian books, Rayhana."

Her sarcasm edges towards exasperation. "Baba, Ibn Zyad is vizier of *dhimmi*. He composed the book in honor of our caliph. Reccimund—Ibn Zyad—has very interesting ideas on weather patterns, and Córdoba's agricultural calendar—even hygiene. I am learning a lot, and besides, there is nothing Christian about it. His Arabic is flawless."

The frown budges only slightly. "Yes, well, there are better things for a young woman of court to be engaged in. Go ride horses with your brother. Or play some chess. Or find some female friends your age to entertain."

Her lips flirt with a pout. "The girls my age talk only about court intrigue, Baba. That and fight over who is the handsomest man in the Royal Guard. Women of court are so tedious." She realizes she herself is frowning now and abruptly changes course, a sloop expertly tacking in a stiff headwind. She rises and comes to him, wrapping her arms affectionately around his chest, squeezing tightly. The tension between them evaporates. She looks up and offers a playful smile, then sticks her tongue out to chide him.

Mid-smile, deep dimples unexpectedly open in her cheeks, instantly lending her beautiful Arabian features an adorable, little-girl quality. The man relents, and despite his best effort, cannot help but grin.

"Crazy girl. You will be the death of me, Rayhana. At least promise me that you will go riding."

She steps back and grins coyly. "Certainly, Baba. After I finish the book."

He shakes his head side to side with faked disapproval but cannot suppress his grin.

On a whim she decides to press her luck. She beams, then says, "Baba, have you given more thought to my request?"

His grin evaporates and his hands return to his hips. "Rayhana, you know that women are not allowed access to the Rare Books Library except under very special circumstances."

She doesn't respond, just continues to flash her brightest, best smile. "It would mean so much to me, Baba. I have read through all of our library, Baba, many of the books twice!"

Her smile weighs on his will, producing a heavy sag in his spirits. He sighs with the recognition of just how defenseless he is against the wiles of beautiful women. A lion at court, a lamb at home. Her mother's daughter, that much is certain. He attempts to muster some sense of authority, then says, "Very well, Rayhana. But only in a private reading room. And only three days a week." He pauses to raise his index finger for emphasis. "And I must approve of the books you read. In advance."

Her dimples fade momentarily then return as she begins to eagerly nod.

"Fine. I will talk to the royal librarian to see what can be arranged. It may take some time, so please be patient. For once."

She is giddy with excitement. "I love you, Baba! Thank you, thank you, thank you!" She hugs him again.

"Crazy girl. Please see that Durr brings a suitable divan to the courtyard. Young women of your state do *not* lie on the brickwork, Rayhana." He shakes his head again with resigned dismay, certain his request will remain unheeded, then heads on for another busy day in the law courts and arguments he knows he can win.

Her dimples return as she watches him leave, then vanish without a trace with the fading of her smile. She lies back on her floor pillow, rests her leg upon the opposite knee, opens the book above her, and finds her place, content to be alone with the magic of the words cast wide upon the page.

The royal librarian has cleared room on his ample desk for his protégé, who sits on a floor pillow to his right. The golden flames of the oil lamps have been lengthened by two and extra tapers have been brought in, their foray demanding excellent lighting. Master and apprentice each have a thick volume laid open in front of him, as well as two unequal stacks just beyond; one examined, one not. Both men lean close to the pages, peering intently, their index fingers lightly touching the stiff vellum, slowly tracing the tightly scrawled Greek symbols from left to right as they sift for clues. The postures of the two mirror each other, the older man using his left hand, the younger man his right. The room is bound by an understood silence, the only exception the cracks and crinkles of the turning of the ancient vellum sheets. The tension in the room is palpable, the air pulled taut with anticipation of unknown words, the promise of new discovery.

Without looking up, Samuel says, "This is one of the volumes from the *Hippocratic Corpus*. We have two complete copies of the entire set already." He closes the codex and sets it on his taller stack and sighs wearily.

Zafir looks up. "Yes, so is this one. More Hippocrates." He closes the volume, sets it on his taller stack, then luxuriously stretches into a ball-fisted, taut Y and yawns loudly.

Samuel purses his lips, sighs, then mutters, "I was so hoping for something new this time." Only two books remain on his unexplored pile.

"Patience, Master Samuel, one never knows." The two exchange a warm smile. They share a deep love for the hunt. Zafir lifts his final volume. His eyes widen as he examines the spine. He has intentionally saved the best for last. "Ahhh ... Aristotle. Good, Levi was right." Samuel anxiously looks up. There is obvious water damage but not catastrophic. Zafir opens it gingerly, thumbs through the first few pages. His finger stops. He frowns, then says, "*The History of Animals*. Our third copy." Zafir closes the book.

Samuel returns to his own thick codex. "This is also Aristotle." He turns the first vellum sheet and reads, then frowns. "Ummm ... another *Metaphysics*, I am afraid." Both men sigh in unison as he sets it on his tall stack.

The last book is the damaged volume. Samuel begins to chew his cheek. He slides it forward then lifts it for inspection. On the spine there is no indication of what lurks within. He says, "No label. Unusual." He continues to stare at the codex from different angles as Zafir looks on, then opens the leather cover. The bindings have failed and the entire front section of the manuscript is missing. He looks more closely, noting the jagged cut marks, which he silently indicates to Zafir. It appears that the section has been violently ripped from the book with a crude instrument of some sort. Samuel's disgust with anyone who would dare disfigure a book is instantaneous and unmistakable. He shakes his head sadly. He gingerly explores further, turning the book over and lifting the back cover. A large back section has also been ripped out. Only the thin middle portion remains.

Samuel says, "This poor codex has seen better days." Zafir nods. Samuel moves back to the front of the book. The title pages are gone, but on the upper left corner of the inside of the leather binding a faint set of markings can just be seen. Samuel leans closer and slides the taper in. There is a hastily scribbled identifier in crude, sprawling lettering, placed there presumably to identify the contents after the title pages were ripped out. The scribbles are faded, the first few letters unreadable. Samuel leans even closer. Oddly, the lettering is Latin, not Greek. "… otle's *Opticae Thesaurus.*"

Samuel's right eyebrow instantly lifts into a question mark as he says, *"Book of Optics?* Aristotle's *Book of Optics?"* He looks up and exchanges an amused glance with Zafir, who takes this as an invitation to move closer. Samuel picks up a dry reed as a pointer. "Look. Latin, not Greek. I wonder why?" He stares into space. "Aristotle's *Book of Optics* … I have never heard of such a book." He and Zafir exchange an anxious smile.

Zafir offers, "Perhaps the Latin was added by the Romans before the Great Library burned?"

"Perhaps …"

Samuel looks now to the first page of the widowed middle section. Beginning in the upper left, he traces with his reed, haltingly translating the Greek aloud:

"Problem 37. On the creation of the …"

Samuel halts, wrestling with the translation. Zafir leans in and offers: "'True Form.' I assume Plato's 'Theory of Forms.'" Samuel nods and begins again.

"Problem 37. On the creation of the True Form of any object using a …"

He stops again, frowns, and points for Zafir. Zafir pronounces, "'Darkened Chamber.'" Samuel re-reads the entire passage.

"Problem 37. On the creation of the True Form using a Darkened Chamber."

The two exchange matching eyebrow question marks, then quick, excited smiles. The game is afoot. Samuel presses onward, stopping three times for Zafir's guidance on word choice:

"Propositions:
1. All material objects possess both a True Form and a Shadow Form.

2. Only the True Form embodies the definitive essence of the object.

3. The True Form always exists in mirror inversion relative to the object. (Here proved.)

4. The human eye only perceives images which are non-inverted relative to the objects which generate them.

Theorem:
The human eye is incapable of perceiving True Forms, and thus human perception of the world is finite and limited to Shadow Forms.

Proof of Proposition 3:"

Below these words is a dense collection of inked drawings, highlighted with lines and arrows. The geometrical scribbles seem to have been applied furiously, the spontaneous outpouring of a pulsing mind, not the deliberate copying of an ancient manuscript by a scribe. Barely legible Greek words are scribbled here and there at odd angles. Several words are scratched out then rewritten, then scratched out again and another word substituted.

A long arc links the top drawing to a larger, three-dimensional sketch of a rectangular box below it. On one face of the box a tiny circular hole is indicated. To its right is a crude drawing of the sun with dark irregular blotches inked carefully onto it, and a straight line with an arrowhead pointed at the circular hole on the box. Samuel whispers, "A darkened chamber?" As his narrowed eyes track from drawing to text to drawing, Samuel's frown deepens. He turns the page. More of the same.

Zafir points to the very bottom of the second page. Written in bold red ink is the phrase, ὅπερ ἔδει δεῖξαι. He translates, "'What was required to be proved.' The author clearly feels he has proved Proposition 3. 'The True Form always exists in mirror inversion relative to the object.' What do you suppose he means by that?"

Samuel shrugs, then slides his reed to the lower right corner of the page. The faint scribbles in Latin are barely discernible but were obviously made by the same hand that placed the inscription on the inside cover. There are only three faded words, the first two in Latin, the last in Greek: *Camera Obscura. Eureka!* Samuel mouths the words. "Darkened Chamber ... I have found it!" He begins to chew his cheek again. Silence settles in now as master and apprentice struggle unsuccessfully to digest the mystery unveiled before them. They slowly re-read the text of Problem 37, carefully studying the drawings as they go; amazed, confused.

Samuel breaks the trance. "I have never seen anything like this from Aristotle, Zafir. Never. Every volume we possess is a careful copy by a meticulous scribe, a neat rendition of a finished piece." He shakes his head side to side. "This volume ... reads like a work in progress, a draft of some sort. An original working notebook, maybe?" The two look hard at each other, their serious expressions melting first into sly grins then precipitating two sharp bursts of delighted laughter. The thrill of the hunt.

Zafir boasts, "My, my, wait until the caliph hears of this!"

Samuel's smile fades. "Not so fast, my boy, not so fast. We need to understand what we have here." He thumbs through the book. More of the same. Numbered problems then furious geometrical scratchings interspersed with barely-legible marginal scribbles. He consults the bottom of the last page. "Problem 55. Problem, but only part of the solution. I wonder how many there were in total ..."

Zafir replies, "Judging by the original thickness, surely a hundred at least."

"Yet if it was a working notebook, the back section may not have been completely filled."

"True."

"Well, let us make the most of our eighteen, then. We will begin by translating all the problem statements."

Zafir lifts a paper tablet into place, hurriedly fingers Samuel's reed jar for a freshly sharpened point, then slides an ink pot to within easy reach. The two hover together over the scribbled secrets of the ancient codex like expectant fathers as they begin the meticulous task set before them.

Gifts

The mouthwatering mélange is impossible to ignore. The intoxicating aromas join forces and heave as they struggle to lift the lids on the ceramic crocks imprisoning them. First, the raucous bouquet of delights shyly peeps to make sure the coast is clear, then they sashay voluptuously into the air, producing rumbles and growls and grins in the five people seated about the large oak table. Under separate banner are roasted spring lamb with fresh rosemary and salt; a slow-cooked stew of braised kid with root vegetables; sliced beets and pearl onions sautéed in butter; boiled chard with pink radishes and pine nuts; pungent fresh spring greens dressed in spicy olive oil and tossed with dried cherries and slivered almonds; and an assortment of honey-drenched dried fruits.

The room is silent, still, but full of expectation and bated breath. A quick glance to the window marks the setting of the sun behind the distant ridge line, the bright yellow orb fading to a deep burnt-orange glow as the day exchanges places with the sleek diamonds of the night.

She holds a thin taper to the golden flame of the oil lamp until it catches, then turns and lights first one and then the other candle set on the table in front of her. Beside the candles are two braided loaves, a thin white cloth nestled upon them. A pitcher inside a matching basin rests beside the loaves to her left. Six places are set.

Her wavy, nut-brown hair approaches a black hue in the flattering lamplight, touched here and there by gentle flecks of gray. She was clearly attractive in her youth, but in that magical manner that only a certain kind of love favors, she has grown beautiful with age, burnished now to a deep, warm, satisfying glow. Her girlish figure may not have survived the years unscathed, but her body has grown fuller over time, more sure of itself, her curves lengthening in an especially satisfying way. Nature's kind reward for the burdens of childbirth.

She waves her hands above the flame once, twice, three times, then covers her eyes and begins in a soft, silky voice. "Barukh atah Adonai, Eloheinu, melekh ha'olam asher kidishanu b'mitz'votav v'tzivanu l'had'lik neir shel Shabbat." *Blessed are you, Lord, our God, sovereign of the universe, who has sanctified us with His commandments and commanded us to light the lights of Shabbat.*

The others answer in unison. "Amein." *Amen.*

She uncovers her eyes and looks anew at the lit candles, her deep, honey-almond eyes widening as if she is seeing the light for the very first time. The corners of her mouth lift into a lovely, unselfconscious smile as she turns to her husband. He returns her nod with a jovial wink.

Samuel lifts the ornate silver goblet high and continues in Hebrew, "And there was evening and there was morning, a sixth day. The heavens and the earth were finished, the whole host of them. And on the seventh day God completed his work that he had done and he rested on the seventh day from all his work that he had done. And God blessed the seventh day, and sanctified it because on it he had rested from all his work. Blessed are you, Lord, our God, sovereign of the universe who creates the fruit of the vine."

The four respond in kind. "Amen."

"Who made all things exist through His Word."

"Amen."

"Blessed are You, Lord, our God, King of the Universe, who sanctifies us with His commandments, and has been pleased with us. You have lovingly and willingly given us Your holy Shabbat as an inheritance, in memory of creation because it is the first day of our holy assemblies. In memory of the exodus from Egypt because You have chosen us and made us holy from all peoples and have willingly and lovingly given us Your holy Shabbat for an inheritance. Blessed are You, who sanctifies Shabbat."

"Amen."

Samuel takes a sip from the goblet and passes it to his wife, who repeats his motions. The wine circles the table in silence.

Samuel now lifts the pitcher and pours cool water first over his left hand, then over his right, as he says, "Blessed are you, Lord, our God, King of the Universe, who has sanctified us with His commandments and commanded us concerning the washing of hands." He dries his hands then passes the pitcher and bowl to his right. Each repeats the prayer as they wash then passes the pitcher and bowl.

Samuel lifts the cloth from the two challah loaves and raises one up, saying, "Blessed are You, Lord, our God, King of the Universe, who brings forth bread from the earth."

"Amen."

He tears a small piece from a loaf then passes it to his right. When all have pieces they bow their heads in unison and silently eat the morsel.

All seriousness evaporates from the room. Samuel smiles broadly and opens his arms wide in greeting. "Welcome, Levi, my dear friend. Lord, bless poor Zafir who is never on time! We invite the angels of Shabbat to join us." He turns to his right and lifts both palms to the woman standing beside him. "We give thanks to my dear wife, Rebekah, who brought forth our dear daughters into this world, who cares for us and our home with such loving devotion, and who has worked hard all day to prepare the Shabbat feast for us." She offers a pleased smile as she continues to stare down at the table. The younger girl, six, giggles. The elder daughter, just turned twelve, remains serious, prim.

"Amen."

Samuel raises his voice, "Let us feast together and remember our great blessings!" The pent-up anticipation erupts in a burst of cheerful laughter and bright chatter until the first forkfuls again hush the table.

Several minutes later there is a light knock. Both girls rise and race to the door, the elder girl catching herself at the last moment and stopping just short.

Rebekah chides them. "Girls!"

The younger daughter flings open the door and runs into the arms of Zafir, smothering her giggles into his chest. Zafir laughs loudly then bends down and kisses her on top of the head. "And how is my best girl today?"

"Fine, Zafir. Why are you always late?"

The young man laughs again. "My apologies, Sara, I forgot that I was racing the sunset. Will you forgive me?" He grins.

Her playful smile is contagious as she scolds him with her finger. "Just this once."

Her sister steps forward. "Sara, let Zafir pass." A month ago she, too, would have rushed to hug the young man, but times seem to have changed. She steps forward demurely and curtsies. "Are you well, Zafir?"

Zafir tilts his head quizzically. "I am wonderful, Miriam. I have had a magical day, thank you." He steps forward and kisses her familiarly, first on one cheek then on the other, then steps past her into the room, her bright blush lost on all but her mother.

Rebekah chastens them, "Girls, please, Zafir is hungry."

"My apologies for being late, Master Samuel. I lost track of the time."

Samuel chuckles his quick forgiveness then says, "No matter, no matter. We Jews know the precise moment of sunset better than you Muslims, so I am afraid you are at a disadvantage, my boy. Besides, Levi reminded me that you would never miss a free meal!"

Zafir laughs loudly.

Samuel, Levi, and Rebekah step forward to greet the young man, and after affectionate hugs and back-slaps, the six settle back into the feast amid light conversation.

Intrigued now, Rebekah discreetly studies Miriam. The girl cannot take her eyes from Zafir, hanging on his every word, laughing just a little too loudly at his jokes. As Rebekah continues to observe her daughter she shakes her head and sighs. When she finally catches Miriam's eyes, she widens her own in silent query. Miriam blushes scarlet and glues her gaze to her plate. The corners of Rebekah's mouth lift into an amused grin.

The three men are alone now, reclining on divans circled tightly for intimate conversation around a small table crammed with hot mint tea and sweets.

"And so?"

Samuel exchanges a conspiratorial grin with his protégé over his steaming cup as Zafir greedily chews on a dried honeyed apricot. "And so, what?"

Levi sighs heavily, familiar with the game. "The cache, Samuel. The papermaker's cache?"

Samuel's grin widens. "Ahhh ... the cache. I had forgotten about that. Well, perhaps a trinket ..."

Zafir chuckles, enjoying the amusement. "Or two ..."

"And ...?"

Samuel smiles and says, "You tell him, Zafir."

The young man's amused grin sags into seriousness. "Well, twenty-six of the codices are fine examples of ancient Greek volumes. We suspect them to be authentic, tracing back to the Library at Alexandria. The great physicians: Hippocrates, Polybius, Galen, Dioscorides. And some of the major playwrights: Sophocles, Euripides, Aphareus, several others. And there is indeed some Aristotle."

Levi brightens with anticipation.

Zafir continues. "Alas, we have copies of all twenty-six already in the Royal Library."

Levi frowns.

Samuel joins in. "Abu al-Qasim may want to consult the medical treatises to check his old volumes for accuracy of translation."

Levi sighs as his eyes sadly slide to the floor. "Yes, I suspect he will." He lifts his eyes once more. "But there was also the broken codex, the twenty-seventh, the one with all the drawings. What of it?"

Samuel exchanges another conspiratorial grin with Zafir. "Oh, yes, I forgot about that one. The poor broken codex, bless its soul. Well, it appears to be of some minor interest, actually." He is obviously enjoying this revenge on his friend.

Levi's eyes dance between both men. He starts to impatiently wave both hands in tight circles to speed up the conversation. "Well? Well?"

Zafir continues. "We believe it is Aristotle. But a volume Samuel has never seen before."

Levi sits up straight and leans forward attentively.

Samuel says, "Sadly, the front and back sections were forcibly ripped out, but there is a working title scribbled on the inside cover, in Latin. Aristotle's *Opticae Thesaurus. Book of Optics.* Numbered problems and their solutions. There is no *Book of Optics* in the known canon of Aristotle, Levi. Elaborate geometrical solutions with copious annotations. Interestingly, it seems to be a working journal of some sort." He hesitates to build the fever. "I believe it may be Aristotle's own working journal. Maybe. Written in his own hand and fully annotated by the great master. If so, it is a dream come true."

Levi whistles then laughs. "My, my ... a trinket, you say?" He slaps his knee. "In his own hand? Are you sure?"

Zafir chimes his caution. "No, not sure. There is much translation and cross-checking to be done before we can be positive. Samuel and I recorded all of the problem statements today. Eighteen. The first is strikingly original, something the Latin annotator labeled 'Camera Obscura.' Darkened Chamber. He seemed quite interested in Aristotle's proof. We are not sure what it means yet, but the ideas are definitely new. At least Samuel has never seen them. Something about artificially creating a true form, the true image, of an object using a darkened chamber and the implied limitations of human perception."

"Interesting ..."

Samuel responds, "And possibly dangerous. You understand the implications of images in Islam. We must treat this delicately until we know more."

Levi considers for a long moment then answers, "Yes, I agree."

Samuel locks eyes first with Levi then with Zafir to garner seriousness. "The existence of the twenty-seventh codex will remain a strict secret. For now." Both men nod their acceptance of the pact. The room falls silent as the three weigh the many possibilities.

Samuel says, "I had also thought to bring in Zaheid to assist us. His Greek is excellent, and his expertise in matters of science surpasses the three of us combined. Besides, adding a Christian perspective to two Jews and a Muslim will round us out, help us appreciate all potential angles. Agreed?"

Both men respond, "Agreed."

Samuel now changes the subject to lighten the mood. "I learned at the Vizier Council yesterday that we are to have visitors."

Levi answers, "Oh? I had not heard. Who?"

"A diplomatic delegation from the Holy Roman Empire. Emperor Otto II is sending his personal envoy to Córdoba, one Peter Strobel. And with him is a monk from the Cluny Abbey in Burgundy. Brother Cleo. Supposedly the most accomplished scholar and physician in the whole empire."

Zafir grimaces.

Samuel continues. "It seems the emperor wants Brother Cleo to learn all that he can of Arabic medicine from Abu al-Qasim. Herbs and potions, surgical technique, wound treatments; everything."

Levi arches his eyebrows as he replies. "This should be interesting. Do they speak Arabic?"

"Evidently Brother Cleo does, at least some. He spent time with Reccimund when the caliph sent him to Otto I's court several years back. Reccimund speaks highly of him." Levi nods.

Zafir asks, "What do they want with us?"

"It seems Peter Strobel has requested that the Royal Library and its staff be placed at their disposal, to assist with translations, to retrieve needed volumes. Busy work. Of course, the caliph secretly wants us to teach them some culture while they are here."

Levi laughs as Zafir frowns. The young man says, "A distraction and a waste of time. We have more pressing business."

"I agree. Nevertheless, the caliph desires it. We are at their disposal."

Zafir offers only a resigned nod while Levi smiles indulgently at the younger man's impatience. Master and apprentice, two of a kind.

"They are to arrive in three days, I believe. After Shabbat I will speak with Zaheid and arrange a late-night meeting for the four of us to plan our attack upon Aristotle's secret bastion."

This brightens Zafir's mood a bit, producing a reluctant smile.

Rebekah sits on a stool in the bedroom brushing her luxurious dark tresses by candlelight, her left hand lifting her thick hair off the back of her neck while she methodically works it with the brush.

Samuel silently eases in behind her, leans down and gently breathes into her ear as he reaches around her and cups her full breast.

She starts, then smiles. "Yes, Husband?"

He ignores her, sliding her nightgown down off her shoulder to kiss the nape of her neck. She shivers but remains silent.

He whispers, "Shabbat is a time for rejoicing, Rebekah, for enjoying the gifts we have been given."

She tilts her head, amused, then coyly smiles. "And what gifts would those be, Husband?"

He chuckles. "Why, the gifts of your beautiful body, Wife." He works his way across her bare shoulder, her eyelids drooping a little more with each press of his lips. Abruptly, she playfully giggles, then rises and turns, moving into his familiar embrace.

She is nestled into her favorite spot between his arm and shoulder, teasing the wispy hair on his chest. These two relish the sacred sanctuary of their canopied bed. He traces his fingers over the sumptuous curve of her full hips, back and forth, back and forth. The single taper casts deep shadows across the room that dance and flit in time to the flame's flicker.

She is the first to break the trance. "Miriam is in love."

Samuel lifts his head to see her face, incredulous. "In love?"

"Yes."

Samuel frowns. "With whom?"

"Guess."

"Rebekah, you know I hate guessing games."

"Guess."

A silent tug of war ensues, but uncharacteristically, she gives in first. "Zafir."

Samuel lifts his head higher to see her better. "Zafir?"

She looks up into his eyes. "Yes, Zafir."

He snorts. "Rebekah, Zafir is twice Miriam's age."

"Exactly twelve years older, yes."

"She is only a child."

"You need to pay more careful attention, Samuel. She is a young woman. Her first bleeding moon was six months back."

"Miriam is in love?" He shakes his head in confused dismay. "Zafir? He is ancient compared to her."

"Samuel, how much older are you than me?"

Silence.

He reluctantly whispers, "Ten years." He is frowning again.

She smiles. "Zafir is unaware that she is growing up, and he clearly does not see more than the little girl he has known all these years. Still, he must be sensitive to Miriam, delicate with her feelings. I do not wish to see her hurt, Samuel. Will you speak with him?"

More silence, then a resigned, "Yes, I will speak with him, Wife."

"Thank you, Husband."

The Shining City

The two men straddle their mounts on the high edge of the Sierra Morena's last gasp before it melts into the broad alluvial plain, mesmerized to silence by the vivid scene set before them. One is clearly a well-placed gentleman of the court. He is dressed in a silk robe of royal purple, the sleeves and bottom of the robe a red silk strangled in embroidered gold filigree and inlaid with decorative pearls and fired enamels.

His companion sits in striking contrast, a study in plain black; flowing woolen tunic, cowl attached to the scapular hugging his shoulders, all held together with a simple rope belt at his waist. A large gold cross hangs from a heavy chain around his neck. The unmistakable dress of a Benedictine monk.

Both men shield their eyes from the dipping sun as they scan the horizon, stopping here and there to exchange words of amazement. Stretching before them as far as the eye can see are irregularly shaped rectangular fields, some pale green with foot-high spring wheat, others darker green with neatly stitched rows of cool-weather vegetables, some fresh-tilled and painted in with a pleasing contrast of warm browns. Some fields lie fallow, filled with a playful verdant patchwork of thick, lush grasses mixed here and there with contrasting riots of crimson and yellow from clover and mustard greens.

There are wide expanses of orchards all puffed up and proud in their white glory, the blossoms of the pears, lemons, apples, plums, cherries, and almonds perfuming the air with a delicate scent. The less easily cultivated lands around rocky outcrops are ruled by squat olive trees, their silvery-green leaves shimmering in the late afternoon sun, the masses of tiny white blossoms swollen and ready to pop.

Temporary wooden fences boxing the fallow fields corral livestock as they happily graze the lush grass. In return for this succulent bounty they agree to drop their sweet earthy manure to be worked into the soil as fertilizer for next year's harvest, then are sent on to the next lush paddock needing their attention.

Wide irrigation channels track the boundaries of the rectangles, worming their way back to the source of the life's blood of these fertile lands, the Guadalquivir River. The deep green meander of the wide waterway traces from left foreground at the base of the ridge line into the hazy distance at the far right, seductively twisting and bending its way to the horizon. *Dhows* under full sail dot the river like honeybees, feverishly racing perishable goods to market, joined here and there by flat river barges plodding under their heavy burdens.

As the monk points west to the horizon at their far right, the gentleman leans in his saddle to better follow his sight-line, finally glimpsing their quarry. "Córdoba."

The monk responds, "According to Sister Hroswitha, the 'Ornament of the World'." The two lock eyes, but only one smiles.

Even from a league the great city is impressive. Hovering over a sharp bend in the Guadalquivir, the two dozen towers set into the high city walls can be easily seen. The bulk of the city is nestled on the north side of the river, but the city has overflowed to the opposite bank, linked by the wide span of the massive Roman-era stone bridge, the Puente Romano.

A rampart surrounding a large tower camps at the end of the bridge opposite the city, suggesting a garrison. Their squinting eyes track in tandem back across the river to the city proper as they try to make out more detail. There is a tall spire just north of the bridge, taller than the towers set into the city walls, and more ornate, less defensive looking. The monk lifts his finger again to point. "That must be the *minaret* of the Great Mosque." The gentleman remains silent but frowns.

The monk raises his finger up and to the left, pointing into the distance. "Madinat al-Zahra, the Shining City." A tiny ivory smudge jostles with the heat wrinkles hugging the rise of the ridge line several leagues beyond Córdoba.

The gentleman turns dour. The silence pulls tight then stretches uncomfortably, releasing a derisive, "The palace of the infidel. May God protect our souls." The monk responds with a puzzled look then a shrug.

The remainder of the entourage is stopped a dozen paces behind the two men: three men-at-arms, their squires, a standard-bearer, four servants, three pack horses, and their Arab guide. The standard-bearer's pike stands precisely vertical and tall, the light silk colors snaking lazily in the refreshing mountain breeze. The double-headed black eagle set upon a gold background is unequivocal on the travelers' place of origin: the Holy Roman Empire.

The monk points down and to their right at the small dust cloud dogging four riders half a league down the road. "We have visitors." The gentleman nods somberly as he locates the riders. Their welcoming party is closing quickly, the month's journey at an end. The monk turns in his saddle and speaks haltingly in Arabic to their guide, who nods, then spurs his horse into motion and sets off down the hill.

"I bid you a warm welcome. *Bishop* Reccimund sends his greetings and glad tidings. I am Monsignor Alonso al-Rahib, his *Vicar General.* I will serve as your host and personal guide while you are with us in Córdoba." The man's smile is easy and warm, sincere. He is dressed in the plain brown robe of a priest. His Latin is understandable but tinged at the edges with an unusual accent.

The gentleman is stiff in his saddle, on display, intent on projecting his state. He responds in a formal tone, his Latin precise and impeccable. "I am Peter Strobel, Ambassador of His Royal Majesty Otto II, Emperor of the Holy Roman Empire. I am here to meet with Caliph al-Hakam II." He lifts his palm to his companion. "This is Brother Cleo of the Benedictine Abbey at Cluny. He seeks an education in Arab medicine." This last sentence has a slight bite to it.

The monsignor ignores the ambassador's formality and tone. "Yes, yes, Brother Cleo. Reccimund speaks very fondly of you. And I have read your work. A true pleasure. Córdoba is honored by your presence."

The monk returns the smile. "A blessing upon you, Monsignor Alonso, you are kind. Abbot Maiolus sends his warmest regards from Burgundy."

"Good, good. Shall we?"

The entourage falls in behind the three as they begin to walk their horses down the switchback leading out of the mountains, Monsignor Alonso between Brother Cleo and Ambassador Strobel to allow easier conversation during the remainder of the journey.

"I thought we might talk some about Córdoba. I can answer any questions you may have."

Strobel replies with a curt, "When will we see the caliph?"

Alonso's smile fades. "All in good time, Ambassador, all in good time. Such matters cannot be rushed in Córdoba."

Brother Cleo attempts to deflect the tension. "How many people live in Córdoba, Monsignor Alonso?"

Alonso's face brightens. "Please call me Alonso. Well, the last census, two years back this June, put the number at two hundred and ninety thousand. The largest city in Europe."

Brother Cleo whistles. "By far. Impressive. And the libraries, tell us about the libraries."

Alonso beams with obvious pride. "Cordoba's libraries are remarkable. Beyond remarkable. The caliph is a great patron of the arts. The Royal Library alone contains over four hundred thousand volumes, the largest collection west of Baghdad. They are organized by subject matter and housed in seven different buildings."

Both visitors offer only shocked silence. The largest secular library in Europe resides at the University of Paris and contains just over four hundred volumes. Cluny, which owns the largest monastic library, contains six hundred and seventy-three books.

Alonso continues. "There is the Library of Quranic Commentary, the Hadith Library, and the Sharia Library, all adjacent to the Great Mosque and convenient to the law courts. These three are the largest. Then there is the Poetry Library, the Library of Architecture, and the Mathematics Library, all within the Alcazar. This is where you both will stay. Then there is the Science Library and, of course, the famous Library of Medicine. Within Madinat al-Zahra is the Rare Books Library. The caliph holds his favorites close." He smiles.

Brother Cleo breaks the silence. "Excellent. I assume Abulcasis frequents the Library of Medicine?"

"Indeed he does, Brother Cleo. Abu al-Qasim, Abulcasis, is the royal physician to the caliph. A brilliant man and a teacher of great renown. You will like him." The two men exchange grins. "Beyond the Royal Library, there are an additional seventy odd smaller libraries within Córdoba proper that enjoy the caliph's patronage. Princes, even merchants and artisans, all collect books, and most have personal libraries within their homes. There are hundreds of copyists and scribes within the city and schools to train the next crop of translators."

Strobel responds, "Fascinating. Who pays for all this?"

Alonso laughs. "Taxes maintain the Royal Library and fund its acquisitions."

Strobel offers a sour retort, "Taxes on Christians, you mean."

Alonso's smile fades once more. "Partly. All People of the Book, dhimmi, do pay a *jizya* tax to live within Córdoba. Both Christians and Jews. But all citizens are taxed by the state, regardless of religion. Part of that tax goes to the Royal Library. But it also funds hospitals, homes for the poor, schools, even churches and synagogues."

Brother Cleo responds, "Interesting. So your congregation is able to worship in peace?"

"Within reason, yes. We may not attempt to convert, that is strictly forbidden, and we are subject to Sharia Law like all

Muslims, with several exceptions. But our churches are tolerated, accepted even. The same for Jews."

Peter Strobel remains silent, but he is frowning.

Alonso continues, "Bishop Reccimund sits on the Vizier Council, the caliph's Council of Ministers. He is vizier of Dhimmi, advisor on the caliphate's dealings with both the Christian and Jewish communities. And Samuel al-Tayyib, the royal librarian, is a Jew. As you will see, for any person with unique skills, there are few artificial ceilings imposed by religion in Córdoba."

Brother Cleo is pensive. "Very interesting ... and to my mind, quite refreshing." He offers a generous smile.

Strobel's face is set into a rigid mask, frown lines carved deep into plaster.

Brother Cleo is accustomed to rising before sunrise for *Prime*. He has washed his face, dressed, and reclines now on a floor pillow with his *Breviary* open on his lap, the single lit oil lamp spilling a meager but serviceable glow across the room. He has always enjoyed sunrise, a still and peaceful moment before the world awakes. This morning he is distracted, however, unable to focus on the familiar readings of the *Divine Office*.

From the Alcazar, where he and Strobel are quartered, to the Great Mosque is no more than a hundred paces. Their adjoining rooms on the third floor of the palace provide a generous, expansive view of the city. The Great Mosque is set prominently in the center foreground, a fact that Brother Cleo realizes is surely no coincidence. He can't help but smile as he imagines Strobel's disapproving frown.

As the monk tries once more to refocus his attention on the task at hand, a melodic sound weaves its way effortlessly into the room, commanding his attention. He looks to the window. A man's tenor, nasal in tone. An Arabic song. The words are difficult to untangle from the melody, but the song is unusual, magical; somehow beckoning. The man's fluid voice alternates between long sustained notes and a rapid undulating rhythmic trill. Then it stops. A moment later it begins once more, more urgent now in its summons.

Brother Cleo smiles with his recognition. The *adhan*, the Muslim call to prayer. He rises from his pillow and steps to the window, curious now. As he parts the curtains, the city is still locked in a pre-dawn ghostly gray. He looks to his right and scans the horizon, locating the faint red glow marking the spot where the sun will momentarily rise. He looks back to locate the source of the song. As the melody springs back to life, his eyes track to the top of the minaret set on the far left side of the Great Mosque. It is the tallest structure in the city. Brother Cleo cannot make out the *muezzin*, but the voice betrays the location where he must be standing. The massive dark monolith of the Great Mosque looms large beneath the prayer caller, the enormous doors open to welcome the thousands of the faithful.

Brother Cleo shakes his head in wonder, enthralled by the first sunrise of his first full day in a Muslim city rich beyond his wildest dreams with books filled with ancient lore.

Cravings

"Close your book and come sit with me, darling."

The boy, perhaps twelve, grudgingly looks up from the page, eyes his mother wearily, and returns to his reading.

"Hisham? Come." She pats the silk divan. "Come, my darling."

The boy rolls his eyes as he sighs, marks his place and closes the book, then rises and slowly crosses the room, collapsing heavily on the end of her divan, resigned to his torture. The light in the room is generous, softened by the warm glow of the alabaster-paned windows, polished thin enough to permit the passage of light, but blind to prying eyes. His hair is blond like his mother's, eyes bright gray, his features a pleasing blend of Arab and Basque.

There is an effeminate air about him somehow, perhaps the result of having lived his entire life sequestered behind the high walls of the royal harem, denied the raw pleasures of rough play with boys his own age. He is a child of books and imaginary worlds, and though he is approaching the threshold of puberty, he remains a pet of scheming eunuchs and concubines, a loose straw caught in the headwind of his mother's ambitions.

Her beauty has ripened gloriously with the years, a lush plum hanging heavy with sweetened juice; long blond curls, striking blue eyes, still very much the voluptuous Basque princess that Caliph al-Hakam II was so taken with in his youth. She remains silent as she stares at her son, appreciating, calculating. "Hisham, I believe the time has arrived for you to begin serious preparations for becoming caliph. You must learn the arts of leadership, my darling; administration, politics ... even war." She cocks her head just so as she admires her work.

The boy grimaces. "You know that such things hold no interest for me, Mother." The pitch of his voice matches his feminine aura. "I will study Sharia Law and the *Hadith*. I can already recite most of the *Quran* from memory. Besides, Baba is young. He has told me that there is no need to begin my training." His eyes silently plead.

"Yes, well, it is clear that your father is not interested in giving you a proper education in matters of state. Trust me, it is past time for you to begin. Therefore, I will see to it myself."

The distinctive knock at the door is muted, delicate, somehow tender. Mother and son break their stare and look to the sound. Her eyes brighten; his dim.

"Come, Jibril."

The door opens, permitting a small-boned wraith to slip effortlessly into the room. The man's effeminacy is visually arresting: his features attractive but decidedly girlish, his nails painted heavy purple to match his eye shadow. He is dressed in the long, flowing silk robe of a court princess, his hands and feet decorated with elaborate henna art like a bride at a royal wedding. His stride is feminine, the citrus-musk perfume stepping one pace to his front as he glides forward, declaring his presence. The head eunuch of the royal harem.

His voice is soft, slippery. "You sent for me, Sultana?"

"Yes, Jibril. Hisham and I were just discussing his education."

The eunuch tilts his head as he weighs her words, delicately sniffs the air, then offers a thin smile of understanding. "Wonderful news, Sultana."

She looks back to her son with narrowed eyes. Her tone sharpens. "Hisham, leave us." The boy now seems reluctant to move. Her tone flexes into a strung bow, the message unmistakable. "GO." The boy wilts, then rises, crosses the room to retrieve his book, and without meeting either of their stares, slinks out under drooped shoulders, the slamming of the door straining the limits of court decorum.

The silence afterward lingers.

She looks at the eunuch. "My son is not happy."

"Apparently not."

"I need your help, Jibril."

"Your wish is my command, Subh." He extends his arms outward, palms up, as he bows with mock ceremony, then nestles into the divan beside her with a telling familiarity.

"Hisham's education will require dexterity on our part, Jibril. Significant dexterity."

"Subh, you know that the caliph will fight this. He fears that a well-trained heir is something of a threat. Ironic given that Caliph Abd al-Rahman, may Allah rest his soul, was meticulous in training him for rule from a very young age." Jibril pauses to dredge for a memory. "As I recall, Subh, al-Hakam was on jihad with his father against Count Fernan Gonzalez when he first set his eyes upon you."

She lowers her eyes. "Those were better times."

"It is odd to me that our caliph is willing to put his lineage at risk. He is not a young man, as you know. And he has only one son. Should he pass from this world before Hisham is fully trained ...." The eunuch curls his lips provocatively. "Due to some unfortunate accident at court, say, or a riding mishap ... his legacy will be in jeopardy, the kingdom in peril. A dangerous gamble, in my opinion. One never fully knows the silent ... ambitions that roam Madinat al-Zahra." He offers a wry smile.

"I have given him his only son, yet he pays me no homage. None." She frowns. "I endure the mockery of the royal concubines —especially the young men. I have put up with his ... perversions long enough. It has been years since he has even touched me ... thank God for your attention to my ... needs."

The eunuch lays his henna-painted hand upon her thigh and begins to trace a circle with his thumb. "I live to serve, Subh." That wry smile returns.

"Try as he might, he will not deny me my due, Jibril. Mark my words, my son will be caliph. With or without my husband's consent."

The silence stretches taut.

Softly, he asks, "What exactly do you have in mind, Subh?"

They lock eyes. "I have in mind to seduce Muhammad ibn Abi Amir."

The eunuch arches both eyebrows. "Interesting ..."

"I will seduce him, and in exchange he will manage my accounts. That will pay him handsomely, and importantly will gain him entry to the royal harem. In return he will secretly instruct Hisham in the ways of rule while he is here. I will see that he is amply ... compensated."

"Very interesting—if dangerous." Jibril considers their victim. "Ibn Abi Amir is a handsome man, that much is sure, and of solid Arab lineage. He is intelligent, an expert in Sharia. And he is on the Vizier Council, though only in a minor role. A widower. Rumor has it that he enjoys the ... company of his female slaves. Important to us, he is of modest means. He needs gold if he is to rise in power at court." The eunuch muses. "It is not clear to me, however, that he could be tempted by a taste of the caliph's wife, even if he stood to benefit from her gold. It will all depend on his ambitions. Few things can be kept secret at court forever, Subh, and discovery would mean his certain death—after an elaborate emasculation, I am afraid." He stares into space as he calculates. "Perhaps with the right inducements ... but risky, very risky." He locks eyes with the sultana. "An intriguing plan, Subh, that much is certain."

"I want you to contact him, Jibril. Discreet channels, of course, should we feel the need to back away. Use Bundar. We must think of a way to lure him to the royal harem under the cover of night so that we might secretly meet and I can offer him my ... proposition. One he cannot afford to refuse."

The head eunuch beams now. "Subh, you know how I so enjoy a challenge."

She returns his smile. "Indeed I do, Jibril, indeed I do." She reaches down and slides his hand between her thighs.

Sutures

The priest and the monk stroll the short distance from the Alcazar to the Royal Hospital, a large, two-story building nestled near the city center. It is an hour past sunrise, the air still cool and fresh, pleasantly moist. Under the sun's intense yellow stare, dew vapors waft upward from the terracotta roof tiles of the buildings, sucked into the intense blue of the sky. A spring day filled with promise.

As the two enter the generous square they stop to admire the scene. The bustle and sounds of the vibrant city are awakening as dozens of hand carts moving to market rattle along the stone streets. Merchant wares are racked in elegant displays at the edges of the square, boards hastily chalked with specials of the day. Vendors tweak their merchandise, straightening here, rearranging there, picking a piece of lint, polishing a smudge with a moistened thumb.

Others loiter about in groups of twos and threes, idly conversing with their neighbors, catching up on gossip, slurping tea, laughing at bawdy jokes. The communal oven was stoked long before dawn, its bed of coals thick with crimson embers. Baking is in full swing already, the tenders shuffling the loaves a dozen at a time on flat wooden paddles in and out of the enormous masonry oven as the long line of customers continues to build. The heavenly aroma of fresh baked bread fills the square.

As the two men begin to weave their way through the throng, Cleo resumes his relentless barrage of questions, Alonso patiently answering one by one. At Cleo's insistence, they converse in Arabic. Cleo's command is fluid, then halting, as he trips on a difficult word or phrase, loses an idiom, then fluid once more as he pushes on through. He clearly has a gift for language. Alonso occasionally switches to Latin to clarify a point, then resumes in Arabic. Rarely does Cleo need a second pointer to hurdle the same stumbling block. A few more weeks and he will be accented but fluent, Reccimund's able tutelage of two years past shining brightly through the cracks.

Years of monastic life force Brother Cleo's hands behind his back, his eyes glued to the ground as he listens, absorbs, nods his understanding. He poses a follow-up question for clarification before moving on to their next topic. Alonso seems unaware that his hands carry half the conversation. The two men smile often, stopping now and then to share a laugh, dodge a cart, or stop to admire a vendor's wares. They obviously enjoy each other's company.

"So how many medical students does Abu al-Qasim instruct?"

"It varies, but he is intent upon training all of the caliphate's physicians, or at least those that work in the caliph's fifty hospitals. I would guess that at any given time there might be twenty, perhaps twenty-five, in training." Alonso stops to chuckle. "He calls them his children. He personally selects each one. Their basic instructions last one year, followed by a specialization of six months, then an apprenticeship with a senior physician for another six months. But their education is continuous. As soon as Abu al-Qasim feels they are ready he sends them forth to begin their service, but he visits each of them regularly to observe their technique and give them pointers. And he requires them to attend special refresher demonstrations to teach them the use of new instruments he has developed or show them new surgical procedures."

"Amazingly efficient. It is no wonder Arab medicine has advanced so quickly."

"There will be a demonstration tomorrow afternoon in the Royal Hospital." He halts, forcing Cleo to stop. "Abu al-Qasim has invited you to attend, Cleo. You are to be his honored guest."

Cleo beams. "Excellent. Excellent! Thank you for arranging it, Alonso."

"It was Abu Al-Qasim's idea. He is anxious to meet you, you know."

"The feeling is mutual." They resume their stroll. "I have heard rumors that he is writing a medical encyclopedia."

"Indeed. He calls it, *Katib al-Tasrif.*" Cleo is obviously struggling with the translation, so Alonso switches to Latin. "The Method of Medicine."

"Ahhh, I see. Good. How far into it is he?"

"Good question. Last I heard he had finished several volumes, but that was some time back. You will have to ask him." Alonso smiles, then lifts his palm to direct Cleo down the narrow street to their right.

The attendant remains mute as he leads them down the long narrow corridor, the only sound the quick *click-clack* of his wooden heels upon the marble floor. Closed doors line both sides of the corridor at every third step, the sequential Arabic numerals on the door placards rising as they pass; odd to the left, even to the right. Evidently, patients' rooms. It is still early and the corridor is empty, the morning bustle of nurses and physicians not yet commenced. As they pass through a tall double door the hospital's architecture changes; the regular array of doors replaced now with widely spaced, much larger doors, presumably opening into bigger rooms.

Alonso leans in and whispers, "Surgical theaters." Cleo nods.

They exit the building through an iron-covered exterior door into a small interior courtyard, turn right, pass through a narrow tunnel into a second, smaller courtyard, then turn left. They suddenly hear the muted but crisp rhythmic *ping ... ping ... ping ...* of a hammer working a piece of steel on an anvil.

The melody grows steadily louder as they approach a sliding door on the far corner of the courtyard, then abruptly halts, as if suddenly privy to the presence of intruders. Their guide grips the handle on the door, slides it open, then indicates that they should step inside. As they cross the threshold, the attendant steps back, slides the door closed behind them, and departs, his task complete. They have found the royal physician.

The room is dim. The two clerics stand motionless, letting their eyes adjust. The room is small and cramped with the feel of a cluttered workshop. Tall benches line the walls to their left and right, piled deep with books, all manner of blown glass vessels, dozens of pieces of scrap metal of various shapes and sizes, even a stone grinding wheel.

To their front, at the far end of the room, stands a rather frail-looking, gray-bearded man, his foot furiously working a floor bellow, pumping air into the open-faced charcoal furnace. The blackened chimney yawning above him exhausts soot from the room.

The man wears a leather apron and has a woolen mitt on his left hand, which is holding a thin, curved iron rod, its end buried in the crimson embers. With each step on the bellow, the spurt of fuel produces an echo pulse of pleasing crimson brightness. The man is not looking at the embers, however, but instead is intently studying a sheet of paper on a high table immediately to his right, his index finger resting on a drawing of some sort. To his left is the anvil, the source of the song, a large bucket of water set beside it. Next to these is a wide table decorated with a neatly arranged collection of hammers in various shapes and sizes, some massive, some tiny; a collection of files; and various other bending and shaping tools. A master metal-worker's toolkit. The only tidy spot in the entire workshop.

The two clerics exchange a smile, then Alonso clears his throat and says, "Master Al-Qasim?"

The man looks up from the drawing but does not seem to fully register the source of the disturbance. As he stares blankly at the wall his rhythmic foot pumping does not change pace.

He tries a little louder, "Master Al-Qasim?"

The foot pumping abruptly ceases and now the man swivels his head to locate the intrusion. A warm smile follows. "Ahhh, Monsignor! Good, good, I have been expecting you. Just a moment. Forgive me, I was lost in thought." He extracts the piece of iron from the fire, at its end a flattened loop of glowing orange. He steps to his left and dips the iron into the bucket to a truncated hiss and a burst of steam. He sets the object on the anvil, removes his mitt, then shuffles forward to greet his guests.

The smile has not left the man's face. "You must be Brother Cleo of Cluny. Welcome, welcome!" He spreads his arms then shrugs. "Excuse my mess. This workshop is my one indulgence. My children clean it but I just cannot seem to keep it neat. I have heard much about you, Brother Cleo. Welcome to Córdoba!"

Cleo bows and says, "Master al-Qasim, the honor is most definitely mine. What you have done in the medical arts is nothing short of remarkable. I hope to learn much from you."

"Yes, yes. Well, my children do most of the real discovery here. They do indulge me and let me play from time to time. Please, call me Abulcasis. That is the name I am known by in Europe, yes?"

Cleo smiles. "Indeed it is. I am afraid we have few masters of Arabic in the empire. Call me Cleo, please."

"Well, Cleo, your Arabic is quite passable. You have had good teachers."

"I have, indeed. First Bishop Reccimund, and now the monsignor, though he is a relentless taskmaster!" All three laugh.

Silent smiles settle upon the men. Finally, Cleo says, "I am amazed that you are skilled in the metalworking arts."

"Ahhh ... well, I have a great love for inventing new surgical instruments, you see. It is both my hobby and my passion. Fortunately, my children indulge me." He motions Cleo forward. "Come, look at my latest creation. Come, come." His excitement is contagious. Abulcasis shuffles to the anvil and lifts the forged object and hands it to Cleo. Alonso observes with a grin; he knows that the game is afoot. The monk studies the object. The piece stretches fingertip to elbow and is bent into a soft curve along its length. Halfway down the length, the metal angles sharply away from the shaft and parts into a swayed, flattened loop. The curves are precise but pleasing, somehow elegant.

35

"Can you guess its function?" He flashes an impish grin.

Cleo remains silent as he rotates the object in his hands and considers its possible purpose. Alonso's grin widens. The monk offers, "I would say some sort of grasping tool, but it seems too large for a surgical instrument."

Abulcasis is smiling, clearly someone who takes delight in all manner of surprises. "Good. Close, very close. It is not complete yet, you see. There will be a matching piece that mirrors this one, and the two will be joined at a hinge, with handles added. And it still must be ground smooth and polished." He pauses to allow this new information to sink in. After the silence stretches to a full minute, he gleefully says, "Give up?"

Cleo sheepishly grins. "I give up."

"It is an instrument for use in childbirth." The physician's hands are on his hips, his back straightening as he rises on his tiptoes. His triumphal stance.

"Ahhh ..." The monk looks puzzled.

The physician reaches for the object, grips the end of the instrument where the handle will go, then grips its imaginary twin and flexes the object about its future hinge point. It is clear now that the gentle curve of the loop is matched to the size of an infant's head, the sway of the shaft precisely designed to conform to the soft curves of internal female anatomy.

"It is designed to slip inside a woman who is struggling with a breech baby, to provide additional leverage on the baby's head during childbirth."

The monk blushes bright scarlet with the revelation. Alonso cackles. Abulcasis beams.

Cleo reluctantly chuckles. "I see. Yes, I see it now, yes." Abulcasis hands him the instrument again. He rotates it appreciatively, its intended function now obvious. He nods his head. "Ingenious. Clever, very clever indeed." He looks up to the royal physician. "But do you not risk injuring the child in such a procedure."

Abulcasis turns serious, all teacher now. "Any crude attempt to forcibly extract a baby from the womb can do great harm to both mother and child. In such births, death for both is the most common result. Even if the baby is pulled free, its brain is often damaged. With this new instrument, I think I have found a way to safely extract the baby without harming either mother or child." His glee is unmistakable. "Like all new surgical instruments, however, it must be carefully tested and refined. I have practiced this on corpses already to get the size and shape correct, and I have a patient presently nearing term upon which I will soon attempt its use."

The monk blanches. "Corpses?"

The patient teacher returns. "Cleo, even the ancient Greeks practiced their medicine on human corpses. It is the only logical way to refine surgical techniques. Animals will just not do. In the end it is the best way to serve our patients, to preserve and protect life." He grins. "Though it does present certain logistical challenges."

"Fascinating. This is not done in Europe. I would like to hear more."

Alonso raises both hands in surrender. "Gentlemen, I am afraid I must meet Bishop Reccimund shortly. He is just back from Granada. Master al-Qasim, may I leave Cleo in your able company?"

The royal physician beams. "Certainly, certainly, we are only beginning here. There is much for us to talk about. Give my best wishes to the bishop. And tell that rascal he owes me a visit. Now go, go!" He shoos Alonso.

Cleo chimes in enthusiastically, "I would be delighted to stay."

"Excellent. Then I bid you both a good day." Alonso turns to leave. As he slides the door closed behind himself, he grins approvingly. The two men are already hunched over the table studying the drawing of the instrument, Cleo's endless questions beginning to predictably unfurl. Abulcasis, the consummate teacher, delights in his new pupil's thrill of discovery. His hands flare and dance with drama as the myriad of explanations commence.

"I have good news, Ambassador. I have just come from a meeting with Bishop Reccimund. He tells me that an audience with the caliph has been arranged."

A long, exasperated sigh is followed by a prickly, "When?"

"Two days hence."

Strobel sneers. "Well, it is about time. I must tell you, Monsignor, that I have never been forced to wait for an audience with any ruler in Europe. Never once."

Alonso nods consolingly. "I understand, Ambassador, I understand. You must appreciate that the ways of the Umayyads are different from the rest of Europe. The caliph maintains a more ... eastern attitude towards meetings. I am sure the caliph felt that a certain ... formality was required. One fitting for the

Ambassador to the Holy Roman Empire. And that takes time to properly prepare, as I am sure you would agree."

Strobel sniffs the air as he frowns. "A poor excuse."

Alonso presses on. "The caliph has requested that Brother Cleo join us. He would like to hear more about Cluny Abbey." Strobel's frown deepens measurably, but he remains silent. "We will be summoned by a royal herald and escorted to Madinat al-Zahra. The Shining City is a league and a half's journey from the Alcazar. There you will meet not only the caliph, but also his entire Vizier Council. And tour the Royal Gardens, of course. They have a collection of most unusual plants and animals, you know." The ambassador's eyes narrow with suspicion. "Trust me, Ambassador, your visit will prove worth the wait."

"We shall see. I have seen all the finest courts of Europe."

"I can assure you that the Shining City has no equal."

The answering frown remains firmly anchored.

The room is arranged as a compact amphitheater, the ceiling rising far higher than one would naturally expect for a building this size, lending the space an oddly exhilarating, dramatic air. Four tightly-turned, semicircular terraces rise steeply from the white marble floor, one lifted high above the next, providing unobstructed views from any vantage point. On each terrace rests a neat arrangement of fluffed cotton floor pillows, offering comfortable seating for thirty.

At the center of the circle rests a large wooden rectangular table waist-high off the marble floor, and to either side two smaller, shorter tables. Upon one rests a diverse collection of metal instruments neatly arranged on a bleached linen sheet, some recognizable, some not; knives, pliers, thin-bladed saws, an array of clamps and tweezers, various sizes of hooked and bent needles, small spools of threading. The other table hosts a collection of two dozen blown-glass jars and bottles of varying shapes and sizes, some containing clear infusions of herbs, others partially filled with brightly colored distilled elixirs; several shades of pale blues and burnt yellows, even bright cherry. Beside the glasswork are stacks of thick cotton cloths, a basin of water, and a single table lamp with a blue-tinged, golden flame.

Around the central table on the three sides facing away from the circles of the amphitheater, lamp trees stretch high, their smokeless flames lending a steady radiance to the entire space. Save for the absence of actors and an audience the room could easily be set for a Greek tragedy or a poetry recital, perhaps the long-awaited performance of a famous lute virtuoso.

At precisely one hour past noon prayer, a bell down the hall sounds three times, and not a minute later the double door to the room swings opens, admitting a steady stream of well-groomed, bearded young men in plain gray robes. Their demeanor is universally serious at first glance, but a second study reveals a playful edge, their conversations familiar but hushed; expectant and excited.

A quick laugh by one is mock-shushed by another, an elbow to the ribs in the back row is passed man-to-man until the last in the chain grimaces and points accusingly at the leader staring nonchalantly at the ceiling, eliciting chuckles that slowly catch fire then spread. Suddenly, a wad of paper arcs high in the air, squarely striking the Lord-of-the-Front-Row on top of his head, producing sharp cackles.

A moment more and the room might devolve into mayhem, but beyond their view the doors creak open once more and a familiar shuffle instantly silences the room, though not before the last paper wad is launched. The tight ball again plunks the Lord-of-the-Front-Row to perfectly timed, barely squelched giggles, just as the royal physician enters the circle of the theater beside a strange man dressed in somber black.

Abu al-Qasim stops as the paper wad rolls to his feet. His head pivots ominously in slow motion as his eyes scan the crowd for the marksman, the scowl heavy upon his face. Their eyes remain glued to the royal physician, all humor and grins sucked from the room. He scrutinizes them for a moment more with a frozen frown, then breaks into a warm smile. The deep affection the pupils share for their teacher relights their faces.

He lifts his palms affectionately as his smile widens, then he nods his welcome and begins their cherished mantra, "My dear children."

They respond with one voice, "Our beloved master."

"Healing is your life's work."

The chorus says, "We will do no harm."

He replies, "You will honor your patients."

"No matter their station."

Together they chant, "Amen."

The monk is awestruck.

Abu al-Qasim lifts his palm to his companion and says, "Children, we have a special guest with us today." An expectant pause follows. "Brother Cleo from the Benedictine Abbey in Cluny.

Brother Cleo is a scholar and a healer and he is here to learn our medical techniques. Please make me proud." He beams.

Cleo bows. "I am honored to be with you."

Abu al-Qasim dramatically rises up on his toes as he continues, his excitement blossoming. "Today, I have selected an interesting case for us. Our patient is suffering from an acute obstruction of the intestine. A young man about your age." Several shift uncomfortably in their seats. "Without surgery he may die. Mishandle our instruments and we risk an infection that will surely kill him. You will see me use a heated iron to cauterize small blood vessels in his gut. Proper sterilization against infection will prove key in this case." He widens his eyes. "And of course there will be a refresher in proper wound suturing with catgut, a skill that many of you still need to practice, I am afraid." He pauses. "You will watch and you will learn, children, and then you will take turns practicing these procedures while I observe your technique. Alas, your unfortunate patient is to be a ... she-goat." Heavy groans echo off the walls.

It is an hour past midnight and the Rare Books Library in Madinat al-Zahra is fast asleep. The narrow hallway weaves its way through the maze of windowless rooms in the sequestered North Wing, a place off-limits except for a privileged few. The passage is lit only by the array of small octagonal skylights scattered high above, the full moon casting tight, angled columns of ghostly eerie glow upon the polished marble floor.

The man wears a concealing black robe and a black turban, his deeply-bronzed face and hands smudged darker still with oil-moistened charcoal. The intruder is frozen into a statue, listening intently for any hint of danger. Satisfied, he eases from the protection of the shadow, his slippered feet gliding on the slick marble as he eases around a pale column of moonlight and turns to peer past the doorway into the room.

The space is tight, the walls lined with floor-to-ceiling book cases, each crammed full with dusty volumes. A low-slung oval table surrounded by floor pillows is the only piece of furniture in the room, the pale octagonal moonbeam centered upon its dark surface as if by design. Bundar looks up and registers the unkind leer, then silently curses the sultana for her decision to launch a sortie under the stare of a full moon.

He sees that the hallway resumes its trek through the labyrinth on the opposite corner of the room. The man works his way between the angled beams then pauses at the shut door and cups his ears to listen. Nothing. His fingers move to the door latch with practiced dexterity, opening it without so much as a whisper. He slips around the corner and vanishes.

Three rooms later the intruder has reached his destination at the farthest end of the North Wing, now deep in the bowels of the Rare Books Library. Near the end of the hallway he sees the thin slit of soft lamp-glow oozing from under the closed door. He cups his ears and focuses. He can hear muffled voices. A hint of a smile settles on his face. The sultana's information was correct. As always.

The risk of discovery is acute now and his heart begins to race. He carefully works his way from shadow to shadow until he reaches the door. He leans close. The voices are louder now but he frowns as he realizes that he still cannot follow the conversation. Against his better judgment, he leans farther still to rest his ear upon the cool wood. The Arabic words come into sharper focus, but after a moment his frown returns as he realizes that his vantage is still imperfect.

The thick leather-bound codex from ancient Greece creaks its arthritic Coptic binding to whisper a gentle query about the unexpected visitor. Alas, his immediate neighbors only speak Arabic and Hebrew. From four books down, however, a heavily accented but passable reply thankfully emerges. The fluttered whisper of gossip begins to spread among the upper shelves.

"Aristotle was obsessed with vision. You recall --- ----------- -- --- ----- ---. -- makes sense to me that he would ---- -- --------- --- ---- -- ------ ---- ------ ------ of Forms."

The speaker is obviously pacing. When he faces the door, the intruder can make out his words. When he stops and turns, the words are lost. But he knows the voice. The Jew, al-Tayyib, the royal librarian.

A second person chimes in, "I say we test his proof of Proposition 3 by building our own darkened chamber. We have his design, more or less. What do we have to lose ... besides our beauty sleep?" Three distinct chuckles answer him. Four men. This one is young and clearly facing the door. The three must be seated around the table while the Jew paces.

A third person answers in unintelligible mumbles, "-- ----- ----- -- ---------." Facing away.

He guesses that the others must be al-Tayyib's assistants but fails to match voices with faces.

A fourth person. "I suspect it would ultimately have to be tested in daylight. That clearly presents logistical problems."

The Jew answers. "Perhaps we can begin at night with - ------ -- - ----, --- ---- decide upon our next steps. I think ..."

The hushed whispers from the upper shelves have grown furious now, a hotly contested multilingual debate on their best course of action. A moment more and the whispers damp out, evidently a decision made. The silence stretches tight.

The sharp slap of the volume on the marble floor is piercing in the stillness of the night, as startling as a close thunderclap on a cloudless summer day.

The voice in the room abruptly halts.

The intruder's panic is instantaneous, his eyes white with terror. But he is a professional and reacts at lightning speed, his motions quick and fluid as a leopard. He race-slides down the short hallway, and hand gripping the door jamb, swings himself into the previous room, heart pounding, and freezes into a wall ornament, his needle dagger now drawn across his chest.

There is a metallic double-clank of the door lock, then the sliver of lamp-glow under the door widens into a triangle, spilling light into the hallway. Samuel steps cautiously forward, suspicious of the empty passage. His eyes settle on the volume. He steps three paces down the hallway, lifts it from the marble floor, and rotates the book to read its spine.

"Galen of Pergamon." He nods his head approvingly then mutters, "How on earth did you get here, my friend?"

Samuel raises his eyes to find its home, his right eyebrow lifting as he meticulously examines the open slot for clues. His eyes track down the hallway. He frowns his distaste for unsolved puzzles as he begins timidly to step down the passage, the codex now tucked under his arm. He leans forward to peer into the room. Nothing but pale moonbeams. He chews his cheek in silence then shakes his head, sighs, and turns, retracing his steps.

"It was nothing. A book fell from the shelf."

Zahra

The three men walk their horses side-by-side behind the mounted herald and his two flanking standard bearers. The entourage exits the Alcazar and turns left, then soon approaches Córdoba's southwestern gate. Monsignor Alonso rides between Brother Cleo and Ambassador Strobel to make conversation easier, mirroring their entrance into the city two weeks back.

The trek to Madinat al-Zahra along the *Almunya* Way is a two-hour journey at their slow gait. The Almunya Way is not the most direct route to the royal palace, but rather the most splendid, the views carefully arranged to overwhelm and confound visiting dignitaries; calculated to impose a lasting impression.

There are laws forbidding a gallop on the Almunya Way, the lead-up to the Shining City decreed to be savored, slowly dissolved on the tongue like a sweet almond-honey morsel. Madinat al-Zahra is set like a gleaming white jewel chiseled into the rising brown hills of the Sierra Morena, perfectly placed to both amplify its ornate luster and express its command of the entire Guadalquivir valley.

The men are dressed in their finest attire, Cleo in Benedictine black, Alonso in priestly gray, Strobel puffed and plumed in his royal purple, red, and pearl-studded gold filigree. A small but elaborately wrapped package is strapped to the back of Strobel's saddle.

The three navigate the defensive double-switchback tucked within the tower topping the enormous city gate, arriving finally outside of Córdoba's imposing defensive walls. Guards pace the ramparts high above. The sun tracks behind the riders, its prying glare suddenly frustrated by the high wall. Daybreak was two hours ago, the herald oddly insistent upon the exact timing of their departure, an obvious calculation of some sort.

The Almunya Way is paved with precisely-fitted thick slabs of cut limestone, following the manner of the Romans who first settled here. Hexagonal stones are set deep and interlocked on a deep-layered bed of finely-crushed rock. Raised white marble curbs line the road and regularly-spaced culverts permit proper drainage. The Almunya Way is easily wide enough for five riding abreast. It is a road that would engender an appreciative nod from the architect of the Via Appia in Imperial Rome.

Just beyond the gate, as the expanse of the scene comes into full view, the herald stops to allow the visitors to absorb the amazement laid before them. Beyond a thin buffer on either side of the Almunya Way, as far as the eye can see is a rich tangle of buildings, all manners of sizes and shapes, abutted or with narrow streets between them. A metropolis outside the metropolis. Sprinkled throughout are prominent, high-walled compounds surrounding nests of two- and three-storied buildings, each compound with at least one tower, many with several. These expansive walled enclaves have the feel of fortresses. It is as if Córdoba did not end at the main walls in the usual manner of cities, but instead spilled beyond into a crammed patchwork of miniature city states.

As the two visitors continue to absorb the view, Alonso offers some explanation. "Each walled compound you see is called an 'almunya.' In Arabic, 'munya' means 'wish.' Think of them as country estates. They are elaborate retreats for the aristocracy of Córdoba, for royals and merchants, lawyers, even clerics. They leave Córdoba with their families to get away from the hustle and bustle of city life and court intrigue. To relax.

"Each almunya has its own private gardens, fountains, orchards, even stables. Some even have small mosques. The Arabs, especially, guard their privacy and insist upon enjoying a regular measure of reflective seclusion. Of course the towers offer expansive views, not only of Córdoba, the river, and Madinat al–Zahra, but also of their neighbors." He chuckles. "There is a competition of sorts for the tallest tower, the best view, the choicest building site, the lushest gardens. The Arabs insist on privacy, but they love to spy on their neighbors from behind drawn curtains. Elaborate belvederes for discreet viewing of neighbors are essential to any well-conceived almunya."

The two men remain silent in their awe. The wealth involved in the display is staggering. Finally, Strobel manages, "How many almunyas are there?"

"Hundreds, certainly. They span the distance between the city walls and Madinat al-Zahra, with the most expensive located along the banks of the Guadalquivir." He points to the sharp bend in the river to their left, in which nestles an especially plush almunya with a half-dozen towers. "That is al-Naura, the original almunya of Córdoba, built by the caliph's father, Abd al-Rahman III, to mimic the famous almunya in their homeland, al-Rusafa, the ancestral almunya of the Umayyad clan. Abd al-Rahman III is the original builder of Madinat al-Zahra." He points farther down the river. "And that is Arha Nasih, Caliph al-Hakam's almunya."

His finger tracks inland and rises. "See the almunya in the far distance?" The two men squint then nod. "That is the famous al-Rummaniyya of the vizier of the Royal Treasury, Durri the Small. Famous for its fish farms."

Strobel complains, "I could not see any of this from my room in the Alcazar."

"That is no coincidence, Ambassador. As you will come to appreciate, the Umayyads relish surprises for their guests. This is the first of many today, as you will soon see."

Strobel and Cleo exchange an uneasy glance.

To their left is the hunter green of the river, the harbor lined by docks and storehouses for transported wares, dozens of dhows and various vessels tethered tightly to the river's edge, workers busying about loading and removing cargo. Lifeline to the city.

Their eyes track back to the Almunya Way itself. To either side, set every hundred paces, are trees the like of which neither visitor has ever seen. Tall and gangly with branch-less trunks, topped by a fluff of spiky plumage high above.

Cleo breaks his silence. "Unusual trees. What are they?"

"The Arabs call them 'palms.' Imported at great expense from the land of the Umayyads at the far end of the Roman Sea. A reminder of the desert and their Arab ancestry, I suppose. Palms produce delicious dried fruit called 'dates.' Dark and intensely sweet. You will like them." He smiles.

The herald and the standard bearers resume their measured pace along the Almunya Way. The three men follow suit, in silence, the eyes of the two visitors darting right to left and back again as they struggle to absorb the scene.

A stone's throw ahead, the palm-lined road angles sharply away from the river and begins its slow rise into the hills towards the Shining City. As they round the bend, the herald stops once more as a dozen trumpets begin to sound off to the right. Madinat al-Zahra can now be seen rising in the distance to the front. Their first clear view of the Shining City, all gleaming white.

Alonso is grinning as his companions' mouths fall open with surprise. Along both sides of the road, and stretching into the distance, are members of the Royal Guard, set precisely seven paces apart. The Royal Guard is gloriously attired in flowing bright red robes with gold piping and gold sashes, jeweled dagger scabbards hanging at their waist. They stand at attention, tall and erect, expressionless, their ceremonial swords gripped with both hands in front of their chests and held high in the air.

As the trumpet anthem fades, Strobel looks at Alonso and whispers incredulously, "Do they stretch all the way to the palace?"

"Indeed."

"But that would require thousands."

"Indeed."

Cleo begins to chuckle with childlike delight. "Remarkable. Truly remarkable."

At that moment, a small army of young girls dressed in pure white robes, with olive skin and flowing raven locks, flit into the road from both sides in front of the entourage, not a whisper among them. Some of the girls pull white silk brocades from their woven baskets and fling them into the air, continuing this over and over as they move forward along the road, their baskets replaced by attendants as they are emptied. Other girls have baskets filled with red ochre flower petals, which they also launch into the air by the handful as they skip down the road. The entourage resumes its slow march in pursuit, the Royal Guard set as stone statues marking their passage. The horses clop upon limestone painted now in white and red ochre, the colors of the caliph.

Cleo continues his gleeful chuckle. Ambassador Strobel looks awkward and pinched, trapped between awe and the stiff formality mandated by his station. Alonso just grins.

The Almunya Way is now pointed squarely at Madinat al-Zahra, still half a league distant, but she is coy and only teases her voluptuous delicacies into view bit by bit. It is clear already, however, that Madinat is huge, a city in itself, its high white walls stretching east to west at least a quarter of a league. They cannot yet see what is behind the walls, except for the terracotta tiled roofs of the tallest buildings on the far side of the city that tiptoe into view as the palace gains altitude up the slope. Where the Almunya Way meets the Madinat's white wall they can see a large double gate with massive defensive towers set to either side. Dozens of red banners snake in the soft breeze. Evidently, their destination.

As the entourage works its way along the road, the visitors begin to relax and enjoy the scenery. The Royal Guard has become an ignorable fixture of their journey, and even the swarms of girls that continue silently to spray the road with red ochre and white no longer command their attention. An occasional head pops into view through a slit in the window curtains from the closer almunyas with a view of the road. The faceless heads assess the entourage for a moment then slide back into the shadows, seemingly uninterested.

To their right an elevated, open-arch aqueduct angles diagonally into view as it follows the gentle downhill slope from the mountains to the river. At regular intervals, small spillways controlled by levered wooden gates tap into the main flow and the cool water rushes down narrow troughs into the ground to disappear into buried culverts. The prominent sound of rushing water betrays the volume of the flow, and a soothing aquatic hiss seems to seep from the ground everywhere around them.

Cleo says, "Tell me about the aqueduct. It looks Roman in origin."

"Yes. That is one of the branches of the massive aqueduct system that feeds Madinat al-Zahra, the almunyas, even Córdoba itself. The locals call it the Aqueduct of Valdepuentes. It winds many leagues into the upper reaches of the Sierra Morena. At its source there is enough water to form a small river, then it breaks into dozens of feeder aqueducts like this one. Its construction does in fact date to the Roman era, though the Arabs have extensively refined it and extended its reach. As you will see firsthand, water is treasured here, and is an essential feature of the architecture throughout Madinat and Córdoba, presumably due to its scarcity in their homeland. All the palaces and almunyas, even most homes and businesses, enjoy indoor plumbing, complete with flowing water latrines."

Both visitors lift their eyebrows incredulously. They had assumed that the latrines in the Alcazar were for privileged guests.

"Water is tapped from the aqueducts then diverted into underground culverts and distributed in lead pipes. The latrine water ultimately empties into the river well below the city, while the house water is diverted after its use to power fountains and irrigate gardens and orchards. You will not find a cleaner or sweeter smelling city in Christendom." This observation is not lost on the two visitors. European cities reek of sewage and refuse, producing an unbearable stench in the summer swelter, and indoor latrines are virtually unheard of, even at court.

A massive arched stone bridge comes into view. The wide, cascading stream is spanned in the Roman style using carefully-cut rectangular white limestone blocks, *ashlars*, formed into an unusual self-reinforcing horseshoe arch, a feature that is decidedly un-Roman.

"This is called the Bridge of Maria Ruiz. The Umayyads are accomplished builders."

Cleo queries, "Who was Maria Ruiz?"

Alonso shrugs.

As their mounts clop up and over it, Cleo admires the stonework. "Exquisite construction. It will last a thousand years."

Alonso smiles. "No doubt."

The ambassador answers with a frown.

The Almunya Way terminates into a large circular plaza paved in white marble and ringed by the Royal Guard. Hundreds of the bright red soldiers adorn the ramparts of the white palace walls, their silent watchfulness purposefully menacing.

The entourage stops behind the herald just as they enter the plaza, the visitors' tension wrung tight as their hearts begin to race with nervous energy. The conversation fades as the monk and the ambassador survey the scene.

Alonso breaks the trance. "This is the Bab al-Sura, 'Gate of the Statue,' the formal entrance to Madinat al-Zahra." He lifts his palm to direct their eyes to the central feature of the plaza, a large square basin of unusual green marble. In the center of the shimmering water, raised high on a pedestal, is a life-sized gilded sculpture. A standing woman, posed suggestively, one hand playfully on her hip, her other arm outstretched, beckons with her hand. She is nude, her pleasing feminine curves more than generous, her enticing golden curls trailing down her back to her ample bottom. The nipples on her full breasts are pronounced, stiff. Her lips are parted seductively, as if she is wooing her lover. A Greek Siren.

Alonso is discreetly observing Cleo as the monk appraises the sculpture. The closer the monk looks, the deeper his blush grows; but he does not avert his eyes.

Alonso laughs loudly. "Meet Zahra. Talisman of the Shining City. She is the namesake of Madinat al-Zahra, of course." He turns to the Ambassador. "Zahra means 'shining' in Arabic, and 'madinat' is 'city.' The Shining City. Zahra was the favorite concubine of Caliph Abd al-Rahman III and later became his wife. Ironically, a Christian princess from the Navarre. Legend has it that the caliph was so taken with her that he promised her the world's largest jewel if she would join his harem. Madinat al-Zahra is the result." He chuckles. "Or so the story goes. In any case, she was quite a woman, as you can easily see. Supposedly, the sculpture is a true likeness."

Cleo just nods and blushes. The ambassador predictably frowns, then mutters under his breath, "Obscene."

Cleo asks, "Is she still alive?"

"No. This is all that remains of Zahra. Needless to say, she has both her admirers and her detractors. The *imams* despise the display of flesh, of course. But the royal court and the caliph believe she brings luck to the city, and she is thus revered ... though most will not admit this publicly. Personally, I rather fancy her!" He laughs loudly.

Behind the fountain, the heavy metal gates begin to creak open along a vertical slit but stop when the split is just wide enough for a man to pass. The visitors stiffen in their saddles.

A middle-aged man strolls out. His gray-flecked beard is neat, close-cropped. He wears a purple silk skullcap and is dressed in a purple woolen cassock trimmed in black silk. Around his neck hangs a pectoral cross. A large gold ring with an inset ruby adorns his right hand. The attire of a bishop. The man smiles warmly as he approaches the entourage.

Alonso makes eye contact with the bishop and nods, then says to his companions, "Shall we dismount, gentlemen?" He makes the introductions. "Bishop Reccimund. May I present Ambassador Peter Strobel of the Holy Roman Empire."

Strobel bows and answers in his finest Latin. "Excellency. The emperor sends his warmest regards." Reccimund responds with an amused grin.

"Please convey my best wishes to the emperor. Forgive my delay in meeting with you. I have been away in the south on the caliph's business. I am pleased to say that he has provided funds for the renovation of the church in Granada." Strobel does not respond but his demeanor oozes disapproval.

Alonso continues, "And you know Brother Cleo of Cluny." The bishop's smile widens as he steps forward and hugs Cleo, who can't help but laugh.

Reccimund switches to Arabic. "And how is my star pupil? Practicing, I trust!"

Without hesitating, Cleo responds in flawless Arabic, "I am having a marvelous time in Córdoba, Excellency."

"Oh, you know better than that, Cleo. I am simply Reccimund, no more."

Cleo chuckles. "Very well, Reccimund, very well. Alonso has been a wonderful host. I have met Abulcasis, a marvelous teacher, and I have already experienced a surgical demonstration. The Arab advancements in the medical arts are extraordinary!" His smile grows wider, all boyish enthusiasm. "And I have experienced the *hammam*." He gushes, "Twice. Remarkable!"

"That was only a taste, Cleo, only a taste. We have so much to show you. And how is Abbot Maiolus?"

"Very well, thank you. He still brags to anyone who will listen about the cache of books you brought him on your last visit." Reccimund responds with a bright cackle. "He sends his warmest greetings."

"I have prepared another cache for him, even bigger this time. Some Arab love poetry I have translated, and of course my new book, the *Calendar of Córdoba.*"

Alonso clears his throat to remind Reccimund of their guest.

He turns to Strobel and switches back to Latin. "My apologies, Ambassador. I had forgotten that you are not conversant in Arabic. A pity." Strobel struggles to straighten the growing downward curl of a frown. Reccimund opens his arms in welcome. "You are both in for a treat today, gentlemen. I will be your host as we tour the Shining City. But first, we are expected at a formal audience with the caliph and his Vizier Council. You will be amazed at the palace. A great many surprises await you. Come, come, they are expecting us. Come."

He leads the men to the crack in the gate. Just as the four step into Madinat al-Zahra, an unusual horn sounds from somewhere deep in the palace, not with the shrill of a trumpet, but instead with a regal, deep-throated bellow in a pitch so low they can feel it in their guts. The Horn of Isarfil.

Rumblings

"Tell me of Algeciras, Imam. My parents are well?"

Muhammad ibn Abi Amir and Imam Abd al-Gafur recline on divans set in a tight V for intimate conversation. A small triangular table fits elegantly in the gap between, permitting easy reach of the silver tray of dried dates and roasted almonds. The imam first inhales the honey-mint tendrils rising from his cup, then touches his lips to the tea, delicately sipping to avoid a burn. He pops several almonds into his mouth and crunches. Ibn Abi Amir sips wine from a crystal goblet, patiently waiting for the imam's reply. The atmosphere is relaxed, familial.

The imam finally stops chewing and looks up. "They are in good health, Muhammad, good health. Your father is a daily fixture at the mosque these days. You heard that he finally stopped his law practice?"

"Yes. Mama wrote to me."

"He has time at last to help me at the madrasa." The imam chuckles. "He relentlessly quizzes my young pupils on their Hadith, and their memorization of the Quran. And he hawks over my legal assistants to ensure a proper preparation of our documents for court."

Ibn Abi Amir smiles.

"Your mother ... well, your mother is the same. She prays for you each day, Muhammad, and the children. Especially Rayhana. She wonders aloud when you will return to Algeciras and bring her grandchildren home."

Ibn Abi Amir's expression hardens. "Madinat al-Zahra is my home now, Imam, you know that. Our caliph requires my services."

The man searches for the right words, his tone softening. "She also insists it is time for you to marry again, Muhammad. It has been six years since Rayya passed, may Allah bless her sweet soul. She says the children need a mother."

Ibn Abi Amir's face freezes into a mask, but he does not respond.

The imam chooses a safer subject and deliberately brightens his tone. "You have done well for yourself, Muhammad. The grand imam speaks highly of you. Imagine, only five years in Córdoba and already a vizier on the caliph's council. Impressive."

A whiff of tension slides between Ibn Abi Amir's words, stiffening his syllables. "A very minor vizier, Imam. One thing I have learned is that power at court requires gold. And many well-connected friends. Of the former I have precious little; of the latter, well, let us say that my list of friends is growing by the day."

The two fall silent.

Ibn Abi Amir forces himself to relax. "How long will you be staying in Córdoba?"

"Several weeks. I have some research to do in the Sharia Library. I need background material on several interesting cases."

"I see. I will speak with the royal librarian to ensure you have access to all that you need."

"Thank you, Muhammad, that would be most helpful." The imam's eyes track to Ibn Abi Amir's hand. "I see that you are drinking wine now ..."

Ibn Abi Amir eyes his goblet. The stiffness between his syllables returns. "Watered-wine, Imam. It is customary at court."

"Yet, forbidden by the prophet."

"Well, when at court, Imam, one must sometimes bow to the wishes of one's superiors."

The imam nods. "Perhaps ..."

"The caliph himself partakes. Córdoba is not Algeciras, Imam."

"Yes, I had noticed ..."

At that moment, the door to the room flings open violently to a feminine squeal. She races across the room for the door on the opposite side, curls flying, laughing hysterically, her younger brother giving frantic chase. They are clearly oblivious that their father is entertaining a visitor.

Ibn Abi Amir instantly rises, hands joining his hips as he shouts, "Rayhana! Khalil! What is the meaning of this?" The imam is beaming, completely amused.

The two come to an abrupt, wide-eyed, sliding halt, and then panic sets in when they see their father's face. And then his guest. Rayhana tries to squelch her laughter but it trails off in jerks and jolts, lapsing first into a dimpled grin, then settling into a forced mock-serious expression as the two of them stand at rigid attention in the center of the room.

The son clears his throat. "My apologies, Baba." He looks at his sister and scowls. "Rayhana stole my letter from a ... friend. I was ... uhhh—trying to—retrieve it." Rayhana is staring at the floor, wrestling with her grin. In her hand is a crumpled piece of paper.

Their father relaxes, but he does not attempt to hide his disapproval. "Khalil, I expect more of you. Rayhana, you know better. Give the letter back to your brother. Now."

She sheepishly hands it over, then blurts out, "But Baba—"

He raises a hand to stop her. "Rayhana. This is finished." His eyes widen to make sure she doesn't mistake the message.

He turns to their guest, who has now risen, smile intact. "You both remember Imam Abd al-Gafur. He is visiting from Algeciras. He has brought news of your *jiddo* and your *tetta*." Khalil and Rayhana smile and bow.

The imam chuckles. "My, my, how you children have grown. He levels his palm at his waist. Khalil, you were a child when you left us. Now look at you! Dear boy, you have grown into a young man! You look just like your jiddo; the spitting image." Khalil meets the imam's eyes, obviously pleased. "And Rayhana! What a beautiful young woman. No doubt the young men of court are absolutely dazzled." She blushes deep scarlet and settles her eyes on the floor. "And where is Salim?"

Ibn Abi Amir answers, "Salim boards at the madrasa in the city. He is second year. He comes back for a brief visit once a month."

The brother and sister dare not move without a formal dismissal, but they are clearly straining to vanish.

Ibn Abi Amir makes them suffer a long moment of tense silence before he offers his reprieve. "Khalil, Rayhana, you are excused. Behave yourselves. And tell Hayal that the imam would like more tea."

As Rayhana brushes past her brother, she discreetly pinches him on the back of his arm then speed-walks for the door. He flinches, then gives chase. Fortunately, this last exchange is lost on Ibn Abi Amir as he returns to his seat, but the imam takes it all in with a chuckle.

The two men settle back into their divans.

"The children have grown up, Muhammad. I feel old." He sighs. "Five years seems like an eternity. Rayhana is as beautiful as her mother. How old is she now?"

"She will be eighteen next month."

"I am surprised she is not yet married."

Ibn Abi Amir frowns. "Trust me, Imam, the girl has no interest in men. Her only love is reading. Books, always books."

The imam laughs. "She is a smart girl, Muhammad, what do you expect? You should see that she is educated. What harm can it do?"

Ibn Abi Amir's expression hardens. "She is educated enough. Her life is already spoken for. When the time comes she will help me solidify a key alliance, join my family to a powerful benefactor; preferably an old and rich benefactor. I must have gold. I have my eye on several patriarchs already. Her beauty will play well in that chess match."

The imam's eyes widen with surprise as the lines of his smile fade, but he remains silent. He sighs heavily. "Rayya would not approve, Muhammad."

As the two lock eyes, Ibn Abi Amir's expression becomes cold, dangerous even. "Yes, well, Rayya is gone. I have to think of what is best for my family now. When the time comes, Rayhana will walk the path I choose for her. Mark my words, Imam, the family Abi Amir will soon be a force to be reckoned with in Madinat al-Zahra."

Rayhana is dressed in a long white cotton gown and her bedclothes, and sits, back rigid, on a short stool as her lady-in-waiting works a brush through the tangles of her long brown curls.

"Your hair is so tangled, Rayhana." The woman shakes her head. "As usual. I should braid it during the day when you are out so we could both avoid this mess in the evenings."

Rayhana winces as the brush pulls through a knot. "Yes, Durr."

"You are a young woman now, Rayhana, and your looks should matter more to you. I see the young men of court stare as you pass."

Rayhana frowns.

"Yet you show complete disinterest. Which only increases their curiosity, of course." Durr grins. "Moths to a flame, my dear. Mark my words, soon they will find their nerve and come calling."

Rayhana changes the subject. "Durr, guess what I learned about Khalil today?"

Durr frowns at the familiar tactic but relents. "Tell me."

"He has been writing letters to the elder daughter of Durri the Small, the vizier of the royal treasury. Maryam. And she wrote him back! Khalil pretends she is only a friend, but I can tell he has feelings for her. And her words were encouraging."

"If she is leading him on without her father's permission, she plays a dangerous game."

"Mmm ... Mama always told me I would be free to marry for love, as she and Baba did."

Durr stops brushing. "Rayhana. That was a long time ago. And we were in Algeciras then, not Córdoba. Court life is different and you should know that. Here, marriage arrangements are made to seal political deals, to join families in alliances."

Rayhana hears the change in her voice, looks over her shoulder, and sees Durr's serious expression. She smiles. "Do not worry, Durr, I have no intention of marrying any time soon."

Durr's expression does not relax but instead settles into troubled concern. She begins to brush again in silence.

Rayhana lies on her side, head propped in her palm, the heavy volume splayed open on the edge of her floor mattress. The lamplight lends a soft, intimate glow to the room. She devours the words a fistful at a time, lost in the dunes of the Egyptian desert. It is late in the evening, her permitted single hour of bedtime reading stretched beyond two.

"Let me guess, Rasha, reading again?"

She frowns at the interruption but catches herself and turns to her father, smiling at his pet name for her, 'young gazelle.' "Yes, Baba. Ibn Abd al-Hakem's *History of the Conquest of Egypt, North Africa and Spain*. Fascinating stuff. I am beginning to understand how our family ended up in al-Andalus."

Her father's face is expressionless. "A worthy subject. Our Arab roots are long and deep, Rasha." He eases into the room and settles cross-legged on the floor beside her mattress.

She marks her page and closes the codex, then rolls over to the edge of her bed, palm back on her cheek. "It was good to see Imam Abd al-Gafur. I had forgotten what he looked like."

"Well, it has been five years, and you were young." He falls silent.

She studies his face. "You seem preoccupied, Baba. Is anything wrong?"

He forces a thin smile, but he is obviously troubled. "No, Rasha, I am fine." Silence. "I have been thinking about your future, Rayhana ... and about Algeciras ... and days of old." More silence.

Then she adds, softly, "And Mama."

He looks up. "Yes, and Mama. I know you miss her."

Rayhana's voice flushes with emotion. "Yes." She falls silent as she imagines her mother.

Ibn Abi Amir gives her space then straightens his back and offers his rehearsed words. "You are a woman now, Rayhana. And already well beyond the age of marriage. I will begin to look for a suitable match for you."

Her face hardens as her nostrils flare. She sits up and faces him. "But I am not ready for marriage, Baba. Not nearly ready. And besides, I have not found anyone that even remotely interests me. Boys at court are so tedious."

The tension rises in the room, his body stiffening with resolve in the face of open dissent. The lamp flame flickers its surprise at the quick turn of emotion. "Daughter. Listen carefully. I will be the one to choose your mate, not you. You will marry when I feel the time is right. And that time is sooner, not later. You will obey my wishes and honor your family."

Her face flushes with anger as her heart begins to pound, but wisely she holds her tongue. When she recovers her composure, she says evenly, "Mama assured me before she died, Baba, that I would be free to marry for love." She can't keep her voice from rising. "And only when I decided I was ready. She promised, Baba, she promised!"

He hardens into iron. "She was not in a position to promise anything, Daughter. I will wed you to whomever I feel best serves the interests of our family."

She is livid but does not respond. After a brief wrestling match she loses control, shakes her head violently, and blurts out, "Then I will marry a *saqaliba*! I trust that meets with your approval, or must I also bow to your sacred Arab bloodline?!"

His command of his temper is normally steadfast, but he is seething now and hisses, "How dare you! No daughter of mine will ever marry a slave, no matter his station at court. Do not even joke about such things. You owe your life to this family, Rayhana, and to me, and you will act in ways that honor the family, AND ME!" He rises without another word and strides from the room, slamming the door behind him.

Her eyes are full and her hands are shaking, the dragon of despair curling close and resting its heavy claws upon her shoulders. She has not tasted such dark hopelessness since her mourning of her mother's passing. As her tears begin to streak her cheeks she pleads with a whisper, "Mama, I need you. Mama, come to me. Come to me, Mama. Please." She pushes the codex roughly onto the floor and buries her head into her pillow as she sobs.

It has grown late and still he sits. The muffled cries from Rayhana's room have mercifully ceased. The home is silent as a graveyard, but the stillness is strung tight, infused with discomfort.

Ibn Abi Amir frowns as he realizes that he has been stuck on the same page for twenty minutes with still no inkling of the nuances of the legal argument presented. He marks his place and closes the book, then turns and searches the deep gold of the lamp flame for some unseen hint at life's mysteries. He resents the fact that unhappy females can evoke such unease in him. He sighs heavily and wills himself to a lighter mood, in need of some interesting distraction.

A moment more, then, softly he calls, "Hayal?" Slightly louder, "Hayal?"

His slave emerges in her bedclothes, slipping silently in from a side door. "Yes, Master?"

He motions. "Come."

She hesitates for only an instant.

"Come, Hayal, my tea is cold."

He studies her as she approaches; the long blond hair, the full breasts, those lovely hips. A fine investment. Her eyes remain glued to the floor, pleasingly submissive as always, allowing him ample room to drink in her generous curves. He wonders to himself why all women can't be so demure, so obedient. He feels the familiar stirring, the pleasant gnaw of desire in his gut, as he recalls the faint blond down gracing the small of her back, the pleasing stiffness of her nipple between his lips.

As she reaches for the teapot, he unexpectedly raises his hand to meet hers. She freezes. He tenderly holds her delicate fingers and begins to lightly stroke her index finger with his thumb. She reluctantly looks up into his hungry gaze, her face expressionless.

He swallows hard, then says, "Hayal, I am retiring to my room now. Please bring my tea to me there."

She pauses just a moment longer than necessary, then softly says, "Yes, Master."

The silence has stretched to three days, one-word answers to direct questions the extent of their conversations; otherwise nothing. Her brother is away for the evening and the two of them are stranded at the table in silence. He studies her, resentful of the torture she so easily brings to bear. Just like her mother. Decision made, he straps on some cheer, ready to hoist the white banner. "Rasha?"

She looks up from her plate to meet his gaze but does not respond, her expression blank.

"I have some good news for you."

Her heart begins to pound as she anticipates the hammer-fall.

He casually smiles, trying to lighten the mood. "I spoke yesterday with Samuel al-Tayyib, the royal librarian."

Rayhana relaxes her shoulders, her dilated pupils fixed on her father, her face unreadable.

"He has made arrangements to allow you access to the Rare Books Library ..." He lets the words trail off, hoping to elicit a favorable response. To no avail. He adds, "According to the rules of our original agreement, of course. You may begin tomorrow."

She continues to stare at him then drifts back to her plate as she weighs his words. She sees through the obvious ploy, of course. She does not look up again but a moment later whispers, "Thank you." She lifts a forkful of food to her mouth.

He smiles at the predictability of the miniscule size of the morsel she tosses back but is confident that his foot is now safely wedged in the door.

Ibn Abi Amir stops his nervous pacing to thumb the sleep from his eyes. "Tell me again exactly the words he used."

"He said, 'I have a message from my master that must be placed directly into the hands of your master. No one else.' I said, 'And who is your master?' He replied, 'The guardian of the royal harem.'"

"How did he find you?"

"I was coming back from a midnight meeting with some of our ... eyes in the city. I rounded a corner and there he was, blocking my path, silent as an assassin. I drew my blade but he raised his hands in peace and spoke his words. Then he handed me the scroll and vanished. I came straight here."

"Good, Aslam. You did well."

Ibn Abi Amir stares into space as he considers Aslam's report. The thin scroll remains clenched in the palm of his hand, unopened. He brings the scroll close once more so he can study the unbroken seal.

"Jibril al-Azhar. Head eunuch of the royal harem. Someone to be respected, Aslam, feared even. A powerful ... man. He has eyes and ears throughout Madinat al-Zahra and the city. This is odd. Troubling. What would the head eunuch of the royal harem want with me, I wonder?" He breaks the seal with his thumbnail, unrolls the thin scroll, then reads the precise dots and swirls of the finely-wrought Arabic calligraphy. Aslam discreetly holds his position at arm's length, affording his master privacy.

Peace be upon you and your family. A friend desires a meeting with you to discuss a certain business proposition. Due to its sensitive nature this meeting must take place in the royal harem, and as you can imagine, will require the utmost discretion on your part. I will guarantee your safe entry and return. Have your man deliver your reply to my man at the same time and place tomorrow evening. Instructions will follow when appropriate. I look forward to your favorable reply. J.

Ibn Abi Amir reads the scroll twice, then steps to the table and lights the edge of the paper on the lamp flame, dropping it to the marble floor when the black edge racing ahead of the golden spurts of flame reaches his fingers. As the flame flickers out, he grinds the ashes with the heel of his boot. He again stares into space as he absorbs the many implications, then begins to pace to steady his thinking.

"Interesting, very interesting. Aslam, we are done here. Come see me late tomorrow morning. I must carefully consider my reply." As the man turns to leave, Ibn Abi Amir adds, "Not a word to anyone of the encounter or the scroll."

Aslam nods, insulted that his master would feel the need to state the obvious. He turns and slips from the room back into the black stillness of the moonless night.

Eden

As the Gate of the Statue creaks closed behind them, the four men step through a smaller secondary, horseshoe-shaped door into a large rectangular chamber bathed in twilight. Reccimund leads, followed by Cleo, Strobel, and then Alonso. Strobel carries the small package, which he tucks into a hidden pocket within his robes. The only illumination in the room comes from a lattice of narrow slits that span the ceiling high above them: pour holes for boiling oil and Greek fire should the outer gates fail.

To their front is a solid ashlar wall, giving the illusion of a dead end. Reccimund leads them through a small exit door to their right. The room shrinks into a head-high passage only wide enough for two to stand abreast. After four paces the passage turns left, then left again, then right, broadening once more into another large, dimly-lit ashlar chamber before exiting through a metal-reinforced horseshoe gate into the bright sunlight. The classical Umayyad defensive tower-gate architecture, impregnable under assault.

The men pause to let their eyes adjust then begin to twist their heads to study the scene that unfolds lavishly before them. Two dozen red-plumed royal archers look down from above, expressionless, their unstrung ash bows strapped at angles across their backs, quivers on both shoulders chock-full of iron broadheads, the red-feather fletching matching perfectly their uniform piping.

A white marble road five paces wide and set orthogonal to the outer walls of Madinat al-Zahra leads due north into the palace grounds, the Royal Guard at their statue-best once again lining either side of the path, but much denser now, as if to announce the nearness of their final destination. The marble road is arrow-straight, stretching for five hundred paces before it ends at another gate, this one set in a tall, distinctive red ochre and white striped horseshoe arch on the extreme right side of another high, white ashlar wall, obviously a walled inner compound of some sort. Some distance behind the wall, tiled roofs tease the eye as they climb up the wide terraces cut into the slope.

Reccimund explains, "The secondary wall surrounds the Alcazar, the royal palace. To the front of the Alcazar are the Royal Gardens and a pavilion known as the Hall of Treasures. We will visit that first. On the terrace behind are the many buildings of the royal court, including the Hall of Abd al-Rahman III, where our audience with the caliph will take place."

Cleo asks, "What sorts of buildings occupy the royal court?"

"Well, besides the Hall of Abd al-Rahman III, there is the Royal Treasury, the Rare Books Library, the villas of the Vizier Council, the caliph's suites and his various audience chambers, and the Royal Baths." He grins. "And of course the Royal Harem." Cleo blushes as Strobel sneers.

Reccimund points just to the right of the horseshoe gate. "The Alcazar even has its own private mosque for the royal family and their favorites. Just there, see?" Cleo nods. "It is known as the Aljama Mosque. Of course there are dozens of administrative buildings required to run the kingdom. Some of the more important are within the Alcazar, but most spill out into the *medina*. The royal mint is there, for instance."

He sweeps his hand to their right. As the medina stretches up the terraced slope, it reveals a dense, endless maze of multi-storied buildings leaning in over narrow paved streets. The buildings are constructed from the white limestone ashlars quarried nearby, with terracotta roof tiles. The white buildings have a neat, manicured look, giving the remarkable appearance from the river of a gleaming white city set high upon a hill. Occasional public squares break up the building maze, each adorned with a flowing fountain, stone benches for lounging, stalls for vendors to hawk their wares, and clutches of skinny cypresses straining for the sky.

The medina is crammed into the entire eastern half of Madinat al-Zahra, ending abruptly at the upturned flattened hand of the city wall and truncated on its western edge by the marble road upon which they now stand. The buildings are meticulously decorated, flowers spilling luxuriously from window boxes, a strong preference given to stately red ochre geraniums mixed with waterfalls of white leadwort: colors of the caliph.

People busy about their work, narrow pushcarts clogging the streets and squares, but while the medina is crowded with traffic, it exudes a relaxed, comfortable feel, issuing an invitation to browse and chat. The smell of fresh leather rests heavy in the air, mingled with baking bread, roasting meats, drying herbs, and the faint, pleasing gaminess of animals.

Reccimund allows his visitors time to absorb the scene set before them. "The medina of Madinat al-Zahra is a small, self-contained city. Everything that Córdoba has, Madinat has also, though in miniature. Come, you will see." Reccimund motions them forward.

As they begin to walk, Cleo asks, "How big is Madinat al-Zahra?"

"There are nearly three-hundred *arpents* bounded by the outer walls."

"And how many live here?"

Reccimund smiles at the monk's natural inquisitiveness. "A good question, Cleo. I would guess maybe five thousand live and work in the medina with another three hundred in the Alcazar. And a garrison of Royal Guard, which are said to number four thousand."

Cleo whistles.

Strobel frowns.

As they continue their walk, Reccimund sweeps his hand to the left to guide their eyes. "The Royal Orchards. Almonds, cherries, pomegranates, pears, apples, olives, vineyards ... and of course date palms, a specialty of the Umayyads, as I am sure Alonso told you." He points. "Beyond are paddocks for horses, forests for game, even fish farms. The royal court does enjoy its cuisine."

Cleo points. "What is the large run of buildings at the far western wall?"

"Garrisons, stables, and parade grounds for the Royal Guard."

As the men approach the second wall a penetrating, guttural roar issues off to their left from just beyond the walls of the Alcazar. Cleo and Strobel halt, their eyes wide with surprise. A million years of instinct orchestrate their movements. The roar is unmistakably proud, a throaty greeting of a large carnivore in search of its prey. A second later there is an answering roar. Cleo and Strobel involuntarily take a step back. Reccimund and Alonso exchange grins.

Reccimund breaks the tension. "One of the caliph's many surprises. He keeps a zoo of rare animals. A hobby of his. You just heard his pair of African lions. He calls them the 'King of Beasts.' Alexander and Xerxes."

Strobel and Cleo look confused and wary. They have no idea what a lion is, but their imaginations easily visualize a beast with enormous fangs and a taste for men.

Reccimund and Alonso laugh. "You will see. Not to worry. They are kept safely within a high-walled compound surrounded by a moat. Come." Cleo attempts an awkward chuckle, and reluctantly the men begin to move forward once more.

———— ◎ ————

The long accompaniment of the stoic Royal Guard ends at the horseshoe gate, subtly amplifying the anxiety Cleo and Strobel already feel, as if their protection within this strange place has been lifted, exposing them to danger. This cleverly timed transition from a sense of relative security to being suddenly ill at ease is no coincidence, the intent obvious to all but first-time visitors. The four are suddenly on their own. They move through the gate and step into another walled compound, this one arrayed on a single flat terrace, a perfect square two hundred paces on each side. Not a single person is in sight.

Cleo's mouth drifts open. He nervously whispers, "My God ... Eden."

Strobel is wide-eyed but silent.

The entire walled space is a lush garden paradise, precise in its layout and fastidiously manicured but flowing, unstudied in its elegance. It is opulent but restrained with a hard-to-define but profound sense of complete harmony and peacefulness. Birds produce a cacophony of merry chatter, their heads snapping in unison to track their unexpected guests, the morning gossip suddenly growing enthusiastic, bawdy.

Reccimund explains, "To Muslims, the walled secret garden is a cherished concept. To them it is an image of paradise, called *al-Jannah* in the Quran. 'The Garden of Eden' to you and me. Al-Jannah means both 'garden' and 'secret place.' The Islamic garden is a sanctuary, a place to rest, to balance the heart, mind, and soul. But it is also a place of worship, where one comes to meet God in paradise on Earth."

Cleo gushes, "Extraordinary."

The powerful floral-citrus perfume of the star-covered oranges lies heavy in the air, sweet and intoxicating. There are all manner of trees, squat and bushy mingling with tall and skinny, many unknown to the visitors. Head-high cherries, almonds, and plums are bathed in an explosion of white blossoms. There are endless close-cropped myrtle-hedge mazes exhaling their musky spice, large canopied ferns, hundreds of fragrant white roses set into carefully tilled beds. Wisteria slithers up trellises set along the walls, their tendrils trailing plumes of bright purple that spill an ethereal scent of violet-infused honey. Gardenias and white lilacs lend their delicate sweetness to the heavenly aroma.

There are dozens of fountains, water everywhere, the pearly tinkle soft and pleasing, but when joined together they produce an eerie but very soothing aquatic hush upon the entire garden.

Narrow, marble-lined troughs contain tiny mountain-cooled crystal clear rivers that link the pools of the fountains, the plumbing masterfully arranged to maintain a gentle but steady flow from north to south through the entire complex, cooling the landscape.

Benches are arranged at ideal vantage points to encourage contemplative lingering, and here and there thick cypress privacy hedges ring tiny alcoves, the squat bubbling fountains set between the two small stone seats cleverly designed to shroud intimate conversation, gentle words of wooing, the soft chorus of lovemaking.

Pea gravel paths wind their way through the gardens, intersecting the more stately right angles of the larger marble paths that bisect the square, delineating the four quadrants of Eden. Roman busts atop marble pedestals mark the junctions where paths meet then depart. Nude Roman sculptures of gamesome sprites and nubile goddesses peek timidly from between hedges. Not a leaf or a pebble or a blossom seems out of place.

A narrow peninsula as high as the outer walls is attached to the center of the north wall, jutting out into the garden where it supports a rectangular building. Clearly an intended focal point. Marble steps lead from the garden up to the peninsula on its south side, issuing an invitation.

The men turn left on the narrowed marble path just inside the gate and walk westward along the outer wall, absorbing the scene in silence. They then turn right at the precise center of the south wall and head north to the steps of the elevated peninsula. They can see now that at the border between the peninsula and the north wall, perhaps fifty paces behind the first building, sits a second more massive structure ringed by floating red ochre and white horseshoe arches, where it lords over the entire walled garden compound. Evidently, their destination.

As the four men climb the marble steps out of Eden, the building slowly comes into view, the terracotta tile roof, followed by running red ochre and white striped horseshoe arches set effortlessly upon marble columns, then finally a white marble floor.

Directly in front of them is a large square pool, the water rich and dark. The pool could be knee-deep or a league-deep. Between enormous lily pads, dozens of bright white blooms are luxuriously unfolded atop tall stalks. A school of hand-length iridescent orange fish rise in unison to greet the visitors, their thin oval lips opening and closing in tight syncopation as they beg for food. In the center of the pool a large black amber lion with pearl eyes is suspended above the depths, its paws resting in the cool dark water, liquid dribbling from its exaggerated fangs. Two smaller square pools sit on the east and west sides of the building, hugging the edges of the peninsula.

Oddly, the building set before them is completely open on the north and south ends, allowing visual access, and evidently meant to be walked through: some sort of visitor's pavilion. There is a large central nave with smaller side naves on either side. The contrast between the shaded interior and the bright sun makes it difficult to discern the contents of the room from this vantage point, though it is clear that the floors are crowded with irregularly-shaped objects.

At the north end of the room, farthest from them, is the silhouette of a standing man. His arms are spread wide in an open-palmed U, as if inviting the visitors to enter, but he is a frozen statue, mute.

Reccimund leads the visitors around the pool to the entrance of the pavilion. As they slide into the cool shadow thrown by the jutting roof extension, the contents of the structure sharpen into focus, bringing the men to a halt. Cleo's mouth slides open once more, but this time he is driven to silence. Strobel, not given to surprises, gasps then stammers, "Sweet Jesus ..."

The central nave is arrayed with dozens of large oak chests lining the narrow walkway, the elaborately carved, ornate lids opened to reveal their precious contents: gold *dinars*, by the tens of thousands. The chests are filled to the brim then haphazardly spill their treasure to the floor, which is literally awash in gold pieces. In the left side nave are more chests, these overflowing with silver *dirhams*. There are waist-high pyramids of stacked gold and silver bricks, dozens of blown glass vases filled with massive rubies, emeralds, sapphires, and diamonds; a collection of ornate gold crowns with inlays of precious gems; a long, low-slung table adorned with priceless jeweled daggers and swords; tall jars of rare perfumes from the east; bolts of the finest spun silks, whites and blues and reds, all elaborately embroidered with pure gold thread. The right side nave is lined with bookcases filled with leather-bound volumes—hundreds of precious books.

The casual display of wealth is staggering, disarming. The combined treasuries of all of Europe would not equal a tenth of the wealth arrayed before them, and the unstated but distinct impression is that this is only a taste of the caliph's royal treasury. Not a guard in sight.

Their companion at the far end of the room has not moved a muscle. They see now that he is dressed in a floor-length, flowing red robe of many layers, the silk adorned with a spider web of gold embroidery, wide gold piping, and looping gold cords. Into his wide golden belt is tucked a jeweled dagger. His head is wrapped in a bright white turban. Again, the red ochre and white motif of the caliph. The man is middle-aged, deeply tanned, and his gray-flecked beard is close-cropped and neat. His appearance is unmistakably regal, a caricature of an oriental despot. His face is expressionless, unreadable, his eyes resting upon the visitors but betraying no agenda or thought.

Without warning, his chest expands as he inhales, then he releases a deep baritone, projecting a rich announcement in precise Latin, "Behold the treasure of al-Andalus. Witness the glory of the Umayyads!"

Inexplicably, Strobel lowers himself to one knee, bows his head, then gushes, "Your Royal Highness, I bring greetings from Emperor Otto II of the Holy Roman Empire." Reccimund and Alonso turn to decipher Strobel's unexpected motion, then break into grins when they see his posture. Cleo seems unsure whether to join his companion or not, but chooses to remain standing, though he seems unsure of himself.

The despot's face remains stern for a moment longer, then breaks into a grin, followed by a widening smile. His shoulders begin to shake with his growing chuckle, then more violently with his boisterous laugh, his head finally tilting back to roar. Strobel looks up sheepishly.

As the despot's shoulders still, he once again composes himself to say in his precise Latin baritone, "You are mistaken, sir. I am Jawdhar, master to the royal jewels and the caliph's falconer. I am but a slave of the caliph."

Strobel flushes bright scarlet and awkwardly rises, muttering under his breath. The grins glued to Reccimund and Alonso fade.

The debunked despot continues, "Come, gentlemen, the caliph and his Vizier Council await you. Please follow me." He motions the men forward, turns, and leads them through the pavilion, the only sound the metallic jingle of boots slipping and sliding on a bed of loose gold coins.

The transition from shadow to bright sun constricts their pupils into a momentary blindness and they draw their hands up to line their brows. Before them is a much larger square pool, also filled with fish and blooming lilies. A duplicate statue of Zahra rises from the depths at its center, the dark water lapping at her golden calves. A large green bird with blue and red plumage and a curved black beak rests upon her shoulder, eyeing them.

Across the water is the horseshoe-arched entrance to the formal reception hall. The distinctive red ochre and white striped arches are suspended on ornately-carved marble columns. The building is single-storied but tall, suggesting a cavernous interior. The outer walls are plainly decorated, creamy white except for the colored arches. Their eyes are drawn to the roof line, an unusual joining of two dozen vaulted wooden pyramids, somehow suggesting a Bedouin clan camped beside a desert oasis. A larger tent at the far back center of the roof rises above the others to ensure visibility and is covered in hammered gold, its brilliant reflection burning into their eyes. The use of precious gold to gild a roof sends an unambiguous message.

As with the pavilion, the interior of this building is darkened by the contrasting light outside, effectively masking the details of its contents. In the far depths of the room they see an eerie pulsing red glow, as if spawned by a bonfire. But this is clearly an illusion, since there is no obvious chimney on the building, or smoke.

As the entourage eases around the thin edge of the pool, Zahra's bird turns to keep a watchful eye upon them. The deathly stillness of the scene gives the unmistakable impression that they are being observed and measured. Beads of sweat dot Strobel's forehead. His armpits have begun leaking and his heart is racing.

The men enter the building through a transverse entry nave. The guards are suddenly back in attendance, but these men have a very different look than the Royal Guard. These knights are from the caliph's famed Slavic Guard, his personal bodyguards, a private army. Originally brought as slaves from the eastern mountains by Caliph Abd al-Rahman III, they are the best trained knights in Europe, both feared and respected. They are fawned upon at court with food, women, and lavish gifts, courtesy of the caliph. Their shoulder-length blond hair is the giveaway, a token of admission and a badge sported with great pride. Blue eyes are the rule in the Slavic Guard, not Arab brown, and their sculpted bodies compare fairly with the marble statues of the ancient Greek Olympians. Once they were Slavic slaves, saqaliba, but brought to an Arab land long ago. They are devout Muslims now, knights of position and power, and fanatically loyal to the caliph.

The ornate hilts of their drawn broadswords are held tightly to their belts and angled skyward. Their careful arrangement in the outer nave funnels the entourage into the audience chamber. The blue eyes of the Slavic Guard are fixed to the floor, as if oblivious, but each man exudes a sense of spring-cocked readiness to react in an instant should the occasion warrant it or the caliph flick his head to summon them to action.

The visitors pass into the audience chamber, a large interior nave adjacent to two smaller side naves, each separated by a run of floating horseshoe arches. Their guide stops to let their eyes adjust, and the visitors begin to study the room. Every surface is covered by impossibly dense, *arabesque* designs carved into the smooth plaster, lending an exotic, oriental feel to the space. The walls and columns are alive with the dancing red glow, the interplay of light and shadow mesmerizing.

At the far end of the room, a horseshoe arch inset into the wall frames a simple wooden folding chair upon which a man is seated. High above him rises the pyramid of the tent they saw from outside. Hammered gold covers the inside of the tent as well, lending the illusion of a solid gold roof. To either side men are seated on large pillows, legs folded, four to the left and three to the right, with a matching but empty fourth pillow. The Vizier Council. The side naves are bare, but each inset wall arch opens into a shallow niche containing a tall, cylindrical, paper-thin alabaster vase filled with fragrant white lilies.

The pulsing blood-red glow envelopes the room, preventing them from making out much detail of the viziers. The visitors' eyes are drawn to search for the source of the obscuring light. In the center of the room rests a circular marble floor basin, a man's height across. The basin is filled to the brim with liquid silver that quivers and shakes as if alive. A round black pearl as big as a baby's fist hangs just above the surface of the shimmering pool as if miraculously floating in midair. At every fifth heartbeat, the pearl magically dips down into the silver surface then rises back, inducing gentle ripples in the basin that playfully tease the light, producing the uncanny modulation of red.

Quicksilver is far more precious than gold, and much rarer. Even the most famous of alchemists in Europe might only possess a thimbleful of the magical flowing metal. The visitors' eyes follow the red beam upward at an angle to a short curved track of palm-sized red lenses set into the angle of the roof. Mystery solved. Cleo sees that the design cleverly accounts for the sun's seasonal progression in the sky. He calculates that the angle of the sunbeam must be precise in its alignment to the quicksilver, dictating a window of fifteen minutes, perhaps twenty, each day when the room is filled with dancing red light. Given that their journey began three leagues away and early in the morning, the required timing for this display is truly impressive.

As the visitors continue to stare hypnotically at the shimmering quicksilver, the light abruptly disappears, returning the room to its natural dim hue. The effect is unsettling, the silent stillness of the room quickly approaching oppressive, as if tuned to produce anxiety and awe in the visitors. No one moves.

As they wait for some unknown signal, Cleo and Strobel study the seated men. The viziers look their parts. Their expressions are solemn, unreadable. They are dressed in elaborate attire, robes bright with blues, reds, and yellows. Two wear white turbans. The men all have close-cropped beards. All but the man third to the right of the caliph are middle-aged or older. To a one they exude an air of keen intelligence, their eyes sharp and alive. Several seem impatient with the wait; others amused, perhaps curious. The man second to the left of the caliph looks to be the oldest of the lot. He wears an ornate, curved *scimitar* with a matching jeweled needle dagger tucked into his leather belt: the unmistakable confidence and swagger of a battle-hardened knight.

Interestingly, the caliph himself is dressed plainly, in stark contrast to the false-despot, the Royal Guard, and even his viziers. A simple, buttoned white tunic, a tan over-jacket, and a white turban. He is middle-aged, his face a deep olive tone, with a close-cropped, gray-flecked beard and mustache. His dark almond eyes sparkle. This man does not seem given to easy smiles. He has the look of a scholar rather than a king, one more at home in a library than in the royal court.

The despot steps back at a right angle and lifts both arms, one palm raised to the seated man and one to the visitors, then commences in his authoritative baritone, "The ambassadors from the court of Emperor Otto II of the Holy Roman Empire." He pauses, then begins discernibly louder, "His Royal Highness, Caliph al-Hakam II, son of Abd al-Rahman III, the great al-Nasir. Second caliph of al-Andalus, sultan of Córdoba, lord of the glorious Madinat al-Zahra, elder of the Umayyad clan, protector of the written word, champion of truth, defender of the faith. May Allah smile upon his reign."

The echo stretches for three seconds. Still no one moves. Reccimund whispers to Strobel and Cleo. "It is time to move forward and formally meet the caliph and the Vizier Council. Come." The visitors' hearts are pounding.

Alonso stays where he is, but Strobel and Cleo follow Reccimund as they step around the quicksilver floor basin and take their station side-by-side five paces in front of the caliph, at the center of the shallow V of the Vizier Council. The Royal Guard flanks the sides of the nave all the way to the back wall. Reccimund moves to the right and seats himself on the open floor pillow, leaving the two men stranded.

Strobel gets it right this time, bowing deeply, then gracefully sliding to one knee. Cleo follows his lead. He begins in Latin; slowly, precisely. "Your Royal Highness, I bring greetings from Emperor Otto II of the Holy Roman Empire. I am Peter Strobel, personal envoy of His Majesty, Emperor Otto II, and Ambassador to the Empire." He lifts his palm to his left. "This is Brother Cleo of the Abbey at Cluny, in Burgundy, who has come to learn the medical practices of Abulcasis." He hesitates, then adds, "Abu al-Qasim." He stops, wondering whether the caliph understands him.

Unsure, he continues, "We are honored by your generous hospitality. Madinat al-Zahra is a remarkable tribute to the glory of your kingdom." He holds for some response. Nothing. Growing desperate, he stands and retrieves the small package from beneath his robes.

The eyes of the Slavic Guard instantly rise from the floor, their coiling muscles invisible except to a practiced eye. Strobel places the package in both palms in front of his chest and stretches it forward, the universal sign of a gift. Reccimund rises from his pillow, accepts the package with a bow, then turns and slowly walks to the caliph, placing it in his hands with a wry smile that the visitors cannot see.

As Reccimund returns to his pillow, the caliph begins to meticulously unwrap the small package, his expression one of a child who delights in surprises. As he removes the wrapping, his eyes widen. When he lifts the leather cover, a spontaneous half-smile eases onto his face. Without looking up he says in lightly-accented Latin, "A Christian Psalter. What a wonderful gift." He is soft-spoken, his voice slightly effeminate, scholarly. He thumbs through the pages with obvious delight. "The craftsmanship is excellent and the illustrations exquisite. Tell me about it."

Strobel relaxes, surprised that the caliph speaks Latin, but relieved nonetheless. "Your Highness, it is called the *Trier Psalter*. It contains the Book of Psalms, as well as hymns and canticles. Quite rare in the detail of its gilded illustrations and use of vibrant colors. From the emperor's own library. He learned of your interest in Christian and Jewish scriptures from Bishop Reccimund and thought you might enjoy an addition to your collection. It was created by the monks at the Abbey of Reichenau, near Trier."

The caliph is still thumbing through the pages, his delight obvious. "Beautiful. I have several Psalters, but none with illustrations so lovely. Please express my thanks to the emperor for his fine taste."

Strobel bows, feeling more in control of the situation. "With pleasure, Your Highness."

The caliph finally looks up as he sets the book upon his lap. "Ambassador Strobel, Brother Cleo, welcome to al-Andalus. Your presence honors us. May I present my Vizier Council." He lifts his palm to his right. "Jafar al-Mushafi, my grand vizier." The turbaned man somberly nods. Strobel responds in kind. "General Ghalib al-Nasiri, my military vizier. Durri the Small, vizier of the royal treasury. Samuel al-Tayyib, royal librarian and vizier of books, whom you have already met." Samuel smiles warmly. The caliph shifts his palm to his left. "Master Abu al-Qasim, royal physician and vizier of medicine, whom you also know." Abulcasis nods and chuckles his response. "Arib ibn Said, vizier to Constantinople. Muhammad ibn Abi Amir, vizier to Africa." Ibn Abi Amir offers a curt nod. The youngest of the viziers by at least ten years. "And last but not least, Rabi ibn Zyad, whom you know." Reccimund smiles.

Strobel bows. "The pleasure is mine, gentlemen."

The caliph continues, "I trust your quarters in the Alcazar are suitable?"

"Indeed, Your Highness, most luxurious. The splendor of Córdoba is legendary in all of Europe. Brother Cleo and I are deeply impressed. And Madinat al-Zahra is a treasure beyond words."

The caliph's face remains expressionless. As if suddenly made aware of the monk, he shifts his eyes to his right. "Ibn Zyad speaks very highly of you, Brother Cleo. As does Abu al-Qasim. Your natural curiosity and your openness to new ideas are unusual for a Christian from the north. Quite refreshing."

Cleo smiles and bows his head as Strobel wrestles with a frown. "My only hope, Your Highness, is that I do not bore them with my endless questions."

A hint of a smile from the caliph. "My royal physician has never been bored a day in his life, Brother Cleo. He thinks up new surgical devices even as he sleeps." Abulcasis and Cleo both laugh.

The caliph looks back to Strobel. "Ambassador, as you know, I sent Ibn Zyad to the court of your emperor's father, Otto I, to open dialogue between our kingdoms. In my view that exchange was beneficial to both parties." Strobel nods, clearly pleased at the diplomatic turn in the conversation. "I would like to resurrect that agreement with Emperor Otto II. And expand it. I propose an exchange of a delegation of scholars, lawyers, scientists. There is much we can learn from each other. In my view, opening dialogue and fostering a mutual respect and tolerance is the key to peace and prosperity for both our kingdoms."

Strobel responds, "A noble sentiment, Your Highness. I will convey your generous offer to the emperor. I am sure he would be most open to the idea." The caliph nods, satisfied.

The lines on Strobel's face tighten. "If I might, Your Highness. There is one request the emperor did wish me to convey." He pauses to precisely frame his words, then continues. "He would welcome your assistance in a certain ... delicate matter." The caliph is a blank slate. He nods as an invitation for Strobel to continue.

"It seems, Your Highness, that African pirates continue to raid our shipping in the Roman Sea, and even the coastal cities of the Empire. Toulon and Marseille have been at their mercy for some time now. Anyone captured by these corsairs, sailor or not, is sent to Africa to be sold into slavery. They have grown so emboldened of late that they even sailed up the Rhone River and attacked Lyon." Strobel pauses for a response. Getting none, he continues. "This flagrant disregard by the pirates for the Empire's property, its borders, and its people is growing worse. The emperor wished me to inquire whether Your Highness might be able to help bring a halt to such barbarous raiding." Strobel holds for a response.

The caliph takes a full minute before he says, "As you may know, Ambassador, these corsairs, while followers of the Prophet, are lawless brigands with rewards of gold upon their heads. They have raided my own merchant ships, even my ports. They have no honor or loyalty, and they respect no borders. Algeciras and Málaga have been at their mercy for some time. Even Cádiz. Unfortunately the pirates are based on the coast of Africa belonging to the Fatimid Empire, beyond the reach of al-Andalus, I am afraid."

Strobel licks his lips then presses his case. "I understand, Your Highness. But the emperor has recently learned that Córdoba has grown ... interested in Africa."

The caliph's expression hardens. Jafar al-Mushafi and General Ghalib discreetly exchange a glance without moving their heads.

Strobel continues, oblivious to the clues. "The emperor felt that perhaps with a foothold in Africa, Your Highness might be in a unique position to ... aid us in our defense against these pirate incursions. It would be an assistance for which the emperor would pay handsomely. In gold, of course." The caliph actually frowns before his features return to stone. Reccimund sighs.

The silence stretches out, growing uncomfortable. At last, the caliph says, "Ibn Zyad. I believe you promised our visitors a tour of the treasures of Madinat al-Zahra." It is obvious that the audience has ended. As Reccimund rises from his pillow, Strobel raises his brows, first confused, then perturbed. He instinctively frowns, and his mouth opens as if to challenge the dismissal. Cleo touches Strobel's sleeve to check his actions. Strobel's mouth closes. The two formally bow, back away three paces, then turn and exit with Reccimund behind them. The caliph continues to study the men as they depart, the frown back upon his face.

Discoveries

4 June 975.

The two have wound their way deep into the twisted maze of
the Rare Books Library. He leads, his gait easy and comfortable,
clearly at home in these jeweled caverns. She can barely manage
to suppress her giddiness. Her head cranes and swivels and darts
to take in the marvels as she passes. She spontaneously halts
here and there to hurriedly scan a label, finger a binding, then
rushes to catch up. He intuits her every move and cannot help
but smile at her childlike excitement.

He stops outside a nondescript wooden door. "And here we
are. Come, my dear, you will enjoy this." He opens the door for her
with a crisp metallic snap and indicates that she should enter. As
she timidly steps inside, her head tracks floor to ceiling, then she
pivots on her heel, surveying treasures beyond her wildest
dreams. Her face is nothing but dimples.

Her guide watches her absorb the space, clearly deriving great
pleasure from what he sees. "We have six rooms that make up the
Library of the Ancient Greeks within the Rare Books Library. This
one contains our collection of Greek literature, poetry and a
portion of our mathematics holdings. Small, but exquisite. Your
new home." He laughs. "Trust me, Rayhana, you will enjoy this
room. Many of my greatest treasures rest here."

She is effervescent. "Oh, Master al-Tayyib, I am so grateful. I
have longed for this day."

"Intense curiosity and an insatiable desire to learn. Well,
these are my greatest inspirations. Seeing those qualities in a
young woman? Now that makes me happy!" He beams as she
laughs. "I have two girls of my own, you know, Miriam and Sara.
Dear girls. Smart, like their mother. I am afraid the three of them
dance circles around me while I plod about." He chuckles. "Even
so, those three are my great joy."

She likes this man.

Samuel turns more serious. "Tell me, Rayhana. Your father
seemed reluctant to allow you entry to the Royal Library. He
insisted that you be confined to a single room under strict rules of
privacy. Evidently he fears allowing anyone to know that you can
read! While I will admit that few women have studied here, there

is certainly ample precedence. Zahra herself roamed this building!"

She smiles.

"Your father also made some ... unusual requests." Her smile fades. "I am first to seek his permission for any books you desire to read," Samuel shakes his head in disbelief. "It seems the man has a strong preference for histories of the Arab peoples." She winces; he laughs. "I assured him, of course, that I would scrutinize everything you read to protect your innocence."

Her pained expression deepens.

"Between you and me, my dear, your father's reading tastes are woefully narrow. What you read in this room will remain between the two of us. Do I make myself clear?"

She beams her response.

He lifts his palms, "So, Rayhana, tell me. Do you read Greek?"

She blushes and looks to her shoes before returning to meet his gaze. "I am afraid I do not, Master al-Tayyib. Several Arabic dialects. And Persian. Some Latin."

He nods appreciatively. "A worthy accomplishment, my dear, given your father's ... preferences. There is no need for Greek here. All but the most recently acquired books have been translated into Arabic." He points to the shelf. "See? The original to the left and its translated twin nestled beside it."

He rubs his palms together with anticipation. "So, where to begin?" He steps to the bookcase and begins to peruse with his index finger the titles on the head-high shelf. "I was thinking ... I was thinking ... I was thinking ... yes, here it is. One of my great loves. We call this codex the *Ambrosian Iliad*. We have other copies of the *Iliad*, but this is my favorite. The *Ambrosian* is a rare illustrated *Iliad*, over five hundred years old. From Constantinople." He fondly touches the codex, then gingerly lifts the translated twin from its home and hands it to her. Her eyes widen with anticipation as he smiles his approval.

"Herodotus tells us that the poet's name was Homer. He lived almost fifteen hundred years ago. The *Iliad* is an epic poem, you see, the most famous poem from ancient Greece. Homer splendidly recounts the events of the great war between the Greeks and the Trojans. The war was fought over Helen of Troy, supposedly the most beautiful woman in the world." He smiles. "Though I dare say you are a close second, my dear." He laughs as she blushes.

"I would encourage you also to examine the original codex. Take time to study the elegance of the Greek script and the wonderful detail and color of the illustrations." He muses for a moment then slyly grins. "Should your father ask, you spent your time with Ibn Khordadbeh's *Kitab al Masaslik wal Mamalik*. Alas, Persian, not Arabic, but a boring treatise on roads and kingdoms, so he should still approve." He chuckles.

"What else? You will be undisturbed here, so make yourself at home. I have meetings to attend, but I will come for you for noon prayer." He grins. "Your father's orders."

She beams. "Thank you, Master al-Tayyib, you have made me very happy."

"The pleasure is mine, Rayhana. I cannot wait to hear your opinion of Homer!" He turns to leave.

The door snaps shut and she is deliciously alone. She places the volume on the low-slung oval table in the center of the room then looks up into the array of octagonal skylights. She smiles. Not a cloud in the sky. She turns and lifts the *Ambrosian Iliad* from its niche and lays it on the table beside the translation. She opens the binding on the original, her heart racing as she studies the beautiful reds, greens, blues, and golds of the first full-page illustration. The woman at the center of the picture has long blond tresses. She whispers, "Helen."

Too anxious to begin reading, she stands and circles the room, pronouncing the names of the Arabic translations as she goes, completely mesmerized. Her fingers move with a deep satisfaction, caressing the leather bindings, touching the odd lettering of the ancient Greek.

High above her, a whisper of delirious approval leaks from Euclid's *Elements*. The thick codex frantically flexes his leather covers to distract his neighbors from their tedious morning discourse, alerting them to the rare feminine presence within their secret domain, a world made stiff by the logic of symbols, a world punctuated by parallel lines and intersecting circles. A hushed, appreciative chorus soon races along the geometry shelf, but then trails off into a transfixed silence, bound in a net cast wide by the awesome power of a beautiful woman to strike dumb the calculating mind. Moths to a flame.

"Brother Cleo, may I present Levi al-Attar, royal purveyor of books. There is a not a codex alive that can escape his eager pursuit." Levi smiles and bows. "My able assistant, Zafir Saffar, royal translator. A genius with ancient Greek." Zafir nods. "And last, but not least, Zaheid al-Nasrani, knower of all things knowable." Zaheid laughs. "Zaheid is our man of science. And our token Christian." Samuel, Levi, Zafir, and Zaheid all laugh loudly. After only an instant of delay, Cleo joins the fun.

"The pleasure is mine, gentlemen. You are very kind to take the time to meet with me. I am certain you are all quite busy." There is an amused twinkle in Levi's eyes as he catches Zafir's quick grimace.

Samuel answers for the group. "Well, the work of a library is never done, that much is true, but even so, we are at your disposal, Brother Cleo. Assisting a fellow lover of knowledge and books is never a chore for us." Samuel smiles warmly.

"Thank you. I am indebted."

The five fall into a comfortable silence.

Samuel says, "Brother Cleo, I understand that Abu al-Qasim is in Madinat today. Levi has recently brought us several volumes from the *Hippocratic Corpus*. Master al-Qasim wants to cross-check our existing manuscripts against these new ones. For consistency. I thought Levi might introduce you to some of the more famous Greek medical treatises we have in the Rare Books Library and then take you to visit with Abu al-Qasim."

"That would be splendid!" The man's obvious enthusiasm is endearing.

"Good, good. Levi, when you are finished, please join us in my study. I have a matter I need to discuss." Levi nods. As the pair exits the room, they hear Cleo launch into his famous rapid-fire questioning. "Exactly how many volumes are there in the *Hippocratic Corpus* and when were they ..." Then they are gone.

Samuel grins. "I like him."

Zaheid nods his head in agreement, "Genuine enthusiasm never disappoints. Even though he is a cleric I detect a refreshing lack of dogmatic ... rigidity." He chuckles. "I wish I could say the same for Ambassador Strobel. I met with him yesterday. The man positively exudes condescension. You can smell the arrogance seeping from his pores." All three laugh.

Samuel lowers his voice. "Gentlemen, urgent matters await us. Zafir, Zaheid has some interesting ideas on how to design our replica of Aristotle's camera obscura."

"Yes, well, they are only ideas at present. I need to make some more calculations. I am recalling a discussion on the use of cut crystals and mirrors to redirect light rays. Years ago. I believe it was in the writings of Theon of Alexandria, if I am not mistaken. My sense is that his ideas may serve us well in our own design."

Samuel says, "Zafir, please locate the codex and meet us in my study. I forget exactly where it resides. Try the mathematics room first, then the Egyptian collection. Or it may even be in one of the Greek rooms."

Zafir nods and departs. A moment later, Samuel's eyes widen. "I forgot to tell him about our secret guest." Zaheid's eyebrows lift into question marks. "Ibn Abi Amir's daughter is studying the Greek poets. Three mornings a week." Samuel frowns. "The father is an odd man, hard to read." He muses. "Unsettling, somehow ... it surprises me still that the caliph chose him to join the Vizier Council." The frown evaporates. "But the daughter is a complete joy. Bright girl, quite beautiful. And delightfully ecstatic to be given the chance to explore our treasures. You will like her." He chuckles. "I started her out with the *Ambrosian Iliad*." Zaheid nods appreciatively. Samuel shrugs. "Oh well. If Zafir stumbles upon her he will have to figure out what to do."

As the two turn and make their way to the door, Samuel rests his arm affectionately across Zaheid's shoulders. "Come, my friend, you must educate me on the science of light."

The single-mindedness of Zafir's search propels him through the door before he realizes the room is occupied, his sudden surprise jerking him to a sliding, awkward stop. His startled exhale of "Ahhh!" skips across only three heartbeats before settling into irritation at the interruption of his hunt.

Her eyes are wide with terror as they leap from the page to join the explosion of curls launched by the recoil of her head. Her sharp gasp suggests a child caught in some calculated act of willful disobedience. Unnerved, she rises from her floor pillow, then involuntarily takes a step back.

The strained silence of guarded appraisal stretches out.

Finally, his accusatory, "Who are you?"

She straightens her back. "Who are you?"

He frowns, lifts his chin a notch, then announces, "I am Zafir Saffar, royal translator. I work for the royal librarian." A honed edge of conceit lies loosely buried somewhere under these last words. He widens his eyes into a mocking query.

The flare of her nostrils is barely perceptible. Her eyes narrow. "I am Rayhana Abi Amir." She lacquers on her own conceit. "My father is Muhammad ibn Abi Amir. Of the caliph's Vizier Council. I was told I would not be disturbed."

His frown returns. "Not disturbed? What are you doing here? The Rare Books Library is forbidden to visitors."

Her expression hardens. "I have permission to be here."

An incredulous, "Permission? From whom?"

Her stare is challenging. "Master al-Tayyib, of course."

He oozes intense skepticism. "I was just with him. He made no mention of you."

She shrugs with a fake casualness. "Nevertheless, he brought me here."

An impatient, "Why would he bring you here?"

She quizzically tilts her head just so, her half-smirk somehow unmistakably questioning his intelligence. "To read."

The line of his exaggerated sigh precisely marks the standoff. As he considers his options, his eyes track to the table and the two splayed codices. Decision made, he adjusts his tone to be more welcoming. "I am sorry to have startled you." She nods her acceptance. "What is it that you are reading?"

Satisfied, she matches his tone. "Master al-Tayyib started me on the *Ambrosian Iliad*."

In spite of himself, he smiles. "I love the *Iliad*."

The dam inexplicably breaks, the water streaming through the thin cleft with a mighty gush. "I have only just started, but it is a complete joy!" Her enthusiasm is instantaneous and contagious, her Arabian beauty magically flaming up as if lit by a thousand candles. He is struck dumb, mesmerized by her transformation. His emerald eyes cling desperately to her lovely face in a feeble attempt to steady his legs. She is running full-stride now. "Homer's poetry is so different from anything I have ever read! Exquisite! Nothing in Persian compares." She grows more animated, her hands beginning to adorably lift and dance in time to her accelerating words. "The Muses! How clever! And how interesting that the Greek gods enter the plot and mold events to suit their whims. And Achilles ... I love the way he stands up to Agamemnon to end the plague. But poor Briseis!" She stops for a breath, and as her grin widens dimples suddenly dive into her cheeks, completely unanticipated, taking his breath away. His eyes have not left her face but he hasn't heard a word she has said.

He shakes his head to clear the cobwebs. "Sorry ... Achilles?"

She shakes her head, confused, oblivious of the mesmerizing spell she flings about so casually. A second later her dimples return. She waits for him to catch up.

He focuses. "Yes. The *Iliad* is, uhh ... an ancient ... mmm ... story." He clears his throat. Never once has he been at a loss for words. He takes a deep breath and searches for footing. "But its many themes are so remarkably contemporary. It is as if it were written yesterday." Thankfully, some solid ground. He presses on, his words carefully meted. "Homer explores the nature of glory and respect and wrath; and the ultimate tragedy of war. He speaks of homecomings, and man's fate in the world. Homer has much to teach us about living. Samuel may have told you that the *Iliad* comes from an oral tradition. Homer's recited version predates by hundreds of years the written version. And as you say, his verse is exquisite ..."

He stops as he becomes acutely aware that she has been studying him. They share strained smiles, locking eyes for an instant longer than necessary.

He clears his throat again, something he never does. "When I ... interrupted your reading, I was searching for a book for Samuel. Master al-Tayyib. Theon of Alexandria. A book on geometry and optics. I was not able to find it in the mathematics room or the Egyptian collection. I think it may be here ..."

She nods, amused.

"Samuel is waiting for it ..."

"I see. Please, continue your search. I will rejoin Achilles." They both try for casual smiles but don't quite get there.

As he steps past her, the hint of citrus spice presents itself. Her perfume is subtle but impossible to ignore; regal somehow, yet utterly feminine, his beloved bitter orange blossoms buried somewhere beneath her clothes, dabbed upon her warm olive skin. Sublime, weak-kneed intoxication. He swallows hard, inexplicably woozy as his heart begins to race. He slows to steady himself then methodically slides the ladder toward the center of the bookcase, directly behind her. He begins to climb, ridiculously self-conscious, wondering if she is watching but afraid to turn around. He forces himself to begin perusing the bindings, resuming the search for his elusive quarry.

She has taken her seat on the floor pillow and leans in over the codex, elbows on the table, chin glued to her folded hands. She finds her place. Five minutes later she is still on the same sentence.

"Ahhh, found you!"

She stands and turns to watch as he descends, codex in hand. She is beaming.

He laughs as he shows her the book. "An Egyptian caught hiding among the Greeks."

"I am glad you were able to find it."

"Yes. Samuel will be pleased."

Silence. They each hold their positions, seemingly afraid to break the trance.

"Well, I should be going. It was nice to meet you ... Rayhana." He offers a warm smile.

"The pleasure was mine ... Zafir." She blushes.

With a pleased nod, he turns.

As the door snaps shut she stands motionless for several moments, the quick exchange of expressions almost comical; amused grin to confused grimace to satisfied smile, then back again. She sighs deeply then takes her place on her pillow once more, elbows on the table, chin on her folded hands. But this time she stares straight into space, ignoring the siren's call of the ancient codex.

The whispers high above have managed somehow to jump two shelves down and one bookcase over into the literature section, arcing around behind her. Predictably, the prim mathematical murmur shifts to a more lively and disjointed exchange. One poet begins to expound upon feminine beauty, another on the delicious tortures of young love. Three playwrights slide themselves to the cliff-edge to peek over and see what all the fuss is about, joining in a shared nod of appreciation. A bawdy rejoinder is tendered from one of the comedians, eliciting a barely stifled cackle further down the shelf.

Her eyes narrow as she lifts them towards the ceiling. Instantly the upper shelves still, the books leaning back into the shadows. She holds her breath to sharpen her hearing as she scans the upper reaches. Nothing. She shrugs, then finds her place once more and settles back into Homer's magical incantation.

The three men are hunched over the codex laid open upon Samuel's desk. Zaheid points with a reed to a place on the page. "It seems clear to me that there must be a mathematical relation ..."

Silence. By habit, when his gears are whirring, Zaheid will wait for a query before continuing.

Samuel gives up with a heavy sigh. "Mathematical relation?"

Levi grins.

Zaheid continues, "Yes. Between the size of the hole and the required dimensions of the chamber."

Samuel nods. "Yes, I can see that. Good."

"But should the hole match the shape of the chamber, a square, or can it be round, or even triangular? Does it matter? I am not yet sure. Theon of Alexandria may be able to help us."

There is a metallic double-clank of the latch and then the door swings open. Samuel abruptly closes the codex and the three lean back, attempting varied looks of casual indifference.

When they see that it is only Zafir, they relax with a collective sigh. Samuel says, "You should have used our standard knock, my boy. We thought you were the ghost of Zahra." He chuckles.

Zafir grimaces. He does not forget such details. "Yes ... I am sorry, Samuel." He recovers by holding up the codex and offering a lame smile. "Zaheid, Theon of Alexandria can run but he cannot hide." The three older men laugh.

Samuel says, "Good, good. Where did you find him?"

"Not in the mathematics room or the Egyptian collection. Somehow he found his way to the Greek rooms, hidden among the geometers."

Samuel silently nods, studying his protégé.

Zaheid nudges Samuel then says, "Mmmm ... find anything else of interest in there?"

Zafir actually blushes, a first.

Levi's eyes widen, instantly curious.

Zafir quickly recovers by looking down to examine the binding of the codex. He looks up. "No one told me Ibn Abi Amir's daughter was reading there. Last I heard the Rare Books Library was off limits to ... visitors." His tone at the end is all wrong, oddly strained somehow, twisted too tight.

All three men stare at Zafir, intrigued. The young man is again inexplicably examining the leather binding.

Samuel tries to deflate the tension. "It is my fault, my boy, my fault. I should have warned you. Her father made a special request I could not easily refuse. It is only three mornings a week. And she will be gone by noon." He smiles. "She is delightful. Bright."

Zaheid adds with a sheepish grin, "And beautiful."

Zafir still refuses to meet their gaze. "No matter. All is well." He mumbles, "We talked about the *Iliad*." Zafir never mumbles. He shakes his head side to side, his expression unsettled, confused.

Levi is absolutely enthralled.

Crossings

The smell of rain is unmistakable on the evening breeze. The parched fields of the Guadalquivir Valley sigh, content at the promise of some relief from the merciless summer swelter. The wilted plants tilt their heads back and yawn widely, hoping to catch a few cool drops to slake their misery. Sleepy cattle stare stupidly at the dark horizon as they register the line of storms, then swish their tails, bored, and bend down to tear at the emaciated grass.

The low rumble of thunder can just be heard. The jagged slashes of lightning are pinned to the distant crags of the Sierra Morena, the pulsing copper-gold flashes unveiling the raised-arm menace of the bulging thunderheads, first there then vanished, only to reemerge a moment later, the swollen monsters now three steps closer.

It is an hour past midnight, late for a summer storm, but a welcome diversion for their perilous journey.

The leader wears a fitted black robe and a long black turban pulled tightly around his head, his hands and face smudged to a matching hue with oiled charcoal, joining him to the darkness. His flitting ebony eyes and his silent, fluid gait, cautious pauses followed by quick, decisive movements, betray a careful training in the arts of stealth and deception. Bundar has made this dangerous journey many times.

The follower seems far less comfortable. His fine robe is better suited to the law courts than a late-night foray into the forbidden quarters of Madinat al-Zahra. He struggles to keep up.

The leader approaches the entrance to the narrow alley sliced between the buildings. His movements are feline. Just beyond is the guard station, their last hurdle. The lit windows indicate life within, but only a single royal guard stands watch over the entrance to the royal harem. The sentry paces mechanically, first towards them, then away; towards them, then away. The leader measures the cadence. Satisfied, he raises his hand and motions. He frowns at the labored breathing of his companion, the undisciplined weakness of his unguarded breath. The black wraith whispers. "We are at the guard station. When I give the sign, we move, quick and silent."

The storm is close now. A sharp cut of lightning produces an expectant wince in the follower. He looks skyward, anxious. The leader counts the seconds to the throaty rumble to gauge distance. There is time. The wind is picking up; a prelude. The lush, moist scent in the air shouts RAIN! but not a single drop falls. A convulsing bright flash suddenly illuminates the two men pinned to the wall for what seems like an eternity, then they are erased.

They move.

The leader and the follower bend around the corner. They cling to the edge of the alley, weaving into the eaves of the doorways as they slide forward. The windows above them are dark, but the leader knows there are many sleepless eyes in this area of Madinat. He raises a hand to halt the follower, listens as he scans, then motions him forward.

Another bright flash freezes the two into place and then finally releases them. The heavy guttural rumble rattles the window panes above.

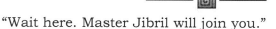

"Wait here. Master Jibril will join you."

Ibn Abi Amir nods.

The black wraith slides across the foyer and into the central hallway then disappears.

Ibn Abi Amir's heart is pounding. An automatic death sentence awaits any uncut male discovered in the royal harem. To steady himself he inhales deeply, holds it, then exhales.

He swivels his head. The foyer of the royal harem is expansive. Tall ceilings with two skylights and marble floor. No windows. He sees for the first time the two heavily-armed statues standing to either side of the horseshoe-arched door. Eunuch guards dressed in all white. Their eyes are pinned to the floor, but their hands rest upon the hilts of their broadswords. The walls are decorated with a raised white arabesque set upon a polychrome palette of reds. Ornate, standing silver oil lamps; elaborate hanging silk tapestries. White flowers decorate waist-high enameled ceramic vases. A red ochre and white striped horseshoe arch hovers over the entrance to the central hallway. The recesses of the hallway are dimly lit, cavernous. There is a hint of sweet incense in the air.

The place is devoid of human sound; only the sustained rumble of muted thunder and the soft whistles of swirling wind can be heard. The first solitary drops of rain plop heavy upon the glass of the skylight, quickly tire of the languid pace, then join forces to fall in thick sheets, the torrent producing a sustained aquatic *sushhh* within the foyer.

He waits.

A court princess slips effortlessly from the hallway into the foyer. Petite. Flowing silk robe, heavy makeup. Hands and feet painted with henna art. The face is girlish but clearly male, his features youthful, babyish even. As the eunuch draws closer the sweet citrus-musk announces his presence. Jibril al-Azhar, head eunuch of the royal harem. By all accounts not one to be toyed with. His spy network is rumored to be the most extensive in the city.

"Muhammad ibn Abi Amir, vizier of Africa. Welcome to the Royal Harem." The eunuch lifts his palms and bows deferentially. "I trust your journey was uneventful." His voice is soft and feminine, silky, but with a dangerous edge lurking somewhere within.

"Yes."

"Bundar is skilled in the arts of darkness." He looks up. "Thankfully, some much-needed rain."

"It is a pleasure to meet you, Jibril."

"The pleasure is mine, Muhammad." He lifts his palm to the hallway. "Come, let us talk."

Jibril stops mid-sentence and looks up. Ibn Abi Amir's eyes follow. They watch silently as two young men approach. One carries a tray with two glasses of wine, the other dried fruits and nuts. These two do not have the demeanor of servants, however. Their attire is odd. Both are shirtless, revealing sculpted chests. Their features are chiseled; exceptionally handsome young men. Greek gods. These two are clearly not eunuchs. Ibn Abi Amir is confused. As he continues to stare he is shocked to see that their gauzy cotton trousers are shear and revealing. Both men's erections are massive, impossible to ignore. Ibn Abi Amir's eyes widen as he recoils.

As the two set their trays down, their leers are aimed squarely at Ibn Abi Amir, something that would never be tolerated in a servant. One winks. The two turn and strut to the door.

Silence.

Jibril waves his hand dismissively. "Concubines. They serve at the pleasure of the caliph. Fatik and Muhja, two of his favorites." Jibril's voice is matter of fact, his expression unreadable.

Ibn Abi Amir's mouth opens to speak, but he remains silent. His mouth closes. So the rumors are true. "I see."

More silence.

"Tell me about your friend, Jibril." His tone edges towards impatience.

A thin smile slices the eunuch's face. "Our friend, Muhammad, our friend. The sultana. The wife of your caliph. You may call her Subh."

Ibn Abi Amir can't completely hide his surprise. The reason for the strange meeting location is now obvious. The sultana is forbidden to leave the royal harem. "She has a business proposition ... for me?"

The eunuch's smile widens. "Indeed she does, Muhammad." He licks his lips. "One, I suspect, that will interest you greatly. On multiple levels."

The silence stretches out as Ibn Abi Amir considers this new twist.

"But I will let her tell you herself. Come, you must meet Subh. She is a remarkable woman."

"Sultana. May I present Muhammad ibn Abi Amir, vizier of Africa."

Ibn Abi Amir bows. "My lady, I am honored to meet you."

She studies him just long enough to make him feel self-conscious then abruptly smiles. "Please. I am Subh. It is a pleasure to finally meet you, Muhammad. I have heard so much about you." All formalities are dropped.

The room is lit by a dozen well-placed candelabras, the warm glow designed to be especially flattering. He appreciates instantly that the rumors are well-founded. The caliph's wife is a beautiful woman; voluptuous. Her long, wavy blond curls dance in the flickering light. The Umayyad caliphs are celebrated for their preference of blonds. Piercing azure eyes. Her makeup is elegant and subtle; impeccably applied. A single black dot adorns her right cheek, a tiny mole, but inexplicably its precise placement adds magnificently to her allure.

He is shocked to see that she wears bedchamber clothes; a fitted white silk gown, sheer to within a hair of transparency. Bare shoulders except for thin straps. Her nipples are hard, impossible to ignore as they strain against the thin silk. He has to will his eyes away from them. He swallows hard to steady himself.

"Please, let us sit." She indicates the only divan in the room.

Jibril bows. "Sultana, Muhammad, I will leave you." He bows. The snap of the door latch seems impossibly loud. Ibn Abi Amir's heart pounds. He has violated every court protocol he can think

86

of. In the royal harem with the caliph's wife, alone in her bedchamber. Instant death if caught.

She is already seated and has turned to face him, her back against the silk pillow. Her breasts continue to torment him. He sits, as far away from her as the divan allows, but is forced to pivot to enable conversation. He crosses his leg, then uncrosses it, crosses it again. A hint of a smile brushes her face.

She studies him. "My spies told me that you were a handsome man, Muhammad. I see now that they are given to understatement."

He looks to his lap then gathers himself and looks up. "Jibril indicated you had a business proposition for me, Sultana." She raises a finger, forcing him to add, "Subh."

"My spies tell me that you lost your wife six years ago. Rayya, an Arab beauty from the deserts of Africa. She contracted a tragic illness in Algeciras while you were away studying in Córdoba. By the time you got home she was gone, leaving you with three motherless children. That must have been difficult. You moved your children to Córdoba soon afterwards, to the chagrin of your family. Your family dwelling within the royal palace is modest but comfortable, appropriate to your status as vizier to Africa. A minor role to be sure, well outside the Golden Circle, but you do know Africa, and you do have contacts in the *Maghreb*. You are respected in the law courts. You are a shrewd business manager, skilled in the arts of trade negotiation. You do have modest connections to the wealthy merchants in the city ... but I would be careful before I trusted those imbeciles. They will betray you in a heartbeat. Your spy network is ..." she searches for the right word, "... meager." She widens her eyes. "At best."

Silence.

"You select your female slaves for their looks, and of course they are ... encouraged to minister to your needs. Quite understandable."

His eyes narrow.

"You have two sons, the elder a student of only modest intellect, studying in the grand imam's madrasa. The younger son stupidly flirts with the daughter of Durri the Small. I would be careful there. Durri does have a temper when pressed."

His face is a frozen mask.

"And you have a daughter." She smiles. "The smartest of the lot by a wide margin. Lives to read. Old to still be unmarried, though. My guess is that you intend to use her as a bargaining chip, to entice some old patriarch with gold to spare and an appetite for young virgins. Not an unwise move given that she inherited your wife's looks. I am told she has begun frequenting the Rare Books Library. I would watch the Jew al-Tayyib carefully if I were you." She sighs. "There is something about the man that I just cannot bring myself to trust."

Silence.

"Your spies are thorough, Subh."

She waves a hand dismissively. "I pay them well, Muhammad. Though confined to the royal harem, Madinat al-Zahra is my dominion. I think of it as my personal playground." She flashes a coy smile.

"Is there anything else I should know about myself?"

"Well ... you have both a great desire and a great need for gold. Your connections are growing, to be sure, but they remain very limited. Your influence is poised to expand, but alas, only if you can locate enough gold to make it so. You are ambitious, Muhammad. I like that. You have many talents and ample potential. You would not be here tonight if you did not." They lock eyes.

"Your proposition?"

She turns matter of fact. "I want you to manage my accounts, Muhammad." He would never have guessed this. "As you can easily infer, my holdings in al-Andalus are ... extensive. You will keep my books and provide me with regular reports. You will have free rein to buy and sell as you please, provided you deliver me a healthy profit, of course. I am eager to expand in the south, even in the Maghreb." That coy smile returns.

His heart races but his face remains unreadable. "I see. And in return?"

"And in return, you will receive the gold you covet. Three hundred gold dinars per month, plus ten percent of all profits on my accounts. In gold."

Silence.

Her blue eyes bore into him. She licks her lips. "And I require an additional favor."

He lifts his eyebrows, inviting her to continue.

"It concerns my son, Hisham. Your future caliph, Muhammad. You will provide Hisham with private lessons in the arts of governance. The elements of court law, business, and financial accounting, certainly, but also instruction in how to manipulate the merchant class and how to deal with the imams and other troublemakers. You navigate those dangerous waters with ease. Hisham must learn the intangibles required for effective rule as our future caliph."

This, then, is the real proposition. And a dangerous one at that. "Surely Caliph al-Hakam intends to provide his son with such training. Why do you need me?"

She frowns. "You would be surprised, Muhammad, at the things you do not know about our caliph." He nods, recollecting the scene with Jibril. "He neglects his own son. The boy will not be ready when the time comes. Unless we act. We must protect the Umayyad caliphate, Muhammad, and ensure the safety of the dynasty. We owe the people that much."

Silence.

"The caliph will never permit me access to his son, Subh. The boy's home is the royal harem. With you." He raises his hands and shrugs. "I am forbidden entry."

"Precisely. That is why you will visit me weekly for a reckoning of my accounts. The caliph will indulge me that if I insist. Jibril will guarantee the safety of my virtue while I am in your presence." Now her grin is wicked.

"Regular visits to the royal harem to settle your accounts. A ruse to enable time with Hisham ... so that I can ... educate him. Against the caliph's will. Very risky."

Another coy smile. The man is refreshingly bright. She nods. "Well?"

He studies his lap as he muses. It is the opportunity he has long desired. Dangerous, yes, but filled with promise. Imagine, a chance to mold the future caliph. "Five hundred dinars, fifteen percent of the profits I earn for you, and five thousand arpents of land."

She laughs. She would have been disappointed if he hadn't bargained. "Four hundred dinars, twelve percent, and I will throw in ten thousand arpents ... near Algeciras if you like. My final offer."

His stern expression brightens. "Done."

She beams. "Excellent. It seems your fortunes are about to change, Muhammad ibn Abi Amir."

She rises up on her knees and leans forward, cutting the distance between them. He is surprised by the impropriety but freezes in place. Her blue eyes dance as they bore into him. Her gown folds open as she leans close, exposing her breasts. He cannot restrain his eyes. Stiff, darkened nipples crowning sublime milky softness. He swallows hard as his heart pounds. As he raises his eyes to meet her gaze, she slides her right hand forward along his thigh, stopping an inch from his groin. He doesn't move a muscle. An exaggerated licking of her lips is followed by a breathy whisper, "The caliph ignores my needs, Muhammad. I ache for a real man. Ache."

There is a sharp double knock and Jibril enters the room and abruptly halts, averting his eyes. Subh leans back. Ibn Abi Amir flashes the look of a trapped animal and awkwardly stands, trying to arrange his robe to hide his stiffness. Unsuccessfully.

Jibril clears his throat. "My apologies, Sultana. The rain has stopped. Bundar says that the time is right for Muhammad's exit."

Ibn Abi Amir looks positively rattled. He struggles to gather himself and moves to join Jibril.

"Muhammad?"

He stops and slowly turns. "Yes, Subh?"

"Next Thursday, an hour after noon prayer. I am counting the moments."

A curt nod and the two are gone.

She is stretched out on her divan, luxuriating.

Jibril comes and sits on the floor at her feet. Neither can suppress their grins.

"Your timing was impeccable as always, Jibril."

"It would seem that you aroused the poor widower, Subh. Shame on you."

She laughs. "I am afraid so. And what did he think of Fatik and Muhja?"

"Oh, I would say Ibn Abi Amir will not soon forget the sight. A revelatory instruction in several important matters. Size, for instance." She laughs. "I fear our two Greek gods were indulging in a bit of fun before they entered all hard and glistening."

She smiles, satisfied. "Marvelous. You followed our conversation?"

"Every word. He is ours."

"Muhammad ibn Abi Amir will be thinking only of me when he gives up tonight and awakens his maid to sate his stiffness."

"No doubt, poor man. We must play him carefully, Subh."

"Yes. He is not stupid. And unbridled ambition is always dangerous. But, expertly managed, he will serve us well, Jibril. Hisham shall have his education. You and I will share the boy's throne. Queen and Regent."

Jibril responds with the sly smile of a serpent.

"Come, darling, you must tend to my needs."

The eunuch slides her gown up and bends to softly kiss her ankle. He touches his tongue to her calf and traces a moist curve up along the inside of her thigh. She leans back further, pulls her gown to her belly, spreads her legs as she arches her hips, and closes her eyes. She conjures a new face as she begins to pant.

Circles

22 September 975.

Caliph al-Hakam, his grand vizier, Jafar al-Mushafi, and his military vizier, General Ghalib al-Nisiri, the Golden Circle, step from the crimson glow of the warm room of the royal hammam, drop their towels one by one, then arm their way into the red ochre cotton robes the bath eunuchs raise in waiting. A second set of eunuchs steps forward to sash them tightly then kneel to install silk slippers.

With the trio properly attired, a third set of eunuchs approaches to offer each man a cup of chilled, watered wine. The Golden Circle is mute, but the two viziers have just spent a vigorous half-hour in the steamy heat of the hot room informing the caliph of the latest happenings. As usual, Jafar does most of the talking with General Ghalib adding a clarification or opinion here and there. The caliph absorbs. With this prelude, the Golden Circle now expands to include the larger circumference of the Vizier Council.

Jafar raises a palm and says, "Shall we, Sire?" The caliph nods and the three exit through the horseshoe arched doorway into the cool anteroom of the royal hammam. General Ghalib trails, his limp noticeably painful; a wince measures each step.

The anteroom of the hammam is the favored setting for the caliph's intimate audiences with his viziers. The air entering from the opened windows high above is refreshing, with an unmistakable crisp hint of fall, a welcomed balm to their scalded-pink skin. The light has changed from a dim, misty crimson to a subdued, soft daylight glow cast by the dozens of translucent alabaster windows that ring the compact, elegant room.

Eunuchs busy about bringing wine and morsels to the viziers, who are seated on floor pillows gathered tightly about the caliph's divan. In the center of the circle a marble floor fountain gurgles and splashes in a pleasing manner, its hidden purpose to quash all conversation from prying ears. A tickled guitar accompanied by the soft melodic hum of a young male voice echoes from somewhere unseen, mingling effortlessly with the whispers of the seated guests and the bubbling fountain, casting a soothing spell over the entire space.

Seated are: Rabi ibn Zyad, vizier of dhimmi; Abu al-Qasim, royal physician and vizier of medicine; Durri the Small, vizier of the royal treasury; Arib ibn Said, vizier to Constantinople; Samuel al-Tayyib, royal librarian and vizier of books; and Muhammad ibn Abi Amir, vizier to Africa.

As the Golden Circle enters the room the whispers cease. The viziers bow their heads deferentially but remain on their floor pillows. General Ghalib motions the eunuchs from the room with a brusque flick of his wrist and a dour grimace, producing an immediate scurry. The song evaporates. As the last eunuch slips out, the grizzled old man jerks his head at the four royal guards stationed by the door, who bow and exit, taking up their places immediately outside. No one is to come or go.

General Ghalib and Jafar exchange a glance then sit. Ghalib's grimace is chased by a sharp hiss through clenched teeth as he eases himself down.

Jafar begins. "Gentlemen. Our topic is foreign affairs. Several interesting events bear our collective consideration. Speak freely." He clears his throat. "As you are aware, we have received a diplomatic entourage from the Holy Roman Empire. Ambassador Peter Strobel from Magdeburg and Brother Cleo from Cluny. The former, predictably tiresome; the latter, quite refreshing." There are whispers of concurrence before he continues. "The caliph has asked Samuel to extend them every courtesy in the Royal Library."

Samuel smiles.

"Brother Cleo has been especially eager to absorb Abu al-Qasim's mastery of medicine. Evidently, an able student."

Abu al-Qasim vigorously nods his approval.

"We intend to use their visit to launch closer trade ties and a new cultural exchange with the Holy Roman Empire. Rabi ibn Zyad will organize this and coordinate. What we began with Emperor Otto the Great, we must continue with his son. The caliph feels it is our best defense against Christian incursion from the north. The Empire must come to see us as an equal, an essential trading partner. And, of course, as a source of learning and knowledge that they desperately covet." Jafar pauses to make eye contact with the caliph, who nods.

Jafar continues. "You may not have heard that young Otto has recently married. Interestingly, to the niece of our friend Emperor Tzimisces of the Byzantine Empire." He looks to the vizier to Constantinople. "Some details please, Arib?"

Arib ibn Said straightens his back. "Otto the Great negotiated a marriage contract for his son with the Byzantines prior to his death. A thinly veiled attempt to reunify Western and Eastern Christendom. Young Otto, known to those close to him as Otto the Red for his flaming hair, married Theophanu, Emperor Tzimisces' niece. She is twelve, Otto sixteen. An attractive girl, educated. There are rumors of budding love. No children yet, I am told."

Rabi ibn Zyad says, "I am surprised the pope did not fight the two emperors' brazen attempts to further marginalize Rome."

Arib ibn Said lifts his hands helplessly. "How could he? As you will recall, the elder Otto was instrumental in Pope Benedict VI's election. Rumors say Benedict was handpicked, the emperor's chosen pawn. Otto bought the cardinals he needed, discredited those against him, and threatened the rest. Rome trembles. It seems the pope has now been effectively imprisoned in Castello Sant'Angelo, under the pretense that it is the only place in Rome safe enough from brigands for a pope to effectively reign. Otto's doing, no doubt. Out of sight, out of mind." Several chuckles.

General Ghalib interjects, "As you know, the Byzantines are our strongest ally in the east. Tzimisces has proven to be an able general, and this new alliance may serve us well. After liberating Thrace and the lower Danube, he has turned south and invaded Mesopotamia. By all accounts, his campaign against the Abbasids is going well. It seems that Caliph al-Muti quivers in his palace in Baghdad." Laughter echoes through the group. "Tzimisces vows to capture Jerusalem and the rest of the Holy Land and return it to Christendom. I am confident he possesses the means." He pauses. "The loss of Holy Jerusalem is not something we desire, of course. Nevertheless, the harder Tzimisces presses the Abbasids, the better for Córdoba. One caliph is enough for Islam, and that caliph is Umayyad, not Abbasid, by Allah's Will." Smiles circle the room.

Caliph al-Hakam finally speaks, his voice soft and feminine. "And let us not forget that the Byzantines sent me the gold and mosaics to complete the mihrab of the Great Mosque. It is a crowning glory and a fitting tribute to Allah by a Christian emperor. I have seen to it that the Great Mosque has no rival anywhere and never will. The Byzantines have proven time and again that they value Córdoba as an ally." All around are nods of agreement.

Jafar motions to Arib ibn Said to continue. "Young Otto brought his bride to Rome for a post-nuptial ... blessing. With little fanfare, Pope Benedict crowned Theophanu Holy Roman Empress. A significant development. Despite his youth, Young Otto seems quite adept at politics."

Jafar takes over. "In short, the Holy Roman Empire and the Byzantine Empire draw closer together each day. We must work to ensure that Otto follows Tzimisces in assigning the appropriate value to Córdoba and what she represents to the West."

Rabi ibn Zyad adds, "Young Otto seems eager to befriend us. His diplomatic mission suggests that he desires to walk in his father's footsteps. It is a path we can easily encourage."

Jafar responds, "Yes, I agree. As a first step, we will propose a Córdoba delegation composed of diplomats, theologians, scholars, and physicians, who will travel to Magdeburg in the spring and stay for a year at Otto's court. And we will invite a larger entourage to Córdoba. We will press for not only diplomatic and economic dialog, but an expansive cultural exchange."

The caliph frowns. "Otto may be adept like his father, but it seems his ambassador needs some lessons in decorum."

Laughter is the reaction.

General Ghalib responds, "Certainly Strobel's lament of the African corsairs' flagrant incursions on their coastal cities and merchant vessels has merit. We, too, are feeling the same pressure. The devils have struck as far west as Cádiz. Just last month they captured and burned several ships in port and threatened to torch the city unless an offering of gold was made. Frustrating. How we best deal with these pirates is not clear." He grimaces as he shifts the position of his leg.

Durri the Small replies, "Still, Strobel's offer of gold for our help was a brazen insult to the caliph."

General Ghalib snorts, then says, "Yes. A despicable lack of manners."

Rabi ibn Zyad responds, "Do not judge him too harshly, gentlemen. Strobel lacks finesse, that much is clear, but only because he does not yet know our ways. Give him time, he will come around. He is bright, and I suspect, quite cunning. Played carefully, he can serve us well."

General Ghalib looks dubious. Heavy sigh. "In any case, these corsairs strike unimpeded from harbors beyond our control. This must end."

"Fatimid harbors, General." The first words from Ibn Abi Amir. "The corsairs strike us from Fatimid harbors. With Fatimid support and Fatamid encouragement. We will have no peace while they rule the Western Maghreb."

Eyes turn to Ibn Abi Amir. Jafar says, "Please continue."

"In my view, we must exploit their only real rivals, the Idrisids, a loose confederation of Berber clans living in the Rif Mountains. Fight fire with fire. Devout followers of the Prophet, praise his

Holy Name. They lack culture, to be sure, but are capable warriors and ruthless in battle. Expert horsemen. From what my sources tell me, better than any in al-Andalus."

General Ghalib sniffs, then grimaces, but remains silent.

Ibn Abi Amir continues, "Alas, the Berber clans of the Rif remain disorganized, unable to offer any coordinated resistance to the Fatimids. For now." He pauses to gauge his audience. "The Berber clans fight each other ceaselessly: blood feuds over simple insults, petty squabbles for power, stolen horses, women—the usual. But, properly honed, I believe they are the key to cutting the legs from under the Fatimids and putting an end to these corsair raids." He looks about the room. "This would demand diligence and substantial finesse. And gold, of course. The Berbers are deeply skeptical of our motives. And they resent our more ... tolerant approach to Islam."

General Ghalib scoffs, "The Berbers hate us. They would never ally themselves with Córdoba."

Ibn Abi Amir's reply is matter-of-fact. "The General is correct, the Berbers do hate us. But they envy us, too, just like the Fatimids. The Berbers must first be subdued by the sword, then molded to serve our needs. They are a warrior people with deep traditions, and they will respect us only when they are forced to respect us. We must earn their trust."

Jafar asks, "Their leader?"

"Nominally, Sultan al-Hasan ibn Guennoun. Weak and ineffective. He will never unify the mountain clans. The Fatimids have pushed him back into the Rif. He hides in Hajar an-Nasar, a cliff-top fortress."

General Ghalib interrupts, "I know the place. Eagle's Rock. East of Larache, high in the Rif. Well protected."

Ibn Abi Amir continues, "At present, the Fatimids seem content to lock Ibn Guennoun away in the mountains. Meanwhile, they provide safe haven to the corsairs in the ports of the Western Maghreb. Corsairs who grow fat with booty. Sad to say, the new Fatimid ruler, Sultan al-Muizz, is building lavish palaces with Córdoban gold."

Durri the Small frowns.

The caliph softly asks, "What would you suggest, Muhammad?"

Ibn Abi Amir takes a deep breath. "An expedition, Sire. We send an army under General Ghalib's command to ... convince Ibn Guennoun that we would make an excellent ally against the Fatimids."

General Ghalib scowls. "Attack Hajar an-Nasar?"

"Yes, General, but with help. I have recently made contact with Ibn Guennoun's chief rivals, the Banu Birzal, the largest Berber clan not part of the Idrisid confederation. They rule the Rif south of Tetouan.

"Their leader is Sheikh Hamid al-Tariq. A natural leader I am told, and a formidable man. Given proper respect and support, I believe he will serve our needs. A blood feud exists between Ibn Guennoun and al-Tariq. We can exploit this. I am afraid Ibn Guennoun's time as an Idrisid sultan will be short lived."

General Ghalib interrupts again. "How do you know all this?"

Ibn Abi Amir shrugs. "My ear is always to the wind, General."

He is answered with a scowl.

Ibn Abi Amir remains silent until the caliph motions him on. "Sire, first we befriend al-Tariq and the Banu Birzal, then together we march on Hajar an-Nasar and defeat Ibn Guennoun, something he knows he could never do alone. We then install al-Tariq as the new sultan of the Rif Berbers. I am confident he can unify the Berber clans. As a friend, Córdoba will ensure that al-Tariq has ample gold to buy the favors he needs to solidify power. When the time is right, we will unleash his Berber army on the Fatimids. They will break from the Rif like lightning and capture the most important ports of the Western Maghreb: Larache, Tangier, Ceuta, al-Hoceima, Nador, perhaps others. It will be no secret to the Fatimids, of course, who wags the Berber tail. Our desire for an end to the corsair raids will become known by back channels."

Silence.

"The Berbers are a formidable fighting force, Sire. And after decades of oppression, they will jump at the chance to spill Fatimid blood. Trust me, they will more than occupy the attention of the Fatimids. Córdoba will gain an important ally in the Maghreb, and an important buffer between us and the Fatimids. Suitably occupied, the Fatimid appetite for supporting corsairs will quickly wane. Even Emperor Otto will be in our debt, Sire." He looks about the room. "Who knows? Perhaps we may decide to rule the Maghreb ourselves when all is said and done. A simple cut of the puppet's strings." He smiles. "Only if we decide there is a pressing need to bring Umayyad culture to our needy brothers in Africa." Approving nods are the response.

Jafar turns to Durri the Small. "What would it cost us to finance such an ... expedition?"

The royal treasurer waves his hands dismissively. "Depending on the size of the army, a pittance. The treasury is flush. Six million gold dinars and eight million silver dirhams. We could send a small army, say four thousand knights, for half a million dinars, perhaps less, even assuming no booty. And the return on that investment would be handsome, assuming they put an end to the corsair raids. I would also find a way, of course, for Otto to properly compensate us for our trouble. By discreet channels, obviously."

The caliph responds, "An interesting idea, Muhammad. I will give your ... suggestion some thought." He glances first to Jafar and then at General Ghalib.

Jafar clears his throat. "One last topic for today. The Christians in the north. General Ghalib?"

Ghalib frowns. "It seems that Christian lust for our lands in the Upper Marches has flared once again. Garcia Fernandez, the new Count of Castile, has begun offering noble status to anyone in the gentry who is willing to provision a mounted knight. My sources tell me he is secretly training an invasion force."

Arib ibn Said asks, "Who?"

Rabi ibn Zyad responds, "Eldest son of the Count Fernan Gonzalez of Castile. He is known as 'White Hands.'"

Ibn Said queries with his eyes.

Ibn Zyad grins. "Skin pale as a ghost. Hair white as an old man's; sky blue eyes. The man stands out in a crowd."

The men break out into scattered laughter.

General Ghalib adds, "His father was a thorn in our side for decades. Thankfully, fate had its way and he has gone to meet his maker. Alas, the son appears to be cast from the same mold. Garcia is ambitious, well trained in the arts of war. And from all appearances he seems to be a capable tactician. This new threat must not be taken lightly."

Jafar says, "The caliph has decided that Córdoba should send an unequivocal message to Count Garcia before he begins meddling in our affairs. General Ghalib will oversee the raising of a thousand troops in the Middle Marches. They will be sent to garrison Medinaceli in the border lands between al-Andalus and Castile. The troops will first refortify the castle then become visible around the region. That should serve as a deterrent at least temporarily." He turns to Durri the Small. "We will need resources to hire and arm the troops."

The vizier of the royal treasury smiles. "Of course."

Rabi ibn Zyad says, "Would it be helpful for me to plant seeds in political circles within Castile that Córdoba has no intention of ceding lands without a fight?"

General Ghalib nods. "Yes. But carefully, Rabi. Garcia must come to his own conclusion that we will not hesitate to rally forces for *jihad* should the need arise. He must realize that we have the means to match any army he might envision raising."

Jafar looks around the room. "Good. I believe that is all for today, gentlemen, unless there are any questions."

The caliph interjects, "Samuel. Word has come to me of a new shipment of books from Constantinople."

Samuel grins. "Indeed, Sire. Twenty-seven volumes of ancient Greek, apparently from the Great Library of Alexandria before it was razed. Most are in good condition. A bargain by any stretch, Sire. We have copies already of those we have examined to date, but Abu al-Qasim is pouring over some of the medical volumes to check for consistency against our extant volumes."

The caliph looks at Abu al-Qasim.

The royal physician answers, "I have already come upon some interesting differences in translation, Sire. We may well learn something useful."

"Good." He looks back to the royal librarian. "Samuel, I would enjoy seeing a sampling of the books. When you have completed your cataloging, of course."

"Certainly, Sire." Samuel bows.

The caliph smiles. "By the way, please complement Zafir. *Lysistrata* is a treasure! I could not stop laughing. Let us hope that the women of Córdoba do not learn from the Greeks."

Samuel's delight is unmistakable. "Indeed, Sire, the Greek plays are magnificent. I will pass on your kind words. Zafir will be pleased to hear that you enjoyed it."

Jafar pulls them back to business. "Anything else?" He pauses. "Good. Our meeting is adjourned."

The viziers rise in unison. The Golden Circle remains seated.

Jafar softly says, "Muhammad. Could you remain a moment? We would like a word. In private."

Ibn Abi Amir nods, his face expressionless. He stands still as a statue as the others move silently to the door. His heart is pounding. Ibn Abi Amir has never been alone with the Golden Circle.

The quiet is leaden, tortuous. The caliph begins, "Your ideas about the Maghreb intrigue me, Muhammad." He pauses. "Your presence within the Vizier Council has been ... beneficial. Though you are young, your ideas are well considered and have merit. The grand imam was right to nominate you for the position."

Ibn Abi Amir bows. "Sire, you are too generous. I live to serve you and the kingdom by any means I possess."

Jafar and General Ghalib study Ibn Abi Amir intently.

The caliph continues, his demeanor a studied indifference. "The sultana visited me this week, Muhammad."

Ibn Abi Amir's face is frozen, unreadable.

"She made a most unusual request." He offers a long pause. "It seems that the sultana would like you to personally oversee her accounts and assets. It would require you to manage her holdings in the kingdom, both here in Córdoba and also in the Middle and Upper Marches. She requested weekly meetings to seek your advice and discuss your planned acquisitions."

Ibn Abi Amir frowns. "Me, Sire? I do not understand."

"I have always indulged the sultana with ample resources, Muhammad. To date those have prospered. She is a wealthy woman. But it seems she desires to expand into the south now, especially in Algeciras and Cádiz, perhaps even the Maghreb. She feels your expertise in legal and trade matters, and your many connections in the south, would serve her interests well."

"Sire, I am honored by the sultana's request, truly. But I am afraid that is quite impossible. As you know, I am far too busy in the law courts in my service to the grand imam. And, of course, I have my diplomatic demands from Africa. I am afraid I simply do not have the time to take on another role. I would be happy, of course, to suggest someone who would suit her needs."

The silence stretches. The eyes of Jafar and General Ghalib have not left Ibn Abi Amir's face.

"I understand, Muhammad. But the sultana was insistent. It must be you. As you might imagine, keeping the sultana happy is no small matter. I would consider it a personal favor."

Ibn Abi Amir bows. "Certainly, Sire. Your wish is my command."

The caliph smiles. "Thank you, Muhammad. I am in your debt."

Jafar says, "As you might imagine, Muhammad, these weekly meetings will present some logistical challenges, given that the sultana is confined to the royal harem. I will arrange things with the head eunuch so that the intrusion on your other duties is minimized."

"Thank you."

"While you are within the royal harem a chaperone must accompany you at all times."

"Of course."

"I will have her account ledger brought to you today so that you may familiarize yourself with her holdings. I believe the sultana would like to meet you in person this Thursday. I will send the details shortly."

Ibn Abi Amir nods.

Jafar waves his hand in dismissal. "That is all."

Ibn Abi Amir rises, bows to the caliph, and exits.

The silence inflates.

Jafar sighs. "The sultana's request is most unusual, Sire. I find myself wondering what her true agenda is. As we all know, she is a shrewd one. Every decision she makes is the result of a complicated set of calculations."

The caliph frowns. "Yes ..."

General Ghalib grumbles, "I do not trust him."

The caliph replies, "He has fresh ideas, Ghalib, and those ideas are useful to us. I think he is right about the Berbers, by the way. They are the key to the Fatimids." He pauses to muse. "Still, I will grant that he is a difficult one to read."

Jafar adds, "And let us not forget his connections to the grand imam."

The caliph nods. "Have him watched. Discreetly, of course."

General Ghalib seems satisfied. "I will put my best man on it."

The caliph's mood measurably brightens. "Jafar, can you please summon Jawdhar? I would like to fly my falcons today. Have him meet me at the northern gate in one hour."

"Certainly, Sire, I will see to it."

Tangles

With a practiced touch he presses down firmly on the door handle as he lifts the metal latch, opening it without a sound. He sidesteps the preferred creak of the floorboard and slips into the room. He stops to survey the scene. The pink-orange glow of sunrise kisses the window pane, releasing the muted grays that bind the room. There is a chill in the air. In the distance the sweet lament of the muezzin can just be heard.

She lies on her side facing him, tucked into her usual fetal position like a child, the heavy quilt pulled tightly to her chin. Waves of dark brown spill out across her pillow, framing her lovely face. Her breathing is steady and even.

He steps to the side of the bed and raises the nub of blue flame on the oil lamp to a warm yellow glow. She doesn't stir. Her features are perfectly relaxed, peaceful. As he studies her he spontaneously smiles. He sees that her eyes beneath their lids are still, her dreams departed.

He rests the steaming cup of tea on the table beside her then bends down and kisses her lightly upon her cheek as he whispers, "Good morning, beautiful." He tenderly kisses her again. "I love you." His kisses explore her face; cheek, then forehead, then eyes, and finally lips.

She stirs and whispers, "Good morning, Husband."

He rolls her onto her back and eases down beside her on the bed.

"My Rebekah, a princess worthy of King Solomon's court."

A mock smirk. "You have been reading too much, Husband."

Samuel laughs. "Only stories of love, my dear, only stories of love." He folds back the covers and eases his hand beneath her gown to cup her full breast.

She starts. "Your hands are freezing!"

He grins as he retreats. "A small price to pay, my love." He laughs. "I brought you tea, darling."

The corners of her mouth lift. "Thank you, Samuel."

"I brought you kisses, darling."

She grins. "Thank you, Samuel."

"I brought you a profession of love, darling."

Her grin widens. "Thank you, Samuel."

He lifts his right eyebrow into an exaggerated query.

She giggles. "NO, Samuel!" She pins his hand.

He leans in and they first rub noses, then touch lips.

"I love you, Husband."

"I love you, Wife."

Their cherished morning ritual draws to a close.

Rebekah sits up, tucks her knees to her chest like a little girl, yawns, and launches a giant feline stretch. She lifts her tea, cups it with both hands to warm herself, then delicately sips. "Tell me about your day."

He sighs. "The usual. Meetings, meetings, and more meetings. Hopefully with some time squeezed in for my beloved Aristotle. We continue to pour over this broken codex. Fascinating stuff. I am convinced it is Aristotle's personal working journal. A unique window into the man's mind. His genius leaps from the pages, Rebekah, but frankly, I do not understand much of what I read. Yet. He thinks in images, and he proves his propositions as a geometer would, which can be confusing. But with Zaheid, Levi, and Zafir at my side, who knows, perhaps we will learn some secrets soon. The mechanics behind his camera obscura still elude us, but it seems Zaheid has found some help among the ancient Alexandrians. I think we are close." He chuckles. "Zafir is not so sure. Our dear boy is always the skeptic."

She touches his arm. "Did you talk with Zafir?"

"About?"

Rebekah frowns. "Miriam, Samuel. You told me you would."

"Ahhh ... the love affair."

She punches him.

"Yes, yes, I spoke with him. You were right, of course, the boy had no clue. He thinks of her as a little sister, no more. Not to worry, Zafir has promised to be mindful of her feelings."

"Good." Her expression turns serious. "Your little girl is a woman now, Samuel. This is only the beginning, you know. If not Zafir then some other young man. She is a pretty girl. You do realize they will soon come calling."

He frowns. "I suppose, I suppose. May heaven help me. All I can say is that they better be serious readers. I plan to interview each one!"

She laughs. "Tell me more about this girl Zafir met."

Samuel shrugs. "Rayhana Abi Amir. The daughter of the vizier to Africa. Ibn Abi Amir is a strange man, hard to read. But his daughter is a joy. Pretty, and bright. She reads in the Rare Books Library three mornings a week. Her love of books is contagious and heartwarming." He chuckles. "Talks with her hands. Quite endearing. And she has these wonderful dimples, perfectly hidden except when she smiles." Samuel pauses as he recollects. "Zafir stumbled upon her unexpectedly last week while searching for a book. Afterwards, the boy acted very odd, suddenly forgetful. There is not a forgetful bone in Zafir's body, Rebekah. And he mumbles whenever the topic of Rayhana comes up. Mumbles! Zafir!"

Samuel offers an exasperated exhale and raises his voice, incredulous. "He even blushed when Zaheid made a joke about the girl. Have you *ever* seen Zafir blush? Our boy tries as best he can to avoid the topic altogether. Of course, Zaheid and Levi have no intention of allowing that."

Rebekah has not stopped grinning. "I assume it is obvious to you?"

"Obvious to me? What should be obvious to me?"

"Love, Samuel. Our Zafir is in love."

Samuel looks confused, then frowns as he shakes his head. "Love? *Love?* For Yahweh's sake, Rebekah, he just met the girl!"

Her grin is fixed. "What did you feel when you first saw me, Samuel?"

Silence.

"There is such a thing as love at first sight, Husband."

"Mmmm ..."

She leans forward to kiss his cheek. "I expect regular reports."

He stares into space, bewildered.

She studies him. "Zafir will always be your protégé, Samuel, nothing will change that. But he deserves the love of a woman, a family of his own."

He exhales wearily. "I suppose ..."

As her grin slowly relaxes her honey-almond eyes dilate with the dance of a new song. She reaches for him. "Come to me, Husband."

The dark square is tucked into the hanging tapestry at eye level, hidden in a tight loop of calligraphic swirl. The embroidered silk covering the neat incision through the wall has been opened to a size no bigger than a thumbnail, sufficient to permit a single prying eye. From just a pace away the peep-hole disappears into the weave, blending effortlessly into the text of the love poem. The field of view is deliberately narrow, centered on the sultana's divan.

An ebony eye stares out, the boundary between the thin ring of the iris and the dilated pupil erased to a continuous midnight hue. The quick blink of painted lashes is the only betrayal of life hidden behind the wall.

The contrast between the milky porcelain of her skin and his dark olive torso is arresting, the striation of light and dark pulsing with urgency as their twined bodies writhe and stretch and bend. Blond curls are scattered everywhere, her legs scissored about his waist, toes curled tightly.

A soft sheen of sweat traces the curve of his spine. He softly groans as he thrusts into her, attacks her deliciously pale neck. Her perfume is dabbed in several strategic places and it drives him wild. She stretches her head back to beckon him, then seemingly tries to escape his urgent kisses and bites, then invites him once more, teasing him.

She pants but is otherwise silent through it all. As usual. There is an unseen smile from behind the wall; confident, knowing. The eye is amused by all the acrobatic antics, no more.

As the man's motions become more urgent, however, her body suddenly tenses and a cry slips from her mouth, softly at first, then more forcefully, almost against her will. The voyeur is startled, and responds by pressing his eye more tightly to the peep-hole. He has never before seen a look quite like that on her face. Vulnerable? He grimaces.

The man's groans begin to lengthen and become more vocal. She cries out again, this time almost as if in pain, and then she calls his name, first a clenched whisper, then louder, more emotional, "Muhammad ... Muhammad!" A final wrenching convulsion and he collapses onto her, stilling the writhing tangle.

They lie motionless, his face buried in her neck. She stares at the ceiling. As she begins to play with his hair a satisfied smile eases onto her face. She playfully runs her fingers down his back, exploring, and doesn't stop until he shivers. She laughs. He lifts his head, kisses her deeply, then abruptly slides from her and reaches for his robe. She remains as she is, her body sprawled in all its glory. Her cheeks and breasts glow a soft rosy pink. She has lost five years, perhaps ten. The smile remains.

She watches him dress.

He clears his throat. "I trust my report was adequate, Subh?"

She laughs. "Oh, more than adequate, Muhammad. My only regret is that I did not arrange for a daily accounting." He smiles in spite of himself. She continues, "I will send for Hisham when you are ready. He can join us here."

Ibn Abi Amir frowns. "No. I have decided that our lessons will be conducted in private."

Silence.

st cultivate a trust between the two of us or else these lessons will mean nothing to the boy. That cannot happen with you or Jibril, present. And I do not want to be in your bedchamber. We need privacy, in a room where he feels comfortable."

She studies him. "Very well. You may use the library down the hall. The boy practically lives there."

He nods.

She reaches for the bell beside her and dingles it. Two quick knocks and Jibril enters. He does not even register her nakedness. Ibn Abi Amir frowns. The eunuch says, "Sultana?"

"Please see that Hisham is brought to the library. He and Muhammad will meet there. And have tea delivered as well."

"Certainly, Sultana."

Ibn Abi Amir says, "Jibril, I will need a map of the Maghreb."

The eunuch looks puzzled but replies, "Certainly, Muhammad. I would be delighted to show you to the library."

The sultana studies her new lover as he leaves, but he does not look back.

Ten minutes later Jibril enters without knocking and takes up his station at her feet. She has not moved.

"I do not like this privacy arrangement with Hisham, Subh. Too many unknowns."

"I agree. Can you have a peep-hole installed in the library?"

"Yes, but it will take time. I will see that it is ready by the next meeting."

"Good."

The silence stretches out.

"You feigned your pleasure quite impressively, Subh. I am sure he never suspected. You even had me convinced for a moment ..."

Her gaze is vacant, unreadable. "Yes, well, some things are important to a man."

The eunuch offers a thin smile. "Indeed." He rests his henna-painted hand upon her thigh and begins to trace a small circle with his thumb. "Shall I tend to your needs?"

She turns away. "No. Leave me."

His smile collapses. The circling thumb instantly freezes and his expression hardens into a mask. He whispers, "Very well." He stares at her for a moment more, waiting for her gaze, but it doesn't come. He rises and leaves the room.

———— 🔲 ————

Zaheid beams. "My memory never fails me. Theon of Alexandria did indeed experiment with Aristotle's camera obscura, I am sure of it!" He proudly taps the splayed codex.

Levi, Zafir, and Samuel lean close. Only dense text.

Zaheid indicates the precise place on the vellum and slowly reads the ancient Greek. Zafir translates to Arabic as he goes. "Candlelight passing through a pinhole will create an illuminated spot on a screen that is directly in line with the aperture and the center of the candle."

Samuel replies, "Do you think he learned of it from Aristotle's journal? Perhaps it was his hand that inscribed the page with 'Eureka!'"

Zaheid shrugs. "Unknown, but it seems plausible. After all, Theon clearly frequented the Great Library."

"Yes, but it was razed during his lifetime."

"Correct. But I am confident he is writing about Aristotle's camera obscura. He utilized the instrument to deduce that light follows straight lines. Note that Theon explicitly says he uses a pinhole for the aperture. So my thinking was all wrong. There is no need for us to worry about the shape or exact size of the hole; it must only be small compared to the dimensions of the camera. We can use a sharp nail to make a tiny puncture."

Levi interjects, "Still, it would make an interesting experiment to see what effects the size of the hole make on the resultant image."

"Agreed. Theon does not mention this, but it is certainly a logical experiment. He does say, however, that the color and perspective of the candle are perfectly replicated on the screen. Inverted, of course. Aristotle's true form."

Samuel says, "Levi, have you completed the construction of the camera?"

"Nearly. Zafir secured the materials we need from the royal book binder two days back."

Eyes turn to Zafir.

"I told him I needed them to make some repairs on the new shipment of books we received. A dozen sheets of paste board and three sheets of binder's leather. He does not suspect."

Samuel replies, "Good. By the way, the caliph now knows of the cache's existence. No details of the Aristotle journal, of course. We should assume, however, that the whole of Madinat al-Zahra is now aware of our cache."

Levi chuckles.

"The caliph wants to examine the codices himself when we have completed our cataloging." Samuel looks to Zafir. "He adored your translation of *Lysistrata*. Well done, my boy."

Zafir smiles, clearly pleased.

Levi continues, "The camera's panels have been cut to size according to Zaheid's instructions, edges honed and fitted, and the interiors painted black. Zafir and I will assemble the camera late this evening with glue and nails. The final touch will be to make this pinhole."

Zaheid says, "I think I would first thin the paste board in the center of the front panel to make that easier. And do not use glue on that front panel so we can easily try different apertures."

"Understood."

Samuel says, "How will we see the image formed inside the camera?"

Zaheid slides a large sheet of paper from under the codex, a precise set of plans. He points with his reed. "The camera is small enough to fit on the table. We will place the candle here, with the flame on the same level as the pinhole." His reed moves right. "The image should appear here, on the back panel of the camera. On this side of the camera we will cut a small flap that can be bent outward to view the screen."

Samuel nods. "Yes, good."

Levi grins. "We should be ready tomorrow evening."

Zafir says, "Where should we test it?"

Samuel responds, "The small reading room adjoining the mathematics collection should do nicely. When you finish tonight, bring it there. Cover it with a sheet and see that the door is locked."

Zafir acknowledges with a curt nod.

Zaheid points an impish grin at Zafir. "I assume that room is free of beautiful maidens? The Sirens' song makes it so difficult for me to concentrate. If we cannot find beeswax, you will have to lash me to the mast like Odysseus."

Levi offers a matching grin.

Zafir blushes but does not respond.

Samuel scolds Zaheid with his eyes and lets the room settle. "Tomorrow evening we will gather at midnight for our first test of Aristotle's Problem 37."

Spirals

3 December 975.

The knock is barely audible but distinctive. Two quick taps, a pause, one tap, a longer pause, a final tap.

Instant dimples.

He slips into the room then pivots, leaving his head stranded in the hallway as he continues his survey of the long corridor, first left, then right. Satisfied, he retrieves his head to study the door latch. He places both hands on the hardware at precise points as he gingerly closes the door, muting the normally loud, metallic double-snap to a whispered tick.

He pivots once more then mock frowns. "The Rare Books Library is forbidden to visitors. Why are you here?"

She quizzically tilts her head just so, her half-smirk somehow unmistakably questioning his intelligence. Their shared joke. "To read." Her dimples return as he laughs loudly.

"Good morning, Rayhana."

"Good morning, Zafir."

She is seated on her pillow, back straight, palms cupped in her lap, codex predictably open in front of her on the low table. A notepad, reed pen, and inkwell are set beside it, a half page filled with dots and dashes and squiggles.

The cream of her cotton robe is the perfect foil for her warm olive tones. Her amber starbursts sparkle. Two mother-of-pearl combs pull her dark curls from her face, but the barely restrained mass feverishly resists, the tresses getting the better of the tug-of-war. Wispy spirals of dark brown waterfall adorably onto her cheeks. Somewhere close an intoxicating hint of orange blossom floats.

To his chagrin, his heart begins to pound. As usual. He swallows to steady his legs and reminds himself not to clear his throat. His grin bears a decidedly self-conscious stamp. He tries for a casual tone and almost gets there. "And what does Samuel have you reading this week?" He clears his throat.

Her face magically brightens, a transformation so stunning he has yet to get used to it. "He thought I should begin some of the Greek plays."

Zafir's excitement is instantaneous and barely contained. "Really?! The Greek plays are my specialty, Rayhana. Tragedy or comedy?" He steps forward and plops down across from her, his anxieties thankfully vanished. His elbows hinge to the table as he rests his chin on his balled fists and begins to memorize her face.

She beams as she lifts the codex and shows him the spine. "Tragedy. Euripides' *Trojan Women*. He thought the connection with the *Iliad* would be interesting to me ... and a good introduction to Greek tragedy. Zafir, it is so heartbreaking ... after Troy falls, all the women are forced to serve as concubines to the conquerors. Cassandra is given to Agamemnon, Andromache to Achilles' son." She takes a deep breath. "Queen Hecuba has learned that her daughter Polyxena was sacrificed at the tomb of Achilles. And poor Astyanax. Just a boy ..." Her eyelids fold shut. Remarkably, a single tear slides down each cheek. She turns her face from him to erase them with her thumb. "Forgive me. The story is just so real and so terribly sad."

His eyes have not left her face. He understands perfectly. "There is nothing to forgive, Rayhana. The women of Troy suffered terribly, and Euripides wants us to relive that horror with him, to taste the tragedy so we might better appreciate the awful waste of war. Supposedly, he wrote the play during the Great War of the Peloponnese after the wholesale slaughter of the innocents of Milos by the Athenians. Euripides wanted to remind all Greeks that they had forgotten what suffering was like."

"I have never read anything quite like it."

He smiles. "No. The Greek tragedies are wonderfully unique. Aristotle was the first to speculate on their origin. As he recounts in his *Poetics*, tragic theater is believed to have evolved from a religious rite associated with Dionysus—Bacchus to the Romans— the God of wine and reverie. The *Dithyramb* was a chorus of male voices used in that celebration, and somehow those songs evolved into spoken characters caught within an unfolding tragic drama. He said the first performances were held in Attica but they quickly spread across Greece."

"When were they written?"

"Euripides wrote just after the Greek Golden Age, almost fourteen hundred years ago."

"Amazing." Their shared smile lingers. "Was he the first tragic poet?"

"Actually, no. Euripides followed Sophocles. Aeschylus was the first we know of. Euripides' innovation was to focus more on the portrayal of the feelings of his characters, the torment and suffering of those caught up in real human events. He strives for realism."

"Yes ..."

Their eyes linger on each other until they become aware of the fact, then each awkwardly looks away, she to her codex, he to the upper shelves. There is a flurry of quick movements high above, but he misses the action.

An idea strikes Zafir and he returns to her. "How much do you have left in the *Trojan Women*?"

She rejoins him. "Not much. I am sure I will finish this morning."

He beams. "May I have the honor of selecting another play for you?"

Those glorious dimples. "Certainly."

He leaps up to the bookshelves, where he hurriedly scans the titles with a barely contained enthusiasm. She turns to watch him, amused.

He speaks as he scans. "What I would like you to try, Rayhana, is an example of a Greek comedy. Aristophanes." He turns to catch her eye. "My favorite of the Greek comedians!"

She grins.

He returns to his task. "A master of the use of satire as a weapon. You will love him!"

She laughs.

"Where are you hiding? Show yourself, sir!" He hurriedly moves to the next shelf. "Ah ha! Found you!" He extracts the volume, turns, and without thinking, sits down next to her, shoulder to shoulder, drops the codex on the table between them, and proudly thumps the codex with his finger. "Aristophanes. *The Wasps*."

Her expression shifts from wide-eyed surprise to an amused grin.

As he becomes painfully aware of her proximity his heart starts to race once more. He clears his throat then mentally kicks himself. "I ... umm ... consider *The Wasps* to be, uhh ... Aristophanes' finest work." There is a massive pause. "His ... mmm—masterpiece."

Her amusement grows. She casually leans to let her shoulder brush his, producing an electric tingle that causes him to flinch. "This is wonderful, Zafir, thank you." She opens the cover to read the title page and stops. "Oh my ... you actually translated this?" As she turns to him, she becomes instantly aware that they are close enough to kiss. Her heart begins to race.

He slowly lifts his gaze from the codex to find her sparkling amber starbursts. His head is swimming. He swears he can feel the heat from her body. As those spirals continue their exquisite torture, he desperately wills his eyes away from them, only to have them lock onto the soft swell of her breasts. He can hear his pulse in his ears. He takes a deep breath to gather himself. "I did, yes ..." He offers a sheepish grin. "Royal translator? It was two years back. I hope you find it enjoyable, Rayhana. *Wasps* is one of my favorites ..." The orange blossoms are so close.

She does not acknowledge him. Her eyelids droop as she leans harder into him and tilts her head ever so slightly upward. Without thinking, he lifts his hand to touch her cheek and cannot resist twisting his index finger into a spiral. Her eyes close. He leans into her. Their lips slowly touch, then part, then touch once more, then linger, then finally part. She opens her eyes to his warm smile. She grins shyly then licks her lips and her eyes retreat to her lap.

Their shoulders remain glued. An overwhelming desire to kiss her throat washes over him. He has to swallow hard to chase it away.

She abruptly looks up. Her casual tone is almost convincing when she says, "Good ... I now have my Wednesday reading settled."

His emerald eyes burn into her. Her head wilts to her lap again and after a moment she shyly says, "That has never happened before, Zafir. I will treasure the memory."

He lifts her chin to meet his gaze. "As will I, Rayhana. Thank you." He chuckles to inject some levity, finally feeling his legs. "You must forgive me. For some reason I get stupid and forget how to speak when I am around you."

She laughs.

"And I clear my throat for some odd reason I have not yet been able to figure out." He shakes his head in dismay.

Mock concern fills her face. "Yes, I thought you might have an illness of some sort." They both laugh and fall into contented silence.

"I must know more about you, Rayhana. Please."

First, a curious expression, then she shrugs. "There is not much to tell, really. I grew up in Algeciras. My jiddo and tetta live there still. And many of my cousins, of course. I have two brothers; one older and one younger, both here in Córdoba."

"You are Arabian."

She grins. "Yes. As I am often reminded, Baba's family traces its roots all the way back to Damascus. To the time of the Prophet."

He knew it. One of the desert beauties of legend. "How long have you lived in Córdoba?"

"Almost five years now."

"What brought you here?"

She looks back to her lap. "While we were still in Algeciras, my mother passed away unexpectedly while my father was studying here in the madrasa of the Great Mosque. We were devastated. I was devastated." When she looks back up, two tears course down her cheeks. Like a little girl, she smears one with her palm, the other with her fist.

"I am so sorry, Rayhana. What was her name, your mother?"

She sniffs and composes herself. "Rayya. She was from the Maghreb. Near Tetouan. I was very close to my mama." She exhales the lingering pain. "After she passed, Baba moved us three to Córdoba. Against Jiddo and Tetta's wishes."

"I have not met your father."

"Baba is a good man. But changed. He loved Mama so. Now there is a deep sadness within him, a wound that refuses to heal. He pretends it is not there, but I can see it. It makes him very stern sometimes, and unforgiving. But when he was in Algeciras with Mama, he was filled with laughter and joy. I know it is still inside him somewhere." She pauses. "His promotion to the Vizier Council was a dream come true for him. It was a position Baba craved. We moved into the Alcazar late last year."

"I am glad you did."

She smiles. "As am I." She relaxes into a coy grin. "Until last week, court was very boring." They both laugh.

"Samuel is not sure what to make of your father. He says he is difficult to read." He hesitates. "He also said that your father refuses to provide you an education."

Her face collapses. "That is true. I had to beg and plead for him to allow me just to read in the Rare Books Library. I am given no formal tutors. What I know I have learned on my own."

Zafir frowns. "Why would he not want you educated?"

Her chin begins to quiver as her eyes fill. "Mama always told me I could marry for love, when I was ready. She promised me. But Baba told me that he will choose my husband for me. Very soon. I know in my heart that Baba is planning to marry me to some old man so that he might gain influence at court. Such a man does not want an educated wife, only a slave." A choked gasp slips from her throat. "My father will sell me for gold, Zafir, to the highest bidder." Her tears melt him into a puddle.

Zafir's mouth slides open, then his face reddens. "He cannot do that!"

She wipes her tears. "Of course he can. And he will. He knows the law better than anyone."

He grasps both of her shoulders, and turns her to face him. "I will not allow it! I will NOT allow it, Rayhana!"

Their eyes remain locked as they fall silent, some sort of unspoken declaration made. He releases his grasp. They face each other now, knees joined.

"You were not born in Córdoba either, were you?"

Their hands find each other.

"No. I was born in a distant land, a place called Caratania."

She shakes her head.

"Nearly three hundred leagues to the northeast, on the eastern border of the Holy Roman Empire." He smiles as he recollects. "A beautiful land, Rayhana. High, snow-covered mountains filled with mighty oaks and elms and giant maples." His hand paints a picture. "And in the fall colors like you have never seen, reds and yellows in a thousand shades." His excitement is contagious.

She grins as she studies him.

"And crystal streams, filled with trout. Waterfalls like you have never seen, Rayhana. And green, everywhere green."

Her grin widens. "Like your emerald eyes. I have never seen anything like them."

He laughs.

She continues, "How did you end up here?"

He falls silent as his body tenses. His cadence slows. "When Emperor Otto invaded our lands, Karnburg, where I lived, was sieged and after six months, razed." After a long, weighty pause, he continues. "My parents were murdered."

She gasps. "Oh my ..." Her eyes well up.

"My father was a court chamberlain, a brilliant man. A good man." His face falls to his lap. His voice becomes strained and then begins to quaver. "My sisters were ... raped ... in front of me."

Two tears escape her dam.

He can't bring himself to look up. "We were sold into slavery, Rayhana. They were sent to Saxony. I went first to Bavaria, and then to Paris, and finally Córdoba. I have never seen them again."

She tightens her grip on his hands and whispers, "How old were you?"

A heavy sigh. "Twelve. I am ..." He can't seem to mouth the words. "I am ... saqaliba, Rayhana."

Stunned silence.

She forces herself to smile. "You have done very well for yourself, Zafir. How did you end up working in the Rare Books Library."

He takes a deep breath and exhales the memory and finds her eyes. "When we were brought to Córdoba, two dozen of us, they separated us according to our ages and skills. Those boys that could not read and write were sold to merchants and farmers. The girls were sold as household servants—or worse. The two youngest boys were forced to become ... court eunuchs."

She gasps.

"Fortunately, I had passed the optimal age. Because I was educated I was sent to work for the royal book binder. I worked there for two years."

"I see."

"One day Samuel surprised me while I was reading a codex in ancient Greek." His face becomes more peaceful as he recollects. "My father taught me ancient Greek. My first love."

She smiles.

"Samuel was intrigued. Mastery of ancient Greek is rare in Córdoba. He arranged for me to begin my training as a royal translator. Thankfully, I advanced to the top of my class. First, I learned Arabic and was taught the Quran and Hadith. Two years later Samuel chose me to serve as his assistant, and I have been with him ever since. I owe my life to Samuel, Rayhana. He is a father to me."

"That is an amazing story, Zafir."

"It is hard to believe it was twelve years ago. I consider myself Córdoban now. And my Arabic is as good as anyone I know, even you."

She grins.

"I have embraced Islam, though there are times when I forget my prayers."

As she nods her agreement and points to herself, they share a laugh. He stares off into space, pensive. "But to this day, when the spring rains come and the waters flow, I think of the beautiful mountains of Caratania ... and my lost sisters."

There is a crisp double-knock and a turmeric-yellow statue fills the doorway. The whites of their eyes are enormous, the shock writ large on their faces almost comical. Their backs involuntarily stiffen as their legs draw up, releasing the kiss of their knees, and their twined hands discreetly withdraw to their laps. Zafir awkwardly stands and steps back from her.

"Ohhh …" Samuel's expression shifts from a warm smile to surprise, to puzzlement, to a classic raising of his bushy eyebrows as he tries to decide what is going on. He attempts to glue his smile back on. "Mmmm … I did not realize you were here, my boy. Rayhana, I trust Zafir was not disturbing your reading?"

"No, Master al-Tayyib, not at all. Zafir was simply explaining the nuances of Greek tragedy. I was confused on several points." There is something in her voice that is not quite right.

"Well, certainly Zafir knows his Greek plays, my dear. Do *not* let him get started on the comedies or he will never shut up."

The three laugh loudly.

"Well, I am afraid it is time for noon prayer, Rayhana. Enough reading for one day." He turns his gaze to Zafir. "We will meet this afternoon … about our project."

Zafir's expression is matter-of-fact. "Yes. At three. I will check with Levi for an update."

Samuel's gaze lingers, his right eyebrow raised high at his protégé, who dodges the query and looks away.

High above, three volumes of love poetry lean dangerously over the precipice, waiting to give the signal. When the door double-snaps shut, the fuse is hastily lit and a bawdy chorus of "HUZZAH!" in a half-dozen ancient languages spills from the upper shelves.

Eagle's Rock

The two elegantly-curved divans are placed in mirror image, close enough to permit intimate conversation while maintaining a comfortable distance. Two cups of hot mint tea rest on a slender table between them. Beside them sits a thin, rolled scroll balanced in the clutches of an ornate silver holder.

The room is compact, cozy even, circled by floor-to-ceiling bookcases stuffed with ancient codices. A careful survey at the arrangement of the shelves is enough to reveal that these books are read. Ibn Abi Amir reclines on one divan, a thin, leather-bound ledger opened and turned face down on his thigh. Any decent book binder would shame him for his abuse of the spine. As he lifts his cup to take a sip, undulating tendrils of steam sway as if caught in a gentle breeze. His face is expressionless, but his almond eyes are piercing and alive.

With the soft knock his eyes track to the door, but otherwise his face does not move. Jibril motions the boy into the room. The boy hesitates when he sees the seated man. Jibril coos then softly presses his palm to the boy's back to encourage him forward.

"Hisham, may I present Ibn Abi Amir, vizier of Africa. He is a good friend of your mother."

The boy remains silent, wary.

Ibn Abi Amir does not speak but sets his tea down and indicates the adjoining divan with his palm. The boy does not move. "Leave us, Jibril."

The eunuch barely suppresses a grimace but bows and retreats.

When the door closes, Ibn Abi Amir studies the boy for several moments, then says, "Please join me, Hisham, I have something I must show you. Something you will find quite interesting." He again indicates the divan.

He continues to study the boy as he shuffles forward, eyes glued to the floor. He looks his age, twelve, but there is a softness about him that is mildly distasteful. No doubt the result of a sheltered life among concubines and eunuchs. And an overbearing, scheming mother. This one has never ridden a horse or wielded a sword or drawn a bow. Made for the library, not for leadership. No wonder the caliph refuses to train him. Ibn Abi Amir's heavy sigh carries a hint of disdain.

Blond like the mother, but his face is an intriguing blend of Arab and Basque. The slight twitch of his upper lip betrays Ibn Abi Amir's disapproval of this sordid kind of corruption of ancient Arab bloodlines.

As the boy approaches, he looks up. Giant, steely-gray eyes; serious eyes. Ibn Abi Amir thinks they are his best feature.

The boy sits and gazes at his hands folded in his lap. Ibn Abi Amir ignores him. He lays the ledger face-down on the table then unlocks the latches of the silver holder, lifts the scroll, and begins to unroll it. The pleasing crackle of the old vellum lures the boy's eyes.

"You know the Maghreb?"

The boy barely nods.

Ibn Abi Amir pinions the vellum using both cups of tea. Even an incompetent mapmaker would cringe. "Show me Fez."

The boy considers, then leans forward and lowers his finger to the map.

"And Bou-Admed?"

The finger slides to the coast.

"Hajar an-Nasar?"

The boy's gray eyes meet Ibn Abi Amir's, then move back to the map. His finger slides west into the Rif Mountains.

"Tell me about Hajar an-Nasar."

The boy hesitates. "Eagle's Rock. A mountain fortress. Stronghold of the Berber Idrisids." The voice is soft, feminine.

Ibn Abi Amir nods, satisfied. Clearly, the boy reads. The silence stretches as he calculates his next move.

The boy's eyes have not left Ibn Abi Amir's face.

"Within a year the Idrisids will declare fealty to your father and attack the Fatimids. I will be the one to arrange it."

The boy's eyes widen.

Ibn Abi Amir's eyes move to the ledger, luring his quarry. "A full accounting of your mother's holdings. Impressive, I must say. Gold, silver, jewels, books, substantial lands in the Middle and Upper Marches, silent partnerships with a dozen Córdoban merchant families. Your father is very indulgent."

He notices a tickle at the corners of the boy's mouth.

"Care to see?"

The boy reaches for opaque composure but in the end is unable to suppress his curiosity. It is there for all to read. Ibn Abi Amir makes a mental note. A defect to be corrected.

He opens his palm in invitation. "Go ahead."

The boy lifts the ledger by its corners, as if afraid it might burn his fingers. He opens it and begins to peruse the first page. As Ibn Abi Amir studies him, the barest hint of a grin emerges.

"I am now the keeper of your mother's accounts, Hisham. I am authorized to buy and sell as I please, provided I return a profit. She is especially keen to acquire lands in the south." He pauses. "And in the Maghreb."

The boy lifts his eyes to Ibn Abi Amir's face.

"Your mother has great plans for you, Hisham. She wishes to see you become caliph ... to succeed your father."

The eyes grow wary.

"This you understand, of course ... and secretly desire." He pauses to let the words sink in. "Yet you pretend to be interested in only the Quran and Sharia Law." He studies the boy's reaction as he calculates. "Your father has refused to train you for leadership. Why?"

The boy looks away as he whispers, "I am an unworthy heir."

"No." The boy looks back to Ibn Abi Amir. "Your father fears you, Hisham. He sees your destiny as the greatest caliph of al-Andalus. Therefore, he denies you that path to preserve his own legacy. History is filled with many such examples."

The boy is now the one calculating.

"Hisham, your mother asked me to teach you what you need to know to be a great caliph. I have agreed." The two lock eyes. "If your father finds out, he will have me executed." The statement is matter-of-fact.

The boy recognizes the simple truth of the words and appreciates the man's candor.

"There is much for you to learn, obviously. But I thought we might start by allowing you to choose our first investment in the south. It would have to be well-researched, of course. Somewhere near Algeciras, perhaps, or even Cádiz. Somewhere that would not attract undue attention. For obvious reasons, your mother prefers to acquire her possessions ... discreetly. You will locate the land and set a fair price, Hisham. I will serve as your sounding board, but you will make the final decision. Together we will draft the legal documents and conclude the transaction. You will share in the profits. Then we move on to the Maghreb. There will be bribes to be placed among the Idrisids, of course, and Fatimid lands to acquire once they are conquered by our new Berber allies. Eagle's Rock shall be ours, Hisham."

The boy's eyes sparkle with an uncharacteristic eagerness. He nods.

For the first time, Ibn Abi Amir smiles. "Come sit beside me, Hisham, there are some entries I suspect you will find particularly interesting." He pats the divan as the boy rises to join him.

Collage of Silence

The thin strap of midnight silk covers his eyes, the color a close match to his cropped beard and wavy hair; a stark contrast to his pallid, ghostly skin. Not a day past twenty, and fit. The silk mask is his only privacy. His pathetic, wilted penis crouches over stillborn twins buried in a nest of black scriffle.

His alabaster thigh is splayed from groin to knee, the awful cut made precisely, lovingly, his body folded open for the world to admire. The outer muscles of the leg have been carefully severed and laid back like cut cloth to reveal the magic of the inner machinery. The absence of blood is striking, surreal.

Abulcasis rises up on the balls of his feet as he conducts the orchestra. His hands dance a complicated jig as he speaks. Heads among the terraces nod. Cleo stands rigid beside him, the ever-attentive pupil. The old man turns and reaches for an instrument. He grasps it loosely in his hand, rotates it for all to admire, then works its action back and forth as he explains its intricate design and function. Eyes are glued to his every word. Several break their stares to hastily scribble notes, then leap back to their master, fearful of missing a morsel.

Abulcasis issues instructions to his assistant. Cleo reaches for the table and lifts an instrument, inserts, then spreads it to widen the wound, coaxing into view the narrow streak of reed-sized tubing Abulcasis is after. He does not stop speaking to the wound as he maneuvers his instrument. Cleo hovers, angles his head for a better look. The instrument clamps onto the tube, closing but not severing it. Remarkably, as Abulcasis releases his grip the jaws remain locked on the tube. Among the terraces, several nod their heads appreciatively, others exchange nervous glances; one more tool to master. The maestro is free now to reach for his blade. He begins to methodically expose the length of the tube as it makes its long run to the knee, conversing with the wound as he exposes it.

The Upper Marches are brutal in winter, the cold winds from the northern mountains merciless in their bite as they sweep the high plains. The distant rumble of thunder lifts the shepherd's head. He instinctively two-hands his crook and with a quick glance accounts for each of his sheep grazing the spare scruff within the narrow draw. He turns and stares to the north. The thunder grows louder. He frowns, puzzled. He eases into the meager cover of the scrub brush and crouches, acutely aware that he is dangerously exposed.

He sees the pulsing steel tip of a pike rise from the horizon. Then the unmistakable blood red on white as the banner snakes and snaps in the breeze. The Cross of St. James. Christians. He sinks to his knees, turns to check once more that his flock is safely out of sight, then freezes. The first knights rise into view, mercifully angling away from him to the southeast.

He has never seen Castilian cavalry this close to al-Andalus. One lead rider, a bannerman, then a column five wide, a noisy jangle of gleaming plate and mail, maces and broadswords; the suck and blow of the massive mounts, jets of cloud pulsing from their huge nostrils. The cavalry charges onto the plateau at full gallop, the rolling thunder pursued by billowing plumes of dust. Riding hard, but for where? As the tail of the beast finally comes into view, he quickly counts. Two hundred, give or take. He studies the leader. The knight's visor is down, but the shepherd's eyes are instantly drawn to the unnatural bone-white hands jerking and slapping the leather reins against his dappled gray mount. Count Garcia Fernandez of Castile. White Hands.

The burst of light from the taper begins in a limpid sky blue, is exchanged for burnished copper-gold, then sighs upward into an opaque elegant cone of piercing yellow. As the bent tip of the blackened wick intersects the edge of the inverted teardrop of noon sun, there is a glowing pinprick of brilliant orange. The gentle undulation of heated air ripples above the radiant bulge, echoing the rim of molten fire. Occasionally a thin wisp of wriggling black soot feathers into the waves and vanishes. The taper and its magical offspring live and breathe, an organic union, the courageous barter of Prometheus for a slice of warm, bloody liver.

The flame offers the only light in the small room, but in the absence of moving air it stands tall, slender, and proud, casting sharp angles of shadow into the upper shelves. Books of a precise thickness are laid flat to anchor the polished silver of the ornate candle holder. The flame rests at the edge of the round table and is aligned with the tiny hole in the face of the box erected on the far side of the circle.

The four men are knotted together, children at play with their new toy. Their expressions are serious, eyes fixed to the closed flap of the camera. A tense, expectant air fills the room, the leaden weight of anticipation, a pleasing gnaw in the gut. No one dares to move.

After a final glance from flame to pinhole, Zaheid leans forward and lifts his hand to open the tiny flap on the side of the camera. Breaths are held. He leans farther still to partake of the camera's hidden treasure. The other three study his face for some hint. Zaheid stares, mesmerized. His eyes widen as his mouth falls open, then his face relaxes, only to be traded for a beaming smile and a vigorous nod. He turns to Samuel and silently mouths, "Eureka!"

High on the shelf above them, an ancient, battered volume of Euclid's *Elements* peers from the shadows, mildly curious. His crust crackles as he flexes to take in the odd scene. He sniffs, then scoffs, unimpressed with their discovery.

The door opens, first a sliver to test for sound, then decisively to permit quick passage. The door closes, returning the corridor to its slumber. He turns and listens as he scans for signs of life.

The hood of his robe is pulled forward over his face to obscure his identity. He is silent in his silk slippers. The corridor is washed in a muted gray, the wicks of the oil lamps turned to blue nubs for the stretch of the long night hours.

Satisfied, the man hugs the wall and flows forward. His movements suggest a secret knowledge of this place. He stops just short of the first door and listens, then slips past to the second door, pausing, then moving on. As he approaches the third door, he reaches up, and with both hands folds back his hood. He lays his ear to the door. After a quick glance in both directions he caresses the latch into a hushed double-tick. He holds his breath as a triangle of warm light cuts the floor and widens. The man slides through and the door closes without a trace.

Diagonally across the hallway a silk tapestry hangs, the dense arabesque a jungle of stems and leaves in endless waves of repetition. An inky pupil stares from a folded leaf, the quick blink of painted lashes the only hint of fauna among the dense foliage.

A trio of tapers set upon a stand beside the large canopied bed bathes the room in a seductive, warm glow. The floor fountain in the center of the room bubbles and froths its soothing murmur, the silky-wet sounds somehow sensual, arousing. Behind the bed-curtains of wispy lace a pair of Greek gods reclines upon pillows. These bronzed beings are too beautiful for clothes, athletes lifted mid-Games from slopes of mighty Olympus. That, or Titans.

Oceanus and Hyperion, perhaps? The gods' expressions are haughty; hungry.

The caliph's robe drops heavily to the floor. He parts the lace and slips inside.

The doubled tier of arches floats upon marble columns slender as a young girl evoking a dense forest of date palms ringing a lush oasis in the Syrian Desert. The trees are endless, stunning in their uniformity, the view from any vantage upon the floor identical. The Umayyad horseshoe arches, commandeered from the ancient Visigoths and raised to perfection, are visually arresting in their alternating bands of red ochre and white, the colors of the caliph.

The doubled arches join forces to disperse and break the weight of the low ceiling producing a complex play of light upon shadow, sound upon silence, a paradox of intimacy bounded by such a vast open space.

There is some magical architectural abstraction at work in the forest of Umayyad palms, a labyrinth without walls, a spatial arabesque of red ochre and white that shouts its metaphor, the infinity of Allah. The worshipper praying at any location in the giant structure resides at the very center of the cosmos, a mirror to Allah's desired union, Creator with his creation, at one instance of time, at one location in space, there to stretch out in all directions, for all eternity. This is a temple of prayer. This is a communion of souls.

The floor of the great space is a sea of woven hemp, the shifting sands of an endless desert. Rows of the prostrate faithful stretch straight as arrows, hundreds times hundreds. Their foreheads and palms are flat to the sand, the ocean of souls gathered in perfect symmetry about the breathtaking *mihrab* of Byzantine gold and cobalt mosaics, a pathway opened to Mecca.

The grand imam proclaims, "Subhana rabbi al-a la wa-bi-hamdih." *Glory to my Lord, the Most High, the Most Praiseworthy.* Thousands of whispers coalesce in echo. Again. A third time. Then the grand imam says, "Allahu Akbar!" *God is great!* A deafening roar answers. Hundreds times hundreds rise into a kneeling posture as a single organism.

The man's turban is sloppily wrapped, stained from neglect, his grizzled, unkempt beard flecked with gray, his shoulders swayed into an uncomfortable arc from years of bending over the fruits of his labors. His calf-skin apron is splotched and sliced from decades of use.

One would guess him to be ancient, but he is much younger than he appears, the eager glint in his eyes the giveaway. The hint of a satisfied smile is permanently written on the man's face. Either he delights in his work or is amused by some timeless irony. That, or perhaps he is a bit crazy. Or all three.

Here is an artisan of the highest caliber, twelve years an apprentice, twenty-three now as a master craftsman in the workshops of the royal book binder. He is in love with his creations to the exclusion of his looks and his hobbies—even his family. He lives for his work.

He sits on his high stool, hunched over the object of his current affections. He skillfully threads the tiny needle, pulling the flax wire tight above him. His hands are steady as a stalking leopard. He lovingly lifts the folded and pressed section of paper sheets from his workbench. Bringing his eyes close, he begins to work the needle into the minute puncture in the fold, rapidly sewing in lock-stitch to the other end. An elegant knot, then a smart cut with his blade to trim the excess.

He lowers his needle and raises the section to study it from several angles. He opens the text-block to test the snugness of his work. Pleased, he threads a larger bore needle and again pulls the flax wire tight. He gingerly lifts the swelling volume, carefully fits the new section into place, then begins a new row of lock-stitch orthogonally across the spine, joining it to its sisters for eternity. To his left rests the richly tooled binder's leather glued to paste board that will soon bless the finished codex.

The book binder's satisfied smile never wavers.

His elegant, flowing robe is finely wrought and expensive, the attire of a Berber sultan: full black beard stretching to his chest, crimson turban expertly wrapped. The dagger in its bejeweled sheath is stuck into his wide leather belt, joined by a priceless scimitar of Damascus steel that hangs precisely at his side. His ebony eyes are serious; dangerous. There is little doubt he knows how to use his weapons.

He paces the ramparts of Hajar an-Nasar, impatient for news. He stares down upon the burnt-brown crags lording over the etched spider web of valleys. The unforgiving Rif Mountains. The slopes are devoid of trees, the lonely clumps of scrub the only tones not close cousins of sand and soil.

The Berber's training presses his gaze to logical ambush points in the sharp angles of the valley, ideal defensive positions for thwarting a Fatimid invasion. He squints to assess the watchtower on the nearby peak; sated, he moves on. A lone eagle drifts lazily, rung upon the rein of a wimpling wing, scanning for a careless jackrabbit, a viper curled in the thin shade of a boulder, a wayward lizard.

The Berber's head lifts west to the horizon to the thin streak of cobalt—ocean. He returns to the south to continue his survey. His eyes burn for a sign. There. His ebony gaze locks onto the tiny swirl of dust at the far end of the distant canyon. He cannot see the riders, only the billowing tan smudge. A thin smile slices his face.

The stack of Greek comedies, their usual fare, has been pushed to the side of the table; her love of geography has come calling. A map folio lays open on the table before them, the large sheet of pale vellum brilliantly decorated with blues and reds. The Maghreb. She talks and talks, lingering over points on the map to add a footnote here, an unappreciated tidbit there; Tangier, Larache, Fez, Al Hoceima, Bou-Ahmed, Tetouan, Hajar an-Nasar. She raises a question, answers it herself, then hurries on with the next lesson. He cannot help but smile.

He kneels, she sits. He leans hard against her for a better view, gluing their sides, reaches forward then thumps the map as he tenders his question. She giggles her answer, scolds him, then resumes the lecture, on to the next city. Their bodies do not part.

His chin is above her shoulder. His eyes escape the map to explore. The heavenly indentation between her throat and collarbone, the wispy V of dark down that graces the nape of her neck as it dives for cover, the delicate curve of her lashes. He can barely restrain himself from fingering the loose brown spiral that takes delight in taunting him so. The battle lines are drawn.

As her hands flit about to make a special point he inches forward with feigned interest to savor the soft swell of her breasts as they slip beneath the folds of cotton, warm olive skin curving magnificently under white. His heart races.

As he tilts his head to breathe in her hair, that intoxicating mélange of orange and spice steps forward. He barely nudges an errant curl with his nose.

The teacher races merrily along, oblivious.

A discreet shift of his shoulder against hers and he finds her ear. He loses the battle, the steamy whisper of breath his white flag of capitulation. Her words halt mid-sentence, punctuated only by the droop of her eyes.

Lesson over.

Another whisper of breath, better directed. She shivers, electric fire dancing deliciously down her spine. He lifts her chin and rotates her face. The dimples have vanished, her lips just parted enough to permit her shallow, quickened breath. Their chests pound in tandem. Her amber starbursts ringed in honey brown lock onto his emeralds to renew their unspoken pledge, then fold closed.

Their lips touch at a point, with a timid delicacy, linger, then part, only to rejoin more forcefully. He breaks their connection to slide his knee between hers to turn her. His hands slide down her arms at a deliberate pace, shoulders to elbows to bare forearms to soft hands, his destination a tight twining of fingers for some feeble measure of restraint. As he leans forward her eyes are still closed.

The kiss flares, bursting into a life of its own, the damp heat spreading between them insistent, urgent. A riot of tingles and silver sparkles begin to jump between these two at a dozen points. He kisses her harder, presses himself against her. A pleasure murmur slips from her, the incantation magically releasing their imprisoned hands.

The frantic race commenced just after dawn, and even now, at mid-morning, it is obvious to all who the winner will be.

Sailors rush about the deck readying for battle, a haphazard distribution of their meager supply of swords among the healthiest, a hasty arrangement of chests and barrels for some measure of protection against the infidel marauders' arrows. Others climb the rigging, checking and rechecking ropes and knots that they already know are cinched tight.

Praying for a miracle.

The pursued flag bears the double-headed black eagle set upon gold, colors of the Holy Roman Empire. At the stern the captain stares towards Africa, helpless. He barks at the man beside him, who rushes for the crammed hold with his orders, then turns and eyes his sails; half full, no more. He grimaces, then returns to his pursuer.

Behind, no farther than a skilled javelin throw, is the flagless *dromon*, the oared sailing galley preferred by Barbary corsairs. The galley is smaller than the merchant, sleek and low to the water, the cut of its sails sharp and angular. There must be fifty oars jutting from each side, operating as a single living being; lift-forward-scoop-pull, lift-forward-scoop-pull. The life of a chained galley slave; row or die. The captain can just hear the muffled cadence of the row-master's hammers. Relentless.

He can clearly see dozens of turbaned heads gathered at the bow, the gleam of their scimitars bright flashes against the climbing sun. Bowmen decorate the rigging. The swirl of the grappling hooks make tight circles in the air, arc high, then disappear into the cobalt before being reeled back. Practice.

He mops the nervous sweat from his brow, chews his cheek until it bleeds. He turns and sights along the bowsprit, scans the horizon east to west. Landfall is a thick line of green now, steadily swelling, but he knows they will never make it.

The man's Latin script is impeccable, the tight black letters regular in form and size, densely packed. Any scribe would be pleased. His posture is prim, erect. The writing flows elegantly across the parchment, the words benign: People met, places visited, books examined, various foods, architecture, commerce. At the end of the page he signs his name with a flourish that is clearly practiced and proud.

Your faithful servant,

Peter A. Strobel
Emperor's Ambassador

He sets his quill down and carefully blots the page, blowing upon it just to be sure. He retrieves a small vial of liquid from an interior pocket, examines it, shakes it vigorously, then opens it. He inhales. Cloyingly sweet. He lifts a second quill, this one much finer. He dips into the vial and begins to write between the heavy black lines.

Deer-England-Apple-Red Majesty. Wealth beyond wildest dreams. Exchange delegations. Treaty.

He stops, lifts the page to examine the words as they dry. The gray letters fade to a light smoke, then a faint smudge, then are gone. The toying of a mischievous *genie?* He holds the paper at several angles to be sure, flips it over. Satisfied, he nods, dips his quill and begins his second line.

No success corsairs. Misplayed. Underestimate caliph. Learning. Confirmed goals Africa. Loved gift.

The words disappear one by one, the line erased.

Caliph aiding Byzantines over Abbasids. Sends gold. Unclear how. Jerusalem will fall.

Long enough for a sigh, then vanished.

Córdoba Christians renegades. Impure Eucharist. Arabic Bibles. Jews in high office. Many slaves.

A dozen heartbeats then not a single trace.

Count Garcia Fernandez Castile biggest threat Córdoba. Suggest covert support, pressure Upper Marches. Progress.

When done, he peruses his work then folds the letter, lifts his sealing candle, dribbles the hot red wax, sets his ring upon it, and presses.

Treacle

7 March 976.

Jafar's hands are clasped behind his back, fingers circling his wrist, eyes on the floor. Pacing clears the man's mind, sharpens his calculations. The caliph reclines on his divan, staring into space, pensive. General Ghalib grimaces from his pillow, his bad leg stretched out to ease the awful ache.

The Golden Circle.

General Ghalib growls, "I will arrange his death; a simple matter."

Jafar stops to frown. "No, too messy. You underestimate Madinat's inability to hold a secret, Ghalib. The logical inferences and the implications will be obvious to anyone with a single connection at court and a flake of intelligence."

"An accident if you like, then, clean. I have just the man."

"No, we must be clever."

A weary sigh leaks from the caliph. "Tell me once more, Ghalib."

General Ghalib is short on patience. "What more would you like, Sire? He enters her bedchamber alone. Not once, not twice; each week. For months now. You can rest assured they do not play chess, Sire." He issues a wet, rattling cough. "Must I spell it out? The bastard beds the sultana!"

The caliph winces.

Jafar injects some calm. "I have made inquiries, Sire. This managing of her accounts is only a ruse for her games. He buys land and makes investments, yes, but that is a front. There is no longer any doubt that he ... visits the sultana without escort. My new eyes in the harem leave no room for debate in the matter. I am afraid Ghalib is correct."

The caliph stares into space, his expression blank. "Seducing my vizier? Bold, even for her. Why this betrayal?" He shakes his head. "Jibril must be involved."

General Ghalib answers, "That painted wraith is into everything. Trust me, he helps arrange the trysts. It is time we dealt with that cunning spider once and for all." He draws his hand violently across his throat.

Jafar waves his hand dismissively. "I am more worried about the time he spends with Hisham while in the royal harem. Who knows what poisonous treacle he pours into the boy's ears. I suspect that is where the threat lies. Her adultery is only a tool, a game to garner allegiance, no more. She does not love him. She lusts after power, she always has, and now has found an unlikely accomplice. With proper training Hisham can be a dangerous weapon to wield against us, Sire. She knows this."

General Ghalib raises his voice. "Treason is what it is!"

Jafar stares at the caliph as he frames his question. "You are certain that Fatik and Muhja are not involved?"

"I am sure. Beautiful boys, but stupid." He sighs wearily. "Why would he risk so much for her sake?"

Jafar shrugs, "It is a timeless tale, Sire. Gold certainly; as you know, he has little. But even more so, power and influence. Pride is what drives a man like him, I am sure of it."

General Ghalib adds, "That, and carnal lust. An even more timeless motivator." Another wet cough.

Jafar sniffs. "We must be cunning, Sire." He glances at Ghalib and emphasizes his point with his eyes. "And subtle." Jafar lowers his gaze, locks his hands behind his back, and resumes his pacing. The man's formidable machinery begins to whir in the silence.

The air is tight, heavy.

As he halts and pivots to face the caliph, his face brightens. His arms fall loose to his sides, then his right hand rises to the level of his head, a single finger waggling at the sky. The caliph's gaze meets his grand vizier.

Jafar says, "We must ensure that he travels with the army to the Maghreb."

General Ghalib frowns. "Forget that. He has already refused me. He insists his new duties require his presence in Córdoba. He tells me he will write me a letter of introduction to al-Tariq. Arrogant goat turd!"

Jafar offers a sly grin. "I envision a change of plans." He becomes more animated as he speaks, the knots of tangled web unraveling quickly now. "The caliph will appoint him *qadi* of the Maghreb. Logical, given his role as vizier of Africa and his legal training. After all, the man has knowledge of Berber laws and tribal traditions. As the caliph's legal authority in the Maghreb his presence will be required by Ghalib's army when it strikes for Africa. He cannot refuse. Removed from court by legitimate means, and no one will be the wiser. She will be powerless to prevent it. Hisham will return to his solitude and his books."

Silence.

Jafar continues. "The Rif Mountains are a long way from Córdoba, Sire, and even her networks will be stretched to a thread and snap. She cannot protect him there. Who knows what may happen in that dangerous wasteland ..." He offers Ghalib a serpent's smile.

The general's scowl relaxes as he signals his approval. "Good, I like it. We march for the Maghreb in four weeks, perhaps three—as soon as the weather warms. I will keep an eye on the devil until we reach the Rif. Battle is a risky business. I am afraid he will suddenly find himself at the vanguard of our army without an escort when those famous Berber ambushes rain down upon us. The desert mountains can be such a cruel and unforgiving place." His grin widens then twists into something sinister.

Both men rest their eyes upon the caliph and wait.

Finally, a somber nod. "Very well. Arrange it."

Perspective

Giddy with their risk taking, the couple can barely stifle their hushed giggles as they slip and slide down the hall in silk stockings, him pulling her along by their joined hands. His face grows serious as he halts to peer around the last corner. All clear. He lifts his eyebrows to query her one last time and is answered by dimples. They race hand-in-hand to the far end of the hallway until their sliding stop doubles them over with silent hysterical laughter. He fumbles for the key as he glances over his shoulder to shush her. The clank of the door latch is impossibly loud, then they are through.

Two dramatic exhales. Safe. He relocks the door. They exchange a quick, triumphant glance, then bright, knowing smiles. Their fingers remain glued.

She surveys. Yet another cozy reading room, similar to her second home. The array of octagonal skylights high above provide good light. As usual, the shelves are crammed floor to ceiling with ancient volumes. Upon the table in the center of the room rests the boxy contraption he has told her about, stared at by a pair of sleeping candles several feet away.

With a flourish of his hand he pronounces, "My lady. May I present our camera obscura."

She curtsies, her grin stretched wide.

He releases her hand to gesture as he begins his lecture, instantly the serious teacher. His pupil lifts her shoulders to sober up. "Our knowledge of this magical contraption grows. The image produced by the camera is truly remarkable. A mirror of what the eye perceives, but upside down. Exactly as Aristotle claims. He argues that this is the True Form, the image Allah created, and he offers it as proof of the existence of the Shadow Form, with its implied limitations on human perception. Remarkably, the image the camera produces has a life of its own, a third dimension. Samuel calls this 'perspective'.

"We have experimented at length using candles. Zaheid thinks that it should be possible to trace a line from the flame's edge directly to the edge on the image, and thus prove the straightness of the light rays; their perfection of form. Theon of Alexandria claims as much, but we have yet to figure a way to test this directly."

Her eyes have not left the camera. She is mesmerized. She whispers, "Tell me more."

"Well, the size of the pinhole determines the brightness of the image, but if you make the hole too large, the sharpness of the image fades. Make it too small and the image dims." He studies her.

She stands rapt as she dissects what she sees. She edges forward and angles her head to examine the orifice, exchanges a quick glance between the candles and the hole, then nods approvingly. "How do you view the image?"

Zafir indicates the small cloth flap. "The opening must be small so as not to disturb the interior. The image is projected onto the back of the box."

She smiles irresistibly. "May I?"

"I am afraid there is nothing to see. The room must be pitch black and the candles lit. Alas, the camera is a slave to the night."

She ignores him, leans close, lifts the flap tentatively, as if it might suddenly bite, then presses her eye close.

Her sharp gasp is instantaneous, startling him. "Oh my ... How incredible!"

He assumes she is making fun of him, but the excitement painted on her face makes him curious. He smirks. "You cannot see anything during the daylight, Rayhana."

With a coy grin, she beckons him with her finger.

He shrugs and sidles up to her, folds himself to peer into the tiny window.

He jolts as if scalded. "Oh my!"

She laughs loudly.

He leans in once more, dubious. "This makes no sense." She joins him at the magical portal, their cheeks pressed together to permit each a view from a single eye. Buried within is a perfect panoramic picture of the bookshelves, upside down and inverted, so bright and sharp he can make out the titles on the spines. Floating in the air in front of the shelf is the pair of sleeping tapers. The perspective produced by the contrast of foreground to background makes the image seem real enough to reach out and touch.

They slowly unfold in tandem as they rise, faces serious, dazzled. She steps to the rear of the contraption to study it.

"What?"

She raises her eyebrows. "Thinking ..."

He joins her, curious now.

"What if we replaced the back panel of the camera with a piece of polished paper, or perhaps sheer silk. The light would leak through, and then we could view the image from the rear ..."

"Mmmm ..."

"We could even trace the outline of the image onto paper."

He is nodding now. "Yes ... yes—of course! Excellent, Rayhana!"

They stare at each other, faces serious with the awe of their discovery. The corners of his mouth lift only a hair, but this instantly tickles her lips into a slow, radiant blossoming, her dimples digging deep for glory. Without warning he hugs her, lifts her from the floor, swings her side to side, slinging her giggles.

"Praise Allah! Wait until Samuel sees this! Rayhana, you have discovered that the camera obscura can produce a daylight image! An amazing daylight image! A whole scene, and with even more perspective! And a clever way to view it and capture it!" They laugh at her triumph then fall silent as they simultaneously recollect the real purpose of the visit.

He sets her down, bends his knees to equal their heights, eases his hands around the small of her back, and pulls her tight against him. He kisses her hard. Soon the timeless chorus of love-murmurs awakens the silence. A moment more and a duet of weighty sighs and soft groans punctuate the room, the unmistakable mark of a mounting tension made raw and throbbing by months of kissing and touching.

If these lovers had bothered to reexamine the scene captured by the camera, they would have witnessed three volumes of poetry wiggle their way forward from the shelf to lean over the precipice and take in the stunning view.

Farewells

Master and apprentice sit side-by-side on the divan, twin ledgers opened in their laps. Their backs face the entrance to the room, obscuring their expressions from the prying orb in the wall hanging. They know that they must lower their voices to whispers if they wish to remain unheard.

The master's arm rests across the shoulders of his apprentice.

The boy's gentle shake betrays his tears. There is a stiffness to the man's gestures, however, a comfort to the boy, certainly, but with an odd sterility to it.

The boy sniffs. "Must you go?"

"I am afraid I must. Your father wills it."

"Why?"

"I am to be qadi of the Maghreb. It is a great honor."

"When will you return?"

He hesitates. "That is hard to say." He considers his words. "It will be for some time, I am afraid. The journey is long, and there is much to be done. At least six months, perhaps a year."

The boy's lower lip quivers. "Oh …"

"The time will pass quickly, you will see. And I will write you. You will continue your education, of course, and together we will relentlessly pursue our acquisitions. You have done well thus far and I expect more great things from you." He smiles. "You make me very proud." He lowers his voice to a whisper. "You have memorized our private key?"

The boy nods.

The man's normal voice returns. "Expect regular letters. I will be leaving books for you to memorize. You will be quizzed upon my return." He squeezes the boy's shoulders to lighten the mood.

The boy manages a weak smile.

The master drops to a whisper again. "And what is our word, young sir?"

The boy answers with a soft kiss of breath. "Eagle's Rock."

They lock eyes. The boy says, "I will miss you."

The man smiles. "I will miss you, too."

There is a long pause and then the boy says, "Will you bring me a gift?"

Ibn Abi Amir laughs loud. "Oh, you can depend upon that, Hisham. A gift fit for a caliph!"

The two are intertwined upon her divan, darkened olive shades woven with milky porcelain, flesh pressed against flesh, limbs penetrating limbs. He lies on his back, she on her side, clinging to him, pulling him close. Her ear rests over his heart, her knee scissored across his groin, arm tucked across him, cinching him tight.

The tapestry hanging on the wall has been replaced, this one minus the peephole and heavy enough to suppress sound.

He enjoys these quiet moments after their desperate love making. He never ceases to be amazed by the hunger a week's absence produces in her. When he entered her lair she didn't utter a word, just flung herself into his arms, her eyes begging him to devour her. His news has preceded him. As expected.

He has memorized every inch of her glorious curves, understands better what she desires than she does herself. It took only moments before she was crying out her pleasure, breathlessly calling his name over and over.

If she could see her face during these moments, she would berate herself for putting herself at his mercy. She knows better.

He plays her like a fine instrument. He methodically slides his fingers up and over the generous curve of her hip on the journey down her beautiful thigh. She inhales, holds her breath. He pauses at the damp, silky warmth behind her bent knee, the soft swell of her calf, her slender ankles. She frees her pent-up sigh when he reaches her toes.

He stares at the ceiling as he silently considers her, his eyes growing cold, steely. How easy it was to tame her, he thinks. The markings of a lioness still, but I have filed her fangs flat with the months of unbridled ecstasy. Soon I will cut her claws to the quick and they will bleed. And she will not give it a second's thought until it is too late. He realizes he pities her plight. But not enough to alter his plan.

She is helpless against his touch. She twists her hips to press against his pelvic bone and begins to writhe like a cat in heat. His calculations continue as she moves on him. He is already stalking the Maghreb, coaxing the Banu Birzal, rehearsing their approach to Eagle's Rock, the games that must be played, the promises to be made and broken, the bribes to be pressed into both reluctant and eager hands.

Her tortured groans finally garner his attention. He reluctantly pulls himself from the desert, lifts her on top of him, joins their bodies, then begins to pluck her taut strings for the hundredth time. It has become something of a game to him. He loves to study her at the exact moment her azure eyes lose focus and she cries out. He muses that he could strangle her at that very instant and she would not resist.

A half hour later, sated at last, some measure of sanity returns to her, but her tone is so tender and laden with emotion that Jibril would have trouble recognizing her. "I will miss you, Muhammad. How will I manage without you?"

Ibn Abi Amir hears the growing love in her words. As he squeezes her against him, his thin, satisfied smile rises to the ceiling. He is amazed at how much pleasure he derives from breaking her.

He thinks: She believes she is free still, but I own her now. She will willingly do my bidding.

The schemer schemed.

"I will miss you, too, Subh." His tone is similarly weighted. "You must be strong in my absence, darling." He considers his words. "I do not want Jibril or anyone else near your divan while I am away. You belong to me now, Subh, and only me. Do you understand?"

Silence.

He raises his voice. "Promise me, Subh."

Softly, she agrees, "I promise."

"The time will pass quickly, darling, you will see. All unfolds according to our plan. You have done well, Subh. The clues were found, your husband knows everything now." He laughs derisively. "Suddenly I am qadi of the Maghreb. Imagine. They do not understand the power they have bestowed upon me, the danger I represent to them. Stupid fools. It can only have been Jafar's idea."

"It is fitting to see them insist upon you assuming the mantle of their own undoing."

"Yes ... Hisham's time approaches. Our time approaches, my darling." He smiles, satisfied. "Soon, very soon."

"Ghalib will try to murder you in the desert."

He laughs. "Of course."

Concern slips into her voice. "Do not underestimate him, Muhammad. I cannot protect you there."

"I will handle Ghalib, Subh."

Silence.

Emotion embraces her words. "I will miss you so. I am not sure I can bear it." He feels a warm tear on his chest. His thin smile returns.

"You must, darling. I will write to you. Jibril is not to know our private key, Subh. Our secrets will remain between only us. Promise me."

"I promise."

"If all goes well, look for my signal during the summer, after Hajar an-Nasar falls. You must be very careful. No one must ever suspect. Ever."

"I have already secured the poison. A most unusual one from the east. A single application is all that is needed, and it will take months to work its magic. By the time he is ill no trace will remain. No one will ever know."

He squeezes her to him. "Good. When I return you will be free of this prison, Subh, and we will be together forever."

Her voice quavers. "Yes, Muhammad, yes ..."

"How long will you be gone?"

"At least six months, perhaps a year."

"I see ..."

"Salim is the elder of the family, Rayhana, his word will be final in my absence. You and Khalil are to obey him. I will send him instructions by letter, and he will report back to me."

"I see ..."

He studies her. "Rayhana, when I return from the Maghreb I will arrange your marriage."

Her expression wilts. She pleads, "Baba—"

"Rayhana. We have had that discussion. It is past time."

She blurts out. "I have met someone, Baba!"

His expression hardens. "Met someone? How did you meet someone? You shun the men at court."

Her face blossoms. "In the library, Baba. His name is Zafir. He is a royal translator, the protégé of the royal librarian."

Ibn Abi Amir frowns. "The Jew."

Her tone stiffens, "Master al-Tayyib, vizier of books, Baba."

"My orders were clear, Rayhana. You were not to be disturbed while in the Rare Books Library. It sounds like I need to have another conversation with al-Tayyib before I leave."

Her tone turns frantic. "It was not Master al-Tayyib's fault, Baba! He has been so kind to me. Zafir was searching for a book for his research. We met, that is all, I swear. We talked about books. He is very learned, Baba, you will like him. He specializes in the translation of ancient Greek texts to Arabic. Master al-Tayyib says his Greek is the best in Córdoba. Even the caliph reads his translations. Zafir has a bright future at court, Baba."

Ibn Abi Amir's tone turns vicious, "Greek? Who cares about Greek? Arabic is the only language for us!"

"Baba. Meet him, please, I beg you. You will like him, I know you will!"

"No, Rayhana, I will not meet him. I am off to the Maghreb." He weighs what to tell her. Decision made, he says, "When I return from Africa, Rayhana, I will be bringing a Berber prince with me. For you."

She gasps.

"You heard me. A Berber prince. A man of great faith and power, a man of honor. He is to be your husband. We will join our Arab bloodline to the most regal Berber clan, the Banu Birzal. Allah will smile upon your many children."

Her face grows ugly. She screams, "BABA!"

The slap is completely unanticipated. Her head recoils with the blow and she slips beneath the waves of silent shock, her eyes instantly filling. The hand print on her cheek is already a deepening red and the bright sting pulses on in blinding flashes. Her stunned stare sinks to the floor.

He seems confused over what he has just done, livid still, but mixed with an embarrassed remorse. He has never before struck his daughter, not once. His voice quavers momentarily, "The matter is closed, Rayhana." Then his strength returns, "and you WILL obey my wishes. It is done." He turns and leaves.

She collapses to the floor under a heap of sobs.

Aslam's eyes are on the floor, head bowed as he listens.

Ibn Abi Amir stares into space as he whispers his instructions. He halts, frowns, then hisses his final words with more emphasis. "I want it all. Where he comes from, his family, his friends, his teachers, who he knows. Everything." He has to will his balled fists to relax, then exhales his temper to regain composure.

Aslam's eyes rise to meet his master, followed by a crisp nod. "I will see to it, Master." He turns to depart.

"Aslam?" The man turns back. "Be discreet."

He nods once more and departs, hurt that his master insists on stating the obvious.

Responsibilities

Algeciras, **14 April 976.**

The room smells of death. Imam Abd al-Gafur whispers, "He collapsed two weeks ago in the madrasa. He has been like this ever since. He slips in and out of consciousness, but when he is awake he does not seem to know where he is or what has happened. Three days back he stopped eating. He is no longer making water. The physician says his time is close. I pray that his passing will be a peaceful one, *inshallah.*"

"Inshallah."

"I am glad you are here, Muhammad. I have prepared his burial plot and blessed the shroud your mother chose. All is ready when the time comes." He pauses. "There must be peace between you two before he passes, Muhammad. Your mother waits in her room."

He smiles weakly. "Thank you."

The door closes and the two are alone.

Ibn Abi Amir's eyes fill. The old man lying on the bed is but a shadow of his father, the proud lawyer, a qadi loved by the people of Algeciras. They could never agree on anything, except the importance of Sharia Law, but even there each man's interpretations differed radically, the father more liberal and forgiving, the son more conservative and judging. They crossed swords constantly. When the son left for Córdoba after Rayya's passing they parted with bitter words, and have not spoken in five years.

He looks out the window past the harbor to the cobalt sea beyond. "Where have the days gone, Baba? I have missed you." Tears streak his cheeks.

He steps forward and kneels at his father's bedside, lifts the old man's limp hand, kisses the back of his palm, then touches his forehead to the spot.

"Baba." Louder, "Baba!"

The old man's lashes flutter, then open, struggle to focus, then trace a confused search of the ceiling.

"Baba!"

The old man rolls his head to the voice, but there is no recognition. He looks but he does not see.

"Baba, Muhammad is with you. Muhammad, Baba. Your boy."

A hint of a smile quivers onto the old man's face. A breathy sigh, "My son ... my beautiful boy."

Ibn Abi Amir chokes back a sob and kisses his father's hand once more. "Yes, Baba, your son. I am here. I am here with you, Baba."

The old man's smile grows. "*Alhamdulillah.* My son has come home to me." His eyes close, but the smile remains. A breathy whisper, "All is well, all is well now, Alhamdulillah."

Ibn Abi Amir leans close. "Baba ... I love you. You will be proud of me, Baba. I am vizier to the caliph, Baba. And now qadi of the Maghreb. A qadi like you, Baba, like you. Soon, Baba, our family will rise in power, you will see, to great heights. One day I will rule all of al-Andalus, Baba, you will see, and my name will be spoken with respect for a thousand years. You will be proud of me, Baba ... so proud."

The old man does not stir. Ibn Abi Amir lays his ear to his father's chest and begins to sob.

She studies him as he tells her about court life in Córdoba and his many accomplishments. His pride and ambition weave seamlessly through his words. She recognizes it, sees him as only a mother can see her children, flesh from flesh, life from life. But there is something more, something new, something she cannot quite place. She muses: He has not aged a day. Still beautiful, but so serious. Where is that warm smile, the laughter, the tender affection that beautiful Rayya coaxed from my boy's hard heart? Her worry lines deepen. "It sounds like Allah's favor has smiled upon you, my son. Tell me about the children."

Silence.

"Salim is a fine young man, Mama. He studies at the grand imam's madrasa at the Great Mosque. It is a great honor for our family, Mama. He will be a lawyer, like Baba and me. Someday a qadi, perhaps." The pride returns.

She nods. She knows this already from Imam Abd al-Gafur.

"Khalil is a spitting image of Baba. But he enjoys court life more than his studies."

She grins.

"There is hope. He is bright. I intend to send him to the madrasa when he is of age. If there is a future for him, it will be found there." He frowns. "I am afraid he has an eye for the pretty girls."

She smiles. "Like his father."

He falls silent.

"And dear Rayhana. Tell me about my beautiful Rasha. Such a mirror of her mother, may Allah rest her soul."

He looks away, only for an instant, but this does not escape her.

So the imam's words are true, she silently acknowledges. She intuits the answer as only a mother can.

"Rayhana does nothing but read, Mama. That crazy girl will be the death of me ..." He sighs. "She will have nothing to do with court life. The young men steal desperate glances as she passes. She could have any of them with the snap of her fingers but could not care less." He grunts his displeasure. "That girl has a will of iron, Mama, a will of iron."

She laughs. "Like her mother."

His eyes soften for only a heartbeat. He whispers, "Yes ... like her mother." He collects himself. "I arranged access to the Rare Books Library for her. I would like to see her educated. That seems to have satisfied her, praise be to Allah. For now."

"Are there no wedding plans?"

"Not yet."

His face is expressionless, but she sees his lie.

"There is no rush, Mama. I will look into it when I return from the Maghreb. I am certain that someone suitable can be found in Córdoba."

Her voice softens, "Son, Rayya promised her she could marry for love. As you two did."

"I know, Mama. The girl reminds me often. It shall be so."

More lies. The emotion wells up in her chest and her heart begins to break.

"And how about you, Muhammad? Five years is a long time. You must remarry—it is time. For yourself, and also for the children."

He stares into space, then whispers, "No, Mama. I have tasted love and been broken for it. Never again ..."

She is not sure who this person is. Where has my boy gone, she wonders. Her plea is gentle, motherly, "Muhammad ..."

His expression hardens into stone. "No more, Mama. I must leave for the Maghreb."

She gasps. "Your father ..."

"I have made my peace with Baba. General Ghalib is ready to sail and he insists I remain with the army. As qadi of the Maghreb I have duties, Mama, surely you see that. Responsibilities, Mama. Baba would understand that." He rises.

She is silent, but her eyes have filled. A single tear spills from each dam and races down her cheeks. He moves to her and kisses her, but he refuses to meet her flooded eyes.

"I will see to Baba's papers before I leave and make sure that all is in order for you to live comfortably." Boyish excitement steals his voice. "And you must come see the land I purchased for the family. Ten thousand arpents, Mama. The wealthiest merchant in Algeciras could not do better. Even a view of the sea." Now she refuses to meet his gaze. Duly chastised, his expression settles into stone once more. "My duties will keep me in the Maghreb, Mama. Six months, perhaps longer." He leaves without another word.

Her chin sinks to her chest as she cries.

Bargain

"Will the weather hold?" The tone is gruff, impatient.

The captain nods. "I believe so, my lord. The squall should remain safely to the west."

General Ghalib snorts. "Do not 'believe so,' Captain, know so. Much is at stake. I do not like being on the open ocean."

The captain straightens his back. "The storms will not challenge us, my lord. The sea will remain rough but of no serious concern to the fleet."

Ghalib looks west. A squat, thick band of charcoal masks the joining of sun to water. He turns east. Wispy striations of breathtaking pink stretch across the sky. Below, the thin, jagged line of nut brown marks the coast, thankfully always in sight. He answers with a curt nod then turns and limps down the deck of the *shalandi*. The cruel sea air tortures him, producing a wince with each step.

The Arab horse transport is a variant of an oared *bireme* galley with a wider beam, a deeper draft, and an extra mast. The horse stalls run bow to stern to equalize the weight, thirty all told, with slung bunks below deck for the knights and their gear.

The horses are restless, their eyes white and skittish. Ghalib frowns his disapproval. He knows that with this chop and roll the mounts will soon be queasy. It will take a day for them to find their legs again. He raises his eyes past the stern. The armada contains thirty-five *shalandi*, fifty plodding infantry galleys, twenty cargo merchants, and an escort of a dozen faster *dromons* protecting their flanks; too formidable for meddling corsairs, and safely away from any Fatimid patrols, who rarely venture past the Pillars of Hercules.

Ghalib looks up. The two angular *lateen* sails are full, but he knows the real work is done by the oarsmen. The relentless pounding of the oar hammer is annoying, but they are making good time. They should be in Larache by mid-morning, noon at the latest.

He stops to stroke his stallion, a midnight black Arabian of impeccable lineage. He slides his hand into a pocket then pulls out a treat. Whiskered velvet lips tickle his palm. The grizzled warrior sprouts a rare grin. "Soon, Taneen, my dragon, the caliph will own this squalid desert. You, sir, shall make me proud." The horse raises his head regally. "Steady, boy. We will be off this dung heap by the time the sun is high." The stallion whinnies in answer. General Ghalib's smile widens.

Sultan ibn Guennoun stands on the edge of the roof of the stone tower rising above the castle keep, the highest point in Hajar an-Nasar. His legs are spread for stability and his robe whips and snaps in the stiff wind. The updraft is strong enough to force him to lean forward to find his balance. One hand rests upon the hilt of his scimitar while the other strokes his long black beard; a nervous habit. The late afternoon sun is in his eyes, but he does not attempt to shield them; he only squints, narrowing his ebony pupils to fine slits. A man of the desert.

A single step forward and he would plunge five hundred feet to the valley floor. He enjoys the danger of this particular vantage, and the view is unrivaled. He studies the coast at the horizon. "You are sure?"

"Yes, Sire, the Umayyads. A thousand horses and perhaps three thousand infantry and supplies. They landed at Larache three days ago and have set up camp across the river, near Lixus." The courtier stands back from the edge several feet but still seems uneasy.

"Did the Fatimids oppose the landing?"

"No, Sire. But the Fatimid garrison is small. Or perhaps they do not feel threatened by the Umayyads."

"Perhaps ..."

He clears his throat. "I have heard rumors, Sire."

"Speak."

"Sire, my sources tell me they aim to march on us, not the Fatimids."

"Why us? The Fatimids are their enemies, not the Idrisids."

"I do not know, Sire." He pauses. "Perhaps the caliph desires a winter palace in the Rif for vacation." His eyes sparkle, but the sultan does not seem amused.

"What do they expect to do with such a puny force in these mountains? Take Hajar an-Nasar?" He scoffs. "The Arabs are fools."

"Certainly, Sire. Should I prepare the troops?"

"Not yet. Let us see if they aim to challenge us directly. We have plenty of time. But I want to know the moment they move."

"Of course."

"Who leads them?"

"Ghalib al-Nasiri."

The sultan nods. "The caliph's military vizier. Interesting ... never send a boy to do a man's work. I look forward to facing that old scoundrel in battle. I will have his head on a platter."

"Sire, they have also brought a man they are calling 'Qadi of the Maghreb.' Muhammad ibn Abi Amir. An Arab from Algeciras."

He turns. "Surely they know the Idrisids will never answer to an Umayyad qadi."

"One could never accuse the Umayyads of being timid, Sire."

"The cisterns and granaries are full?"

"They are, Sire. We could withstand a two-year siege, longer if required."

"Good. They do not have enough troops for a serious siege. The Umayyads are soft. Wait until they taste the Rif summer. Their lips will crack and their tongues will split from thirst, and then the sandstorms will fill their mouths and silence their blasphemy. When the Arabs beg for mercy, I will gut them and leave them for the jackals, then make water on their bleached bones." He falls silent. "Send word to the clans. And tell Omar I have a special task for him. We should arrange a greeting from the Rif to get these Arabs' attention."

"What of the Banu Birzal, Sire? We could use their horsemen."

"Forget the Banu Birzal. Those swine will never join us. Al-Tariq would rather see the Arabs rule the Rif than me." He spits in the dust. "Make sure your spies watch him. I do not need the Banu Birzal making mischief while an Arab army bears down upon me."

The courtier nods, then turns and leaves, relieved to be away from the precipice.

The sultan continues to survey the west, wondering what game the Arabs are playing this time.

The paper scroll is resting on Ibn Abi Amir's desk when he returns to his tent after noon prayer. The guards saw nothing, which pleases him.

Meet me at midnight tonight in the village under the cobbler's sign in the medina, two alleys up from the wharf. Come alone.

No wax seal. Maghrebi dialect, but the calligraphy is precise, practiced. An educated man. He examines the paper for any other markings. Nothing. He angles the lower right corner of the paper close to the candle flame, careful to heat it without catching it on fire. He studies the dull yellow glow that seeps through the paper.

Still nothing. A moment more and a faint doodle appears then darkens into an insignia he knows. As he withdraws the paper from the flame the marking fades into oblivion.

As he stares into space, Ibn Abi Amir smiles. Banu Birzal.

He hires a young boy that afternoon to show him the village. After visiting the mosque, the wharf, and the market, they pass by the cobbler's sign. There is a deep alcove in the front of the shop that offers protection from the alley. Public, but private. He does not wish to pause to give away his interest so he simply memorizes and moves on.

After dinner with Ghalib and evening prayers, he retires to his tent for letter writing. He is anxious about what is coming but not enough to burden his sleep. It amuses him, really. These major turning points, this grand plan he has hatched increasingly seems to be written in the stars, the Blessed Will of Allah. He walks a scimitar's edge to be sure, but his confidence slowly but surely grows, a wheat seedling nurtured by a warm spring rain, top-heavy already by the swelling promise of a bountiful harvest.

He passes no one in the medina. The village sleeps. He can hear faint activity down at the wharf; the rustling of gear, a hammer slapping a wooden wedge, the slippery hiss of rope racing through a bolt, empty boxes being stacked. Fishermen readying their dhows for a pre-dawn sail.

A dog yaps, then stops, then unleashes a barrage of explosive barking. He hears the man's curse, the sharp yelp of the animal, then silence. Another curse.

He looks up. The stars are spectacular. The air has cooled, and is quite pleasant now. The day was hot, a presage to the coming summer swelter he knows will soon beset them. The unforgiving heat of the Maghreb is legendary.

As he passes through the deserted market stalls, faint smells of the day's activities linger still. He stops, lifts his chin, and inhales, sifting the different scents woven together in a tangled mesh. Spices; most he knows, a few he does not. Grilled lamb, baked bread, a mélange of citrus, all bathed in the moist brine of the sea air. The effect is pleasing; it reminds him of market days during his boyhood in Algeciras. He continues his journey, walking slowly, confidently. He does not want to arrive early or appear anxious.

He is dressed as a qadi, the fine black robes of the law courts. He has added a black turban to his wardrobe. Less common in Córdoba, unnecessary for a man of his station, but quite important in the Maghreb, especially among the Berbers. His ear is finely tuned to local customs these days. He is unarmed.

He scans as he walks, absorbing everything. He turns the corner and stops. The alley oozes a dim glow cast by several haphazardly placed oil lamps. Deserted. The cobbler's sign is halfway down on the right. The darkened recesses of the alcove are blocked from his view.

He takes a deep breath, whispers "Inshallah," then casts his die and resumes his leisurely pace. He folds his hands behind him to accentuate the fact that he is unarmed, but also to assume a posture befitting the qadi of the Maghreb.

He stops under the sign, looks down the alley one last time, then turns to scan behind him. Satisfied, he steps into the shadows. As his eyes adjust he sees the menacing statue of carved dark stone. Ibn Abi Amir bows, but does not speak.

The man is tall for a Berber, imposing even in twilight. He looks to be Ibn Abi Amir's elder, but by how much is hard to say. He is dressed in the fine flowing robes of a wealthy Berber knight. Perhaps the Sheikh he seeks? Unlikely, though he looks the part.

The curved scabbard of the scimitar hanging at his side is impossible to ignore. The man's palm rests on the head of the hilt, but his fingers are relaxed and open by desert custom; welcoming but not foolish. There is little doubt he is familiar with the use of his blade. A bejeweled needle dagger is stuck in his belt at an angle permitting it to be instantly drawn if required. The man's beard is long and untrimmed, the rule among the desert clans. Elaborate turban.

His face is expressionless, unreadable, but his ebony eyes are alive, filled with pride and hints of menace. Desert eyes. This man is clearly a leader of some sort.

"I am Muhammad ibn Abi Amir, Caliph al-Hakam II's vizier to Africa." He hesitates, then adds, "I am qadi of the Maghreb."

Silence.

He continues, "I received your message. And your insignia. I am pleased to see that my letters were received. Thank you for coming."

The silence begins to grow uncomfortable.

"I wish to speak with Hamid al-Tariq, Sheikh of the Banu Birzal. Can you arrange this?" Ibn Abi Amir's Maghrebi dialect is flawless. He waits.

A deep baritone finally answers him, rolling out ponderously, the slow movements of a desert life. The voice is one of command,

and matches the menace latent in his eyes. "I am Jafar al-Tariq. Hamid is my brother, may Allah protect him. I am commander of the cavalry of the Banu Birzal, by Allah's will the favored clan of the Maghreb."

"I am pleased to meet you, Jafar. My contacts spoke of you with respect." The man ticks his head, no more. He studies the Berber knight as he calculates the best angle of attack. Ibn Abi Amir continues. "The Banu Birzal are the rightful rulers of the Rif Mountains and the Idrisid Kingdom. It is a pity that Sultan ibn Guennoun rules in your brother's place."

The hate woven through the Berber's words is jarring. He hisses, "Sultan ..." He spits. "That dog duped the desert clans with his empty promises. He betrayed my brother and broke his solemn word. His life is forfeit. He knows nothing of desert war, Qadi of the Maghreb, or how to organize the desert clans into a real fighting force. When the time comes, the Fatimids will pull him limb from limb, devour his troops, and spit out their bones. He will take the Idrisid Kingdom to his grave with him. The desert clans will perish. I shall curse their folly, then weep."

"Yes, they will perish." Ibn Abi Amir continues his study. "Unless the Banu Birzal join forces with the Umayyads to capture Hajar an-Nasar and wrest power from him before it is too late. I, as qadi of the Maghreb, will install your brother as the legitimate sultan of the Idrisids. The Banu Birzal will rule the Rif, and all the Berber clans will unify under the Banu Birzal banner and fight as they were meant to fight."

Now he is the one being studied.

That lovely baritone answers, "Tell me more."

"The caliph has sent a thousand of his finest mounted knights and three thousand infantry and archers under the command of General Ghalib, whom I am sure you have heard of."

Jafar interrupts, "Mounted Arab knights are no match for desert horsemen."

"That I will concede ... but they are a capable fighting force nevertheless. Ghalib knows battle tactics, Jafar. Unfortunately, his army is too small to take Hajar an-Nasar by direct assault. Unless ..."

"Unless?"

"Unless the Banu Birzal have spies within the fortress that can aid him. Show him the best routes of attack, warn him of ambushes. Poison their cisterns, perhaps, or loose rats into the grain stores; maybe even open a gate deep in the night when the time is right." He stops. "But that would require the Banu Birzal to have infiltrated Ibn Guennoun's army, to already be inside Hajar an-Nasar."

The thin line of the Berber's white teeth are his only answer. Desert warfare is a ruthless game.

"Good. I suspected as much."

"Why would the Córdoban caliph wish the Banu Birzal to rule the Idrisids? Berbers have no love of Arabs and would strike any hand that meddles in the Rif."

"There is only one reason for the caliph's interest, Jafar. Like you, we believe the Fatimids must be driven from the Maghreb, pushed back into the eastern desert where they belong. We share the same goal as the Banu Birzal. The Fatimids are a threat to al-Andalus, and to the caliph's rule ... and of course to his gold. The Idrisids, under Banu Birzal leadership, are the only ones in the Maghreb that can rid us of the Fatimid scourge. The Umayyads will support you with gold, with arms, and all the legal means at our disposal to ensure your brother's legitimate rule of the Berber clans. Your men will do the fighting, not the Umayyads. When the Fatimids are gone, the Banu Birzal will rule the Maghreb as a friend of the Umayyads. You will possess the splendor of Fez, all that the Fatimids have built. In return, you will protect the caliph's southern flank and put an end to the corsair raids that scourge our merchants." He stops to let Jafar absorb.

Jafar finally replies, "For any hope of sustained success against the Fatimids, all the mountain clans must be unified under my brother and properly organized and armed."

"Precisely. As qadi of the Maghreb I can formalize that unification and give it legitimacy by decree of the caliph. Hamid al-Tariq will be sultan of the Idrisids, Jafar, and you his general. The clans will follow the Banu Birzal to war. With Ibn Guennoun gone, the Idrisids will be feared in the Maghreb once more. Then the Fatimids will tremble; they will be the hunted ones."

Silence, and then, "Guennoun belongs to me and my brother when the fortress falls. To deal with as we see fit."

It is Ibn Abi Amir's turn to smile. "With pleasure."

"I will arrange a meeting with my brother when you arrive at Hajar an-Nasar."

"Good. Jafar, one more thing. Since arriving in Larache there have been threats made against my life. It seems that there are those that do not relish an Arab qadi ..."

"That would include most of the Berbers of the Rif. And, of course, the Fatimids."

151

Ibn Abi Amir smiles. "Exactly. But without the authority of the qadi of the Maghreb, there will be no legitimacy extended by the caliph to your brother ... when the time comes."

"It is dangerous to wander alone at night, even near the cities, Qadi of the Maghreb. Any Berber knight could soak the desert sand with your blood before you blinked your eyes."

"As could you, Jafar ..."

"As could I." His hand tightens on the hilt of his scimitar. The Berber's ebony eyes burn into Ibn Abi Amir, searching for any hint of mischief, any buried deceit. His hand relaxes. "You are brave, Qadi of the Maghreb, to meet me alone and unarmed. No Berber would dare risk the kiss of my dagger under his ribs. I have killed more men than you have known."

Ibn Abi Amir detects a whiff of respect seeping into the Berber's voice, which pleases him. His bold actions this night will soon be known among the clans, the stuff of desert legend.

Jafar continues, "You must take care who prepares your food and those you choose to ride with." He pauses. "I will assign two of my best men as your personal bodyguards. Trust them with your life, Qadi of the Maghreb."

"Thank you, Jafar, I am in your debt." He bows. Ibn Abi Amir is conscious of the heavy pouch filled with gold dinars inside his robe, but decides the message it would send would spoil the moment. The right time for bribes will arrive soon enough.

"Look for them at first light, two days hence. Suktan and Tahir."

"When will I meet your brother?"

"When the time is right, Qadi of the Maghreb, you will know."

Ibn Abi Amir bows once more then extends his right hand, palm up, and in Berber custom, the two clasp forearms as brothers.

"Wine?"

"No. Now that I am in the Maghreb, I have adopted the local customs. The Berbers are much more observant Muslims than we are, General Ghalib. They offend easily when it comes to perceived insults to the Prophet or to Islam. As qadi of the Maghreb, my piety will be carefully scrutinized."

Ghalib grumbles, "Suit yourself." He takes a deep sip of his own wine.

Ibn Abi Amir says, "When does the assault begin?"

"In three days. We have nearly assembled all of our supplies, and my scouts returned from Hajar an-Nasar last night. They have located water on the north side of the base of the mount and an acceptable staging area. We will take the canyon route to save time. The fortress is formidable, perhaps impregnable. The Idrisids are aware of our presence and are readying their fortifications. No doubt they have plenty of food and water to withstand a siege. They seem to know that we are after Ibn Guennoun, not the Fatimids."

"The Berbers are not stupid, General."

"Debatable. They chose Ibn Guennoun, did they not? He could not fight his way out of a wheat sack. Without Hajar an-Nasar he has nothing. The Fatimids will feed his bones to the jackals after the first real fight."

Ibn Abi Amir nods, then falls silent. "I have made contact with the Banu Birzal."

General Ghalib's head snaps up, pursued by a scowl. "I was to be informed before that happened."

"More accurately, the Banu Birzal made contact with me. Late last night I awoke to find a Berber knight standing in my tent."

Ghalib scoffs, "In your tent?"

"Yes, in my tent. Your guards are lax, General Ghalib; blame them, not me."

The general's scowl does not waver. "And?"

"Jafar al-Tariq, Commander of the Cavalry of the Banu Birzal. Importantly, brother of Hamid al-Tariq, Sheikh of the Banu Birzal." Ibn Abi Amir stops. The General impatiently waves his hands to push him on. "I am pleased to say that they have accepted our offer, General. The Banu Birzal have well-placed spies within the fortress that will aid your assault, perhaps even open the gates when the time comes so you can walk in unchallenged. I am certain the Berber clans will rally around the Banu Birzal once Ibn Guennoun is gone. He did demand Guennoun as a prize when the fortress falls, a spoil to do with as they wish. I said yes. I assumed you would approve. It seems there is a blood feud between Hamid al-Tariq and Ibn Guennoun, something the desert Berbers take quite seriously. We can exploit that."

General Ghalib grunts. "How do we make contact with their spies?"

"We do not. They will contact me and arrange things once we reach Hajar an-Nasar. He was emphatic, however, that they will only deal with the qadi of the Maghreb, no one else. It seems they have great respect for Sharia Law and uphold the absolute authority of my jurisdiction in all legal matters. Quite refreshing, actually."

General Ghalib studies him.

"Oh. He also told me that as qadi of the Maghreb I am entitled by Berber custom to personal bodyguards. He seemed concerned for my safety, given that the Berbers have a special dislike of Arabs, and the land is wild between Larache and Hajar an-Nasar. As you know, the desert is a dangerous place, General. I could not refuse without insulting him. They will arrive tomorrow morning. Only two. I will pay for their food and supplies, of course."

Ghalib has not broken his intense stare. "Of course."

The distant warble of the muezzin's song begins. "Ahhh ... join me for noon prayer, General?"

Ghalib waves his hand impatiently. "Another time. I have work to do."

As Ibn Abi Amir rises and exits, Ghalib's cold stare follows him through the tent flap.

Dances

Samuel opens his eyes, rested and instantly awake. Not a single sound disturbs the tranquility. The orange-gold sunrise leaks into the windows high above their floor mattress, asserting its will upon the slinking pre-dawn gray. He has awoken at first light since he was a boy—he loves the whispered promise of sunrise, Yahweh's tender renewal of his steadfast love for his creation. Another day of wonder to behold and savor.

He sifts the wispy streams of growing light, is fascinated by the subtle mixture of rich hues evolving and strengthening as they creep down the wall, deepening in gold tones minute by minute. He instinctively knows from what he sees that it will be another beautiful day, cloudless and warm. He sighs, deeply content. He relishes the Sabbath, the only morning he permits himself to lounge in bed after sunrise.

She lies on her side facing away from him, curled into the fetal position he finds so endearing. He turns and snuggles against her, molds his body to hers, his knees folded into the bend of hers, the tops of his feet married to her soles. He breathes in her dark brown curls then carefully eases his arm across her, trying hard not to wake her.

They made love the night before. He smiles. Not the frantic wrestling and desperate contortions of their youth. No, a deliberate and practiced exploration of velvet clefts and glistening facets set to the sighed songs of love; drawn out slow into a thin, taut wire of sweet agony, twisted tightly until just before snapping, held there quivering for a ridiculously long time, then mercifully released in a long, heavy gush to their gasps of adoration. Her eyes always well up afterwards, spill with the sheer intensity of the joy they have just shared. Infinitely more satisfying than their youthful fumbling. This is something they have grown into over their many years together, polished now to mirror sheen, cherished as a precious jewel in their celebrated life as one body, one soul.

He feels himself stir and can't help but press himself harder against her with the inevitable result.

She shifts, yawns, then tenses into a feline stretch.

"Good morning, beautiful." He kisses her cheek.

"Good morning, Husband."

His tone turns playful. "I trust you slept well?"

He can't see her face but knows she is grinning. "Like a baby. Something kept me up late last night, the most unusual dreams. So realistic."

He chuckles. "I enjoyed you."

"I enjoyed you enjoying me."

"I love these mornings, Rebekah. Nothing to do, no place to be, only us."

"Yes ... Yahweh's great gift. We are blessed, Husband."

They fall into contented silence.

"You were right, you know."

She grins again. "Which time?"

He squeezes her tighter.

"About Zafir."

Her tone brightens. "Tell me."

"He loves the girl, Rebekah. The boy is absolutely smitten."

She rolls over to face him. He relaxes onto his back and now she snuggles in against him.

Her smile is radiant. "And ..."

"I told you about how I surprised them in the library."

"Yes."

"It was obvious even then that something was going on besides reading."

"As I told you. And ..."

"We talked yesterday. He lingered until Zaheid and Levi left my study, then fell silent. It was obvious he had something he needed to say, but he just sat there like a stone. I had to coax it out of him. He began that infernal clearing of his throat, then that stupid mumbling. Poor boy spoke to the floor the whole time."

She giggles. "And ..."

Samuel sighs. "Well, first he apologized for deceiving me. I pretended ignorance—I did not have the heart to tell him you had figured it out long ago. Then he professed his feelings for Rayhana."

She chides him. "You men! His words, Samuel, his words! What did he say? His exact words."

"The poor boy is in agony, Rebekah. I am afraid Cupid has turned him into a pin cushion."

Her glee is unmistakable. "Samuel! What did he say?"

"Mmmm ... you know I have trouble recalling conversations, Rebekah. Let me see ... once the boy got rolling he could not stop. 'I have never met anyone like her. She is so beautiful and so smart. She loves all the things that I love, my beloved Greek plays, the *Iliad*.'" He stops.

"GO ON!"

He flashes a playful smile. "Those dimples are like daggers in my side! I never know when exactly they are going to appear." Rebekah giggles and motions him forward. "Let me see, what else? Oh! Those first few times I was around her I could not breathe, and my heart did nothing but pound. I still sometimes say stupid things when I am around her, but it amuses her now. We talk for hours and hours about everything; about nothing. We just want to be together.' The boy sees her every time she is in the library now. It seems they have worked out some sort of ... plan."

Rebekah grows animated. "Talk for hours and hours. He has kissed her. Definitely."

"Judging from where they were sitting when I surprised them, I would wager so."

"How joyful, Samuel! Our Zafir is in love, and more importantly, his love is returned. It reminds me so of our early days, Samuel. You never knew what to say. I was dying for a kiss and practically had to beg you for it!"

He laughs. "There is more. Zafir confessed that he showed her our camera obscura. I have to say I was taken aback. I raised my voice and he cowered like a scolded puppy. But then he told me her ideas. The girl is bright, that much is obvious. She figured out things none of us have been able to. Daylight images, Rebekah! The camera is capable of producing daylight images. Imagine! Who would have guessed? And she suggested a way to view the images more easily. Can you believe it?"

She grins. "Of course I can."

Samuel sighs. "Well, I put the boy's mind at ease. Instead of the four of us working on it, there will now be five. And with her father gone to the Maghreb, there is less to worry about from him, at least for now."

"With no chaperone they must be very careful, Samuel. There are so many prying eyes at court."

"Yes, I agree." He pauses. "Even if they do follow protocol, Ibn Abi Amir is going to make trouble over their relationship, Rebekah."

Concern edges into her voice. "What do you mean?"

"Well, from what Zafir said, the father told Rayhana he intends to marry her to the highest bidder to advance his position at court. He lusts for gold, that much is common knowledge in Madinat. Ibn Abi Amir is a strange one, and getting stranger by the day. Evidently, she tried to tell him about Zafir, but he would hear none of it. In a fit of rage, he struck her."

Rebekah gasps.

"Hard to imagine. Thank goodness the man is gone. Hopefully when he returns we can talk some sense into him. We have to try. Perhaps I can approach the caliph for advice—he has always liked Zafir. These two belong together, Rebekah. Rayhana is despairing and Zafir is saying silly things; dangerous things. He says he will oppose the father."

"He loves her, Samuel, what do you expect him to say?"

"The man scares me, Rebekah."

"We must help them, Samuel."

"Yes, we must. We will."

"I would like to meet Rayhana. How about inviting the two of them to dinner? She can bring her brother as a chaperone, if that will make it easier."

"I will mention it to Zafir. I am sure he would like that. She has no mother, no one to talk to, and it sounds like she needs someone to listen to her ... and to give her some good advice."

The choir's rhythmic chant of the *Offertory* is glorious. The complex echoes weave into a tonal harmony that drifts effortlessly into the upper reaches of the basilica where the reverberations stretch wide and hover only to evaporate into the haze of sweet frankincense whisked into heaven by angels. The chant is solemn and reverential, but the competing melodies are precise and bright, deeply joyful; God's beckoning whisper spoken straight into the hearts of the kneeling faithful.

Brother Cleo's eyes are closed as he listens. He smiles, content to bask in the presence of such mastery. Peter Strobel kneels beside him, lips pursed with impatience, disapproval of something, of everything, written large upon his face.

The chant ceases, but the notes linger on for several seconds. Bishop Reccimund raises his arms, palms up, and begins the *Preface* with "Sursum corda." *Lift up your hearts.* The congregation answers. The Mass works its way inexorably towards the apex of Holy Communion, using scaffolding already nearly a millennium old.

When the Preface prayers are concluded, the chant of the *Sanctus* begins with the men's ponderous baritones. They are quickly joined by the boys, who effortlessly gather in the highest notes to broaden the choir's register.

Sanctus,
Mundi fabricator et rector.
Sanctus,

Unice ipsius patris et equalis dominus.
Sanctus dominus deus sabaoth,
Mundi qui culpas almis flammis mire detergis.
Pleni sunt celi et terra gloria tua.
Osanna in excelsis ...

When the Sanctus chant ends, the lovely melody lingers, reluctant to vacate the welcoming space. The smile has not left Brother Cleo's face. It pleases him deeply to know that the Gregorian Mass, a staple at Cluny for some time now, has found its way to Córdoba, to the Basilica of Saint Acisclus, a Christian conclave in a city of Muslims. This version of the Roman Mass is different, to be sure, a cousin not a brother of what is practiced in the rest of Europe, but pleasing in its own way. As he has learned, Córdoba rarely copies anything word for word, much preferring to absorb, then alter; to produce something creative and unique.

The Córdoban Mozarab Mass is no different. By the caliph's decree, Christian worship is welcomed by the city, encouraged even, and the fourteen churches of greater Córdoba are full on Sundays. An Arabic Bible is used for the readings, since virtually all Córdobans speak Arabic, while only few are fluent in Latin. And while the prayers of the Mass are said in Latin, as mandated by Rome, depending on the priest, it is more often than not a heavily Arabic-inflected Latin, intermixed with local dialect, a verbal mélange referred to by Córdobans as "Latinia." Reccimund's Latin is excellent, if slightly accented, but even he infuses Latinia into his Masses.

Peter Strobel most assuredly does not approve of what Córdoba has done with his Mass. The use of an Arabic Bible offends him mightily, the words on his Lord's lips forced into the infidel's tongue! And the abuse of proper Latin he finds inexcusable. He has wondered aloud to Cleo many times whether these Masses are even valid, much less approved by Rome. His expression is inevitably one of mild surprise when Christ's True Presence does in fact melt upon his tongue. He embraces the Grace, but remains wary of some sort of cruel trick lurking in the shadows, some sleight of hand ready to dupe him.

As the Sanctus nears its end, Reccimund begins the *Canon* in a hushed voice, which lends his words weight. He ends with, "Per ipsum et cum ipso ..." The congregation listens to the priest's familiar, *'Through him and with him,'* verse and responds, "Amen."

Reccimund bows, joins his hands in prayer, closes his eyes, and looks up at the crucifix, then begins his solo chant of the

Pater Noster. His lovely voice, rich and resonant, carries the Lord's Prayer beyond the rafters. The Mozarab Mass presses on.

After communion and his final chanted prayer, Reccimund turns and faces his congregation, then lifts his hands. The congregation bows.

Veni, sancte spiritus, Et emitte caelitus, Lucis tuae radium. Veni, Pater pauperum, Veni, dator munerum, Veni, lumen cordium.

The congregation responds, "Amen."

Reccimund unexpectedly beams and switches to Arabic. "Dear brothers and sisters. Peace and blessings be upon you and your families."

He is answered with one voice, "And upon you."

Strobel turns to Cleo and frowns, then queries the monk for a translation using only his eyes, which is rendered flawlessly.

Reccimund continues, "Our Lord has blessed us beyond measure, dear friends, and today we give back some of that sweet goodness. As a reminder, this afternoon we will join with our Muslim and Jewish brothers and sisters in a work of mercy. A new hospital is being built for the laborers and their families across the river. We need your hands, dear people! Bring tools, bring food to share, and bring your families. We will join together with Córdoba's faithful and honor our shared God, our blessed common roots. Please meet here at the basilica at an hour past noon." His smile widens. "Be prepared to sing as we march, my friends!"

Excited murmurs kick up.

Reccimund motions the congregation to rise. He makes the sign of the cross as he booms, "In nomine patris, et filii, et spiritus sancti." The people follow his motions through the Sign of the Cross and respond with a boisterous, "Amen!"

As the people begin to file into the streets a geyser of conversation erupts. There is nothing pinched or glum about the Mozarab Mass.

Strobel is still frowning.

Aslam still questions the wisdom of his master leaving him in Córdoba. His pensive grimaces give him away. The Maghreb is a dangerous place and trusted friends are rare. He has no choice but to obey, of course. Ibn Abi Amir assured him that being his eyes and ears in Madinat al-Zahra was far more valuable to his safety than a personal bodyguard in the desert. Still ...

Ibn Abi Amir's spy network has grown fat over the past months, thanks to the riches lavished upon him by Subh. The goal? Facts painstakingly obscured from prying eyes; but more importantly, ugly rumors and whispered gossip, unseemly dalliances, even outright slander. Inside knowledge to be wielded as a dagger under the ribs. The jewels most sought? Scandal fodder of any sort; adultery by a wife of privilege, the taking of a servant maiden by a master, or better still, the taking of some unsuspecting boy. The breaking of Sharia Law, sins that would embarrass or destroy, provide leverage when the time is just right. All more than worth their weight in gold. And Ibn Abi Amir doles out his gold lavishly, saving nothing for himself or his family.

The hazards? The inevitable game of cat and mouse. Knowing with certainty which spy is most loyal to whom, inferring partial versus whole truths behind any given piece of obscure information, knowing when to believe and when to doubt and when to seek a second source. Hardest of all, knowing the proper price to pay for a juicy morsel. It is a dangerous game, to be sure. Subh, supremely gifted in such matters, has contributed greatly to Ibn Abi Amir's education, even gone so far as to share some of her most trusted sources. She is a fool to do so.

The lion's share of Aslam's time is now spent in secret rendezvous with their eyes in Madinat and in the city. He keeps careful records of whom he pays what and writes his master weekly detailing the juiciest tidbits, all safely buried within their secret code.

Ibn Abi Amir's war chest grows by the day, by the hour. The prizes he most fancies are surprisingly not found in Madinat al-Zahra, but among the powerful merchant families of Córdoba, the economic engine driving the enterprise and wealth of al-Andalus. Such men, for the most part, are kept safely outside the tight reins of power in the royal court within Madinat al-Zahra and the immediate sphere of influence emanating from the Golden Circle.

The square is bursting with activity, the pleasing sweaty bustle of market day on a warm spring morning. The throngs of shoppers swarm the stalls rimming the square, crowding around carts laden with fresh vegetables of all shapes and sizes, rows of spices, a patchwork of bright color set into conical mounds poured neatly into large crocks, embroidered silks and bolts of cotton cloth, silver and gold jewelry, ceramics and farming tools, and of course countless books.

The air itself is an epicurean delight, the tendrils of smoke from braziers brimming with the mouthwatering aromas of roasted meats, steaming baked bread, endless kettles of simmering stews. The air is alive with impassioned haggling, sliced here and there by hearty laughter, delicious gossip whispered into the backs of hands by both women and men, the bright sounds of children running and playing, the pained bleats and cries of caged animals soon to meet their fates.

Aslam's pensive grimace returns. He is after something specific this day and has made the journey to Córdoba himself. He has at last received the tip he needs from a seasoned informer, a book binder, his ancient shop buried deep in a dark alley winding away from the large square adjacent to the Great Mosque.

Aslam melts into the crowd. His dress is unremarkable, his face common. There is not a single person, who if later asked, would recall his presence. He is master of his craft.

He picks his way across the square, stopping for a slice of roasted kid and a thick slice of bread to soak up the bloody juices. He locates the spot the informer indicated, and after a quick survey for danger, turns and makes his way down the tight alley. The crowd thins out and the light dims. Here there are more expensive shops and grizzled artisans, few of whom will bother to haggle. He finds the shop easily and lingers outside until the sole customer leaves, then he steps though the door and studies the room.

The binder's shop is tiny, cramped, somewhat disheveled. All around are shelves of books waiting to be worked on, stacks of leather, pressed binding boards, spools of thread, a side table with a neat collection of metal instruments. There is a pleasing organic smell of freshly tanned leather laced with pungent hints of animal glues, stains, and ink. An old man, the binder, sits upon a high stool, hunched over the thick codex on his workbench. He stares through a giant lens, a fine pick in his hand. Alone. He glances up as Aslam enters his shop but pays no heed. He has been at this far too long to push his wares. Those that can appreciate art will know it when they see it. He returns to his task of picking diseased thread from the spine of the old codex.

"You are skilled, sir. Beautiful work."

The binder looks up but does not speak. A statement of the obvious. A slight tick of his head is the only response he gives. He returns to his task.

"I was told by a ... friend that you know the royal book binder."

The man looks up again but does not speak.

Aslam places his outstretched hand upon the workbench, which the binder registers with a flick of his eyes.

"I seek information on an apprentice of the royal binder. From several years back." Aslam withdraws his hand, leaving a neat stack of three gold dinars. "A young man by the name of Zafir Saffar. Do you know him?"

The binder studies the gold, his expression unchanged. He reaches for a swath of cotton cloth, picks it up, then lays it over the coins to hide the bargain struck.

He returns to his work. "I know him."

"He spent two years with the royal book binder."

The binder picks thread as he whispers. "Yes. He has a gift for the binder's art. Alas, the royal librarian learned that he spoke Greek and ended the apprenticeship. He now works for Master al-Tayyib, the Jew, as a translator."

"That is him. He is not of Arab descent, is he?"

"No."

"What can you tell me about his family? Do they live in Córdoba?"

"He has no family."

"What happened to them?"

The binder hesitates. "I do not know." Aslam senses the man is lying. "I was told al-Tayyib is his only family now."

"I have seen this Zafir Saffar. Unusual green eyes. He looks European to me. Perhaps from the eastern mountains? I have heard rumors from my—friend, that he may in fact be saqaliba." There is an odd bite to the word, as if he fears he will be sullied by simply uttering it. "What do you think?"

The man looks up from his work, studies Aslam. "That, I do not know." He returns to the spine.

Aslam guesses it is another lie but cannot be positive. "He has the look. Not the hair, but definitely the eyes. Those odd emerald eyes."

The book binder shrugs.

"Does he ever come to the city?"

"When he worked for the royal binder, he would visit me from time to time to buy some special leather or fancy binder's board. The royal binder appreciates my art. But he comes no more. He lives and works in the Rare Books Library in Madinat al-Zahra now. He has little need for the binders' art."

Aslam frowns. A dead end. "I see." He tries another angle. "Do you ever send shipments directly into Madinat al-Zahra? To the royal binder, or at least to his workshop?"

"Occasionally."

"Do you take those yourself?"

"Of course. Who else would I send?"

Aslam nods. Better news; a possible card to be played. "If you hear anything more about Zafir Saffar, anything at all, I would appreciate knowing." Aslam slides a small piece of folded paper onto the workbench. The name of the informer and his address. A single gold dinar is tucked inside the paper.

The binder looks up, ticks his head, then returns to his task. When he looks up again, Aslam is gone.

The narrow canyon snakes its way through the toothy pinnacles of the Rif Mountains. This maze of twisted canyons is the only direct route to Hajar an-Nasar from Larache, but its reputation as a killing ground is known across the Maghreb. General Ghalib's army is guided by local Berber clansmen they have bribed, but there is no denying that this is an ambusher's paradise. No more than five horses can ride abreast in most places, stretching the cavalry column out to a dangerous length.

The sides of this canyon rise vertically to a hundred-fifty feet, in some places higher, and the path twists and turns so often that they have no view of what is coming next until it is in their faces. A ribbon of azure high above dogs the tight curves of their journey.

This is a land of long, eerie shadows, of sudden rock-falls that startle and spook; of quick, nervous glances over the shoulder. This is a parched land, devoid of green; of raging torrents birthed by ferocious storms that arrive instantly from nowhere, black and menacing, that drop their imprisoned water in sheets so thick it cannot be seen through, then disappear. The one respite of canyon travel is that the troops are shielded from the relentless blistering sun. Ghalib's army has been at this drudgery now for two uneasy days.

The horses are jittery and their riders understandably wary. It is as if the whole of the Rif was designed for defense against invading armies. Their progress is slowed by the deep powdery sand that finds its way to the bottoms of the canyons, miring the wheels of the supply carts and slowing the infantry stuck behind the cavalry. The gritty flour finds its way into their clothes, their tents, even the food they eat.

General Ghalib rides at the front of his army. He recognizes the danger he has placed his men in. He has no choice, if he is to reach Eagle's Rock quickly, and timing is everything in this sortie.

He is no stranger to calculated risks and does not hesitate to put his army in harm's way. But he scowls his distaste, barks his commands angrily at his lieutenants, then snaps like a rabid dog if questioned. His men cower under his withering glare, but there is an unstated respect for his skills of command. The man does not lose battles.

The army is moving too slowly, with no room to maneuver if attacked, and he does not trust their Berber guides to choose the right path to safeguard them. His patience wears thin.

As the canyon bends sharply left for the twentieth time, General Ghalib sees that their prison mercifully broadens out into a massive oblong cauldron with more modestly sloping sides, and the deep sands shift to firmer rock. He mutters to himself, "Finally ..."

As he exits the canyon into the sun, he squints into the piercing brightness then looks skyward to the west. Across the broad ravine, just where the trail leads back into another clenched canyon, vultures turn in elegant, tight circles about a cylinder rising high into the sky. Dozens of scavengers preparing for a feast.

Ghalib raises his arm and barks his command to halt the column, which percolates in a series of shouts echoing backward along the canyon walls.

Ibn Abi Amir, a hundred paces behind Ghalib in the middle of the cavalry, looks up, curious. He can see nothing. He makes eye contact with his bodyguards, first to his left, then to his right. Both men draw their scimitars and expose their dagger hilts.

Ibn Abi Amir says in dialect, "Suktan. What is happening?"

"I am not sure, Qadi of the Maghreb. Perhaps an ambush."

"Are we in danger here?"

Suktan and Tahir lock eyes and come to a silent agreement. Tahir says, "Unlikely, Qadi of the Maghreb." He lifts his chin and closes his eyes as he gently inhales. "I can smell blood on the air. Fresh, but not too fresh. The Idrisid dogs have already done their work and gone."

Ibn Abi Amir's eyes widen. He slowly inhales but can detect nothing but scorched desert smells.

Ghalib turns and motions to his vanguard. Fifty knights spread into a defensive formation and move forward slowly on their mounts. Their weapons are drawn in unison with a single crisp metallic hiss, gleaming like bright shards of flame in the late afternoon sun.

Their horses are white-eyed; ears twitch this way and that, several spook and rear and have to be whipped back into line.

Sweat begins to course into the eyes of the knights as their hearts pound.

Ghalib slows as the awful carnage comes into view. He motions his men to stop then moves forward alone. He surveys the slain members of his advance scouting party: two dozen of his most trusted and seasoned knights led by two of their Berber guides, riding a half-hour ahead of the main army. Clearly the ambush was a complete success; whoever did this is long gone.

He looks up; the whirling vultures are impatient. Several of the giant birds are perched already on the clefts above the slaughter, their mottled, misshapen heads and black, beady eyes staring down upon the carnage. The bravest among them silently glides to a landing in a flush of black feathers, tucks its giant wings, then begins to awkwardly hop toward the nearest knight. What was elegant in flight is pitiful on the ground. Ghalib waves his arms and shouts to spook it. The bird reluctantly launches, the massive wingspan swooshing the air as it struggles to climb. The other birds stare stupidly from their perches, too lazy to respond. Or too hungry to care.

Ghalib scans the canyon walls and sees the series of ledges rising on either side aligned like bookshelves. An ideal position for an ambush. He sees that large boulders were dropped off the cliff behind the scouting party to prevent them from returning to the open space and safety of the cauldron. The canyon bends out of sight a stone's throw beyond the ambush. Hidden horsemen would have emerged to block their escape while the archers did the real work. It is apparent that it all happened so quickly his knights had little time to put up much of a fight.

There is a sweet metallic scent in the air, organic and moist; the unmistakable smells of the slaughterhouse. This terrible heat will quickly turn it to a choking stench. Ghalib swallows hard as he comes closer. He whispers to Taneen, "Barbarian swine." He rubs the stallion's neck to steady him.

The dead knights have been stripped of their armor and clothing, as well as the arrows that killed them, then flayed with a butcher's skill. Hands, feet, and faces a ghostly white, limbs and torsos a sickening deep crimson. The sand under their skinned bodies is a black, oily mess. There are shocked, terrified expressions on the dead men's faces. Men he trained; men he has ridden with for years. Their mouths are stuffed with their own genitals. Every man has been emasculated. Ghalib hawks, then spits, to avoid vomiting. His blood begins to boil.

He counts the bodies. All twenty-four. The two Berber guides are missing. Predictable, he thinks. They must have played some role. Ghalib curses their families. No horses have been killed. Clearly their archers knew their business. All the weapons are gone.

He turns his mount, Taneen, and walks back to his vanguard. His knights' faces are grim with understanding. "Ambush. They are all dead. Inform the cavalry that we will camp here tonight. I want your best guards at both canyon entrances and climbers along the tops of the walls. Clear those boulders and gather a detail to help with burial of the bodies. And find the imam, we need his services."

He hisses, "And spread the word. There is to be no mercy for any Idrisids we come across, here or at Hajar an-Nasar. No prisoners. None." He looks back at the carnage, then faces his riders once more. "If a single vulture so much as touches one of my men, I will have your heads." He kicks Taneen hard and canters back to have words with the remaining Berber guides.

Convolutions

Magdeburg, Saxony, Kingdom of Germany, **2 May 976**.

It is a glorious spring morning, alive with new birth after the interminable winter; giddy with promise. The morning air is still chilled and crisp, but hints of the day's coming warmth are everywhere. Lovesick birdsong, profuse and boisterous, joins the male prancing and pleading beset by the indifference of demure females. There is not a wisp of cloud to be found, and the sky's hue is piercing, like shining from shook foil, an achingly pure Platonic Form of the color azure.

The last of the winter's snow was three weeks back. It was a difficult winter in Saxony; cruel. The palace still shivers, the cold, damp stonework of the castle stubbornly resistant to the fires roaring within the massive yawns of the fireplaces. Several forests have been pillaged for a modicum of comfort.

Otto II, Otto the Red, Holy Roman Emperor, sits at his writing desk in front of the double window. He is young, but thanks to his father's diligence, already a seasoned politician and veteran general at nineteen. Otto the Great worked for years to ensure a smooth transition of power to his redheaded boy.

The drapes have been pushed back and the heavy shutters thrown open wide to invite the streaming sunshine in to play, coaxing spring's glory to an easy entrance into the dim caverns of the castle. Otto can feel his spirits lifting already, his enthusiasm returning for the intricate game of running an empire. The campaigning season lies just around the corner, and he is still young enough that the thought excites him.

His diplomat Peter Strobel's letter lies on the desk, the seal broken. Otto stares out the window deep in thought. Below him lies the Elbe River, its usual deep hunter green exchanged for the hue of tilled earth, gorged by the generous rains. The dense forest on the far side of the river is still translucent but dabbed in with a pale-green hazy paint hinting that the swollen buds have finally begun to pop. The blooms of the apples, pears, and cherries cannot be far behind. Jonquils by the thousands spill along the river's edge, a carpet of brilliant yellow trumpets.

There is a quick triplet of knocks at the door. Otto does not register it at first, but after another set he reluctantly turns.

"Come."

The massive oak door splits and the chamberlain slips through, then bows.

"Your Highness, Bishop Dietrich of Metz has arrived."

The emperor smiles. One of the few Saxon nobles he can trust. His father's most valued advisor in all matters of state; now his. "Excellent. Send him in, send him in."

The chamberlain bows and withdraws.

The voice is subdued and silky, the voice of a studious man. "Majesty." The bishop bows. He eschews the clerical formalities of his considerable station and is instead dressed as a common priest; dull woolen grays, knotted rope belt, a silver pectoral cross. There is understated elegance to the man's mannerisms, a holdover of his days at court before adjourning to the safety of the monastery.

"Dietrich." The emperor's smile widens as he rises. He greets the bishop with a kiss to each cheek, followed by a tight, unbecoming hug. It is evident that their affection is genuine and mutual. Otto indicates two seats by the window.

"It is good to see you, Majesty."

"Yes, Dietrich, I have missed your company."

The bishop smiles. "As have I, Majesty." He grimaces. "Metz can be so tedious, especially in winter. Saxony will always be my home." He forces a smile back on his face. "Theophanu and the baby are well?"

"They are, yes. Theophanu has nearly recovered from the birth. Her father sent her childhood nursemaid to care for her, which is a comfort. Sophie howls through the night, but she grows like a weed." The emperor beams. "She has my hair ... and her mother's temper!" The young father's pride is irrepressible.

They both chuckle.

"I am sure a boy will be next, Majesty."

"Let us hope so. The sooner I have an heir the better. I am afraid the Saxon nobles will continue to nip at my heels until that day. They still distrust Theophanu."

"That is to be expected, Majesty. She has no German blood. But give them time, they will come around. As I have said many times, both to your father and now to you, making an ally of the Byzantines is the lynchpin to the Empire's stability. You have done well by marrying her."

"Yes ..."

The bishop studies the young man with an amused grin. "You look fit, Majesty. Marriage suits you."

Otto's expression turns uncharacteristically self-conscious, almost embarrassed. "She and I are ... suited for one another."

So the stories are true, Dietrich thinks. Love. And she is fertile. Excellent news for the empire.

Otto's confidence returns. "Spring has come at last." His grin widens. "The apples will soon be blooming. Theophanu loves apples."

"Yes, praise God for spring. I have never seen so much snow. It has been a terrible winter; our people have suffered."

Otto turns pensive. "Yes ... my father taught me how to control many things, but, alas, not the weather."

The silence is comfortable.

"And where will your campaigns take you this spring?" There is a hint of irony in the bishop's tone.

"Thankfully, those cursed Danes are beaten. Harald Bluetooth is safely tucked back into his castle now. I hold his children ransom and will have their heads if he attempts to break our treaty. I do not expect more trouble from him, at least this year."

"And what of Bavaria?"

Otto sighs. "Henry is imprisoned in Ingelheim and Bishop Abraham in Corvey. The rest of his conspirators scattered back to their rat holes. But I have their names. Despite what you said in your letter, I still believe I should have had all of their heads."

"Mercy can sometimes be a more potent weapon than wrath, Majesty."

"Mmmm ..."

Dietrich continues, "Thank God for Bishop Poppo's spies, Majesty. I did not think Henry had the brains for such an involved plot."

"No. It seems Swabia was the final straw that broke my cousin's back. Alas, Swabia is a morsel he shall never taste. I am still amazed he surrendered without a fight."

"Indeed, unexpected. It seems the threat of excommunication can still be a powerful weapon, if not used too liberally." He muses. "I suspect Bishop Poppo would relish being named a cardinal, Majesty ... when the time is right. He so loves the color scarlet."

Otto laughs. "It is already arranged."

"Good. I would suggest, Majesty, that you consider ... reorganizing the southern German duchies or it will only be a matter of time before Bavaria rises up again in rebellion."

"Agreed. Please draw up some plans, Dietrich."

The bishop ticks his head. "With pleasure, Majesty."

"Tell me about Rome."

It is the bishop's time to sigh. "What a mess. Pope Benedict VI is now interred in the catacombs of Saint Peter's Basilica, God rest his soul. I am pleased to say, however, that Count Sicco has had his way. The bribes and threats were interminable, but in the end, effective. The Bishop of Sutri is our new pope, Majesty. The Papal College of Cardinals elected him three weeks back."

"Good. I assume he understands who arranged his election?"

The bishop grins. "Of course, Majesty."

"What name?"

The bishop tenders a coy smile. "Why, Benedict VII, of course, Majesty. We must continue the fine tradition of Holy Roman Popes." Otto laughs. "His first act as pope was to excommunicate Cardinal Ferrucci. That scoundrel is now under house arrest in Constantinople. Count Sicco arranged it all. We will not hear from him again."

"I was told that Ferrucci took the Vatican gold with him."

Bishop Dietrich smiles. "Yes, I am afraid so. Rest easy, Majesty, Count Sicco has already secured it. It is on its way to Magdeburg as we speak. Alas, not as much as I had hoped." His smile widens. "Still, it is a pity our new Pope Benedict has no gold of his own to buy favors. It seems he will just have to depend upon Saxon generosity, Majesty."

Otto offers a rueful smile. "A pity, indeed. Good work, Dietrich. Always the master."

The bishop nods, clearly pleased with himself. "You are too kind, Majesty."

They fall silent once more.

Otto looks up. "I received a letter from Strobel."

Another grin. "Ahhh, and how is our starched ambassador faring among the infidels?"

"Predictably, he is scandalized by all things Moorish. He says the Mozarab Mass is no longer Christian and is afraid the bread the priest consecrates may be impure. It seems their bibles are written in Arabic." Dietrich laughs.

"But, Córdoba is wealthy beyond measure, that much is sure. Awash in gold. We will renew my father's diplomatic exchange and expand it. A new treaty on trade should follow."

"Excellent. We need Córdoba, Majesty."

"Yes. The caliph is a shrewd one. It seems the Moors do have designs on Africa but they will not help us with the corsairs, at least not yet. I misplayed that hand. It seems we offended them by offering gold for their intervention."

"I see. A pity."

JOHN D. CRESSLER

"Strobel is confident that time will heal the insult. The caliph is allied with the Byzantines against the Abbasid Empire, even supports Tzimisces financially, though how he gets his Arab gold to Constantinople without it being noticed is anyone's guess." He shakes his head. "Imagine. Muslims paying Christians to kill other Muslims. Strobel believes Jerusalem will fall to Tzimisces."

"Interesting. More reason to tighten the Byzantine alliance, Majesty. I assume your wife still has access to inside information from Constantinople?"

Otto nods.

"Good. Please let me know when the final push for Jerusalem begins, Majesty. The pope may try to rally the people against the Byzantines if they take Jerusalem. You know how we Christians just cannot seem to manage to get along. I will alert Count Sicco to insist upon calm from the Papal pulpit. Perhaps a threat to send the new pope to Castel Sant'Angelo like we did his predecessor ..."

"Excellent idea." Otto turns pensive, then says, "Strobel seems to think Count Garcia of Castile is the biggest threat to Córdoba. He thinks we should try and exploit that to our advantage. Offer covert support, encourage Christian pressure on the Moors in the Upper Marches."

"Interesting ... what we most need from the Moors, Majesty, is their gold. Preferably by expanded trade and taxes. But if there are other means available, we should at least entertain them. These campaigns of yours, Majesty, great as they have been in expanding our borders and securing loyalty to the empire, have depleted your treasury. Even with the addition of the Papal gold, we lack the means for a protracted war against any capable enemy. And as you well know, France will likely be next. It is only a matter of time before the Duchy of Lorraine bursts into flames. The place smolders already. The rumors I hear from Paris concern me, Majesty. France is not likely to give up Lorraine without a fight. I suspect war will be sooner, rather than later. We must be ready and solvent."

Otto frowns but nods his agreement. "What do you know of Garcia?"

"Count Garcia Fernandez. They call him 'White Hands.' Elder son of Count Fernan Gonzalez of Castile and Queen Sancha Sanchez of Pamplona. Pale as a ghost. But formidable. He is supposed to be very ambitious and, like his father, a hater of all things Moorish. With the father dead he now controls Castile. I have heard rumors that he is making lords of any gentry that will provide knights for his army."

Otto responds, "A dangerous game."

"Indeed. Still, a proven means to raise an army. As we both know."

They exchange grins.

Dietrich muses out loud. "Mmmm ... publicly invite strong relations with the Moors by offering a diplomatic exchange and a new trade treaty, while privately aiding their chief enemy in the region. Perhaps the caliph would pay handsomely if we could use our influence and manage to intervene and stop the Castilian incursions in the Upper Marches ... the idea is growing on me, Majesty." He falls silent, with Otto's eyes now glued to him. "This would have to be delicately framed, of course, and the means of our covert support safely beyond discovery. Still ... it is an intriguing proposition. Let me give it some careful thought."

"Please do."

Captive

Zaheid works his thin blade carefully into the seam, rocking it back and forth with delicate pressure to slip it into the joint. There is a sharp crack of the glue as a thin crevice opens between the body of the camera and the screen then begins to move along the seam in front of the blade as he slides his tool forward. Halfway across he stops and squints to examine his work.

Behind him and to either side, hands on their knees and leaning over each shoulder, Samuel and Levi look on with serious expressions.

Zaheid purses his lips as he concentrates. Satisfied, he continues. He reaches the corner, withdraws the blade, then repeats the process on the other side. "I hope that you are right about this, Rayhana. We spent a lot of time constructing this camera."

Zafir and Rayhana exchange glances. Rayhana is fidgety, nervous. Zafir grins to reassure her. "She is sure, Zaheid."

Samuel waves his hand. "Onward, Zaheid, I am not getting any younger!" He turns and smiles at Rayhana.

After another minute, a single loud snap releases the back panel. Zaheid lifts the board and examines the edges, then traces his thumb along the body of the camera, noting several rough patches. He lifts his gritted woodblock and massages the edges to smooth them. "Excellent."

They rise as one, pleased with their work.

Rayhana opens the folio on the table and withdraws a single sheet, pinches each side and holds it up for the others to examine. "I asked the calligrapher for an extra deep polish on the paper, so thin and smooth that light can pass right through. Zafir trimmed it to fit to the camera dimensions."

Levi asks, "What is the best way to attach it?"

Zafir answers, "I crafted a wood frame to support the paper. It has a beveled edge that will pull the paper tight as it is fastened to the camera. I have drilled holes through the wood so it can be easily tacked to the camera body. That way we can change the paper as needed."

Zaheid and Levi nod their approval.

Samuel says, "Good. Shall we? Make way, Zaheid. Back, Levi, back." Samuel parts the sea then motions Rayhana forward.

She slides between the men, cradling the wisp of paper. She kneels down and places the thin sheet against the opening at the back of the camera, aligns it, then stretches each thumb and finger to four points to ready it for the frame. "A perfect fit."

Zafir picks up the frame and kneels down behind her. Her dark curls are everywhere, and the faint hint of her perfume makes him woozy. He stops, looking confused as he struggles to balance decorum with necessity. With his left hand he awkwardly works the frame underneath her outstretched arms, and with the other reaches over her other arm to grasp the corner of the frame. He hesitates, trying to decide how to do this without actually touching her. He gives up and leans into her to complete the move. She grins as she pushes back to steady him. He visibly flinches as their bare forearms touch.

Zaheid nudges Samuel. The three men cannot stop smiling.

Zafir swallows hard and concentrates on steadying his trembling hand. The contact point between their arms refuses to stop pulsing, but he manages to anchor the paper with the frame.

Zaheid picks up the tacks and the tiny hammer and places the first in the drilled hole in the upper left corner. "Ready?"

She answers for them. "Ready."

A quick tap, then another at the bottom left. Zaheid switches sides and taps the other two tacks home.

Samuel says, "Good. Let it go."

As Zafir releases the frame, the paper remains tight as a drum.

Rayhana beams. "Perfect."

Zaheid is impressed. "Excellent, Rayhana."

Her excitement is contagious. "We should now be able to view the image from the back. All of us at one time. And for experiments, we can make marks on the paper to study the precise dimensions of the image produced by the various combinations and placements of the objects we project."

Samuel blurts out, "The girl is a genius! You should learn from her, Zafir. I would suggest paying careful attention to everything she says and does."

Rayhana dimples.

Zafir blushes.

Levi beams.

The crisp knock prompts a hushed exchange of passwords. One of the red-robed Slavic guards opens the heavy door to a crack, while the other stands cocked, hand on his sword hilt, out of sight of the visitor. Satisfied, the bodyguard stands down, turns, and makes his announcement.

"Sire, the sultana has arrived."

"Good. Show her in."

She crosses the room with a feline sashay. She owns wonderful curves and understands perfectly how to accentuate them. "How nice to be out of my dungeon, Husband. Your suites are so much plusher than mine."

The caliph frowns. "Subh, we both know that is not true."

She is her normal voluptuous self; long blond curls pulled back from her face with a silk ribbon, prominent breasts barely constrained by her tight, revealing gown; eyelids painted to highlight her brilliant blue irises; deep-ruby lips. As non-Arab looking as one could imagine finding in Córdoba. Evocative, as always, and beautiful.

With Ibn Abi Amir gone, the aura of her pent-up sexual tension shimmers about her, somehow lending a steely edge to her movements, a too-tight coiling of some unseen internal gear that may suddenly explode if improperly handled. It radiates a third presence; it moves beside her, sits when she sits, jabs her mercilessly when she twists her hips the wrong way. She seems more dangerous, more reckless. More desirable.

Al-Hakam can feel the man's presence, almost smell him. He wrinkles his nose with distaste. While he has no desire for this woman, being cuckolded is another matter altogether. He thinks: Soon, Ibn Abi Amir, very soon. The sands of the Maghreb thirst for your blood. He forces himself to smile as she curls luxuriously into the adjoining divan. A barely perceptible groan escapes her lips as she crosses her legs. Her husband takes note.

"Thank you for the invitation, Husband." She insists upon reminding him constantly of their failed relationship. "Tea and conversation are always a welcome diversion from my tedious prison life in the royal harem."

He ignores the bait. "You look well, Subh."

She cannot resist toying with him. "You are kind, Husband. I have had so much trouble sleeping these days. All I do is toss and turn. You must see if Abu al-Qasim can create a potion for me."

Though he has never been her equal in verbal jousting, he returns her taunt with his own barb. "Certainly ... I knew you would enjoy it if I invited my brother and his wife to join us."

Her time to frown. "Al-Mughira is so tedious, Husband."

He grins triumphantly. "He is my only brother, Subh."

She resigns herself with an "Mmmm ..." as if that fact is somehow debatable.

They lapse into silence; she calculating, he anticipating her next move.

He guesses right.

"You would be so proud of Hisham, Husband. He has finally broken away from his interminable religious studies and has developed a keen interest in investment. And geography. Imagine!"

"Really?"

"Yes, a most unexpected turn of events. Our son is suddenly asking me about my land holdings and where they are located, and he now knows the Middle and Upper Marches so well that you would think he was born there. He insists I show him everything on a map. It seems he has grown especially interested in the southern lands of al-Andalus; Algeciras, Cádiz. Parched wasteland to my eyes, but he sees their potential. And he has begun to fancy the Maghreb. The Maghreb! Our son even asked me for an allowance so that he can dabble in the markets, begin some investments of his own. Can you believe it?"

He hesitates. "What did you tell him?"

That cunning smile. "Well, how could I refuse? He is our only son, after all. The more he learns about investing, the better he will serve the kingdom when he is caliph. Surely you agree he needs to be a good steward of Córdoba's wealth?"

Al-Hakam remains silent as he studies her face.

She continues, seemingly oblivious. "I must say, with Ibn Abi Amir managing my accounts now, I am unusually flush." She smiles. "With gold."

The caliph's face hardens at the mention of the man's name.

She pushes on gleefully. "That man is a genius with money. He definitely has a golden ... touch. I am directing the profits Ibn Abi Amir makes me to a special account for Hisham—strictly for the boy's amusement, of course. Our son just purchased two-thousand arpents near Algeciras, overlooking the sea. You should be proud, Husband. Our son has talent." She sparkles.

There is another knock at the door and a moment later the Slavic guard announces, "Sire, al-Mughira ibn al-Nasir and his wife."

The caliph smiles warmly as he rises to greet them. "Brother, Fatima." The two men warmly hug. He kisses Fatima on both cheeks.

Subh does not move from her divan. "How nice to see you both." There is a condescending edge to her tone, subtle but unmistakable.

Her flagrant lack of manners does not surprise either of them. Fatima and al-Mughira share a lament of al-Hakam's weakness in bringing the blond Basque witch to glorious Madinat. A youthful vice, trouble from day one. Al-Mughira thinks: Praise Allah that he keeps her chained up to prevent her meddling at court.

"It is always so nice to see you, Subh." There is a hollow ring to al-Mughira's words. There is no love lost between the sultana and the caliph's brother.

"Sit down, Brother. Sit, Fatima." The caliph indicates the empty divan. He turns to his bodyguard. "Please have Nuh bring tea and sweets."

Subh frowns.

A short while later a bronzed, sculpted god enters from a side door bearing a large golden tray loaded with a steaming tea pot, cups, and sweets. He sets the tray down on the table and begins to prepare the tea service.

Subh scowls at her husband's new lover; an addition to the royal harem last month, a purchase from Persia; an obvious ploy on his part to punish her. She abruptly uncoils and rises. She snaps, "Leave it where it is."

The young man freezes at the sharpness of her words and looks helplessly to the caliph for instructions.

Point made, she adjusts her tone. "I would be delighted to serve our guests, Nuh. You are dismissed." She slinks to the service table, wide eyes trailing her.

The caliph grimaces. "That is fine, Nuh, you may go." He hesitates, then smiles. "I had forgotten how much the sultana enjoys serving me." Fatima grins. The caliph does not take his eyes from the young man until he vanishes through the door.

Subh has her back to the three as she readies their mint tea. She carefully pours the four cups, then adds a spoonful of light-tan cane sugar to each and stirs until it is dissolved.

She turns and brings the first cup to the caliph, bows, and says, "Your wish is my command, Husband." She casts a withering smile.

He remains silent as he sifts her for mischief. He has learned the hard way to appreciate the importance of suspicion in dealing with his wife.

Al-Mughira says, "Have you heard from General Ghalib and the army?"

"I have, yes. Three days back. The army arrived safely in Larache, unopposed by the Fatimids, praise Allah. They have begun their march to Hajar an-Nasar. They should be there by now, I should think. Plans have been laid out and orders issued. All is well."

"May Allah grant us a quick victory."

"Inshallah. What news from the city?"

"Ahhh ... the normal bickering between the merchant families in all matters of influence and wealth. It never changes. Who should defer to whom, who gets to set the market price, who has the most beautiful almunya, the largest library. The usual. But business is good, coffers grow full, and Córdoba's trade expands. Our silks and ceramics and paper are in high demand everywhere, even as far as Constantinople.

"Good. I intend to sign a trade treaty with the Holy Roman Empire. Europe's markets should open to us. The kingdom will prosper."

"Yes, I had heard the rumors. This is a good thing, Brother. The merchant families will welcome the news. I will spread the word."

The caliph nods his approval. "And the spring crops?"

"The fields have been plowed and sowed. The winter rains were generous, so we have plenty of water for irrigation. All expect a generous harvest."

"Excellent."

She serves as they talk. When she has finished with the tea and offered each some sweets from the tray, she curls back into her divan. As the tedious conversation between the caliph and his brother drags on, her eyes begin to roam about the room, settling finally on the tea service resting upon the table.

The thin, smoky tendril wriggles as it escapes the spout of the gold teapot, but once free of its prison, its struggles abate and the smoke begins to diffuse, floating limply, helpless as it evaporates. A final gasp of surprise at the crushing irony, then the ghostly snake vanishes into thin air, gone forever. She is mesmerized. Captivity gives life; freedom brings death.

As she studies the teapot she begins to calculate, the voices sliding away into oblivion, stilling the air. She focuses her roiling energy to a sharpened point and conjures Ibn Abi Amir's face. A moment later a thin smile slides across her painted lips.

Cleo looks up from his codex, suddenly recalling a question he meant to ask Alonso earlier. "Tell me about the saqaliba?"

"Ahhh ... saqaliba. I wondered when you would ask. A delicate subject, I am afraid."

"So I assume. At first I thought they were simply household slaves. But now I am not so sure. I have heard mention that many at court are saqaliba, even the caliph's bodyguards, and some hold high office, which seems to be a contradiction, at least to my understanding of slaves."

The two men are alone in the reading room of the Library of Medicine. Alonso is thumbing through the *Hippocratic Corpus*. Cleo is riveted by Galen's description of the Antonine Plague, which he devours. Abu al-Qasim is due to meet them shortly for a question and answer period, followed by a surgical demonstration in the afternoon.

"I understand the confusion." Alonso marks his page and closes his codex. "Where to begin? The Córdoban slave trade actually began with Caliph Abd al-Rahman III, Caliph al-Hakam's father. He conceived of the saqaliba as a means to solidify his power, and importantly, fill out the ranks of his army. It turned out to be a quite shrewd move, the repercussions of which are still felt today.

"After Abd al-Rahman III wrestled control of al-Andalus from the rival clans, he turned against the Christian kingdoms. What the Arabs call 'jihad,' holy war. He was constantly on campaign to push the Muslim borders northward and secure Córdoba's rule."

"Yes, as I recall, he fought against León."

"Correct. León first, and then Navarre and Aragon. He sacked Pamplona in the Basque lands." Alonso grins. "That is where the sultana hails from. Young al-Hakam was on his father's campaign and decided he wanted a Christian princess as a prize. She had to be blond, of course." Alonso rolls his eyes and Cleo laughs. "But León was always the caliph's bitterest enemy. King Ordono, then his son Ramiro. Formidable enemies.

"A combined Christian force finally managed to defeat Abd al-Rahman III decisively at the *Battle of Simancas*, in the Upper Marches. The spring of 939, if memory serves. After that the caliph never again commanded his army but left the business to others. Eventually the borders were stabilized, mostly from exhaustion on both sides, and a measure of peaceful standoff has endured ever since."

"The caliph's army was a slave army?"

"In many ways, yes. Arab commanders, and with troops from Muslim clans in the south, but the bulk of the troops were mercenaries, and many were slaves."

"Where did he get them?"

Alonso nods. "Back to the saqaliba. Literally, the Arabic word for 'Slav,' which refers to the peoples of the mountain lands east of the Holy Roman Empire."

"Yes ... northeast of Venice."

"Precisely."

"As Otto campaigned to expand the boundaries of his empire eastward, he encountered fierce resistance. To impose his will, after each new conquest his army would execute the warriors, then take their young sons and daughters and sell them to the slave markets; first to the Abbasids, but then to the Umayyads.

"Predictably, to avoid the condemnation of the Church, Jews were employed as financiers and acted as middlemen in the transactions. Much gold exchanged hands. The practice turned out to be an effective weapon against Slav rebellion. Their families were decimated, and those lands under the emperor's control remain largely docile to this day."

"I see ... so the caliph paid gold for young boys and girls. I assume the boys were then trained as soldiers for the army."

"For many roles, actually. The army, certainly. The Slavic Guard, the caliph's private bodyguards, are all saqaliba. A very prestigious position with many rewards. The saqaliba were also sold into various trades and apprenticeships."

Cleo frowns. "And some were turned into eunuchs."

Alonso sighs. "It is true. That legacy of using eunuchs at court has a long history with Arabs. Strange as it seems to us, it is a widely accepted practice dating back a millennium and is found in all of the Muslim kingdoms."

"Does the practice continue today?"

"It does, yes."

"How about the girls?"

"They were mostly sold to wealthy merchants as maids, ladies-in waiting, cooks, even artisans. Sometimes mistresses."

Cleo blushes. "Do any of the saqaliba remain Christian?"

"Very few. They learn Arabic, of course, and are raised in Muslim households. It is quite natural for them to convert."

"I see ..."

"The important thing to understand about the saqaliba, Cleo, is that they do not remain slaves forever. At least most do not. And by law they are treated well. The wealthy merchants of Córdoba have an accepted tradition of rewarding good service with freedom. Even as saqaliba, they are then able to rise in rank in society according to their talents, just as anyone else.

"All in Córdoba are treated equally with respect to social mobility; Muslim, Christian or Jew. Arab, Mozarab, Berber, or saqaliba. The caliph's Vizier Council contains a Mozarab, a Jew, and a saqaliba."

"Remarkable. Have I met any saqaliba?"

"Mmmm ..." His eyes brighten. "Yes, in fact you have. Samuel al-Tayyib's protégé, Zafir, is a saqaliba. But free now as you know and esteemed at court. Oh, and General Ghalib is a saqaliba."

Cleo is incredulous. "General Ghalib is a saqaliba?"

Alonso smiles. "He is. He rose through the military ranks unimpeded by his ancestry."

They fall silent as Cleo absorbs this.

"So many fascinating contradictions ..."

Alonso continues. "That does not mean that prejudice is nonexistent here. There are elements of society, among conservative Arabs especially, who lament the power of the saqaliba at court, and they also dislike the fact that Christians and Jews are treated with esteem. But the caliph, to his credit, has made it amply clear that the rules of vertical mobility in Córdoban society will continue as they were under his father. And for the most part those rules continue to work well."

Cleo looks serious, pinched. "This gives me much to consider, Alonso. Thank you."

Alonso tries to lighten the mood. "Come, my friend, all will be well." He beams. "I have it on good authority that Abulcasis has a new surgical instrument to quiz you on."

This produces a grin. Cleo has been looking forward to surgery all week.

Reins

9 July 976.

The night air is still as death, sharp and biting, a cruel contrast to the glowing furnace of the day, known only as *hariq,* "consuming fire", to the locals in the Rif Mountains. Cold nights like this beckon the carpet vipers to slither under bedding, the widow-maker scorpions to wander into unsecured boots.

The night is moonless. A sea of sparkling light adorns the dome high above, the pulsing diamonds parted by the thick ribbon of milk slathered from horizon to horizon. Every half hour or so a quick-tick of fiery emerald zigzags then vanishes.

A lone she-wolf points her nose to Polaris and howls her stoic agony, an eerie lamentation for her lost mate. The only movement of the Abyssinian owl is a tandem blink of its giant orbs as the oblivious sand rat skitters into view. A sleek rush of feathers, then nothing until the truncated screech as needled hooks puncture the tiny skull, lifting the wriggling fodder from the ground.

Ibn Abi Amir awakes a dozen times each night to the strange desert sounds, imagines he hears footsteps when none are there. He tosses and turns till first light.

The army has been encamped at Hajar an-Nasar for over two weeks now, dug in for siege. Ghalib's expeditionary sorties on the castle have proven disastrous, every canyon an ambush in waiting. Tensions remain high, fear floats on the baked air. Orders are barked, not spoken.

Despite his protests, General Ghalib insisted that Ibn Abi Amir pitch his tent with the other officers, an easy stone-toss from his own. Keep your enemies close. Suktan and Tahir never leave the man's side, taking turns standing guard through the chilled nights. True warriors of the desert, they insist on sleeping next to their hobbled horses under a simple tarp. They scoff at the Córdobans with their plush tents and luxurious carpets, their cushioned bedding and silk pillows. Soft and weak.

Ibn Abi Amir is awakened by the tingling numbness of his toes. He sits up, blind, and fumbles for another blanket, which he tucks in around his feet. He pulls his covers tight to his chin and curses the night. By mid-morning he will be sweating; freezing again by midnight.

Three hours before sunrise he finally drifts off, but his sleep is poisoned and restless, his dreams full of dark omens.

His eyes spring open when he feels the line of cold steel press against his throat, but he remains motionless even as his heart begins to pound. He can see nothing in the tent. Pitch black.

The whisper is barely audible. "You need better bodyguards, Qadi of the Maghreb. I could spill your blood with a flick of my dagger and no one would ever know who came calling for your soul. You are brave, Qadi of the Maghreb. That, or foolish."

"Brave and foolish, Jafar. I wondered when you would come. Suktan and Tahir?"

"Outside. Dress quietly. I would prefer not to have to kill any of Ghalib's guards."

"Yes, that would be unfortunate. Where are we going?"

"To meet my brother. He will decide your fate in the Rif." He pauses. "You will behold the power of the Banu Birzal. If all goes well, you will celebrate this day forever, Qadi of the Maghreb. Tread carefully."

"I am ready to meet my fate, Jafar."

"You will ride with Suktan. Your eyes will be bound until we reach camp. The path to the Banu Birzal must remain lost."

"I understand. Let us make haste."

The journey seems to have stretched half the night, though Ibn Abi Amir knows it could not have been more than two hours. He shivers under his travel cloak. Not one word has been uttered since they left Hajar an-Nasar.

The only sound announcing their passage is the sudden burst of horse clop as the six riders move from sand to rock. The dense clatter of echoed sound is knotted and teased by the maze of canyon walls then swallowed by the silence as their mounts step one by one back into the thick silt and move on in single file.

A short while later, they stop.

Suktan quietly announces, "We have arrived, Qadi of the Maghreb. Let me help you down."

As Suktan unties the cloth, the scene unfolds. They are in a large oval canyon, a steep-sided wash basin an arrow's shot across. Not unlike where the terrible ambush occurred. Ibn Abi Amir is reminded of the Roman amphitheater at Leptis Magna. Jagged fissures in the rim of the basin offer entry and exit to riders.

The world is muted and gray, but the night is clearly done. All but the brightest stars have evaporated. He turns to his right to note where the sun will be born after it wrestles free of its bindings behind the crags of the Rif. At least another half hour until the warming sunrise. It is a chilled twilight world of shadows and sharp angles, of burnt-brown and umber.

Hundreds of large Bedouin *bayt*, one tent per nuclear family, cover one whole side of the amphitheater, arranged in neat symmetry, first by patriarchal groups linked by marriage, called *goum*, then by *ibn amm,* cousins of multiple generations. All are kin, ruled by the ancient Bedouin honor codes of *Sharaf* and *Ird* for males and females; blood oaths that bind the clan. All are subject to the decrees of Sheikh Hamid al-Tariq.

The hobbled horses of each family are kept close, to be mounted in an instant should the need arise. Ibn Abi Amir can see the silhouettes of the Berber knights on the canyon rim. Dozens of lookouts are posted high above. His presence is known.

He first hears then sees the dozen riders approaching. Ibn Abi Amir takes a deep breath to steady himself.

The secret camp of the Banu Birzal.

Hamid and Jafar al-Tariq are spitting images of one another, except that Hamid's untrimmed beard is flecked with gray and crow's feet tug at the corners of his eyes. An ugly scar begins on his forehead, parts the eyebrow, then curves outward down his cheek. The kiss of a scimitar.

He is tall like Jafar, with those intense, smoldering ebony eyes. Hamid's robes are more elaborate than his brother's, trimmed with gold lace and cord. His is the only bright red turban; the rest are black.

The ruby-encrusted silver scabbards of the Sheikh's scimitar and needle dagger are priceless, the blades almost certainly of the finest Damascus steel. The mighty warrior-king of the Rif. The journey to behold this face has been a long one. Fate will decide the rest.

The knights to either side of the Sheikh rest their hands on the hilts of their scimitars, fingers opened in desert fashion, but there is not a single welcoming face to be found. Ibn Abi Amir wonders if he has made a fatal miscalculation.

Jafar's deep baritone breaks the silence, "The qadi of the Maghreb, brother."

Sheikh al-Tariq does not answer at first, preferring to continue his study of the Arab.

"My brother has spoken of you." The sheikh matches his brother's baritone; a voice used to command. "He believes you possess the means to restore the glory due my people." There is a skeptical note in his tone.

Ibn Abi Amir waits, expressionless.

"It is a dangerous game you play, Qadi of the Maghreb, an unarmed Arab in a Berber clan. You are brave, something we Berbers respect. But I must warn you, one false step, one misspoken word, and you will never leave this canyon alive." Desert pride wraps around his words. "You must know that the Banu Birzal have no love for the caliph of Córdoba, Qadi of the Maghreb.

Ibn Abi Amir calculates, then speaks. "Nor do I, Sheikh al-Tariq."

The silence tightens.

Hamid al-Tariq's expression shifts oddly as his chest begins to lift and heave as he tries to fight the eruption brewing within. A chuckle slips past his lips, then a stifled bark, finally a roiling, boisterous laugh. He begins to rock on his heels as his head tips back and he roars to the morning sky. The Berber knights join in, and suddenly the barren desert is an amusing place, a land of cackles and hoots.

Despite himself, Ibn Abi Amir grins, then reluctantly chuckles. He bows deferentially to the sheikh. A game.

"Did I scare you, Qadi of the Maghreb? By clan law you are an honored guest among the Banu Birzal. Come, let us share tea and sweets, then you must behold the skill of our cavalry. There is none finer in the Maghreb or al-Andalus. Afterwards, we will feast and talk business. Come, Qadi of the Maghreb, come."

The sheikh and Ibn Abi Amir are seated on Persian carpets laid out on the sand. Bodyguards stand at attention in a semicircle to their rear. The warmth of the sun on his back is welcomed, but Ibn Abi Amir knows that within two hours he will be soaked with sweat. The sweet luxury of the royal hammam in Córdoba feels like an ancient memory.

The sheikh indicates his cavalry formation across the basin. "Now you will understand the power of the Banu Birzal, Qadi of the Maghreb." The man's pride is unmistakable.

Ibn Abi Amir nods. He has been waiting for this moment for many months and wonders now whether his imagination has gotten the best of him. How good can this cavalry possibly be?

The demonstration begins with a cavalry parade. Jafar and three lieutenants lead the parade forward at a slow trot, then turn and move past the sheikh and Ibn Abi Amir. Three columns of mounted knights, each five riders wide and twenty deep, moving as a single creature. The sheikh beams. The horses are small by European standards, but sleek and well-muscled; no doubt fast.

There is an obvious precision to the movements of the cavalry; no horse out of line, all locked in perfect step. The riders grip their reins but do not seem to use them to command their mounts. Clearly, they are a well-drilled fighting force. But parade is different than battle.

The Berber knights are heavily armed: scimitars at their hips and daggers strapped upside down to their upper-left arms for quick access. A special holster fixed vertically to the backs of their saddles carries four throwing javelins and a longer, heavier jabbing lance. A strung longbow is tied to each saddle, with a quiver of arrows in easy reach. Each man holds a heart-shaped, boiled-leather shield.

The knights' armor is minimalist, chain mail hauberk under flowing crimson robes, heavy felt cloak, and tight black turbans concealing all but their dark desert eyes.

Ibn Abi Amir muses inwardly: Far more weaponry than Ghalib's cavalry, whose knights don either a single lance and broadsword or else bow and arrow, never both. But can they effectively use them?

As the parade angles back to its starting point, Jafar and his lieutenants circle round to the viewing carpets and remain mounted.

Jafar announces, "Whenever you are ready, Brother."

The sheikh smiles and nods.

Jafar circles an up-pointed finger in the air and instantly the front five riders from each column erupt to a gallop, each group of five moving in tandem with the others. One group branches left, one right, and the last charges ahead in the middle. Each knight in the middle column readies his javelin, while the two flanking columns lift their bows and nock their arrows at full gallop. The knights' motions are effortless as they shift their reins and ready their weapons. These horses are fast, the flicks of sand from their hooves slinging high into the air.

Ibn Abi Amir looks to his left at the five targets, each a man-high bundle of cloth tacked to wood, propped erect and spaced at three paces apart.

As the cavalry charges, the center throng pulls ahead of the flanking columns and at the last moment breaks hard right into single file in front of the targets, as elegant as a dance move. Just past their turn they launch their javelins. A second later the flanking columns bank left and right, releasing their arrows together. The three-headed hydra rejoins and slows to a canter as they move back to their ranks.

Each target sports a still-swaying javelin and two arrows buried in its chest.

Ibn Abi Amir actually gasps at the remarkable demonstration of cavalry prowess. He whispers, "Remarkable ... I have never witnessed such skill." The display impresses him beyond his wildest dreams.

Both Sheikh Hamid al-Tariq and his brother laugh loudly. "Behold the Banu Birzal, Qadi of the Maghreb. No army can stand before us."

Stunned silence.

"How many mounted knights like this can the Banu Birzal field?"

Jafar boasts, "Two thousand, Qadi of the Maghreb. What you see in the canyon is only a taste. For safety, the clan is broken into quarters and camped several leagues apart."

Ibn Abi Amir nods his head as he calculates. Enough. More than enough.

Jafar looks across the amphitheater and again circles his up-pointed finger in the air. The next group of riders explodes, the formation different this time, six staggered tiers in a relentless rolling wave.

As they close rapidly on their quarry, Ibn Abi Amir's expression remains blank, but his eyes have widened.

Hamid and his brother, Ibn Abi Amir, Jafar's two cavalry commanders, and the clan imam sit on a large carpet in Bedouin fashion inside the Sheikh's massive tent, the communal feasting platter laden with steaming food placed in the center of the circle so it can be easily reached by all.

Desert food is prepared to be eaten by hand. Skewers of grilled chicken and lamb, braised goat, thick yogurt, hard cheese, a tall stack of flat bread for dipping and pinching food, dates and olives, herbed chick peas with olive oil, sliced cucumbers and melons, and boiled rice sautéed with onions and hot peppers then tossed with yogurt and lamb and topped with pine nuts; wild berries, toasted almonds, honey, and jams for dessert.

The meal is meager by Córdoban standards, but tasty nonetheless, and filling. Despite his initial distaste, Ibn Abi Amir has quickly grown used to eating with his hands from a communal plate. He dresses as a Berber, eats as a Berber, and speaks flawless Maghrebi dialect. They respect him for it. A true qadi of the Maghreb.

They feast in silence by desert custom. To speak would be rude. When they finish, Hamid puffs his chest out and burps loudly, then beams. One by one the others follow, Ibn Abi Amir last. He has practiced his belches, refined them.

"A feast fitting of the qadi of the Maghreb, yes?"

"I have had no finer in the Maghreb, Sheikh. I am honored to be included at the table of the Banu Birzal."

Jafar smiles, obviously pleased at the way things are progressing.

Hamid claps his hands and servants instantly arrive to remove the meal. A second set brings small wash basins and towels to each man to clean himself. A third set then arrives with steaming sweet mint tea, and when finished, they depart, leaving the tent empty except for the circle of cushions.

Hamid's satisfied expression abruptly shifts to seriousness. "Good. Let us talk business. How goes the Arab siege of Hajar an-Nasar?"

Ibn Abi Amir grins. "I am afraid, Sheikh, that General Ghalib has met with no success. None whatsoever. Ibn Guennoun's ambushes have been frequent, and the sorties made against the castle proper have all been easily repulsed. Any Córdoban unlucky enough to be captured is first tortured, then flayed alive. Fear stalks the camp as the knights wither in the desert heat."

The sheikh tilts his head to the sky and roars.

"Qadi of the Maghreb, Ghalib will not defeat the Idrisids. He does not know the desert, and he does not respect our ways."

"No, he does not, Sheikh. To his peril. He will never capture Eagle's Rock without the Banu Birzal."

"The Banu Birzal can deliver Ibn Guennoun and the castle with the snap of my fingers. When the time is right. And, of course, for the proper price."

"Yes ..."

"That price is your legal declaration that the Banu Birzal is the legitimate leader of all the Rif clans, with a decree issued to all clans to rally under my banner. The clans will respect your authority, Qadi of the Maghreb."

The sheikh turns to the imam, who nods his agreement.

"We will then gather and train an army to defeat the Fatimids." The sheikh pauses. "But this will require gold, Qadi of the Maghreb, much gold."

"All of these things shall be yours, Sheikh, you have my word.'

The sheikh studies him. "Among the desert clans, Qadi of the Maghreb, a man's word is his most precious possession; his *Sharaf*, his honor. When it is given, it is binding unto death."

"You have my word, Sheikh."

Hamid nods, satisfied.

"Here is what I would suggest, Sheikh. Let Ghalib languish for another two weeks. He must fully appreciate that he has no hope of capturing Hajar an-Nasar without the Banu Birzal."

Jafar smiles.

"I will then inform Ghalib that Jafar will meet with him to offer your plan. You must not bring Ghalib into your confidence, Sheikh—he is a viper and must be handled delicately. The man aims to kill me as soon as I have delivered the Banu Birzal and Hajar an-Nasar falls."

Hamid frowns.

Jafar's answer is matter-of-fact. "I will release his soul tomorrow if you desire it, Qadi of the Maghreb. Say the word and it shall be so."

"No, not yet, Jafar, not yet. Sheikh, your price should be this. Deliverance of Hajar an-Nasar for ten thousand gold dinars and my decree legitimizing Banu Birzal rule. You get to keep Ibn Guennoun, of course, as a prize. There is to be no negotiation of price. Ghalib will balk but he will pay. He has no choice."

Silence seeps into the circle as Hamid considers the offer. His eyes settle to his lap as he strokes his beard.

"In the end, Sheikh, Hajar an-Nasar will fall and Córdoba will be victorious over the Idrisids, and the Banu Birzal will reign over the Rif as a friend of the caliph. The Maghreb will be yours to rule, and all will prosper ... all except the Fatimids. Their blood must color the desert sands."

Silence.

Hamid looks up. "And what of the future, Qadi of the Maghreb? What happens after we possess the Maghreb and the gold is expended and the Fatimids are gone? What then for the Banu Birzal? Do we return to our desert ways?"

This is the moment Ibn Abi Amir has anticipated. His fate, his future, rests upon the edge of a dagger. He takes a deep breath, then casts his die.

"This is the future I see for the Banu Birzal, Sheikh. When Hajar an-Nasar falls, the caliph will recall General Ghalib and the army to Córdoba to honor the Umayyad victory. He does not intend to leave without taking my life. To thwart Ghalib's plan, I will be whisked away into the desert canyons in the middle of the night, nominally to attend to lingering legal matters with the clans. I will simply disappear.

"Some months later, when the qadi of the Maghreb returns to Córdoba, he will have with him one thousand of the best Banu Birzal cavalry. And their families. A Banu Birzal army under Jafar's command. I will assure the caliph that they have been sent by you as a token of your appreciation, Sheikh, and they will be formally dedicated to the defense of the city, to ease any concerns at court. The Banu Birzal will make their home in Córdoba." He hesitates. "In truth, the Banu Birzal will be the fist of the qadi of the Maghreb."

All eyes rest upon Ibn Abi Amir, but no one speaks.

"Through me, Sheikh, the Banu Birzal will gain a voice at court. And power. I will see that the Banu Birzal pursues jihad against the Christians in the north and that they taste many victories. The Banu Birzal will help me banish the weak, tainted faith that flourishes in al-Andalus. Together we will honor the memory of the Prophet and banish the Jews and Christians from the kingdom. The Banu Birzal will profit wildly. You shall have gold beyond belief. The destiny of the Banu Birzal, Sheikh, lies in rich al-Andalus."

Silence follows.

"Córdoba will fuel the expansion of your kingdom in the desert. The Banu Birzal shall be both a people of the desert and a people of Córdoba." He stops and one-by-one locks his eyes on each man, then continues. "The people of al-Andalus will whisper the name Banu Birzal with fear and respect for generations to come, Sheikh."

Hamid has not stopped stroking his beard. He frowns. "Bold words, Qadi of the Maghreb, very bold words. But can it be done?"

"Yes, Sheikh, bold words. But true words. It can be done, you have my word. Place the Banu Birzal at my side and together we will secure the future of your people and honor the Prophet."

The quiet returns. A line has been crossed and Ibn Abi Amir can only embrace the fate that follows.

The wait is interminable. Decision finally made, the sheikh slaps both palms upon his knees. "We have a saying in the desert, Qadi of the Maghreb. 'I against my brother, my brothers and I against my cousins, my cousins and I against strangers.' What you desire shall be yours, but only under one condition. You must become Banu Birzal. You must join with me as my blood kin, and as Jafar's blood kin. Then, together as brothers, we shall stand tall against the caliph and al-Andalus."

Ibn Abi Amir's eyes sparkle. Clearly, an anticipated move. He feigns ignorance. "Blood kin, Sheikh?"

Hamid leans towards Jafar and whispers something. Jafar listens then nods.

"You have no living wife. You will marry my youngest daughter, Qadi of the Maghreb. You will be my blood kin, a member of the Banu Birzal clan. Ulla, my desert flower, my pride and joy, is the most beautiful of my girls. She is just past her first bleeding moon. She is of age. She shall be yours."

Ibn Abi Amir's expression remains blank. "I would be honored, Sheikh, to be your blood kin, to join the Banu Birzal. Let it be so."

All in the room beam and nod their approval. The sheikh reaches out his right hand, palm up, and in Berber custom, the two clasp forearms as brothers.

"The joining of our families will be a glorious day, Qadi of the Maghreb, a celebration like no other."

"Yes ... it will bring me great joy, Sheikh. I grow tired of the life of a widower."

"A man is not complete without a woman at his side, Qadi of the Maghreb. The Prophet said as much."

"I have one request, Sheikh."

Hamid issues an invitation with his eyes.

Ibn Abi Amir proclaims, "From this day forward, Jafar shall be known to me as 'al-Andalusi.' He will be respected by all, and he will feared by all." He pauses. "And when we rule Córdoba, Sheikh, al-Andalusi shall be wed to my daughter, Rayhana, the most beautiful maiden in Córdoba."

The sheikh roars. "A most excellent idea, Qadi of the Maghreb! Jafar has only one wife. He is man enough for two! It shall be so."

Jafar beams. "I place my scimitar at the command of the qadi of the Maghreb of the Banu Birzal, my brother and my kin." Ibn Abi Amir reaches out with his right hand, palm up. He and al-Andalusi clasp forearms as brothers.

The circle is closed, the fate of al-Andalus sealed. The history of the next five hundred years is set in motion by this single spark, fortune's merciless arrow loosed upon time and events, stretching taut to eternity's distant horizon, the life and the death of many great peoples.

Words

Dinners are served late during the summer months in Madinat al-Zahra, well after sunset, and out in the courtyards under the stars. As the day dies, the cheery glow outlining the peaks of the Sierra Morena fades from bright rose to burnt orange, then a final slash of purple before the sun surrenders its reign.

The stars sense their opportunity and begin to tiptoe in, at first in shy dribbles, then in bumptious hordes. Having found their places they commence their self-important, gloating sparkle, diamonds spilled across the sky. The moon is a sickle.

There is a hint of a breeze, no more, but the Córdoban summer evenings are usually kind, the night air cool and refreshing, a welcome relief from the day's unbearable swelter.

Evening meals are light, as befitting heat-tempered appetites. Skewers of roasted chicken and lamb, served warm but not hot, sliced beets and pearl onions bathed in cellar-chilled vinegar, a salad of fresh greens tossed with spicy olive oil and sprinkled with dried cherries and slivers of roasted almonds, fresh-baked bread and butter. Diluted wine for the men, mountain-cooled water for the women and children.

The meal is served picnic style upon a large Persian carpet unrolled beside the gurgling fountain. Small oil lanterns set atop poles bathe the scene in a soft, pleasing glow.

Gathered on their pillows are Samuel, Rebekah at his side; their two daughters, Miriam and Sara; Levi; Zaheid and his wife, Iuliana; Zafir; Rayhana ,and her younger brother, Khalil— nominally her chaperone, though he couldn't care less about such formalities.

Rebekah effortlessly directs the pace and topics of conversation as she observes, striving to ensure that Rayhana feels comfortable and welcomed. As they eat, the group's talk is steered about; events in the city, upcoming poetry recitations, the lack of rain and the relentless heat, tidbits of harmless palace gossip, what is new at market.

With impeccable timing, at a natural lull she asks Levi what is in store in the way of new book acquisitions, predictably stirring the men to wax poetic on their personal wish lists—a topic they never tire of debating. Rayhana listens, but her grin and the bright sparkle of her eyes makes it clear she shares their excitement for books.

Thankfully, Zafir seems at ease and has obviously figured out how to speak normally in the girl's presence. Rebekah muses that his increased comfort around her is telling of their relationship. Yes, they have kissed.

Rayhana is radiant. Those dimples are adorable, unexpectedly diving deep into her cheeks then vanishing, only to reappear a moment later, fanning her allure, as if the deep creases have a will of their own. A beautiful young woman and clearly smart. It is easy to see why Zafir is smitten. Rebekah likes her already.

As the meal progresses, Rebekah studies the couple discreetly, noting the quick darting glances jumping between the two, the knowing smiles directed at their laps at some shared secret, some inside joke. With feigned casualness, they rest their hands on the carpet between them, no more than an inch part, and when the center of conversation moves safely across the carpet away from them, the tips of their fingers kiss, then part, kiss again, then retract to the safety of their laps.

Rebekah has to fight to suppress her grin. The couple's body language is rehearsed and precise. Responsible and careful— which is good. But in the end, such things are difficult to shield from a seasoned eye. Rebekah sees it all, carefully folded and pressed and tucked away, but impossible to hide. It scratches then pierces the surface here and there despite their best intentions. Rebekah savors this new knowledge. She takes a deep, satisfied breath as she smiles. Love.

Miriam has obviously given up on Zafir. Instead, she now moons over Rayhana's handsome younger brother. Rebekah smirks at the predictability of it all. Thankfully, the boy seems oblivious to Miriam's attentions. No doubt he has his mind set upon another. Whispers at court point to Durri the Small's elder daughter, Maryam; from what she knows, an unwise choice.

The debate rages on. Zaheid insists that the Royal Library is weakest in science, especially optics and mathematics, and that is where Samuel's acquisition priorities should lie for the fall. Levi has a soft spot for medical treatises and mentions a conversation with Abu al-Qasim regarding rumors of some new books by Galen that have surfaced in the east; like so many volumes, once lost to history but now suddenly found. Samuel eggs them on, teases them, accuses them of preposterous demands. Zafir makes his usual plea for Greek literature, especially more plays. Round and round it goes.

Rebekah interrupts with mock frustration, "Enough! You men and your books! You are boring our guests." Sara frowns and nods her agreement. Miriam has her dreamy eyes locked upon Khalil waiting to echo his response, which does not come. Rayhana grins as Rebekah continues. "And poor Iuliana ... I am sure she hears enough of such things at home, Zaheid. Surely it is time for tea and sweets." She turns to Rayhana. "Would you mind helping me, Rayhana?"

"Certainly, I would be happy to."

Zafir drinks her in as she leaves, then turns and rejoins the fight. Predictably, Zaheid insists on one last point before the matter is closed, and they are at it again.

Rebekah sets the kettle on the fire to boil and begins to arrange the sweets on the tray. She turns to Rayhana and smiles. "Love suits you, my dear."

Rayhana blushes deep scarlet and somehow seems fascinated by her shoes.

Rebekah's smile widens. "Do not worry, it is obvious only to one with an eye for such things. I have never seen Zafir so happy, Rayhana. You suit each other perfectly. Zafir is like a son to us, you know, and what makes him happy, makes us happy. Samuel and I are both very pleased at this new and unexpected direction in his life."

She shyly looks up. "Zafir loves you both so deeply. Your approval matters a great deal to him. And to me."

"Zafir is a fine young man, Rayhana." She winks. "Someone to build a happy life with."

Dimples. "Yes ... we are blessed."

Rebekah's smile relaxes. "Yes, richly blessed."

"I never thought about love ... until I met Zafir. But I knew that very first moment, that first painfully awkward moment, that there was a magical spark between us, some sort of destiny at work."

Rebekah's smile returns. "It was the same for me." She resumes setting the tray with sweets. "You must be careful at court, my dear. The eyes and ears of Madinat are everywhere. Gossip fancies the missteps of young lovers."

"Yes, I know ... we try to be careful. We meet in my reading room in the Rare Books Library, nowhere else."

"Good. Your reputation must not be put at risk." She finishes with the tray then turns to the kettle, which is just beginning to steam. She readies the teapot.

"What does your father think of this?"

Silence.

Rebekah turns.

Rayhana's eyes have filled and her chin is quivering. Her giddy joy has vanished, the burdens of the real world suddenly shocking and raw. She slowly shakes her head. "Baba said ... Baba said ..." She chokes back a sob. "He said ... he said he will marry me to some ... Berber prince ... from the—the—the desert!" The tears are streaming by the time her shoulders begin to shake. "Mama promised me I could marry for love. She promised!"

Rebekah's mothering instinct is spontaneous. She moves forward and hugs the girl to her. "Shhh, shhhhhh ... I did not mean to upset you. Shhhh, Rayhana ... shhhh ..."

Rayhana's voice quavers as she says, "I tried to tell Baba about Zafir, I tried. He would not listen. I do not know what to do. What am I to do? What will become of us and our love?"

"Do you know when he is to return to Córdoba?"

She sniffs against Rebekah's chest. "No. Baba writes only to Salim. It has been three weeks since the last letter. He says only that things 'go well' in the Maghreb."

Rebekah continues to rub the girl's back as she ponders. She leans back now so that they can lock eyes. "Listen to me."

Rayhana sniffs again and nods.

"We will find a way. Do you understand me?"

A weak nod answers her.

"Samuel and I will help you, Rayhana. I am not sure how just yet, but do not worry, we will help you both. All will be well. I promise."

Another sniff and a stronger nod. She hugs the older woman as a little girl would embrace her mother.

"Time to smile now, young lady." Rebekah makes a funny face, which elicits a hint of a grin.

Rayhana wipes her tears with the back of her hand and sniffles once more for good measure, then exhales heavily to regain her composure and shakes her hands.

"Good girl. Let us bring the tea and sweets. Once those crazy men stop arguing they will wonder where we are. Come, you carry the tray."

The man lifts the quill, dips it carefully into the vial and begins to insert his precise script between the heavy black lines.

Dawn-Eager-Angel-Royal Majesty. Ghalib Caliph's army Maghreb. Hajar an-Nasar siege.

He lifts the page and watches the words fade into nothingness. A hint of a smile. He dips his quill and resumes.

> *Time right WH invasion. Attack Medinaceli, Gormaz. Both weak.*
> *Córdoba defenseless. Nervous.*

The line vanishes.

> *Suggest more gold WH mercenaries. Made contact spy Castile.*

Strobel blows, inspects his work, then neatly folds the letter, lifts his sealing candle, dribbles the hot red wax, sets his ring upon it, and presses.

A resigned sadness frames the boy's face, lends its weary sag to his shoulders, a lazy shuffle to his gait. He has never felt so lonely. His one nibble of adventure was yanked from him forcibly in an awful instant. He reels from it still. He retreats to the only thing he knows, his books. He occasionally revisits the ledgers of his new holdings, but his heart is just not in it anymore.

There is a soft knock at the door and his mother appears. Predictably, she does not wait for his invitation, just barges in. He watches her cross the room. His heart begins to pound, a machine beyond his control, trained by years of her merciless manipulation of his young life. She looks tense somehow, pent up. Maybe vexed by something someone said or did. Or failed to do. He cannot be sure; he is never sure with her.

She stops and stares as if undecided. She frowns. "I could not read this with my key. That can only mean he left a separate key for you." She stretches out her arm dramatically, releases the opened letter onto his desk. She turns and leaves without another word.

The boy stares at the crumpled paper. Finally, some news from the Maghreb. As he sits up and straightens his back, a grin of anticipation slips onto his face. He has memorized the key, of course, has no need of a crib sheet. He extracts a sheet of paper from the drawer, places it in front him, then lifts a reed pen from the holder and inks it. With his thumb and forefinger he pins the letter open, then smoothes its wrinkles.

A full page of precisely rendered dots, dashes, and swirls. He instantly recognizes Ibn Abi Amir's elegant hand. His grin widens into a full smile. He finds his place and begins the laborious transcription process to recover the words of love he so longs to hear.

The grand vizier looks up from his desk. "Yes?"

"My lord, Faiq al-Nizami and Jawdhar have asked to see you. Privately."

Jafar frowns, puzzled. Odd combination. Faiq is master of the Tiraz, the caliph's textile factory of the medina and also master of royal courier service; Jawdhar is master of the royal jewels and master of the caliph's falcons. The two are more than competent in their privileged roles and are dependable allies of the caliph. Together, these two are the unofficial, though undisputed, leaders of the saqaliba of Madinat al-Zahra. Consummate players in the royal court.

The roles of the saqaliba at court are many and varied, ranging from the Vizier Council, to the caliph's Slavic Guard, to all manner of artisans, to physicians and poets, to concubines and eunuchs. A substantial fraction of the population of Madinat. These two are masterful purveyors of court gossip, famously adept at handling intrigue. They live for information; covet it.

"Did they say what they wanted?"

"No, my lord. Only a private audience."

His curiosity now engaged, he says, "Very well, send them in." He stands to receive the two men.

"Faiq, Jawdhar, I trust you are well?"

Both men bow, followed by a tandem refrain. "Very well indeed, thank you, Jafar."

Jafar indicates the pillows, and the three men sit. "May I have tea brought?"

Another tandem refrain. "Thank you, no." Twins.

"And how are things with the Tiraz, Faiq?"

"Business is booming, Jafar. A massive set of orders from Constantinople. Our latest tableware. The green, white, and black motif; you may recall it." Jafar nods. He owns some himself. "My artisans will be hard pressed to fill the order by the beginning of the fall."

"Good, good. I assume your price will include a handsome donation to the royal treasury?"

"Oh, rest assured, Jafar, rest assured."

The men all smile.

Jafar turns his head. "And the caliph's jewels are safe, Jawdhar?"

That deep baritone replies, "You may depend upon that, Jafar." He chuckles. "It took my staff nearly a week to store and catalog the display of the caliph's treasure we laid out for the Christian ambassador. That poor fool has never beheld so much gold. You should have seen his eyes."

They all smile, satisfied.

"And the caliph's falcons?"

"Eager for the hunt, most eager."

The silence stretches long enough to turn awkward. Jafar's curiosity increases with each strained second. He wonders: What are these two after?

Faiq finally begins. "We wish to bring a matter to your attention, Jafar. Something we freely admit we do not know the whole story behind." He glances at Jawdhar. "Yet ... it was something my duties as master of the royal courier service allowed me the privilege to ... notice. A delicate matter, I am afraid ..."

Jawdhar adds, "A private matter, yes."

"You may depend upon my discretion, gentlemen."

The two saqaliba look at each other for confirmation, then Faiq begins. "It seems that Ibn Abi Amir has been sending letters to Córdoba from the Maghreb."

"And why would that be surprising?"

"His letters are coded for secrecy."

"Yes. A prudent practice for important communiques. I would do the same."

"He writes to his elder son."

Jafar raises his eyebrows. He is beginning to tire of the chase.

Faiq continues, "He also sends a sealed letter pouch to his servant, Aslam, a man we hear interesting ... rumors about. Hidden carefully within the letter pouch are other sealed letters. It seems Ibn Abi Amir also writes to a number of important merchants in the city. Some of the richest and most influential merchants. Some of whom have ... questionable allegiance to the caliph." He pauses. "Abd al-Kabir, for instance."

"I see. I presume you maintain a complete list of their names?"

Faiq offers only a thin smile.

Jawdhar says, "There is more, Jafar."

"Please ..." he leads on, finally getting to the meat.

"He also sends letters that his man delivers to the royal harem ... twice now ... to the sultana."

Jawdhar adds, "We found that ... puzzling."

Jafar considers his words before responding. "There is a simple explanation. Ibn Abi Amir is now keeping the accounts of the sultana's holdings and is assisting her with her investments. With the caliph's permission, of course."

The response is in tandem. "I see ..."

Faiq continues. "We were not aware of this arrangement."

"Well, as you might imagine, the caliph does not desire this to be common knowledge." He uses his eyes for emphasis.

"We certainly understand. You may depend upon our discretion, Jafar."

"Is that all, gentlemen?"

More silence.

Faiq answers, "Interestingly, the last dispatch for the royal harem, which arrived only two days ago, also contained a letter addressed to someone else ..."

"Oh?"

"It was addressed to young Hisham."

Jafar's inability to completely mask his surprise is noticed. "I see." He recovers quickly. "I assume you could not decode the contents?"

Jawdhar replies. "No."

Faiq continues, "If we might be so bold, Jafar."

"Please."

"The fact that Ibn Abi Amir is sending coded letters to the caliph's only son strikes us as ... unsettling. The caliph's deep reservations about the boy's worthiness to succeed him are well known in Madinat, Jafar, at least within the circles of the saqaliba."

Jawdhar adds, "As are the sultana's skills at sowing seeds of discord."

Jafar chews his cheek. "Yes, I understand. You may rest assured, gentlemen, that I will bring this news to the caliph's immediate attention. I know he can depend upon your utmost discretion in this matter. And I am sure he will also welcome any other information you may have the occasion to learn regarding Ibn Abi Amir's letter writing habits."

Both men bow their heads then rise.

She lies curled on her divan, her marvelous curves exaggerated beneath the silk that strains to contain them. His transcribed letter lies folded across her thigh. She stares into space as she considers his unexpected words. She has never allowed a man to command her this way. She welcomes it, she resents it; she loves him, she hates him. And always that dull ache that torments her ceaselessly, day and night. He must have known when he exacted her promise. How is it that he controls her so easily from so far away?

She bites her lip to focus, then frowns at her weakness as she muses: So unbecoming of a woman of my means and stature to be beholden to a man like him.

But she is helpless to resist, cannot erase his face from her mind's eye, cannot help but conjure the sweet caress of his hands upon her body, the feel of him inside her. She crosses her legs tighter in a vain attempt to quell the ache.

She lifts the letter and reads it slowly once more, savors the titillation of Ibn Abi Amir's bold words, then curses his power over her. How dare he command her so! She lays the letter back down.

Her heart is pounding now.

In the end, she does his bidding, his first command to trace a soft arc around the generous swell of her breast then brush the hard nipple straining against the silk with the backs of her fingers. Her eyes droop then close as she sighs heavily. It has been so very long. As instructed, she slides her hand under the silk. It crosses her warm belly to press the throb between her thighs. Her motions are answered by a soft, tortured groan, then her familiar pant. She sees him smile from the desert in her mind's eye, welcomes him into her arms to work his strange magic. She gives herself to him, is powerless to resist him. She whispers his name, "Muhammad ... Muhammad—"

"Subh, I have news from the Maghreb that will interest you—" He abruptly halts as she violently twists away from the door.

Her face is pure venom when she turns to confront him, her face flushed, hardened into bright anger. "You MIGHT have the decency to knock, Jibril."

The eunuch is speechless. It has been years since a knock was required before entering her bedchamber. He stammers, "My ... apologies, Subh, I did not mean to—to—surprise you ..." He is still wrestling to recover his composure.

She hisses, "You mean, Sultana."

"My apologies, Sultana, I did not mean to surprise you." He is a portrait of fluster.

She sits up and begins to smooth her gown, mold her features. The tempest calms. "What is it you want?"

"May I sit, Sultana?"

In ancient times he would have knelt before her and stroked her legs as they conversed in quiet tones. She slides her feet back to indicate the opposite end of the divan.

He hesitates, then sits, resigned to his fate. He realizes that even in his absence his rival's power grows. He has come to loathe

Ibn Abi Amir. He has to will the frown from forming on his face. Softly, he begins again, "I have news from the Maghreb."

She remains taut and expressionless, a coiled snake.

He continues, "Hajar an-Nasar will fall. Apparently, the fortress will be delivered by spies of the Banu Birzal, who were somehow able to infiltrate the Idrisid ranks. I must admit, I was skeptical Ghalib could pull it off."

"Where did you hear this?"

"I have eyes on Ghalib's staff. The attack is imminent."

"Muhammad is safe?"

The eunuch hesitates. "Yes."

Her expression softens. "Thank you, Jibril."

"You are welcome, Sultana."

"Subh."

He breaks into a thin, effeminate smile. "You are most welcome, Subh." His mood brightens. "There is more. It seems a new shipment of saqaliba has just arrived in the city from the Holy Roman Empire. From the lush mountains of Caratania. A dozen boys and two dozen girls. I managed to request three of the youngest boys for service in the royal harem. The appropriate bribes were carefully placed, to turn the key and open the lock."

"Naturally ..."

His smile widens. "My request has been granted, Subh." Glee is painted to the corners of his face.

"Their fate is to meet your ceremonial dagger?"

He flips his wrist dismissively. "Of course. My new protégés, Subh, think of it! Finally, some new royal eunuchs for me to train. It has been so long, so very long." He rubs his hands together. "How exciting! And I even get to select which ones!" He beams like a little girl. "I think I will have one of each color: a blond, a brunette and a redhead. I will introduce them to you before the gelding."

She nods, seemingly disinterested.

It is not the response he sought. He studies her as he calculates. He whispers, "Subh, I would be happy to tend to your needs. Despite my ... limitations. You know that I am skilled as a lover. I miss our times together, my darling. Let me satisfy you." He rests his henna-painted hand upon her foot.

She jumps as if seared by a branding iron, jerks her feet away from him, her expression one of unadulterated disgust.

He recoils in horror, instantly aware of his miscalculation. He silently curses his stupidity.

"Leave me. Now. Go. GO!"

The eunuch rises and slinks out like a whipped puppy.

Tides of Time

2 August 976.

The night is moonless and impossibly cold, the sky an orgy of pulsing energy. A streak of fiery emerald slices the heavens then vanishes. It is three hours before sunrise, the genie's hour; the hour of treachery, of revenge. The castle is fast asleep, the silence deafening.

Rats dither about in slippered feet, nosing into crevices after dropped morsels of grain and crumbs of bread. Rodents own the desert night and are oblivious to the two-legged masters of their abode of hewn stone, wary only of the all-seeing orbs of the lurking owls. Somewhere outside the castle walls a jackal lifts her head and cries for her mate. A moment later her lover answers from a distant ridge.

In the canyons far below, sporadic campfires ring Eagle's Rock, the timeless signature of siege.

Sentries pace the castle ramparts, vaporous wraiths under a direct stare, changing to discernible shadows of human forms with peripheral vision.

There has been no major action for two weeks now and the sentries grow bored and careless, resentful of their unlucky assignments. After all, everyone knows the fortress is impregnable, the Umayyads best of all.

The air is bone-chilling at this altitude, the icy breeze whistling around the corners of chiseled stone, prodding cracks in the shuttered windows, content to worm its way into the folds of the knights' robes. The sentries shiver, pull their cloaks tighter, then stamp their feet to relieve the numbness in their toes and stave off the relentless drowsiness. They stare to the east, forlorn, silently beckoning the warmth of the sun. They will begin to curse it by noon prayer.

Near the back gate of the fortress, the hint of the lone sentry is just visible as he paces atop the high wall. A twin sprouts behind him and silently closes in. The two shadows hug for a brief instant, then one collapses. A moment later the second shadow vanishes, leaving the rampart empty, the approach unguarded. At a dozen strategic points around the castle, the same scene is repeated within a span of a dozen breaths.

203

Muted whispers, a rustle of feet, then a soft *clank-clank-clank*, followed by a heavier *clunk* as the gate locking mechanism is worked. The massive doors creak open.

More hushed voices whisper, the cool metal hiss of a scimitar being drawn; first one, then dozens. Padded footfall begins to move through the gate into the fortress.

Silence.

Five minutes later, a distant rumble tickles the castle mount. A coming storm? The rolling thunder coalesces and grows in strength, and when it makes its final turn a hundred yards outside the fortress walls, there is little doubt of its source; horses at full gallop.

By the time the alarm bell begins its rude, metallic clang, the Banu Birzal cavalry is sluicing through the gate, wave after wave screaming their shrill battle cry, *"Allahu Akbar! Allahu Akbar!"* as they pass into Hajar an-Nasar uncontested.

The castle's fate is preordained, the tides of time playing out cruelly, the matter settled before it has a chance to begin. The desert exacts a terrible wrath upon the vanquished. Horrible screams begin to pierce the darkness as panic sets in.

Blood will be spilled, and spilled handsomely.

Disgust is written into the folds of Ghalib's weary face as he approaches his prisoner. The general looks haggard and pale, his lids heavy from lack of sleep, his limp more pronounced than usual. He frowns as he surveys his quarry then shakes his head as if he cannot quite believe that his prisoner managed to cause him so much grief. He lifts his eyes and scans the carnage in front of the keep. Bodies are everywhere, many headless, and the rich scent of blood is heavy in the air. The sweet reek of the butcher shop.

The prisoner has been stripped naked and drawn into a taut T by his captors, his feet bound together and fixed to a stake driven into the earth, his hands stretched out and anchored to two heavy posts, then cinched tight enough to make the man cry out. His pathetic, pallid body is frozen in place.

The sun has been up for an hour, the colors at the horizon already having passed from soft, tender pinks to hardened, angular yellows. The air has stilled and is quickly warming. By sunset the hundreds of Berber bodies will bloat unnaturally then split like gourds, releasing a poisonous brew that will foul the breeze for days on end.

The vultures are up early, a dozen already beginning to climb into loose, lazy circles high above the decimated castle. Avian gossip spreads like the wind, and within the hour news of the coming feast has reached halfway across the Rif.

At the prisoner's feet lies the severed head of his henchman, Omar, the man's eyes facing the cloudless sky, still open in shocked surprise. Beside Omar, the heads of several courtiers rest upright, as if buried to their necks in the dark, blood-slickened dirt. The work of the Banu Birzal. The heads will soon be piked and set upon the main gate of Eagle's Rock for all to behold.

General Ghalib begins the ordeal with a bitter taste in his mouth. "Sultan ibn Guennoun. At last we meet."

Silence.

The man's ebony eyes burn, the smoldering hate wafting upwards to join the lingering tendrils of smoke scattered among the ruins of his lair.

Ghalib continues to stare at the man.

The sultan hisses, "I might have known the Umayyads would use Banu Birzal scum to betray me. You would never have taken Hajar an-Nasar by force of arms, Ghalib."

"We would never have taken Hajar an-Nasar ... yet here we stand, victorious, Sultan."

"You Arabs have no honor." He spits at the ground.

General Ghalib laughs. "Actually, Sultan, there is not a single drop of Arab blood in my veins. I am saqaliba, the caliph's slave." His laugh settles into a thin smile. He studies his prisoner, amused. "I am afraid history is not kind to the vanquished, Sultan. Your Idrisid bones will be picked clean by the vultures then scattered in the desert sands. A month from now your wives and your children will have trouble recalling your faces. A year from now, your people will have to think hard just to remember your names. A century from now Hajar an-Nasar will slip into legend, its location lost to history, you and your people forgotten." He pauses to let this sink in.

"I am afraid the reign of the Idrisids has come to an end, Sultan. There is a new leader of the Rif. Hamid al-Tariq of the Banu Birzal." He lifts his hand to his right to indicate the approach of the two brothers and their dozen bodyguards. Ibn Abi Amir walks behind them, flanked by Suktan and Tahir.

Sultan ibn Guennoun struggles against his ropes but cannot move. There is pleading in his tone as he says, "Ghalib, you are an honorable man, the caliph's vizier. You cannot hand me over to this barbarian. The Berber tribes will pay my ransom. The caliph will have gold for my release."

General Ghalib sighs. "I am afraid a deal has been struck, Sultan. Your life has been spoken for. No ransom will be made." He pauses. "Perhaps you should have considered the possible consequences of your actions before you had my men skinned in the canyon." He turns to leave, followed by a half dozen of his officers.

Sultan ibn Guennoun opens his mouth for a retort then slowly closes it. His heart begins to pound as his executioners approach.

General Ghalib says to the Berber brothers, "He is all yours. Your gold will be delivered tomorrow. My troops will begin our preparations to occupy Eagle's Rock."

Hamid al-Tariq and al-Andalusi nod.

"Ibn Abi Amir, you should come with me, this will not be pretty."

Al-Andalusi replies, "No. The qadi of the Maghreb must pronounce judgment on the condemned. He must witness firsthand the fate of those who violate Sharaf, the honor code of the desert tribes."

Ibn Ami Amir says, "I will stay, General."

"Suit yourself." General Ghalib shrugs then walks on and begins barking orders to his officers and pointing in different directions to spell out the tasks at hand.

They are by the main gate fifteen minutes later when they hear the first quick, startled scream. Ghalib and his officers look up in unison. The officers exchange nervous glances. A longer, anguished scream follows, then a man's desperate plea for mercy. An extended silence then an awful scream so piercing it turns the heads of the Córdoban knights on the castle walls. Sobs and blubbering follow.

General Ghalib shakes his head and mutters, "Get me out of this cursed land and back to civilization." He begins to bark orders once more, chased now by curses to quicken the steps of his men.

The awful screaming continues for well over an hour before it mercifully fades, then ceases.

The sky above the castle is thick with a vortex of swirling black feathers. Hundreds of red-rimmed, beady eyes scan the battleground, impatient to quell their stomach rumbles.

General Ghalib paces the castle keep as he reads the letter. His senior officers look on, anxious for news, but smart enough to hold their tongues until spoken to.

The old warrior stops, shakes his head, curses, then resumes his pacing. His limp is exaggerated, excruciating, yet he refuses to sit. He seems to welcome the pain.

He stops again and turns. "The caliph has recalled the army to Córdoba. He wishes to celebrate our victory over the Idrisids. It seems I am to be given the honorific title, 'Sword of the Caliph.'" He frowns. "Trouble is brewing in the Upper Marches. White Hands has made his move. Clearly, the man has spies in the kingdom and knew that Córdoba's army was away in the Maghreb.

"He invaded with five thousand cavalry and eight thousand infantry. He has defeated our mercenary army at Medinaceli and has moved south and laid siege to Gormaz, our fortress at the Duero River. He will be hard-pressed to take Gormaz, but they are short of troops and stores, so one never knows. Predictably, all of al-Andalus is already in a panic. We will refit in Córdoba and then move north to lift the siege and drive White Hands back to Castile where he belongs. I punished the father, and I will soon punish the son."

The officers break into a dozen hushed conversations.

Ghalib's second-in-command, Ahmed al-Qadir, says, "What of Eagle's Rock?"

The room quiets.

"We will leave a garrison. Two hundred men. More than enough to repel any Fatimid meddling. No Banu Birzal will be allowed unescorted within the castle walls; Hajar an-Nasar is an Umayyad fortress now. I do not trust these Berbers, especially now that they have gold to play with. Any news on the clan gathering?"

"They are to meet next week. I am told they will formally elect Hamid al-Tariq of the Banu Birzal as their leader. They will sign a treaty to join the Rif clans and begin to organize an army to fight the Fatimids." He hesitates. "Or so Ibn Abi Amir says."

Ghalib frowns. The name alone pains him.

A gruff, "Where?"

"Chefchaouen. A day's ride."

He considers. "I see. I want Umayyad representation at the meeting, Ahmed. And I mean representation besides that of Ibn Abi Amir. You go, and take a hundred of your best men with you. I want a clear message delivered that gold and arms come only with agreement to the caliph's demands. I will draft an agreement for al-Tariq to sign."

Ahmed nods.

The officers' eyes are glued to their commander.

"Begin preparations for our departure. We march for Larache in two days, gentlemen. Ahmed, send word of our need for dromons. Through discreet channels. We do not need a visit by corsairs on the voyage home." He lifts his eyebrows for emphasis and locks eyes with his officers. "I want no surprises on our journey back to Córdoba. Not a whisper of our plans or schedule to the Berbers. Understood?"

A collective, "Yes, my lord."

"Dismissed."

The officers turn to leave.

Ghalib motions to his second-in-command.

When the others are out of earshot, Ghalib says, "At sunrise tomorrow go to Ibn Abi Amir's tent, bind him and bring him to me. Take a dozen men in case his bodyguards resist. I have no more need of that man's help."

"Understood." Ahmed turns to leave.

"And, Ahmed?"

"Yes?"

"Have his tent watched. Discreetly. I want to know when he farts or makes water. Understood?"

"Consider it done."

General Ghalib resumes his painful pacing as he calculates his next move. Finally, the waiting is over. A thin smile settles onto the man's grizzled face. There is a debt to be paid.

"What do you mean, gone?"

"He and his two Berber bodyguards have vanished."

"The guards you posted?"

"Their throats were slit. All four. All of Ibn Abi Amir's belongings have been removed from his tent. It must have happened deep in the night."

Ghalib stares at Ahmed, his mouth twisted into a grimace. "Damn the scoundrel! I should have anticipated that move. I must be getting too old for this." He shakes his head with disgust.

"Should I send troops after him? He must have gone to the Banu Birzal camp. We can track him."

Ghalib shakes his head. "He is not that stupid. Besides, we do not need to provoke a fight with al-Tariq, at least not now." As Ghalib ponders his options Ahmed patiently waits. These two have been together for years.

"It seems that we will have to leave the qadi of the Maghreb in the desert after all. For now. However, select your best man. Someone of Berber heritage who speaks Maghrebi and looks the part. Take him with you to the clan gathering, and insist to al-Tariq that he remain with the Banu Birzal as the caliph's personal representative. That should keep him safe."

Ahmed smiles. "I know just the man. Salim. He was born in Tangier. Good with a dagger."

"My orders may well cost him his head, Ahmed. Do you trust him?"

"He is completely loyal. He will do as I command."

Ghalib nods. "For now, he is to blend into the camp and go unnoticed. Weeks from now, when all is settled and the army is gone, Ibn Abi Amir will emerge from hiding. When that time comes, Salim will murder him while he sleeps. Understood?"

"Perfectly."

"Good, make it so."

His letter arrived mid-morning and was instantly decoded. She has read it a dozen times now and memorized his instructions. She folds the letter across her thigh as she considers their odds. So it begins. She lifts the paper to read it one last time, then holds it over the candle and watches it curl into the golden flame. She does not release it until she feels the burn sting her fingertips. She lifts the small bell from her side table and jingles it twice.

A moment later, the door opens and the eunuch enters and bows. "Sultana, your wish is my command."

"Tell Jibril to arrange a meeting for me with the caliph. For tea. There are some things we need to discuss. Tomorrow morning, if possible."

"Certainly, Sultana." The eunuch bows and closes the door.

As Subh stares into space, a slight smile tickles her cheeks then fades. The die is cast.

As she continues to stare, she traces a wide arc across the lovely contour of her breast. She shifts her hips. As she touches her finger to her tongue she conjures his face and professes her love. Her heart begins to race.

Professions

She suddenly stops and frowns. Her frustration obvious, she grabs the mass of dark curls tormenting her, hastily pulls it up, and pins it at the top of her head to keep it out of her way as she works. By the time her arms are back at her side, the cadre of conspirators has already successfully plotted their escape, the wispy springs spilling one by one down her cheeks, bouncing jubilantly in their new-found freedom.

His eyes grow large. He is riveted, dumbfounded, by how sensual a woman handling her own hair can be. He would sell his soul to weave his fingers through that dense brown forest. He swallows hard to steady himself.

He becomes obsessed by the dark downy V that begins at her hairline then works its way deliciously downward towards the nape of her neck. He is helpless to will eyes away from it.

She is lost in her work, completely oblivious. She uses a string to position the first candle exactly four feet from the pinhole of the camera then uses a ruled straight-edge to place the second taper exactly six inches to the right of the first. She adjusts it to make sure the angle is true.

He watches only the V.

Satisfied, she glances up at him and smiles, then moves to the back of the camera to study the screen. She purses her lips as she concentrates, barely able to contain her excitement. As the image sharpens, her smile widens. She looks up and beams, mouths an excited barrage, and motions him over.

It takes all his willpower to find her face again. He nods and takes up a position behind her so they can study the screen together.

She chatters on and on, her hands dancing as she goes. She lifts a charcoal pencil then kneels down, her eyes glued to the camera's screen. She uses her index finger to indicate the first candle flame, then the second, instructing him as she moves. She boldly proclaims her expectation of the distance between the two flames, then holds her straight-edge to double-check. She is right, of course.

He chuckles, lamely nods his agreement.

With the soft pencil she carefully marks the positions of the two life-like bulbs of yellow. She rises and moves around the table to the front of the camera.

His eyes follow her hips. As she turns and leans forward to adjust the taper he is just able to glimpse the soft swell of her breasts. He swallows hard, his heart racing.

Using the straight-edge, she slides the outer candle to twelve inches. She retraces her steps and repeats the same marking process on the screen, then returns to slide the candle to eighteen inches.

He makes some comment. She playfully scoffs then comes back to the screen and kneels down once more and instructs him on what she expects to see.

This time he kneels behind her to match her sight-line, but his eyes are not on the screen at all, only on the dark, downy V. He leans forward and kisses the nape of her neck.

Her hands instantly freeze and the lesson abruptly halts.

He kisses her neck again, more forcefully now, then touches his tongue to the point of the V and traces an arc to her bare shoulder. She turns her head slightly so he can find her ear. He sucks her earlobe between his lips and softly exhales.

She shivers.

He eases his hands beneath her arms, over her hip bones, and finally onto her stomach, then pulls her hard against him. Their breathing is quick and shallow; matched. His hands inch upward to cup the heavy swell of her breasts. They release a duet of deep sighs.

Behind the tapers' flames and out of sight, two fat encyclopedias, desperate for some news, any news, have ratcheted a thin volume up between them. The little codex claws and strains, then finally gets the glimpse it seeks. Hushed whispers begin to percolate among the lower shelves, drowned out by the exquisite tortured song of love.

Day by day their love grows more emboldened, less constrained by artificial boundaries and barriers. Heaven knows it is impossible to sequester such things in tiny sealed rooms forever. Love yearns to boldly proclaim, to shout to the heavens.

This is foolish, of course, especially in a place like Madinat al-Zahra, which treasures its juicy gossip like a delicate morsel, first sucked and savored, then crushed mercilessly between the teeth.

But such are the ways of young lovers. Emotion trumps logic, pounding hearts trample calculations. Feelings rule the day. Samuel and Rebekah would not approve, of course. If they knew.

These two hold hands as they dance and flit from reading room to reading room, all shushes and barely suppressed giggles. They own the Rare Books Library. Suddenly he simply must show her his favorite haunts, his most precious books, the prizes of the caliph's collection—even his room. She devours it all, giddy with their daring.

And so they check that the coast is clear, then they dash.

He reveals the many secrets in the catacombs running beneath the Rare Books Library, the niche of books forbidden by the grand imam to be made public, the lost volumes only Samuel and his most trusted companions know about and have squirreled away, the books that many in Córdoba would barter half their fortunes to possess if they but knew of their existence.

They sit facing each other, their floor pillows touching. His elbows are propped on his folded legs, his eyes locked to her face, concern written deeply into his features.

She talks and talks.

He listens.

This is no discourse on their experiments with the camera obscura or an interpretation of a new Greek comedy she has just read. Her expression is weary and burdened. When she pauses he adds a comforting word, reaches out to squeeze her hand to reassure her, then beckons her on.

After a long pause to gather herself, she continues. She grows more animated as she goes, her hands lifting and dancing in time to her voice. She abruptly halts. Her eyes fill and her chin begins to quiver.

It breaks his heart.

She tries to speak but cannot. A single tear traces a neat line down each cheek. Her head collapses forward like a felled oak.

He takes both of her hands and whispers her name. "Rayhana."

Her face does not budge from her lap. She tries to speak through her tears but cannot quite manage.

He interrupts with her name once more, now more forcefully. "Rayhana!" He squeezes her hands.

She shyly looks up. Her face is a wet mess, and her chin still quivers uncontrollably.

He smiles, then says, "I love you, Rayhana."

She gasps sharply, then her dimples flash, then she starts to cry harder. But these are tears of joy. She quavers, "I love you, too, Zafir, with all my heart. With all my heart."

His eyes well up. "I will always love you, Rayhana. Always."

"I will always love you, Zafir."

"Listen to me."

She sniffs as she wipes her tears. Their eyes are glued to one another.

"We will find a way, Rayhana. Do your hear me?"

She weakly nods.

"We will find a way. I promise, Rayhana. We will be together. No one can stop that, not even your father. No one."

She practically leaps into his arms. The two young lovers embrace as if tomorrow was only a dream.

Durr faithfully escorts her charge to the entrance of the Rare Books Library on the three days of the week the girl lives for. Samuel has long since ceased to meet Rayhana and escort her to the reading room, deferring instead to Zafir, who has graciously agreed to fill in for his master.

When they catch sight of each other they wrestle with their body language but do manage to maintain a semblance of decorum when in public view.

And the eyes of Madinat are watching closely; of that, you can be sure. He bows, she curtsies.

Very stiff.

Very starched.

Very proper.

The eyes of Madinat do a double-take, no more. There may be a fleeting seed of suspicion, it's true, a hint of unbridled passion, but certainly no proof of wrongdoing. But then, when did juicy gossip ever require proof?

Durr knows, of course. How could she not? Rayhana has not confided as much just yet, only a hint here, a thinly veiled reference there, but some things are obvious to a woman who has known you since birth. She is indulgent with the girl, gives her two extra hours in the afternoon before she retrieves her and heads home.

Durr is elated but secretly worries. How could she not? She knows Ibn Abi Amir and what he is capable of, has seen it firsthand.

Once alone they kiss and touch, then decide on their plans for the day. Mostly it is talking for hours on end about everything, about nothing. Books, of course, and the camera certainly, but also gossip from Madinat al-Zahra and the city, religion, politics, poetry, even the weather. She loves to hear his childhood memories of Caratania. When conversation wanes they exchange wicked looks then flit to another room and begin anew. Their hushed giggles are incessant, the air around them electric, drenched in unsated passion.

Then kiss and touch some more. Besides talking, they read; some favorite codex of his, or some forbidden fruit he knows will interest her. She devours everything within reach. They dissect the hidden meanings together in staccato bursts of twined interruption, chased by longing smiles, even occasional disagreements on the author's intent, which inevitably end with bright laughter and a kiss.

Samuel is patient with his protégé's absence on these days, knowing full well the boy will work half the night to catch up on his duties. Rebekah scolds him when he forgets and complains about Zafir's inattention.

They know better. They know better than to tempt fate. Of course they do. And yet, here the two lie, side by side, on his bed, in his room, door locked, reading Aristophanes. A bawdy comedy, no less. What could they be thinking? It begins innocently enough. It always does.

She is on her stomach, her legs bent at the knee, feet high in the air, crossed and swaying like a little girl. Her elbows are on the floor mattress, her chin resting on her balled fists. Her hair is loose and unruly, just as he likes it. The mass of curls buries her shoulders then spills down the sweet inverted arch at the small of her back.

He lies on his side, single elbow on the mattress, balled fist on his cheek. With his free hand he teases her curls.

The splayed codex lies in front of her. She reads, he listens; or tries to. He catches himself and interrupts here and there to make a point. She giggles adorably when she stumbles on the poet's ribald phrases. He can only laugh. He has read the comedy a dozen times and could recite long passages from memory. Between comments he memorizes the outline of her face. She seems oblivious to the spell she weaves.

He casually pulls a tress into a horizontal line as he straightens an especially fascinating curl.

She reads on.

He lowers the taut curl into the small of her back, as if to measure its length, then abruptly releases the spring. His fingers remain, however, and settle instead of departing, beginning to explore. His thumb joins in, slows to savor the soft indentation at her spine, then continues to map the terrain.

There is a slight pause in her reading, no more.

His eyes are locked on her generous curves, mesmerized by how beautiful her body is. He is entranced by her olive-toned calves, up high in the air, bare from ankle to knee. His fingers rise up and out of the inverted arch to begin their downward journey at a snail's pace.

She trips on a word, begins again, trips once more, then stops altogether. Her legs slowly fold down to the mattress. Her eyes droop, then close, but she does not resist.

He continues to explore with a delicate touch. He grows bolder with each inch he traces. He begins to slide down her thigh, finally resting on the silky back of her knee. He lingers.

She is amazed that knees can be so ridiculously sensitive. She tenses with pleasure and curls her toes, her head sinking to the mattress, eyes closed. She exhales heavily through parted lips.

As he begins to trace an exquisitely slow backwards path, her robe and silk slip follow along, guided by his thumb, exposing her lovely olive thighs, inch by delicious inch. As he moves, his finger begins to edge closer to the line that joins her legs, coaxing them apart.

He has imagined this a dozen times, a hundred, but is unprepared for the tortuous intensity of the ache it produces. His heart is pounding, his breathing quick and shallow.

As he inches upward, she sighs, then is helpless to prevent the soft groan from slipping from her.

She loosens the lock on her legs, allowing him to dip his fingers. His touch grows bolder still.

Her hips seem to develop a mind of their own. First, they tense, shift subtly, then they twist away from the pleasure, then back up and into it. She begins to writhe.

His hand freezes. He leans down and whispers into her ear. "You are so beautiful, Rayhana, so beautiful. I love you."

A strained whisper, "I love you, Zafir."

Her feminine murmurs and sighs thicken the air and grow in intensity.

Knock, pause, *knock-knock-knock*, pause, *knock*.

Her soft groans cease as her head pops up.

Animal fright jumps into their eyes.

He jerks his hand away as if branded.

215

Someone attempts to open the door but finds it locked. The distinctive knocking pattern repeats.

There is an explosion of curls and she is up smoothing her robe. She looks terrified.

"Zafir? It is Levi." A little louder he repeats, "Zafir?" Pause. "Samuel needs you. Something has come up. Zafir?"

He holds his fingers to his lips to silence her. She is a caged animal, trapped.

His voice sounds unnatural, awkward, and tense. "Thank you, Levi." He struggles to even out his voice. "Tell Samuel I will be there in a moment ... I have to take care of a few things first."

Silence.

"Certainly." Long pause. "I will wait for you in Samuel's study."

His voice is more his own now. "Thank you, Levi."

They remain as they are, staring at the door, listening to his footfall recede.

Their heads pivot in tandem to stare into each other's eyes, their expressions stony and serious. She whispers, "Do you think he heard us?"

"No." He does not look especially confident.

They remain motionless for almost a full minute, then they simultaneously burst out in silent laughter, double over with hysteria and relief. The kiss that follows is urgent, their insistent, weighted sighs twisted into a tight twine then pulled taut and double-knotted by their throbbing ache.

It begins innocently enough. It always does.

Conquests

7 September 976.

The ceremonial plaza, a narrow rectangle between the Great Mosque and city wall lining the Guadalquivir River, is packed tight by the citizenry of Córdoba, a dense collection of Muslims, Christians, and Jews, all convened for the triumphal return of the victorious Umayyad army from the Maghreb. Even the visiting foreigners cannot help themselves and join the throng to gawk. Those that cannot fit into the square cram the Puente Romano, the ancient Roman bridge that spans over the deep green river just opposite the Great Mosque. Dhows by the hundred are moored along the river within earshot, their decks awash in people.

A thousand cavalry and five hundred infantry dressed in their finest ceremonial uniforms are arrayed in tight formation on the grounds of the Alcazar just to the west of the plaza.

The semicircular platform for the dignitaries is set into the steps of the Great Mosque, the red-robed Slavic Guard lining the edges. On the left side of the platform are dozens of imams, qadis, and mullahs. To their right are Abu al-Qasim, Samuel, and the remainder of the Vizier Council, Faiq al-Nizami and Jawdhar, a clutch of the more important court officials from Madinat al-Zahra, and all manner of decorated officers. Brother Cleo and Peter Strobel huddle with Reccimund.

On the eastern side of the platform overlooking the plaza is a small elevated stage where the Caliph al-Hakam, the grand imam, Jafar al-Mushafi, and General Ghalib stand.

The richest families of Córdoba have front row seats in the plaza below the stage, their distance from the caliph rank-ordered by a complex set of calculations based on wealth, influence, networks, levels of patronage for the arts, and, inevitably, bribes pressed into eager palms. Merchants and commoners crowd the edges of the plaza and spill out onto the bridge. Rumors are thick in the air; no one seems to want to miss out. It is rare these days for the caliph to abandon Madinat al-Zahra for the city. Rare indeed.

Excitement is alive in the air, driven by a steady drone of conversation. It is a party atmosphere, though tempered by the distant sound of war drums from the Upper Marches. People are nervous, especially the rich merchant families who fear the impact of war on their customers, their trade routes, and of course their purses.

It has been thirty-five years since the Battle of Simancas, and while those intervening years have not been devoid of conflict, a truce of sorts between al-Andalus and the Christian kingdoms in the north has prevailed, a mutual understanding that economic prosperity is preferable to the press of more ideological pursuits. Evidently, no more.

The grand imam raises both arms to signal that the caliph is ready to begin. The crowd is boisterous but the buzz stubborn.

"Salaam. Shalom. Peace." The caliph's voice sounds uncharacteristically weak. Jafar studies him, first puzzled, then concerned. The caliph waits for silence so he can be heard by all. The drone begins to slowly taper off then finally dies out.

"Citizens of Córdoba. As you have no doubt heard, our magnificent army, under the leadership of General Ghalib, has been victorious over the Idrisids. The mighty desert fortress of Hajar an-Nasar has fallen, my friends. The Umayyads are again respected and feared across the Maghreb!"

The crowd roars.

"Soon the Fatamid Empire will be driven back to the east where they belong. The Rif Mountains will once again belong to Córdoba and speak Andalusi. Córdoba will prosper, my—"

The caliph halts. He looks confused, dazed. He begins to wobble.

Jafar reaches out a hand to steady him, his concern now clearly visible. "Sire? Sire?"

The caliph recovers and smiles weakly. He whispers, "I am fine, Jafar, fine. Odd. I suddenly felt very woozy, but it has passed."

Jafar nods, but the concern does not leave his face.

"Córdoba will prosper, my friends." His voice strengthens. "Once again, Baghdad will tremble when they hear the word Umayyad! Córdoba will be the true heart of Islam!"

Another excited roar leaps up to dance before it calms.

The caliph scans the crowd expectantly then raises his arms dramatically, palms up. "From this day forward, people of Córdoba, General Ghalib will be known to all as Sword of the Caliph. In recognition of his many accomplishments, General Ghalib will receive the almunya of my grandfather, al-Naura, and the ceremonial scimitar of my father, Caliph Abd al-Rahman III, may Allah rest his soul."

Hushed awe spreads through the crowd.

Jafar presents the bejeweled scabbard on a red silk pillow to the caliph. The caliph lifts the sword and unsheathes it with a cool, metallic hiss. He points it vertically in the air for all to see. "Behold, *Saif al-Haqq*, Sword of Truth, the sword of the Umayyads, the sword of Damascus, the sword of glorious al-Andalus!"

General Ghalib bows deeply and receives the sword from the caliph with two hands, then bows once more. When he rises, he flirts with a smile.

The crowd applauds wildly.

The caliph waits for calm. "People of Córdoba! My people. You have heard the rumors from the north. The rumors of war."

Mouths close and the crowd stills.

"General Ghalib will refit his army and march to relieve our garrison at Gormaz. The Sword of the Caliph will have no rest until he reminds White Hands who owns the Upper Marches. Do not fear my friends: we will smite this Christian menace, we will drive the Castilians from our land. Long live al-Andalus! Long live Córdoba! Long live the Sword of the Caliph!"

The crowd roars its approval. "Sword of the Caliph! Sword of the Caliph! Sword of the Caliph!"

Only a trained eye could detect his slight tentativeness with his horse. He rides well but not well enough. Yet. His daily training regimen is relentless, and at his own request his instructors give no weight to his station, spare him no pain. They grant him no mercy when he is exhausted.

He has been at this for over a week now. The man learns, and he learns quickly. He still walks awkwardly from the angry blisters opened and weeping on his rear. His awkward gait about camp is a constant source of good-natured teasing by the warriors of the clan, but their mocking is affectionate as if he is simply a late-comer to a right-of-passage that each of them, as young boys of the Banu Birzal, had to endure in order to exit puberty and assume their rightful positions as knights of the clan.

The formal attire of his office has vanished, for now, replaced with a chainmail hauberk under his billowing crimson robe, a heavy felt cloak, and a black turban. The attire of a low-ranking Banu Birzal cavalryman. Here, one must earn the privilege of donning an officer's robes. He carries a boiled leather heart-shield and a scimitar. His dagger is strapped upside down on his upper left arm in Berber fashion. That is all; he is not yet ready for arrows or javelins and focuses instead on learning to ride in tight battle formation with minimal use of his reins. As he has been repeatedly told, his horse must feel his commands before they are needed.

Al-Andalusi gallops hard at his side as they approach their target for the tenth time that morning, Suktan and Tahir a horse-length behind. They form a tight quartet. At the last possible moment, the four turn as one, breaking hard left then immediately hard right, passing just to the rear of their quarry. He gauges it perfectly this time with a double-flick of his rein, then swings backward and up with his sword as he passes the target, neatly slicing off the straw man's arm at the shoulder.

As the four slow to a canter, Ibn Abi Amir pumps his fist in the air like a triumphant youth and shouts out his victory loud enough to echo off the canyon walls.

Al-Andalusi draws close and offers a congratulatory slap on his shoulder, then proceeds to point out the dozen things he could have done better. Suktan and Tahir grin their approval.

A massive cheer erupts from the mounted cavalrymen watching the display. The devotion of the Banu Birzal horsemen to the qadi of the Maghreb swells by the day. Their drilling is incessant also, the thousand Berber horsemen molded now into an emphatic iron fist of unparalleled mobility, unprecedented in its lethality. They are soon to cross the narrow ribbon of cobalt separating the Rif from the soft underbelly of plush al-Andalus. Very soon.

Al-Andalusi is impressed with his understudy's progress. Within a few weeks, not months, Ibn Abi Amir will be ready to command the Banu Birzal force.

As the four slow to a walk, Ibn Abi Amir turns to al-Andalusi and smiles warmly. "Again, my brother."

The Berber grins. "Anything for the qadi of the Maghreb, anything."

Al-Andalusi turns to face their army, raises his fist, and shouts, "Allahu Akbar! Allahu Akbar! Allahu Akbar!"

The thunderous roar answers him, "ALLAHU AKBAR! ALLAHU AKBAR! ALLAHU AKBAR!"

The four horsemen jump to a gallop in tandem, launch a spray of the Rif's fine sand high into the baked air, turn, and once again begin their attack.

The Golden Circle emerges from the crimson steamy mist, the drape of hot vaporous tendrils swirling about them before breaking up as they pass into the cool air. The three men are quickly robed in red, refreshing watered wine soon gracing their hands. They adjourn to the three divans arrayed in a tight ring within the cool anteroom of the royal hammam.

Ghalib is deeply tanned. He looks ancient but still formidable. He winces as he sits, but his leg seems better, no doubt a benefit of the rough kneading of the bath attendant.

Jafar flicks his head and the bath eunuchs and bodyguards vanish. The room is still, pleasingly quiet. He studies the caliph, the worry lines cutting deep into his face. The man is pale and he looks unhealthy.

"Sire, how are you feeling?"

The caliph seems lost in thought. He slowly looks up. "Weak, Jafar. I am afraid I do not feel myself today."

Jafar and Ghalib both study him.

Jafar says, "I will send for Abu al-Qasim when we are finished, Sire. He should be able to brew a potion that will help you regain your strength."

A foggy, tepid response. "What? Oh ... yes, perhaps that would be good. Thank you, Jafar."

"Sire?"

The caliph tries to focus.

Jafar continues. "Sire, we must decide upon what to do about Ibn Abi Amir's letter."

"Letter?" He struggles to make the connection. "Yes ..."

General Ghalib says, "That scum has some nerve. He is practically dictating orders to you, Sire. To you! His caliph!" He scoffs, "Qadi of the Maghreb. He is not to be trusted. The man is dangerous, Sire, and the longer he lives, the more risk he brings to us."

Jafar frowns. "I agree that he is not to be trusted, Ghalib. And it is a shame that the plans we laid were not realized."

Ghalib scowls.

"Still, with the Christian invasion from Castile and the Upper Marches under siege, perhaps we should not be too hasty to refuse an offer like this. Imagine, one thousand of the finest Berber cavalry at our disposal. He says that the Banu Birzal will be placed under the caliph's direct command to defend Córdoba against any Christian threat."

Ghalib hisses, "He says ... he says ... yes, the man SAYS many things. But WHAT he says is not to be trusted. I have watched him closely, Jafar. I have seen how he operates. The Rif is his playground now. His actions are never benign, even if they may seem to be. He has a motive, of that we can be sure."

"Yes ..." Jafar stands, locks his arms behind his back, and begins to pace. "What of the assassin you left in the Banu Birzal camp? Any word?"

"None. I would not put the chance of success very high. To his credit, Ibn Abi Amir is careful and cunning. He anticipated my every move at Hajar an-Nasar, and just when he realized I no longer needed him, he was gone." He frowns. "Heaven help my assassin when those barbarians get their hands on him. I have seen their work up close." Ghalib stops to stroke his beard before he continues.

"Ibn Abi Amir seems to hold some odd sway over the Berbers. He speaks their language, he adopts their ways." He grimaces. "Suddenly, Ibn Abi Amir is the most conservative Muslim in Africa. He never misses prayer, and he shouts the five pillars of the faith from the mountaintop. He is ready with a quick curse for the Christians and the Jews and wonders aloud why they are given free reign by the caliph. Treason. He has even given up wine, and wears a black turban like the Berbers."

Ghalib locks his eyes first on the caliph, then on Jafar. "The man changes himself to suit the needs of the moment. Means to an end. The question is, what end? Human chameleons are always dangerous, Jafar, you know that."

"Indeed. Caution is certainly warranted. Sire?"

The caliph seems more coherent now. "I understand the concern, gentlemen, and I share it. And Ibn Abi Amir did breach protocol with his impertinent letter. Still, having Berber cavalry at my disposal for defense of the city will calm the fears of Córdoba. With Ghalib and the army away fighting White Hands at Gormaz, the city could become a tempting target for León or Navarre. If we plant the appropriate rumors in the north, the Berber cavalry could be used to our advantage to sow seeds of doubt among the Christian kingdoms. Even with Ghalib and the army away, they would think twice about marching on a Córdoba guarded by fanatical Berber cavalry itching to renew jihad."

Jafar grins as Ghalib frowns.

Ghalib says, "Dangerous, Sire. I do not like it; too many unknowns."

The caliph responds, "Let us not forget, Ghalib, my Slavic Guard can ably defend Madinat al-Zahra in your absence. The Berbers are no risk to the royal court. There will only be a thousand of them, after all."

General Ghalib offers only a weary sigh, but he is clearly not happy.

Jafar says, "I agree. How about this, Sire? When the Berbers arrive, we stage an elaborate ceremony of welcome and then insist that they swear personal allegiance to the caliph publicly as Córdoba looks on."

The caliph replies, "Good, good, I like that."

General Ghalib seems resigned. "I would recommend not telling Ibn Abi Amir of this twist until he is here and is helpless to prevent it. The man must be carefully watched, Sire."

The caliph and Jafar nod their agreement.

"And the Berbers must not be allowed to set up camp anywhere near Madinat al-Zahra."

Jafar answers, "No, definitely not. We could construct a settlement for them across the river so they have no easy access to the city or Madinat."

Ghalib chimes in, "We would need to refortify the Puente Romano to prevent a crossing."

Jafar replies, "Yes. We should establish a new garrison on the other side of the Guadalquivir. That should send Ibn Abi Amir and his Berber horsemen a clear message."

Ghalib says, "At the Roman Tower. Easily defended."

The caliph muses, then says, "Good. Make it so. Jafar, draft a letter to Ibn Abi Amir. Leave out all of the details we have discussed."

"Certainly, Sire."

"And Ghalib?"

"Yes, Sire?"

"A quick victory at Gormaz. Let us put an end to the ambitions of White Hands once and for all, and remind him of Córdoba's authority. I want you back in the city by the end of the year."

"It shall be so, Sire," he assures the caliph without a hint of doubt.

"Good. It is settled, then."

As the caliph rises his knees begin to quiver. As his eyes lose focus, his legs buckle and he folds to the floor. Jafar rushes to his side as Ghalib shouts for the Slavic Guard.

Ceremonies

The man lies face up on the scorching sand, spread eagle and naked, his joints cinched tightly with rope, then staked. A thin strap of leather crosses his forehead and is anchored to the earth on either side so that he cannot move his head. A fly caught in a spider web.

He has been this way for almost two hours now, and already the ghostly pale of his exposed flesh has been exchanged for a seared red. Thin rows of blisters mark the lines where his back, bottom, and legs touch the sand, swelled tight as gorged ticks.

His only view all morning has been the deep blue of the sky. But as the sun has relentlessly climbed in the sky to torment him, its blinding molten gold forces him into a tight squint. Sweat pools at the corners of his eyes, bloats, then spills its sting, forcing his eyes to blink away the torment. He squeezes his eyes shut for a brief reprieve, only to reopen them a moment later to begin the process anew.

The only evidence that he is not alone is the hushed cadence of hundreds of voices reciting the *dhuhr* prayer somewhere off to his right. He struggles to turn his head but cannot.

The man's face is a portrait of unadulterated terror. His eyes flit anxiously right and left, up and down, close then reopen. No one. Nothing. Only the soft tones of recited noon prayer that are somehow menacing, building to some kind of climax.

His heart pounds. He softly groans.

Abruptly the prayer halts. The sting of sweat forces his eyes to pinch close. He hears the silky crush of leather upon sand, the footfall of dozens of approaching knights.

He begins to whimper. He feels it before he sees it. Cool shade upon his face. A miracle. Someone uses a cloth to gingerly wipe his face. Drops of water are dribbled onto his cracked and peeling lips. He licks desperately with a swollen tongue and is answered with the mercy of a single sip. He opens his eyes.

Ibn Abi Amir stands above him to his left, al-Andalusi to his right. Dozens of Berber knights gather round the spread-eagle man.

Al-Andalusi begins, "You have Berber blood, Salim, but you have been corrupted by the blasphemy of the Córdoban Arabs. You have violated Sharaf, Salim. You have betrayed the qadi of

the Maghreb. You have betrayed the welcome of the Banu Birzal."
He stops and spits on the man. "For this you shall die a horrible
death."

The man begins to blubber.

Contempt drips from al-Andalusi's words. "You coward! You
shame the Rif, Salim, with your lack of courage to face your
chosen destiny. How could you ever imagine we would not
discover your plan? I will not corrupt my dagger with your blood.
Instead you shall suffer long and you shall suffer much."

Al-Andalusi turns to his right. "Cover his eyes."

As the world goes black, the man cries out and begins to beg.

He feels a thin stream of sticky cool plop heavily onto to his
belly, puddle into a slick mess, then trace an arc to his groin. It
smothers his penis with sticky wetness and then crisscrosses his
upper thighs, back and forth, back and forth. A sweet floral smell
permeates the air.

The man struggles against his bindings, but he cannot move.

"Honey, my friend, precious desert honey. A shame to waste it
on your poor soul, I will concede, but there is a fine point to be
made here. Think back to your childhood in Tangier, Salim.
Surely you remember the famous soldier ants of the Rif. Not the
small stinging brown ones. No, the big black soldiers as long as
the joint on your little finger. The ones with the big ripping
pincers. Do you recall, Salim? During the cool of the night they
emerge from their nests and travel as an army in search of prey.
Their queen has a keen taste for flesh." He pauses to let the
horror sink in. "They can strip the meat from a goat's bones before
the sun rises. I have seen it many times, Salim."

The man whimpers.

"Quiet, coward." He spits again. "It seems that the queen of
the soldier ants also has a sweet tooth, Salim. The elders tell me
that she can smell honey from a league away and will march her
army over any terrain to find it."

Silence.

"Tonight, the queen and her soldiers will come calling for you.
I cannot say exactly when, I am afraid, but rest assured, come for
you they will. We will guard you to ensure that the jackals are
kept safely away. By morning, however, the only trace left of you,
Salim, will be your bones, which I will crush to dust and scatter to
the wind."

"Please, Ibn Abi Amir, have mercy! Protect me from these
barbarians! Mercy, Ibn Abi Amir! I was only doing General
Ghalib's bidding. You know he wanted you dead. I have a family,

Ibn Abi Amir, children! Please! Grant me Allah's mercy!" The man breaks into thick sobs.

As the cries dull to a whimper, Ibn Abi Amir softly says, "There is no Ibn Abi Amir, Salim. There is only Qadi of the Maghreb. And he is now Banu Birzal."

The men gathered round shout out, "Long live the qadi of the Maghreb! Long live the qadi of the Maghreb!"

"Goodbye, Salim. I will pray for your soul."

"Save me, Qadi of the Maghreb, save me!"

Ibn Abi Amir and al-Andalusi turn for camp. Not another word is spoken. The desperate pleas continue for another half hour, then weaken, then finally dry up, swallowed whole by the scorching heat.

It is just before midnight when they hear the first startled scream, a jolt of sharp surprise. The desperate begging resumes. Within fifteen minutes the sounds have risen to a piercing caterwaul of agony. After some time the screams turn hoarse then weaken, but don't cease until two hours before sunrise. Several final anguished spurts disappear into the chilled night breeze.

By first light the boiling black mass has begun departing for the safety of their tunnel lair. The white bones remain staked in the sand, the joints still strung tightly. A shock of tangled hair, black and frizzled against the fleshless skull. The greedy stragglers, gorged and heavy, emerge from his eye sockets, the sweet taste of brain still pink and fresh on their pincers. They sniff the wind then scurry to catch up with the galloping horde.

The room is awash in the pleasing soft tones thrown by dim candlelight. The menagerie of shadows cast by the flickering flames leap and sway seductively upon the carved arabesque walls. The room is quiet, ceremonial, a held breath laden with anticipation.

Jibril is dressed in his most luxurious finery, flowing silks and golden lace, accented by his exquisite collection of jewels and gold. His elaborate makeup is a striking collection of purple and crimson and umber, his hands and arms a lacy spider's web of henna art, all coils and tight swirls, a calculus of patterns.

There is a breathless excitement in Jibril's movements, the thrill of unopened gifts, of hidden surprises. He fusses about, checking and rechecking, straightening and shifting, removing a faint smudge from polished wood with a moistened thumb.

Three divans are arrayed in a line in the center of the room, flanked at each end by a towering candelabra. These divans are miniature in size, too small to fit adults; something one might see in a child's room.

A tall, slender table rests to the front of the divans. On it rests a carefully arranged collection of objects: a codex opened to a marked page; an oil lamp with a blue teardrop of flame; a blown flask half full of some viscous amber liquid; three small crystal cups; an enameled golden bowl studded with rubies; three curved needles threaded with a long strand of catgut; and a miniature ceremonial dagger. The dagger's sheath is ornate and bejeweled, the workmanship exquisite. A priceless heirloom with bloodlines tracing to ancient days when Damascus was still ruled by the Umayyads.

Jibril fidgets with his arrangement of the table for the third time. Satisfied, he lifts the dagger and carefully pulls the blade. His eyes widen as the mirror sheen lengthens. The shape of the blade is unusual. A thin, curved ribbon of steel. The ground cutting edge is on the inner curve of the blade, not the outer. Most unusual.

As he lightly touches his thumb to the ribbon to test its edge, the tip of his tongue sneaks between his lips, coaxed forward by his ecstasy. He presses just enough to raise a fine line of blood, then releases. Razor sharp. His heavy sigh is laden with the sweet satisfaction of conquest, almost sexual in its intensity.

The deep, pleasing resonance of a ceremonial gong sounds once, twice, three times, then the door to the room opens. Three red-robed eunuchs of the royal harem enter with a formal stiffness, followed by three young boys dressed in white silk gowns, blond, brunette, then redheaded, then another eunuch. The door closes to three additional gong strikes, the rich reverberation lingering in the air then evaporating. Shadows dance upon the walls.

Jibril opens his arms in welcome. "Welcome to the Royal Harem of Madinat al-Zahra. Tonight, a great honor will be bestowed upon each of you."

The boys look angelic, their eyes wide, their postures stiff and tentative. They cannot understand a word he is saying.

Jibril's smile is magnificent.

"You boys have been chosen for a special life, a life that is forbidden to all but the most worthy. A life of wealth and honor, a life of privilege and luxury. You will wield great power. You will be envied. You will be feared."

The boy's expressions have not changed.

Jibril steps towards them and motions with his palm. "Please, recline upon your divans."

The boys' wary eyes follow his palm. Jibril becomes more insistent, guiding the blond boy to the divan, then arranging him. Two of the eunuchs guide the other boys to their divans.

Jibril surveys. Satisfied, he says, "Good, good. Please relax." He turns to the table and pours the viscous amber liquid into each of the three crystal cups. Three eunuchs each lift a cup and bring it to the boys.

"Drink, drink." Jibril mimes his desire. The boys stare nervously at their cups, but after another urgent instruction and a nudge from the eunuchs, they drink the sweet syrup. Smiles sprout on the boys' faces. They lick their lips. Delicious.

"Excellent ..." Jibril returns to the table, lifts the codex, and begins to recite the *Rite of Passage, the Way of the Eunuch*. As his lips move feverishly, the boys' eyes begin their leaden droop. Heads nod then bob, each jerk widening their eyes for only an instant, only to droop once more. Soon they cannot hold their heads up. The eunuchs guide them back against their divans. Their eyes fold closed.

Jibril comes to the end of his recitation and pauses for a response. The six eunuchs of the royal harem answer in unison, "So let it be done, let the honor of the chosen life begin. Amen."

Jibril closes the codex and lays it back on the table. He lifts the dagger, withdraws the blade, then permits it to kiss the swaying blue flame. He slides it back and forth, back and forth. He glides to the first divan, kneels, and affectionately strokes the boy's wispy blond hair. Then he traces a slow arc across the boy's cheek with the back of his finger. He delicately shifts the boy's legs, lifts his silk gown, and leans in with his dagger.

A half-hour later, the ceremony has ended and the boys are taken back to their new homes, three small but plush rooms in the royal harem that they will occupy their entire lives.

Jibril is alone now with the dancing shadows. He cradles the golden bowl in both hands, his eyes adoring its hidden treasure. Six wet, grayish-pink, tiny egg-like orbs, each delicately laced with blood vessels. One could mistake the bowl for a sparrow's nest.

The eyes of the head eunuch of the royal harem are wide, awestruck, the tip of his tongue pressed tight to his ruby lip.

By Bedouin custom, the formalities of the wedding ceremony, the *nikah*, take place at sunrise, but the celebration lasts until midnight—and only then will the marriage be consummated. The morning, afternoon, and evening are filled with lavish feasting, celebratory games, the rich rhythms of Bedouin music and song, seductive veil dances by lithe young women, back slaps and ribald teasing, bright laughter and frivolity. How ironic that a people with such capacity for quick and deadly violence can so enjoy a good party.

Bedouin wedding feasts are a rare time when young men and women of the clan are permitted to gather and mingle, exchange shy, furtive glances from the safety of their respective male and female throngs. The bolder ones will begin to flirt, perhaps even offer whispered words of promise and desire. It is here that the beginnings of commitment are made, that stirrings of love and union are first floated then tested, often to later blossom. Parents watch that decorum is obeyed but silently smile at their sons and daughters as they tiptoe into the circle of life.

As the evening begins to ripen, the festivities shift in tone. Musical instruments are laid down and families begin to drift one by one to the bonfire to listen to the embellished stories of the elders of the clan. Young, dewy eyes widen with the stretch of hands and exaggerated tones of the clan's revered ancient leaders. The crack and pop of the roaring fire sends sparks shivering into the pulsing diamonds high above. The night chill draws people closer to the thick bed of crimson coals.

The young people have heard these stories dozens of times, of course, and know many of them by heart, yet they beg the elders for more. The birth of the universe, the first difficult days of the clan, the many victories over their rivals, their heroes, the cherished elders long since passed, even the clan's tragedies and betrayals. So grow the rich, collective knots of memory of the desert Berbers, the legacy of the Banu Birzal, the new rulers of the Rif Mountains of the Maghreb.

Ibn Abi Amir has ascended the ladder of respect within the clan. His opinion is sought, his answers valued. The married women wink and whisper as he passes; he is a handsome man, after all. The knights puff up proudly under his compliments, and the girls approaching marriageable age swoon then giggle from behind tent flaps. The qadi of the Maghreb is Banu Birzal now, and he will be defended at any cost with the clan's blood.

At midnight, under great fanfare, husband and wife are paraded in their wedding regalia by torchlight in and among the clan's hundreds of tents to bless the clan with new life. The two are followed by hundreds of trilling revelers to Ibn Abi Amir's tent, the wedding tent, conveniently removed a stone's throw from the edge of the clan for some small semblance of privacy.

When gathered, the whistling and cheering throng lapse into silence and sprout satisfied smiles. Ibn Abi Amir formally bows to the clan elders, thanks Sheikh Hamid al-Tariq for the great gift of his daughter, looks skyward with open palms and gives praise to Allah, then turns and leads his bride into the tent and closes the flap behind them. Satisfied, the clan turns for their tents.

He sighs his relief. Finally, some peace. The sounds of the crowd begin to grow fainter then disappear. He crosses the expansive tent and lights a single oil lamp beside his bed. A soft dusky glow fills the space. He removes his outer robes, then turns and looks back at the entrance to his tent. She stands motionless where she entered, eyes glued to the carpet. By Bedouin tradition, a new wife must be formally invited into her husband's tent. And his bed.

She wears the finest white silks the clan possesses, thankfully not the drab black robes of clan females. Still, even a common merchant in Córdoba would possess better. Her face is carefully obscured; has been since the beginning. A lacy silk veil mutes her features, carefully crafted to burnish her allure, to create mystique.

He studies her. She is tiny as a rabbit. Gold dinars from his wedding gift, the *mahr*, are woven into the silk veil, the long jangles completely surrounding her head. She wears an emerald-studded gold bracelet he brought from the goldsmiths of Córdoba. There is no finer jewelry in the Rif.

Ibn Abi Amir sighs again, more heavily now. Ulla. The favorite daughter of Hamid al-Tariq, Sheikh of the Banu Birzal. Now the wife of the qadi of the Maghreb. His wife. The burden of it all weighs on him.

She is a child. Easily five years younger than Rayhana, perhaps more. He recalls the shiekh's words: *Ulla, my desert flower, my pride and joy, is the most beautiful of my girls. She is past her first bleeding moon; she is of age. She shall be yours.*

Past her first bleeding moon ... Ibn Abi Amir frowns. What to do? His machinery begins a complex set of calculations as he weighs his options.

She is a statue of silk and gold.

Decision made, he crosses the room and extends his palm to her. She tentatively places her small hand in his, but her eyes remain glued to the carpet. "Come, Ulla, you are welcome in my tent."

Her eyes do not budge. He steps closer to her, and with both hands lifts the veil of coins from her face.

An exquisite desert flower. He sees now that her father did not exaggerate her looks.

He methodically removes the combs from her hair, first one then the other. Midnight ringlets spill down her back. He studies his new wife. A beautiful girl. He nibbles his inner cheek as his breathing quickens. He lifts her chin with his finger and her eyes meet his for the first time. His pupils widen then are swallowed whole by her molten ebony. Here is the stuff of desert legend. The timeless, convulsive thrill of a beautiful young Bedouin virgin.

His heart begins to race. "You are welcome in my tent, Wife."

After a long pause the girl speaks, her voice surprisingly steady and confident. "I am honored to be your wife, Qadi of the Maghreb."

Ibn Abi Amir frowns. "To you, Ulla, I am only Muhammad."

She shyly nods. "I will serve you well, Muhammad. I will tend your tent and prepare your meals. I will bear your sons. They will be feared knights of the Banu Birzal, and their names will be whispered with awe around the clan bonfire for generations to come."

A satisfied smile eases onto his face. "Come, Ulla, you are welcome to share my bed. I shall have none but you, my desert flower. Come, Ulla, let me teach you the ways of love. Come ..."

He leads her across the tent. Under the soft glow of the lamp he begins to slowly undress her.

The narrow web of alleys between the city walls and the river are absolutely mobbed, the air charged with reverie; the heady thrill of a long-anticipated festival finally come. Each person has been supplied a small red ochre and white flag tied to a long pole. The colors of the caliph.

General Ghalib and the army break camp at sunrise at Madinat al-Zahra to begin the journey north to the Upper Marches, to Gormaz. The red and gold clad Royal Guard stand at attention on both sides of the Almunya Way the entire distance between Madinat al-Zahra and Córdoba.

As the lead element of the cavalry reaches the city, they turn and begin to cross the Puente Romano across the Guadalquivir, thousands of flags begin to frantically wave back and forth, back and forth, a sea of slashing color. Thunderous cheers ring out then march alongside the long column of troops.

Toddlers are lifted onto shoulders that rotate here and there at the many wondrous sights. The City Watch crowds Córdoba's walls closest to the river to get a glimpse of the famous Sword of the Caliph.

The scene is packed, tight with emotion. Here are Córdoba's best troops marching off to defend the kingdom with their lives. Scarfed mothers spontaneously burst into tears at the tense majesty of the moment. Fathers stand erect and proud, their arms gathered round their families protectively. Elder sons stand rapt, eyes wide with awe, dreaming of a day when they too might fight for Córdoba's honor. Their sisters, at least those of a certain age, exchange furious whispers behind opened palms as the sea of handsome young men file past.

The army is stretched into a thin line reaching nearly all the way back to Madinat al-Zahra: six thousand cavalry, nine thousand infantry, and two thousand archers, then hundreds of supply wagons and a thousand rear-guard cavalry. The troops look fresh and groomed, ready to battle Satan himself.

General Ghalib, in his finest ceremonials, leads the way atop Taneen. As he passes, rolling echoes of "Sword of the Caliph! SWORD OF THE CALIPH!" ring out, then dog him. He ignores the crowd, as usual, his famous grimace chiseled into stone, eyes stern and locked forward. He is thinking already about his options for attack and how best to break the siege leveled upon Gormaz by White Hands.

"Allahu Akbar! ALLAHU AKBAR! SWORD OF THE CALIPH! SWORD OF THE CALIPH!"

Schemer Schemed

21 September 976.

The man is ghostly pale, his cheeks sunken, his eyes hollow and vacant. He looks a decade older than his sixty-one years.

Abu al-Qasim slides his hand under the man's head and gently lifts it. "Sire, you must drink. I have prepared my famous brew, just for your pleasure." His voice turns playful. "It is widely held by my children, Sire, that my brew tastes so awful that it can scare disease from the body."

The man's vacant eyes focus slightly, and a hint of a smile tickles the corners of his mouth.

Abu al-Qasim chuckles affectionately. "Who am I to argue? Good, Sire, good. Two more sips and we will be done."

The slurps are crude and unbecoming.

"Excellent, Sire. Now you must sleep. You will feel better when you awake, I promise. Then, more of my tasty brew." He chuckles again.

The caliph's gaze begins to blur and his eyes droop then close, are forced open once more against their will, then close for good. His breathing is shallow and quick.

Abu al-Qasim continues to study the caliph's face. He stands and turns to Jafar. The royal physician's expression says it all.

Jafar takes a deep breath then exhales. "Tell me the truth."

"The caliph is dying, Jafar. I have never seen any disease quite like it. No fever or chills, no tenderness in his organs, no jaundice, no wound or infection. Just this general malaise that slowly but surely grows worse. Much worse now, I am afraid." He hesitates. "He is barely producing water, and he cannot hold solid food down. My brew will sustain him for a while, but only for a while." Another hesitation. "His organs are beginning to fail."

Jafar opens his mouth to speak then closes it.

"I am not sure what else to try, Jafar. I am at the limits of my powers."

"Would surgery be possible? Perhaps he has some parasite within him."

"Two weeks ago, yes. Today, no. He is too weak. If I open his body it will kill him." Abu al-Qasim muses. "No, I think rest is all that can be done. Rest."

233

Jafar is lost in thought. He folds his arms behind him as he stares at the floor and calculates. He looks up. "Do you think it is possible the caliph was poisoned?"

Abu al-Qasim's eyes widen. "Poisoned? The royal kitchen has an army of tasters, Jafar. How could he have been poisoned?"

"I have no idea. I was just curious of your opinion ..."

Another weary sigh. "This has none of the signs of any poison that I am aware of. Those favored by assassins are quick acting, leading to paralysis of the breathing muscles. Some will ruin the liver over several weeks. But that produces jaundice, which he does not have. It has been months now since the caliph first complained of feeling ill. He shows none of the symptoms consistent with a poison."

"Yes, I understand. Still ..."

"My knowledge of poisons is admittedly limited, so I cannot be sure, but it does not appear to me to be the case."

"I see. Thank you, Abu al-Qasim. The caliph values your loyalty and expert medical attention."

"I am the caliph's humble servant. The kingdom owes the man a great debt. As do I. It is time for us to pray, Jafar. We must pray that Allah in his great mercy and compassion rid our beloved caliph of this terrible malady."

"Prayer. Yes ..." Jafar looks distracted. He looks up and into the royal physician's eyes. "The caliph's dire condition must remain a secret at court, Abu al-Qasim. For now. Contingency plans must be put into place."

The royal physician nods soberly. "I understand."

"Your father is ill." Her tone is matter-of-fact.

The boy's eyes slowly rise from the page. His mother reclines on her divan, reading. She has not even bothered to look up.

"What ails him?"

"Abu al-Qasim does not seem to know."

The boy's voice tightens. "Is it serious?"

She hesitates before answering. "Yes, I am afraid it is."

The boy closes his book and sits up straight. His eyes have not left her. Finally, she looks up.

"Why did you not tell me sooner, Mother?"

She flicks her hand dismissively. "I did not want to worry you, Hisham." She licks her lips. "But I have just learned that his condition worsens. I thought you should know."

The boy whispers, "Will my father die?"

Her azure eyes bore into him. "Come sit, Hisham. It is time for a serious talk." She indicates the end of her divan. "Come ... please. We must talk, Hisham."

The boy hesitates, but in the end, he rises and takes up his station at the end of her divan. She has not moved a muscle. She studies him in silence, her face devoid of all emotion. His eyes wilt to his lap under her gaze.

A hint of a smile is her only response. "Your father will die, Hisham. Soon."

When the boy looks up his eyes are filled.

She studies him.

"What will become of us, Mother?"

A single tear spills, first from one eye, then the other.

She fights to keep her disgust from showing. Her voice rises slightly with a tinge of bite. "What will become of us?" She frowns, then takes a deep breath, exhales her bile. "You will assume your rightful place as caliph. THAT is what will become of us, Hisham."

The boy's lower lip is quivering now and tears are starting to stream. "But I do not wish to be caliph, Mother." He sniffs. "I do not have the training."

She sits up and slides close to him. His eyes wilt back to his lap. She forces his chin up and turns his face to hers. Her eyes are dilated, crowding her piercing azure into a thin, neat circle.

She smiles. "Hisham."

He sniffs.

"As sultana, I will serve as your regent until you come of age." She studies him. "Ibn Abi Amir will help me train you for your future role as caliph. He will be our ... partner in ruling the kingdom until you are ready. Do you understand what I am saying?"

The boy's voice brightens. "Will the Vizier Council permit this?"

Her smile widens. "By your decree, son, it shall be so. You will be caliph, and your word will be final. The Vizier Council will bend their knees to you, Hisham. All of al-Andalus will bend their knees to you."

The boy has ceased crying. He wipes his eyes. "Can we please leave the royal harem?"

She laughs loudly. "THAT, dear Hisham, shall happen on the first day of your reign!"

He nods and smiles weakly. "When will Ibn Abi Amir return from the Maghreb?"

She beams. "Soon, very soon, my love. All will be well, you will see. He will teach you all you need to know about being caliph.

The people will adore you, Hisham; you will be a wonderful caliph."

The boy's eyes grow. "He said he would bring me a gift from the Maghreb."

She laughs again. "Yes, Hisham, Ibn Abi Amir will come bearing many gifts. For both of us."

The boy's smile widens.

The three men sit cross-legged on silk pillows in a tight ring about the bubbling floor fountain. The flowing water provides a lovely artistic accent in Jafar's library, but its principal function is to prevent eavesdropping.

The three have exchanged pleasantries over tea for twenty minutes now; trade delegations, acquisitions, poetry readings, Gormaz, the usual. Jafar allows the conversation to die a natural death then dismisses his servants with a flick of his wrist. The silence inflates, mingling playfully with the aquatic gurgle.

"Faiq and Jawdhar, I have asked you here this morning for a serious conversation ... a conversation requiring the utmost secrecy and discretion. A delicate matter concerning the caliph."

The two answer in tandem, "You have our solemn word, Jafar." These two seem unfazed. They are completely at ease with secrets.

"Gentlemen, you have heard rumors that the caliph has not been feeling well for some time now."

The saqalibas nod as one. Their rumor network is the best in Madinat al-Zahra.

"I am afraid I have ... cultivated the rumors to obscure the truth. In fact, the caliph is gravely ill, and he worsens by the day." He pauses. "Abu al-Qasim does not hold any hope for the caliph's recovery. His organs are beginning to fail."

This produces genuine surprise.

Faiq grimaces, then shakes his head and says, "We had no idea it was that serious, Jafar."

"That was by intent, Faiq. As you can understand, if the enemies of the caliph sense a power vacuum looms, the kingdom would be at grave risk. Very dangerous, especially with White Hands on the march and Gormaz under siege."

"Of course. A prudent decision, Jafar."

Jawdhar says, "If I might be so bold, Jafar ... is there any evidence of foul play? As you know, Ibn Abi Amir continues to write covert letters to the most ambitious merchant families in

Córdoba. We have it on good authority that he seeks to ally himself with those families ... against the caliph."

Faiq adds, "And he continues to write to the sultana and the boy."

Jafar shrugs. "Abu al-Qasim does not think it was poison, but who can be certain?"

Silence.

"Gentlemen, the caliph has been very clear about one thing. He does not wish Hisham to assume the role of caliph should he pass from this world. He feels the boy is too weak and does not possess the skills needed for able leadership of al-Andalus. The caliph fears he would bring the kingdom to ruin."

Their tandem response is matter-of-fact. "We agree."

"And there is the matter of the sultana. If the caliph dies, it seems obvious that Subh will attempt to assume the role of regent to rule in the boy's place until he is of age. An extremely distasteful proposition, given her ambitions."

A collective, "Agreed. Extremely distasteful."

"What I am proposing, gentlemen, is that the caliph's brother, al-Mughira ibn al-Nasir, assume the role of caliph in the event that al-Hakam dies." He pauses. "I have already spoken with al-Mughira about this. He has agreed to serve if required."

Silence.

Faiq lowers his voice and speaks slowly and precisely. "Jafar, breaking the defined rules of succession of the Umayyad caliphate could be considered treason. The sultana will howl, of course, but I worry more about the merchant families in Córdoba. They would relish any excuse to rise up against Madinat al-Zahra. They have no love for al-Mughira, that much is sure, and Ibn Abi Amir has been steadfast in fanning the flames of discontent within the city."

Jafar replies, "I agree. That is where your skills are most needed. If this transition is to occur peacefully, we must have the support of the Vizier Council, the support of the Slavic and Royal Guard, and the support of the saqaliba in the positions of highest power within Madinat al-Zahra. And the blessing of the grand imam, of course. If we are united, gentlemen, and have the backing of the military and the imams, mullahs, and qadis at court, Córdoba will be compelled to acquiesce."

The spittle-splash of the floor fountain grows loud in the lingering silence.

Jafar continues, "I can deliver the Vizier Council. Sadly, Ibn Abi Amir's absence will prevent him from voting." He smiles wryly. "And the Slavic Guard will respect the caliph's wishes. The grand imam will require finesse, but I am confident I can convince him that it is in his best interests to anoint al-Mughira as caliph. The question is, can you deliver the saqaliba within Madinat al-Zahra, especially the Royal Guard? Those who do not wish to be involved must at minimum remain neutral and must not interfere."

Jawdhar says, "Does Ghalib know?"

"Yes. He understands there are no other options. With the Christian threat looming, a smooth transition of power to a capable leader is of paramount importance, especially now. He is with us, and the army will follow Ghalib."

Faiq and Jawdhar exchange a quick glance. Faiq says, "We can deliver the saqaliba of Madinat al-Zahra, Jafar. And the Royal Guard will stand with us. Al-Mughira shall be the chosen successor to Caliph al-Hakam II."

Jafar nods. "Good. Then it is done."

Jawdhar says, "How long do you expect the caliph to live?"

"Difficult to say. A week, perhaps two." Jafar shakes his head. "Not long. We must move quickly, gentlemen. No one must know when the caliph dies. Al-Mughira must be secretly sworn in before we make the announcement to the city."

Faiq says, "Agreed. What of the sultana and Hisham?"

"They will be exiled quietly to some remote location. I am pursuing connections in Majorca that should suit our needs."

Jawdhar adds, "And Ibn Abi Amir? He could make trouble for us."

Jafar smiles. "I have it on good authority that Ibn Abi Amir will not leave the Maghreb until the new year. He is presently training a cavalry force to be placed in the service of the caliph against the Christians. By the time he arrives in Córdoba al-Mughira will already be caliph. Ibn Abi Amir and his Berber cavalry will be required to pledge their fealty to Caliph al-Mughira or return to the barren desert of Africa."

A tandem nod. "Excellent."

The day is clear and pleasant, the swelter of the summer heat tempered by a refreshing edge of coolness. The air is still, the scene tranquil. A dust cloud loops and rolls in the distance, rising from behind the distant ridge rimming the western edge of the Vega de Granada. The cloud begins to boil forward towards the city, gaining heft and lengthening. One by one, the field laborers stand erect as they notice the odd storm. They lean lazily on their spades, curious.

A throaty rumble of thunder rises from behind the ridge and grows steadily in intensity. Several laborers cup their ears then mouth an explanation to their neighbors. Nods are exchanged. Tense expressions slide onto the men's faces but they do not otherwise move.

As the dust cloud breaks over the crest of the ridge, the red ochre and white banners of the caliph come into view. The two lead riders raise their right arms, slow to a trot, then halt. It takes a full minute for the rolling thunder to dissipate. The clot of dust begins to settle.

Al-Andalusi surveys the valley. "What city is this?"

Ibn Abi Amir replies, "Granada." He points to the small fortress at the end of the long, narrow promontory to the east. "See the castle?"

Al-Andalusi nods curtly. "Not nearly as defensible as Hajar an-Nasar."

"No, it is not. Granada is small and poor compared to Córdoba, but important to al-Andalus, nonetheless. The city was settled first by the Romans, then the Christians. Muslims have lived here since the original Maghrebi jihad, over two hundred and fifty years now. Granada is famous for its fine silks and ceramics. And its food." He lifts his palm to the verdant Vega.

"How many live within the walls?"

"Perhaps ten thousand. The Jews joined the Christians and Muslims a hundred years back and the three now live together within the city. A common model in al-Andalus, my brother, courtesy of the Umayyad caliphs."

Al-Andalusi spits. "The Banu Birzal do not believe that Christians and Jews should be permitted to live among the faithful, Qadi of the Maghreb. They corrupt our purity."

Ibn Abi Amir shrugs. "I do not disagree, al-Andalusi. Still, the Sultan of Granada is well-regarded by the caliph."

"How long before we reach Córdoba, Qadi of the Maghreb?"

"If we ride hard, four days."

Al-Andalusi's eyes sparkle. "Qadi of the Maghreb, the Banu Birzal live to ride hard."

Ibn Abi Amir smiles. "Let us make haste, then. The wagons can follow later with their escort. The end of Ramadan approaches. We may even make *Eid al-Fitr* if we press—Córdoba during the Sugar Feast festival is a sight to behold, my brother. Let us water our horses in the Darro River then turn west and push for Córdoba."

Al-Andalusi pivots in his saddle then pumps his fist in the air. "Banu Birzal! We ride for glory! We ride for jihad! Long live the qadi of the Maghreb!"

"ALLAHU AKBAR! ALLAHU AKBAR! ALLAHU AKBAR!"

Ibn Abi Amir and al-Andalusi exchange knowing smiles then kick their stallions to life. The lead column explodes forward, folds over the ridge, and spills into the Vega, the dust cloud dogging their route once more. The rolling thunder of a thousand Berber cavalry rumbles to life and roars out onto the plain.

Promises

They are in their usual places: side by side on their plush floor pillows, shoulders kissing, hunched forward over the thin, leather-bound codex, two sets of elbows resting on the table. Her fingers are meshed, supporting her chin; his fists are balled, glued to his cheeks.

Her eyes race right-to-left, right-to-left, as they move quickly down the page. She reads faster than he does, so from time to time he is forced to skim to keep up. Her expression is one of rapt awe.

He takes great delight in her obvious joy. This is her first opportunity to devour *Antigone*. Sophocles is a consummate master of the Greek tragic form; Zafir's favorite after Euripides. This translation is his and, as with others, he knows long passages by heart.

While he makes a show of chasing her down the page, he indulges himself frequently with a clandestine study of her face; the soft lines of her cheekbones, the wisp of down gracing her earlobes, the perfection of her lips. And always those dangling spirals of brown that are impossible to tame. He is careful not to attract her attention, and after months of training he has grown skillful in maneuvering only his eyes to savor her while she reads.

She has happily melded with the neat Arabic script on the page, oblivious. She releases the lock of her fingers, turns the page and flattens the paper with a crinkle, then resurrects her pedestal. Her eyes have not wavered from the codex. The quick right-to-left tracking resumes unabated. She is clearly enthralled by the story.

He grins. He removes his left fist from his cheek, unkinks it, then allows his hand to wander, a finger casually twisting into a spiral of brown at her temple.

She does not seem to notice.

Emboldened, he releases the spring and lightly traces the curve of her ear.

She absentmindedly shakes her head as if to shoo a fly.

He blows softly.

She lifts her head and sighs, mildly annoyed. "Zafir ..."

He feigns complete innocence. "Yes, Rayhana?"

She turns to face him. "Zafir, it is *Ramadan*. Remember our agreement, please." Her grin sprouts then blossoms. "Focus, my love, focus."

"No kissing or touching." He sighs. "Thirty days is a long time, Rayhana."

"*Eid al-Fitr* is only three days away," She replies with an impish grin. "Pray to Allah for strength, Zafir. Only three days."

He smiles. "Three days is an eternity, Rayhana."

She shoulder-bumps him in a mock scold, and they both laugh.

"This is a fascinating story. Can we please read?" She uses her eyebrows to exaggerate her response.

He nods and rejoins his fists to his cheeks. Her eyes bore into the words. He resumes his chase. He will begin studying her face again before ten minutes have passed.

She turns the page. King Creon has just learned that Antigone defied his edict and buried Polyneices, a capital crime. Creon is livid that she, a Greek woman, would challenge his authority as King of Thebes. He accuses her; she offers no denial. Antigone proclaims Creon's edict unjust and immoral and her own defiant actions to be in keeping with the will of the gods. Creon sentences her to death.

Rayhana gasps.

Zafir turns to her, sees that her eyes have welled up.

"Rayhana?"

Tears spill, then her lower lip begins to quiver.

"Darling?"

Without looking up she slowly whispers, "I ... am ... Antigone." The pause stretches. Her voice quavers, "My father is King Creon."

He hugs her to him. "No, Rayhana, no." He realizes too late that she might interpret the play as a commentary on their plight. He thinks: Wait until she sees how it ends.

He sighs. "Rayhana. Sophocles uses his story to comment on the tragedy of unchecked pride and the dangers of tyranny to a free society. Antigone is in the right, of course; Creon will come to regret his decision."

She doesn't seem consoled. Her shoulders softly shake as she starts to cry.

"Come, my love, let us take a break." He marks the page and closes the codex, then turns her to face him.

She sniffs. "I am scared, Zafir. What will become of us? My father will bring a Berber prince with him from the Maghreb, I know he will. What will we do then, Zafir, what will we do?"

He pulls her head tight to his chest. "Shhhhh ... shhhhh ..."

It breaks his heart when she cries like this. He holds her to him in silence to allow the storm to pass. A final sniff and a heaving gasp, then she quiets.

He whispers, "We will marry, Rayhana. Your father cannot prevent us from being together. Samuel and Rebekah will help us find a way. Samuel has already written to Imam Abd al-Gafur and requested an audience. He is due in the city for Eid. Your father will not return until the new year. We have time."

She hugs him tighter.

He lifts her chin, emeralds penetrating amber. "Before Allah, Rayhana Abi Amir, I profess my love for you." Their eyes well up as one. Zafir's voice quavers, "I betroth myself to you, Rayhana, my beloved. I will love you and cherish you for all eternity. I join my life to your life, my heart to your heart, my soul to your soul. May Allah bless our love and our marriage."

Their eyes are inches apart, bound tightly together, pupils dilated wide, midnight wells a thousand leagues deep. Their souls are stripped bare by the intensity of their love, conjoined by Grace. Emerald spills into amber starburst to produce a third striking color, brighter and bolder than either alone, flecked with shimmering sparkles of gold and silver, the colors of young love.

Tears spill from her eyes. Her chin quiver resumes as she whispers, "Before Allah, Zafir Saffar, I profess my love for you. I betroth myself to you, Zafir, my beloved. I will love you and cherish you for all eternity. I join my life to your life, my heart to your heart, my soul to your soul. May Allah bless our love and our marriage."

Their foreheads lean in to touch.

The codex sees it first, the shimmer of blue that begins to gather in wispy tendrils about them, mist upon a mid-winter's pond. The blue aura thickens and stretches, begins to dance across their shoulders, playfully flit about their heads, circle their joined hands. The book holds its breath tight, dazzled by the strange sight.

The love in the room grows heavy and palpable, a third presence. At the dense center of the quivering aura a strike of blue flame suddenly leaps between their hearts, the radiant flickers delicately lingering upon the lovers.

Their foreheads remain glued, the rhythm of their laden breath, the pounding of their hearts running now in perfect lockstep.

"My beloved."

"My beloved."

"You must believe that Allah will help us find a way, Rayhana. We WILL be together, my love. Say it, Rayhana, say 'I believe.'"

"I believe."

He nods. "It will be our secret word. Our bond."

"I believe, Zafir, I believe."

This thin codex will have a grand yarn to spin upon reshelving; professions of love and commitment, of the strange aura and the dancing blue flames. Soon the tale will be common knowledge among the Greek playwrights. It will not be long, of course, before the poets get wind of it; they always do. They will bend and poke it for clues, twist and stretch it, then lay it flat to the page to fit the opening lines of their next great love poem.

There is a hint of chill on the soft, cottony breeze. The judges of the tug of war between summer and autumn will soon raise the arm of a new victor. The sky is clear and the stars bright, the waning moon a thin sickle low on the horizon. The Shining City slumbers. The shadows in the alleys are long and deep, a playground for those eyes in the city that never sleep.

Though they have met dozens of times, they rarely exchange more than a quick whisper. Their ebony eyes can say it all.

These two are skilled at their profession; masters of the art of misdirection and stealth, of discreet observation, the press of gold into palms, of veiled threats. Both are experts with a blade, each experienced in slipping a needle dagger up under the ribs and into the heart or slitting a throat. They are feared by the few who know of their existence. And rightly so. These two are dangerous men, though only if cornered—or commanded. They much prefer to flit from shadow to shadow unseen, tending to the networks that are the eyes and ears of their masters.

Aslam has no love of Bundar, that much is certain, but he does respect the man's art. Aslam possesses Berber roots, and there is an off-putting taint about his counterpart, the wraith of the royal harem, an Arab, a rank air of condescension. This innate claim of primacy offends Aslam. It is as if the royal harem were Bundar's private domain, Subh and Jibril his to command. Aslam is certain that the man will learn soon enough who rules whom. The thought amuses him; he savors it like a honeyed morsel.

Aslam whispers, "For the sultana." Bundar nods. There is a quick pass of a thin parcel from robe to robe, then the two vanish into thin air.

A moment later, a block away, a dog yaps once, twice, then is silent.

These two have laid their prayer mats side by side, oriented towards the *qibla*, ready to begin their *dhuhr salat*. Each has performed *ghusl*, the ritual cleansing, using a basin he keeps filled in their favorite reading room.

It was her idea that they share prayer when together to mark Ramadan. They both are obedient to Ramadan's mandate of fasting from food and drink from sunrise to sunset, a wearying task, but in the end a cleansing one.

The faint echo can just be heard through the open skylights above them, the hypnotic song of the muezzin atop the minaret of the Aljama mosque in Madinat al-Zahra.

As they turn and face Mecca, their expressions become serious. They stand erect, raise their hands, palms out, at shoulder level, and begin quietly together, as a single voice, "Allahu Akbar."

They lower their hands to cover their hearts, right hand over left.

"Subhanaka allahumma wa bi hamdika wa tabara kasmuka wa ta'ala jadduka wa la ilaha ghairuka." *O Allah, how perfect You are and praise be to You. Blessed is Your name, and exalted is Your majesty. There is no god but You.*

"Audhu billahi minash shaitanir rajim." *I seek shelter in Allah from the rejected Satan.* "Bismillahir rahmanir rahim." *In the name of Allah, the most Gracious, the most Merciful.*

And so it begins.

They bend over and rest their palms on their knees, their words flowing now in perfect rhythm. They stand erect once more, then lower themselves to the mat and bend over to touch their foreheads and palms to the floor.

"Allahu Akbar."

They recite three times, "Subhana Rabbiyal A'la." *How Perfect is my Lord, the Highest.*

They rise up on their knees, lips in steady motion, and utter a final triplet of "Subhana Rabbiyal A'la" and another "Allahu Akbar."

245

And then it starts all over again.

At the end of their second *Rakah*, they whisper to their right and then to their left the intoned conclusion of salat, "Assalamu alaikum wa rahmatullah." *Peace and mercy of Allah be on you.*

They rise, express their satisfaction with only their eyes, then roll up their mats. They have grown to cherish this shared prayer time, this holy moment, the love of Allah binding their growing love of each other.

Her hands begin their dance as she bubbles, "So I have an idea, kind sir."

He raises his left eyebrow in mock query.

"Yes. An idea for our afternoon reading. It is a story with which I am afraid you may be quite unfamiliar." She grins coyly.

He beams, intrigued. "I see. Unfamiliar, my lady? I must warn the fair maiden that I have read a great many books."

She laughs. "Alas, I fear, kind sir, this one you have not yet come across."

His grin is fixed to his face. "Perhaps the fair maiden might have pity on me and tell me the title?"

Her grin blossoms as she cups her palm, leans in, and begins to whisper into his ear.

His amused expression grows with each hushed murmur. He roars.

"Indeed I do not know the book, my lady. Pray tell, how did my lady hear of this treasure from the Rare Books Library's collection of love poetry?"

He cannot take his eyes off those adorable dimples.

"Why the codex itself made the request, kind sir." Her tone is at once coy and playful.

His eyebrow voices his incredulity.

"It is true, kind sir. You see, the poor codex begged me to bring you. It seems his verses pine to be spoken aloud. And they must only be spoken by the lips of lovers."

A grin. "I see. Then let us not keep the poor poet waiting. Shall we, fair maiden?" He lifts his palm.

She curtsies. "We shall, kind sir."

They have nearly exhausted the experiments that can be conducted with their camera obscura: the size of the pinhole, the distance between the pinhole and screen, the shape of the interior chamber, the distance and location between the point on the object and its corresponding image point and the angles between —Rayhana's specialty.

The five of them stand in a semicircle at the back of the camera perusing their latest brainstorm. They study the image in silence. Set upon the paper is a neatly reproduced white and black chessboard, but the parent chessboard has been carefully tilted away from the camera at a precise angle, lending the image an eerie third dimension. As the five look alternately between the parent and its child, their smiles widen. The shades and perspective of the image are uncanny in their realism.

Zaheid says, "I have been reading Ibn Sahl. Fascinating stuff ..."

Silence.

Samuel gives up first. "Ibn Sahl?"

Levi grins.

"Ibn Sahl. Persian mathematician. He has done some interesting work with mirrors based on Ptolemy's early work on polished iron. Using blown glass and lead. He claims he can bend light." Zaheid pauses. "I was thinking ..."

Silence.

Samuel flops his arms at his side. "Thinking?"

"Thinking. Perhaps a mirror placed within the camera might prove useful for turning the image right side up."

Zafir replies, "Interesting. How?"

"Well, my boy, the ray of light from the object enters the pinhole as usual. But if we place a flat mirror at a precise angle inside the camera the ray will instead be reflected upward. So the image would be located on the top of the camera, not its back. According to my calculations, such an image should be non-inverted."

Rayhana's smile grows as she nods. "Yes, yes, I see it! If you trace a ray from the top of the object it will be reflected in the mirror to the bottom of the screen. The same for the bottom of the object. The image should flip, top to bottom." She reaches for a reed pen, inks it, and hurriedly sketches on the paper tablet. Samuel and Levi lean in and begin to nod.

Zaheid continues, "But the angle of the mirror would need to be precise. To achieve this effect without distorting the shape of the image, the distance between any point on the mirror to the back and top screens would need to be identical.

Zafir's excitement grows. "Forty-five degrees. Yes, I can see that."

Zaheid grins his approval. Samuel and Levi seem less confident in the conclusion but pretend otherwise.

Rayhana adds, "The mirror would have to be perfectly smooth so as not to corrupt the quality of the image."

"Correct, my dear. The experiment would indeed require an exceptional mirror. And it would need to be large enough to fill the chamber."

Zafir adds, "Or we could simply build a smaller chamber to fit the mirror we have."

Levi says, "There is a mirror maker in the city I have had dealings with. His mirrors are small and round, but very high quality. He works with the best glass blower in the city. He uses a technique first utilized by the Romans; gold leaf on the back of polished pieces of blown glass. The largest I have seen are about this big." He holds up his hands to frame the distance. "Perhaps he could make it bigger and cut it into a square for us."

Zaheid says, "That, or even a rectangle would be ideal."

Levi muses, "It will be expensive ..."

Samuel shrugs. "Sometimes the pursuit of new knowledge requires deep pockets. Before you stands a willing patron." He puffs out his chest. "Go commission us a mirror, Levi."

They all smile.

Rayhana offers, "If only there were a way to permanently capture the images we produce. We would be able to make much more precise measurements and calculations. That chessboard is about as complicated an object as possible for performing tracings upon paper."

Zaheid replies, "An interesting thought, my dear. I stumbled across something along those lines just yesterday that got me thinking."

All eyes are now on Zaheid. Predictably, he stops.

Samuel sighs heavily, then widens his eyes as he circles both hands in the air. "And?"

Levi grins.

"Dioscorides. You know the man; Greek pharmacologist and botanist. First century Rome?" He pauses to survey but sees only blank stares.

De Materia Medica?"

Samuel knows this five volume encyclopedia. "Of course ... Dioscorides." He rolls his eyes at his friend's idea of drama.

"Dioscorides performed a number of interesting experiments on *bitumen* obtained from the Dead Sea region. He called it Judaicum bitumen; claimed it was better than Roman bitumen." He widens his eyes before continuing. "And that it had magical properties ..."

Levi asks, "Of what sort?"

They are riveted now.

"Well, that is where it gets interesting. This is what Dioscorides did. First, he dissolved a small quantity of Judaicum bitumen in lavender oil, then, in a darkened room, he carefully painted the solution on a thin sheet of polished silver and let it dry. When set, he covered it with black cloth and brought it out into the light. When he was ready, he quickly exposed the silver sheet to the scene he wished to capture, then covered it with the cloth once more. Back in the darkened room, he removed the excess bitumen by painting it again several times with lavender oil, carefully dabbing it clean each time." He pauses. "Dioscorides claimed that a faint ghost image of the scene remained on the silver. Permanently."

Rayhana is all dimples.

Zafir asks, "Was the ghost image right side up or upside down?"

Zaheid frowns. "Good question. He did not say."

Samuel asks, "What proportion of bitumen to lavender oil?"

"He did not say."

Rayhana chimes in, "How long did he expose it?"

"He did not say."

Samuel groans. "Did he speculate on how it worked?"

"No, he was at a loss. And Dioscorides had a fine mind."

They muse in silence.

Levi interjects, "The Greek Fire utilized by the Byzantine navy is said to be a form of liquid bitumen. Samples should not be hard to obtain ... with a well-placed bribe or two. Perhaps even some Judaicum bitumen. Lavender oil is commonly used to make artist's oils, so I am sure we can get that in the city." He grins. "And Samuel has plenty of silver, as we all know."

They laugh.

"Your patron approves. Let the magic begin!"

The night is cool and crisp. Autumn's advance is inarguable now, the deal done, the hard press and windy bite of winter on the Upper Marches not far behind.

The full moon is bright enough to throw a sharp shadow. The rock promontory rising abruptly from the plain glows in the twilight. Along the run of the peak are magnificently sculpted limestone ramparts, blue in the moonlight from this angle. Darkened outlines of the sentries atop the walls stand out clearly.

Just beyond the juncture separating the angled slope of the castle mount from the river plain are elaborate fortifications; stone barriers, crude fences made of wooden stakes and logs, breastworks dug into the dark earth. Cooking fires are scattered among square tents, stretching back from the castle mount a stone's throw. There, another line of heavy fortifications. A neat, double ring. Hundreds of fires. The fortifications on the plain run east to west then bend round the plug of a mountain; a ring of fire surrounding the castle mount. The unmistakable signature of siege.

The castle of Gormaz is impressive by any reckoning. The thirty-one-tower stone edifice was built by Abd al-Rahman I, the first caliph of Córdoba, as a bulwark against Christian incursion, certainly, but also as a reminder to the rich and ambitious Muslim landowners in the Upper Marches to mind their manners. The castle is narrow and long, hugging the contours of the stone crag that serves as its foundation.

Just north of the Duero River, Gormaz hovers above the plain like a king upon his throne. The castle was built upon Roman ruins, but its massive red ochre and white Umayyad horseshoe-arched gate betrays its Arab lineage. The view to the north, to the Christian lands of Castile and León, is impeccable.

Gormaz has never been taken by force of arms. But White Hands, like his father, has always believed that there is a first time for all things. He has nearly twenty-six thousand troops under his command. He aims to send a message to Córdoba, one that cannot be misinterpreted: *I am coming for you. I am coming.*

Blessed Eid!

29 September 976.

It is a breathtaking fall day, the sky a pristine dome of crystalline azure, the luxuriant light glowing with the earthy tones of autumn. Warm still, but exceptionally pleasant.

It is a grand day for a festival. Eid al-Fitr has finally arrived, a glorious exclamation point to mark the end of Ramadan's wearying demands. Eid has neatly aligned with the beginnings of fall, its lateness this year a consequence of the fluid drum beat of the lunar calendar as it slides against the seasons.

The clench of Ramadan's abstinence, at first a bracing slap but ultimately cleansing for the penitent, impatiently awaits Eid's tilt of the scale from subtraction to celebration.

Eid has a special hold upon the people of Córdoba, the high-water mark of the city's many festivals. The caliph spares no expense. He opens his coffers, the sweet jingle of coins cast wide for the city's pleasure. Eid is the caliph's time to remind the world that Córdoba remains Europe's richest city. Religious affiliation matters little this day, nor does ancestry or station. All partake in the glory of Eid. Peter Strobel and Cleo each receive special invitations from the grand vizier himself. Strobel predictably scoffs at first but eventually succumbs to Cleo's insistence that they must not miss the caliph's legendary Eid festivities.

This year might have been different, of course. The siege at Gormaz still weighs on the psyche of the city. But General Ghalib and his army are on the march now, first gathering forces in the Middle Marches then moving north to punish White Hands. Everyone knows that Ghalib never loses a fight. Never. With the caliph ailing in secret, Jafar has decided that this year's Eid must top them all, a distraction from the coming storm still unseen over the horizon. Yes, a lavish festival is just the distraction he needs.

Eid revolves around a feast like none other; unusual delicacies imported from across the known world, many horded weeks in advance, months even. Sweets and morsels of all shapes and sizes, fruits swelled tight with luscious juices, the plush velvet of citrus flesh.

All manner of creatures from sea and land, tracked and netted or speared, then prepared with a deft touch using fine salts and spices aplenty. The city will be awash with delectable scents tacked onto the breeze; the sweet smoke billowing from sizzling meats, simmering soups and sauces, bread hot from the ovens slathered with butter scooped fresh from churns.

And the entertainment is beyond measure. Storytellers by the dozens will spin their fat yarns with widened eyes and outstretched arms as huddled children alternately cower, then beam. There will be poetry readings, recitations of ancient words, mimes, songs of a hundred types, and the exquisite tickling of strung instruments by consummate masters.

There will be dancing, of course. Especially cherished are the veil dances of desert lore, set to the quick-tick of tambourine, pipe, and drum, and offered up by the city's most beautiful young women, selected and specially trained for these jealously-guarded roles.

Here is the stuff of legend among the crowing, back-slapping young men of the city. Their false bravado is amusing to the married folk, who see the truth and cannot suppress their smiles; these young men would melt into a puddle if a single dancer but dropped her veil and locked her almond eyes upon one of them. Boys in men's bodies.

The nubile young women enjoy the attention, of course, as well as the power their curvaceous sways hold over their adoring audience. It is all harmless enough given the safety of the obscuring silks. Yet later, as the evening deepens, words will be exchanged among the bolder. Veils will be dropped and identities coyly revealed, shy promises tendered, delicious hints of implied trysts that may or may not actually transpire. Such is the way of young love.

Córdoba is a city of performance, of showmanship, of bragging rights and virtuosity. It is customary to save one's best for the glory of Eid.

Young men and women of marriageable age are granted permission to intermingle under watchful eyes. Here is a time when connections are made and deals are struck between families.

The faithful rise long before dawn, giddy with the promise of the day's events. By custom, they eat a quick breakfast of dried dates. The throngs first make their way to their local hammams; squeaky clean is the rule for Eid. The women are all smiles and giggles. Teeth are cleaned, hair is braided, expensive perfumes lavished, not dabbed; elaborate henna art applied to hands and feet. The men are more subdued but are unable to suppress their satisfied grins for the party that beckons. It is Eid, after all, and the air is thick with excitement and the coming revelry.

First, the formalities. The city's elite will gather before dawn in the Great Mosque for communal prayer; rich merchants and their beautiful wives and daughters, lawyers and clergy, court functionaries, and high ranking officers. The remainder of the citizens will fill their neighborhood mosques. The faithful will drop their offerings of silver coin for the poor and needy, the *Zakat al-Fitr*, into massive ceramic vases as they pass through the mosque entrances. Men and women will be separated into roped sections, men at the front, women at the back.

After the muezzin sounds his sweet lament, the *Salatul Fajr*, the special dawn prayers of Eid will commence, solemn and reverential. The grand imam will address those gathered among the forest of double-arches within the Great Mosque.

At the end of the Eid service, as the faithful depart, the tight solemnity will lift in thick sheets and the anticipation will begin to boil up and over. Warm hugs and double kisses, grins and bright laughter will first ring out, then blossom. "*Eid Mubarak! Eid Mubarak!*" "Blessed Eid! Blessed Eid!" Families will slowly move to their homes to change into festival attire then spill back out onto the city streets and squares to begin the celebration. By tradition, the festival will not end until midnight.

And what of Madinat al-Zahra? Well, Madinat has an Eid celebration all its own; there is no equal in the east or the west. What is lavished upon Córdoba will be quadrupled in Madinat; quintupled. Baghdad would blush at the waste of gold.

Rules are relaxed, rare delicacies offered; watered wine will flow. There will be a cacophony of virtuosic displays tendered. The realm's very best will be invited to Madinat al-Zahra with great fanfare; music, song, poetry, dance. Careers are made at Madinat's Eid.

By tradition, the caliph tosses handfuls of silver coins, his Eid gifts, *Eidi*, into the throngs of gleeful children, who scamper about in chase of shimmers. All of the caliph's gardens are opened, only once per year, to create a giant playground for those of the royal court. By nightfall, Madinat will gleam under a thousand torches, the great glow visible from miles away.

The Slavic Guard is the only contingent still on duty, but even they will discreetly confine themselves to the outer walls and entrances, and partake of the fine food brought to them on silver platters. The Royal Guard and the palace workers in the medina are given the day off to play in Córdoba.

For those of the royal court, Salatul Fajr will transpire in the Aljama Mosque just beyond the caliph's residence. Predictably, there is a pecking order for seating among the double-arches within the modest-sized mosque, by station and rank. Unlike in the Great Mosque, where the grand imam's word holds sway, the women of court are allowed to sit with their men, whole families gathered together.

By tradition, a respected imam of the realm is invited to preside. As luck would have it this year, Imam Abd al-Gafur of Algeciras has accepted the honor. He slipped into Madinat the evening prior.

Unlike in Córdoba, Zakat al-Fitr here is offered in gold, not silver. The contents of the enormous vases could purchase a small kingdom, or, as in this case, fund the caliph's fifty public hospitals for the entire year.

The Vizier Council is led in by the bedecked Slavic Guard with great fanfare and plume. By tradition, the caliph and his council attend the Eid service together and are seated in a special area near the mihrab. Jafar, as grand vizier, leads the entourage in, as expected. Even Samuel and Reccimund are present to pay their respects. Only General Ghalib and Ibn Abi Amir are missing, but the reason for their absence is known to all.

Oddly, however, the caliph is nowhere to be seen—a fact that escapes no one. "So the rumors are true. The caliph is ill, too ill for Eid!" Furious whispers are passed behind opened palms. "The caliph's ailment must be serious after all."

Subh is not allowed out of the royal harem, of course, a decree of the caliph dating back many years. Instead, she is forced to worship in the royal harem's tiny oratory mosque with Jibril and the other royal eunuchs, that perfumed and painted group bolstered now by three unnaturally docile young boys.

Even Subh enjoys a small triumph, however. Beside the caliph's empty seat in the Aljama Mosque sits tender Hisham, bejeweled, robed in red ochre and white, the caliph's colors, looking befuddled and dazed. Jafar was opposed to allowing the boy's presence, but as the grand imam was quick to remind him, at least one member of the royal family is required to proclaim the solemn end of Ramadan and the joyous beginning of Eid.

To trump her chess move, Jafar has invited the caliph's brother, al-Mughira, to sit on the other side of the caliph's vacant seat. The subtle message will be lost on all but those most in need of receiving it.

Zafir kneels midway back in the mosque. Rayhana is tucked neatly on the edge at the rear, Durr and her brother beside her. These two have found each other's eyes, of course, a sweet sinking of emerald into amber. Nothing more, not even a hint of a smile or a dimple. Their secret gaze is invisible to all but the most practiced of eyes. But then, Madinat al-Zahra is a city of practiced eyes.

It is impossible for these two to flaunt their love. They know this. Of course they do. Rebekah has reminded them both repeatedly: "It is the Eid festival, yes, and restrictions are relaxed, yes, but this is Madinat al-Zahra, and al-Zahra craves her gossip almost as much as her gold. You must be exceedingly careful."

Still, love will find a way, it always does. A plan was hatched weeks back, how could it not be so? Their love has not yet seen the light of day, chained instead within the windowless realm of the Rare Books Library. Such love knows no bounds, needs no excuse to struggle for its freedom. Such love craves bright sunlight, an open sky, the pulsing diamonds of a clear, moonless night.

A plan. Yes. They have picked it over and parsed it, relentlessly, for any weaknesses or oversights. Folded, then opened, then folded once more. It is a neat plan, though not without risk.

They rehashed it for the final time yesterday. Eid steps close. As they rehearse the details, their hearts pound with their daring then they turn giddy and double over with laughter.

At unexpected moments these two suddenly lapse into silence under the weight of their love. They each swallow hard as the dancing tingle races up and down their spines, as the sweet fluttering gnaw sets up camp in their stomachs.

He whispers his plea, "A kiss, just a kiss."

She stays strong, reminds him of their Ramadan pact then smiles. "Just one more day. One. Only one."

He suffers happily, content to finger the dark spirals falling on her face, stroke the lovely curve of her cheekbone.

Deep in the night, though, as the genies begin their prowl, they each toss and turn in their beds, their hot, damp throbs relentless as they dream of the rich possibilities of a garden tryst.

There are times when such dreams spill into the waking hours. They wrestle their exquisite tortures. In vain, of course. These two have vivid imaginations, after all, honed to a razor's edge by love-stoked desire. Their love pulses with a maddening energy all its own.

"We will need your help." Her tone is casual, matter of fact.

She has changed into her festival fare, a lovely, cream-colored gown of the finest silk, a dozen gold buttons spaced from neck to ankle, and cobalt piping and gold lacework weaving down the sleeves. The gown is close-fitted, and while the cut leans towards the modest, it does not pretend to be shy about her curves either. Tiny gold hoops for her ears and that ethereal orange-spice perfume dabbed in strategic places. By this point she is a master at torturing Zafir.

She is seated in front of her mirror in her bedroom as Durr puts the finishing touches on her hair. Their final agreement was a simple pinning with mother-of-pearl combs trailing into long, loose curls gathered only twice by a thin ribbon of cobalt. She looks absolutely radiant. The soft, pleasing glow of love.

She has intentionally waited until the last minute so that Durr would have no time to fret over the details, deduce all the risks.

Durr looks up from her work and into the mirror to lock eyes with her mistress. "My help?"

"Yes. Zafir and I will need your help."

"Ahhh ..." Durr ignores Rayhana's smile, remains stone faced.

"We have a plan."

Durr scoffs. "A plan?" Concern seeps into her expression. She can guess where this is going.

"Yes. A plan for this evening for the two of us. For Eid."

Durr sighs wearily. "Rayhana ..."

"Durr, it is Eid!" A tinge of exasperation seeps through and stains her voice.

"Yes, it is Eid. And this is Madinat al-Zahra, Rayhana. You know your father would never approve of your meeting Zafir, especially not alone."

An edge of disdain cuts into her voice. "Baba is in the Maghreb, Durr, and will be for months. He will never know."

She widens her eyes emphatically. "And your brothers?"

"My brothers have their own plans for Eid, and they do not include me. You know they will never notice if I go missing for a few hours, Durr."

Silence.

Durr's tone turns serious. "Aslam will notice."

A meted whisper of a response. "Yes, Aslam will notice."

Another sigh, even heavier this time. "I do too much for you two as it is."

Rayhana brightens. "And we are grateful, Durr, truly." She pleads now, "All we want is time alone outside of the library dungeons. To let our love see the light of day. Just once. Is that so much to ask?"

Durr looks back to her work without answering and resumes fiddling with the best placement of the hair combs.

The silence inflates.

Without looking up, Durr says, "Tell me."

Rayhana smiles brightly.

Madinat al-Zahra is a thick mob of merriment; food and wine and dancing and song and games and recitals; of all manner and kind. The steady drone of commotion and throngs of people at play, sharp shrieks of *oohs!* and *aahs!,* sudden peals of laughter, pleasure gasps of surprise and delight, exaggerated groans as rare delicacies touch lips and then are dissolved upon tongues.

Eid in Madinat is an orgy of performance, a feast for the senses. Zahra would be proud. Visitors to the city are absolutely amazed at the sheer scope of the festivities—and the cost. Cleo cackles with delight at each new spectacle he witnesses, and even Ambassador Strobel manages to smile a time or two. The streets and squares are packed with the privileged of court, suddenly free to roam the vast palace grounds; toddlers tugging on their parents' sleeves, pointing and shrieking at this or that miracle as their proud mothers and fathers beam their approval; the pure glee of wide-eyed children set free upon a carnival stage to race about and explore with their brothers and sisters; the quiet pleasure of elderly couples strolling arm in arm as they quietly compare this year's Eid to the days of their youth; excited gasps at the throaty roar of the caliph's lions, the exotic cries of dozens of strutting peacocks, the eerie cackle of the slinking hyenas. And woven among it all, the demur looks of eager young women unleashed upon the game of flirting. Of course.

Clutches of ripening beauties flit about, all furious whispers and giggles, diving and ducking under the furtive glances and shy grins sprouting from the knots of young men of privilege that weave and bob about them. The young men's lanky bodies are stiff with the self-consciousness of youth, but they are bold enough when gathered in a pack to race about, nipping at the girls' heels. The timeless pursuits of youth. Madinat at Eid is a rare treat for such dances.

———— 🌀 ————

Rayhana and Durr stroll about, arm in arm, enjoying the beautiful weather, marveling at the lavish spread of entertainment. As they move through the crowds, men, both young and old, turn their heads to drink her in as she passes. Conversations quiet mid-sentence, mouths open, subtle nods and eye-flicks are made in her direction. The old men offer an appreciative smile; the younger ones swallow hard.

Here is the desert beauty of Arab legend, fitting for the glory of a poem, some ancient *ghazal* penned in bold red ink and gilded with gold. She is oblivious to the stares, as usual, has no inkling of the spell she casts about so freely.

At the close of a mid-morning lute performance, Rayhana and Durr come upon Samuel and Rebekah. Zaheid and Iuliana are close by and the six gather to chat. Hugs and double-cheek kisses all around.

Samuel beams. "My, you look lovely today, my dear."

Rayhana blushes. "You are kind, Samuel, thank you. I love Eid. Where are the girls?"

"Good question! Knowing Miriam, flirting with the boys, no doubt. That is why we insisted she take Sara with her!"

They all laugh.

Rebekah studies the girl. She knows without being told. She asks with her eyes about Zafir. Rayhana's dimples flash and she looks down.

Rebekah leans close and whispers. "Please be careful, Rayhana, Zahra watches. Please."

She soberly nods her response.

Samuel says, "Rayhana, I have arranged a meeting with Imam Abd al-Gafur for tomorrow. I will plead your case. Delicately."

Rayhana's eyes well up. She whispers, "Thank you, Samuel, thank you. What would Zafir and I do without you all?"

Zaheid tries to steer the mood to shallower water. "Rayhana, I have some news from our experiment."

Iuliana frowns, then elbows her husband. "Eid is not a day for science talk."

The corners of Rebekah's mouth hint at a coy grin. "I am afraid I lost that battle long ago, Iuliana."

Rayhana smiles, the desired result.

Samuel puffs up his feathers. "Let the man speak, Wife. The girl knows more about what we are doing than anyone; blame her, not us!"

They laugh.

Zaheid clears his throat, then continues. "My dear, you were right about the proportion of lavender oil. I was using way too much. Yesterday I was able to obtain a lasting image. Extremely faint, but unmistakable. After Eid, you and I will resume our experiments."

Her face brightens with childlike glee. "That is wonderful news, Zaheid! We are close now, very close."

Grins all around.

Rayhana asks, "Where is Levi?"

Iuliana mock frowns, then points across the courtyard. Levi is playing a coin toss game. Zaheid calls his name. When Levi responds with a wave, his expression tells it all; he is losing badly.

They laugh.

Rayhana and Durr offer cheek kisses and hugs, then the two depart. Rebekah's gaze follows the girl until she turns the corner. There is concern in her voice as she says, "I am worried for them, Samuel. They must be very careful."

Samuel's expression turns serious. "Yes. I have warned Zafir. Much is at stake now."

"Do you think Imam Abd al-Gafur will help them?"

Samuel considers this for a long moment, then finally shrugs. "Unclear. I hear good things about the man, but defying Ibn Abi Amir is asking a lot of anyone. We shall see ..."

After lunch, Rayhana and Durr turn a corner and practically collide with her brother, Khalid, his Maryam in tow. After Khalid's shocked surprise and Maryam's blush fades, he mumbles an awkward introduction and a perfunctory "Eid Mubarak," then moves on.

Rayhana has long ago stopped teasing him. She now understands far too much about such things. Khalid and Maryam must be careful as well; Durri the Small has his own eyes sprinkled about Madinat.

Thankfully, she will not see Salim today. He and his friends from the madrasa have opted to remain in the city to celebrate there. One less concern to worry about.

Mid-afternoon, as they stand listening to a poetry recital, he catches her eye from across the courtyard. By careful intent they have avoided each other all day. Zafir acknowledges her with a single wink, no more. She looks down, unable to check her smile.

Durr, who has a sixth sense for such things, looks to their left and sees the young man. She frowns and guides Rayhana by the elbow on to the next performance down the narrow alley.

Zafir moves off in the opposite direction and disappears into the crowd.

As they exit the courtyard she whispers to her mistress, "Please stick to your plan, Rayhana, that is risk enough."

Duly chastised, the girl nods and says, "Forgive me, Durr."

He is tucked neatly into a doorway, his back to the cool stone. He has foresworn all black, his working color, traded it for a bright festival robe that will not attract attention.

He sees it all, of course. The wink, the dimples, Durr's quick acknowledgment of the boy's presence, their hasty retreats.

Something is up, that much is certain. He waivers for a moment, trying to decide if he should just corner the boy and explain life to him in terms a saqaliba can understand—the point of a dagger. But no rush, that time will come soon enough. He knows his master would tell him to forget the boy and safeguard Rayhana. He leaves his lair and melts into the crowd.

The day grows late. He watches the two women enter the public latrine building. Aside from the one encounter it has been uneventful work, his job an easy one. Aslam eases into a doorway across the courtyard to wait. He scans the crowd with a practiced eye. He sees many he knows; some he receives information from, some he holds information on.

Nearly ten minutes pass. Durr exits the building. Alone. Aslam stands erect, instantly alert. He scans the crowd in both directions. Rayhana is nowhere to be seen.

Durr moves down the street with the throng of people headed to the performance stage, obviously not waiting for her mistress. Aslam gives chase, moving as quickly as he can without attracting attention.

As she turns the corner he reaches for her arm and grabs her. She jumps with surprise, shock painted large across her face.

"Aslam! What are you doing?" She tries to compose herself. Unsuccessfully. She is clearly terrified of the man. "Let go of me, Aslam."

He tightens his grip on her arm and pulls her into a doorway. "Where is she?"

"Where is who?"

His fingers dig into her flesh.

She winces. "You are hurting me, Aslam."

He hisses, "Where. Is. Rayhana, Durr?"

"Oh. We ran into Rebekah al-Tayyib in the latrine. She wanted to introduce Rayhana to a friend of hers, a poet. She told me she would meet me later for dinner at the pavilion."

His tone is menacing. "She did not exit the building, Durr. Where is she? Tell me NOW!"

"She went out the other entrance, Aslam. On the side alley. The one that leads to the poetry stages. She left with Rebekah."

He releases her. Other entrance. Side alley. Aslam curses his error. He hisses, "I will deal with you later." He turns and moves upstream against the crowd to find the second entrance to the latrine.

As Durr rubs the pain from her arm a hint of a grin slides onto her face.

The burnt-orange sun bloats as it sinks into the horizon and is impaled upon the crags of the Sierra Morena, releasing gasps of purple and crimson. Wisps of brilliant pink cirrus clouds stretch out in thin fingers across the sky. A breeze begins to stir. The wonderful night beckons Eid forward. The festival will continue for many hours more, the last of the revelers not reaching their beds until well after midnight.

As dusk settles in, torches by the thousands begin to be lit, and soon the play of shadows upon the walls lends an ambiance of magic and mystery, of ancient charms and alchemy. A potion is mixed, and the pulsing diamonds are summoned to join the festivities. Pinpricks begin to peek through the graying dome one by one. When eyes are laid upon the scene below, the dim flickers blossom into brilliant jewels, smiles writ large upon their faces.

Young children are deposited in their homes with nursemaids and the crowds begin to age. Watered wine flows at night in Madinat; couples slide closer together as they walk. Kisses will be stolen in the twilight gardens by lovers young and old.

Eid's poetry by night will edge towards sweet rhymes of desire, whispered pleas of longing; the troubadour's songs a wistful remembrance of young love blossoming under desert palms beneath a starry sky. Veil dances will grow bolder, the curvaceous sways of the beautiful young virgins more adventuresome and teasing. The perfumed night air of Madinat al-Zahra will shimmer and sparkle.

Gormaz

The Sword of the Caliph is within a four-hour hard ride of Gormaz castle, but he dare not move ahead of his infantry and supply train. He knows he cannot push too hard during daylight hours, else the dust cloud will be a sure giveaway of their position. He has timed the march so that the army should arrive just before midnight, plenty of time to prepare weapons and form ranks for a dawn battle. He aims to attack before their full strength is known and counterattacks can be planned.

He approaches from the southeast, threading his way between the arid rolling hills of the Upper Marches. It is a barren land of scrub oaks and dense thickets of bushes and narrow ravines, devoid of good cover for hiding the advance of an army of this size, though his scouts insist that their presence remains undetected.

Ghalib has fought a dozen different enemies and he appreciates better than any that one never knows exactly what to believe in war. Looks are always deceiving. He hopes for surprise, yes, but knows that he will need some luck.

The weather is unusually warm for the end of September, summer's last gasp before it surrenders for good to winter's pillage.

Lifting a siege is never a trivial matter. His scouts have painted a grim picture; it is obvious that the Christians know what they are doing. White Hands is dug in around Gormaz's compact castle mount in a double ring, the inner ramparts designed to repel a breakout attempt from above, the outer ramparts designed to thwart a relieving assault from the plains.

Ghalib knows the fortification well. He has read Julius Caesar's *Gallic Wars*, after all, memorized the great Caesar's innovation in siege warfare at Alesia in Gaul, the thousand-year-old stroke of tactical brilliance seared into his psyche.

His gamble is that White Hands can be lured out of his lair to a pitched battle on the Plains of Gormaz. When the armies are engaged, a trailing cavalry force will swoop in and punch a quick hole in the double-ring to relieve the surrounded castle. It is a gamble, he knows, but he sees little alternative. Gormaz does not have the troops or stores to withstand a siege of any length, and a direct assault is unlikely to penetrate the outer rampart at full garrison. He must first draw the Christians out.

Ghalib sighs. He knows that if Gormaz falls, the Middle Marches will offer little resistance to an invading Christian army. The path from Gormaz to Córdoba will be paved with gold. Córdoba is a juicy plum, too tempting for White Hands to ignore. There is little room for error.

As General Ghalib traveled north he crisscrossed the arid wiles of the Middle Marches, calling on dozens of rich landowners loyal to the caliph. He has gathered an additional two thousand cavalry and three thousand infantry, courtesy of Durri the Small's chests of gold coin and Jafar's notations on who owes the caliph favors and who can be best threatened.

He has gathered mercenaries, most with only meager training, but useful numbers for the coming fight nonetheless. He will use them as fodder for bogging down the Christian center while his veterans attempt to turn their flank. His reserve cavalry will attack in a staggered pincer move on the opposite side of the castle, safely hidden from view of the main battle, then make a neat sword-slice through the Christian fortifications.

Such a tactic did not serve the Gaul commander well, of course, but, then again, Vercingetorix had no knowledge of Caesar's mind, and no means to draw him out from behind his fortified ring. Ghalib has never flinched from rolling the dice; therein lies much of the secret of his many successes as commander of Córdoba's army. Calculated boldness is usually decisive. Caesar knew as much.

Assuming the castle garrison commander has any brains at all, Gormaz will seize the opportunity and erupt through the breach and roll up the enemy from within. White Hands would be a fool to stay and risk an assault from their combined forces.

But there lies the rub. The commander of Gormaz, a man Ghalib knows to be an able tactician, was killed in the first battle with White Hands. Ghalib has no clue who is now in charge of the Gormaz garrison and no means to get a coded message to him with his orders. He knows he will need some luck.

Few have successfully challenged Córdoba's army with Ghalib in command. Not a single major defeat under Caliph al-Hakam II, and none since the Battle of Simancas under his father before him. Thirty-five years and counting.

Ghalib shakes his head. Count Fernan Gonzalez of Castile and León, White Hands' father, was the nemesis of the caliph's own father. A man never to be taken lightly. Never. Ghalib hisses, "Christian bastards, just cannot leave the Upper Marches alone."

All indications suggest that White Hands learned all that his father knew, and then some. General Ghalib understands better than any that White Hands will be a formidable opponent on the field of battle. He has money, and his army is well armed and trained.

General Ghalib mutters, "Still, thirty-five years of victories should count for something." He checks himself and scowls. He knows well, of course, that history means nothing in battle. Armies live and die by a single mistake, a slight miscalculation. He needs luck.

He leans down and pats his stallion's neck, whispers into his ear. "Come, Taneen, time to teach White Hands some manners." The horse whinnies, then rears. The old man laughs loudly.

"You are positive it is him?"

"Yes, my lord. A grizzled old man on a jet-black stallion."

"How far?"

"A three hour hard ride, my lord. But they are moving slowly, staying with their supply wagons."

"As would I, as would I ..." He bows his head, folds his arms behind him, and begins to pace. His officers know better than to interrupt his calculations. They simply stare at the man's shoulder-length shock of white hair, the color of sun-bleached bone, a mirror of his ghostly pale skin. He can't be over twenty-five, but he exudes the serious demeanor of a veteran commander.

White Hands stops and looks up. "Ghalib aims to arrive by night to hide his numbers. He will attack at dawn. How many?"

The officer pauses, knowing that his commander does not suffer inaccuracy. "I make it at least eight thousand cavalry, my lord. Ten thousand infantry, give or take, perhaps two thousand archers. They are well supplied."

Silence.

"You are sure your men were not observed?"

"Positive, my lord."

The ghost nods and resumes his pacing. The gears are whirring again.

He stops. "Fewer than I would have guessed, Enrique. You are positive that his army was not split?" He looks up, locks his eyes on his officer. Piercing blue crystals bore into the man. "A secondary force, perhaps? Cavalry hidden in reserve? Ghalib likes to do that, you know."

The officer does not flinch. "No, my lord, only one army. I sent riders out five leagues to both the east and the west, then had them circle around behind the Moor army. Nothing in reserve, my lord."

White Hands nods his approval. "Good, good. Well done, Enrique, well done." He bows his head, resumes his pacing.

Five minutes later his officers have not shifted their positions. The air tingles with expectation. Still the man paces.

Another minute and abruptly the ghost stops and raises his head, a death-mask of chiseled white marble, completely unreadable. "Ghalib's plan is now known to me."

The men exchange nervous glances.

White Hands abruptly breaks into a wide smile. "We shall greet the Moors with a surprise of our own."

He turns to his adjutant and barks, "Bring my map, Alfonso. Quick, man, there are plans to be made! Time is wasting!" He turns to his second-in-command. "Don Diego, prepare the defenses and send word to the troops to strengthen the outer ring on the southeast side of the castle mount. That is where Ghalib will strike. Get the cavalry in their armor and ready to mount at my command. Let us ride to victory over the Moors, gentlemen. Carry the day and Córdoba is ours!"

The elite Moor cavalry ride five abreast in three perfect columns, each five hundred strong, the two sides of the pincer flanking the battering ram. The cavalry moves slowly to quell dust as they snake their way along the shallow wash between the two squat hills. They are approaching their launch point at the edge of the final low rise that obscures them from view. A well-trained archer could almost reach the siege fortifications from here.

Their hope is that they are visible from the castle mount but not from the Christian ramparts. General Ghalib has impressed upon his second, Ahmed al-Qadir, that the key to their victory lies in surprise. "You must puncture the ring before they know what hit them, Ahmed. Strike fast and strike hard. Let the garrison roll up their defenses from the inside, then gather your men and ride in support of us on the plains. I will need you to carry the day."

Each column is led by the red ochre and white banners of the caliph so that their identity is obvious to lookouts on the castle walls.

A simultaneous raising of left hands from the lead officers in each column slows then halts the cavalry. Final orders are passed back as killing tools are lifted and readied. These men are seasoned veterans, but their hearts pound as they whisper prayers for protection for themselves and their comrades and stroke the twitching ears of their mounts.

Ahmed gives the signal and hoof thunder roars to a deafening volume as the dust billows up into thick clouds.

"ALLAHU AKBAR! ALLAHU AKBAR! ALLAHU AKBAR!"

As planned, General Ghalib's troops have formed into ranks and silently marched into position, ready to fight by first light. Their presence quickly becomes known as the darkness surrenders to gray, setting off a frantic scramble within the Christian fortifications. Alarm bells begin to sound as the ramparts of the double ring fill with helmeted heads and drawn bows.

Ghalib stubbornly holds his position, his army's posture issuing an unmistakable challenge for a pitched battle. As anticipated, White Hands cannot refuse and keep his honor, and as the golden beams of the breaking sun began to slice up the arid landscape, his glistening cavalry file out by the hundreds from their northern gate, followed by supporting infantry and archers.

Ghalib can only smile. He waits patiently for them to form ranks. The only courteous thing to do in such matters.

Just before the battle commences these two eye each other across the plain, Ghalib on his midnight mount, White Hands on his dappled gray, each surrounded by their bannermen and officers. Messengers stand ready to rush orders to the units as the battle unfolds.

The Sword of the Caliph turns left, then right, lifts mighty *Saif al-Haqq*, the "Sword of Truth," into the air, and shouts, "Allahu Akbar!"

A thunderous roar answers him, "ALLAHU AKBAR!"

"Allahu Akbar!"

"ALLAHU AKBAR!"

"Allahu Akbar!"

"ALLAHU AKBAR!"

They charge.

The battle rages on the Plains of Gormaz, the two armies locked in a death grip. The fighting is hand to hand across a wide front, a quivering dense mesh of flailing bodies. Slender columns of gleaming cavalry leisurely amble about then suddenly change directions and charge hard, puncturing the mass to work their awful violence.

Archers on both sides launch volleys of weeping black darts that rain indiscriminately on both friend and foe alike. The veterans know to keep one eye up for the black rain. They lift their shields above them at the last instant, absorb the arrowheads, then lower their shields and resume fighting until the next volley arrives. The poorly trained, however, tend to miss on their timing, and instead look up to take an arrow between the eyes.

The fields are slick with bright crimson mud.

The center of each line is a dense tangle of death, a mayhem of broken bodies and truncated screams, a surreal waking nightmare. Spiked maces smash skulls and sling splattered brains; broadswords whir and slash about frantically, cleaving arms and splitting heads in shocking bloody sprays.

Strange, demented yelps vie with heaving grunts. Stallions howl as they are disemboweled by pikemen, then tangle and trip over their slimy entrails, falling upon their stirruped masters with an awful metal crush. Infantrymen rush upon the grounded knights and wriggle their needle daggers through locked helmet visors, puncturing disbelieving eyes as their blades sink into brains. A quick scream and the work is done.

Heaves and groans, curses and shouts, ping upon ping upon ping. All bathed in a fine crimson mist, the sweet metallic scent of fresh blood ladled heavy upon the crisp morning air.

As the field steadily lays claim to stacked cords of the vanquished, voices soften; the begging of the maimed, muted cries for mercy, the quiet calling out for mothers and wives. Limbless veterans mewl like infants.

Crossbow bolts bury themselves feather-deep in the necks and haunches of wide-eyed stallions. The wounded monsters twist away from the biting agony, limbs stuttering across the fallen bodies to the ugly melody of crushed steel plate and horrible screams.

The Moor mercenaries manage to clog the advance of the more heavily-armored Christian knights, as designed, but pay dearly for it. Their ranks are quickly decimated.

General Ghalib limps hard as he paces and stops to look anxiously over his shoulder for some positive sign of the cavalry's attack on the siege ring. A flag from the castle. Smoke. Something! He grimaces and turns to his adjutant. "What is delaying them? They must break the ring while the battle rages. I need support! Support, damn you! WHERE IS MY CAVALRY?! Ride to them and bring me some news. Find Ahmed! GO! NOW!"

White Hands begins to exert his will upon Ghalib's center and the mercenary lines evaporate now at an alarming rate. In desperation, the Sword of the Caliph issues orders for his reserve cavalry to be split, half to come forward to bolster his collapsing center, the other half to swing wide right and make for White Hands' flank. He sees now that he must turn their flank for any hope at victory.

The commander of the Moor cavalry miscalculates badly, and his end-run races unaware into arrow range of the Christian siege ramparts. Suddenly the air is streaked thick in black slivers of death as horses and knights begin to fall, first in ones and twos, then by the dozens, then hundreds.

Too late, General Ghalib sees the mistake, but can only offer a curse. Instead of turning back, the cavalry is caught up in the fever of battle and foolishly continues to press their case. By the time they reach White Hands' flank not more than two dozen Moor knights remain, and these are quickly cut to the ground.

This fight is getting away from Ghalib, and getting away quickly.

Horns sound in the distance. Again. A third time. From the southwest, to their rear. As they snap about, Ghalib grimaces as his officers exchange puzzled looks. A dust storm billows at the edge of the distant hill. The horns sound again, louder now. Cavalry. He sees them as they begin to break from the dust. The banners tell it all. Red cross on white.

He stares in disbelief. With his reserves already committed, and without Ahmed's cavalry, he has nothing left to blunt this new assault. He barks his orders. "We must collapse our left and draw back into a defensive arc, else they will route our flank and it will be over. QUICKLY!" The command post erupts into desperate action.

He turns at the sound of a horse bearing down on them. The mount pulls up in a banter of legs and dust. His adjutant slides from his saddle and races to him.

"My lord, our cavalry has breached their fortifications. We have breached the ring!"

"Both rings?"

"Both rings!"

"Why no sign from the castle?"

The adjutant looks pained. "My lord, the garrison has not left the castle walls to support us. They did not strike from inside as planned. No one came, my lord, not one. Our cavalry is barely holding on. Ahmed is dead."

Ghalib is incredulous. He opens his mouth, then closes it. He turns back to the southwest. The cavalry continues to spill from the hillside onto the plain. A thousand horses at least, maybe two. He hisses, "Mark my words, I will have the head of whoever commands Gormaz. The fool has murdered us all!"

Ghalib's shoulders droop as the weight of the awful recognition settles on him. His luck has finally run out. Defeat. "Gentlemen, this fight is over. Sound retreat. We have only one option left. Make for the breach with all haste. Gormaz's walls are our only hope now. Use the cavalry on the left flank for rear-guard. Get as many men into the castle as you can."

"But the army will be trapped, my lord."

The Sword of the Caliph's glare is withering. "You think I do not appreciate that! Either we retreat to the castle or the army perishes. MOVE!"

He looks back at the advancing cavalry. He sees it will be a race against time; the stragglers will be cut down.

He shakes his head and hisses a final curse upon White Hands. "Bring Taneen! Quickly!"

Eden Redux

The black veil covers her head and is pulled tight around her face, sliding around her shoulders then draping to her waist, all but hiding her fine silk gown with its cobalt piping and gold lace. She is unnoticed, all but invisible in the growing darkness. The intent, of course.

He comes often to the Royal Gardens with Samuel and Rebekah and the girls, a privilege enjoyed by the Vizier Council. He has scouted their spot for weeks now. The two of them practice matching stride lengths in the safety of the long hallways of the Rare Books Library, he awkwardly shortening his to match hers. It is comical to watch, more often than not devolving into hysterical laughter.

She, too, has been here before, but with her father gone these many months, the maze of paths has become vague in her mind's eye. She follows his instructions to the letter, carefully counts her strides, timed to the cues he has insisted she memorize. *After you enter the southeast gate, thirty-seven paces due west, then hard right, twenty-six more, until you pass the inset marble fountain, then turn right once more ...* She grins.

She forces herself to walk slowly, naturally, pretend that she is a middle-aged mother out to admire the caliph's gardens as she steals a moment of peace away from the demands of her clutch of children.

The Royal Gardens are a place for couples on the evening of Eid, and the throngs thin out and disperse to enjoy some privacy.

The escape went just as they planned. No sign of Aslam. But she knows she stands out as she moves, and he will not have given up the chase. Fortunately, the couples she meets have eyes only for each other and don't bother to wonder why a woman in *hijab* wanders the Royal Gardens by herself in the deepening night.

The drone of Eid can be heard in the distance; a chorus of baritone singers, the pumping silvery jangle of struck tambourines, the soft melodic pluck of a lute trio chasing an anguished reed pipe, all woven together in a beautiful tapestry until it ends abruptly in a sudden roar of applause. A moment later, the quick *tick, tick, tick* of drum sticks and the music begins again, more urgent now, greeted by rowdy whoops and hollers; no doubt the musicians have been joined by the swaying hips of veiled young virgins.

The party continues unabated, but the vast Royal Gardens are quiet now, a tranquil respite: the trickle of flowing water, the pearly tinkle of fountain splash, the dance of shadows upon elaborately carved stucco walls, the breeze gently rustling the branches of the desert palms.

The magical garden is dense and lush with all manner of plants and shrubs and trees, wide carpets of close-cropped grass, giant ferns set beside deep pools of black water, their feathery fronds interlocked, forming a neat, opaque canopy thick enough to stop a heavy rain; flowers bloom by the thousands.

The garden is a rich assortment of lovely exotic scents, all overlaid with splashes of fragrant rose and gardenia cast upon the breeze. There are dozens of sculpted privacy alcoves of precisely trimmed cypress hedge, each inset with small benches ringing bubbling fountains. A torch has been lit at every junction in the maze of intersecting paths, but the light is swallowed whole by the lush foliage, casting the entire garden complex into a dim twilight punctuated only by the eager diamonds pulsing high above.

Her heart pounds with their daring. She is helpless against the sweet gnaw in her stomach that forces itself upon her, the aching clench tightening with each step she takes. She repeats the words that Rebekah has taught her from the Hebrew scriptures, a mantra to steady herself. An ancient declaration of love from the "Songs of Solomon."

> *My beloved is mine and I am his.*
> *My beloved is mine and I am his.*
> *My beloved is mine and I am his.*

She has made six turns, weaving her way to the far northeast corner of the Upper Royal Gardens. It has been some time since she has passed anyone. She comes to another junction. Shadows from the lone torch scatter into the foliage and vanish. She stops and listens. A pleasing cacophony of fountain tinkle, nothing more. She turns to her rear. Alone.

Satisfied, she turns left. The narrow stone path transitions to pea gravel as it bends back around to the right. To the left of the path is a head-high wall of manicured cypress hedge; to the right, a compact orchard of a dozen miniature cherry trees. Zahra's snow. The soft crunch of her sandals upon the gravel is perfectly timed to her whispered cadence, "sixteen, seventeen, eighteen." She stops.

271

At her left is a neatly cut keyhole in the cypress wall.

Her dimples flash in the twilight.

She checks behind her once more, then slips through and disappears.

No luck at the poetry stages. Clearly a ruse. He curses Durr's name for the tenth time and circles back to the latrine, but she is nowhere to be found. Vanished.

He stops to reconsider.

A full minute transpires before the lightning strikes.

He thinks: Of course! The Royal Gardens. How could I be so stupid?

He moves quickly now, weaving in and out of the throngs. There is time still, he is sure of it.

She steps through the keyhole and stops to absorb the scene: a tiny courtyard with a cozy lover's bench facing a bubbling fountain. Just beyond is a compact, kidney-shaped pool of black water hugged on three sides by a dense carpet of plush grass. The spill of the privacy fountain dribbles down a narrow marble trough and sighs into the pool.

A dozen fish rise on cue to greet her, quick flashes of brilliant orange in the pale light, their mouths a syncopation of oval kisses. She smiles then unwinds her black shroud, folds it, and tucks it away. She continues to study the space. The opposite side of the pool is canopied by the elegant fronds of a trio of giant ferns, the dense pale green feathers bowing almost to the ground, forming a neat carpeted tent just high enough to kneel within.

Just as he described. Her heart races.

"My beloved."

She smiles and turns to her left.

Zafir steps from the shadows.

She whispers, "My beloved."

The couple he has startled is at first flustered, then resentful of the intrusion. A serious lapse of Eid protocol.

He apologizes once more and asks again in his most polite voice. "My wife, have you seen her? Please, sir."

The couple exchanges a quick glance. The young man says, "We passed such a woman twenty minutes ago as we exited the Upper Royal Gardens. Black head scarf. She may still be there."

He bows politely. "Thank you, sir. My apologies again for disturbing you. Eid Mubarak."

The young man grunts, "Eid Mubarak." They watch him as he moves quickly down the path, turns right, disappears.

They resume their passionate kiss where they left off.

"You are so beautiful."

She slides into his arms. "I have missed you so. Alone at last."

"Aslam?"

A coy smile. "I am afraid poor Aslam is still wandering about Madinat. It seems he is totally lost. I fear the man may be chasing a ghost all night long." She laughs.

He holds his finger to his lips. "Shhh ... we must be very quiet now, Rayhana."

Their expressions turn serious. He leans down and they kiss, tender and lingering. At the tops of their heads a flash of radiant blue flame shimmers into the air then relaxes and curls into a warm glowing aura resting upon their shoulders.

As the kiss becomes more urgent, he bends his knees to equal their heights, slides his hands to the small of her back, and pulls her tight against him. The duet of pleasure sighs begins to intensify. She locks her foot around his bare ankle, the heat from their bodies mingling deliciously.

They begin to twist and contort where they stand, welding their bodies into a conjoined sculpture. A moment more and they finally catch themselves and push away, flushed and panting. Their eager eyes are locked and dilated. A hint of a smile brushes his features. Their shoulders begin to shake, then they simultaneously double over in silent hysteria.

He exhales loudly. "Thirty days ... Ramadan was an eternity."

Her breathless answer, "Yes, an eternity. But now it is Eid, Zafir. And our love has been released from its prison within the Royal Library. I LOVE the gardens at night."

"Yes, finally free. Look up, Rayhana."

They lose themselves in the orgy of stars.

She whispers, "What a lovely night to be alone."

He turns her face and they lock eyes. "What a lovely night to lie with my beloved."

Her eyes well up. "I love you so."

"You are my life, Rayhana, all I have ever dreamed of, all I have ever wanted."

He breaks the trance with a mischievous grin then indicates the bench with his palm. "Shall we sit, gentle lady? With your permission, there is a matter I wish to discuss."

Her dimples frame her playful smile. "Why, kind sir, how bold of you. A matter to discuss? Pray, have you written me a poem, perhaps some clever words with which to sway my favor?"

He laughs and pulls her, giggling, to the bench.

They sit, hand in hand, shoulders and thighs and feet kissing, staring at the dawdling fish in silence. Without looking up he says, "I have something for you, Rayhana." His tone has turned oddly serious.

She looks up, curious.

He reaches under the bench, retrieves a small package.

She radiates the instant glee of a little girl. "Eidi?! For me?"

His expression remains serious, prompting her wide grin to slowly close. He hands her the gift. She looks up for confirmation to indicate that she should open it.

A soft crinkle of paper and she gasps, then whispers, "Oh my ... oh my, Zafir? The *Ambrosian Iliad*! Our first book ..." She looks up, eyes brimming.

He tightens the knot of their hands.

She asks with wide eyes and an incredulous whisper, "How?"

"I spent these past months copying the text myself. I hired an artist in the city to duplicate the illustrations from the original. With Samuel's blessing, the royal bookbinder agreed to do the final assembly. The binding is as fine as any to be found in the Rare Books Library. It is a perfect copy of the original."

As she thumbs through the illustrations her mouth drops open. "Oh my ... it is a magnificent Eid gift, Zafir, thank you. Thank you!"

He lifts her chin and turns her head with his thumb and forefinger. "No, Rayhana, not Eidi."

Her eyes grow wide.

"Mahr. My wedding gift to you, my love. This very night we shall marry."

Her chin begins its quiver, then her eyes begin to leak their liquid treasure. Two neat tears slide down her cheeks. "I desire nothing more. But what of Imam Abd al-Gafur? What of the nikah? Samuel told me he is hopeful he will agree to marry us."

"And so he shall, when the time comes. But tonight, my love, this very night, we will come humbly before Allah and proclaim our love for each other, and beg for his Grace, that he might bless our union." His voice begins to quaver. "I will marry you this night, Rayhana, my beloved, if you will have me."

Her quaver matches his. "I will marry you this night, Zafir, my beloved."

They stand, hand in hand, emeralds melting into amber.

Zafir whispers, "In the name of Allah, the Merciful, the Mercy-Giving, praise be to Allah, Lord of the Worlds, may prayer and peace be upon the Prophet Muhammad, his family and his companions." He pauses. "I, Zafir Saffar, marry you, Rayhana Abi Amir, in accordance with Islamic Law and the tradition of the Messenger of Allah."

Their eyes are locked to each other, tears flowing down their cheeks. As they offer their words of commitment, the rich blue glow of the aura pulses in the small courtyard, the fish wide-eyed and amazed.

"With Allah as my witness, I accept Rayhana as my beloved wife. I will love and cherish her for all eternity. May Allah grant us his great Grace."

Her chin quiver returns. She whispers through her tears, "With Allah as my witness, I accept Zafir Saffar as my beloved husband. I will love and cherish him for all eternity. May Allah grant us his great Grace."

A shower of brilliant blue sparks leaps between their hearts. The poor codex stranded on the bench heaves and twists, manages to flip open its cover for a better view.

Zafir says, "May Allah bless our union with all that is good and holy."

They both whisper, "Amen."

The silence stretches as they savor the awesome moment under the shimmering blue glow, hand in hand, hearts joined and pounding, eyes locked to the other.

Her dimples fill with tears of joy as these two break into giddy laughter. He hugs her and lifts her into the air, swings her side to side, slinging her giggles. As the motion slows then stops, she looks down upon him and they grow serious once more. She recites the Hebrew poem,

My beloved is mine and I am his.
Awake, north wind,
Come wind of the south!
Breathe over my garden,
And spread its sweet smell.
Let my beloved come to me,
Let him taste its rarest fruits.
I shall give him the gift of my love.
Come, my beloved, come.

She whispers, "Come, my Zafir, my beloved, let us lie together as husband and wife."

As he leads her by the hand around the pool, the mesmerized school of syncopating kisses treads water atop the jet-black depths. They flick-swish their pectoral fins in perfect time to precisely rotate in tandem as they track the lovers' movements, their bulbous eyes wide with awe.

The deprived codex has managed to wriggle to the edge of the bench, trying desperately for some semblance of a view, any view at all, but before he can catch himself manages to slide off the edge, landing with a truncated grunt in the pea pebbles, chased by a tirade of Greek curses.

Zafir lifts the feathered frond of the fern canopy with an eager smile and beckons his wife with an uplifted palm. Her radiant dimples disappear beneath their wedding tent.

He comes to yet another torch-lit junction, this one a three-way split. He moves silently as a stalking leopard, slippered feet upon cool white marble.

He looks up. Through the foliage he sees that the northeast corner of the Upper Royal Garden walls is not more than a stone's throw away. He curses the infernal maze of confusing paths. Which way? He cups his hands behind his ears, takes a deep breath, listens. Only the muted drone of Eid festivities. Once more. His eyes dart left. A girl's giggle? He takes another deep breath, holds it, listens. Nothing. Once more. Still nothing.

He can sense their presence. He turns left as he continues the hunt.

The aura of love fills the fern tent with a blue-hued twilight. Zafir has spread a fine quilt upon the plush carpet of grass.

There is only height enough to kneel, and they face each other, a foot apart. Their breathing is quick and shallow, their hearts pounding in their chests, pounding, pounding. Their expressions run to serious, as if suddenly aware of the magnitude of the holy journey upon which they are to embark. Their arms remain at their sides as they continue to stare into each other's eyes, content to let the moment stretch.

"Ana behibek." *I love you.*

"Ana behibak."

He leans over, lifts the hem of her gown and begins to finger the gold buttons, slipping them from their home one by one as he works his way slowly upward.

Her heart pounds.

He is at her breasts. Three more. Two. One. Her gown folds open, only the cool sheer of her silk slip between them now. He stops and begins to undress. She watches him remove his cloak and shirt, then lean to his elbow to take off his sandals, pants and undergarments. Her eyes widen with the reality of what she has long imagined.

He is kneeling once more. She helps him with her gown, lifts the silk slip above her head, then giggles as he wrestles desperately with her bosom wrap. She guides his trembling fingers to the pins and helps him unclasp them. The release of her beautiful breasts elicits an amazed gasp of awe. She answers with a smile.

He slides closer to her, but still they do not touch. He reaches for her long tresses, pulls the thick bundle of curls to her front. He removes the combs one by one, then unties the top cobalt ribbon, then the second, releasing the thick bundle of dark curls. They need no coaxing now that their freedom is won. He gathers her tresses and brings them to his face, inhales her.

"Praise Allah, I swear you smell of heaven ..."

Her dimples dive deep, then her face relaxes to serious once more and they vanish.

He lifts her hair and slides it back over her shoulder. She tips her head back, shakes it once, then twice, a ridiculously seductive motion that makes him swallow hard. They join hands. He lowers his eyes to drink in her curves, feasting on the vision he has dreamed of for so very long. He tentatively lifts his hand, his fingers still trembling, traces a wide curve around and under the heavy swell of her breast.

Her lids grow heavy as she exhales. With his thumbs he brushes her nipples, transforming them into rose statues set upon perfect curves carved from flawless alabaster. Her stiffening is a siren's call impossible to resist. He leans forward, and with a breath of moist warmth, takes a statue between his lips to gently caress it.

A pleasure leaden sigh leaks from her. Her eyes fold closed of their own accord.

Without releasing her, he slides his hands around her and cups her bottom, then feathers his fingers around her glorious hips and down her thighs to the back of her knees, those glorious knees. She shivers and can't keep from bending forward as her groans inflate the tent.

He slides closer still, then pulls her against him.

He lifts her chin. "Look at me, Rayhana."

She opens her eyes.

"I will always love you, Rayhana. You are my beloved, my angel, my life."

Her whisper is breathless. "I will always love you, Zafir."

Her eyes close again as she parts her lips and licks them wet, inviting him. He kisses her now, softly, tenderly, the moment exquisitely stretched out to a thin hot wire twisted taut, so taut, with roaring passion.

As he eases her down to their wedding bed, she folds open. He hovers above her on his elbows, eye to eye, his hands cupping her face. "I do not want to hurt you."

She whispers,

Let my beloved come to me,
Let him taste its rarest fruits.
I shall give him the gift of my love.
Come, my beloved, come.

Emerald and amber dissolve into a simmering puddle as he eases into her; a quick gasp, a clenched exhale, an exaggerated pleasure-sigh, then a soft feminine groan commanding his echo to obey.

She wraps her arms tightly around him, locks her feet to his ankles, and lifts her knees to draw him deeper within her, sculpting the timeless, magnificent image of two becoming one.

What has been months in the making, a sweet tortured agony, a slow roasting of frayed nerves upon a spit set close over crimson coals, the sweet clench of the relentless, a throbbing ache with a mind all its own, slows now, slows to a savored eternity as they walk hand in hand into love's sublime dance.

The blue aura flares, sizzles and sparks, a giant pulsing bundle of convolved energy.

The constellations high above lean desperately into one other, straining to see the young lovers through the dense canopy, yearning for a glimpse of the coming miracle, just a glimpse.

The liquid silk pressing in upon him becomes too burdensome to bear and he begins to move in her, slowly, so slowly, urged on by her tortured refrain of love murmurs. The taut glowing wire twists tighter, then tighter still, begins to sing like a plucked cord on a fine lute.

His movements quicken. Their eyes have never left each other. He sees her amber starbursts first widen with surprise then lose focus, then offer only sweet pleading. She tenses and arches her back to escape the boiling cauldron, curls her toes in desperation, then yields to the gush of ecstasy as she enfolds him and begins to cry his name, "Zafir, Zafir. Zafir! Zafir!"

The molten fire imprisoned behind the stone dam bears down hard upon him.

"Yes, Rayhana, yes ... I love you, Rayhana, Rayhana ... I love you, Rayhana ..."

Still they cling desperately to each other's eyes. Tears are spilling from hers now, her pupils giant midnight cauldrons. She sees the waves crest high above her, knows now that they intend to devour her whole then drown her. She gasps once, twice, then surrenders herself. She arches as she cries out, but this time moves back up and into the pleasure as it crashes down hard upon her. "Zafir, I love you, Zafir, Zafir! I love you ... Zafir!"

A thin sliver of jagged crack reveals the crimson glow of the molten fire behind the dam. The welling up of a single scalding drop, only a dewdrop. As it squeezes through, the sweet crumble of mortar, the collapsing of mighty stone, the irresistible torrent sweeping down upon them and over them and in them and through them.

His motions slow, then cease, their eyes still locked to each other. Their hot panting quiets.

The molten fire burns within her now, charged with life's greatest mystery, trumpeted for the stars to witness and record upon heaven's great scroll. The inexplicable of inexplicables, the incomprehensible obvious, the sweet quiver of love's ecstasy staked tight within the circle of the Holy Sublime. Here is the golden ring of Divine Love, its million suns focused down onto the polished spark of new creation.

They are both crying, the sheer intensity of their lovemaking spilling over them, crushing their senses flat with a joy so deep, so weighty, that it lies well beyond the reach of words.

How could it not be so? Here is a love of the rarest order.

It is twenty minutes later when they first hear it.

He is on his back, arm around her; she curled tight against him, knee scissored across him. They are still, enjoying the pleasing fountain tinkle as they savor their first moments together as husband and wife.

The soft crunch of a slipper eased down upon pea gravel; muted, a hushed gruffle flushed into the breeze. A moment more, then another crunch.

She hears it first, tenses, then whispers, "Listen."

He hears it now. He pulls her tighter, finds her ear. "Someone is coming." The crunches grow louder, punctuated by long moments of silence between.

He can hear her fear break through. "Aslam ..."

A gentle, "Shhh ... he cannot see us in here. We are safe."

She hugs him tighter still as they listen. The sound is nearing the entrance to the courtyard. The soft crunch arrives at the keyhole entry, then ceases.

Silence.

Their hearts are pounding. She leans close to his ear and breathes, "The codex."

They exchange a quick, nervous glance. He raises his finger to his lips.

One crunch closer. A second. A third.

Silence.

He is in the courtyard.

The fins on the school of fish freeze in place and the orange streaks slide back into the black depths. The stranded codex holds its breath.

It feels like an eternity before they hear the soft crunch once more; receding now, and quicker. One step, a second, a third, a fourth, then a slow meted movement on down the path. They do not move a muscle. All they hear is the muted drone of the festival laced with the quiet gurgle of the bubbling fountain.

They both exhale in unison.

She whispers. "It had to have been him."

"Yes."

"Surely he saw the codex."

"Somehow he must have missed it."

"Should we leave?"

He shakes his head. "No. We will stay here until just before Eid ends. It may be some time before he gives up." He squeezes her tighter to him.

Her coy, dimpled grin spreads. "We must stay here until Eid ends? What should we do with all of that extra time, Husband?"

A mock frown. "I am not sure, Wife, do you have any ideas?"

She releases a cute, muted squeal as he pulls her on top of him.

"Shhhh ..."

He slides her knees up his side, then encircles her back and pulls her to his chest. His hands drift to her hips, their shared gasp the only indication that he finds her.

Her eyes turn lazy and droop as she leans down to kiss him, a thousand dark spirals curtaining their faces.

An hour later they are dressed, smoothed and put back together, the flush of their cheeks the only hint of their tryst.

He leans down to retrieve the codex. "How did you end up here, little brother?" He lifts the volume and sees that from his angle just inside the keyhole, Aslam's view of the codex would have been blocked by the stone bench.

She nods her understanding. "Praise Allah."

"Yes, praise Allah. That was close."

Zafir edges to the entrance and carefully looks in both directions. Nothing. He turns back to her.

"Shall we return to the Eid festival, Wife?"

"You are forgetting something, Husband."

He smiles, then leans and kisses her deeply. When her knees begin to bend and she cannot suppress her groan, they push away from each other, smiling.

"You are a goddess, Rayhana. You drive me CRAZY!"

She giggles, takes his hand and webs it to hers, and the two lovers begin their casual stroll back towards the waning festival.

Their kiss outside her villa is long and lingering.

"I love you so, Zafir."

"You are my angel. I will be counting the moments until tomorrow morning in the Rare Books Library, Wife. Perhaps we can spend some time looking for a lost volume in the crypt."

She grins coyly. "Yes, I believe it may take quite a while to find the codex we are looking for, Husband."

He laughs loudly.

One more lingering kiss and they part. He drinks her in as she slips inside the gate, then he turns for home.

He winds his way back towards the Rare Books Library. His thoughts are on her, of course: her fabulous curves, their lovemaking. He smiles as he whispers, "My desert goddess," and shakes his head in disbelief. He has never been so happy.

The throngs are thinning quickly now and the streets are almost empty. Alas, fabulous Eid is over. Normal life will rear its head with the coming sunrise. He begins to hum a favorite childhood tune while he walks.

As he turns the corner he is yanked violently into a shadowed alley and grunts as he is slammed to the stone wall, which is more than happy to claim his breath. The man's forearm pushes his chest tight to the stone. He feels the cool press of steel against his throat just under his jawbone.

Aslam is back in his working clothes, a study in black. Zafir is pinned fast to the wall by a shadow.

He whispers a hiss, loaded with menace. "Flinch and I will gladly bleed you out, boy."

Zafir's eyes are wide with terror, his heart pounding. He gathers himself, manages some semblance of a challenge. "What is the meaning of this? I am a royal translator, a servant of the royal court under the caliph's Royal Librarian, Master Samuel al-Tayyib. You will answer to the caliph for this!"

"I know who you are, boy. Saqaliba. I also know that you stole the maidenhead of my master's daughter this very evening."

He is instantly livid. "How dare you! Rayhana is my wife, you scum."

His sneer is ugly. "Your wife ..." he scoffs. "You are a fool, boy. The girl is spoken for. You can be sure she will never marry a saqaliba." His grin is sinister. "You may have picked her fruit, boy, but rest assured, she will soon be wedded to a Berber prince. She will spread her legs for the Banu Birzal and birth a dozen Berber warriors. You will see soon enough."

He presses the steel enough to draw a thin line of blood. Zafir winces. Aslam leans close. "Listen carefully, boy. You and Rayhana are no more. You are nothing. If I ever see you within a stone's throw of the girl again, ever, I will geld you. Personally." He spreads Zafir's thighs roughly with his knee and presses on his groin. "If you value these you will stay away from her, understand?"

Zafir's heart is pounding but he remains silent, his eyes furious. Blood is beginning to trickle down his neck.

Aslam's knee relaxes then shoots upward. He releases his blade and backs away laughing.

Zafir sees only bright flashing needles of white light He doubles over as he sputters and coughs, gags, then vomits. He groans his agony as he wobbles with his elbows glued to his knees, struggles to find his feet. He paws the empty space and eventually finds the wall to steady himself. He exhales the rolling waves of nausea as he gingerly rises.

The wraith is gone.

Terror jumps into his eyes. "Rayhana! RAYHANA!"

As she enters the courtyard she stops, the smile on her face a league wide. She looks up at the heavens and laughs, hugs herself and spins about, then laughs some more. It is the happiest day of her life.

"My beloved ... my husband ... my Zafir."

She can't erase the grin from her face. She eases the door open and steps into the foyer. She listens. Nothing. They are all already in bed. She turns and quietly closes the door, sets the lock, and then pivots.

"Rasha."

She jump-yelps. Her terror is instantaneous, the force of the shock striking her dumb, draining her face of blood.

Ibn Abi Amir steps from the library into the foyer, an odd smile screwed to his face. "Rasha ... I thought you would be happy to see your father after all these months away." His frown deepens with each step closer. "Clearly, you were not expecting me." He stops and studies her, his smoldering ebony eyes stripping her bare.

She withers, lowers her gaze.

He hisses, "Eid at night without a chaperone, Rasha? What were you thinking? Have you no honor? You have shamed our family, Rasha, you have shamed me." He shakes his head, his disgust obvious.

The silence is deafening.

"Come, Rayhana, we have guests. There are two people you must meet." His voice would cut through stone.

Her head jerks up, eyes wide with fright, reduced now to a scolded child. She is pale as a ghost. Her eyes fill and her lower lip begins to quiver.

Ibn Abi Amir's command voice. "Brother, come. Come and behold the most beautiful ... virgin in Córdoba." The word catches in his throat.

Al-Andalusi steps into the foyer and slowly surveys her from head to toe, his expression greedy, a wolf sniffing among lambs. That booming baritone admires, "She is a desert flower, Qadi of the Maghreb, the most ravishing girl I have ever laid eyes upon. She will make a fine second wife. Our babies will be beautiful and strong, mighty warriors for your Banu Birzal army."

Her world pixilates, the voice turns tinny and distant. Thousands of tiny black daggers fill her pupils, her world edging first to gray and then to smoke then fuzzing into a haze of gauzy pinpricks. She folds like a rag doll to the floor.

Shadows

She is on him as he closes the door, enfolds him in a stranglehold of porcelain limbs, a python set upon an unsuspecting fawn. She laughs, she cries, she pulls his face to hers and smothers him with kisses; she desperately buries her tongue in his mouth then bites his lip as she pulls away, drawing blood. Just for good measure.

He seems surprised at her ferocity, but he shouldn't be. Her hunger consumes her every waking moment; has for many months now. He created this, did he not? Each new letter was inked with some erotic command and hints of growing love; but only hints. It grew into an addiction she has grown powerless to resist. He has broken her as he would an errant pony, though she is only vaguely aware of this. Fool.

She deceives herself into thinking she can regain some semblance of self-respect by proving her mastery over his body. She is intent on making him pay for his letters, punishing him for the torture he has inflicted upon her. A pathetically naive goal; this battle is long over.

He gives in to her, of course, why would he not? He lifts the succubus and carries her to the divan where he bends her and folds her and fills her, until she immodestly cries out his name over and over. It all seems to amuse him.

A quick moment of rest is all she permits him. She is not done with him yet, is eager to extract her price, and she understands well how to wield her body as a weapon.

She strokes him back to life then swallows him whole. She is satisfied only when she has stolen his helpless groan of her name. Then she pins his arms down and straddles him for more. His impenetrable ebony eyes lock onto her as she rides him, watches as the ecstasy steals the focus from her piercing azure orbs and she cries out again.

Their lovemaking grows so loud that the whole of the royal harem surely hears. But she is beyond caring, and so is he.

Afterwards, she lays her cheek on his chest, her legs scissored tight and locked around him, imprisoning him. They both glisten with sweat, hearts still thumping hard.

She ponders this man she both loves and hates ... and fears. His close-cropped beard has long vanished; it is full now and

285

stretching down his neck, a kinky mass of black scraggle. Different, but she likes it. He is deeply tanned, a creature of the desert now, and dresses as a Berber, not an Arab; a simple robe and black turban. The monotony of the color makes him look serious and intimidating; she guesses that is his intent.

He is more handsome than she remembers but looks more like some wayward tribal *mullah* than a member of the Umayyad caliph's Vizier Council. Qadi of the Maghreb. Without his clothes he is still beautiful, of course, distractingly so; addictively so.

But a feeling nags at her. Something about him has changed, something subtle that she can't quite place. Something.

She shifts her knee to reach for him, but he locks her wrist.

"No more, Subh." He chides her. "Give me time, woman."

She laughs loud. "I have missed you so, Muhammad. We have been too long apart."

"Yes."

She unleashes a devilish grin. "I may never get enough of you, you know."

He releases a shadow of a smile. "I am here now, Subh. You can have me as much as you like. Every day, every hour of every day. I am yours."

She snuggles tighter to him, satisfied.

They fall silent. She is thinking thoughts of love, of marriage, of ruling the kingdom as husband and wife; he is thinking of the new settlement for his Banu Birzal across the river, of battle tactics, of bribes still to be placed.

Her words are matter of fact. "My husband is dying."

"Yes. You have done well, Subh, very well. No one suspects. How soon?"

"Very soon. Days. It seems that even Abu al-Qasim, my husband's great healer, has given up hope."

"Good. Then we are ready."

"There is a plot you should be aware of, Muhammad." Her voice edges towards concern.

"Tell me."

"It seems that Jafar has made an alliance with Jawdhar and Faiq. They aim to name al-Mughira as my husband's chosen successor when he passes."

He knows all about this, of course. His spy networks are far larger than hers now.

"General Ghalib?"

"He is with them."

"And al-Mughira has agreed to serve?"

"He has."

"Do they have the support of the Slavic Guard?"

"Evidently so, yes, at least the officers. Jawdhar and Faiq are still working to arrange it all."

Silence.

"And the grand imam?"

She hesitates, having reached the limits of her information. "I am not sure."

He knows they have not secured the grand imam. Alas, their fatal flaw. A legitimate caliph cannot be appointed without the grand imam's consent.

"I will deal with it."

"How?" She is surprised by his nonchalance.

More forcefully he says, "Subh, I will deal with it." He changes the subject and relaxes his tone. "How is Hisham?"

"He is well. He misses you. The boy has grown sullen and no longer tends to his investments. He is once more lost in his books and his fantasies. I insisted he take part in the Salatul Fajr service for Eid, just to spite Jafar. He hated it. If Hisham is to be caliph, Muhammad, he will need a strong regent to marshal him. He has so much to learn."

"Yes, he does. Two strong regents, Subh."

Her bright laugh is filled with delight.

"I will see the boy soon enough. Tell him that the qadi of the Maghreb will expect a full reckoning of his accounts. And tell him I have a gift for him."

She mocks him. "Nothing for me, Qadi of the Maghreb?"

He squeezes her. "I just gave you the first part of your gift, Subh." She laughs. "Are you ready for the second?"

He lifts her chin and pours his molten ebony into her sockets. She is helpless to resist as his hot lava sears her brain.

She can only offer a breathless, "Yes, I am ready ..."

"I love you, Subh."

Her eyes brim then spill. The woman's legs have been crudely broken, bloody roots the final vestige of the sharp fangs she once sported and enjoyed sinking into wriggling flesh.

"I love you, Subh. We shall be married, and then we shall rule as Hisham's regents, as equals. Al-Andalus will be our playground, my love."

Her voice quavers, "I love you, Muhammad, more than I have ever loved anything or anyone. I desire nothing more than to marry you." Tears of joy stream from her.

His smile, which by any reckoning ought to be tender and warm, is thin and stretched; it seems too smug, too satisfied. Not a smile of love, but a smile of conquest, of triumph.

He lifts her hand and squeezes himself with her fingers. She groans. He emits a steely whisper, "Do not speak, Subh, not a single word. Do just as I say, and do only what I say."

Her lip begins to quiver.

"Roll on to your stomach and up onto your knees.

She hesitates.

His whisper hardens. "Do just as I say, and do only what I say."

She does. She is silent. She obeys.

"Good."

Her thighs are trembling.

At the very end he permits her to speak, but only the words he feeds her. This time, as her gaze fades to vacant, she cries out, "I love you, Qadi of the Maghreb! I love you, Qadi of the Maghreb! I love you, Qadi of the Maghreb!"

"Who?" Jafar is incredulous.

"Muhammad ibn Abi Amir, my lord."

Jafar exchanges a nervous glance with Jawdhar and Faiq, who are both wide-eyed.

"But that is impossible. He is in the Maghreb until the new year."

The Slavic guardsman is adamant. "It is him, my lord. He has a Berber with him. They are unarmed. Ibn Abi Amir says he wishes to see you. He says the matter is urgent."

Silence.

Jafar begins to pace as his mind whirls. The guard stands motionless, awaiting instructions. Jawdhar and Faiq are having a conversation with their eyes.

Jafar stops. "Interesting ... tell him ... tell him I would be happy to receive him. Give me ten minutes then show them both in."

The guard turns and departs.

"Well, well ... shrewder than I would have guessed. The man is a schemer, that much is sure."

Jawdhar's lovely baritone asks, "What do you make of this, Jafar? This could complicate our plans considerably."

Faiq adds a nervous, "Very considerably. He will oppose us. He will demand Hisham be named caliph."

Jawdhar adds, "And he has the grand imam's ear."

Jafar responds, "He does not have the Slavic Guard, gentlemen."

Jafar resumes his pacing, arms folded behind him. "A mere complication. Though, I will concede, one that must be managed very carefully. If he is in Córdoba, then the Berber army is in Córdoba. Untimely. He must have gotten word that the caliph is ailing. Subh would be my guess. It is a good thing that our fortifications on the river are nearly complete. Put the Slavic Guard and Madinat's garrison on high alert and make sure our gates are secure. The Berber army must not be allowed to cross the river. Alert the City Watch and send orders to the captain of the Puente Romano to see to it."

He stops to lock his eyes on them. "Be discreet. I do NOT want a panic, here or in the city. Spread the word that the caliph has invited the Berbers here to accept their pledge of fealty against the Christian incursion. No more, no less. But let it be known that this was the caliph's plan all along."

Jawdhar and Faiq nod in unison.

"If only we had some news of Ghalib. We should have heard something by now."

"What a pleasant surprise, Ibn Abi Amir, a pleasant surprise indeed. We did not expect you until the new year."

Both visitors are dressed in formal Berber attire, their robes and turbans midnight black.

"Yes, that was my plan, Jafar. But then I received news that the caliph was ailing. With the Christian siege at Gormaz hanging heavy upon the kingdom, I assumed that the caliph could use the services of the Banu Birzal sooner rather than later."

"You assumed ..." The words hang heavy in the air.

"I sent a letter to the caliph telling him of the change of plans. Has it not arrived?"

Jafar studies the man's stone mask. "No. It has not."

"My apologies, then. In the caliph's last letter he extended an invitation to the Banu Birzal."

The only reply is a cool, "Yes, he did."

Ibn Abi Amir turns to his left and lifts his palm. "May I present, Jafar al-Tariq, brother of Hamid al-Tariq, Sheikh of the Banu Birzal. Jafar is commander of the Berber army. He is known to all as al-Andalusi."

The Berber bows deeply.

"Al-Andalusi ... an interesting choice of names for a Bedouin prince of the Rif Mountains."

The Berber's command of Andalusian dialect is modest, thickly accented. His baritone is deeper even than Jawdhar's. He bows once more. "I am honored to meet you, Grand Vizier Jafar. The qadi of the Maghreb has told us much about you and the great glory of Córdoba. The Banu Birzal will dedicate our lives in service of the caliph."

Silence.

Jafar replies, "Qadi of the Maghreb ... yes, and I have heard much of the Banu Birzal. Much." He turns. "May I present Jawdhar, master of the royal jewels and the caliph's falcons, and Faiq, master of the Tiraz and the royal courier service."

Both men nod as they are introduced.

Ibn Abi Amir says, "What news of the caliph?"

Jafar pauses before he answers. "The caliph is ill, as you know. Fortunately, Abu al-Qasim is nursing him back to health. He has concocted some secret elixir. He believes the caliph should fully recover by the end of the year, perhaps sooner."

Ibn Abi Amir looks relieved. "Praise Allah. Perhaps we might see him? Al-Andalusi would like to kneel before the caliph and pledge the fealty of the Banu Birzal."

"A most excellent idea, Muhammad. Though I am afraid that is impossible just now. Soon. In the meantime, the caliph has arranged land for the Banu Birzal to make camp. Across the river."

"Across the river ... I see."

"Yes. The caliph felt that the grazing land was better there. And certainly there is more space to spread out."

"Yes." Muhammad smiles thinly. "I noticed the new fortifications on the far side of the Puente Romano."

"For protection against the Christians, of course."

"Of course. Al-Andalusi will see that the army and their families are settled in quickly. Any news of General Ghalib?"

Another slight hesitation. "We expect news of victory any day now. Gormaz is a long journey by courier."

"Yes, a very long journey."

The fortress located at the entrance to the Puente Romano on the far side of the Guadalquivir River has been hastily erected, but it is formidable nonetheless. Time only for earthen walls and wood, but the impressive stonework of the ancient Roman Tower rising high above the bridge serves to anchor the fortification and lend it an air of intimidation.

Unconventional in design by Arab standards, the fortress has been fashioned to repel a large cavalry assault. Moats; breastworks lined with thick nests of steel pikes funneling approaching riders into lethal fields of fire by archers and crossbowmen; wide, saw-tooth trenches dug deep and paved with short spikes that would give even a trained jumper serious pause before urging his mount to leap.

The garrison manning the defensive edifice is small, only three hundred troops, but the intended purpose is obvious to anyone with an ounce of military training. The message sent is one of distrust, of wariness. The fortress is meant to salve the festering suspicions of Córdoba's rich citizenry, suspicions triggered by the Berber army now camped upon the city's doorstep.

The deep green of the Guadalquivir ambles, slow and ponderous, stuffed as usual with a flotilla of dhows, barges, and sailing craft. The river brings life to the city, and business is good.

Fall encroaches; the weather cools, becomes crisp; the shadows in the Shining City begin to lengthen.

The spires of the Roman Tower provide the ideal vantage point to keep a tight watch on the birth of the Bedouin settlement sprouting in the hastily re-purposed fields and orchards hugging the far side of the river. A thousand horsemen and their families, perhaps six thousand Berbers all told. A tiny fraction to add to the city's population, to be sure, but these immigrants are different. They do not socialize, they do not even attempt to fit in. The city notices.

There is nothing haphazard about the layout and organization of the tent city. Within a day it is erected, communal ovens and cooking fires assembled, and defensive barriers and guard posts set into place. The horses graze on the pastures beyond but are guarded day and night. Stallions are the life's blood of a Bedouin clan, more valued than a young wife.

The people of Córdoba are a welcoming lot, it is in their spirit. They are used to accommodating foreigners, but they have never known people like the Banu Birzal. Tents? In Córdoba?

The wives of the Berber knights, clad in either full-length, black *chador,* or perhaps even face-obscuring black *burqa*, most unusual in this cosmopolitan city, cross the Puente Romano to venture to market, their dark eyes fierce with desert pride but also wary and distrusting. They keep to themselves, eyes rarely straying, and speak only when spoken to.

The market vendors exchange whispers, some discreet, many not. Children point and snigger. The Berber language is all but unintelligible, the dialect and accent odd to such cultured ears. The foods they prepare are different; less refined, more primitive. They shun delicacies as wasteful and weak. Books are of little or no interest, poetry an indulgence of the rich. They do not partake of watered wine or other elixirs; relaxation towards any of the proclamations of the Prophet is unthinkable.

The Córdobans are incredulous. Who ARE these barbarians? Judgments are rarely spoken directly but nevertheless are levied.

The Berbers smell of sweat and animals and smoke, enough to give offense in the tight quarters of the market squares to the meticulously bathed and perfumed Córdobans. There are no hammams in the desert, after all, and only rarely are there streams to bathe in. Water is a precious resource, for drinking, cooking, and *ghusl*.

The Banu Birzal quickly learn to make use of the Guadalquivir's vast treasures. The women string up sheets and shrouds by the hundreds between the trees at the water's edge. For privacy. The citizens of Córdoba are aghast. "Use the hammams, for Allah's sake! Why won't they use the hammams?! What is with these desert Berbers?!" The unmistakable whiff of prejudice hangs heavy in the air.

The clan settles in, rituals are reestablished, tent mosques, complete with anointed muezzin, are carpeted and dedicated. The *adhan* sounds across the Guadalquivir five times a day, a faint echo to the Great Mosque. All men and boys of the clan attend Friday service, but the women and girls are not permitted to join them, and instead use separate tents for their own private worship services.

Young women of marriageable age are carefully shielded from view by elaborate burqa shrouds whenever they are outside the family tents. The fear is of unwanted distraction to pure male thoughts, the arousal of wanton eyes, the dreaded sin of lust.

Women here live in a world of black cloth, of drapes and coverings and hides, except when sequestered in the privacy of their family tents. They eat only after their men are sated and exist to serve, to praise, to cook, to sew, to bear and raise children, to run the household, to please when their men require pleasing. They are respected for this, of course, and valued. Most embrace their roles with a fierce pride.

Quiet Quranic recitations, inevitably masculine utterings, can be heard late into the evenings in the lamp-lit tents of the Berber camp. The Banu Birzal are a devout people, fiercely so.

Atonement

2 October 976.

The knock is gentle and restrained; feminine. She looks up from the *Ambrosian Iliad*, her treasured mahr, a portrait of all-cried-out, weary sadness.

The door creaks open. "Your father has summoned you. He says he must speak with you."

"My father must speak with me? Speak with me?" The tone mirrors the picture. "My father despises me, Durr." Her eyes grow wary. "Is the ... Berber still here?" She chokes on the word.

"No."

"And Baba's ... wife?" She can barely say the word.

"No. They are both gone."

Her tears are not distant. "She is a child, Durr. What could Baba be thinking? She could be my little sister."

"Yes."

"Where are my brothers?"

Silence.

"Durr?"

She looks down. "Your father found out about Khalil and Maryam."

"Aslam ..."

"Yes. He is being sent to Almería. Tomorrow. To join the garrison there."

Rayhana gasps. "Khalil, a knight?" She is incredulous. "He has never held a sword in his life!"

"Your father seems to think it will help him remember his duties to the family. Evidently your father has plans to find him a Berber bride."

"And Salim said nothing?"

"Salim has been forbidden to leave the madrasa, Rayhana. He is not even permitted to write."

"Dear Allah, help us."

Silence.

"Your father wants to talk to you, Rayhana."

Her tone turns scathing. "I have nothing to say to my father, Durr, nothing."

"Please, Rayhana. Do not antagonize him. That will only make matters worse."

She is incredulous. "Worse, Durr? Tell me, how could I make it worse?"

She has no answer.

She stands before her father, eyes resting on the floor.

He ignores her as he continues signing papers from behind his desk, scolding her with silence.

Minutes pass.

Without looking up, he says, "You disappoint me, Rasha. You were raised better."

She looks up.

"So smart, yet so stupid. I made it quite clear you were not to see the boy again. You have brought shame upon us all. Shame." The word bites like acid.

He sets his reed pen down, then looks up and studies her as he frowns.

She meets his gaze.

"Reading in the Rare Books Library? Reading, Rasha? You met with this boy, alone without a chaperone. Many times. All these months." He shakes his head. "I can only imagine what went on." He sighs. "I failed you, daughter. I made your sin quite possible. Me!" A stiff, ironic laugh. "Believe me, I have prayed to Allah for forgiveness, and have vowed to right my wrong." He continues to study her. "Saqaliba?" The word is hissed. He shakes his head. "Aslam found it all, of course. How could you stoop so low, Rasha?"

Her jaw muscles tense as her nostrils flare, but she remains silent.

"Well?"

She takes a deep breath to steady herself then speaks with a carefully meted tone. "I love Zafir, Baba. With all my heart and soul, I love him. I tried to tell you this before you left. Zafir and I love—"

He scoffs. "Love ... you know nothing of love, daughter."

She pleads, "Baba ... Have you forgotten your beautiful Rayya? The love you felt for Mama. Baba, remember Mama? I learned of love from you two! You two!"

His expression does not change, but his eyes fill.

"You married Mama for love, Baba, for love. She told me this many times. Those long months you were away studying, Mama and I talked about your early life together, the love you two shared. She told me how you courted her, Baba, the poems you wrote, the love letters. How you loved each other more than life itself. That is all Zafir and I want, Baba. That is what Mama wanted for me. You know this. Baba, YOU KNOW THIS! Please understand. Please remember. Please ..."

His voice softens to a whisper. "Your Mama left me, Rayhana, left me when I needed her most. I cried until there were no more tears. My heart shriveled to dust then scattered in the wind. Your Mama is gone, Rayhana, she is no more, only a distant memory."

Two neat tears slide down her cheeks. "She lives on in me, Baba. Mama lives on in me."

"No, Rasha, my beautiful Rayya is gone forever." As he blinks his tears away his face hardens into a stone mask; his voice firms. "I have worked for many years to make a name for the Abi Amir family, to make our fortune, to earn the respect we deserve. We are on the verge of greatness. The name Abi Amir will be whispered in homage for a thousand years, Rayhana, you will see." He stops. "You have a part to play in that, daughter, a large part. The family of the qadi of the Maghreb must join with the Banu Birzal clan of the Maghreb. Both you and your brothers. As blood kin. I have married the Sheikh's daughter. You will marry al-Andalusi, Rayhana. He is an honorable man, and he will make a fine husband."

Her shoulders begin to shake. "Baba ... no, no Baba." She looks upward as she lifts her hands, pleads to the heavens, "Mama, hear me. Mama, help me!"

"It shall be as I say, Rayhana."

She sniffs loudly and straightens her back. Her tone turns defiant. "Does ... al-Andalusi know, Baba, that I am no longer a maiden. From what I hear, the desert Berbers are quite insistent ... they only marry virgins. It is said that young Berber brides must bring a white silk cloth on their wedding night to prove their purity to their husband and the clan. A red-stained flag to fly on the wedding tent." She is breathing hard as the tears spill from her. "Tell, me, Baba, did 'little sister' bring her white cloth when you consummated your child-marriage in the desert?"

Ibn Abi Amir stands and slowly walks towards her. His face is flushed, fists clenched, a steaming kettle set to explode. He stops in front of her.

She readies herself for the coming blow.

He takes a deep breath, unclenches his fists, then steps back.

She taunts him. "Not going to strike me, Baba? I thought that was how Berber men treat their women when they dishonor them."

His voice is icy. "Sadly, you know nothing of Berber honor, Rayhana. You disgust me ..." He is out to punish her now. "And do not worry about your wedding cloth, Rayhana. I am sure Ulla will be happy to lend you hers so that our family honor is preserved." He wears a thin, cruel smile.

She blurts out, "Zafir and I have already married, Baba!"

His eyes widen.

She smiles ruefully. "Yes, Baba. Married. Zafir and I exchanged our wedding vows in the presence of Allah just before we lay together. He proposed, I accepted. He presented me with my mahr, and we exchanged our vows. We are married now, Baba, married."

The purveyor of the law courts considers her words.

He smiles. "Then perhaps you would be kind enough to show me the *nikah*, Rayhana? I would like to see who signed the wedding contract in my absence."

Her face falls.

He sneers. "And who would dare serve as your *wali*, Rayhana, tell me who?"

Silence.

He scoffs, "Married ... married to a saqaliba? Never. You are an Abi Amir. You are a sinner, girl, no more and no less." He aims to draw blood. "A whore, Rasha. You are just a whore."

She gasps. Who is this person that used to be her baba? Who?

"You must atone for your sins, Rayhana. You must atone." He examines her as he would an insect before pinning it to a display board.

She withers under his scrutiny, senses the ax before she actually sees him lift it.

"From this moment hence you are confined to your room. Under lock and key. As atonement, you will knit me a prayer shawl to wear into battle. From the finest Granadine silk. Durr will teach you the stitches. Only when you have finished it to my satisfaction will you be permitted to leave your room. After that, you will not leave the villa until your wedding day. Your marriage to al-Andalusi WILL be consummated, of that you can be sure."

She seethes. "You CANNOT hold me here against my wishes, Father. You WILL NOT hold me here."

He laughs. "Cannot? Will not? Dear Rayhana, I have every legal right to do so. Let us not forget that I am your father. Sharia Law is on my side. I have already instructed Aslam and my Berber bodyguards to see to your ... care personally. Trust me, you will not leave our villa without me knowing."

Her anger smolders, a pile of glowing embers starved for fuel, ready to burst into flames at the slightest invitation.

He studies her, enjoys watching his words worm into her and gut her. "Oh, and Aslam has been instructed to geld the boy if he shows his face. Your saqaliba lover will either return to his books willingly or he will join the royal harem as its newest eunuch."

She screams her fury as loud as she can.

He laughs once more, then his face sets firm with resolve.

Durr pours the heated water into the shallow basin. The steamy tendrils linger momentarily, then vanish. Her voice is tender, barely above a whisper. "I brought you fresh linens to bathe."

"Thank you, Durr." Rayhana's response is listless, resigned. For the first time in her life she has been denied the luxury of daily hammam. She never realized how much she took bathing for granted. There is little pleasure to be had from a tiny washbasin. She manages the best she can.

Durr looks like she has something to say but hesitates.

"What, Durr? Tell me."

"I was wondering if you wanted me to teach you the stitch work. For the ... prayer shawl."

Rayhana's eyes fold close. "No, I cannot bear it just yet, Durr." She sighs heavily as she wills them open. "Give me time, Durr, I need time."

"I understand."

Her eyes fill. "Durr, you must give me something to hope for. Please. Something, anything."

"I am trying, Rayhana. My every move is scrutinized."

Silence.

Durr inhales then exhales loudly. "I saw Rebekah at the market this morning. The vendors on the west side of the market square in the medina, just where you said. I did not approach her, but I am sure she saw me. We were being watched. Aslam."

Rayhana's face brightens as she whispers, "Praise Allah. Praise Allah!" Her hands lift and begin to dance as she calculates. "Of course! I will prepare a note, Durr. Something that can be rolled in a miniature scroll. It must be tiny, so tiny as to be almost invisible, easily hidden between two outstretched fingers. Next time, you will decide to buy what Rebekah is buying and stumble upon her. You will greet her as if it is a complete surprise that you met." She widens her eyes. "It has to be a surprise, Durr. Aslam will be watching and he will be suspicious. He may even approach you both to challenge you. You must be ready for this."

Durr slowly nods looking extremely wary.

"As you are standing beside Rebekah, you will let the scroll drop from your fingers into her market bag. But she must see you do this, and Aslam must not."

"How?"

"We will practice, Durr, we will practice. You will see, it will be easy." She beams, she is reborn. "Rebekah should be at market again on Friday. She will need to shop for Shabbat. Will you help me, Durr? Will you help us? Please, Durr!"

Silence fills the room.

In just a whisper she consents, "We must practice."

Rayhana smiles. "We WILL practice, Durr, we WILL practice!" She hugs her mistress, freeing a startled giggle. "A plan, Durr. We have a plan!"

The caged bull paces as the words erupt from him. Rebekah sits, stoic, a portrait of motherly concern. Samuel frowns at the floor as he listens.

"He has her locked in her room! She cannot leave for any reason. She bathes in her room, eats in her room, has to use a chamber pot. A chamber pot! He insists she atone for her sins by knitting him a silk prayer shawl. A PRAYER SHAWL!" He hisses. "The bastard! And she is confined to the villa until the wedding day with this Berber monster, someone they call al-Andalusi." He stops, clenches his fists then releases them, resumes his pacing.

Samuel looks up. "Sit, boy, you are making me anxious."

Zafir stops, grimaces, then reluctantly drops heavily into the chair. A second later he is up again, pacing.

"She has told me I must stay away, that Aslam has been instructed by Ibn Abi Amir to—to ... geld me if he finds me with Rayhana again."

Rebekah gasps. "Dear Lord ... What has the world come to?"

Samuel tries again. "Sit, Zafir. Please."

As the boy plops back down; his shoulders sag and his chin folds to his chest. His voice quiets as he says, "What am I to do? What am I to do? I cannot live without her. I WILL NOT live without her. What am I to do?" He chokes back a sob and covers his eyes with his hand. His shoulders begin to shake as he cries.

Rebekah rushes to him, cradles him as she would a young child. "Shhh, Zafir ... shhh. It will be fine, it will be fine, shhhh ..."

The room grows quiet.

Samuel says, "I met with Imam Abd al-Gafur, Zafir."

Zafir looks up.

"He is sympathetic to our cause but wary of defying Ibn Abi Amir. Understandable. He promised that he would consult with Rayhana's grandmother about the matter and seek her counsel. I cannot imagine, that with this new turn of events, their sympathy would not grow for you two. I will write to him today and get the letter to Algeciras by the fastest rider. I am sure he will help us, Zafir, I am sure of it."

Zafir's eyes are still full. "Thank you, Samuel."

Rebekah chimes in, "And at least Rayhana was able to get word to you, Zafir, that is something. Durr will help us."

Zafir sniffs. "Yes, that is something." His face brightens. "Rebekah, will you help me get a message to her. Please?"

She doesn't hesitate, "Of course I will, Zafir, of course I will."

Samuel frowns. "Aslam is a dangerous man, Rebekah. I hear all sorts of awful rumors about him. And Ibn Abi Amir now has two Berber bodyguards that do not leave his side. I do not think sending a message to Rayhana would be a wise move."

Rebekah's eyes lock onto her husband. She speaks calmly and slowly, but her tone is unmistakable. "Samuel. I WILL help, Zafir, and I WILL help Rayhana, no matter the danger."

Samuel sighs with the finality of his wife's tone. He has heard it a thousand times and doesn't even bother to try and counter her. "Very well, but you must be very discreet."

She smirks. Always the obvious with this one.

He turns to Zafir and lifts his finger to scold. "And you, Zafir, you are NOT to go near her villa, under any circumstances. Let us keep you in one piece. Understood?"

The boy nods.

Rebekah muses out loud. "How to get a message back to Rayhana while Aslam watches us ... hmmm. An interesting challenge ..." She twists her fingers into her curls as she stares into space.

Silence, book-ended by two masculine breaths held tight.

She beams. "Ahhh! I have it!" She looks at Zafir. "A silk prayer shawl, correct?"

"Yes, he insisted upon the finest Granadine silk. Why?"

She beams as she nods. "Easy!"

Ghosts

11 October 976.

The workshop is dark. Sheets of darkened paper have been tacked to the insides of the windows to squelch any adventuresome slivers of leaking light. A single oil lamp with an unusual green flame, some alchemist's fancy, hangs outside above the plain wooden door, the only marker for the location of the meeting. The street lamps have been extinguished in both directions.

A nondescript warehouse on a nondescript alley that worms deep into the working quarter of Córdoba's medina, close to the docks on the Guadalquivir. Such men as these would never be seen here by light of day, for this is a section of the medina for those who heave and grunt and sweat. This is a land of harbor workmen, of dhow captains inspecting their fresh hauls, of ceramics and tableware in the process of being stacked, wrapped, and crated by laborers, of warehouse clerks who first catalog then barter and sell for their masters, of dock-hawks who negotiate the best shipping rates to Constantinople, of tax collectors. This is where Córdoba's commerce is gathered and priced, then boxed and transported to the far corners of the earth.

No, these men come under the cover of night, prompted by a simple note saying, "Your presence is requested for an important meeting that concerns your family's interests." Below is written a day, a time, an address, in a simple scrawl of Arabic, then sealed with red wax using a stamp labeled *AA*—Abi Amir.

This is a gathering of a sizable fraction of the leaders of the most powerful merchant families of Córdoba. These are businessmen, rich beyond measure, who intend to stay that way no matter the whims that may emanate from Madinat al-Zahra or the current caliph.

They arrive one by one, flanked by the inevitable bodyguard, some with a matching pair. Aslam emerges from the shadows to greet each merchant by name. He acknowledges their bodyguards with a curt nod, then politely whispers that only the merchants are allowed inside.

The bodyguards look wary and touch their masters' arms, a sign of caution. A correct response. But the merchants know

Aslam, and after a close scrutiny of his face for hints of danger, they offer a shrug of agreement then slip inside. The bodyguards sullenly slide back into the shadows to wait. They do not speak to each other; a professional courtesy.

Aslam has come to know much about these merchants in the many months of Ibn Abi Amir's absence from the city. By now he has a chest full of incriminating evidence; juicy gossip about their families, miscellaneous tidbits that may or may not be accurate, but are useful nonetheless.

Meanwhile, he brings them news from the Maghreb, whispers from Madinat, inside information that can lend them a trade advantage. He discreetly offers gold for information about their colleagues, friend and foe. He allows the plans of his master's secret arrival in the city with his Berber army to be known a day in advance, and he delivers this meeting invitation personally. Aslam has earned their trust, and has to spend only a tiny fraction of it now to secure their entry without bodyguards.

Ibn Abi Amir has invested a large amount of energy, and most of his gold, in cultivating these connections to the most powerful merchant families. Here is the real power base that drives the caliphate of Córdoba, the Umayyad Empire. A caliph requires taxes to govern, vast heaps of gold—and trade furnishes the lion's share of that wealth. The merchants have no philosophical bone to pick with the Umayyads, why would they? Business is good; better than good. Even after taxes, these men have grown rich beyond their wildest dreams.

They build lavish towered almunyas outside the city walls, fill up their libraries with rare volumes they never read, become patrons of the arts just to garner respectability, then quietly buy up land in thousand-arpent increments in the Middle and Upper Marches. They collect sailing ships by the fistful, candy to be swallowed. Oh, the games of the rich.

True, Caliph al-Hakam II has been overly concerned these past years with acquiring books and fostering the arts, with building hospitals and making the dhimmi feel welcomed and valued. Few new trade delegations and exchange treaties have been granted. A pity. The merchants may frown their disapproval, even grumble among themselves, but these are pragmatic men; businessmen. Provided the caliph's actions do not impact trade and the lavish profits they have come to expect, little is done. The relationship is symbiotic.

The caliph rarely leaves Madinat now to visit Córdoba, and even more rarely consults with these powerful men before he acts;

a snub that is noticed, certainly, and in many instances, resented. Still ...

But these corsair inclusions that have begun to increasingly plague the ports and hamper trade routes across the Roman Sea are another matter entirely. This troublesome pirate meddling costs them dearly in merchandise and people, and has crossed the serious threshold of affecting their profits. The frowns and grumbles have shifted to curses and accusations.

The caliph seems impotent to halt the pillage of the corsairs provoking a deep discontent that festers among the merchant families. And now this Christian incursion at Gormaz. What next? From their gossip it would seem that White Hands and his army were camped right outside the city walls. Nerves are frayed, fingers are waggled, the grousing grows louder.

Ibn Abi Amir has fed this malaise, of course, stoked the fires of discontent at every opportunity, in every imaginable way. "Something should be done. Something must be done! This is simply unacceptable. Al-Andalus is being poorly governed. Al-Andalus is in peril."

Within, the room is dimly lit, the circle of thirteen pillows filled by graying tycoons swaddled in the finest gold-embroidered silk robes, their hands and necks adorned with precious jewels, rings and pendants from Persia and the Orient.

Ibn Abi Amir sits among them, the youngest man present. Al-Andalusi sits at his side, their Berber mantra of plain black robes and turbans offering a stark contrast to the bejeweled merchants.

Suktan and Tahir, his Banu Birzal bodyguards, are the only two men in the room that are armed. The feminine curve of their massive scimitars hang loose at their sides, their ornate dagger cases sunk into their sashes. They stand back in the shadows in opposite corners of the room, pillars of menace. The merchants grimace upon entry, but in the end, Ibn Abi Amir's bodyguards are easily ignored. It is Ibn Abi Amir, after all. There is trust here.

When all are assembled, Ibn Abi Amir begins. "Welcome, gentlemen."

Murmurs.

"You received advanced word from Aslam of my unplanned arrival in Córdoba. Certain ... events have forced my early return, but all is well."

More murmurs.

"As you know, I have brought a Berber army with me, gentlemen, an army like none other. A Berber army that will be placed in the service of the caliph. A Berber army that can and will defeat White Hands should the need arise. A Berber army that will safeguard the city and protect your trade routes within al-Andalus. They are the Banu Birzal, the masters of the Rif Mountains, the most formidable warriors ever to gallop across the rich soil of al-Andalus."

The merchants nod their approval.

He lifts his palm. "This is al-Andalusi, gentlemen, the brother of Sheikh Hamid al-Tariq of the Banu Birzal, and leader of the army."

Al-Andalusi nods. "He is my brother now, gentlemen. I am blood kin to the Banu Birzal. I am Qadi of the Maghreb."

Incredulous whispers.

"Al-Andalusi, my brother, is now your friend. He can be trusted, as you trust me."

The oldest among them strokes his long beard as he listens. Abd al-Kabir, the undisputed leader of the group. "And what of the corsairs, Ibn Abi Amir?"

Grumbles of concurrence.

"Soon the Banu Birzal will drive the Fatimids out of the Maghreb and back into the east where they belong, Abd al-Kabir, and the corsairs will have no ports from which to strike your shipping. The Banu Birzal have already unified the Idrisids of the Rif and are organizing for battle as we speak. They have the caliph's backing, and his gold. The conquest will take time, but the wheels of war are already in motion. By this time next year, gentlemen, your trade routes will be free of corsairs. On that, you have my word."

Abd al-Kabir nods his approval, joined by a pleased chorus. As the room quiets, tension fills the space.

Abd al-Kabir says, "And tell us, Ibn Abi Amir, what turn of events prompted your early return to Córdoba?"

Silence.

Ibn Abi Amir's gaze circles the gathering. "The caliph is dying."

A flare of shocked whispers ignites the circle.

When the room settles, Abd al-Kabir says, "We know of the caliph's illness, Ibn Abi Amir, but we have been assured by the grand vizier that he is on the road to recovery. Abu al-Qasim has been treating him. He did miss Eid al-Fitr, it is true, but he will be well by year's end."

Ibn Abi Amir's voice turns icy. "Jafar is lying. The caliph will be dead within a week, at most two."

Shocked silence.

"There is more. When the caliph dies, Grand Vizier Jafar, with the backing of Faiq and Jawdhar and the Slavic Guard, will attempt a coup. They intend to banish Hisham and his mother and name Caliph al-Hakam's brother, al-Mughira, as successor to the Umayyad caliphate."

The circle roars.

Abd al-Kabir lifts his hands to quiet them, a scowl now creasing his features. "Hisham is the caliph's legitimate heir, and by law the caliph's successor. Al-Mughira has snubbed the merchant families at every turn. He must never be allowed to rule." He inhales, then exhales heavily.

"What they risk is civil war, a terrible prospect for business."

"Yes, Abd al-Kabir, they do risk civil war. Jafar has the tacit approval of General Ghalib. And thus his army."

Grumbles.

"This must not be permitted, Ibn Abi Amir. Think of the implications for Córdoba, for all of us."

"No, it must not be permitted. Stability of the Umayyad lineage must be maintained at all costs."

The silence inflates.

Ibn Abi Amir studies their faces. "Gentlemen, I intend to see Hisham appointed caliph, and I intend to declare my loyalty to him. With the grand imam's blessing, I will serve as the boy's regent until he comes of age, and then I will step back into the shadows. During my regency, I will ensure that your livelihoods remain unfettered and that Córdoba prospers in every way."

Silence.

"And how do you intend to accomplish this, Ibn Abi Amir?"

The qadi of the Maghreb smiles. "With your support, of course, Abd al-Kabir, and the support of the merchant families." He lifts his hands to them. "And with the help of Banu Birzal." He rests his hand on his brother's shoulder.

"Blood is bad for business, Ibn Abi Amir, very bad for business."

"Rest assured, Abd al-Kabir, my actions will be quick and clean. The world will never know that there was a coup attempt. Córdoba will be back to normal in three days, no more, with Hisham in his rightful role as caliph and the people cheering his new reign. Your businesses will be unaffected."

Abd al-Kabir's expression announces his doubts. "But the Slavic Guard and General Ghalib. How will you handle these ... complications?"

Ibn Abi Amir's smile widens. "You must trust me, Abd al-Kabir, you must trust me. There is a plan." He locks his eyes on each of the merchants, one by one, searches their faces for any hint of disagreement. Satisfied, he says, "Not a word to anyone, gentlemen. Go about your business as normal. All will be well."

An acquiescent hush settles in the room.

Rayhana looks up from her reading. She recognizes the timbre of the knock and relaxes her shoulders. The metal lock double-clicks and the door creaks open.

Durr enters then closes and re-locks the door. She carries a small bag.

"Hello, Durr. What did you bring?" Weary resignation clings to her words.

Durr's face is expressionless. "I brought you something from the market."

Rayhana queries with her eyes.

"A bolt of silk, Rayhana. From Granada. The merchant that has his shop on the west square of the medina. The one by the mosque. They say he has the finest silk in Madinat."

The girl's eyes grow wary. "Silk ..." She croaks, "For a shawl."

"Yes, Rayhana. You must begin the shawl. It is time." Durr's tone remains stubbornly upbeat. "I will teach you."

The girl's eyes fill and her liquid gaze settles into her lap.

Durr smiles. "Come, Rayhana. You must see this silk, it is so lovely." She opens her bag and withdraws the small bolt. As white as the finest bleached cotton, the weave perfect and tight, so sheer you can see the lifelines on a palm placed beneath it. She approaches her mistress and lays the bolt on the splayed codex.

Rayhana wipes her eyes and stares but seems afraid to touch it.

Durr whispers, "Unroll the bolt so that you can see it better."

The girl is paralyzed.

More forcefully she repeats, "Rayhana, unroll the bolt of silk."

Her hands rise tentatively from her lap. She lifts the bolt, removes the pins, and begins to unroll it. Halfway through the unraveling something drops out onto the codex. A palm-sized rectangle of silver plate, not much thicker than a heavy foil and polished to a mirror sheen.

Rayhana squints, puzzled.

Durr is beaming.

She tenderly lifts the piece of paper-thin silver mirror and gasps sharply. She angles the object to better catch the light, brings it close to her face. Her mouth opens in disbelief. Her eyes fill once more, but this time their desires are beyond her control and the tears spill down her cheeks. She cradles the mirror with both hands. Her shoulders begin to softly shake. She chokes back a sob, unexpectedly laughs loudly, then begins to wail. Oddly, the girl is beaming through the torrent she unleashes. Tears of joy.

Durr holds her. "A gift, Rayhana, from the one who loves you."

The sobs intensify.

Curious now, Durr lifts the silver mirror to study it more closely. At first it seems only heavily smudged; dirty. She leans closer, then she, too, gasps. She has never seen the like. A faint ghostly image of Zafir, barely visible, but unmistakable. He is sitting in front of a bookcase, his smile large upon his face. She studies the image. He holds a piece of paper in front of him. The bright red squiggles and dots and dashes of the Arabic script read, "Rayhana: my beautiful wife, my beloved, my heart and soul. I believe."

They are both hysterical now.

When the storm finally ebbs, Rayhana says, "How, Durr, tell me how you got this? How?"

"Rebekah, it was Rebekah. At the market yesterday we spoke. She told me to visit this particular silk merchant, and to ask for a bolt of the finest white Granadine silk. I asked why, but she just smiled. 'Tomorrow morning,' she said, 'It must be tomorrow morning.' So I went."

"You did not tell me ..."

"No, Rayhana, I did not want to get your hopes up. You have worries enough as it is."

She nods, then hugs Durr to her.

"On the way home, Aslam stopped me."

Rayhana's eyes widen.

"He demanded to know what I bought. I told him the truth—silk for the prayer shawl. He rudely took the bag and opened it, examined the silk, then gave it back. Rebekah buried the silver mirror safely inside the bolt. He did not find it, praise Allah."

"You are very brave, Durr. My Durr is VERY brave. Thank you, thank you, Durr!" Mercifully, a pair of dimples emerge from their long sequester.

Durr smiles, then frowns. "But what is this, Rayhana? How can Zafir's likeness be captured within a piece of polished silver? I do not understand."

Rayhana laughs loud. "Well, let me just say it has to do with a darkened chamber and some very clever men whom I adore."

Durr looks puzzled, shrugs, and then they laugh together.

Rayhana stares at the image of her husband. She whispers, "My beloved, my heart and soul. I believe, Zafir, I believe."

He smothers the boy in his arms, holds his head to his chest, a cherished son not seen in more than half a year.

The boy basks in the man's affection, his frozen features first thawing, then blossoming, his demeanor miraculously transformed from lifeless to elated.

"I missed you, Hisham."

"I missed you, too."

They hug in comfortable silence.

Ibn Abi Amir says, "You have kept up with your studies? I expect a full accounting of your many investments, young man."

The boy grins. "My ledgers are in order, sir."

Ibn Abi Amir laughs. "You received my letters?"

"Yes. All twelve."

"Our key is safe?"

"Of course." The boy seems proud of himself. Ibn Abi Amir cannot help but smile.

"Good, Hisham, very good."

Sheepishly, he asks, "Did you bring me a gift?"

Ibn Abi Amir laughs. "Yes, Hisham, I brought you a gift. Several, in fact."

The boy beams.

"Close your eyes and open your hands." The boy grins as he cups his hands in front of him. His heart is pounding as he feels the weight press down.

"Now open them."

Hisham studies the object, puzzled. A slab of weathered gray stone. It fills both palms.

"You must guess." Ibn Abi Amir is clearly enjoying himself.

The boy studies the gift. "A stone."

The man laughs. "Yes. But not just any stone."

Hisham looks up.

"A stone from the lintel of the main gate of Hajar an-Nasar, Hisham. I have brought you a piece of Eagle's Rock."

The boy smiles.

Ibn Abi Amir reaches into his robe and withdraws a small scroll. "And the deed to the fortress. You, dear Hisham, are the owner of Hajar an-Nasar now. I have seen to it. The fortress is yours, and yours alone. Your garrison marks the southernmost Umayyad presence in the Maghreb. You rule the Rif, young man."

The boy's smile widens. "My garrison ..."

"There is more." Ibn Abi Amir pulls a bejeweled dagger case from his robe. The case is delicately curved and ornate, the polished silver a spider web of fine engraving, studded end-to-end with rubies and emeralds. Priceless. "This is the ancestral dagger belonging to the great-great-grandfather of Hamid al-Tariq, Sheikh of the Banu Birzal. There is no finer dagger in the Rif, Hisham. The blade was forged in Damascus, the cradle of your ancestors. The sheikh wanted you to have it as a token of the Banu Birzal's eternal fealty to the Umayyads."

The boy's eyes grow wide as he slides the blade from the case with a cool hiss. He whispers, "Mother has never allowed me to have a dagger ..."

"You have one now. Times are changing, Hisham." Ibn Abi Amir's expression grows serious, and the boy looks up at the shift of tone, a wary edge sliding onto his features.

"You will soon be caliph, Hisham. It is nearly time for you to serve your people. Do not worry. Your mother and I will act on your behalf as your regents. We will not leave your side, and we will help you learn to govern wisely." He raises his hands. "You will be free of this ... dungeon." Ibn Abi Amir studies the boy. "The people of al-Andalus will worship you, Hisham, they will worship you. You will be the most powerful person in the entire world. The history books will whisper with awe the name Caliph Hisham for a thousand years."

The boy's wariness evaporates and is replaced with a hint of a smile.

"Come, Hisham, let us talk, there is much for us to catch up on." He puts his arm around the boy's shoulders and leads him to the divan.

Formalities attended to, Ibn Abi Amir says, "We must speak privately, Grand Imam."

The old man dispenses his attendants with a simple flick of his fingers.

The grand imam sits cross-legged on his silk pillow, elbows on his knees. His fine black robe and black turban are an overt acknowledgment of his ancient Berber bloodline. He wears a stern, no-nonsense expression. One can imagine that it would require the grandest of occasions for this man to indulge the world with a smile. He is old. Ancient. The tip of his beard just touches his lap, a solid mass of kinky white. But despite the man's age, the eyes are young, the sparkle within the ebony that of a deeply pious man who is also quite at ease with political maneuverings and court intrigue. He has seen it all. And survived to lead the most powerful mosque in the world.

"It is good to see you, Muhammad." Firm, steady voice.

"I have missed you, Grand Imam." Ibn Abi Amir kneels, lifts the older man's right hand, kisses it, then deferentially touches it to his forehead.

The older man responds with a slight tick of the head, clearly pleased.

Ibn Abi Amir sits.

"You have brought an army with you to Córdoba."

"Yes, Grand Imam. The Banu Birzal will swear their allegiance to the caliph." He pauses. "And to you."

A simple tick of the head.

Ibn Abi Amir continues. "You know of Jafar's plot."

The old man's eyes twinkle. "Of course."

"Al-Mughira cannot be named caliph without your blessing, Grand Imam. Jafar knows this."

"Yes. His bribes have been lavish. Beyond lavish. And he has pledged that al-Mughira's first act as caliph will be to expand the Great Mosque by two-fold. Imagine ..."

"Predictable. And?"

"I have led him to believe that he has my support."

"Good. He does have the Slavic Guard."

"Yes, a minor problem for the qadi of the Maghreb, I am sure."

Ibn Abi Amir smiles. These two know each other well. "Grand Imam, Hisham will succeed his father. I will serve as his regent until he comes of age. With your wise counsel, of course."

Silence.

The old man muses, "What of Ghalib?"

"I will handle Ghalib, Grand Imam."

A simple tick of the head. "There must be no civil war, Muhammad. Order must be restored in the city, and very quickly, or the support of the merchant families will waiver."

"Yes. All is arranged."

"Excellent."

Ibn Abi Amir studies his mentor. "You will have your expansion of the Great Mosque, Grand Imam. It will be Hisham's first act as caliph. And the city will return to Sharia Law as its guiding light. Al-Hakam's blasphemous ways will die with him."

The old man nods appreciatively. He raises a finger, a last point that seems to have been suddenly recalled, though this is an illusion. "These books al-Hakam so fondly collects, the blasphemous stories from Greece, these so-called 'Greek plays,' and these books which try to pry out the secrets of Allah's creation using numbers and rules ... such books trouble me. The Greeks are infidels, and their strange ideas and promiscuous ways have no place in the Royal Library."

309

Ibn Abi Amir considers. "Such books are not worthy of Allah, Grand Imam. Perhaps they should find another home."

A simple tick of the head.

At last, some news from Gormaz. He unrolls the scroll and begins to read. Three sentences in, his eyes widen as his mouth opens, aghast. His eyes flick frantically down the page, right-to-left, right-to-left, right-to-left.

"What is it?" Faiq and Jawdhar share the sentence.

When Jafar reaches the end, his eyes fold closed.

"What?"

Jafar takes a deep breath to steady himself, opens his eyes. "Ghalib has been defeated by White Hands."

Faiq and Jawdhar straighten their backs, alarm painted bright on their faces. They share a surprised, "WHAT? HOW?"

Jafar shakes his head. "The details are sparse. The two armies met on the plains of Gormaz. Something went wrong in the lifting of the siege. White Hands was able to out-flank Ghalib and he was forced to retreat into the castle. Only half of his army could be accommodated." He pauses. "The rest surrendered. Ghalib is surrounded, holed up in Gormaz, under siege himself now."

Shocked silence.

Jawdhar's baritone queries, "Who sent the letter?"

"One of Ghalib's officers who managed to escape during the mayhem. He has had no word from Ghalib but felt he needed to send news to the city so that our defenses could be readied."

Faiq says, "This news must be kept secret, Jafar."

Jawdhar echoes. "A secret, yes. Very important."

Jafar pops up and begins his pacing. He stops and turns. "I agree. But you must appreciate, gentlemen, Córdoba will know of this soon, like it or not. The merchant families have eyes and ears that outnumber the stars. These kinds of secrets cannot be held for long. Hours? Days? The question is, will it be long enough?"

Faiq whispers, "The merchants will panic."

Jafar replies, "Yes, they will. And Ibn Abi Amir will be ready to come to their aid with his Berber army. By that time al-Mughira must already be declared caliph and their pledge of fealty sworn. This is essential to our success."

Faiq and Jawdhar nod.

Jafar says, "Send for the captains of the Slavic Guard. We must prepare for the worst."

Razor's Edge

16 October 976.

The tight line of storms races down the slopes of the Sierra Morena an hour before sunrise, spilling bluster and boom over the city. Remarkably, though, not a single drop of rain. A solid sheet of billowed pewter drifts in behind the drama, bringing with it a steady drizzle just after daybreak.

It has been an unusually wet fall, welcome news to Córdoba's agrarian interests. The Guadalquivir is already back to a healthy swell halfway up its banks, something usually reserved for late winter.

Jafar twitches and groans when the dagger of light splits the blackness, then wakes with a start a second later as the concussion rattles the skylight above his bed. He is fully awake by the time the rolling grumble subsides.

His sleep these days has been fitful and wearying, tossing and turning as his mind churns, up a half-dozen times on a good night. He is forced to catnap during the day to make up the difference and preserve some sense of sanity. Madinat holds its breath, the thump of collective hearts quickened by the uncertainty, the fear of the unknown.

He lies awake, mesmerized by the storm's dry fury. The sky above his bed roils, a convulsed battle of night versus day, the only sounds the shrill whistle of the wind driven deep into the heart of the throaty rumble. Within ten minutes the intensity begins to subside as the line of storms sprints on southward towards the Roman Sea. The soothing smell of rain settles onto the city as the slow drizzle begins to dampen the streets.

Sleep is now pointless, so he rises, dons a robe, and begins to pace the darkness. Plans have been set, honed, and rehearsed dozens of times. Still, he now takes the opposing side, Ibn Abi Amir's side, and searches his own for weaknesses. He inevitably moves to the same conclusion. They walk a razor's edge, and timing is everything.

There is a soft tap on the door. He stops and looks up. "Yes?"

"My lord, it is Bashir."

"Come."

The heavily-armed commander of the Slavic Guard enters and bows. "I am sorry to disturb you, my lord."

"No matter, Bashir, I was awake. What a storm." He looks up at the skylight.

"My lord, you asked me to call you if there was any change. The caliph's breathing has ... altered."

Jafar's focus intensifies. "Altered how?"

"Much shallower, my lord. Raspy and labored. Each breath spaced further apart."

"How much further apart?"

"Three times fewer than me, maybe four. I thought you should know."

"Has he awoken?"

"No, my lord, not once. He is pale as a ghost."

"I see. You did well to come, Bashir, thank you."

"Should I send for Abu al-Qasim, my lord?"

Silence.

"No, Bashir. Send for Faiq and Jawdhar. Have them join me in the caliph's bedchamber. And then go and retrieve al-Mughira. Tell him it is urgent, but no more. I would like you there as well." He hesitates. "No one else is to know about the caliph, Bashir." He widens his eyes for emphasis. "No one."

"I understand, my lord."

"Let me dress, I will be there momentarily. See to the others."

"As you wish, my lord." The commander bows, then turns and departs.

The labored rasp of the man's breathing is unnaturally slow. His time is close. Jafar, Faiq, Jawdhar, and Bashir stand circled round his bed, eyes lowered. Al-Mughira kneels, whispering prayers. A death watch.

The rough scrape of his breath ceases. The men lift their eyes expectantly. The rasping resumes. The men exhale in unison. Ten minutes pass. The breathing stops once more. Remarkably, the caliph coughs, thick and wet. His fingers twitch and then his eyelids flutter open. The men step closer.

"Caliph. Caliph al-Hakam. Caliph! It is Jafar. Can you hear me? It is Jafar!"

The eyes open to narrow slits, struggle to focus, then drift to his grand vizier. The shadow of a grin flickers at the corners of his mouth.

Jafar smiles through his tears. "My caliph. Your time to join Allah has come. Your brother is here, Caliph. Al-Mughira is to be your chosen successor, inshallah, just as you wished."

Al-Mughira kisses his brother's forehead. "Allah's peace be upon you, brother, may your soul find rest in his loving arms. All will be well, brother, all will be well. I will serve as you served, I will continue your work."

The caliph swallows hard. His lips part as if he wishes to speak. He licks his lips then attempts a word, but no sound emerges. Another swallow. He tries once more.

Jafar and al-Mughira lean in.

A whispered breath is all they hear. "Praise Allahhhhhhh ..." The exhale stretches out as the air escapes his lungs, then chooses not to return. His eyes widen, as if surprised by his breath's mutiny. His chest stills.

Al-Mughira and Bashir choke back sobs.

Jafar closes the caliph's eyes. He whispers, "May your soul find rest in Allah's arms, my friend, and may your heart be at peace. Your legacy shall endure."

The stillness presses the air from the room.

Jafar begins in a somber tone. "Gentlemen. It is vital that news of the caliph's death not become known beyond this room. There will be time enough for grieving, but only after Caliph al-Mughira has been sworn in by the grand imam."

All nod, concurring.

"I will personally prepare the caliph's body for burial then send a coded letter to the grand imam to arrange for him to arrive at the Aljama mosque before daybreak tomorrow for the formalities. Bashir will arrange a special escort from the city. When the sun rises over Madinat al-Zahra, al-Mughira will be caliph.

"Faiq and Jawdhar, work with Bashir and his men to see that Madinat is secured against any backlash. Place the garrison on high alert, but be discreet, I do not want to alarm the royal court or the medina. I want the guards on all of Madinat's gates doubled and a special detachment of Slavic Guard for the mosque ceremony. Bashir, have them at their stations an hour before sunrise. There must be no trouble, gentlemen, none whatsoever. We will wrap this transition of power in silk.

"I will send a coded message to the commander of the City Watch that no Berber cavalry be permitted to cross the Puente Romano under any circumstances. After al-Mughira is caliph, I will contact Ibn Abi Amir and arrange an oath of fealty ceremony for the entire Berber army. Then we will use them to deal with White Hands.

Faiq says, "What about Subh and the boy?"

"As soon as al-Mughira is caliph, they will be quietly exiled. She can take the child back to her family in the Navarre, assuming they will have the witch." Jafar looks from man to man. "Work quickly, gentlemen, but work calmly. By evening all of our plans must be set in place. Let us meet at my villa after *maghrib salat* for a final accounting."

They nod curtly and depart.

He sits cross-legged on his silk pillow reading a copy of the letter. His smile grows as his eyes skim down the page. At the end, he stares into space, smile fixed, calculating. A moment later he whispers, "Excellent, most excellent."

There is a soft, stuttered knock at the door, a meted rhythm. Their code.

"Come, Aslam."

The black-robed wraith enters and bows.

"You have done good work, my friend. You are sure that this is identical to the letter Jafar received?"

"It is, Master. The courier had two copies, one for the commander of the City Watch in Córdoba and one for the caliph. It is a pity that Córdoba never received theirs." A sinister grin slides onto his face.

Ibn Abi Amir nods, pleased. "Good, good. Who would have thought proud General Ghalib would ever do me the favor of being defeated by White Hands. My, my, how times have changed. Surrounded in Gormaz castle. It seems the man requires the assistance of the Banu Birzal once again. Let us hope that he is more grateful this time."

Aslam's grin widens. "There is more, Master."

"More?" Ibn Abi Amir rubs his palms together with anticipation. "Do tell, Aslam."

"The grand imam's man delivered a note to me, just after noon prayer." He reaches into his robe and extracts the tiny scroll, hands it to Ibn Abi Amir, then steps back to respect his master's privacy.

"Interesting ..." The qadi of the Maghreb fingers the scroll then carefully examines the seal. Satisfied, he uses his letter dagger to open it. Coded, as expected. He slides his reed and ink pot forward and begins to scratch each letter onto his pad. When he is finished he stares at the words.

Madinat one fewer.
His plan proceeds.
Tomorrow sunrise.

The silence stretches out as the man's formidable calculating engine whirs.

He looks up, his face chiseled stone, unreadable except for the ebony eyes, which are alive and fiery. "Our door has opened, Aslam. Bring al-Andalusi at once. Time is short."

Her eyes fold closed as the letter relaxes to her lap, sending two neat tears rolling down her cheeks. Her whisper is tortured. "My Muhammad is lost to me, Imam Abd al-Gafur, my beautiful boy is lost." She wipes her eyes and looks up. "I no longer know this person. I gave him life, I nursed him, I raised the boy right. Praise Allah his father did not live to see what has become of him." She exhales slowly to steady herself. "How did it come to this? How?" She shakes her head. "Poor Rasha."

Imam Abd al-Gafur looks grim. "When Samuel al-Tayyib first approached me to help I had no idea it would ever come to this, Salma, no idea at all."

"I know ... neither did I." She raises the letter and reads it again. "Rasha loves this young man, this Zafir. And he loves her. These two belong together as man and wife, inshallah. Muhammad knows that Rayya wanted the girl to marry for love. He knows! Instead, she becomes a pawn in his petty power games." She raises her voice. "Marry my Rasha to a Berber horseman? Never! The girl WILL marry for love, mark my words."

"From all that I have heard, Salma, defying Muhammad may not be a prudent course of action. He has grown very powerful. He even brought a Berber army with him from the Maghreb. Madinat trembles, especially now that the caliph is ill."

She scoffs, "I am far too old for prudence, my friend." She snorts. "You are, too!"

He chuckles, then grimaces. "Salma, you are not suggesting what I think you are suggesting."

Her eyes sparkle as the wrinkled corners of her mouth lift, a hint of a grin. "Let us just say that I have a great desire to behold the magic of Madinat al-Zahra before I pass from this world, Imam Abd al-Gafur." The grin widens, turns mischievous.

He shakes his head somberly, as if to chastise her, but then chuckles once more.

"Write to Samuel al-Tayyib. Tell him we will begin arrangements for an unannounced winter visit. To Córdoba, not Madinat. It will be easier to remain undetected there. When we arrive they must find some way to arrange Rasha's escape. They shall be secretly married."

"A dangerous game, Salma, very dangerous."

"I will do what it takes to secure Rasha's happiness. It is the least I can do to honor dear Rayya's memory." She hesitates. "Besides, even the qadi of the Maghreb would not dare harm his mama." She smiles.

"I would not be so sure, Salma." He exhales loudly. "Nevertheless, I shall be at your side."

She beams. "Good. Begin drawing up the nikah documents. I need that fine mind of yours to locate a legal basis for me to serve as Rayhana's wali."

He considers this. "An interesting thought. I would need a case of precedence, Salma, something obscure but still binding. Perhaps if I were able to consult the Sharia Library ..."

"It could just be that the caliph's royal librarian may be able to help arrange that, dear friend."

They both laugh loudly.

"In the meantime, we will need to locate a place to stay in Córdoba, and a means of safe passage that will not attract attention. That may take some time to arrange. Ask Samuel for his help locating a dwelling for us in the city."

"I will write to him today. Let us meet again tomorrow morning and begin our plans in earnest."

"Perfect. Thank you, Imam Abd al-Gafur. Your heart is golden."

The man smiles, pleased with the compliment. He bows deeply and leaves.

She stares into space, conjuring the girl's face. She whispers, "Your tetta will help you, Rayhana. Your tetta is coming, dear girl. By Allah's gracious mercy, all will be well. All will be well."

The misty drizzle continues throughout the day, the sky sad and dreary. Balmy for mid-October. There is something alien in the feel of the weather, a hint of the unnatural, as if the day was stolen from spring then stranded in fall. People moving about the city stop and look up into the gloom of the hammered lead, frown their disapproval, then pull their cloaks tighter and move on about their business.

At dusk the cloud cover retreats along a lengthy dagger slice at the western horizon, chased by the sweep of cool wind from the mountains. Suddenly freed from prison, the sunset flashes a spectacular palette of pinks and oranges and purples. The stars bide their time, eager to come out and play. There is no moon this evening, no need to share the night, and the sparkling diamonds begin to sashay across the sky one by one, all primped and gaudy, eager to loose their menagerie upon the unspoiled heavens.

The cool mountain wind laid against the warm dampness of the heavy air kicks up a thick, soupy fog; impossibly dense, an opaque fluff of cotton. At first the fog hugs the ground, afraid to let go, but it grows with abandon, soon filling ravines to the brim then spilling like water into the next lowest spot. Within an hour, one cannot be sure where it is safe to step. By mid-evening the Guadalquivir is erased. Sight-lines vanish and an odd stillness settles across the landscape.

The hairs rise on the backs of the necks of the royal guardsmen standing night watch upon the palace walls. Unable to see the ground or the river or who might be approaching, they grow edgy and nervously finger their weapons.

A league and a half downriver from Córdoba, the fog is head high across the flat pastureland and thicker over the river. The cool winds driving this mayhem have ebbed. The brilliant dome above pulses with energy, the game afoot. A single oil lamp hangs at the water's edge, its meager green glow swaddled in cotton.

The fleet of dromons is moored to the line of docks on the southern bank of the river, the spires of their masts all that mark their presence. The boats are quiet, lamps extinguished. The chilled fog is so damp you could drink the air. The commander cups his ears and listens. Nothing. He leans to his second and whispers, "You are sure we are in the right place?"

"Yes, my lord, this is it. They will come."

"They will never see our lamp in this damned fog. An hour, no more, then we sail. It is dangerous having this many of my dromons on a river in a fog like this."

His second nods.

Ten minutes later, a muted rumble in the east turns their heads. The rumble swells. Horses.

The commander says, "Pass word to the other boats to prepare their decks. Remember, twenty riders each. I want this done in two trips, no more."

The man begins to bark orders and the dromons come alive. Lamps are lit, gangplanks lowered, the stalls opened and readied.

The rolling thunder grows heavy and close then begins to wane. Still, there is nothing to be seen. The commander stares at the center of the dampening sound. Suddenly, the fog parts in thick swirls as a dozen horsemen emerge, slow to a trot, then walk. They stop at the edge of the dock.

The man in the center speaks in a rich, accented baritone. "My cavalry must cross the river by midnight."

The commander answers, "It shall be so, my lord."

Clench

17 October 976.

It is three hours before sunrise, the genie's hour. The fog has steadily devoured the landscape north of the Guadalquivir. Not content, the white monster scratches and claws up Madinat's walls, erasing all evidence of solid ground beneath. Wispy tendrils of drenched cotton hang frozen above the sea of clouds. The night air is chilled, deathly still, not a single sound of life.

The scene recollects a primordial Earth, but any promise of coming life has been rudely swapped with dread and foreboding. The canopy of pulsing diamonds lights the fog bank with an eerie sheen.

Oil lamps have been lit at every guard station along the formidable walls surrounding Madinat al-Zahra. There are only fifty paces between the flames, but the light, normally comforting, has been reduced by the fog to a nub of dulled orange. Each station can discern its nearest neighbor, but nothing beyond.

The two royal guardsmen manning their post on the southwestern wall are understandably nervous. They have been ordered to stay close to their lamp, eyes locked on the white sea for any signs or sounds of movement. Beside the lamp rests an iron gong should they need to sound the alarm. Each man paces silently to keep warm but does not leave the meager bubble cast by the lamp. The red-clad knights are heavily armed, of course; broadswords, daggers, slung bows each with a large quiver of fine arrows over the opposite shoulder. These knights are marksmen, the best trained in the kingdom. They have been told to expect trouble, but as to when, or what kind of trouble, or from whom, they have no clue. Normally at this late hour they would be fighting to stay awake. On this strange night, their hearts race, eyes wide and alert.

The lonely screech of an owl freezes both men in their tracks. Close. They exchange a quick, nervous glance, then resume their careful study of the fog. They have not heard a single sound all night, and there are no trees within a long arrow's shot of the wall. No place for an owl.

A moment later the owl cries again, closer now. They crouch and remove their bows, withdraw arrows and nock their weapons, then duck walk to the wall to listen.

Only silence.

One knight nods at the alarm bell and with his eyes queries his companion. Prudent, perhaps, but false alarms on edgy nights such as this are a recipe for merciless teasing from their fellow guardsmen.

His companion shakes his head. No.

The owl cries once more, no more than a dozen paces beyond the wall, buried somewhere beneath the clouds.

Despite their training these men are scared. Their wary eyes are locked onto each other now for support, their grips tight on their weapons. The one guard splits his two fingers, points at his eyes, and then waggles his fingers at the cotton sea. The other knight nods. In unison, the two guardsmen draw their bows as they slowly rise then tentatively lift their heads and lean over the top of the wall to peer below.

Nothing. A sea of white.

Two tiny swirls rise from the mist. Each arrow strikes its mark, square between the eyes, just under the brim of their helmets. Each man's bow releases harmlessly into the void. The knights slump over the wall in unison, as if lulled to sleep by some magician's spell, the slender steel arrowheads buried deep in their brains.

The silence is deafening.

Remarkable that so many owls are attracted to fog-enveloped Madinat. Within the span of a minute, the scene repeats itself at six adjacent guard stations.

A roped grappling hook loops over the wall, landing in the soft grass; then two, then four, then a dozen. The ropes are slowly cinched tight, a quick jerk to test the hold, then the twisted wrench of leather bearing a heavy weight.

"The hour is late, Aslam," he says in that condescending, dismissive tone.

"Yes, Bundar, the genie's hour. Sorry to disturb your sleep. Alas, my master has an urgent message for the sultana. I am afraid she must be awoken ... there is important news to be delivered."

The wraith of the royal harem studies Aslam for hints of deceit. Nothing. "An odd night."

Aslam responds, "Yes, this fog is unnatural. I have never seen the like. The palace guards are especially edgy. I had a difficult time slipping through unseen."

Bundar continues to study the man. Aslam has not spoken this many words in the previous six months of their late-night meetings. It leaves him with an unsettled feeling. Some new game? Some hidden agenda? What? But he cannot discern danger, and his sixth sense is finely honed for such things. He nods. "Very well." He extends his left hand.

Aslam reaches into his robe and extracts the sealed letter, displays it to put Bundar at ease, then steps forward and lowers it into the man's open palm. As he releases the letter, he unexpectedly grips Bundar's wrist. A needle dagger flashes forward and buries itself under Bundar's ribs, quick as a lightning strike.

Bundar's eyes are frozen wide with shock, but he does not move, only shutters. He clenches his jaw and tries to lift his free arm to defend himself, but cannot. He exhales, clenches his jaw once more. He stands still as a statue then shutters again. Aslam slips closer and whispers, "You swine, you had this coming. Remember the name, Ibn Abi Amir." He releases Bundar's wrist, which falls limply, then places his hand affectionately on the man's shoulder, and using that leverage he gives a quick thrust upward into the man's heart.

The only sound Bundar makes is an awful grunt. His eyes lose focus as his lids begin to flutter. Aslam eases his dagger free. The two men stand face to face. Aslam's sinister smile widens.

Bundar grunts once more, begins to teeter, then buckles to the ground.

Aslam kneels, pockets the letter, then casually wipes his blade on Bundar's cloak and slips it back into his robe. He steps over the slippery black pool widening around the crumpled man.

The heavy triple-clank of the locking hardware is chased by a soft creak as the southwest gate is eased open, but the sound refuses to carry in the dense fog. The tall, metal-encrusted doors part the thick mist in broad swirls. The black-turbaned man steps outside of impregnable Madinat al-Zahra, lights a lamp, waves the green flame back and forth three times, then extinguishes it. He turns and walks back through the gate. Orders are passed using only hand signs. The Berbers depart in pairs in the direction of the royal palace.

Jibril quietly opens the bedchamber door, steps within, and stops. The flame is turned low for sleeping, the lamp exhaling warm, comforting tones. As his eyes drift across to the three small beds set side by side, a pride-filled, fatherly smile eases onto the head eunuch's face. It has become his habit to check on the boys before retiring. His boys. They are fast asleep, angels at rest.

He can never seem to stop himself from admiring his protégés, a vice he indulges each night. He glides across the room to the bedside of the blond, known now as Umar of the royal harem. His favorite. He drinks in the tender beauty of youth. He can never resist touching his boys, of course, and he leans down to gently brush his finger across the warm silky cheek.

The hairs on the back of Jibril's neck inexplicably rise. His finger freezes as the smile vanishes, suddenly alert. Puzzled, he lifts his head and listens. Nothing. His fingers return to their exploration of the boy's face, then make their way into the blond curls. The satisfied smile returns.

Something grips his hair from behind and violently jerks his head backwards. In the same motion a hand reaches around his neck. A slight tug is all he feels, then his hair is released.

Jibril is unclear as to what just happened. A sharp ping on the floor beside him draws his eyes. His small ceremonial gelding dagger.

Instinctively, he turns to demand an explanation for the rude intrusion. Aslam stands a pace away, arms folded, his ugly smile pulled wide and pinned.

The eunuch's confused expression grows. Jibril tries to challenge the man but inexplicably finds he is mute. He feels moisture on his neck, frowns, then, curious, touches the wetness. His eyes widen with horror as he stares at the crimson dripping from his fingers. He looks back at Aslam and tries again to speak. A gurgle-chirp is all he can manage. He swallows hard and tries once more. Nothing. Abject terror leaps into the eunuch's eyes.

The thin line stretching ear to ear has had enough with patient waiting and erupts violently in one heaving gush, Jibril's white bed clothes instantly exchanged for the caliph's colors.

Jibril panics, his hands flailing helplessly the air. He grabs desperately at his neck to try and stem the flood. His mouth opens and closes, a fish tossed onto the bank.

The awful smile has not left Aslam's face. The gore seems to amuse him.

Jibril's eyes continue to plead for a moment more, then begin to dull. The eunuch's lids flutter their surrender and he collapses into his own slick mess.

The boys have not even stirred.

Her eyes slowly open. She uncurls from her fetal position, rolls onto her back, and listens. A soft knock. She looks up at the skylight. Still night. She frowns. What time is it? Her sleep since he returned has been like death, deep and dreamless. Another knock. There is no rhythm to indicate the identity of the visitor, which is odd. Her eyes track to the door. The knock repeats, louder now, more urgent. She sighs, rolls from her bed, and rises, puts her robe on and moves across her bedchamber to the door. She listens.

Nothing.

She whispers, "Who is it?"

"It is Aslam, Sultana."

She frowns again. In the royal harem? How?

"Where is Jibril?"

A slight hesitation. "Sultana, Bundar brought me here, then went to wake Jibril. I have an urgent message from Ibn Abi Amir."

Silence.

"What time is it?"

"The genie's hour, Sultana. Ibn Abi Amir's message will not wait until morning."

She grimaces her uncertainty. Her hand tentatively rises, freezes midair as she weighs her decision, then continues on. The elaborate locking mechanism clanks once, then twice, followed by a sharp click. She slides the latch then cracks the heavy door. The hallway is dimly lit.

Aslam bows. "Sultana. My apologies for disturbing your sleep." He holds up the letter. "A letter from Ibn Abi Amir. An urgent matter, Sultana. It could not wait."

The wariness has not left her eyes. She pulls her robe tight then opens the door further. She extends her hand and opens her palm.

Aslam deposits the letter, bows.

Subh examines the seal, nods, then closes the door, slides the latch, and relocks it.

Aslam has never before laid eyes upon the blond witch. The succubus is as beautiful as they say. He licks his lips, folds them into that menacing, wolfish grin, then vanishes down the hallway.

Back in bed, she uses her dagger to open the letter. Her lover's hand. Not coded.

My Love—
Our time has come. Your husband is dead. Jafar will attempt a
coup this night. Our plans are in motion. You must wake
Hisham and bring him to your room and set your locks. Do not
open the door for anyone, even Bundar or Jibril. Under no
circumstances are you two to leave your bedchamber. None. By
sunrise it will be over. I will come for you. I love you.
Muhammad

A low grumble stirs on the horizon, grows louder, changing to rolling thunder, then louder still until it becomes a throaty roar. By the time the alarm bells on the walls begin to clang in earnest, the Banu Birzal are pouring through the switchback gate into the Shining City. Hundreds of black-clad Berber riders.

Their terrifying battle cry rings out, "ALLAHU AKBAR! ALLAHU AKBAR! ALLAHU AKBAR!" The Shining City wakes to confusion, panic rushing close behind in a heavy, rolling wave. The juggernaut heads straight up the rise leading to Madinat's garrison.

These two sleep in their normal positions: him behind her, spooned tight into her luxurious curves, hand cupping her breast.

The distant sound of bells opens his eyes. He looks up at the skylight, puzzled. Night. He rolls back from her and cups his ears. Alarm bells? Something is happening.

He turns and whispers, "Rebekah." He shakes her shoulder. "Rebekah."

She groans.

"Rebekah, something is wrong."

She recognizes the concern in his tone and rolls over, alert now.

"Listen."

She hears it now. "Are those Madinat's alarm bells?"

"Yes, I think so. Something is not right, Rebekah." He rises and begins to hurriedly dress.

"What is it?"

"I am not sure, Rebekah, but wake the girls and get them dressed. I am going to see what is happening. Keep the door locked. I will not be long."

"Samuel, you are scaring me."

The royal librarian smiles. "I am sure it is nothing, my love. Relax, I will be back shortly with news." He kisses her head and is gone.

Stranglehold

The bells continue their reverberation near and far, a cacophony of jangle, evoking the call to Sunday Mass from a hundred different churches. Torches are lit by the score along the outer walls in an attempt to barter with the moonless dark for a glimpse of the enemy, but these are of little use in penetrating the head-high clouds firmly camped within the palace grounds and between the buildings.

Inside the villas of the Alcazar, families awaken and huddle at their windows, anxiously peering into the mist, not sure what to do. Small bands of red-robed Slavic Guard race through the alleys shouting orders, telling people to remain in their homes and lock their doors. An ominous, electric tension settles into magical Madinat—the lull before the storm.

Hearts pound.

His feet and hands twitch as he groans his misery. He snaps his head side to side, his tormentors close behind. He runs across a vast, barren plain, the angry mob giving chase. He looks back, sees their sickles and pitchforks raised high. They are gaining ground. He tries to run faster—he must reach the sanctuary. The white cross atop the spire is only a hundred paces in front of him, but as he draws closer the cathedral recedes, always sliding ahead of him. He screams, "Wait! Open the doors! Open the doors! Help me!"

Jafar wakes with a start, panting and wide-eyed with fright. It takes several breaths to realize he was dreaming. He sighs wearily. It has been this way every night for weeks.

He frowns.

What is that? Bells. Alarm bells. Sweet Allah! What is going on?!

He jumps from his bed, his heart racing, throws a robe around himself, and moves to the door and calls for the pair of Slavic guards stationed there. No answer. He calls again. Nothing. He frowns. He releases the latch and tentatively pokes his head out. The alarm bells are louder. He peers down the dim hallway. No one. Strange. He opens the door wider and leans forward to look the other way. He gasps.

Two Berber knights in black robes and turbans stand at attention, hands on their sword hilts, wicked smiles glued to their faces. Two crumpled bodies lie curled at their feet.

Sounds of a pitched battle spring to life to the west of the royal palace and quickly grow in intensity; angular pings of steel-on-steel, the clop of horses' hooves, anxious neighs, curses and desperate barking of orders, terrible shouts and pleading voices punctuated by quick screams.

A burst of bright orange blossoms from the wooden barracks within the garrison tucked into the northwest corner of Madinat. Within minutes the flames stretch into a cylindrical column fifty paces high, double that in width. There is a semblance of eerie sunset glow, throwing a swaying dance of shadows upon the white marble of the buildings within the Alcazar. The Shining City holds its breath in silent dread under the orange-hued clouds.

Royal guardsmen begin to stream in earnestly from the garrison's gate to confront the undetermined menace, swords drawn and ready for action. They slow as they take in the empty sea of fog. Where are the marauders?

On cue, banks of black-robed, black-turbaned knights rise in unison from the mist at full draw, loose their arrows, then submerge, only to rise again a moment later and lock onto new targets.

Each wave of emerging royal guardsmen is snapped to attention, their heads thrown back by the slap of the steel-tipped arrows thumping into their chests. The red-clad warriors disappear in clutches. Confusion, then panic, then sheer mayhem, descends into their ranks as their numbers begin dwindling at an alarming pace.

The sheet of fog is neatly sliced into thick swirls by the Berber cavalry charge as it completes its rise up the slope to the garrison. The thundering horde splits into a three-headed hydra, one veering west to the paddocks of the Royal Guard to ensure their enemy remains dismounted, one heading straight for the garrison gate to join the onslaught, and the third angling northeast toward the gates of the Alcazar. Heavy thunder joins then drowns the awful song of the dead and dying.

The battle at the garrison is over before it has really begun. The Berber cavalry thunders through the open gate unopposed, trampling those in their path. Without horses the royal guardsmen are no match for the mounted Berbers, who select their targets then loose their arrows at will. After several hundred royal guards are quickly cut down within the garrison parade grounds, weapons begin to drop and hands rise into the air. It is the unthinkable: surrender.

Where the Banu Birzal would normally show no mercy to a surrendering enemy, mercy is granted. The battle grinds to a halt, the entire barracks now a roaring inferno, blistering the faces of those within a hundred paces, consuming dozens that are too slow to escape. Those of the caliph's knights that survive are marched, shocked and broken, to a makeshift holding pen for safe keeping.

The cavalry reassembles into ranks then thunders off to the eastern side of Madinat for their next task. Their orders are strict: after the garrison is taken and burned, secure the medina and the royal mint, but do not loot or strike a flame.

She knows the door is locked but tries it anyway, working the handle back and forth. Useless. "Durr. Durr!"

Nothing.

She cups her ears and listens. Bells. Definitely alarm bells. She looks up at the unnatural orange glow seeping through the skylight and frowns.

She presses her ear to the wood.

Nothing.

She pounds on the door. "DURR! DURR!"

She frantically works the handle, then pounds the door once more.

She hears a muted, "Rayhana. Quiet! Shhhhh!" A key is fitted into the lock, a double click, then mercifully the door cracks open.

"Praise Allah! Durr, what is going on? I hear alarm bells. There is an orange glow in the sky, and the sun has not yet risen."

"I am not sure what is happening. A dozen Berber knights arrived a half hour ago. Your father left with them."

"With his bodyguards?"

"Yes."

Rayhana's eyes widen. "Is no one here?"

"I did not see Aslam all evening."

She stares intently at Durr as the handmaid's gears begin to whir.

Durr's expression turns wary. "Rayhana, no. This is not safe."

"I must go to Zafir. Help me escape this dungeon, Durr. Help me, please. Now is my chance."

Durr looks pained and indecisive but finally answers with a nod.

Rayhana quickly crosses the room to her bed, grabs the silver-plate image of Zafir and slips it into her robe, then lifts her mahr and returns to the door with the only two things that matter to her now.

Rayhana steps through her door into the hallway. Sweet freedom.

Durr holds up her palm to stop her then touches her index finger to her lips. She turns and hugs the wall as she slips down the hallway; stops and scans. She turns and motions Rayhana to follow.

Together they peer around the corner into the courtyard. No one. They begin to tiptoe towards the door leading to the front gate and the alley.

"Where are you going?" A child's voice asks. The Maghrebi accent is unmistakable.

They freeze, heads snapping to the sound.

A form, slight and dressed in a black chador, steps from the shadows into the dim lamplight. The child-bride. Ulla.

Durr cowers like a caught thief, but an odd calm settles on Rayhana. She stands tall and still as she studies the girl's approach. Rayhana searches the child for clues.

Ulla meets her gaze, clearly unafraid. The young bride radiates poise beyond her years. Pride of place, no doubt. This is her villa now, after all, her domain.

Rayhana's heart softens.

She thinks: The little sister I never had. Such a beautiful child.

It strikes her that Ulla, too, is the helpless victim of an ambitious father. Wed to a foreigner twice her age for political gain. Property to be haggled over then sold.

It is as if Ulla reads Rayhana's mind. She says, "Do not pity me. Your father is a great man, and our marriage brings honor to my people."

Rayhana's eyes fill as she continues to stare. She feels a strange kinship with this girl. "But what about you, Ulla, what do you want?"

For an instant, only an instant, the girl's lower lip begins to quiver, but this is rudely checked by her quick jaw-clench. Her expression freezes to stone. She says defiantly, "I will bear many sons for the qadi of the Maghreb. Sons who will rule al-Andalus for a thousand years. That is my only duty."

A single tear courses down Rayhana's cheek. She whispers, "I must go to my husband, Ulla."

Ulla stares in silence.

Rayhana reaches for Durr's hand and slowly walks towards the door—and freedom. Her heart is pounding. Without looking back, she pauses, then lifts the handle.

The sound comes from behind her. "GUARDS!"

Her shoulders sink as she releases the handle.

The close quarters and tight, twisting alleys of the royal palace complex are an ambusher's paradise. Recessed doorways, rooftop niches, gaps between buildings all become assassins' lairs. Slavic guards lie crumpled in neat piles of threes and fours, caught unaware as they raced around a corner into a barrage of arrows, dead before they hit the stone paving.

Ibn Abi Amir, in full Berber battle dress, marches with a purpose for the heart of the palace. The qadi of the Maghreb is sandwiched between Suktan and Tahir, his bodyguards, who shield him as they move, scimitars drawn, ebony eyes scanning back and forth, up and down, side to side.

A dozen Berber knights break ground in front of the three, and a dozen more trail close behind. As they make their way through the alleys, the black-robed assassins lying in wait to dispatch hapless Slavic guards or curious onlookers rise from their cover and bow. Hushed, reverential whispers of "Qadi of the Maghreb" dog the entourage as they slice through the royal palace, arriving finally at the villa of the al-Mughira family.

His escort takes up defensive positions in the alley. Without knocking, Ibn Abi Amir opens the unlocked door and steps inside, trailed by Suktan and Tahir. The door closes behind them.

They enter a beautiful peristyle courtyard decorated with orange and lemon trees, beds of roses still plush with lingering fall blooms, several tall decorative vases, silk wall hangings, and a triplet of elaborate fountains spilling into a small fish-stocked reflecting pool. A large and lavish villa, fitting for the brother of the caliph. A thin, wispy mist has settled into the courtyard, but the lamps and torches have been lit as if for a formal open-air dinner party, successfully keeping the milky vapors at bay.

Ibn Abi Amir surveys the scene, then looks up to admire the magnificent starshine. He smiles. No hint of gray; at least an hour before sunrise. Right on schedule.

Four men stand side by side at attention in front of the reflecting pool, hands tied behind their backs: Jafar, al-Mughira, Faiq al-Nizami, Jawdhar. Al-Mughira is still in his sleeping clothes. Standing beside them, Aslam.

Ibn Abi Amir approaches. The two bodyguards swing around and take up their stations behind the four prisoners. The smile has not left Ibn Abi Amir's face. He turns to Aslam. "The sultana and Hisham are safe?"

Aslam replies with a slight tick of his head.

"The commander of the Slavic Guard is dead?"

A second tick.

"Bundar and Jibril?"

Aslam's stony expression is exchanged for a sinister smile. Ibn Abi Amir nods. "Excellent work, my friend."

Jafar speaks first, but his voice is tinny and thin, edging close to panic. Unbecoming for a grand vizier. "What is the meaning of this? How dare you arrest a member of the Vizier Council."

Ibn Abi Amir's voice is calm and level. "The caliph has passed. As you know. You four have conspired to remove Hisham as rightful heir to the caliphate and replace him with al-Mughira. As a simple statement of fact, gentlemen: you have each committed treason."

Jafar's mouth opens to respond but closes without a word.

Ibn Abi Amir continues, "Madinat's garrison has been burned, and the Royal Guard have been killed or have surrendered. All of them. The officers of the Slavic Guard are either dead or soon to be. The Banu Birzal are masters of Madinat now. The caliphate is safe, praise Allah."

Faiq and Jawdhar stare at the ground, stone-faced. Al-Mughira is pale as a ghost. He yelps, "It was their idea! These three approached me! I never desired to be caliph!"

Jafar mutters, "It was Caliph al-Hakam's last wish. The boy is not fit to serve. You know this to be true, Muhammad. Córdoba will suffer at his hands, and suffer mightily. The grand imam agreed with me. He was to be here shortly to bless Caliph al-Mughira's reign. You will have to answer to him."

Ibn Abi Amir shakes his head. "Fool. The grand imam will be here shortly to bless Caliph Hisham's reign."

Once again, Jafar opens his mouth to retort, then closes it. He sees the truth now, alas too late to be of use. Schemer, schemed.

Ibn Abi Amir turns to Aslam. "Bring his family. All of them."

Aslam disappears into the villa. A moment later, Fatima, al-Mughira's wife, emerges, dressed still in her nightgown, their eight-year-old son clutching her waist and their five-year-old daughter locked to her thigh. She cradles their two-year-old son in her arms. She shivers fearfully. Aslam indicates where to stand, then backs away a step. The two older children begin to whimper, but their mother is stricken dumb with shock.

331

Al-Mughira tenses as his family approaches but then finds his fatherly voice and calmly whispers, "Do not worry, Fatima, all will be well. I love you, darling. I love you, children. Be brave."

Ibn Abi Amir proclaims in his command voice, "These four men are guilty of treason. They have betrayed the rightful heir of Caliph al-Hakam II. They have forsaken the will of Allah. They have blasphemed against the Truth."

The four men's eyes are glued to Ibn Abi Amir, who issues a simple nod. Massive Suktan slides behind al-Mughira, and with a flash of hands grabs the caliph's brother with both hands around the throat in a stranglehold. Fatima screams. The children cower. Aslam reaches out a hand to prevent her from moving.

Al-Mughira's eyes bulge as his face turns bright red. He snaps and jerks his neck and shoulders as he struggles against the death grip. Suktan bends his knees, and in a wrestler's stance, lifts the wriggling man from the ground by his neck. His feet begin to dance and kick.

The other three condemned men stand like statues, helpless, staring in abject horror as the man suffocates. They strain at their bindings until their wrists begin to bleed.

His wife and children are sobbing hysterically as they watch their father continue to helplessly wriggle in the air, a hooked fish yanked from the river. His kicks begin to weaken, his shoulder rolls slow, then still. His body relaxes and goes limp. His eyes refuse to close, his awful bloodshot stare fixed and vacant; the jaded eyes of a dead fish. Suktan continues to throttle the man for a full minute more, then releases his purple neck, letting him collapse into a heap. A fecal stench wafts across the courtyard.

Faiq is whimpering now, the front of his robe wet.

Ibn Abi Amir speaks softly to the family, his voice gentle and kind. "I am sorry this was necessary, Fatima. But you and your children must taste the fate of traitors and learn to obey. Do not worry, your family will be well cared for."

She screams, "MONSTER!"

Ibn Abi Amir frowns and flicks his wrist in dismissal. Aslam ushers the sobbing mass back inside.

The three men are frantically glancing over their shoulders to see where the two bodyguards now stand. Ibn Abi Amir turns first to Faiq, then Jawdhar. "Do not worry, that is not the fate in store for you two. You will leave this night by boat for Majorca. There you will live in exile for the remainder of your lives. You will never again show your faces in al-Andalus. Understood?"

The two men issue a joint sigh of relief, then a shared, "Yes."

Ibn Abi Amir nods to Tahir, who leads the two men towards the door. As Aslam returns, he motions him over and whispers, "See that they spend eternity on the bottom of the Guadalquivir."

"With pleasure, Master." He turns and follows.

Suktan is stationed behind Jafar now, who can feel the Berber's menacing presence. His face has developed an odd twitch. Ibn Abi Amir steps close to the grand vizier and begins to study him. His expression is one of amusement. "You look nervous, Jafar. What did you expect for treason, a slap on the wrist?"

Jafar's hate flares as he locks his eyes on Ibn Abi Amir.

"Good, good. You should feel hate, Jafar. Impotent hate."

Jafar hisses, "Get it over with."

"Not so fast, Jafar, not so fast. I need you."

The grand vizier frowns, puzzled.

"Yes, I need you. But there is to be a price for your life. Those of the Slavic Guard who are still alive will swear allegiance to Caliph Hisham or be executed. You will convince them to continue to serve the new caliph. The grand imam will bless Hisham's reign and then you will publicly swear your obedience. You will offer Madinat your example to follow. You will continue to serve Caliph Hisham as grand vizier, but you must ensure that the council remains loyal and honors his desires. I will act as the boy's regent until he comes of age. And I WILL be obeyed. Understood?"

Jafar stares.

Ibn Abi Amir smiles. "You see, Jafar, I am a reasonable man. I have Córdoba's best interests at heart. Do we agree?"

A resigned nod registers Jafar's consent.

"Say it."

Only a whisper, "I agree."

As soon as Samuel enters the alley he realizes that Madinat is under attack, the sounds of battle and the leaping flames from the garrison unmistakable. He does an about-face, retrieves his family, and rushes them into the secure confines of the Rare Books Library.

After settling them, he sets off for Zafir. The boy is sound asleep. Once Samuel explains what was happening, Zafir turns frantic and fights him, insistent on going for her. "She will be fine, Zafir, fine! Listen to me! Ibn Abi Amir is behind this attack, I am sure of it. He will keep Rayhana locked safely in her room until the storm passes." Still, Zafir resists. In the end, Samuel has to slap the boy to get his attention and secure his obedience. "Zafir!

Listen to me, boy! I need you to go for Levi, bring him back to my study. Use our secret knock. Do NOT leave the library. Understood?"

Silence.

"Zafir? I need you to retrieve our friend and bring him before it is too late. I must go for Zaheid and Iuliana. Do you understand?"

Zafir's eyes clear. "I will bring Levi, Samuel."

"Good. Now go. GO!"

Five minutes later, Samuel stands with his wife. "I must try and reach Zaheid and Iuliana, Rebekah."

She stares, then slowly nods.

"I have sent Zafir for Levi."

She nods again.

He lectures her as he moves towards the door, "Three knocks, a pause, then two more, a pause, then one. Got it?"

She tugs his arm, eyes full. "Samuel? Samuel?!"

He turns and they lock eyes, their love burning bright.

"Be careful, Husband."

He smiles. "I am always careful, my darling. Zafir should be back with Levi, hopefully before I return. They will enter through that door. Same knock."

She follows his finger and nods. "Remember, my love, if you do not hear the code, do not open the door, no matter what."

Her features are stretched tight with worry.

He turns and slips into the mayhem.

The heavy walls of the Rare Books Library block all of the sounds of the raging battle, the clang of the alarm bells barely discernible now. The quiet settles in and turns oppressive. Rebekah takes a deep breath to still her racing heart and forces a smile to calm her daughters. Alone with the girls pulled tightly to her, the room is silent. Thankfully, the girls both drift off to sleep.

The minutes pass like hours.

She is startled by a gentle rustle of warbled whispers high up on the shelves behind her. She freezes. Wind? The murmurs spread behind her and grow into a chorus of hushed phrases truncated by a stutter of shushes.

She gathers her nerve and looks up over her shoulder. The whispers instantly cease. She continues to stare at the shelves. Books and more books.

Silence.

She lowers her gaze, a puzzled frown on her face. She rechecks the girls. Sound asleep.

The silence stretches.

A half-minute later, the chorus of whispers flares up again. She whips her head, and on cue, the sound vanishes. She looks down once more, and after a short pause, the whispers re-ignite.

A smile tickles her lips. The books. Samuel's books are speaking, trying to keep her company, ease her fears. He has always insisted that his books are alive, pulsing with ancient stories of love and life, laughter and truth, stories that live on forever within those who read and treasure the words lovingly wrought so long ago. Beneath their covers are cares and concerns, thoughts and dreams, as real today as when they were first inked onto page many centuries ago by their masters.

As with most things, Rebekah has always indulged her husband's whims and fancies, bemused but skeptical. She loves this about him. Yet, she now sees the truth of his tall tale. His books do live. His books do talk. And his books are sowing seeds of comfort in her time of desperate need. They care.

Her smile stretches as she hugs the girls tighter to her and listens to the reverie washing now across the shelves, encircling the room. Why these books have chosen her is a mystery. Perhaps they recognize a kindred spirit; maybe they can sense all that is true and sacred in the feminine heart. Who can know?

She is awestruck as she listens. She hears concerns for what is happening outside, multilingual debates on strategy and preferred courses of action, even a chorus of admiring poets in awe of the arresting image of a beautiful mother lovingly cradling her children beneath her wings. There are sighs and cackles, barbed retorts and pointed remonstrations, even an ethereal trill of three-part harmony gently wafting from the shelves of the Christian psalters.

There is a coded knock on the inner door. She looks up. Zafir and Levi. The smile has not left Rebekah's face. She knows. She believes.

On the journey back, the three skitter and scoot from shadow to shadow, passing neat bundles of hideously punctured Slavic Guard as they move. Samuel raps their code and the heavy wooden door opens with welcoming arms, then slams behind them and is double-bolted.

A tense half hour passes.

Samuel rises from his floor pillow and begins to pace once more, looking up to the skylight for the tenth time. A hint of gray.

He muses silently: Thank the Lord, dawn. He sighs. Only Yahweh knows what this day will bring.

Miriam is awake now, her head in her mother's lap. Rebekah tenderly strokes her hair. "Sit, Samuel, you are making us nervous."

Levi chimes in, "Sit, Samuel, you are wearing a path in the marble."

Zafir sits cross-legged on his pillow, chin on his fists, staring at the floor, sullen, crazy with concern for Rayhana.

Zaheid and Iuliana are cuddled together.

Samuel stops. "Dawn is approaching."

Levi says, "What should we do?"

"I am not sure. We will be safer if we just stay here. At least for now."

The others nod their agreement.

Ten minutes later, there is pounding on the door. Wary eyes snap to the sound. Samuel holds his index finger to his lips, tiptoes across the room, and listens. The pounding resumes, then stops, then resumes once more.

"Open up, Jew! We know you are in there!" Samuel does not recognize the voice, but the menace is obvious.

Another voice joins in, one he does know. "Samuel, it is Jafar al-Mushafi. Samuel, please open the door. We must speak."

Samuel turns to his friends, who helplessly shrug, unsure. Rebekah shakes her head vigorously. He turns back to the voice.

"Samuel. You must open the door or they will break it down. Please. The safety of your family is guaranteed, you have my word."

With few good options, Samuel makes a decision. "Who are 'they'?"

"The Banu Birzal. Ibn Abi Amir's Berbers. The caliph has passed. They now control Madinat. Ibn Abi Amir has promised safe conduct to all of Madinat."

Samuel looks back at the group; they are all standing. He shrugs—there are no good options. "Just a moment, Jafar." He slides one latch, then the other, inserts the key and turns it, then cracks the door.

Standing beside Jafar is Aslam, flanked by a dozen heavily-armed Berber knights. Aslam pulls the door fully open.

"Samuel. Ibn Abi Amir requires the presence of the Vizier Council at Caliph Hisham's blessing. This will be held an hour from now when the grand imam arrives from the city. Please dress and meet me in the Aljama Mosque. Peace has returned to the city. There is no danger."

Samuel does not move, his face expressionless.

Jafar looks behind him to the others. "Your family and friends will be safe, Samuel. Guards will be posted outside. No one will bother them, you have my word."

Samuel reluctantly nods.

Aslam stares through Samuel into the room, a sinister smile stitched to his face. Zafir meets the henchman's gaze with smoldering eyes.

Jafar continues, "Please, Samuel, there is not much time. I still need to find Durri the Small, Reccimund, and Abu al-Qasim."

"Very well. My family and friends will remain here until I return. I accept your word for their safety."

Samuel turns to Rebekah and mouths, "I love you." Eyes full, she taps her heart with her fingertips. A second later, Samuel is gone.

Levi exchanges a quick glance with the Berber guards then closes the door and rebolts it.

Blessing

18 October 976.

The slivers of brilliant gold breaking over the rolling hills at the eastern horizon of the Guadalquivir valley coalesce into shimmering daggers, first to tickle the shrouded landscape into a lulled carelessness, then to violently gut the devil's fog into submission. Day's revenge for night's betrayal. No matter; the ugly work is done: Madinat's bloody destiny has been fulfilled.

Within a half hour the fog bank has passed into memory, settled as swollen dewdrops glued to blades of grass and scraggled branches where they will slowly starve to death then vanish. Wispy tendrils cling bare-knuckled to the Guadalquivir's meander, the last vestige of the awful carnage and the merciless torture unleashed with a vengeance upon unsuspecting Zahra.

The genie's hour of 17 October 976 will long be remembered in Madinat al-Zahra, a rich legend to be told and retold countless times. Predictably, the facts will be exchanged for the fanciful, birthing a tall tale almost defying belief. But happen it did, a watershed moment in the history of al-Andalus.

17 October 976: The night the devil's fog charged in to claim the innocence of the city. The night the Berbers lifted beautiful Zahra's gown and had their way with her. The night an evil genie took a flame from hell and plunged it into the heart of the garrison of the Royal Guard, consuming hundreds while they slept. The night the officers of the caliph's cherished Slavic Guard were beheaded one by one, to the last man, at the top of the steps leading into the royal palace, unleashing a crimson waterfall. The night the caliph's brother was strangled barehanded by a twelve-foot horned demon in front of his wife and children. The night the caliph's vizier to Africa, one Ibn Abi Amir, the qadi of the Maghreb, made his presence felt in al-Andalus.

For decades to come, children young and old huddle wide-eyed around glowing embers as they beg their elders for scary stories and jump and start at the hushed retelling of the nightmare that was 17 October 976, when the devil's fog rolled in to rape the Shining City, then bleed her dry.

The sky is cloudless and crystalline, wonderfully cool and refreshing, the undeniable promise of a fine fall day. The garrison still smolders in the distance, but otherwise calm has returned to Madinat. Berber knights own the ramparts now and man the gates, their ranks stationed at strategic points throughout the royal palace, the medina, the royal mint, the parade grounds, the royal treasury.

Hundreds of broken bodies have been hauled away in carts and will be buried by dusk in shallow graves beyond the walls. The dark blood congealed in lavish splashes on the cream of the ashlar pavers along the alleys and in the courtyards have been sloshed with buckets of soaped mountain water then swabbed down.

And what of Córdoba proper? All is in order. Of course it is. This may seem remarkable, perhaps, except that no detail has been left to chance. Ibn Abi Amir's instructions to the powerful merchants and their minions were precise and explicit—and with their extensive networks, influence, and gold, executed flawlessly.

"Our caliph has passed, may Allah rest his soul. When he died, there was a coup attempt led by Faiq, Jawdhar, and the caliph's brother, and, sad to say, supported by misguided officers of the Slavic Guard. Thanks to the heroic action of Ibn Abi Amir and the Banu Birzal, the coup has been put down and the traitors dealt with. Hisham is safe, praise Allah, and will be anointed caliph by the grand imam this very day. He has pledged to carry on his father's work to the letter, to ensure business as usual. Córdoba's garrison has been ordered by the grand vizier to stand down, and all the gates to be reopened. Praise Allah, all is well. Prepare to welcome Caliph Hisham, citizens of Córdoba, may Allah bless his reign."

"Praise be to Allah. We gather on this sad occasion not to lament the passing of a great man, our dear Caliph al-Hakam II, may his soul rest in peaceful bliss. There will be time enough to mourn." The grand imam looks from person to person.

The gathering at the mihrab within Madinat's Aljama Mosque is small: the grand imam and his attendants, a dozen of the city's most powerful clerics, the Vizier Council, a royal scribe, Hisham and Subh, Ibn Abi Amir, and al-Andalusi. Suktan and Tahir are glued to the walls, eyes scanning for any signs of trouble. Jafar is pale as death, the faces of the Vizier Council strained and grim. Jafar has hurriedly painted in the details for them, explained the lay of the land, as dictated by Ibn Abi Amir.

"We gather to anoint and bless Córdoba's new caliph, al-Hakam's son and only heir, his benefactor and chosen successor."

Jafar grimaces.

"Come forward, Hisham." The grand imam motions to the boy. Hisham is clothed in a simple white robe, the dress of the penitent. He shyly shuffles forward, a young boy looking no older than his thirteen years.

The attendant opens the massive book for the grand imam. "Praise be to Allah, the maker of all things, the ruler of humanity, the giver of life, and one who instructed the Prophet, the one who ordained the role of caliph as designate of the Prophet." He pauses. "Hisham, do you promise to honor and respect the office of the caliph?"

"I do," answers a child's voice.

"Do you promise to protect the Holy Quran and defend Islam with your life?"

"I do."

"Do you promise to be a guardian of the Prophet's wisdom and obey his Hadith?"

"I do."

"Do you promise to perform your sworn duties as caliph to the best of your abilities for the benefit of your people?"

"I do."

"Do you promise to defend the faith, to live a life of righteousness and piety, a life of virtue that will be pleasing to Allah and an example for all Muslims of the realm to follow?"

"I do."

The grand imam hesitates. "Do you promise to obey Sharia Law and defer to the Office of the Grand Imam in all matters of faith?"

Eyes rise among the Vizier Council.

The boy's answer is quick, rote. "I do."

The grand imam raises his hands. "What you have sworn, Hisham, has been so recorded for all eternity. Please sign the Oath of the Caliph."

A second attendant opens a leather folio containing an ornate sheet of neat calligraphy. A glance at the fine work indicates that it was prepared well in advance. A third attendant presents a reed pen, which he inks and gives to the boy. Hisham signs the document. The attendants step back.

The grand imam smiles. "Excellent." He turns to his left. "The caliph's stole and staff, please." He lays the red stole, embroidered in gold, upon the boy's shoulders, arranges it, hands him the staff, then bows.

"In the tradition of Umar ibn al-Khattab, first caliph of Islam, friend and companion of the Prophet Muhammad, I present Caliph Hisham II, third caliph of Córdoba. May Allah bless his reign. Long live Caliph Hisham!"

The small audience responds with polite claps, but nothing more. Subh beams her approval. Ibn Abi Amir's frozen, lifeless expression has not altered through the entire ceremony.

The boy turns to face the Vizier Council. "Gentlemen, these past two days have been difficult for Madinat." His voice has magically strengthened. "I mourn the loss of my dear father, whom I loved, and who loved me." His voice thickens and he stops to compose himself. "As his son and chosen heir, it is time to move forward now. I will continue my father's work, just as he continued his father's work. With your help, I will rule wisely, for the benefit of all. I formally request that the members of my father's Vizier Council continue in their present roles so that a smooth transition can be made. The city must return to peace and calm, and the people must be reassured that all is well."

He hesitates then finds the eyes of Ibn Abi Amir. "Until I come of proper age, my mother will remain at my side with her wise counsel, and Ibn Abi Amir, vizier of Africa, will serve as my advisor and regent in all matters of state. His word will be my word."

Furious whispers flare up then wither.

Though his expression remains unreadable, Ibn Abi Amir is deeply pleased. The deed is done, just as they rehearsed. The boy is learning quickly.

The grand imam turns to Ibn Abi Amir. "Do you accept the role of the caliph's regent?"

"I humbly accept the role of the caliph's regent. I will defend the caliph's honor and his kingdom with my life." He bows deeply.

The grand imam says, "Excellent. The caliph's named regent will be subject to the caliph's word, and bound by the caliph's sworn Oath of Office. There will now be a swearing of fealty to Caliph Hisham in the Hall of Abd al-Rahaman III." He lifts his palm and the group turns to exit. Suktan and Tahir take up positions on either side of Ibn Abi Amir, hands resting lightly upon their scimitar hilts.

As the mosque doors are opened and Caliph Hisham and the grand imam lead the entourage out into the sunlit courtyard, a thundering roar erupts.

"LONG LIVE CALIPH HISHAM! LONG LIVE CALIPH HISHAM!"

The courtyard is packed with people who have come to welcome the young caliph's reign. Hundreds are crammed into the compact space. This crowd is no accident, of course. They have been hired to assemble and cheer, even provided a script of permissible phrases. A useful tool borrowed by Ibn Abi Amir from Caesar's Rome.

Hisham cracks a smile in response to the cheering throngs, then beams, a sight none have ever witnessed on the timid, melancholy boy. His mother is incredulous at the people's enthusiasm. She rejoices in silence: Praise Allah! Tears streak her cheeks. My son is caliph. At last, at long last. His people love him!

Mother and son are oblivious to the deception, of course. They see what they wish to see, believe what they wish to believe. Hisham raises his hand in blessing then bows to the crowd, producing yet another deafening roar. Trumpets across the city begin to blare a regal fanfare. Banners and flags by the hundred, the red ochre and white colors of the caliph wave from the rooftops on outstretched arms.

"BLESS CALIPH HISHAM'S REIGN! BLESS CALIPH HISHAM'S REIGN! ALLAHU AKBAR! ALLAHU AKBAR! LONG LIVE CALIPH HISHAM!"

The black-clad Banu Birzal knights open a narrow alley through the crowd, allowing the entourage to slowly make its way towards the golden-roofed Hall of Abd al-Rahman III, the caliph's throne room and reception hall. As the caliph passes, the crowd bends their knees in a wave that spreads like a wind-blown fire through the Alcazar.

Hisham is enthroned in his father's simple wooden folding chair beneath the red ochre and white striped horseshoe arch inside the Hall of Abd al-Rahman III, his Vizier Council arrayed to either side on their ceremonial pillows as if for a formal diplomatic reception. The Slavic guardsmen who would normally decorate the walls are absent, replaced by Banu Birzal. The highest ranking clerics stand with the grand imam; the rest of the hall is filled with dozens of high ranking court officials and dignitaries, even the most powerful merchants from the city. The presence of this latter group elicits pinched, disapproving expressions from Madinat's old guard.

The room is silent as death; not even a single sneaked whisper. They seem to be waiting for something, some pivotal cue.

A flicker of red draws the eyes of the attendees to the basin of quicksilver. Of course. The ceremonial shiver of the rising sun upon the liquid metal, spilling blood into the room, the colors of the caliph. The giant pearl descends, a spider sliding down its precious weave. The room begins to dance and shimmer.

A courtier steps forward and intones, "His Royal Highness, Caliph Hisham II; son of al-Hakam II, may Allah bring his soul peace; grandson of Abd al-Rahman III, the great al-Nasir, third caliph of al-Andalus, sultan of Córdoba, lord of glorious Madinat al-Zahra, elder of the Umayyad clan, protector of the written word, champion of truth, defender of the faith. May Allah smile upon his reign."

The quiet returns as those gathered stare into the rippling red glow enshrouding the hall. Abruptly the light vanishes. Breaths are held as all wait for what comes next.

The grand imam steps forward, raises his upturned hands to the boy, bows, then begins his proclamation. "Young Hisham has been legally sworn in as caliph of Córdoba. He has signed the Oath of the Caliph, a document to be preserved for all eternity. Caliph Hisham has appointed the vizier of Africa and qadi of the Maghreb, Ibn Abi Amir, as his regent, until he comes of age." He pauses until the furious whispers die out. "All assembled are required to pledge their fealty to Caliph Hisham. This includes the members of the Vizier Council, those who remain of the Slavic Guard and Royal Guard, ranking members of the royal court, all imams and jurists, city delegates, the merchant families represented, and the Banu Birzal clan. Each will swear an oath of *bayah* to Caliph Hisham. Let the oaths of allegiance begin."

The Vizier Council is the first to rise, Jafar leading. He bows to the caliph, kneels at his feet, eyes to the ground, then says, "I swear bayah to Caliph Hisham. Long live the caliph." He rises and returns to his pillow. One by one the viziers do their duty, Ibn Abi Amir last among them, as befitting his low station on the council. The boy smiles as his regent kneels, the affection obvious to all. Ibn Abi Amir answers with a wink.

The fealty ceremony lasts the entire morning, ending just before noon salat. Last are the Banu Birzal, who parade in, unit by unit, to swear their oath. Hushed whispers dog the Berber officers as they lead their knights onto the hallowed ground. They exude the stiff arrogance of conquerors, eliciting wary glances, derisive smirks, and a fair share of resigned awe.

After swearing allegiance to the caliph, each officer turns and bows to the qadi of the Maghreb, who acknowledges with a simple tick of his head. The declaration of dual fealty is not lost on those gathered. Message delivered.

Riders are dispatched to Córdoba to announce the news and reassure the citizens. Arrangements for a funeral procession from

343

Madinat to the Great Mosque are made for the following day, al-Hakam's burial rites to be personally overseen by the grand imam. There is to be a grand celebration afterwards in honor of the new ruler. Oddly, the man of the hour, young Caliph Hisham, will not be invited to his own party.

Spells

"Is that really necessary?" She is incredulous. "I thought the matter was settled." She lifts her shoulders. "The coup is over; al-Mughira is dead."

"I am afraid it is necessary, Subh." His voice is calm and reasonable. He locks his ebony eyes upon her, his expression blank. "I have had reports of dangerous elements hidden within Madinat. Some of the Slavic Guard have managed to escape and must be hunted down. And there are rumors of hired assassins disguised as servants within the royal palace. It is just not safe yet. A few days, no more."

She frowns. "But I promised Hisham we would be free of this prison on the day he became caliph."

"I understand, truly I do. But the royal harem remains the safest place in Madinat, Subh. You know this. Hisham's safety is my only concern right now. Just for a few days."

"But what about my husband's funeral? And Hisham's party?"

"I am afraid it is just not safe, Subh. Let me root out all of the traitors and deal with them properly, then life will return to normal. I promise, my love. There will be plenty of time for parties."

"But—"

His voice hardens, "Subh, you must trust me. And obey."

She wilts and slowly nods her head. "I see ..." A flicker of suspicion lingers behind her eyes. She sighs. "Very well, a few days, then. I will explain it to Hisham."

His tone brightens. "Good. Thank you, Subh."

She frowns, as if she just remembered something that has been nagging her. "By the way ... no one seems to have seen Bundar or Jibril."

He does not hesitate. "They were detained for questioning last night. Expect them back in the royal harem tomorrow."

She studies him. "Good. I was beginning to worry."

"Tell Hisham I will come to visit him tomorrow afternoon and we will discuss his first act as caliph. I have some interesting ideas for him to consider. There is much for him to learn."

She relaxes and smiles. "Yes."

He squeezes her hand as he devours her with his eyes, pouring his liquid ebony into her azure pools. He leans into her and whispers, "Afterwards, we will have the entire evening to ourselves." His eyes sparkle.

Her breathing quickens as her organs begin to melt. She swallows hard.

"I want your best men placed on all the entrances. The child-eunuchs are to be given to families in the city. Aslam will see to the arrangements. The male harem and the rest of the eunuchs are never to be heard from again. No one goes in or out without my permission." He lifts his eyebrows for emphasis. "No one. No matter what she says or offers you or threatens you with. Understood?"

Al-Andalusi seems amused. "Qadi of the Maghreb, the blond witch can cast no spell strong enough to break a Banu Birzal." He beams. "It shall be so."

They are gathered in the Vizier Council chamber, waiting. The men sit in a circle on their silk pillows, silent, heads bowed. The room is solemn, resigned. Two Banu Birzal guards are stationed just inside the door.

A few moments later, Jafar and Ibn Abi Amir enter. The absence of the caliph is striking. Puzzled glances sprout and are passed about the room. Ibn Abi Amir nods the guards out.

Silence.

Jafar begins, "I would like to call the Vizier Council to order. As you know, gentlemen, Caliph Hisham has requested that the council membership remain as it was under his father to help ensure continuity of the realm. Ibn Abi Amir, as appointed regent, will act as the caliph's personal representative at our meetings."

Frowns spread around the circle.

Jafar sits, leaving Ibn Abi Amir standing.

Ibn Abi Amir studies each man, testing the waters for potential enemies to be dealt with. Seeing nothing that gives him pause, he continues. "Friends, Caliph Hisham bids you well. He has decided to remain within the safe confines of the royal harem until all involved in the failed coup attempt are rooted out and dealt with properly. I agree that this is prudent. The safety of the young caliph's life is paramount."

Durri the Small interrupts, "For how long?" There is an edge to the man's tone, which is duly noted.

Ibn Abi Amir locks eyes upon him before answering in a slow, icy voice. "As long as necessary."

Durri replies, "Then perhaps we should arrange to conduct our meetings in the royal harem."

The ice turns steely. "I am afraid that will not be possible." He continues his stare until Durri looks away.

"I have had a lengthy discussion with the caliph on the next steps that must be taken to secure the kingdom. Jafar is in complete agreement."

Eyes track to Jafar, who stares into space.

"The following are the caliph's decrees: First, our first priority is to restore order to Madinat al-Zahra and bring calm to Córdoba. Business must resume immediately with our trading partners. To that end, marshal law shall be maintained in Madinat, at least temporarily. Evening curfews will be imposed, effective immediately, and authorization papers will be required to enter and leave." He pauses to study the room. "Second, the caliph felt it would be prudent to suspend all diplomatic missions to the city, at least for now. This is no time for the prying eyes of foreigners. The delegations from Constantinople, Baghdad, Alexandria, and the Holy Roman Empire will all be sent home. They will be recalled when the time is conducive."

Abu al-Qasim's raised hand is acknowledged with a nod. "Surely Brother Cleo of Cluny might be permitted to remain. He is working closely with me on new medical techniques and is not involved in politics. There is much still to be accomplished there."

Ibn Abi Amir stares at the old teacher. "Agreed. But Strobel must leave. Please ensure that the monk confines his activities to medicine, Abu al-Qasim."

"Certainly. Thank you."

"Thirdly, White Hands must be dealt with, and dealt with quickly. As soon as he hears that the caliph has passed, he is likely to test us and march on the city, which could have disastrous consequences for all."

All nod in agreement.

"The caliph has asked me to lead Córdoba's army to relieve General Ghalib at Gormaz. If they choose to march on us before that happens, I will confront the Christians on the field of battle before they reach Córdoba."

Murmurs buzz throughout the room.

Ibn Abi Amir continues. "To best do this, he has instructed me to send for more Banu Birzal horsemen from the Maghreb to supplement our army. They will swear fealty to the caliph and be placed under my direct command."

Whispers flare.

He turns to Durri the Small. "The caliph requires gold for the Banu Birzal. And, of course, gold to outfit the army. We will also need gold to recruit mercenaries from the estates of the Middle Marches."

"How much gold?"

The silence inflates.

"A million gold dinars. A small price to pay to save the kingdom."

Durri the Small stares at Ibn Abi Amir for a full half minute before he ticks his head affirmatively.

"Good. I will begin preparations immediately. Together, gentlemen, we shall reclaim the calm and prosperity established by Caliph al-Hakam, may Allah rest his soul. Caliph Hisham thanks you for your dedication and service to al-Andalus. Long live Caliph Hisham."

The response is a less than enthusiastic chorus of "Long live Caliph Hisham."

"What do you mean, I am not permitted? Stand aside. NOW!" Her bile is rising quickly. This is the third 'no' she has received from the black-robed creatures stalking her domain. These Berber minions refuse to let her pass, but do agree, reluctantly, to summon al-Andalusi.

A short while later, she tries again, her tone even and patient —no small feat. "What is the meaning of this, al-Andalusi?"

"The meaning, Sultana?"

She explains as if to a child. "For the tenth time. Ibn Abi Amir was supposed to visit the caliph this afternoon. He has not come. I wish to leave the royal harem and speak with him."

"Sultana, the qadi of the Maghreb has issued strict orders for your safety and for the safety of the caliph. Neither of you may leave the royal harem at this time."

She flushes, livid. "How dare you! I am the mother of your caliph. I demand to speak with Ibn Abi Amir! Your caliph demands it! You must obey!"

"Sultana, I am afraid the qadi of the Maghreb is unavailable. His instructions were explicit. You two must remain here. And he is not to be disturbed."

She screams, "HE TOLD ME HE WOULD COME TO ME! HE PROMISED ME!"

Al-Andalusi shrugs, his tone relaxed, amused. "Perhaps you are mistaken, Sultana."

Her face is flushed and she is shaking, nostrils inflating and deflating to a measured beat. She studies the man, her jaw clenched, furious. She raises her hand, grabs the door, and slams it in his face with all her strength. The giant *BOOM!* turns the heads of the guards throughout the royal harem.

His deep laugh rumbles in his chest then grows louder and louder until finally it breaks free. He leans back and roars.

Behind the door, there is a muffled wail then desperate, heaving sobs.

———— ⬚ ————

"My, my ..." He continues his race down the page, eyes flicking back and forth, back and forth. He pinches the letter delicately with his bone-pale, spidery fingers. When he finishes reading, he stares into space. A smile cracks his features and blossoms. "My God. Who would have guessed?" He turns to his adjutant. "Alfonso, you are sure of the source?"

"Yes, my lord. A trusted spy within the city. He is in direct contact with Ambassador Strobel. Impeccable credentials."

White Hands nods. "Excellent." He lowers the letter and begins his pacing. His commanders stare on in silence as the gears whir. Five minutes later the white-haired ghost stops and looks up, his face flush and excited. "The time has arrived, gentlemen. A failed coup attempt, marshal law. A new caliph who is just a boy. The city must be on the edge of panic." He shakes his head. "Yes, our time has come. We will march on Córdoba straightaway."

"What of Ghalib and the castle?"

"Gormaz can wait. We will leave a nominal force to ensure the old Moor stays put. He has no means to break the siege."

He turns to Enrique. "This Ibn Abi Amir who leads their army, what do we know of him?"

"A minor official in the caliph's ruling council, my lord. The caliph's representative to Africa. No military training." He smiles. "A diplomat, my lord."

White Hands cackles. "Oh, this will be fun! The only diplomacy I plan to recognize is a white flag." His commanders chuckle. "Remind me, Don Diego, how much gold is there in the caliph's royal treasury?"

The man beams. "I am afraid I cannot count that high, my lord." More laughter. "There are said to be millions of gold dinars within the walls of the Shining City. Many millions. Ten times that in silver. And entire rooms full of precious jewels."

"Yes ..." White Hands' smile fades, the sun sliding behind billowing storm clouds. The room settles to silence in response.

His expression changes to an ugly sneer. His piercing blue crystals begin to burn with hate.

His cadence is meted, deadly. "I will bleed the Moor army. I will bleed the Moor army, and then I will spill the guts of this Ibn Abi Amir myself. I will burn the Shining City to the ground. I will melt down its tainted Moor gold, and then I will tear Córdoba limb from limb and toss the bloody stumps into the river. We will plunder that city like no one has ever imagined. Not a single stone will remain set in a wall." He hisses. "Their fields will be salted. We will have their city, and then we will have their women. The Shining City and Córdoba must never rise from their ashes. Never. My father ..." His voice cracks. "My father will smile from his grave on the day the Moors are driven into the sea." The ghost stares into space.

Shocked silence fills the air.

His sanity returns, his face relaxes, and the clouds part. He sniffs, his voice now matter of fact. "We march in two days, gentlemen, under cover of night. Prepare the army. Now MOVE!"

His commanders scurry.

White Hands motions to Alfonso, who draws close. "Send word to Emperor Otto the Red and Bishop Dietrich. Tell them ... tell them the Holy Roman Empire's gold has been put to good use. Our army is invincible and we march on Córdoba. Tell them I will repay the debt ten times over by spring."

"Yes, my lord."

"Your fastest rider. And send a heavy escort—I do not want Navarre or France meddling in Castile's business. See to it."

"Yes, my lord."

White Hands stares into space, his piercing blue eyes alive and sparkling.

The man's cheeks are flushed, his lips quivering with fury. "How DARE he?! We have a signed treaty. The emperor will never tolerate such disrespect from an infidel!" Strobel snorts his anger. "The new caliph is a child, for God's sake!"

Monsignor Alonso nods his sympathy. "I understand your anger, Ambassador Strobel, truly I do, but I am afraid there is no other option. Caliph Hisham has decided it is best until his rule has stabilized. He is sending all of the foreign delegations home." He pauses. "This is a delicate time. There is fear that White Hands will march on the city."

This silences Strobel. He knows of the covert gold from Saxony. He turns on Cleo, who stares awkwardly at the floor. "Then why is he staying?!"

Cleo looks up. "Abulcasis received permission for me to remain, but only to study medicine under his supervision. I should be able to write to you, I think, to keep you abreast of events." Cleo smiles, but is answered with a stiff scowl.

Alonso continues, "Even Bishop Reccimund is being sent south to Elvira against his wishes, Ambassador."

"I do not like this." The man is calming some.

"Neither do we, Ambassador, but we live in Córdoba as guests. We must honor the caliph's request. It should only be for a short while. The regent has told Bishop Reccimund that the caliph remains committed to the exchange of trade delegations with the emperor. This is only a delay, nothing more. A few months, maybe less."

"Yes, well ..."

Cleo chimes in, "I would suggest going no farther than Marseille. Just for the winter. You can sail from València. That way you can be quickly recalled when the word is given."

The man frowns for good measure. "Emperor Otto has a villa in Marseille." He sniffs. "I will require the finest dromon in València for the voyage. And I only sail under the colors of the empire."

Alonso replies, "Of course, Ambassador. I will see to it personally."

351

Repentance

4 November 976.

The knock is slight, feminine. A miniature Quran, no larger than an opened palm, is splayed before him. He has copied it by hand. It never leaves his person.

The knock comes again. He marks his place and stares at the door. He knows the knock.

Softly he offers, "Come."

The latch lifts and she steps inside, then stops. She bows.

"Rasha." His tone is surprisingly tender.

She is hesitant. "I have a gift for you, Baba." Her voice is restrained, meek.

He stares, silently calculating. She lowers her eyes deferentially. Decision made, he says, "I have missed you, daughter."

She raises her eyes. "Durr told me that you will be leaving with the army for Gormaz."

"Yes. Just as soon as our reinforcements arrive from the Maghreb. Two days, perhaps three."

Silence.

"I wanted you to have this for your campaign." She offers the gift. "May Allah protect you on jihad, Baba." Draped upon her raised hands is the flowing lace of an embroidered silk prayer shawl.

His smile is genuine, his pleasure obvious. He stands and circles the desk. "Come to me, Rayhana."

She steps forward. Her eyes are lowered, the gift outstretched.

He lifts the shawl and admires it. "This is beautiful work, Rasha. Durr has taught you well. Thank you, I will cherish it."

Her eyes remain glued to the floor.

He raises her chin with his finger until their eyes touch. "Let there be peace between us, Rasha." He pauses. "I said words that I regret. I am sorry."

"As did I, Baba. Forgive me."

He folds his arms around her, hugs her to him. It is a scene that was quite common during her childhood. He, the proud and affectionate father; she basking in his warm, safe embrace.

He leans back from her with a pleased smile, hands affectionately upon her shoulders. His unguarded expression is a revelation. "The world has changed, Rasha. Madinat al-Zahra and Córdoba will never be the same." His tone is soft and introspective. "I am now regent to Caliph Hisham. I will soon be the most powerful man in all of al-Andalus."

"Yes, Baba."

"I will defeat White Hands. I will save the Shining City. Allah's favor has smiled upon the Abi Amir family, Rasha, at every turn of the road. Allah has blessed us richly. Allah will continue to bless us. I have come to believe that it is the destiny of our family. My destiny." He stops to gauge her response.

Nothing but deference as she replies, "Yes, Baba."

He studies her for clues for what finally prompted this softening of his young tigress.

She looks down, tentative. She speaks to the floor, just above a whisper. "I have been thinking about my life, Baba." She swallows hard. "I am ready to agree to your wishes. If you desire it, I will marry al-Andalusi. I will do my duty for the good of our family. For you."

He continues to study her, to sift her words.

His face returns to stone. "And the boy?"

She looks up, her eyes pleading. "Zafir must never be harmed, Baba. His safety is all that I ask in return."

Ibn Abi Amir slowly nods his head. "It shall be so, Rasha. You have my word."

She stares into space. "Our love was a dream, Baba. But only a dream. I see that now. Zafir will find another." Her voice quavers. "Someone better suited to his station, to his kind heart."

He bores into her. "Yes, he will find another. Thank you, Rayhana. Know in your heart that I desire only what is best for you. Al-Andalusi is an honorable man. He will be a good husband to you and a fine father to your children."

"Yes, Baba." She lifts his hand, kisses the back of it, and touches the spot to her forehead.

His pleasure is obvious. "As soon as we return from Gormaz, Rasha, I will arrange the nikah. Until then, you are free to leave your room. The villa belongs to you and Ulla now. You will grow to like her, Rasha, I promise." He opens his palms. "Should you require anything from the markets, I will instruct Aslam to permit Durr to retrieve it for you. Anything at all." He takes her face in his hands and kisses her forehead. "Smile, my love! I will shower you with precious jewels, as befitting the most beautiful princess in the realm. Yours will be the most lavish marriage celebration

Madinat al-Zahra has ever known! You will be the envy of all the women of court. You will outshine even golden Zahra!"

She tries to smile and almost gets there.

His excitement grows. "Al-Andalusi will be elated to hear the news, Rayhana! The man was beginning to give up hope. Come, let us make a formal betrothal. Come!" He leads her by the hand out of his office, down the hallway, then diagonally across the courtyard. He pounds on the door. "Al-Andalusi! Come, brother, I have news for you! Wonderful news!"

Ulla sticks her head out of the door to their bedchamber, curious. Suktan and Tahir, stationed by the villa entrance, raise their eyes to the commotion.

The door opens and the massive Berber emerges. "Brother, what news is so urgent? What news? Have our troops arrived from the Maghreb?"

Ibn Abi Amir pivots and motions his wife forward. "Ulla, come! Come, my darling!" The girl retreats into the bedchamber then reemerges, clothed in her chador.

He raises his hands to the world. "I have great news to share!"

Ibn Abi Amir's joy is infectious. Al-Andalusi and Ulla are beaming like children, and even Suktan and Tahir have donned grins.

Ibn Abi Amir lifts his palm to Rayhana, whose eyes remain lowered. "On this very day, at this very hour, my precious daughter, Rayhana, my dear Rasha, the most beautiful maiden in all of Córdoba, will be betrothed to my brother, al-Andalusi. There will be another blood joining of my family with the Banu Birzal. Praise Allah! PRAISE ALLAH!"

Al-Andalusi nods vigorously. "Fine news, Qadi of the Maghreb, fine news indeed! You have made me a happy man, a very happy man!"

Ibn Abi Amir motions the Berber forward, lifts Rayhana's hand, and folds their hands within his. "On this fine day, in front of these witnesses, humbly before Allah, I, Ibn Abi Amir, qadi of the Maghreb, regent to Caliph Hisham, am pleased to formally betroth my beloved daughter, Rayhana Abi Amir, to my brother, Jafar al-Tariq of the Banu Birzal, known to the world as al-Andalusi. May Allah bless their marriage. May he grant these two the joyful grace of many children." He beams. "Rayhana and al-Andalusi will be married upon our return from our victory at Gormaz!"

Al-Andalusi stares at the girl with hungry eyes. She refuses to meet his gaze. The Berber turns to Ibn Abi Amir. "Brother. May I seal our betrothal with a kiss?"

"You may indeed, brother."

The Berber steps closer, lifts her chin. Rayhana's eyes are full and her lower lip is trembling. He leans down and kisses her. The Berber cackles, "I so love a shy bride!" He turns and beams. "I shall think of nothing but our wedding night, Qadi of the Maghreb, when I get to open this desert flower and drink her sweet nectar! Sons, Qadi of the Maghreb, there will be many sons!"

"It shall be so, brother, it shall be so. But first we must teach White Hands some manners."

"Yes, let us teach the Christian ghost the meaning of jihad! He will taste the wrath of the Banu Birzal! Hear it! He shall taste the wrath of the Banu Birzal! WHITE HANDS WILL BLEED RIVERS!"

The lead elements of the Berber army thunder along the south side of the Guadalquivir River just after morning prayers, a dust cloud dogging their movements. Word is passed and people begin to gather in bulging throngs to observe the arriving army. A trumpet fanfare sounds. Preparations for the welcoming are nearly complete by the time the lead units canter into the Berber camp. Joyful shouts of Maghrebi dialect ring out. Hugs and back slaps and bright laughter mark this reunion of desert kin.

The citizens of Córdoba look on, wide-eyed. Riders are dispatched to the Shining City to announce the arrival.

The army stretches nearly half a league: four thousand mounted knights, hundreds of extra horses, dozens of supply wagons with weapons and food. These are the best trained cavalry units of the newly reorganized Idrisid Confederation, a formidable army, complete with Banu Birzal commanders. These veteran desert warriors look the part; they exude a quiet menace.

Their arrival is heartily welcomed, of course, Ibn Abi Amir has seen to that. Seeds have been liberally cast: "The caliph has invited the Berbers to Córdoba. The Berbers will swear allegiance and defend the city with their lives. Only the Berbers can defeat White Hands." On and on it goes. Coins are pressed into hands to help spread the good word. A reassuring measure of calm settles upon the city. Held breaths are released. Business returns to normal. The ruling merchants nod approvingly as they eagerly survey the swelling Berber ranks. "Now HERE is an army to challenge White Hands. Córdoba is safe, Praise Allah."

The families of the warriors begin to straggle in by late morning. The army's rearguard boasts hundreds of wagons loaded with household goods, children, tents. Behind these come herded livestock, artisans and their wares, bakers, tradesmen, even imams and mullahs and reputed muezzins. An entire culture on the move. The message is inescapable: This journey is one-way. The new arrivals are directed on to the Shining City. The Berber army and their families cross the people-lined Puente Romano and continue on along the Almunya Way. Berber mouths fall open at the impossible sight of so much splendor. By sunset they are setting up a second Berber encampment just southwest of Madinat's outer walls.

The arrival of so many Berber families in Córdoba produces interesting changes. While the Berbers are nominally confined to their two camps, their movements about the city soon become emboldened. What begins as a shy tentativeness around Córdoba's citizens quickly vanishes. A pride of place is exuded. Heads are held higher, eyes are lifted from the ground, stares are returned. Especially by the Berber women. After all, their husbands are the defenders of Córdoba and Madinat al-Zahra, the bulwark of the caliph's new army. Here is the promise of success against White Hands and the Christian invaders.

Each morning the Berber women make their way across the Puente Romano and on through the city gates, arriving at the market squares to both buy and sell. At first, people step aside and gawk. Soon, however, the black chadors and face-covering burqas they don in public become so common in the city that they cease to attract attention. Errant children still point and giggle, as children are wont to do, but the citizenry by and large simply shrug and ignore this new addition to the city's look. Córdoba is a diverse and embracing place, is it not?

Within a day of their arrival, chador- and burqa-clad Berber women are a common sight in Madinat al-Zahra as well, especially within the medina and its burgeoning markets. Disapproving frowns persist among the old guard, to be sure, but the decree issued by the caliph was unequivocal: "Madinat al-Zahra and Córdoba will welcome our brothers and sisters from the Maghreb with open arms."

Word has spread, of course, and Madinat's elite have gathered along the viewing ledges lining the switchback ramped street leading from the Upper Basilical building within the royal palace down to the grand portico and onto the royal parade grounds.

Whispers and nods, shushes and nervous laughs. An expectant air of excitement fills the cool morning breeze.

As the smart, cadenced slap of boot leather upon smooth stone grows in intensity, whispers extinguish one by one and heads turn and stare up the empty street. The footfall grows louder. Backs stiffen, necks crane, the shortest rise on their toes for a glimpse.

Ibn Abi Amir turns the corner first, his eyes staring in front of him, glued to the stone street. The entourage holds tight formation behind him. The man's vacant expression feigns indifference, but he hides his true feelings well. After all, the time to gloat has arrived.

The caliph's regent is dressed in flowing black robes with lavish gold piping and cord—the finest silk and cotton in the realm. Gold Quranic embroidery trails down his billowing sleeves. His only jewelry is a gold ring set with a massive emerald. His red ochre turban and untrimmed black beard suggest a Maghrebi sheikh rather than an Arab noble. A priceless Umayyad scimitar of ancient lineage, crafted of hammered Damascus steel, hangs at his side. A bejeweled needle dagger is tucked in his red ochre belt sash. The man looks positively regal. And dangerous.

Suktan and Tahir flank Ibn Abi Amir, a half step behind, in formal battle attire, fingers resting casually upon their sword hilts, eyes scanning the crowd. Al-Andalusi comes next, dressed as a Berber general, followed by a double file of three dozen of the highest ranking Banu Birzal cavalry commanders.

Not a single Banu Birzal even hints at a smile. The body language of these Berber knights shouts menace and cocked lethality.

The city's elite gape, silent and stone still.

A moment later, the entourage disappears into the next switchback, the rhythmic slap of leather on stone fading. Furious whispers reignite. People begin to make their way to the royal parade grounds as the excitement builds.

When they arrive at the grand portico, Ibn Abi Amir, followed by Suktan and Tahir, split from the group and begin to slowly climb the stone staircase to the royal viewing stand. The remainder of the Berber knights exit the royal palace through the central portico in tight formation.

Crowds continue to fill the rows of seats lining the edges of the royal parade grounds. Hundreds upon hundreds of onlookers continue to stream in, pushing and shoving for a glimpse of the action. Royal guardsmen direct the scene and ensure orderly behavior. As the elite of Madinat catch sight of what lies spread before them, they fall silent, consumed with their awe.

The rich promise of spectacle shivers in the crisp air. The sky is cloudless, a flawless azure crystal.

At the top of the stairs Ibn Abi Amir halts. He has imagined this moment only in his dreams. To his front, at the edge of the precipice, is an enormous open-faced red ochre and white horseshoe arch. Beneath it is set a knee-high, golden pedestal. The royal viewing stand. Reserved for the caliph, of course. He has had a second golden pedestal installed, slightly shorter that the caliph's pedestal, located just to its left. For the caliph's regent. Some matters of decorum must be followed.

He knows that beyond lies the massive parade ground, so large that it would be difficult to sail an arrow across it. He knows what resides there. He knows.

He reaches inside his robe to touch his Quran, which he keeps in a pocket above his heart, then fingers the soft silk folds of his prayer shawl. His lips begin to move as he silently prays. When he finishes, he takes a deep breath, then, eyes locked to the floor in submission to the will of Allah, slowly approaches the royal viewing stand. He steps upon the regent's pedestal and faces the precipice. He raises his eyes.

He cannot keep the smile from his face as he surveys the scene. Here is the stuff of legend. The caliph's army. His army. Eight thousand cavalry, six thousand infantry, and four thousand archers. The formations are tightly arrayed, at attention, in full battle dress, ready to march to glory. Elaborate standards and banners identify the various units. Banu Birzal cavalry to the front, then other Berber cavalry, mercenary cavalry, and finally infantry and archer formations to the rear. Al-Andalusi and his commanding officers straddle their mounts in front of the royal viewing stand. Al-Andalusi holds high the red ochre and white standard of the caliph. The army fills the entire parade ground.

The only sound is the snap of banners snaking in the soft breeze.

Ibn Abi Amir opens his palms and slowly raises his hands.

A thunderous, "LONG LIVE CALIPH HISHAM! LONG LIVE CALIPH HISHAM!" erupts.

An expectant silence stretches out.

Ibn Abi Amir's voice carries effortlessly, a natural voice of command. "Today, Army of the Caliph, my brothers, we march to war to defend Córdoba, to defend the caliph, to defend al-Andalus, to defend Allah." He pauses. "We will defeat White Hands and the

Christians. The caliph's army will triumph! Allah will triumph! Jihad calls upon us, my brothers. Together we will answer with our blood and our lives." Ibn Abi Amir pumps his fist in the air. "Allahu Akbar!"

A thunderous roar answers him. "ALLAHU AKBAR!"

"Allahu Akbar!"

"ALLAHU AKBAR!"

"Long live the caliph!"

"LONG LIVE THE CALIPH!"

"Long live the caliph!"

"LONG LIVE THE CALIPH!"

"We march, my brothers! To victory!"

"TO VICTORY!"

Al-Andalusi raises the caliph's standard, turns his mount, and begins to move towards the gate leading to the Road of Los Nogales and Córdoba. The army will pass the city walls, then cross the Puente Romano and head north to the Marches. The crowds in Córdoba will be massive, unprecedented in size. The people will cheer as they have never cheered before. Ibn Abi Amir has seen to this, of course. The confidence resonating from the city's ramparts is palpable.

He raises his reed pen off the paper when he hears the distant roar. He looks to the window and frowns. He has no need to witness Ibn Abi Amir's spectacle, why would he? He appreciates better than anyone what is happening. He tenders a weary sigh and stares into space.

Trapped, he thinks.

He knows he stands upon a dagger's edge. One misstep and it will all be over. At least with the man gone from the city he has a fighting chance to maneuver.

He dips his pen into the ink pot and resumes his letter. He chooses his words carefully, transcribes them with his memorized key, joins the coded letters to the paper. When he finishes, he signs his name with a flourish, sets his pen aside, and lets the ink dry. He inspects his words, inhales deeply, then blows. He carefully folds the paper, lights his sealing candle, drips hot wax onto the paper, then presses his ring upon it. Jafar al-Mushafi, Grand Vizier of the Caliph.

He takes a big risk, he knows this, but he must alert Ghalib to the true turn of events before Ibn Abi Amir can poison his mind. He must lay out his plan. Jafar entrusts the letter to one of few he can still rely upon, Rashid, a favorite courtier of Caliph al-Hakam, now pressed into the service of Ibn Abi Amir as a personal attendant for the journey north. He repeats his instructions twice. "This must be guarded with your life, Rashid. Place it into the hands of General Ghalib. Burn it if you cannot." He sees in the man's eyes the confirmation he requires, a silent "I will die before betraying the letter or its author."

That is all he can ask. He nods his dismissal, his die cast.

Curtains

16 November 976.

"Better. Try it again, slightly higher pitched this time, maybe a little slower." Durr sits on her floor pillow, the loose pile of black cotton cloth tucked in her lap, needle pushing in and out, in and out. As she works, she speaks to her lap. "Go on."

Rayhana concentrates. "I must go to the market to buy food."

Durr responds, "Closer, but the accent is not quite right." She slowly speaks the sentence with a Maghrebi lilt, her unlikely ancestry retrieved after all these years from its secret hiding place. "See? The Berber accent is unusual. Try again."

"I must go to the market to buy food."

"Better. Again."

"I must go to the market to buy food."

"Again, a little slower."

"I must go to the market to buy food."

"Again."

"I must go to the market to buy food."

"Good. Now a different sentence."

"It is market day in the medina, and I must go and buy food for our table."

Durr looks up. "Very well, then I will accompany you." She looks back to her needlework, cocks her ear.

"That will not be necessary. My sister will accompany me. You must stay and guard Rayhana."

Durr looks up, her grin wide. "Excellent."

Dimples.

She mock frowns. "Now let us continue to practice until it is perfect."

"I must go to the market to buy food."

"Again."

"I must go to the market to buy food."

They both sip tea from their divans in silence, the tray of sweets languishing untouched. Zafir is pensive, quiet. He stares into space, his thoughts far away—his usual demeanor these trying days. Samuel has waited all evening to share the news.

Rebekah insisted that he wait until dinner was finished and she returned from putting the girls to bed.

Inevitably, the dinner conversation migrated to the myriad of implications of their new regent and his Berber army, the many changes thrust upon Madinat's elite, the puzzling absence of Caliph Hisham, the looming threat of White Hands. Sadly, there has been little talk of books these past few weeks, and their work on the darkened chamber has been placed on hold.

As she reenters the room, he winks. She answers with a knowing smile. She settles in beside her husband and the two of them lock their eyes on Zafir, the warmth of their feelings for the young man unmistakable.

He feels their gaze and drifts back from the netherworld. "What?" His look turns suspicious. "What? Tell me. Has something happened? Tell me."

Samuel offers a mischievous grin. "Mmmm ... yes, my boy, something has happened." Rebekah's glee lights the room.

Zafir sits up. "Tell me, Samuel, please. Does it concern Rayhana?"

They both are beaming. "It does indeed."

He slides to the edge of the divan, eyes wide and expectant.

"I received a letter this afternoon." Samuel pauses. "From Imam Abd al-Gafur."

A breathless, "I see," is his response.

"It seems that you and Rayhana have new allies, my boy."

Zafir cracks a shy smile. "And?"

"Evidently Imam Abd al-Gafur and Rayhana's tetta, Salma Abi Amir of Algeciras, are intent on seeing you two lovebirds married."

Zafir looks down. "Praise Allah," he says, in barely a whisper. He looks up. "What did he say exactly, Samuel?"

"Well, it seems that the two of them have arrived in Córdoba."

"What?"

"Yes. They arrived two days back. They are staying in Córdoba to avoid attracting attention. At some nondescript tavern I have never heard of. Over in the Christian quarter, no less. They are safe." Samuel chuckles. "Monsignor Alonso brought me their letter. The imam is a clever one."

Silence.

Rebekah can't resist blurting out the news. "Rayhana's tetta has agreed to stand as wali for your wedding, Zafir. She will sign the nikah for Rayhana. You two will be legally married."

Samuel mock-grimaces as his thunder is stolen, then smiles.

Zafir's eyes well up and he utters an incredulous, "But how can that be?"

Samuel replies, "That is what I said, my boy." He laughs. "Imam Abd al-Gafur seems to think he can find precedence for having Rayhana's tetta serve as Rayhana's wali. Given the current circumstances with the girl's father."

"What sort of precedence?"

"That, I cannot say. He has asked permission to access the Sharia Library in the city. Presumably, he intends to find legal precedence, then craft a nikah molded for that explicit purpose. Something that can stand legal scrutiny. I will have to make arrangements to ensure his access goes unnoticed, but that should be a simple arrangement between myself and the Sharia librarian." He smiles. "If legal precedence exists, it will be in the Sharia Library. There is a whole wing devoted to marriage contracts."

Zafir stands, then sits, then stands again. He mutters, "Praise Allah. Praise Allah."

Rebekah and Samuel rise and come to him and fold him in their arms. His head drifts lower. When he looks up, two neat tears roll down his cheeks. He sniffs. "I had begun to give up hope ..."

Rebekah dabs the corner of her eye.

Samuel's voice turns serious. "Zafir, there is always hope for those who put their trust in God alone. True love will find a way."

Zafir nods, but then his exuberance melts. "But even if Imam Abd al-Gafur finds legal precedence, Rayhana is still locked in her villa. And what about Aslam?" His gaze wilts.

Rebekah cups his chin in her palm and forces him to meet her widened eyes. She whispers, "True love will find a way, Zafir. You and Rayhana WILL be together. Remember your words to her: 'I believe.' She needs your strength now, Zafir."

"Yes ..." He slowly nods his head in agreement.

The tinny metallic jingle of the bell raises his eyes from his book. Another jingle sounds, more insistent. He frowns, marks his page, then rises from his floor pillow and moves to the door. Instinctively, his hand opens a fold in his robe, exposing the hilt of his dagger. He slides the cover of the narrow privacy slit and peers out.

A woman dressed in a black burqa. He sighs and thinks, Desert trash ... The only signs of life are two ebony eyes staring back at him. He frowns. "What do you want?" There is an edge to his tone.

"I have come to see my sister," says the woman in Maghrebi accent.

Aslam stares at the woman, more cautious now. "Your sister?"

"Yes, my sister. Ulla. Wife of the qadi of the Maghreb. I am Jalida al-Tariq of the Banu Birzal, daughter of Sheikh Hamid al-Tariq. Her sister." Impatience laces the girl's words, as if she resents having to negotiate with an imbecile.

The man is a purveyor of suspicion. "My master did not tell me of a sister ..." Despite his bravado, there is a tinge of doubt buried beneath.

"I arrived after the Berber army, just yesterday. Please tell Ulla I am here. My name is Samra. She and I will go to market in the medina."

Aslam hesitates.

A voice from behind him asks, "Is that my sister? Please open the door, Aslam. Samra is a princess of the Banu Birzal."

Aslam turns. Ulla is dressed in a full burqa, not her standard chador she wears within the household. She obviously intends to leave the safety of the villa. He frowns. "My master made no mention of a visiting sister before he left."

"Of course not. We did not expect her to make the journey, but at the last minute she decided to come anyway. Praise Allah, she has arrived safely. Open the door, please."

Aslam continues to stare at Ulla. Something bothers him, but he cannot decide just what.

"Aslam. The door." Her tone is forceful.

His mouth involuntarily curls into a sneer. He thinks: When will these desert women learn their place. He sighs, turns, slides one latch, then a second, then lifts the handle and opens the door.

"Sister! I have missed you so!"

Samra steps forward and the two embrace.

Ulla says, "Aslam, we are going to market in the medina. We shall return for noon prayers, then lunch."

"I will accompany you." His master's instructions were clear.

"No." Her curt response causes him to frown once more. He narrows his eyes and studies her.

She substitutes the fiery edge to her voice with reasonableness. "That will not be necessary, Aslam. My sister will be with me. Besides, you must stay and guard Rayhana."

Aslam continues to scrutinize the woman, but one does not stare down a desert princess. The eyes in the narrow slit return his glare until he looks away.

"Very well." His tone shifts. "Please ensure that you are back by noon prayers. I will have the servant prepare lunch."

"Certainly. Thank you, Aslam."

The two women join hands and move down the alley.

His frown lingers as he watches them recede. He hears, "Tell me of Baba and Mama." Girl chatter ensues. He closes the door, slides the latch, then returns to his floor pillow, opens his book and resumes his reading.

A quarter-hour later he hears the door across the courtyard open. Puzzled, he looks up. Ulla, clad in black chador, steps from her bedchamber. Their eyes meet.

He is at the door before the airborne book slaps hard on the brick flooring, breaking its spine. He frantically works the latches as he slings his tirade of curses, slams the door behind him, and races down the alley, needle dagger drawn.

The hot room of the royal hammam is a cotton cloud, the thick steam smudged with a soft palette of reds from the sunlit glass portals high above. Even though the two men sit only an arm's length apart, they can barely see one another. Their whispers are strangled by the gurgle of the floor fountain. Eavesdropping is impossible here. By intent.

"Tell me."

"That path is blocked, Jafar. He has posted Banu Birzal guards at all of the entrances to the royal harem. Not a single Slavic Guard or royal guardsman to cajole. It is impossible to gain access to Caliph Hisham. Or to even get a message to Subh." Durri the Small wipes his dark pudgy face with a towel.

"Did you tell them that any additional release of gold from the royal treasury requires the caliph's signature?"

"Of course. It seems our Regent fears for the safety of the caliph. Assassins still lurk in the royal palace, you know." His sarcasm is biting. "Alas, vigilance is the word of the day in Madinat."

"No doubt."

"No one goes in or out until he returns from jihad. Strict orders from the qadi of the Maghreb himself." He laughs derisively.

"Did you try to bribe them?"

"What do you think?" His tone is dismissive.

Jafar returns a weary sigh. "I see."

Silence settles upon the cloud.

Durri the Small offers another angle. "How about the grand imam?"

"That way is shut. What he desires he already possesses: Final say in all religious matters of state and a signed promissory to expand the Great Mosque. I have learned my lesson there."

"Yes. Alas, a painful lesson for all of us to endure ..."

Jafar ignores him and continues, "What we need is for White Hands to take care of Ibn Abi Amir for us. Preferably after Ghalib is rescued from his prison at Gormaz."

"Wishful thinking. You did not see the Berber army on the parade grounds. I did. Trust me, White Hands is not prepared for the killing machine he is about to face in the Upper Marches. It will take a miracle for the Christians to triumph over that desert horde. Besides, if White Hands is victorious, he will march on the city."

Jafar nods his agreement. He muses, "What if we approach one of the merchant families in the city?"

"Risky. Ibn Abi Amir has them in his pocket."

"Not all."

"No, not all. But choose unwisely and we are finished."

"Agreed. Do you have an intermediary you trust to make contact? An innocent inquiry. A casual conversation over tea with the grand vizier and the vizier of royal treasury regarding the best means for the kingdom to finance the regent's expensive jihad." He hesitates. "Perhaps we require a temporary loan since the royal treasury cannot release more gold without the caliph's signature."

"Mmmm ... sounds plausible enough." He considers. "Perhaps Mamun al-Numan would be willing to listen to reason. Or even Adi al-Fadl. They have no love of Abd al-Kabir and the way he dictates rules to the other merchant families." His face brightens. "I have a man who could do the job. For a price."

"Good, make it so. We must be discreet until we are sure of their loyalties."

"You insult me, Jafar." His voice is playful. The man's skill in such delicate matters is legendary.

Jafar chuckles. "Your reputation is golden, my friend."

"Give me two days."

He has struggled all morning to concentrate. The ancient Greek codex lies splayed to his left, his paper and ink pot to his right. Three lines of tight Arabic scribbles are all he has managed to read this morning.

Samuel has insisted he resume his work, told him that it will clear his mind. He even commanded the boy to use his own study so that Zafir would not have to work alone in his small room. Samuel left at sunrise for Córdoba to make arrangements for Imam Abd al-Gafur at the Sharia Library. He is due back by mid-afternoon. Levi, Zaheid and Iuliana are to join them for dinner.

Zafir lifts his tea and sips, then grimaces; already cold. He lowers the cup and stares into space. All he sees is her face, her curls, those dimples. He can smell the dab of orange blossom between the swell of her beautiful breasts. His eyes well up and he silently promises: Rayhana ... I am coming for you, my love, I am coming for you.

Rebekah and Samuel have formulated and discarded a half-dozen plans already. She has been unable to get any new messages to Durr since the image on the polished silver. They have received only one note in return. A half-dozen Berber guards are stationed now outside the villa for the entire night. And there is Aslam, of course, during the day. He personally guards the door from the inside. If he must leave on business, he brings four Berbers inside the villa to stand watch.

Zafir can offer only a weary sigh. He thinks: There MUST be a way.

The pounding breaks his stupor. He looks up. More pounding. His eyes track to the heavy oak door as his brow knits.

Boom, boom, boom!

He frowns and thinks: What on earth?

BOOM, BOOM, BOOM! More urgently now.

Zafir muses to himself: Berber knights? What do they want now? His gut flutters. Has Aslam finally come calling for a reckoning? He swallows hard.

BOOM, BOOM, BOOM!

"I am coming! One moment!" He rises and approaches the door. He sets his ear to the wood and listens. Nothing. His heart begins to pound.

BOOM, BOOM, BOOM!

"JUST A MOMENT!" He begins to work the door locks. A heavy double clank, then he cracks the massive door, and leans to see what the commotion is about. His mouth slides open. Two Berber women in black burqas. He frowns. "May I help you?"

The shorter Berber woman pushes the door violently open and leaps into his arms. He recoils as if slapped, eyes wide, but she is latched to him now, her arms wrapped tightly around him, holding on for dear life. Uncontrollable sobs break loose from her and intensify.

367

The other Berber woman pushes into the room behind her companion, closes the heavy door, and begins to frantically reset the locks.

Zafir is incredulous. "What is the meaning of this?" He pries the woman's hands from around his neck, holds her by her shaking shoulders, and tries to stand her vertically. She blubbers and sobs, completely out of control. "Easy, easy. It will be OK. Shhhh ... no one will hurt you here. What happened to you two? Shhhh ... shhhhhhh ..."

The hysterical Berber slowly reaches up and pulls her burqa off over her shoulders and lets it slide to the floor.

Zafir is speechless, eyes and mouth wide, struck dumb by the blistering radiance of a thousand suns. All he can mutter is, "Dear Allah ..."

She leaps back into his arms, her curls flying, but this time they twist themselves into a braided rope, each desperately submerging into the embrace of the other, forming a solitary sculpture. He frantically kisses the girl's wet face, her cheeks, her eyes, her mouth, then back again. She laughs through her tears as he smothers her with kisses, then wails, then laughs again, then wails once more, then squeals with glee.

All three are hysterical now.

"Rayhana! My Rayhana! Praise Allah! Praise Allah!"

She sobs it out, "I love you! I believe, Zafir, I BELIEVE!"

Bludgeons

The terrible weather settles in upon the Marches three days after they leave Gormaz for Córdoba. The fine fall weather has lasted for weeks, crisp and invigorating under a brilliant blue canopy, the shadows growing angular and sharp as the sun slinks southward for the duration of winter. Perfect weather for a campaign.

Then this.

They went to sleep under brilliant stars, but at dawn they woke to a sheet of hammered lead straddling the tops of the rolling hills, the drizzle settling in just after first light, steady and bone chilling. There is little point in laboring to build a fire just to choke on its thick smoke. The knights grumble as they eat their gruel cold and runny, tear and gnaw on jerky tough enough to pull a rotten tooth. There is little talking, only cadenced breath fog as the Christians begin the ordeal of breaking camp.

The temperature continues to drop as the dreary grayed landscape emerges, inviting speckles of sleet to mingle with the rain. The men hurl curses as they look skyward then bark angry orders at their squires. Tents are folded and packed wet, clammy metal plate and ring-mail is lifted and fitted, ice to skin. Heavy felt cloaks are slung and cinched tight against the chill. Weary resignation descends upon the army then spreads unseen like a galloping plague.

Even the horses seem unprepared for the sudden change of fortune. Unhobbled, they stand still, sullen and resentful. Most have to be whipped to move.

By mid-morning the army of White Hands congeals and resumes its long march southward into the heart of al-Andalus, their pace reduced now to a trudge. These forested rolling hills of the Middle Marches are known to conceal many perils, chock-full of opportunities for ambush, but the confidence wafting through the Christian ranks is unmistakable, bordering even on arrogance. After all, these knights have been tested by the best Córdoba can field, and triumphed. Spectacularly. Ghalib is a virtual prisoner now, a prized knight removed from the playing board, and half of the Moors they faced on the plains of Gormaz have chains round their ankles, already marched back to Castile for safe keeping.

True, White Hands has split his army, rarely a wise strategy in war, but he holds a strong hand and he knows it. Just to be sure, he sends out scouting parties to his front and on his flanks so he can be certain when the diplomat, this Ibn Abi Amir, will finally show his face to challenge his push for Córdoba and the Shining City. So far, nothing, but it cannot be long. Another week and they will be at the Puente Romano and it will be over. He relishes the meeting, positively delights at the thought of it. He dreams of bathing in Moor blood, of personally spilling the guts of the diplomat. The man's mood is boyish and giddy, not wary. Why would it be otherwise?

"Come, girls, we are off to market. Girls!" Rebekah drapes her shawl over her hair and arranges it across her shoulders in front of the polished mirror by the door.

Sara bounds from her room, smiling, an eager puppy. Rebekah turns and cannot help but chuckle. "Where is your sister?" Sara answers with a shrug.

Rebekah raises her voice, "Miriam! Please, we are late." She knows full well what the girl is doing.

Miriam emerges, her gait unhurried, her back straight, her long raven ringlets perfectly placed, her teeth polished. Rebekah cannot suppress a double-take. Her child has turned into a beautiful young woman. She sighs and muses: Samuel will never survive the trial that is coming, poor man.

Now that Madinat has settled back into some semblance of normal life, the young men have resumed their calling. Jew, Muslim, Christian, it matters little, the girl attracts them all like moths to a flame. She sighs heavily, as only a mother can.

If only the girl had more substance, cared more about her studies than about which boy at court is the most handsome.

They bring gifts, of course, they sing songs, they recite poetry. It is amusing, really, the stupefying effect that feminine beauty has on the young male mind. Samuel wrings his hands when they ask to see her, then quizzes them mercilessly until they squirm.

Miriam willfully ignores her mother's stare as only a daughter may.

Rebekah frowns. "I am sure that is not my perfume I smell."

"No, Mama." The girl's tone is resentful, dismissive. She refuses to meet her mother's eyes.

Rebekah reluctantly gives in, and after a final sigh, tries to smile. She unlocks then opens the door, turns to her daughters, and with eyes wide says, "Come, girls, we have places to be and things to do. I have a treat for you."

As she turns and steps out of the apartment she is turned around and pushed violently back into the room. She screams her surprise, trips and falls, skinning both knees. The girls yelp in shock, then cower behind their mother as she tries to rise.

The man in black steps slowly forward and surveys the room. His dagger is drawn. "Quiet, Jewess, or there will be trouble." Aslam moves across the atrium, steps into each room, one by one, then comes back and stands before her. "Where are they?"

Rebekah is livid. She hisses, "How dare you lay a hand on me!" She is seething. "You will answer for this, you scum."

He ignores her. "Quiet, Jewess, or I may lay more than my hand upon you." His sinister smile reveals bad teeth. He sees the terror settle into her eyes and is satisfied. He casually examines the two girls, resting his gaze finally upon Miriam. "Another fine looking Jewess, all grown up now I see. Must be almost marriage age. I would hate to have to spoil her for her husband." His tone is drenched in menace. Miriam whimpers. He looks back to Rebekah.

Rebekah pulls the girls to her.

"Once more, and only once more, where are they?"

Silence.

"Where are who?"

"I am not stupid, Jewess. Last chance."

"I am afraid I have no idea what you are talking about. Who?"

"Rayhana and Durr. Where are they?" He takes a step closer to her.

She holds her ground, gathers her courage. "I have not seen Rayhana since Eid al-Fitr. As for Durr, I may well run into her at market—I often do. I would be happy to tell her that you are looking for her."

He studies her, a spider admiring a juicy fly stuck fast in his web. "Where is your husband?"

She fights for a steady voice. "He is the vizier of books and the royal librarian. Where do you suppose he is?" She manages a condescending tone. She wills her back straight and steels herself. "Now you will leave, before I scream for help, and leave now."

Aslam seems amused, then a gruff bark of a laugh. "As if anyone would help a Jewess."

She hisses. "Leave ... NOW!"

He studies the room for clues, then sniffs. He steps forward, locks his smoldering ebony gaze upon her, and says, "Mark my words, if you are lying to me, Jewess, you will pay, and pay dearly." He steps back, turns, and is gone.

Rebekah does not move. Her lower lip begins its quiver as her eyes fill. She clenches her fists to still the tremble of her fingers. Both girls stand beside her, crying. She steps to the door, manages to lock it, then leans forward to rest her head upon the cool wood as she tries to calm herself. She repeats silently, be strong, Rebekah, be strong for the girls. Be strong.

A moment later she turns, her face a portrait of feminine will, her voice solid rock. "Come, girls. Rayhana and Durr need our help. We must find your father. Come now, all will be well. We must hurry. Come, girls."

As he looks up into the impenetrable drab, a bland, mottled gray, slivers of sleet sting his cheeks. He strokes the drizzle from his beard with his gloved hand and wipes it on his cloak. His fingers are numb from the cold. He works his fingers to limber them, reminds himself that the weather is their ally. The rain and mud will slow the Christian wagons and the cold will dampen their spirits.

He turns in his saddle to survey his army stretching back into the distance. Suktan and Tahir straddle their horses just behind him.

We are ready for White Hands, he silently thinks. Our time has come.

The last cadre of mercenaries joined their ranks two days back. They march twenty-three thousand strong, with Banu Birzal commanders and an iron core of Berber cavalry. A mighty fist.

Suktan points westward down the hill. "It is al-Andalusi, Qadi of the Maghreb."

Ibn Abi Amir sees al-Andalusi approaching, his mount puffing and blowing sharp jets of cloud. The Berber's smile is wide. Good news. He thunders up and reins in beside Ibn Abi Amir. "We have found them, Qadi of the Maghreb! My death riders have just returned."

"Excellent, brother. Where?"

"Three leagues from Almuradiel, just north of the mountains. A day's hard ride."

"How many?"

"A force larger than ours, but with far fewer cavalry, more infantry and archers. And dozens of empty wagons. The

Christians seem intent to carry Córdoba's booty back north." He grins.

Ibn Abi Amir considers this. "As expected. Their overconfidence will be their undoing. I do not plan to allow them the luxury of forming ranks. Their infantry and archers will be of little use against us in that country."

Al-Andalusi beams. "Their cavalry will not stand against my desert riders, Qadi of the Maghreb."

Ibn Abi Amir smiles. "No brother, they will not. White Hands has no idea what Berber cavalry are capable of." He muses. "White Hands will try and locate our position, of course. Remain on the lookout for their scouts. He must remain blind, that is essential."

"We have already intercepted two scouting parties, each with a half-dozen riders. They did not live to tell a tale."

"Good. I want you to take your men and scout the Christian position. The rest of the army will come under cover of night. I must have a perfect place for my ambush. Between two mountains in a tight, bent valley so that their lead units cannot easily see their rearguard. We must have plenty of cover. Perhaps with a stream that they will have to stop and ford. Search for the right place and send word.

"We will attack while they march and are stretched out thin. They must not be allowed to form ranks." He locks eyes with his brother. "See to it personally—there can be no mistakes."

"Of course, Qadi of the Maghreb, consider it done."

"Once we are set for ambush, our cavalry will attack from their rear. He will not expect that. Then we will split him in half. It will be over before they know we are on them."

Al-Andalusi nods approvingly. It pleases him greatly that his brother has mastered the art of war. "We will spill a river of Christian blood. This will be the Banu Birzal's first jihad, Qadi of the Maghreb."

"Yes, al-Andalusi, the first of many glorious jihads."

"I have work to do, what do you want?" Despite his pounding heart, Samuel manages to adopt the impatient tone of a master chastising a servant. "Come on, man, be quick about it, I have work! What do you want?"

"Where is the boy, Jew?"

Without a pause, he replies, "If you desire an answer, you will remember your manners. You will refer to me by my proper title, either royal librarian or vizier of books. Your choice." Samuel wears a mask of stone.

Aslam stares him down for a full half-minute, then shows his bad teeth. "Where is the boy, Librarian?"

"If you are referring to Zafir, he is not here. What is it you need? Perhaps I can help?"

"I am looking for Rayhana and Durr."

Samuel's look is incredulous and impatient. "Why in the heavens would I have seen Rayhana and Durr? My understanding is that she is imprisoned in the regent's villa. But you would know that better than me."

"I must ... talk with the boy."

"Talk all you want, but he is not here. I sent him to Córdoba to retrieve a parcel of books for me. A new arrival from Constantinople."

Aslam looks skeptical. "When?"

"I sent him a short while ago. I told him to spend an extra day in the city before returning to Madinat. To hear a recital, do some shopping, maybe relax a bit. He has been working too hard, you see."

Aslam sifts his words. "Where is he staying?"

"The quarters of the Sharia Library. Obviously." That dismissive tone returns.

Aslam stares.

"Next to the Great Mosque."

He sneers, "I know where it is, Librarian."

"I have work to do. Remain here if you must, or go find him, I care not which." Without waiting for a reply, Samuel turns his back and walks across the room to his desk, settles onto his floor pillow, lifts his reed pen, dips in the ink pot, and begins to scribble.

When he allows himself to look up a minute later, Aslam has vanished. He offers a weary sigh. He rises, crosses the room, relocks the door, then walks to the miniature keyhole door set into the wall. "You may come out now, it is safe."

They emerge timidly from the latrine like cave explorers reentering the sunlight after being lost for days; Zafir first, then Rayhana, then Durr. Their faces are ashen, their features drawn tight with fear.

Samuel smiles to calm them, steps to Rayhana, and folds her into his arms. "All is well, my dear, all is well."

Zafir finds his voice and gushes, "You were magnificent, Samuel!"

"I still have a trick or two up these sleeves, my boy." He manages a chuckle. "I am just glad the man did not ask to relieve himself."

At last, some grins.

"He will be back, of course, once he finds out your name is not on the registry." He muses. "For some strange reason you never made it there. And you never picked up my parcel. Shame on you! Perhaps you met Rayhana and spirited her to Córdoba to disappear into the medina." He smiles. "You have always been a troublesome boy, and so headstrong now that you have fallen for a beautiful maiden. I am not quite sure what to do with you, you simply refuse to listen to reason!"

They all laugh.

Zafir says, "But what should we do now?"

"We must find a safe place for you three, some place for you to disappear. Somewhere he cannot go."

Silence.

Rayhana whispers, "The room with the camera obscura."

"Mmmm ..." Samuel nods. "Excellent idea, young lady. As deep in the library as one can go. Aslam would have to come through here, through me. He does not have the authority to search the Rare Books Library, at least not until your father returns." He turns to Zafir. "That is where you will go, at least for now. You will need bedding and food and water, and plenty of oil for the lamps. Some curtains to hang for privacy, perhaps." He lifts his right eyebrow. Zafir grins and Rayhana blushes. "And water and a basin to bathe in. I am afraid it will have to be chamber pots for now. I will have Rebekah bring it all." Samuel beams, "At least you will not want for good reading!"

Mercifully, she smiles.

"Lock the doors, and open them for no one without the secret knock. No one." He widens his eyes. "Zafir, you will not leave that room for any reason, understood?"

The boy nods.

"Rebekah, Levi, Zaheid, and I will begin our work on a serious plan for you two." He sighs. "We will need something bold, something they will not anticipate." He shrugs. "You three think about it as well. We should have a little time, at least until Rayhana's father returns from his campaign. My hope is that Aslam will not try and force his way into the Rare Books Library without his master's command. But one never knows with a man like him."

"I will defend them with my life, Samuel."

Samuel frowns. "No. We must be cleverer than he is, my boy. Violence is never the answer." He taps his head with his finger. "We must outsmart the man."

They nod slowly.

He rests his eyes on Rayhana. "My dear, your tetta has come to help you two. She and Imam Abd al-Gafur are in the city now. I will get word to them that you are safe."

Her eyes fill. She whispers, "Praise Allah ... Tetta has come."

Zafir hugs her to him.

"Good, now you three get moving. I will find Rebekah and bring supplies shortly. Go now, shoo!" He waves them out with both hands.

Favors

It has been a long, wearying ordeal, the day's march ridiculously slow and taxing as they navigate the series of narrow, twisting valleys through the mountains. They have had to cross three streams already, the last deep enough to touch their saddles.

The drizzle has continued unabated for two days now. Relentless torture, wet and freezing, drab and depressing. The army is soaked to the bone and shivering, their spirits sapped. The chainmail and steel plate of the mounted knights is icy and leaden. He has been asked twice now by his cavalry commanders if the men might remove some of their armor to ease the burden. He has refused, of course. This is dangerous country, after all. Instead, he assures them that tonight they will take the time to build fires to dry out and have a hot meal.

The army has to stop periodically to allow the trailing wagons to catch up. White Hands rides near the front of his army, as a general should, his dozen adjutants and his bannermen at his side. He continually scans the high hills hemming them in, the tops of the hills lost in the wispy gray. Forested and opaque, primeval somehow. Unnerving territory, but the only quick passage through the line of mountains northeast of Córdoba.

Once this interminable valley flattens and opens out they will stop and make camp. From what his scouts have told him, it will be only an hour, perhaps, certainly less than two, then they will dry their clothes and have some brandy to warm their hearts. Soon they will reach the Guadalquivir plain where the marching will be easier, then the road to Córdoba, paved in stone by the Romans a millennium ago. Two days more, perhaps three. Certainly this dreadful weather cannot last.

Something continues to nag at the man, however, an itch he cannot seem to find and scratch. No news from his scouting parties—none whatsoever. Very odd, very troubling. He has no idea whether the Moors are a hundred leagues away or just around the next bend. A blind army is a vulnerable army, he knows this all too well. He frowns and decides that he will send out another set of riders at first light, larger this time. He must have news of the diplomat's position.

"Look at me." His concern presses down upon his words. "Rebekah, look at me."

She lifts her eyes. Full still, but mercifully no tears. "I am fine, Samuel, really." She forces a half smile.

He is unconvinced. "That one is evil, Rebekah, and dangerous. No scruples or respect for the rule of law. Swine!" His face flushes. "Threatening my wife and children with violence in my own home. HOW DARE HE!"

She touches his arm to calm him and changes the subject. "So they are in the room with the darkened chamber?"

He takes a deep breath, holds it, then exhales. "Yes. They are safe, at least for now. In the far reaches of the Rare Books Library under lock and key."

"How did she get out without our help?"

He shrugs. "Ask her. They were dressed in burqas. I have no clue how they obtained them or how they tricked Aslam."

Rebekah grins. "My clever girl."

Samuel continues, "I must find Jafar and request royal guardsmen for our door. And for the entrance to the Royal Library, too. He will not take kindly to threats from Ibn Abi Amir's lackey."

"No, I expect not."

"We should be safe, I think, at least until our new regent makes it back from his campaign."

She nods.

"Still, it will not be long until Aslam returns from Córdoba. Take the girls and go home at once. Lock the doors and open them for no one until I come for you. I will use our secret knock."

"No, Samuel."

He frowns.

"I will get what they need from the market and I will deliver it to them. They must have supplies, especially food and water. I will not abandon them now because of Aslam's threats. When I am finished, and only when I am finished, will I take the girls home. I will NOT cower in the face of evil."

He knows the tone well and does not argue.

"Very well, but I am going with you. Until I secure some guards we will not be safe, Rebekah. First, we need to find Levi and Zaheid and Iuliana; they can help us gather what we need. We must be discreet. We will buy the food. They can split up and get the rest. For all I know, Aslam may have someone watching us even now, so we dare not all travel together. We must be quick about this, very quick." He looks to his daughters collapsed in a heap on the divan. "Come girls. Up! We have things to do and places to be. Come, my loves, time to rise."

The snaking mountain brook slithers down the slate ledge, emptying its crystal vigor into the deep, limpid pool with a soothing sigh and a hushed trickle-splash, pausing for a moment of calm on its pilgrimage out of the dark valley. Mountain trout as long as a man's forearm hang in the dark water at a hand's depth, rose-moles all in stipple. Tiny pinpricks dance upon the mirror sheen, the speckled rainbow buried beneath, shimmering jewels. Winter's elegant tranquility, a stilled peace all its own.

First, a muted rumble in the distance, then a rising, throaty grumble, exchanged at last for heavy rolling thunder. The trout flick their tails and disappear into the black. A water strider backs into the shadows as a wood shrew looks up from its nibbling at the water's edge, jaw frozen mid-chew, puzzled. A jackrabbit wriggles its whiskers then darts for the brush. Breaths are held.

From around the far bend a column of turbaned black canters from the trees in tight formation, three abreast, ten then thirty then sixty deep, slicing quickly along the poor road paralleling the stream's meander. The cavalry is headed uphill, back into the mountains towards the dark valley.

The knights' swords and maces are sheathed. Each man holds his reins in one hand, his bow in the other, the fine bend of white ash nocked with an arrow. Two large quivers are tied to either side of their saddle horns for easy reach, three dozen arrows fletched with the black and white feathers favored among the Banu Birzal.

Al-Andalusi rides in the lead. Not a single word is spoken, but their faces are painted grim with deadly purpose.

The thunder rolls past.

The man slurps his tea to ease the burn. "Your man said you required gold to help finance the campaign, that the royal treasury is closed even to you, Durri. Why?"

Durri the Small stares at the floor.

Jafar studies the man sitting across from them, calculating. He answers for the royal treasurer, "Because the royal treasury is now under Banu Birzal guard and the caliph is imprisoned in the royal harem. Not a soul goes in or out, not even us. Without the caliph's signature, no one can withdraw a single dinar from the royal treasury, not even Durri."

The room stills.

Mamun frowns. "I had heard rumors. It seems the regent has a plan for the caliph's gold."

"Indeed he does." Jafar continues to study the merchant for clues of his loyalty—or loyalties. "Ibn Abi Amir intends to rule al-Andalus, Mamun. By himself."

"I see. Of what consequence is that to me? Trade will go on, profits will be made, the city will continue to flourish. The merchant families will grow richer just as they have for the past hundred years."

Jafar pauses before he replies. "Do not be so sure, Mamun. The regent has bartered with the grand imam for his support. The city will return to the strictures of Sharia Law. The lavish festivals that have lined your pockets will cease." He smiles. "Berber temperance does not condone such things. What is commonplace today will be judged lavish and excessive, sinful even." He pauses. "And there is the new tax, of course."

The merchant's eyes widen. Such men fear that word more than the plague itself.

"Yes, a heavy new tax. For the expansion of the Great Mosque that was promised by the regent. Ibn Abi Amir's blood barter with the grand imam. I am afraid the burden is to be levied upon the backs of the merchant families. They are the ones that profit the most from the city's cravings, after all."

Another frown. "I see."

Durri the Small clears his throat. "Actually, Mamun, all we require is a friend."

"A friend ..."

Jafar adds, "Yes, a friend, Mamun. A rich friend with many connections. A friend with influence in the city." He takes a deep breath before casting his lot. "My coup attempt failed due to the grand imam's betrayal of his promises to me. The caliph must be freed from his prison and set properly upon his throne. The boy will continue his father's work and the city will return to normal. Business as usual. This meddlesome regent must be stopped before it is too late, Mamun."

The merchant nods his agreement.

"I have it on good authority that there will be an attempt made on the regent's life as soon as he returns from campaign. A most formidable assassin has already been ... recruited. When the upstart is gone, we must be ready to move on the Berber dogs that have settled into our city. The City Watch must attack and burn the Berber camps. Those scum must be driven back to the desert where they belong. Every one of them."

Mamun muses. "Abd al-Kabir and the other families will not go along with such a plan. Ibn Abi Amir pays them well."

"I am afraid Abd al-Kabir's days in Córdoba are numbered, Mamun. The caliph requires a new leader from among the merchant families. When the caliph's treasury is opened to us, we will pay ten times what the regent offers. Abd al-Kabir's support among the families will dry up overnight. Doors will be shut in his face. You will take his place, Mamun."

The merchant licks his lips.

"What you suggest will require considerable gold and many favors called in. A great many favors."

"Of course. That is why we have come to you, Mamun. Your pockets are deep, and you collect favors like the caliph collects books." This produces a pleased smile.

The quiet stretches out as the merchant considers.

"I have a taste for a new almunya. Perhaps one on the banks of the Guadalquivir, one that has fish farms." He looks at Durri the Small expectantly.

Jafar glances at Durri the Small, who without hesitation replies, "Perhaps al-Rummaniyya would be of interest to you, Mamun. I have the largest fish farms in Córdoba. As you know."

The man beams.

"And noble status for my family. I would be honored to receive a villa in Madinat al-Zahra, one high on the hill. And a seat on the Vizier Council, of course. Perhaps the caliph could create a new position that would suit my skills, say, vizier of trade ..."

"Trivial matters, Mamun. Consider them done."

"You may not enter, my lord."

The pikes form a neat X in front of the man in black, blocking the path. The hands of the pikemen's companions rest on the hilts of their broadswords. Slavic guardsmen.

The man in black hisses, "I am no lord. Now stand aside."

"We have orders, my lord."

The man in black turns back to Samuel. "Speak, Librarian." His voice has turned icy.

"The grand vizier felt it prudent to post guards at the entrance to the Rare Books Library. After all, within these walls lie Caliph al-Hakam's greatest treasures, God rest his soul. Now those books belong to Caliph Hisham. The contents of this library are priceless."

The man in black stares back with smoldering ebony eyes.

"I assured Jafar that guards were unnecessary, but he insisted. I have his written orders on my desk if you would like to see them."

Silence.

"I will bring Berber guards to—"

Samuel raises a hand to interrupt. "I am afraid the grand vizier was quite insistent that only members of the Slavic Guard be used. It is spelled out explicitly in his orders." Samuel lifts his palms helplessly. "You are certainly welcome to consult the grand vizier on this matter. I care not who the guards belong to."

Aslam stands still as a statue, his eyes burning into Samuel. "The boy's name was not on the registry of the quarters at the Sharia Library. It seems he never showed up. I scoured the city for two days. Nothing, not even a trace. I find myself wondering, Librarian, if he ever left Madinat." He looks to the X across the entrance to the library, then back to Samuel.

"I can assure you that the boy is not here. Why would I bother to hide him? He has always been trouble for me. And since he met the girl, even worse. I say, good riddance to them both."

Aslam stares.

"Look, Zafir loves the girl, you know this. After she escaped, perhaps she managed to find him before he left Madinat on my errand. I would not be surprised if they left the city and headed south. I believe she has family in Algeciras. The boy has nothing to hold him here."

Aslam has not taken his eyes from Samuel, his nostril flares his only movement, in and out, in and out, the only hint that he is not carved from stone.

His words are meted, deadly. "When my master returns, I will be back, Librarian." A sinister grin opens on his face. "You better have a hundred guards posted by then. If I find that you have lied to me, Jew, I will open your belly so you can enjoy a slow, painful death. While you are dying I will enjoy your wife and your girls as you squirm in your ropey guts." He hisses, "Mark my words, Jew, I will be back."

Samuel flushes crimson. "How dare you threaten the royal librarian! Leave immediately or my guards will escort you out at the point of their pikes. Now GO!"

Aslam laughs loudly. He ambles to the door, opens it, then vanishes.

The Dark Valley

He raises one hand high in the air and tenses his reins with the other, bringing his dappled gray stallion to a halt. His cavalry travels at a lazy pace for an invading army, no more than a fast walk, but this is all the weather and the terrain will bear. Any quicker and the infantry and wagons cannot keep up, the churned muck sucking down boots and miring wheels.

As word is passed, the vanguard turn in their saddles and look back, puzzled, then follow suit, settling their stallions. The stream, broad and deep, angles across the army's path a stone's throw to the front of the lead bannermen. The welcoming plain is visible now through the dreary gray slush. The last gasp of the mountains is tantalizingly close.

The command trickles slowly back along the narrow valley, disappearing around the bend back to the right. No sightline to the rearguard—a situation that is never comforting. A backward-moving sigh travels down the column, the weary infantry happy for a chance to rest their numb, swollen feet.

He cocks his head as if he hears some strange sound, then frowns. He turns to his adjutant. "Alfonso, something is not right, I can feel it."

"What is it, my lord?"

White Hands lifts his head to the crest of the mountain to his left, then up to the crag to his right, then back to the stream in front. "I am not sure. Something." His stallion whinnies. There is a strain of leather as he leans forward in his saddle and whispers, "Steady, boy. What is it?" The man's ghost fingers stroke the horse's gray mane. The massive animal's ears have a mind all their own, cocking to random angles, freezing, then flitting on, only to lock to another direction. Searching, but for what? White Hands frowns once more. "What is it, boy?"

He turns to his adjutant. "Send a rider to the rearguard and tell Don Lugo to close ranks and be on the lookout. And bring me a dozen fresh scouts, I need more eyes."

"Yes, my lord." Hand signals send a mount galloping down the column. The scouting party assembles, hushed instructions are passed, and the riders canter forward, splash-wade the stream, then move down the valley towards the plain.

383

He scowls at Don Diego, his second-in-command. "Something is wrong, I can feel it. There is no room to maneuver in this damned valley, and it will be impossible to form ranks if we have to fight. I do not like it."

"It is impossible for the Moors to position an army in these mountains without us knowing. The most they might manage is an ambush by a small raiding party. Nothing to worry about." Don Diego raises his hands to the hills. "Look at this mess, my lord. They will have no easier time than us crossing it."

White Hands' scowl remains. "Still ... something is not right." He stares at the slopes for a moment more, then shakes his head as if to clear it, barks, "Alfonso, pass the word back, I want double-time until we are clear of these infernal mountains."

Alfonso responds with an incredulous, "My lord? The men are beyond exhausted."

"I said double-time, Alfonso! Now MOVE! I want those wagons over this stream within the hour."

Don Diego tries to soften the blow. "Spread the word that ale rations will be tripled tonight, and hot food aplenty, but only after we are out of the valley."

White Hands nods his assent.

Alfonso salutes. "Yes, my lord!"

He sends two riders galloping back, one to either side of the column. They shout commands as they move, "Double-time, you dogs, double-time! Triple ale when we reach camp, triple ale! All the hot food you can eat, hot food, boys! Double-time, you dogs ..." Cheers cling to the horse's flicking hooves, slowly fading into the distance, dying out as the riders disappear around the bend.

As the army begins to move, White Hands does not take his eyes from the mountains, his eyes tracking slope to slope. He can taste the safety of the plains, the long sightlines and easy march. The freezing mountain water takes their breath as it rises up their legs to their groins. Just as he and the last of his vanguard make their drenched exit, he hears a shout to his rear, "My lord! My lord, look! Sweet Jesus!" The quiver of panic is unmistakable.

White Hands whips his stallion about. His mouth falls open as he sees the thick black smoke boiling from behind the broad ridge hiding his rearguard. The wagons. His expression tightens and turns grim.

First comes a spontaneous whisper, "So the diplomat knows something about fighting after all." His cupped hands join his mouth to form a trumpet. "Form ranks! Prepare for attack! FORM RANKS, GOD DAMN YOU! FORM RANKS! PASS THE WORD! FORM RANKS!" He races back across the stream shouting orders as he moves.

The scene explodes into frenzy. Commands are being blared by so many officers that a chorus leaps down the valley like wildfire. "PREPARE FOR ATTACK! FORM RANKS! PREPARE FOR ATTACK! READY WEAPONS!" Horses rear and whinny. Dozens of trumpets squawk their shrill calls to the gathering mayhem. Officers gallop back to join their banners, frantically shouting orders as they pass their troops. Slit visors scissor shut. Shields are untied from saddle horns and lifted, maces are made ready for close combat, broadswords are pulled from scabbards in a cool, metallic hiss, their terrible sheen lifted defiantly into the air.

The infantry, the most vulnerable of the lot, scurry about, confused, their movements erratic, frantic, the edge of panic never far when battle comes calling. The black smoke from the rear guard thickens and grows, but no one is quite sure where the real danger lurks. Heads circle, scanning the mountains, grasping desperately for clues.

Don Diego gallops up beside White Hands and has to shout to be heard over the growing storm, "Raiding party?"

White Hands leans close. "His army is here, Don Diego, I can feel it! We must form ranks before it is too late."

"I will see to it personally."

"No. Ride for the center of the column, to the bend, that is where they will try and break us. Their cavalry will come down that ridge from the east." He points. "They aim to cut us in half. I need you there. Forget the wagons, let them burn, just hold the line until I can get the rest of the army across the river. It is deep enough to offer some defense. I will sound trumpets when we are set, then you and your cavalry break free of the fight and join us." He widens his eyes for emphasis. "Leave the infantry if you have to. After we slow them at the river, we must break for the plains where we can stand our ground. But first we must get out of the valley of death, and get out quickly, before they can trap us." The two men grasp forearms. "You must hold the line, Don Diego, so I can safely withdraw the army. GODSPEED!"

Don Diego returns a grim nod, then draws blood with his boot spurs as he kicks his stallion to life with a mighty "HYAH! HYAH!" and races down the column shouting, "FORM RANKS! FORM RANKS! STAND FIRM! STAND FIRM! FORM RANKS!" A dozen officers and a hundred cavalry give chase.

———— 🔲 ————

Death comes from above, high up on the steep, forested slope above the center of the army where the bulk of the infantry reside. Arms lift and point to the western peak. Eyes widen, incredulous. A giant darkened smudge floats into view, coalesces, lingers against the gray, then slides into a silent arc and drops like a diving falcon into the valley, spewing violence indiscriminately. Four thousand steel-nosed arrows are launched in a single volley.

The gaze of the mounted officers follows pointed fingers, then they scream, "SHIELDS! SHIELDS! RAISE SHIELDS! SHIELDS!" Before the first arrows strike home, a second dark smudge gathers behind it and begins its lazy arc.

The infantry whimper and groan like whipped children as they drop their packs into the mud, crouch, and race to untie their circular shields, pulling and yanking with quivering hands. "THESE KNOTS, GOD DAMN THESE KNOTS!" Panic steps closer still as the agony of anticipation crescendos. Only a few of the most nimble succeed in raising their red-lacquered oak protection above their heads just as the needles of death begin to stream down upon them.

The last second of stretched silence is the cruelest of all, then a quick stutter of "fuhhh, fuhhh, fuhhh, fuhhh," of feathers burying into mud, then the cascading downpour arrives with a "FUUUUUUHHHHHHHHHHHHHHH," chased then smothered by an answering cacophony of quick, piercing screams as honed steel pierces thin metal helmets and splits chainmail ringlets, burrowing into brains and backs and shoulders and necks.

A sea of men drops to the muck, decimating the scattered ranks of the infantry and archer companies. Embers of panic spark to wildfire that races through the living. Here, then, is the stuff routs are made of. The second volley claims hundreds more. Men begin to throw their gear and sprint for the trees. Banners lie shamed in the mud, trampled upon.

The officers dance about screaming desperate orders to form into ranks, but that time has long passed, the panic impossible to corral. The haunches and necks of the white-eyed mounts are pin-cushions for fancy feathers. Eerie horse-screams join the fray. Those knights with expensive, tempered plate are saved by their armor, the tips just nicking skin; but many others are not. Of those tucked safely behind their gleaming steel, some are thrown by their rearing, spinning, screaming stallions, only to be rolled upon and trampled into the cold crimson slime.

Don Diego arrives just after the sixth volley lands, the center of the Christian army now a melted mess. "SWEET JESUS!" He hears the battle raging at their rearguard but cannot see around the bend. Thick knots of boiling black billow skyward. A chorus of pings, steel-upon-steel, screams and curses buried beneath hoof thunder, desperate, barked commands, the growing moans and begging pleas of the dying.

He turns to his second. "Take fifty knights and make a stand at the wagons. Do not join the battle. Form a wall to keep them off me while I gather strength here and form a new rearguard. Let the wagons burn. The Moors will attack down the ridge—we must be ready when they come."

The officer replies, "Understood, my lord."

"Time, man, buy me time. GODSPEED!"

The officer hand-signals his commands and the cavalry thunders up the dark valley.

Don Diego watches them disappear around the bend, thinking, not enough. He turns in his saddle, surveys the carnage spread before him, and shakes his head. The infantry and archers are done for, either wounded or dead or scattered to the wind. Mercifully, the barrage has slowed to a trickle; the Moors are not willing to waste more arrows. Their work is done.

The second wave of his cavalry arrives. He turns and shouts, "THE RIDGE! WATCH THE RIDGE!" He points. "PREPARE FOR ATTACK! FORM RANKS ON ME! FORM ON ME!" He kicks his stallion to life.

In the end, Don Diego's defensive stand is of little use. The attack does not come down the ridge but instead from the trees across the narrow valley to their rear. The Banu Birzal cavalry stream from the woods in tight formation, a juggernaut three abreast, at full gallop, just as al-Andalusi leads his cavalry around the bend from the smoldering remains of the slaughtered Christian rearguard. As the two Berber cavalry pincers meld into one mighty fist, a massive cry erupts, "ALLAHU AKBAR! ALLAHU AKBAR! ALLAHU AKBAR!"

Don Diego and his officers turn in their saddles to look behind them. "GOD DAMN THESE MOORS!" He screams, "ABOUT FACE! LOOK TO THE REAR! ABOUT FACE! THE REAR!"

Al-Andalusi looses his arrow at full gallop just as Don Diego reaches up to flip his slit visor shut. Too late. The man's head is snapped back with the sudden impact, the steel sliver entering his skull through his left cheek, not stopping until it reaches the back of his helmet. Don Diego's expression is one of surprised shock. Eyes wide, his mouth opens and closes helplessly. He teeters in his saddle. His eyes dull then flutter as he slides from his saddle and collapses in a heap with a metallic crush. His boot remains trapped by his stirrup, lifting his leg grotesquely into the air. His stallion spooks and races away, dragging the knight behind him until the animal's massive legs tangle on the dead body and both crumple into a broken, rolling mess.

"ALLAHU AKBAR! ALLAHU AKBAR! ALLAHU AKBAR!"

Panic roars down the dark valley.

"I said let them go, brother. This battle is won." The voice is calm, even.

The bloodlust is rampant. "No mercy, Qadi of the Maghreb, the Banu Birzal will show no mercy to the infidel! This is JIHAD!" The Berber is slathered in blood, his ebony eyes greedy for more vengeance, more blood, more death.

The voice gains strength, "Let them go, al-Andalusi! Obey me!"

The Berber glares but does not speak.

"White Hands has lost over half his army today. This battle is done. He can do nothing now but limp back to Castile. We will show mercy, as Allah shows mercy. We will let the conquered go, brother, so that Allah may bless our great victory and smile upon us another day. White Hands will long remember how I vanquished him, how I spared his life. His troops will forever fear Ibn Abi Amir and his Banu Birzal."

Al-Andalusi gathers himself and nods. "As you wish, Qadi of the Maghreb." He hand-signals his officers to stand down, and the word is passed through the ranks. The hundreds of small skirmishes scattered among the broken army begin to ebb as the remaining Christians surrender and lower their shields and swords.

The makeshift Christian rearguard encrusted on the opposite side of the crimson-streaked stream stands its ground as their army continues its ragged limp to the plains. White Hands is nowhere to be seen. He has no infantry or archers left to speak of; perhaps half of his mounted knights are dead or captured. A total rout.

"We camp here tonight, brother, then ride at sunrise for Gormaz. It will be impossible for White Hands to send reinforcements, so the siege will not stand. I would not be surprised if they retreat north before we arrive. Send word to Córdoba of our great victory. Tell them ... tell them there is no victor but Allah."

"It shall be so, Qadi of the Maghreb. There is no victor but Allah!"

Spaces

18 December 976.

A single *tap*, then a pause; *tap-tap*, long pause, *tap*, pause, *tap*. The three look up from their books to the door, then anxiously to each other, the fear never distant. Zafir nods decisively and rises, tiptoes forward, rests his ear upon the cool wood, and listens for any hint of danger.

Satisfied, he softly says, "Orange," in Greek.

Through the door, a muted response of "Star," in Greek. Zafir levers the three metal latches one by one, two-hands the wooden brace to remove it, then props it against the wall and cracks the door.

He is greeted by Samuel's bright smile and twinkling eyes. "And how are my precious prisoners this fine morning?" He chuckles.

Zafir makes an exaggerated bow as he sweeps his arm in invitation. "Your prisoners fare well, my lord."

Rayhana flashes her dimples.

"All is well, my dear?"

"All is well, Samuel."

"Durr, I trust these two are behaving themselves?" He beams and the pair blushes.

Durr's reply is playful. "Alas, I have been forced to scold them at least three times a day, Master Samuel. It seems they have eyes for each other."

All four laugh.

The triumvirate have been locked away for almost two weeks now. So far, Aslam has not returned, but Samuel is certain he and Rebekah are being watched. Fortunately, the Slavic Guard take their roles very seriously. By now, what Ibn Abi Amir did to their officers is common knowledge at court. These men will die before allowing Aslam to pass, that much is clear. Still, time presses down upon them all.

Their quarters are cramped. As a reading room it is a cozy space, book-stuffed walls running floor to ceiling; as a dwelling for three, it is much too confined for comfort. Books have been removed from one set of shelves to make room for their supplies. The reading table that once occupied center stage has been pushed to the side, the camera obscura resting upon it still, a queen upon her throne. A hemp line draped with a sheet bisects the room, then is cut again in the opposite direction to form two topless rectangular tents, the women's bedding in one, Zafir's in the other. The remainder of their meager space allows three divans, each with a standing lamp, and a small round table for meals. Two small braziers are all that are needed to warm the space.

Their captivity is beginning to take its toll upon their psyches. They read, they talk, they pray, they eat, they wash—as best they can without the luxury of a hammam—they tinker with the darkened chamber, they play chess, they sleep; but mostly they read. Then they rise and do the same once more. The days are beginning to run together. At least they do not want for good books. Still …

The lovers' close proximity to each other is pure torture, how could it not be? So close, so far. The sweet dagger of love is merciless. He swears he can feel the heat from her olive skin from across the room. The soft swell of her breasts straining against her cotton robe as she stretches, her dark brown curls waterfalling exquisitely down her back to rest on her bottom just so; they all beckon. No, they torment.

They have entire conversations with only their eyes. The quick brush of his hand across the down on her bare arm as he leans to reach for a codex sends molten lightning racing along her spine. She shivers, tenses her thighs to still the sweet agony, looks to him, her eyes pleading for a kiss, just one kiss. He tries to smile but doesn't quite get there. Instead, he swallows hard and looks away.

At odd moments he leaps up and begins to pace the room like a caged animal. He opens a book but only fidgets. Sit-stand-pace, sit-stand-pace, on and on it goes.

She wakes in the middle of the night twisted into her covers, all damp and throbbing. She listens for his soft breathing, wonders if he is awake, too, wanting her. Separated by only a curtain. So close, so far. Durr, the dutiful chaperone, lies between them, snoring softly, but Rayhana knows well that she is a light sleeper.

They have begun to pass notes. These start as tender professions of love, but within two days their words embolden recklessly, the swirls and dots and lines dancing with latent passion and compelling urge. The words practically write themselves upon the page without their hands or their reeds; declarations of their desires, of the manner of their midnight dreams, of their night together in the Royal Gardens. They know better.

"Rayhana, you should read this codex on medicinal flora of ancient Greece. Fascinating stuff."

She responds with an impish grin. "And you should read this codex on the geography of ancient Egypt, Zafir. Shall we swap?"

They do. They each flip to the marked page, devour the other's words, trying in vain not to steal a glance or throw a wicked grin. Or blush. He swallows hard, she curls tighter into her divan.

Durr witnesses it all, of course, as any good lady-in-waiting should, but she remains silent, pretends to be oblivious. Their obviousness greatly amuses her. She buries her grin behind her palm.

Such is young love.

The smile runs away from Samuel's face. "We received news yesterday." He stops to chew his cheek. "From your father." The stillness solidifies. "It seems his army was victorious over White Hands. A rout. He has moved on to Gormaz to try and break the siege there and free General Ghalib."

Her voice wilts, "I see ..."

Zafir offers, "I feared as much. When should we expect him back in the city, do you think?"

Samuel shrugs. "Hard to say. If the news is accurate and White Hands' army was truly destroyed, he will be unable to defend Gormaz. The siege will be quickly broken. Three weeks, perhaps? Winter travel through the Marches will be slow, but no more than a month, surely."

Zafir and Rayhana exchange a worried look.

Samuel smiles to lighten the mood. "Cheer up, you two. That just means we must fix our plans. Rayhana, your tetta and Imam Abd al-Gafur are hard at work in the Sharia Library. It cannot be long now before they find what they are after."

Zafir offers a resigned, "Inshallah."

"You cannot be in the Rare Books Library when your father returns, Rayhana, that much is certain. Aslam is not one to give up; he will make his presence felt the day Ibn Abi Amir arrives in Madinat."

Her sigh is heartbreaking. "Yes, he will ..."

Zafir grimaces. "The question is, where do we go? And how?"

"Where indeed? So far nothing very workable from our end, I am afraid."

"Nor from us."

Samuel forces a smile. "Rebekah is great at solving such puzzles. Never fear, the answer will come. Cheer up, my dear, the answer will come, as sure as the sunrise."

She looks away.

Samuel changes the subject. "So!" He rubs his hands together like an eager child. "I have some supplies that will interest you three. Dried dates! And fresh towels. And even a cask of sweetened pomegranate juice!"

"They deserve some privacy, Samuel. Just for a little while. Almost two weeks together and not a moment alone, not even a kiss. It is not right. They must be going crazy by now. And poor Durr caught in between."

He knits his brow as he puzzles over her words. "They are not married yet, Rebekah. Or had you forgotten? They must wait for the nikah."

She frowns. "In their eyes they are married. We both know what happened in the Royal Gardens on Eid al-Fitr." Her voice is level, reasonable. "Samuel, you heard Zafir. You held him as he cried when he thought he had lost her."

"Yes ..."

She touches his arm, whispers, "We were still betrothed when we first made love, a month shy of our wedding day. Or had you forgotten?"

He meets her eyes. Pained by the burdens of fatherhood.

"You have seen the way they look at each other. Love, Samuel, a love no less true than our own." She grins, confident. "Besides, they will soon have their nikah."

His answer takes time, but in the end he nods. "Yes. They will soon have their nikah."

"Cheer up! Zafir and Rayhana are our children now, and you are their father."

He admits, resigned, "Yes, I am their father. And Yahweh protect me, YOU are their mother." He forces an awkward smile.

She laughs loudly, then kisses him. "Thank you. And, Samuel? Be discreet. Do not embarrass them. Young love is tender-souled." She widens her eyes to make her point.

He scoffs. "Discretion is my middle name."

She rolls her eyes.

Samuel smiles sheepishly. "Oh yes! Let me see ... right! Durr, I believe I require your help to carry the new cache." He is beaming now. "I left the supplies by the main entrance. *Very* heavy." He winks at Durr. "We may even need to find a cart to help us move it. It will take some time before we get back to the room, I am afraid. At least, say, twenty minutes."

Samuel's grin is gigantic. A blind child could read him from a league away.

Durr giggles. "I would be happy to help you, Master Samuel."

They exit the room, leaving behind two blushes and a pair of dimples.

His listens to the receding footfall, eases the latch into place with a deft touch, and turns to face her. Their grins evaporate as his emeralds gush into her amber. The blue aura sparks to life, dancing lightly upon their heads, onto their shoulders, down their arms, settling like radiant mittens upon their hands.

Those first few minutes when these two arrived the books had such high expectations! Lulled to sleep by the endless days of uneventful tedium, all but the stalwart poets have thrown up their hands and given up hope. On the high shelf behind the lovers, a Persian poet suddenly shifts his stance, casts his sleepy eyes down from above, and does a double-take. Within three breaths a flurry of murmurs breaks free from the poetry shelf, racing along the walls. The codices strain and slide to the precipice to peer down upon the two, satisfied smiles painted upon their covers. Finally!

Without taking his eyes from hers, he intertwines their shimmering blue fingers, reaches their hands behind her to the small of her back, and pulls her tightly against him, freeing a shared sigh. Hearts pounding, breathing shallow and quick; the air stills, the world's spinning slows to a crawl.

He whispers, "My beloved."

"My beloved."

Twenty minutes. An eternity to young love.

Plans

3 January 977.

She serves as his lackey, dresses in drab servant's clothes to avoid attracting attention, her veil pulled tight to her face. She retrieves books by the dozens, hundreds, with the help of the mildly-disapproving staff. She sharpens his reeds, she refreshes his ink pot, she brings him mint tea and sweets, she organizes his notes at the end of each day. When he looks up after hours of reading and can no longer focus, she will lay a kindly hand on his arm and insist he rest.

Their search is mind-numbing. So many books, so many trails that lead them everywhere, nowhere. Tantalizing threads occupy them for an entire day, sometimes two, only to end at a stone wall. A single case beckons a dozen more, those dozen a hundred more, each of which must be tracked to its logical conclusion. Taxing work, that much is certain.

Court records are copious and thorough throughout al-Andalus. They are collected from across the kingdom and bound into codices each week, then sorted, recorded for referencing, and shelved. Over two hundred years of accumulated records since Abd al-Rahman I, the first of the Umayyads, who came to power in Córdoba so very long ago. The Umayyads mandated an approach to record-keeping that rivaled their ancestral Damascus, but Córdoba has long since surpassed that mummified city. Legions of books fill the massive Sharia Library, the largest of the seven buildings housing the vast collections of the caliph's Royal Library in Córdoba.

Within is a myriad of arguments presented to and by countless jurists, copies of the legal documents that resulted, and, of course, trial proceedings. Thousands upon thousands of cases of all manner and kind, verbatim records of the points jurists used to argue and win, or even to argue and lose. An accomplished jurist in Córdoba is considered an artist of the highest rank, worthy of great respect, and much gold.

As cases come and go by the thousand and legal precedents are inevitably set, derivative commentary accumulates as a close companion. The jurists require this to make compelling arguments and must cite the precedence they invoke in court. An entire wing of the Sharia Library is devoted to commentary and interpretation of extraordinary cases; another wing to marriage and divorce documents and proceedings.

Their task is daunting, a needle in a haystack. They work from morning till dusk, stopping only for meals and prayers. They both know they are too old for this kind of work, but at moments of exhaustion they exchange knowing looks. Her eyes well up and he smiles to silently reassure her once again, conveying: What we seek is here, Salma, it will be found.

She tries to smile. Tries.

Thankfully, the official documents Samuel has provided them open all of the Sharia Library with little interference. She is the only female in the library on most days, an enigma to the staff. The fact that a scholarly old imam from Algeciras works side-by-side with an attractive female assistant almost his own age registers odd looks, even some mild gossip, but their constant presence day after day exhausts the stares and whispers and soon they are ignored. After all, hundreds of jurists and their charges bustle about the expansive Sharia Library each day, with little time to dally. In and out, on to court.

The miserable weather broke just after sunrise, the demarcation between pewter cloud and open sky a razor cut stretching from horizon to horizon, the arc of brilliant blue sprinting south, the arctic wind nipping at its heels.

First came the welcomed clearing, but then the bitter cold, a more natural state for the Upper Marches in winter. By noon, the squish of mud that sucks heel and hoof stiffens to frozen mortar.

The icy wind is brutal, a sharp slap upon bare skin, prompting black turbans to be loosed and rewrapped to cocoon faces. Numb fingers are clenched and unclenched inside thin leather gloves as horses spout fog blasts to the rhythm of their stiffened canter. Infantry stamp their feet as they curse in a vain attempt to feel their frozen toes. The Berbers shake their heads in disbelief, wonder aloud why Allah would bless a land so unbearably miserable with such staggering wealth. It makes them loathe the place even more. They long for the comfort of their beloved desert and the gentle kiss of its mild winters.

It is too cold for clouds to care to gather, and instead wispy feathers of ice needles are all that can be managed. The regal azure canopy is streaked in the east with fine white lace.

Sightlines are stretched to many leagues by such weather, and the lone spire of Gormaz witnesses their approach well before they arrive, both those who siege and those who are besieged. Ibn Abi Amir's army rides to within half a league just as the sunset's marvelous spill of molten gold paints the landscape. They set camp and build fires by the thousand to let their presence and numbers be felt.

After the knights thaw out and eat, they set about readying their killing tools for the next morning's work. Bloodlust begins to roil and burn.

This is all calculated, of course, a silent and unequivocated ultimatum. By dawn, the annular siege works and towers, so painstakingly wrought by White Hands, lie empty, the occupation force racing north to Castile to rejoin White Hands' decimated ranks.

Victory without a single casualty. Not one. The Berbers scoff at such blatant cowardice.

The minds have gathered. Levi, Zaheid and Iuliana have been invited for dinner by Samuel and Rebekah. Afterwards, they sink into their divans in the sitting room. After the girls have been put to bed, Rebekah's arrival with tea and sweets announces the beginning of the real aim of the evening.

The conversation rambles about, darting between various stale topics, the festive mood that usually graces their gatherings painfully absent. The evening is full of awkward, strained laughs at favorite jokes and jabs, sustained lulls of pensive nothingness, teasing that is half-hearted at best. Heavy hearts abound. Their shared burden, the cloak of quandary, weighs upon them.

What can we do? What should we do? What?

Thus far, no workable solution.

After a long silence, Samuel interjects, "We must get them out of the library somehow. And soon."

No one bothers to answer. The goal has been posed so often it plays rhetorically. The dense quiet settles in.

Just to break the silence, Levi decides to restate the obvious. "Yes. When Ibn Abi Amir returns, Aslam will return in force. The Slavic Guard will be worth nothing then. It cannot be long now."

Zaheid exhales loudly. "No, not long."

Samuel says, "I was thinking ..." Heads turn. "Perhaps we could move them to the crypt."

Iuliana is aghast. "Where?!"

Samuel, Levi, and Zaheid all chuckle. Levi explains, "He means the storage vaults below the Rare Books Library, Iuliana. We call it the crypt. A catacomb of books for those volumes we either have no room to display or which the caliph cannot prudently claim ownership of. There are many thousands of such books buried beneath Madinat."

Samuel adds, "The crypt is as large as the library itself, Iuliana. Dozens of rooms chock-full of books. The whole place is poorly lit. The crypt is a land of dark, tight spaces, full of crates and cabinets. A maze really, with many places to hide."

Rebekah scolds him. "We have had that conversation, Samuel. Even in the crypt it would only be a matter of time before they are found. Aslam already suspects they are in the library. How long can we continue to sneak supplies in to them without him learning of it? He may already know. No, he will tear the place apart until he finds them, crypt or no crypt. He cares nothing about books, rare or not, and could not care less whether they belong to caliph. Nor will Ibn Abi Amir. He will simply ransack the place and root them out."

Samuel's expression is at first incredulous, but in the end he nods.

She hammers her point. "He will find them in the crypt, Samuel."

Zaheid exhales. "Yes, he will find them."

Silence intrudes once more.

Levi says, "What if we built a false wall in one of the crypt rooms? Some sort of secret panel, perhaps hidden behind the books within a bookcase." His hands begin dancing. "Something impossible to detect when he searches the place."

A welcomed excitement blossoms in Zaheid's voice. "Yes, it could be done. Yes, I like that! Perhaps we could do that in several rooms, move them around if need be, maybe two rooms sealed at both ends with false walls, and a hidden passage connecting them. And an emergency escape route back to the upper level through a trap door."

Rebekah's exasperation colors her tone. "And if Aslam posts guards in all the rooms on all the floors? What then?"

The bracing slap of reality. There is no good answer, of course.

Samuel says, "There will be risks associated with everything we think of, Rebekah. I say we stick with my story. Zafir left on my errand in the city; the two of them met after she escaped; they are gone for good. Hidden somewhere in Córdoba, no doubt. In any case, long gone from the Royal Library and Madinat. We have not seen or heard from them since. And good riddance."

Rebekah frowns. "Aslam is not that stupid, Samuel. And Ibn Abi Amir most definitely is not. Yes, there will be risks, but keeping them here is not the answer we seek, even within a secret room in the crypt. How long can they stay there? Years?" She pauses, looking from person to person. "No. Rayhana and Zafir must leave Madinat. Permanently. They must change their names, melt into the earth and vanish, then be reborn to start a new life together somewhere far away from Madinat and Córdoba."

Zaheid whispers, "What a terribly depressing thought." Melancholy incarnate.

Rebekah's tone turns tender. "Zaheid, Aslam will kill Zafir if he finds him, or even worse. Rayhana will be forced to marry that beast of a Berber, then live in a prison of her father's making. To his mind she has betrayed him twice now. There will be no third."

Zaheid's shoulders sag as his eyes droop to the floor. "But what of our work together on the camera obscura? I need her help ..."

Silence.

Levi asks, "Do you think Aslam has written to Ibn Abi Amir and told him that she is gone missing?"

Rebekah considers this, then says definitively, "No. Aslam fears the disapproval of his master. And he still hopes to repossess her before Ibn Abi Amir returns. He waits for us to make a mistake, to tip our hand. We are watched, that much is sure."

Samuel says, "When Ibn Abi Amir returns there will be much explaining to do, but in the end he will instruct Aslam to use all means to find her, even if he has to spill our blood to do it."

Rebekah adds, "I agree. If she does not turn up quickly, he will not hesitate to have his Berbers torture the answer from us." Faces turn grim. "Before that time comes, we must convince Aslam and Ibn Abi Amir that Rayhana and Zafir have left the city for good, never to return."

Samuel replies, "Even if he believed that, Rebekah, he would hunt them to the ends of the earth."

"Yes, he would. We must be clever. We must convince him that it is futile to hunt for them."

Levi quips, "And how would we do that?"

She takes a deep breath, exhales, then unexpectedly smiles. "This is no more than a chess problem, really."

Skeptical eyes study her for a clue.

"You heard me, a chess problem. One to be analyzed and dissected, then an appropriate strategy formulated and executed. No more, no less." Her smile widens.

Samuel grimaces. "A chess problem? Rebekah, we have two pawns. We have no sultan, no vizier, no knights, no castles, no imams. Nothing. Two pawns and three useless old men."

Zaheid ladles his gloom, "And our opponent has a full board."

Levi echoes, "And knows the game as well as we do."

Rebekah's face solidifies into a portrait of feminine wile.

"In desperate situations, bold moves are required. Boldness is the only thing that holds any hope for our victory in this match. Something so daring as to take them completely off guard. Something they would never suspect, not in their wildest dreams." She has their attention now. After a long pause, she proclaims, "We have been thinking about this all wrong."

Samuel snorts. "All wrong?"

"Yes, all wrong. I have a plan. A bold plan. There is risk to be sure, and it will require some careful research, some very discreet research. Something three old men who know the intricacies of the Rare Books Library might even be able to help with."

Zaheid brightens like a lit lamp.

"If we succeed, Rayhana and Zafir will be free forever, and Ibn Abi Amir will not pursue them." Expectation fills the space. "To begin with, we will indeed construct Levi's hidden room within the crypt. But not as a permanent hiding place." She pauses to heighten the drama. "It will serve as the decoy on our chess board." Eyebrows lift in response. She turns. "Levi, you will have to be discreet, Aslam has eyes everywhere. Can you build it with materials you already have within the library?"

Levi ponders this. "It should be possible, I think, yes. As you know, Rebekah, I relish a good challenge." They exchange grins.

"Excellent. All of our pieces must be set in place before Ibn Abi Amir returns, so we must move quickly."

The energy, thankfully, returns to the air.

She continues. "One more thing. We must all move into the library. It will be safer, to be sure, and we must be able to act quickly when Aslam comes calling. Samuel and I will move into the room off his study."

He interjects, "What of the girls, Rebekah?"

"What of them? They will consider it a grand adventure."

He frowns as he tilts his head at her, but in the end, nods. Of course they will.

Levi says, "Zaheid and Iuliana can stay in my suite. Plenty big enough."

"Good."

Samuel's mouth opens to request more details, but before he can speak, she waves him off and continues. "This is how it will unfold ..."

The man looks positively ancient, his limp bad enough to be distracting. He releases a grimace with each ginger step. The face is drawn and pale, deeply lined, gaunt from lack of adequate food, water, and sleep, his beard almost pure white. A marked change from the last time these two met in the Maghreb. A shadow of himself. His turban and clothes are filthy; presumably there is no spare water for such luxuries within Gormaz. The man stinks of decay. Still, he is General Ghalib, the great warrior, the sword of the caliph, military vizier of the realm. Humbled now, perhaps, by the fickle turn of fate, but formidable nonetheless.

Ibn Abi Amir has waited for him on the plains just outside the siege works. He has no intention of climbing the slopes of Gormaz, of meeting Ghalib on his own turf. No, the great General Ghalib must humble himself and come to him, his liberator, the man who vanquished the foe he was unable to defeat. Ibn Abi Amir has been waiting for almost an hour now, a serious snub. The Berbers hold little patience for such affronts to the qadi of the Maghreb. They grow edgy.

Ibn Abi Amir is content, however, his expression unreadable granite. Suktan and Tahir flank him just to his rear, hands resting easily on their scimitar hilts, eyes restless, flicking about. Al-Andalusi and his Banu Birzal commanders are arrayed to either side in a broad fan, a thousand mounted Berbers in tight formation behind them.

The old man stops five paces away and studies the scene. Ibn Abi Amir remains silent; he will not speak first. In the end, Ghalib relents. "Ibn Abi Amir. Your army is a welcome sight. Pleasing to see the Christians tremble and run scared." He scans the officers, then the cavalry. "By my take, a Berber army."

"Yes, General, a Berber army. Led by the Banu Birzal. This is al-Andalusi." He lifts a palm. "Brother of Hamid al-Tariq, sheikh of the Banu Birzal." Al-Andalusi does not move a muscle.

Ghalib studies the massive Berber and reluctantly acknowledges him with a tick of his head. "I see ..." It is impossible to hide the disgust that tinges his voice.

Ibn Abi Amir ignores the insult, but al-Andalusi does not forget such things. "I routed White Hands in the mountains, General. He is limping north for Burgos as we speak."

Silence.

"I had not heard."

"No, I expected not."

The icy wind whistles eerily.

Ghalib takes a deep breath then exhales loudly. "I am in your debt, Muhammad. Your lifting of the siege was most welcomed.

We were already eating our horses and drinking our piss. We could not have lasted more than a few more weeks."

Triumph, But Ibn Abi Amir's expression is of carved granite. "Caliph Hisham's wish is my command, General."

Ghalib just stares. He sighs and acknowledges the reality of this changed landscape with a stiff nod.

Then, suddenly, the unexpected. Ibn Abi Amir takes a step forward and kneels. "You are Caliph Hisham's chosen military vizier, General Ghalib. I declare my fealty and put my army in your service for the protection of the realm. Long live Caliph Hisham." The Berber commanders kneel as one, and a mighty cry erupts from the assembly. "LONG LIVE CALIPH HISHAM!"

Ghalib is not a man given to surprise, but his mouth falls open, the shock written plainly on his face. His features twist into confusion. He seems to age before Ibn Abi Amir's eyes, looks positively disoriented. The intent, of course.

Ibn Abi Amir rises. "Come, General, you are tired. I will have food brought, then we will talk further in my tent. I have some ideas I would like your opinions on. I will have supplies delivered to your troops in the castle. They will want for nothing. Come, General, all is well now. All is well."

The man's dazed, vacant gaze does not vanish. Ibn Abi Amir gently takes the old man's arm and guides him towards his command tent like a doting young knight escorting his decrepit grandfather.

She arrives with an armload of codices and deposits them atop the growing tower on his desk with a mighty exhale.

No response.

Her hands join her hips. "These are the very last books in the Sharia Library. There are no more. None."

Nothing.

"I should know, I have carted them all. Me." She gives a coy grin.

No response.

She gives up with a playful frown. "I will bring us tea and sweets. No need for you to trouble yourself, let me see to it. Really, I do not mind."

He does not look up from the page, only grunts.

She grins, turns, and disappears.

He seems especially intent on the contents of a forty-year-old marriage contract and the subsequent legal challenge by the father to declare it null and void. He turns the page with a knit brow. His finger rejoins the paper, scanning quickly, right to left, right to left, as his eyes glide down the page. His finger stops and his eyes widen. He leans closer, re-reads the words. He leans back, locks his hands behind his neck and stares into space as he considers the implications.

He releases his hands, reaches to his right, pushes one then two then three volumes roughly aside as he searches for a codex he knows he asked her to bring. He spies it at the bottom of her tower, and without thinking grabs for it, toppling Babel, the helpless spire slapping hard on the white marble.

Scolding frowns sprout on the staff members within earshot.

He sheepishly mumbles his pardon but makes no move to retrieve the lost volumes. He slides his quarry in front of him, cracks it open, thumbs quickly through the contents, then dives in. Within two minutes he finds what he is after; the commentary generated by the final ruling on the forty-year-old case.

His finger joins the tight calligraphy as he reads, his pace accelerating. Near the bottom he stops and smiles. He whispers, "Found you, you rascal."

At that instant she returns with the tea service and dried dates. She freezes when she sees his expression, her face a silent query, a hopeful plea.

He is beaming as he vigorously nods. "I have found what we seek, Salma. We have our precedent."

Her eyes well up. "Praise Allah."

"We have not seen the last of White Hands. Beaten, yes; broken, no."

General Ghalib stares.

"He will rejoin his forces then refit his army, and when spring comes, he will march again. You and I must be ready, General." Ibn Abi Amir studies his quarry. That bewildered, confused look remains firmly entrenched. This is almost too easy. He continues, "As you know General, Gormaz is the linchpin to the Upper Marches. White Hands knows this, too. It must be defended General, never ceded to the Christians."

Ghalib says nothing, just continues to stare.

"Oh, I almost forgot. The caliph instructed me to give you this, General, just as soon as I was able." He reaches into his robe and hands him the thin scroll.

Ghalib examines the seal, breaks it, scans it, then re-reads it more slowly. He looks up. "It seems the caliph desires that I remain in command of the Upper Marches. As a deterrent to

White Hands." The timbre is beyond tired. "He has instructed you to leave five thousand of your mercenaries here to support me and provide me ten thousand gold dinars for refitting my army. You are to return to Córdoba at once with your Berbers. To guard the city. It seems there is a new threat building in Navarre." He hands the scroll to Ibn Abi Amir, who unrolls and reads it.

Ibn Abi Amir smiles. "It pleases me to see that Caliph Hisham shares my high regard for your abilities, General."

"Yes, very pleasing." The general's tone has a caustic edge.

"The Upper Marches must be defended by the best army that Córdoba can field, General." Ibn Abi Amir resumes his close scrutiny of the old man, the gaze of a collector of rare insects. He carefully spreads the wings of his prized new find, then slides his pin through the tender flesh with a soft crunch, anchoring it to his display board. "Defended by its best commander, the man most experienced in fighting the Christians." The old man's limbs pinned firmly in place, Ibn Abi Amir beams with pride over his new acquisition and lifts his palms helplessly. "Caliph Hisham's decision makes perfect sense. The Marches are your territory, General, not mine. You know the place, the people, even the terrain. You know the Castilians and their tactics better than anyone. Caliph Hisham is right. The realm is safer with you guarding the Marches, General. He has grown wise for his age. Long live Caliph Hisham."

Stuck fast to his collector's board, unable even to wriggle a finger, the old man simply stares as he listens, but his eyes begin to burn with hate.

"You are sure this was all?"

"Yes, Qadi of the Maghreb. His death was ... how should I say? Drawn out. I am certain."

Ibn Abi Amir reads the letter once more, the transcribed letters scribbled above each coded word. "Amazing that he would use such a simple code." He sighs. "I am sorry to say the grand vizier has outlived his usefulness to me, brother. Let it never be said I did not offer the man a chance to make things right." He muses. "Durri the Small is a modest surprise. Alas, it seems the man is not as bright as I had assumed. Oh well." He looks up. "Perhaps it is time for these gentlemen to make the *hajj*."

"It would be a great pleasure to help them on their way, brother. I fear it may prove to be a long journey."

"Yes, a very long journey indeed. Send word to the city. We leave at daybreak. I want every citizen of Córdoba out to greet us when we arrive. Let them line the Puente Romano and the entire Almunya Way, from the city to golden Zahra and the gates of Madinat. A welcome like none before, a royal welcome befitting the caliph's triumphant army."

"It shall be so, Qadi of the Maghreb."

"And you, dear brother, shall soon enjoy the most beautiful maiden in all of al-Andalus. It will be a day that the Banu Birzal will long remember, and that Córdoba will not soon forget."

Al-Andalusi flashes a wolfish grin.

Conversations

Rayhana and Zafir are seated together on one divan, hands woven together, faces pinched and tight. Samuel paces, arms locked behind him as usual, back and forth, back and forth. He speaks as he moves. Rebekah sits with Durr; Levi and Zaheid stand to the side. All eyes track expectantly from Samuel to the lovers and back again. A serious conversation.

Samuel drones on. Without breaking stride, he acknowledges Levi with a tick of his head, who grins and shrugs. Zafir and Rayhana nod in unison but do not return the grin. The soliloquy continues for several more minutes. The lovers listen intently, nodding their understanding here and there.

Samuel stops and faces them. Time for the key step of their elaborate plan. He chews his cheek as he selects his words, then spills them in one long gush. Zafir and Rayhana simultaneously recoil, shock then fear painted in broad strokes upon their features. Zafir begins to shake his head defiantly side to side and fires a challenging retort at his master.

Samuel nods sympathetically. He lifts a palm to his wife for help. Rebekah nods, licks her lips, and begins to elaborate. As she continues, the shoulders of the two lovers sag and they lean into each other for support, eyes retreating to the floor in tandem. Rebekah finishes and the room grows still.

Zafir lifts his head, turns to Zaheid, and mouths a challenging query. Zaheid's helpless 'no' is plain enough. Zafir turns and fires another barb at his master. Samuel does not respond.

The silence takes root.

Rayhana looks up and whispers, "I will do it." She meekly nods her resigned agreement and repeats more forcefully, "I will do it."

Zafir looks to his beloved, his concern impossible to hide. "Rayhana, no."

Her eyes are full, pleading. She whispers, "It is the only way, Zafir. It must be."

He frowns. She squeezes his hand to reassure him. Reluctantly, he speaks his agreement. "Very well."

"Impossible. We will never be able to move those with just the four of us. Just look at them!" Samuel's hands are on his hips, his lips pressed into a grimace.

The four of them study the massive oak bookcases in silence, searching for clues.

"I saw an interesting drawing in a book I was reading. Just last week." Three sets of eyes turn and rest on Zaheid. "An obscure commentary. A contemporary of Euclid, no less."

Samuel lifts his eyebrows expectantly.

"On the engineering techniques used by the ancient pharaohs to construct the palace at Memphis."

Nothing more.

Samuel, begins to wave him forward impatiently.

"It seems they were understaffed with slaves and had to find a way to move heavy blocks of stone with only a few men."

He pauses again. Levi is grinning, Zafir is frowning.

Samuel's exasperation takes front and center. "Zaheid, please. I have no patience for this game."

Zaheid's expression is childlike, one of innocent confusion. "Game?" He grimaces his puzzlement then continues. "They developed a rope and pulley system so that two men could move a single block by themselves. Very efficient—saved the pharaoh money. First they lubricated the floor with oil to make it easier to slide the blocks, then they gained an advantage from their elaborate pulley system. We could do a similar thing. Attach it to the frame of the door arch, tie straps around a single bookcase. Two pulling, two pushing. They can be moved."

Levi grows excited. "Of course, yes, I see it. I could easily arrange what we need, hide it in a crate of books that is being delivered. Aslam will never suspect."

Samuel seems unconvinced. "There are six bookcases that have to be moved. And first we have to pry them from the wall."

Zafir chimes in, "It can be done, Samuel. Take the books out first, then slide them forward one by one using Zaheid's pulley, set them back in place. Add a strip of wood to the top and we have a new wall of books. If we do it right, you would never be able to tell there is open space behind. Aslam has not been in the crypt, so he will have no clue that the room is smaller than expected."

Samuel says, "And the entry?"

Levi replies, "The bottom shelf on one will have a removable back panel. Remove the books, slide through, replace the books, then reset the panel from the other side. Done."

Samuel is warming to the idea. "And then do the same thing in the adjacent room?"

Levi responds, "Exactly. Identical to this room. Then we break a small hole through the wall between. It only has to be big enough to crawl through. Zafir, Rayhana, and Durr can move between the rooms with ease. This gives them more space, and importantly, an escape route, should they need it."

He nods. "Good." He touches Zaheid's arm. "Well done. For a Christian." They all laugh. "Zaheid, draw out the pulley system so Levi can procure what we need. Zafir, you and I will begin removing the books. And, Levi, we will need pry bars to loosen the cases from the wall. Let us be quick about it!"

The four scurry about.

There Is No Victor But Allah!

19 January 977.

The lookouts atop the minaret of the Great Mosque begin to wave their red ochre signal flags in slow-revolving arcs, and within four breaths a hundred trumpets begin their regal fanfare. Heads turn, folks raise up on their toes, straining for a glimpse of the man. Where is he?! The excitement grows palpable, rolling like waves through the crowd. Children are wide-eyed with awe. Adults trade giddy cackles, elbow affectionate nudges, exchange silent smiles. "Praise Allah, the city is safe." It is a time for rejoicing.

The Puente Romano is packed with the throngs, a quivering narrow alley down the center of the bridge all that remains open to the arriving cavalry. Toddlers adorn their fathers' shoulders, wives hang on their husbands' arms, smiles heaped upon smiles. Berber women clad in black chador and burqa dot the crowds, their expressions at once serious and expectant. After all, they have had no news of the battle's casualties.

Córdoba's defensive walls bordering the Guadalquivir are topped by the red-robed soldiers of the City Watch, standing shoulder-to-shoulder at attention, pikes held high in formal salute. Riders are launched from the Alcazar down the Almunya Way, shouting to the assembled crowds as they go, "He is coming! He is coming! He is just about to cross the river! Ready yourselves! Make haste! He is coming!"

An official holiday has been declared. All trade has ceased, the sails on the dhows slack. Shops are closed, doors to the law courts locked, hammams emptied out, not a single reed of a single scribe lifted from its holder. The city has turned out in force, and the crowd lining the trek along the Almunya Way from Córdoba's gates to Madinat al-Zahra is a dozen thick to each side. Beautiful young girls ready their baskets of white silk brocades to toss at his feet. The crisp winter air is still, abuzz with fervor, shimmering with anticipation.

Ibn Abi Amir leads his army into the city; why would he not? Al-Andalusi, Suktan, and Tahir are just to his rear. He is dressed as a desert sheikh, in formal midnight black and draping gold cord, his elaborate turban wound tight and proper. No smile, not even a hint of well-deserved pride for his stunning victory over the Christians.

When he reaches the center of the ancient Puente Romano, he raises a hand and stops the army. He surveys the scene and nods approvingly. The trumpets cease and a hush settles over the thousands.

He reaches into his robe and removes his small Quran, raises it high in the air and shouts, "Citizens of Córdoba! The army of Caliph Hisham returns from jihad victorious! The city is safe! White Hands is defeated! There is no victor but Allah!"

A great answering roar erupts. "ALLAHU AKBAR! ALLAHU AKBAR! ALLAHU AKBAR! LONG LIVE IBN ABI AMIR! LONG LIVE THE CALIPH'S REGENT!"

Several dozen ancient codices lie splayed and stacked upon the table at haphazard angles, the telltale sign of a hasty search. This small room in the crypt of the Rare Books Library is reserved for medical treatises not deemed acceptable for public display or perusal. Ancient medical lore from controversial sources, manuals of rare herbs intended for questionable ends, obscure potions, and recipes of a certain kind, lame attempts at alchemy, pagan charms, even poisons favored by assassins. And, inevitably, volume upon volume devoted to the whispered incantations of the black arts.

Precious few know of this room's existence, a number that could almost be counted on two hands. Beyond those, only the wispy vapor trail of legend, of crude inference, of trite suspicions, to be hinted at or alluded to by pretenders seeking some advantage at court. It is well understood by the room's protectors that if the grand imam learned of its contents a formal edict of destruction would be forthcoming, leveled under a charge of blasphemy. Caliph al-Hakam loved books far too much ever to permit such wanton acts against the written word, and so the need for extreme secrecy was born.

Zaheid sits cross-legged on his silk pillow, elbows glued to the low-slung table, fists balled against his cheeks. A large candelabra and two standing oil lamps light the room, the glow of the brazier spilling warmth into the tight space. He stares intently at the book of rare herbs and potions spread before him and tries to decant its odd language. It is slow going. He turns the page and continues to wade through the dense script.

Samuel is on the opposite side of the table on a similar mission. He looks up. "Anything?"

Zaheid does not lift his eyes from the text. "Alas, no. There was an interesting reference in Galen's treatise that seemed to point to this little codex, but so far, nothing suitable." He rubs the tiredness from his eyes with his forefinger and thumb. "You?"

"No, nothing."

Silence.

Samuel continues, "I was thinking that it might be prudent to consult Abu al-Qasim on the matter. He knows the medical literature better than anyone."

"Mmmm. Can we trust him with our ... secret?"

"He is an honorable man." Long pause. "I am not sure we have much choice, Zaheid. Time is running out. If we cannot locate what we need, Rebekah's plan is for naught."

They exchange knowing looks then return to their books.

Ten minutes later they hear it. A faint metallic clang, repetitive and steady, launches in the far distance. A second joins it at a slightly different pitch. A third. A fourth. Now the sound begins to lift and bloom, grow with a life of its own, assert its will upon the still air of the crypt.

Both men cock their heads to listen. Bells. As the sound grows the recognition is undeniable; Madinat's alarm bells. They share an anxious glance, then simultaneously frown as trumpets begin to sound, adding their shrill temper to the growing cacophony. The two men sigh in unison. This is no alarm. Celebration.

The door slams against the wall with a sharp crack. Levi and Zafir slide to a stop on the slick marble. "He is here! Ibn Abi Amir has returned!"

Samuel and Zaheid uncoil and stand. The four look at each other in silence, but the pained anxiety is not difficult to read.

Samuel says, "The rooms?"

Levi answers, "Almost done. We were just finishing the back panels of the bookcases. An hour, perhaps two."

"Good. Zafir, go upstairs and find the women, then help them tidy your quarters. There must be no trace of you three left to find there. Understood?"

Zafir nods somberly but remains silent.

"Levi, after you are done, get the supplies moved into the crypt rooms. Especially food and water. Be quick about it. I want everything ready by sunset. And test the signal system once more for good measure."

No one moves.

Samuel lifts his hands as he widens his eyes. "Move!" Levi and Zafir turn and disappear.

"Zaheid, let us go see if Abu al-Qasim is in Madinat."

"Last I heard, Samuel, he was in the city with Brother Cleo perfecting new surgical techniques. At the Royal Hospital."

Samuel sighs heavily. "I see. When is he due to return to Madinat?"

"I have no idea. You know how distracted the man can get when he works on such things."

"Yes. I will send a courier and see if I can summon him discreetly. We must have his help."

His friend nods.

"Surely Imam Abd al-Gafur and Salma are making their way here already. This celebration is the perfect cover to get them into Madinat. Let us hope they have found what they need in the Sharia Library. This marriage must happen quickly or it will not happen at all. Come, my friend, we must hasten our search."

As soon as the entourage safely passes through Madinat's Grand Portico from the royal parade grounds, leaving the cheering throngs, he leans to al-Andalusi and whispers, "Go find Jafar and tell him that I want the Vizier Council assembled in one hour. Everyone, no exceptions. And, brother? Make sure no Slavic Guard are present, only Banu Birzal."

"Consider it done, Qadi of the Maghreb."

In stark contrast to the raucous celebration still rolling through the streets and plazas of the royal court and medina, the mood in the Vizier Council chamber is somber, stiff, and disquieted. The viziers, arrayed by rank on their silk pillows, are silent. The caliph's divan is empty, as are two other pillows. Four Banu Birzal are posted inside the door. No Slavic guards.

Eyes are drawn up as the heavy door opens. The black-robed sheikh strides in, trailed by Suktan and Tahir. The man positively exudes confidence. The conquering hero, a former clerk of the Córdoba's law courts turned into victorious general and the caliph's regent.

Their stares track Ibn Abi Amir as he crosses the room and takes his seat next to Jafar. His two bodyguards take up their stations, Tahir behind Durri the Small, Suktan behind Jafar. The Berbers stand at attention, black-turbaned statues, eyes downcast, palms resting lightly on their scimitar hilts.

Jafar nervously glances over his shoulder to the bodyguard towering above him, his discomfort growing by the moment. Durri the Small fidgets like a young boy. The rest of the viziers, including Reccimund and Samuel, are pale and drawn. Samuel has no idea what the man knows.

Ibn Abi Amir surveys the room, expressionless, then frowns. "Where is the caliph's physician?"

Jafar replies, "Abu al-Qasim is still in the city, at the Royal Hospital. I have sent for him." The grand vizier's voice sounds tentative, weak.

Samuel lowers his eyes to the floor as he begins to calculate.

Ibn Abi Amir answers with a curt nod.

Jafar has already decided on his course of action. He reaches for an authoritative voice, but the words come out tepid and strained. "Congratulations on your great victory, Ibn Abi Amir." He stops to sharpen his tone. "Your defeat of White Hands was welcome news indeed, most welcome news. The city is once again ... safe."

The bitter irony buried beneath the grand vizier's words is not lost on this gathering. Safety seems like a distant memory.

Silence.

Jafar pauses for a response then continues, his voice steadying at last, "You will be pleased to know that I have drafted a proclamation. Al-Andalus is indebted to you and should honor you properly for your victory, Ibn Abi Amir. I am requesting that you be awarded lands in the south. Five hundred arpents. And twenty thousand gold dinars."

Nothing.

The man blindly plows on, what else can he do? "I assume the caliph will be joining us? The Vizier Council has already approved the proclamation, but we will need the caliph's signature, of course, to remove gold from the royal treasury. As you know."

Ibn Abi Amir sighs heavily then speaks, his voice level and calm, a model of precision. "The caliph will not be joining us. However, he has made his wishes known to me."

Jafar chews his cheek but remains silent. The tension in the room grows stifling.

Ibn Abi Amir reaches inside his robe, dramatically withdraws a folded letter, then scans the room man by man, settling at last on Jafar.

"I have in my possession a letter written by ... the grand vizier."

Jafar opens his mouth to dispute this, then closes it. His posture seems to wilt with the realization.

He silently acknowledges: So, the gamble has failed.

Durri the Small's left eye develops a nervous twitch. He touches his finger to the offense to still it.

"The letter was addressed to General Ghalib. Sad to say, Jafar's letter contains words of conspiracy, words of treason against Caliph Hisham." His gaze tracks to Durri the Small, who refuses to look up. He continues to rub his eye in a vain attempt to still the distracting tremors. "It seems the vizier of the royal treasury was a party to this new treason." Durri the Small's hand collapses to his lap, and the winking eye takes on a life of its own.

A pin drop would seem loud.

"I have brought this matter to the attention of the caliph, as is my sworn duty as regent. He has instructed me to have Jafar and Durri the Small arrested. They will be executed at dawn as traitors. They will be left to rot on the city gates for all to witness, and their names will never again be spoken in the kingdom. When their bones are picked clean by the ravens, they will be ground to dust and emptied into the river so that no trace remains. Their property and fortunes are forfeit. Their families will be exiled from al-Andalus, under penalty of death should they try to return."

Shocked silence. Eyes sink to the floor.

Jafar attempts to lash out with a retort, but it comes out tepid. "And what about due process, Ibn Abi Amir?" He halts to try and inject steel into his words. "You spent your life as a jurist. Has the rule of law ceased to exist in al-Andalus? Well? WELL?"

Ibn Abi Amir lifts his hands helplessly. "It seems the caliph has tired of conspiracy within the royal court, Jafar." He continues, "The caliph has appointed me grand vizier, in addition to my duties as regent. I have also been granted the caliph's signatory power over the royal treasury. I am afraid the services of you two are no longer required."

No one dares speak. The room is stunned, the total lack of precedence for such a bold move is breathtaking.

Jafar tries once more, but it, too, comes out halfhearted and weak. The man is deflating before their eyes. "I ... I demand ... an audience with the caliph. To put my case before him." He straightens his back. "I demand it!"

Jafar is answered with an amused smile. "Demand?" Ibn Abi Amir's eyes smolder behind the mask. "Demand? You shall demand nothing, Jafar. You shall receive the punishment befitting a traitor to the caliph." He studies Jafar as he would a roach he is about to crush under his boot. "You may wish to consider begging for the caliph's mercy for a quick death, or perhaps that the exotic tortures the Berbers have perfected might be brief." He stops to let the words sink in.

"I must tell you, Jafar, the caliph was sadly disappointed by your actions. He put his trust in you, gave you the opportunity to make right your many transgressions. And this is how you repaid him." He signals with a quick tick of his head.

Suktan and Tahir crouch in unison, jerk the two men by their shoulders to standing positions, then twist their arms behind their backs. Both men shriek but do not struggle. Their legs melt into wobbles.

"Just so that we understand one another, Jafar, know that your accomplice among the city's merchant families, Mamun al-Numan, has already been executed, his assets seized." Ibn Abi Amir smiles. "They tell me he cried like a baby when shown the torturer's implements. Oh, I almost forgot, the head of the assassin you took pains to hire will be on a pike decorating the Gate of the Statue by nightfall."

Jafar's lower lip is quivering now, his face white as cotton. A telltale scent draws the eyes of those gathered. A growing circle of pale yellow slowly expands around his right foot. He makes no attempt to step from his puddle.

Ibn Abi Amir shakes his head then shifts his withering gaze to Durri the Small. "You disappoint me, Durri. I thought you were brighter. The caliph had use for your services. Pity." He continues to study the cowering vizier of the royal treasury with disgust. "Your daughter. The one my Khalil fancied. Remind me of her name?"

Durri the Small looks up, obviously confused.

"Her name. REMIND ME!"

The room recoils, the reverberation into the chamber's upper reaches stretching out for seconds.

The man whimpers, "Maryam."

"Ah, yes ... lovely Maryam. Beautiful girl, that one. Easy to see how Khalil fell for her." His ebony eyes burn. "Your Maryam is to be sent as a gift."

The poor man is bewildered. "Gift?"

"Yes. A gift to the corsair brothels in Tunis. They will relish her charms, no doubt. Maryam will make a fine whore."

Tears race down the man's cheeks as he begins to blubber and beg. Such weakness appalls the Berbers, who sneer their disdain. Cowards deserve their terrible fate.

The sheikh's expression turns back to stone, his tone relaxing, even, and straight. "Remove these swine from my presence. They offend my sensibilities. I have the caliph's work to do." He flicks his wrist in dismissal.

Gamble

As the delegation slowly moves across the Puente Romano towards the city, long stares dog their steps. Murmurs of surprise, of shock, even derision, are passed from person to person in the wake of their slow, methodical movements. As the long column of black passes through the city gates and snakes right towards the Great Mosque, shutters are flung open and heads pop out. Children giggle and point, wives lift their eyes to their neighbors across the alley and ready their barrage of whispered gossip.

A curious hush settles in a slow wave upon the central square as the delegation enters and is noticed. Transactions are halted, arms still outstretched; people turn and mouths gape. A few minutes later, as the men exit through the far corner of the square, the normal bustle of market day explodes back to normalcy, the hawking of wares joined now by the steady drone of gossip.

The group does not break stride until they reach the residence of the grand imam, located just beyond the Great Mosque, near the river. The delegation halts. The cohort contains almost fifty men; the imams, jurists, clan leaders, judges, and other high ranking officials from the two Berber camps. All are dressed in stoic black robes and turbans, not a single smile scattered among them. Some clutch Qurans in their hands, others have prayer shawls draped upon their shoulders. The weight of their pious faith settles heavy upon them.

A group of five elders trailing long white beards step forward and are ushered by the City Watch through the iron gates, then disappear into the grand imam's residence.

The senior Berber imam gesticulates wildly with his hands as he paces, then stops, balls his fist, index finger extended, and angrily shakes his finger at the grand imam. The Berber seems oblivious to the impertinence of lecturing the highest ranking religious official in al-Andalus.

The Berber is red-faced, positively livid. On and on it goes. The grand imam reclines upon his divan, patiently listening to the diatribe, his face calm, unreadable. He strokes his white beard from time to time, occasionally nods to acknowledge a point, but says nothing. Only his twinkling eyes betray his satisfaction;

amusement, really. The card he has been anticipating has finally been played. He will pick it up, of course, and use it for his own game. These Berbers are toys to him, pawns set upon a checkered board.

When the Berber imam finishes, the room grows stiff and tense in the silence. The grand imam rises, lifts his palms and addresses the five elders. "Holy ones of Islam, Allah has inspired your words. You are clearly pious men of deep faith, and your sincere concern for the spiritual health of the kingdom honors the Prophet. I, too, share your concerns about the lax ways of the people of Córdoba, especially those in Madinat al-Zahra. They trample the will of the Prophet with their sins."

He is answered with curt nods.

"Gentlemen, I pledge to make your charges known to the caliph's regent. Like you, he, too, is a pious man and strict in his faith. Rest assured. Action will be taken on your behalf."

A chorus of approving grumbles emanates from the party of five. The men bow, turn, and leave without ever once smiling.

The grand imam stands still as he considers their words. A thin crack of a smile slices the deep creases of his ancient face. Their intolerant grievances are just as he anticipated.

"This news disturbs me greatly, Samuel. I am afraid we are all coming to learn exactly what the man is capable of. Jurist, vizier to Africa, qadi of the Maghreb, regent, general. Now grand vizier and royal treasurer both. And from what you say, also a merciless tyrant in his own family. Poor Rayhana. What next? Physician? Librarian? Falconer? Poet?" He shakes his head. "Thank goodness he does not know much about medicine or books." Abu al-Qasim offers a leaden smile, but there is a vacuum for levity in the room that swallows it whole.

"One can only assume that Caliph Hisham has been silenced. Precisely how, I do not know. For how long, I do not know. Hopefully, this is not a permanent situation." Samuel frowns. "The man is clever, that much is sure. And ruthless to any who stand in his way." He sighs. "Poor Jafar and Durri the Small ... with one hand Ibn Abi Amir proclaims his undying fealty to the caliph, while with the other he turns the lock on the boy's prison door. Dear Caliph al-Hakam, Allah rest his soul, would turn in his grave if he knew what transpired in Madinat after his death. His beloved Slavic Guard now a bloodied shroud; his court the private fiefdom of an upstart Arab from Algeciras." He stares into space.

"Poor al-Hakam. Gone just when we need him most. If only he had settled matters beforehand, seen to Hisham's proper training ..."

The words trail into silence. There is no easy answer.

Abu al-Qasim turns to Samuel. "We must both tread very lightly, my friend, or we may be next." He forces a smile. "How can I best help you, Samuel?"

Samuel hesitates, exchanges a look with Zaheid, then glances uneasily at Brother Cleo.

Abu al-Qasim smiles. "Do not worry about Brother Cleo, Samuel. The man is my friend and I trust him with my life. As skilled with a surgical blade as any student I have ever taught. It seems even Christians can have talent!"

Cleo blushes, then sheepishly grins. "I am happy to assist in any way I can, Samuel. You have my solemn word of secrecy."

Samuel seems satisfied. "Very well. We aim to rescue Rayhana and Zafir from Ibn Abi Amir's grasp. Get them out of the city for good so that they can start a new life together. Rebekah has a plan ..."

Samuel stops to let them absorb his words.

Abu al-Qasim is the first to break the silence. "Rebekah is bold, Samuel. That would require a very special potion."

Samuel replies, "Exactly."

Zaheid says, "Samuel and I have been searching the obscure medical and herbal treatises in the crypt of the Rare Books Library for clues. So far, nothing that would prove helpful."

He lifts his hands helplessly. "I am afraid I, too, am at a loss. I cannot recall ever coming across anything such as that. Certainly, any suitable potion would be dangerous to ingest, possibly lethal if not carefully measured and administered. Risky, very risky."

Samuel sighs. "Yes, I know, but it is our only option. All else is set. Yet without the right potion, we have nothing."

"I understand ... let me think on it." Abu al-Qasim's eyes fold closed as he begins his search of the massive encyclopedia within his head.

The room stills as the wheels turn.

"I have an idea." Barely a whisper.

Heads turn to Cleo.

Abu al-Qasim slowly opens his eyes. He smiles. "Tell us, my friend."

"The legend of Farfa Abbey," the monk offers quietly.

Samuel lifts his right eyebrow. "Farfa Abbey?"

"Yes, near Rome. Benedictine, like Cluny. Farfa is one of the oldest abbeys in Christendom. Legend has it that when the Vandal marauders invaded, they attacked the abbey on their way to Rome, with the aim to loot and burn it. When they arrived, they found the abbot and the monks all dead in the abbey church. Over a hundred of them. They had apparently poisoned themselves to avoid capture and torture. A mass suicide."

Abu al-Qasim grimaces.

"This evidently spooked the Vandals. They took the gold from the church and left without burning the abbey. The place survives to this day." He pauses. "Interestingly, records from the abbot himself, and even some of those very same monks that died that day, also survive.

Impatience leaks into Samuel's tone, "So?"

"The date of these records is *after* the Vandal attack. And they stretch on for decades. The abbot and the monks clearly lived to tell their tale."

Abu al-Qasim says, "Interesting ..."

Zaheid asks, "Do you know how they did it?"

Abu al-Qasim smiles. "Some sort of exotic potion, I would guess."

Samuel says, "But what potion?"

Cleo continues, "I am not sure, but there must be mention of it in the Farfa Abbey's Ledger Book. All Benedictine abbeys keep meticulous records of everything that happens to their monks and property. Every decision, every action, both large and small. Such ledgers can span dozens of volumes. We have a copy of Farfa's Ledger Book from that period in the library at Cluny. Very famous ... at least in Benedictine circles. Do you have copies of any of Farfa's Ledger Book here?"

Samuel answers, "Unknown. But we should. There is a whole room in the crypt devoted to Christian record books. We keep those out of sight, for obvious reasons." He looks at Zaheid. "The room in the crypt at the far back—the one to the right."

Zaheid nods. "Actually, the title sounds familiar to me. I may have come across it at some point."

Cleo injects some caution. "Even if we locate it, we are assuming the monks recorded how they did it. It is certainly possible they may not have wanted that known."

Samuel frowns. "Yes, I understand."

Abu al-Qasim nods, "Excellent. Needless to say, we would also need a suitable antidote. But they clearly must have discovered that as well. Let us make our way to the Rare Books Library and see what we can find."

In the late afternoon a bulbous tan smudge appears in the still air at the southern horizon, just south of the disappearing meander of the deep green river. This attracts the attention of the lookouts of the City Watch, who carefully track the ominous dust cloud. Word is passed and alarm bells and weapons are readied. Córdoba anxiously watches and waits.

Two nervous hours later, the dozen riders in the advanced scouting party come into clear view as they approach the city's outer fortifications. They are wearing black robes and black turbans to a man. Outriders from the City Watch are sent to reconnoiter just who and what approaches. Word is sent galloping to Madinat.

When the outriders return, the City Watch stands down with an exhale of relief. Friends, not foes.

The main force arrives by dusk. Stretching into the distance are four cavalry columns, each ten riders abreast and one hundred deep. Trailing half a league back with cavalry escort are the hundreds of supply wagons, and behind those are the families of the cavalrymen. A mobile town.

A new Berber army to swell the Maghrebi ranks of the city. Fresh from victories at El Hajeb, Taza, and El Hoceima, routs of Fatimid forces, Sheikh Hamid al-Tariq of the Banu Birzal, the newly ordained sultan of the Idrisids, flush with capable warriors and plenty of gold, has sent a third Berber army to aid the qadi of the Maghreb in his time of need.

The Berbers are welcomed with open arms.

Pounding

As the burnished golden orb puddles onto the saw-toothed spire of the Sierra Morena, the white marble façades on the buildings of the royal court light up on cue, painted in with a lush palette of purples and reds. The impatient stars begin their hushed, tiptoed dance across the open sky. The waning moon, a perfect half circle cut and pasted just above the eastern horizon, casts a disapproving glare. Venus stands close by, preening. It will be a dazzling night, cold, but diamond-studded. Madinat darkens gloriously.

The pounding on the heavy outer door of the Rare Books Library is aggressive. Samuel looks up from his desk, eyes wide, his inked reed frozen just above the paper.

The pounding ceases. Samuel sets his reed aside and cups his ears to listen for voices but can discern nothing.

The pounding resumes, then stops. The door to their room cracks open and Rebekah's head pokes through. They speak to each other with their eyes. She taps her heart and quietly closes the door. He turns to his right and nods to the six Slavic Guards stationed at the main entrance to the library. They stiffen as they draw their weapons and cock into killing postures.

Samuel reaches under his desk and fingers the two thin cords; one smooth, one coarse. Tied to the end of the coarse cord, and set to swing freely, is a thimble-bell. The two cords slip vertically to the floor, side by side, disappearing into drilled holes.

He gives the smooth cord three quick jerks, pauses, then a final jerk. He counts to six, then repeats this. He withdraws his hands. He can feel the hammer of his pulse in his temples.

The pounding on the door resumes, more urgently now. After a deep breath and a weary exhale, Samuel rises and makes his way to the door. The moment of truth.

The room is pitch black, a finger held to the eye invisible. Their dilated pupils scan the darkness helplessly. He can feel her fear even though he cannot see it. He softly whispers, "I believe," and cinches their four hands tighter together.

"I believe, Zafir, I believe."

Durr sits beside them, terrified.

421

Rayhana releases one hand from Zafir and finds Durr. "All will be well, Durr, all will be well."

Five minutes later they hear voices, thin and muted, just perceptible. He cocks his ear and listens.

Zafir mentally tracks their progress: Already in the crypt? That was quick.

He lifts a hand to cup his ear.

At the end of the long corridor, coming this way.

He frowns. The lives of these three are balanced upon the honed edge of a scimitar blade.

The voices grow stronger, but he cannot make out how many there are. At least two, maybe more. The dim glow of candlelight begins to ease into the room. As the muffled voices approach the entrance arch leading into the room, they cease.

Their three pulses gallop in the silence.

The oil lamps are lit one by one. The room brightens to daylight. From inside the room, they hear his voice. "This is where we keep them." Samuel. "Come out, you three. Come out!" He sounds positively jovial.

Silence.

"Zafir? You do hear me, correct? Come out, my boy!"

Confused, Zafir says, "The golden moon ..."

Their code. "Yes, yes. Dances until dawn. All is well, my boy, all is well."

His suspicion lingers, "Who is with you?"

"For Yahweh's sake, come out and see!"

Zafir looks to Rayhana, who nods. He begins to turn the clasps on the corners of the back panel, removes it and sets it aside. He pulls an arm-length of books from the shelf one by one and stacks them neatly, then crouches to the floor, pokes his head through, and begins to slide his body into the tight tunnel through the lower shelf. Torso, hips, thighs, feet, then he is gone.

She waits with held breath, her heart pounding in her ears. A moment later, she hears his voice, brighter now, absent of fear. "Come, Rayhana, come!"

The girl crouches down and tentatively pokes her head into the tunnel. As she passes through, Zafir helps her up. The boy is beaming. She looks at him, puzzled. He lifts his palm. She turns. There stand Samuel and Rebekah, also beaming, and two others, tucked neatly behind them, hidden from view.

She squints her confusion. "What?"

The woman steps from behind Rebekah.

Rayhana gasps, and within a heartbeat her lower lip is aquiver.

"My dearest Rayhana. My, my, all grown up. You are even more beautiful than your lovely mother, Allah rest her soul. I have missed you so, my little Rasha."

Rayhana's shoulders are shaking uncontrollably now as the tears slide helplessly down her cheeks. She can only whisper incredulously, "Tetta ... Tetta, Tetta, you came for me. You came for me, Tetta ... Tetta ..."

"Come to me, dear girl, come to your tetta." She opens her arms.

Rayhana rushes to her and melts into the warm, safe embrace, her head sinking to her grandmother's shoulder as she sobs and sobs.

"There, there, shhh. All is well, Rayhana. Shhh, all is well. Shhhhhh, come, child ... shhhhhhh ..."

Durr emerges from the tunnel and within a second is a hysterical mess. Rebekah moves to her and holds her tight.

As Rayhana begins to calm, Salma says, "Tell me, Rayhana, who is this handsome young man standing here?"

Rayhana flashes dimples through her tears, sniffs loudly, wipes her eyes, then proclaims proudly, "Tetta, this is Zafir Saffar. My beloved, my heart and soul."

Zafir is beaming like a fool.

"Come to me, Zafir." The three of them embrace. "I have heard many good things about you from Samuel and Rebekah, my boy. But no one said how handsome you were!" Everyone laughs. She motions. "Zafir, this is Imam Abd al-Gafur. After my dear husband, Allah rest his soul, the finest man I have ever known."

Rayhana releases her tetta to hug the imam. "Thank you for bringing my tetta! Thank you! Thank you!" He blushes under the girl's embrace, both pleased and embarrassed, then offers a cute, awkward cackle. "I am afraid I am not used to having so many beautiful women in my life!" They all laugh again.

Salma continues, "Rayhana and Zafir, Imam Abd al-Gafur has found what we were seeking in the Sharia Library. Many days it took us. We have drawn up your nikah in triplicate. One that has legal precedence to stand challenge in the law courts. I shall serve as your wali, Rayhana. You two *shall* be properly married."

Rayhana begins to heave and sob again. Zafir hugs her to him as he smiles and looks at Salma through full eyes. "Thank you."

Rebekah chimes in now, taking charge. "This wedding must happen tonight, you two—there is no time for delay. Zafir, you and Samuel go and retrieve Levi, Zaheid, and Iuliana. And then see if you can get our boy dressed properly!" They all laugh.

"There are preparations to be made. Durr, you can help Salma and me decorate their wedding chamber and ready her clothes. The imam will prepare the documents. She looks at Zafir and Rayhana and raises her finger in mock scold. "And you two! You are not to lay eyes on each other until the wedding, understood?" They answer with smiles. "Now, you men, please go! Shoo! We girls have work to do!"

———◉———

Suktan slowly opens the door, his scimitar half-drawn from its scabbard. Even with the assassin eliminated, one cannot be too careful. He steps through the doorway and begins to scan the courtyard. He nods to the Banu Birzal guards, one to each side of the door, two across the courtyard. He turns back to al-Andalusi and Ibn Abi Amir and signals the all-clear with his eyes, then motions with his head to the guards.

Ibn Abi Amir, led by al-Andalusi and followed by Tahir, makes his way into the villa. The guards take up station outside in the alley, and then the door is closed behind them and bolted.

The man stops and breathes in the comfort of his own home, a welcomed respite from the travails of campaign.

Al-Andalusi says, "It is good to be back in Madinat, Qadi of the Maghreb."

"Yes it is, brother, very good to be back."

Her door cracks open shyly, then flies wide. She leaps out, her black chador flowing as she rushes to him, throws her arms around his neck and smothers him with kisses. He is taken off guard by her boldness, but laughs loudly and is clearly pleased. He lifts her into the air by her waist and twirls her back and forth. "Ulla, my love, I have missed you so!"

"And I have missed you, Husband. We have been too long apart." She smiles coyly.

He lowers her and they kiss long and deep.

Al-Andalusi, Suktan, and Tahir cannot stifle their grins. Berber wives are famous for their lavish affection and are known to be ravenous tigresses within the curtained confines of their husband's tents. The men discreetly look away to afford the couple some privacy.

She beams. "I have news for you, Husband!"

"What news, my desert flower?"

She blushes, then pulls his head down to her lips to whisper in his ear.

His grin grows with each word, ending in a satisfied smile. He leans back, incredulous. "Really? Truly?"

She grins and vigorously nods.

"How wonderful, Ulla!" He turns to al-Andalusi. "My wife is with child, brother. The first of our joined clans."

The Berber nods approvingly. "May you be blessed with a boy, Qadi of the Maghreb. The first of many great generals destined for jihad."

Ibn Abi Amir fits his wife under his shoulder and they begin to cross the courtyard. His eyes track to the hallway leading deeper into the house. There stands Aslam in all black.

He stops. "It is good to see you, my friend."

"It is good to see you, Master." Aslam's voice sounds stiff, formal.

"Bring Rayhana to me, Aslam, I wish to give her the good news myself. She is to be an aunt. And there are wedding plans to be made."

Aslam does not move.

Ibn Abi Amir studies the man's face, an open book to him. "What has happened, Aslam?"

No response.

He lets go of his wife as his grin evaporates and his face solidifies into stone. More forcefully this time he repeats, "I said, what has happened?"

Aslam looks down. "I have failed you, Master."

"Failed me ..."

"Yes, Master."

Ibn Abi Amir frowns. "Rayhana?"

Aslam nods. "She has escaped, Master. With the help of Durr. It is my fault. I fell for the she-devil's ruse. I should have been more careful. I am unworthy of your trust." He refuses to meet Ibn Abi Amir's eyes.

"Where could she have gone?"

Aslam looks up. "I have searched all of Madinat and all of Córdoba. She is nowhere to be found."

Ibn Abi Amir sighs heavily. "She is with the boy ... the saqaliba." He grimaces and looks down as his hands ball into fists. "I was a fool to believe she had changed. A stupid fool."

"Master, I suspect that the Jew, al-Tayyib, has hidden them in the Rare Books Library."

He looks up. "Why do you think that?"

"The Jew claims the boy left him that morning for an errand in the city and never returned. He said he suspects that the boy found her and they left together for Córdoba. But I have found no trace of either of them there. And the grand vizier issued a royal edict to post Slavic guards inside the library. Supposedly to protect the caliph's rare books from harm. I was forbidden entry."

"I see ..."

"I have watched the entrance night and day, but so far no sign of her. However, the Jew and his family have moved inside the library. And his Christian friend and wife as well. Zaheid al-Nasrani. I have asked around. He is known at court and in the city. And al-Tayyib's book purveyor, Levi al-Attar, already lived inside the library, just like the boy. He comes and goes, but lately has been bringing odd things into the library. Rope and wood. And food. The girl and the saqaliba are there, I can feel it, Master."

Ibn Abi Amir considers his options. "The grand vizier is no more, and any that are loyal to him will be dealt with by sunrise. My plans are already in motion both here and in the city. The caliph will officially appoint me to my new role at morning salat. As the new grand vizier, I will formally cancel all of Jafar's standing edicts. Gather your men and be ready for my signal. You will force entry and search the entire library complex. Kill the Slavic guards if they resist."

"What of the Jew and the Christian and the others?"

"Find her, Aslam, no matter what it takes." He considers. "And I want the boy brought to me alive." He turns to al-Andalusi. "I am sure Rayhana's new husband would like to deal personally with a saqaliba suitor lusting after his wife."

Al-Andalusi stands grim and deadly. He snarls, "I will tear the boy limb from limb with my bare hands and drink his blood while it is still warm. Then I will grind his bones to dust and piss on them."

Ibn Abi Amir turns back to Aslam and widens his eyes dramatically. "Do not fail me again, Aslam."

The wraith bows. "Consider it done, Master."

Radiant Blue Flame

It is just past midnight when all is finally ready. The furniture in the room has been moved to the hallway in the crypt, but the room with the false wall is still cramped. Standing oil lamps set in the corners light the space to a pleasing hue while two stoked braziers pump their crimson warmth, erasing the cool clinging stubbornly to the tiled floor. The tunnel leading to the bridal chamber is outlined by the faint candlelight from behind the wall of books.

Zafir and Imam Abd al-Gafur sit cross-legged on white silk pillows next to each other with Salma opposite them. Rayhana is arrayed in her finery on a divan set beside her tetta, her treasured *Ambrosian Iliad*, her mahr, resting beside her. The witnesses are circled about the four, also on pillows: Samuel, Rebekah and the girls, Zaheid and Iuliana, Durr, and Levi.

The alarm cord on the floor above hangs unattended, a calculated risk. The Slavic guardsmen have been instructed to rush word if anything unusual happens, but Samuel is confident that there is little to worry about, at least until morning.

A minor panic ensues after Rayhana's bath and perfuming, when she realizes that all of her fine attire resides in her villa. To her great delight, Rebekah calms her fears with the dramatic presentation of a gold-embroidered, cream-colored silk gown with cobalt piping, her favorite color, and white undergarments of the finest Granadine silk. Rebekah had the wedding set commissioned two weeks back.

Durr makes her usual vain attempt to tame the girl's jumble of glorious curls. She marshals Rebekah's gold combs like an expert and manages to successfully hold the unruly mass at bay above the girl's shoulders then relents to permit it to waterfall magnificently down her back, gathered at three strategic points with cobalt ribbons that match her gown. Rayhana's lovely face is radiant with the rich tones of love.

Rebekah's tiny ornate gold hoop earrings are the only pieces of jewelry Rayhana wears, but her hands and her feet are decorated with elaborate bronzed henna art, as befitting a Muslim bride of high standing. Rayhana chose lines from Zafir's favorite Greek love poem for her hands, and those given to her by Rebekah from the Songs of Solomon for her feet. The three women inked the tight script and then filled in with arabesque designs that elegantly twine around the girl's wrists and ankles, fanning out onto her hands and feet. She is absolutely stunning, the rarest of desert beauties.

Zafir has never paid much attention to what he wears, so weeks back Rebekah insisted that Samuel see personally to the boy's wardrobe for the wedding—which he did, after protest. The groom wears fitted cream-colored pants, a light tan buttoned undershirt; a cobalt sash to match the piping on the bride's gown, and a feather-soft brown suede overshirt with cobalt embroidery running down its pleated sleeves. A design Rebekah first blessed, of course. At first, Samuel scoffs at his creation, but in the end has to admit that the boy looks incredibly handsome.

Zafir cannot keep his eyes off the bride. He struggles mightily to catch her eye, but she demurs and manages to keep her gaze discreetly lowered, taunting him. He detects the subtlest of hints of his cherished orange blossoms; exotic and ethereal. Against his will he conjures the soft swell of her breasts, where he knows she prefers to dab her exquisite perfume. He grows woozy as his heart begins to pound.

There is so much joy within the room that the walls themselves seem alive with smiles.

Imam Abd al-Gafur lifts his hands. "Dear friends, let us begin the wedding ceremony." The room grows expectant as he begins to recite the *khutbah*, the wedding speech. "Praise be to Almighty Allah, the origin of all goodness. We testify that there is no god but Allah and that Muhammad is His true Prophet and Messenger." He pauses. "Almighty Allah created man and woman, each in need of the other for completion of their souls. Allah established the great gift of marriage as a means of uniting husband and wife in a blessed bond of love, a love leading to their mutual pleasure and happiness. As the Holy Quran says, 'He created for you your spouses, that you may live in joy with them, and He has set between you love and mercy.'

"Brothers and sisters, today we are uniting in the bonds of marriage, Zafir Saffar and Rayhana Abi Amir, who desire in their hearts to join together as husband and wife, to be bathed by the many blessings of Allah in His divine benevolence. May Allah fill the lives of Zafir and Rayhana with great joy, and may He grant them peace, health, and prosperity. May their union be blessed with many children. May their love never diminish before the end of time. Peace be upon Zafir and Rayhana."

The witnesses collectively intone, "Peace be upon them."

Salma lifts both palms to Zafir and begins the formal wedding rite. "In the name of Allah, the Merciful, praise be to Allah, Lord of the Worlds, may blessings and peace be upon the Prophet Muhammad, his family, and his companions. I marry you, Zafir Saffar, to my granddaughter, Rayhana Abi Amir, whom I legally represent as wali by special dispensation, in full accordance with Islamic Law and the tradition of the Messenger of Allah."

Zafir bows his head in acknowledgment, then lifts his palms to Salma and responds, "I accept in marriage the young woman that you represent, Rayhana Abi Amir, in accordance with Islamic Law and the tradition of the Messenger of Allah."

Imam Abd al-Gafur says, "Zafir, do you accept Rayhana as your beloved wife for all eternity?"

"Yes, I accept Rayhana as my beloved wife for all eternity."

He turns to Rayhana. "Rayhana, do you accept Zafir as your beloved husband for all eternity?"

Rayhana is all dimples. "Yes, I accept Zafir as my beloved husband for all eternity."

Imam Abd al-Gafur turns to the table, then steps forward and presents an inked quill and the nikah, in triplicate, to Zafir. Zafir signs the three wedding contracts. Imam Abd al-Gafur repeats the procedure, first with Salma, then with Rayhana. He then adds his own name as presider beside the formal citation of the legal precedence invoked for permitting Salma to serve as Rayhana's wali.

One nikah will be filed as usual in the law courts in the city, together with Imam Abd al-Gafur's commentary; one will be kept by Zafir for their future life beyond Córdoba; and one will be hidden by Samuel among the stacks of the library for good measure, so that it may be produced in the event of some unexpected legal challenge later on.

Salma, Zafir, and Rayhana stand, and husband and wife face each other. With full eyes, Salma bows her head deferentially to the couple, then takes Rayhana's hands and places them in Zafir's and steps back. The hands of husband and wife intertwine as emerald gushes into amber. Tears of joy slide down each of their cheeks.

Rebekah, Durr, Iuliana, and Salma dab at their eyes. The girls look on, wide-eyed and impressed. The men beam their pride.

Imam Abd al-Gafur closes the wedding ceremony by reciting the final blessing. "May Allah bless this beautiful union of love with all that is good and joyful and holy." The room resonates with a loud "Amen!" and the scene erupts, coalescing into a single massive hug enveloping the elated couple.

As the congratulations begin to wane, one by one they approach the couple and wish them well. Durr begins to cry as she kisses Rayhana's cheeks. She turns to find the girls and ushers them upstairs. Levi, Zaheid, and Iuliana take their cue, bid farewell to the couple, and leave. Salma folds the two of them into her arms, whispers something that makes them both laugh, then turns, unexpectedly hooks her arm into a blushing but clearly pleased Imam Abd al-Gafur, and departs.

It has been decided that Salma and Imam Abd al-Gafur will stay with the others in Levi's suite, the three men in one room, Salma and Iuliana in the other. For this night, Durr will stay with Samuel and Rebekah. Cramped arrangements all around, but only temporary.

Rebekah steps forward. "You will not be disturbed before sunrise, but after morning salat we must begin our preparations to set our plans in motion." She grins. "We will ring the bell before we come." Rebekah's face is a study in pure joy.

Samuel sports that gigantic smile, arms folded with satisfaction. He stands surveying the young couple, his pride writ large upon his face.

"Husband?"

No response.

Rebekah rolls her eyes at the two of them. More forcefully, "Samuel?"

His smile slowly deflates, his expression all innocence. "Yes, Wife?"

"Do you think perhaps that it might just be appropriate to give these two some time alone?" She widens her eyes for emphasis.

Zafir winks at Rayhana, who grins.

"Oh, yes, right, I see. Well ..." With each word his fluster grows. "Ahhh ... time to leave, I guess. Yes. Of course! Time to leave! Come, Rebekah! What are you waiting for?!"

The three of them laugh, but then Zafir opens his arms, beckoning his foster parents. "Come here, you two." The four of them hug tightly. "You have made us so very happy. Thank you for all that you have done."

Rayhana echoes, "We love you so."

Both Samuel and Rebekah nod through their tears, then smile their farewells. Rebekah walks to each lamp one by one, lowers the flames to nubs, lifts a candle, then slides under her husband's shoulder and the two leave without looking back.

As they walk in silence through the crypt corridor toward the stairs, Rebekah's shoulders begin to softly shake. She chokes back a sob.

Samuel stops and turns her to face him. "What is it, Rebekah? What? Tell me, my love."

She refuses to look up. A quavery whisper is all she can manage. "What if my plan fails, Samuel, what then? What will happen to those two? What will become of Zafir and Rayhana and their love? Yahweh help me, I do not know what I will do if any harm comes to them."

He sighs. "Look at me." He has to lift her chin, her lower lip still trembling under full eyes. "Your plan *will* work, Rebekah. It will." He forces a smile to encourage her, though he has wondered the exact same thing a hundred times over. "And they have tonight together as husband and wife. A glorious night. That is something."

She sniffs loudly and wipes her eyes. "Yes, that is something. I wanted it to be perfect for them." She takes a deep breath and exhales through her mouth to regain her composure. "They must have more than a night, Samuel."

He nods. "Yes, they must."

"Such love deserves a lifetime together—and children."

"Yahweh will watch over them, Rebekah. Yahweh will protect them from harm. We must have faith."

They are all giggles as he chases her through the tunnel, first snatching off her silk slippers as she wriggles through in front of him, then grabbing and tickling her feet to produce a shower of cute squeals. But as they climb off the floor, hand in hand, an awed silence settles upon the two.

The room is lit by a single candelabra set on a small table beside the tunnel leading through the wall into the other false room. A plush floor mattress that just fits the width of the compact space rests against the far wall. The covers are made of the finest goose-down sewn between two layers of exquisitely soft combed cotton pulled back at an angle to reveal fine silk sheets and pillows. Red rose petals implausibly dot the covers. A tangy floral citrus melody steps forward to greet them. Those intoxicating orange blossoms.

They turn in unison to each other, their expressions serious. He steps closer to allow their fingers to kiss. He whispers, "Rayhana, we are husband and wife."

"Yes, we are." She whispers,

Let my beloved come to me,
Let him taste its rarest fruits.
I shall give him the gift of my love.
Come, my beloved, come.

He answers with a knowing smile.

The sacred flame spontaneously ignites the stillness, resting delicately above their hearts. As he takes her hand and leads her to the bed, there is a dancing flare of radiant blue, the fingers caressing the crowns of their heads, settling lightly upon their shoulders, sliding down their arms to their fingertips. The soft golden glow of the tapered candles demurely dims in repose, and the room begins to shimmer in the pale blue hue of love.

At the foot of the bed they stand facing each other. The room convulses once, then twice, as the corks are pulled from the brimming bottles of their crimsoned passion. Breaths are held tight, then exhaled in expectant shivers. Soft love-murmurs echo their whispers of devotion and desire. They step closer still, their eyes widening with anticipation, each locked to the other, circular conduits of midnight black connecting heart to heart, soul to soul.

Their lips brush lightly then join, releasing a shower of blue embers. As their kiss deepens and fevers, he bends his knees and molds himself to her curves. The room tenses, launching a contortion of hands and elbows, arms and hips. Her gown slips to the tiled floor with a feathered flush. Her silk undergarment follows, and finally her bosom wrap, triggering his gasp.

He kneels. She bends forward so he can breathe his moist heat upon her exquisite alabaster. He presses his hands behind her trembling thighs to steady her sway. She answers with a drooping of lids, a single delicious shiver, then a soft, tortured sigh.

A moment more is all she can stand. She pulls him up. Her hands grow frantic, begin to dance over him as they struggle together with his unfamiliar clothes. They manage to sever two buttons before the overshirt surrenders, then both stop to giggle as the shoulder seam of his undershirt rips loudly. Three shared gasps later and his clothes lie in a heap beside hers.

Breathlessly, he whispers, "Wife."

And equally breathless, she responds, "Husband."

"Subhanallah." *Glory to Allah.*

"I will always love you, Zafir. I believe."

"You are my life, Rayhana."

Their motions inexplicably still as if they cannot quite believe that this moment has arrived at last. Time slows as the radiant blue glow flares and flashes in the air above them. She eases into the bed and lays her head back upon the silk pillow, inviting him with her eyes. He crawls forward. These two begin the careful steps of love's convoluted dance, their eyes each now glued to the other as they embark upon this ancient, divine journey.

He rests on his elbows above her, inhales her hair, and gushes, "Praise Allah, you smell like heaven."

She is all dimples. "I am yours."

They share a gasp as he finds her. Her ankles spontaneously lock to his as she eases her knees up against his hips. Their faces are inches apart, molten emerald spilling wildly into puddled amber, hearts pounding, pounding, lungs breathless with expectation.

Their nerves begin to exquisitely fray as they are stretched taut and teased, then twisted tighter still into the ache and throb that first demands then seizes their answering moans. Both struggle mightily to disobey their bodies' relentless command to sprint when they desire most to walk, to leap when they desire most to stand still and steady.

"Rayhana, I will always love you. I will *always* love you."

She wraps her arms around his back and pulls him tighter. Her eyes fill and begin to leak down her cheeks as her lips tremble. "Zafir, I believe. I believe!"

As he begins to move in her, slowly, so slowly, the lidded cauldron rattles the room as it steams mightily then begins to boil over and sizzle. Helpless against the growing ecstasy, these two join hands in desperation and race-walk towards the cliff's edge. They do not hesitate at the precipice, just leap into oblivion. They open their eyes to see themselves ridiculously high above the crystalline blue. Down, down, down, then a wild slash through the surface of the heated sea, the delicious waves of sweet agony curling around them and squeezing, forcing them under. Gone.

They break the surface together with sharp blows of air. They see the recoil of their giant splash rise high into the air above their heads, pause midair for what seems like an eternity, then gush down upon them to drown their tortured senses. As the torrent crashes magnificently over them, each cries the other's name.

"RAYHANA!"

"ZAFIR!"

At that very instant, the world ceases its rotation and time collapses to a single point, the ineffable Origin, sacred eternity folded close and tight around these two, the dazzling pinprick of divine light at once both infinitely small and infinitely large.

Their lovemaking stretches on towards morning, each new encounter an adventure in an undiscovered country; a softening, a ripening, a deepening of rare pleasures. An hour before sunrise they finally drift to sleep, spent, Zafir on his back, Rayhana on her side, her head fitted neatly into the crook of his arm on a bed of brown curls, her body twined tightly into his, feet locked together.

The radiant blue flame, love's shy talisman, has dimmed, but hangs still upon the air, a wispy shimmer.

As the couple sleeps, hushed whispers break free from the highest shelves. No surprise, really. This room in the crypt is filled with obscure love poetry from far lands in the east, words of passion and desire set in ancient Sanskrit upon coiffed vellum by daring poets. Words that have yet to make their way into Arabic for want of a reliable translator.

Lovemaking needs no translation, of course, and the books have eased themselves to the edge for a look, their grins wide and satisfied. They take great delight in the delicious scenes that could just as easily have come from the pages of their own volumes. They whisper on and on in their foreign tongue, but these books are discreet and careful, for in the east it is bad luck to wake sleeping lovers.

She lies perfectly still as if asleep, but she has been observing him for several minutes. He stares at the ceiling, in some other place. Concern slides onto her face. She breaks his trance with a soft, "Good morning, Husband."

He turns his head and they share a smile. "Good morning, Wife."

Neither of them moves, content to let the moment stretch. They lie in silence for several minutes, but she can easily read his worry. "Tell me."

No response.

"Please."

He sighs. "I was thinking about Rebekah's plan."

She nods. She knew as much.

"There are so many assumptions, so many unknowns. It worries me."

"Yes."

His eyes fill. "I am afraid, Rayhana. What if it does not go according to plan? What then?"

"There is no other choice, Zafir. All will be well, you will see."

His voice begins to quaver. "I cannot live without you, Rayhana. I will not. I will never leave your side, never, no matter what happens."

She squeezes his hand and smiles to steady him. "And I will not live without you, Zafir. I will never leave your side. Never. You must believe that our love will triumph. Nothing can part us now, nothing."

A tear spills. "I do believe, Rayhana."

At that moment they hear the faint, melodic cry of the muezzin, high in the minaret above the Aljama mosque. Morning salat. Sunrise. Their magical night has come to a close.

Her voice brightens, "Come, Husband, let us pray together for protection and deliverance. We must seek Allah's gentle mercy and His peace."

"Yes, let us pray together, Wife."

Potions

20 January 977.

He eases the door open and stands still as a Greek statue carved in antiquity, his gaze locked upon his charge. The man's face is blank, unreadable, but his eyes are alive. It takes nearly a minute before the boy looks up from his book. Hisham offers an awkward smile, though he is clearly pleased to see the man he thinks of now as his father.

Ibn Abi Amir breaks into a bright, welcoming smile. "Come to me, Hisham, come!" He opens his arms wide in welcome. The boy timidly rises, hesitates, then races and throws himself into his regent's embrace.

Father and son shed peals of delight. "I have missed you, Hisham!" He lifts the boy, slinging his giggles about the room.

"It is so good to have you home. I have missed you."

"Let me look at you." He holds the boy by the shoulders and surveys approvingly. "I believe you have grown since I saw you last. You are getting tall, young sir." Ibn Abi Amir nods, clearly pleased. "And handsome!"

The boy withers under such scrutiny and blushes scarlet, but the words clearly please him. He mutters, "I have grown an inch, to be exact." A slight puff of his shoulders joins his shy smile.

Ibn Abi Amir laughs loudly. "An inch? I think two! Come, let us sit and catch up, Hisham. Come!" They make their way to the boy's divan, take up their usual spots.

"You have won a great victory for my kingdom."

Ibn Abi Amir's smile relaxes. "Indeed I did." His excitement is youthful. "You should have seen it, Hisham! White Hands riding fast as the wind for the safety of Castile. Coward! I slaughtered half of his army, just like this." He snaps his finger. The boy's eyes widen. "Surprised him in a mountain valley then gutted his army." He sniffs. "After the rout was complete, I allowed him to escape, to limp home, bloodied but alive."

"Why?"

"To teach him a valuable lesson, Hisham—one he will not be anxious to repeat. Other challengers will take heed and word will spread far and wide in the north. Legends will grow up around me. The Christians will not soon forget the day Ibn Abi Amir vanquished White Hands." He stares into space.

"Yes. And Gormaz?"

Ibn Abi Amir turns to study the boy. "White Hands deserted his garrison. They scattered like sheep in the dark of night when they saw the size of our army and realized White Hands would not reinforce them."

The boy smiles, delighted.

"I felt it best to leave General Ghalib in command of our northern forces, at least for the time being. He will serve as a bulwark against the Christians." Ibn Abi Amir grins. "But rest assured, they will not soon challenge him. They have learned well what happens to those who march on Córdoba."

"Yes."

Ibn Abi Amir's tone brightens. "I trust your accounts are in order? How go your acquisitions?"

The boy grins. "Of course my accounts are in order. At this rate I will have more land than Mama by end of the year."

The man chuckles, then he grows quiet. His expression changes from summer to winter within the blink of an eye. The boy sees the transformation and his eyes retreat to his lap for safety. The stillness grows deafening.

"Your Mama ..." There is sadness in the man's voice.

Hisham looks up, concerned.

Ibn Abi Amir's tone is matter of fact. "There have been some unfortunate circumstances, Hisham. Things you need to be aware of."

"I see ..." The boy wilts. A barely audible, "Tell me."

The man sighs, lifts his hands helplessly. "Jafar has colluded with Durri the Small in an attempt to usurp your power as caliph. Yet another coup attempt. Amazing that the grand vizier spurned your gratitude after you spared his life. He even hired an assassin to have me murdered, Hisham. Imagine."

The boy looks up, concerned, but remains silent.

"Both Jafar and Durri have been arrested. Sad to say, they solicited and received support from some of the merchant families in the city. Rest assured—all involved will be punished. Their lands will be confiscated and their gold seized." Ibn Abi Amir pauses, but the boy offers no response, though he surely senses what is coming next.

Ibn Abi Amir lowers his voice. "Hisham, your mother was involved in their plot. With Jafar's help, she was going to push you aside and take over your reign. After I was murdered by Jafar's assassin, she was to assume the role of queen regent. As much as I care for her ..." His throat tightens and he swallows hard before continuing. "As much as I love her, Hisham, I cannot permit any act of treason against you, not even by your mother. I will not tolerate it. The good of al-Andalus, the good of our people, must come before my own feelings for her." Ibn Abi Amir reaches to lift the boy's chin and join their eyes. "I could never allow anyone or anything to harm you, Hisham. You must understand that."

The boy's chin quivers. He offers only a strangled, "Yes."

"Jafar and Durri will be treated as the traitors they are. The same for the errant merchants. They will be exiled from our lands. Forever."

The boy croaks, "And my mother?"

Ibn Abi Amir sighs. "Rest assured, she will not be harmed. But she must remain under house arrest within the royal harem. She will not be permitted to see you, Hisham. Not ever again."

Tears spill down the boy's cheeks.

"I understand your pain, Hisham, I do. But your mother is poison to your reign. She is poison to al-Andalus. And to me." The man's voice quavers, "It breaks my heart to say so, but the truth is undeniable. She has forsaken my love."

Sadness envelopes the boy. "When may I leave the harem?"

He shakes his head. "I am afraid it is still too dangerous, Hisham. You are much safer here. I have it on good authority that Jafar has managed to place other assassins in the royal court. Until we find and deal with them it is just not safe for you, not yet."

A resigned, "I see," is his only response.

Ibn Abi Amir studies the boy as he calculates. "Hisham, with Jafar gone and General Ghalib so far from Córdoba, I think it would be best that you appoint me grand vizier and acting military vizier. At least temporarily. I spoke with the grand imam early this morning. He agrees. It would be dangerous if the Christians perceive any weakness in your court. They know me now, and they fear me."

The boy nods.

"With Durri the Small gone, I will also need signatory power over the gold in the royal treasury. To refit your army. Only until we find a suitable person to take his place, of course. I have brought the proper documents for you to sign."

The boy nods.

The regent smiles, content. "Come Hisham, all will be well. I will look after you. With me at your side, no one can oppose your reign. The people love you, dear boy. They love you!"

The boy nods.

Samuel, Zafir, and Imam Abd-al-Gafur work to put the room back in order: lamps are moved, the circular reading table is slid back in through the horseshoe-arched door, pillows are arranged.

Samuel stops to do a double-take and sees the young man in a new light. Zafir looks different somehow, older. Hands on his hips, Samuel breaks into that gigantic smile; the pleased father. When Zafir finally catches his sight, he blushes, finally smirks a response and rolls his eyes, then looks away. Samuel elbows the imam to share a chuckle. Zafir continues his work, intentionally ignoring them.

Rebekah and Salma fuss over Rayhana, primping her clothes and trying in vain to tame her hair with combs. From time to time they stop and smile, whisper knowing words in the girl's ears, then share giggles as she dimples and blushes. Durr is inside the bridal chamber tidying up. Iuliana has brought additional food and water for the next two days, which she moves into the false room.

Just as the men are finishing, Levi arrives cradling the camera obscura. Zaheid carries a small flash of viscous, pale green liquid, and a small measuring beaker. They all turn.

Durr and Iuliana emerge from the tunnel.

Samuel chimes in, "I felt that our camera obscura would serve as a useful decoy when Aslam comes. He will wonder more about this odd contraption and its use than the position of the book shelves and unnaturally small size of the room." Levi tenderly places it in the center of the table.

Zafir says, "But what will you tell Aslam it is?"

Levi grins, "The truth, of course. It is a scientific model constructed from Aristotle's own notes."

Zaheid continues, "Designed to test mathematical principles from optics."

Levi adds, "We will cover the hole so that it will not project an image. He will not know the difference."

Zafir nods. "I see. Good, I like it."

Zaheid places the flask and beaker beside the camera and steps back.

The room grows tense and still as grins fade. The air seems to thin. Breathing quickens and hearts begin to race.

"The potion." Samuel's tone is solemn.

Rayhana steps forward, lifts the flask, and swirls it.

Samuel continues. "Brother Cleo was most helpful. Zaheid found the Farfa Ledger Book. We had all but three volumes from the entire set. Alas, not translated, but Cleo's Latin is excellent. The ledger of the period in question did indeed contain the monk's recipe, and Abu al-Qasim was able to secure the ingredients ... after some discreet bribes in the dark corners of the city. It is a rare poison, mostly lojana, but with henbane and several others I have never heard of. An odd combination."

Rayhana whispers as she stares at the contents, "Such a beautiful color for a poison." Rebekah lays a tender hand on her shoulder.

"And what of the antidote?" Zafir's words are laced with concern.

Samuel sighs, "Alas, that is our problem. Abu al-Qasim has not yet located what he needs to brew it. Some distant kin to mandrake root. He is headed back to the city this morning to try and locate some. He says he has a fresh lead and hopes to secure what he requires by mid-afternoon. He sounded confident."

Zafir's voice tenses, "And if he does not find it?"

No one answers.

Samuel brushes the obvious aside and continues, "Abu al-Qasim was emphatic that the potion must be carefully measured out, the amount adjusted for body weight."

Zafir asks, "How much?"

"He will not know how much is safe until he prepares the antidote and tries both on an animal."

Samuel takes the flask from Rayhana. "This is a potent poison, unusual in its properties, and it must be treated very delicately."

Rayhana replies, "We understand."

"Keep the flask and beaker on the table in the false room beside the tunnel."

Zafir nods.

Rebekah says, "The plan is set for tomorrow morning. Levi's note will be discovered just after morning salat."

She glances at Levi for confirmation.

"We can expect our visitors shortly afterward. All know their roles?"

They nod collectively.

Samuel says, "We can expect Aslam at any time today, so be ready. He is our first test." He turns to Zafir and Rayhana, then Durr. "You three get back inside your room and reset the books. When you hear the bell, make sure all of your oil lamps are out.

No lit braziers—too risky." He grins at Zafir. "I am sure you two can find a way to keep each other warm."

They answer him with a blush and a pair of dimples.

He dismisses the guards then uses their coded knock to announce himself. He waits.

Nothing.

He lays his ear against the wood but can discern no movement within. He knocks once more, louder this time.

A moment more and he hears the latches on the heavy door being worked, then through the crack orbs of brilliant azure appear. The door opens and he steps in.

"I have been expecting you, Muhammad." Her voice is even and calm.

"It is good to see you, Subh. I have missed you."

"And I you, Muhammad. And yet here I sit, alone, imprisoned in the royal harem. Strange ..."

He does not respond.

"Congratulations on your victory. I never doubted you would defeat White Hands. An overconfident fool. Your cunning suits you well." There is a bite to her words.

He drinks her in, how could he not? The gown is one he had made for her while their heated trysts were in full blossom, surely no coincidence. She was indeed expecting him.

Translucent flowing white silk trimmed with fine gold lace trim, tightly fitted to shout her lovely curves. The neckline is cut low to allow her breasts to strain for their freedom, her stiff, darkened nipples pushing hard against the silk suggesting the sublime milky softness beneath. Those wonderful thick blond tresses, pulled high and woven into an elaborate bun. He studies her hair; an unusual style for her, but alluring. And those eyes, so unusual, so magical. Her rare perfume sews it all together, beckoning him. Her purveyors from the east are said to command a hundred gold dinars for each tiny bottle of the amber liquid.

He admires her beauty as he would an exquisite piece of art, but in fairness, his heart begins to race as he stiffens. The man is not made of stone, after all.

She turns, sashays to her divan, and curls into the corner, her posture seductive, inviting him. He follows, sits, and swivels to face her. He struggles mightily to prevent his gaze from sinking to her breasts—but he is unsuccessful. They have made love on this divan a hundred times, probably more.

"How have you been, Subh?"

Silence.

She sighs. "How have I been? How have I been?!" She laughs ruefully. "I have BEEN miserable, Muhammad. The man I love, the man who professed love for me, the man who was to share the throne with me ... that man—that man has imprisoned me. He has forsaken me. How do you think I have been, Muhammad?" Her words are scorching.

He lowers his eyes. "I understand that it seems unfair from your perspective, but my choices proved ... necessary."

She sneers. "Necessary ... Muhammad, MY spy networks, MY gold, MY influence, MY poisoning of the caliph. I launched your climb. You know this."

"Yes." His tone softens. "The love was real, Subh. I still love you."

Her eyes well up, but she is much too strong to let her tears betray her. She scoffs. "Do you? Do you truly love me, Muhammad?" Their eyes meet. Her azure burns bright. "Perhaps you might then explain your new wife, Muhammad. This Ulla from the desert."

The surprise in his expression is unmistakable, but it vanishes as quickly as it came.

"You take a Berber bride instead of ME?" She screams, "A CHILD?!"

His face hardens. "Your spy networks remain formidable, I see. Impressive, Subh, even for you."

Her rueful smile is a hurt, ugly slash across her face.

"She was necessary, Subh. I had to become blood kin with the Banu Birzal, join our families. It was key to it all, actually. I know you will never understand that choice, but it is the truth. I did love you. I do love you still. I do."

Her face is completely unreadable, but her calculating engines are some of the most formidable in al-Andalus. He knows this, of course.

Her expression softens, then she smiles, invitingly. She reaches up to slide the thin strap of her gown from her shoulder, baring her beautiful breast. She eases her gown up to mid-thigh. She whispers, "Then come to me, Muhammad. Come to me and show me that you love me."

He studies her.

She grows breathless with her desire. Her voice thickens, "Show me your love, Muhammad. Come take me. Please. I ache for you, I ache." Her eyes track to his groin, then back to his face. "I can see your desire. Come take me."

He remains undecided for a moment more then gives in and climbs across the void separating them. He touches her foot, feathers his fingers up her calf. Her lids droop and she exhales heavily. "Come to me, my love." Her thighs part just enough for her treasure to catch his eye.

As he leans in to kiss her breast, she arches her back and opens her legs in welcoming. She raises her hands to the back of her head as if to release the glory of her tresses held fast by the bun. His obsession with her breasts grows; no surprise there. She grips one of her hair combs and eases out a palm-sized needle dagger fixed to its end. She folds the needle in against her wrist to sequester it.

She begins to writhe and groan, something she knows he likes, eases her hands down onto his back. She has rehearsed the coming move a hundred times. When he is paralyzed by the grip of his climax, oblivious to the world, she will push the needle into his brain through the tiny opening just where the spine joins the skull. He will not feel a thing. Slight pressure and a quick sting is all. He will shudder once, perhaps twice, just as he normally would, and it will be over.

Her hand rests now in the small of his back, cradling the needle. As he finishes with her breasts, he unbuttons his trousers and pulls her hips forward for a better angle, pushes hard into her. She gasps, the tidal wave of pleasure involuntarily forcing her eyes closed. An instant, only an instant.

He jerks back from her, raising his elbows to separate her arms, whips his hand around and grabs her wrist. Her eyes flare with shock as she begins to struggle, but she is no match for him. Her hand is forced open as he squeezes harder, the comb-dagger stranded in space, quivering, beyond rescue. He pins her other arm.

Her eyes burn with hate, but she is helpless against him, a fly caught in a spider's web.

He reaches with his opposite hand and rips the dagger from her white-knuckled grip, producing a sharp yelp, then drops it to the carpet. He has not left her the whole while. He studies her for a moment more, the amusement on his face uncharacteristically easy to read.

She says nothing.

He begins to move in her, slowly at first. She struggles against him, livid, but as his motions begin to quicken, her resistance evaporates. Before long she is panting, helpless against the pleasure-torture he wields so skillfully.

His sparkling ebony eyes do not leave her.

The hate melts away as her eyes begin their inevitable loss of focus and she cries his name. He convulses just after her, his timing impeccable as always. He slides from her, then eases back to his end of the divan and re-buttons his trousers, his grin wide and satisfied.

His voice is level. "You disappoint me, Subh. Much too clumsy for a woman with your gifts." He studies her. "You always close your eyes at that moment, you know." A heavy, wistful sigh. "Such a beautiful woman, and so insanely desirable. I will miss you. You could have been my concubine, you know. Though never my wife."

The hate returns to her azure orbs, dilated wide now by love's poppy oil, but she remains silent still.

"Perhaps your spy networks mentioned that Ulla is pregnant."

Her expression betrays her ignorance of that fact.

He laughs. "Yes, I just found out. The first of many sons. She is a wonderful lover, much better than you, actually. So eager to please me. She is young, it is true, but so very lovely, and obedient besides. And her loyalty will never be in doubt, never once. If only I could have said the same for you, Subh."

Her eyes have filled again, but this time they spill. "Muhammad, no ..."

He pronounces judgment upon her. "Subh, from this day hence you will never leave your room again. Ever." She gasps her shock. "You will never see Hisham again or speak with him." Her shoulders begin to shake. "Your lands and fortune will be ceded to your son. You will want for nothing material and will be assigned a Banu Birzal lady-in-waiting that only speaks dialect. I am afraid the days of your spy network are ended." He saves the best for last. "And you will have no male attendants of any kind, not even eunuchs—none whatsoever."

She begins to sob. "No, Muhammad, do not do this to me. Do not, I beg you. No, Muhammad! NO!"

"You will grow old and gray in this room, Subh. Your beauty will fade, and you will never enjoy another lover. Your only company will be your hand, my dear. I would suggest you devote yourself to reading the Quran and the Hadith. Pray, Subh. I fear for your soul. You should devote your life to Allah's will and beg for his mercy."

She screams, "You are a monster, Muhammad! A MONSTER!"

He stands. "I will keep the dagger as a gift. Thank you. I will never again lay eyes upon your face or speak your name." He turns, picks up the dagger, and walks towards the door.

She is wailing now.

He closes the door and ticks his head to summon the Banu Birzal guards. "No one goes in or out without my permission. No one. If she receives any information, of any kind whatsoever, I will have your heads."

They nod. "Your word is law, Qadi of the Maghreb. We will see to the blond witch."

Search

The thunderous *BOOM!* at the door is so loud that the panes in the skylights rattle in response. The echo careens impressively off the walls and floors, slips down the hallway on into the library. A startled Samuel drops the bundle of books he was about to reshelf, then curses. He spins and waves a wide-eyed Rebekah back into their room, mouthing, "STAY THERE! DO NOT COME OUT!"

She closes the door.

The six Slavic guardsmen instantly draw their swords and lock into killing postures. Samuel races to his desk, arriving just as the next *BOOM!* arrives, this one louder still and laced with the brittle tear of splintering wood. The whole room reverberates. He gives three quick jerks to the smooth cord, pauses, then repeats this. He takes a heavy breath, holds it, then exhales. He rises and smoothes his tunic, his heart pounding in his ears.

The next *BOOM!* severs the elaborate metal door locks and loosens the two top sets of hinges anchoring the heavy oak door. Still, it stubbornly stands firm.

Samuel begins to walk forward to greet his visitors.

BOOM! The last run of the battering ram does the job, slinging the door open with a mighty crash.

Knights rush into the room in single file and fan out into a battle wedge. The first ten are archers, arrows nocked, bows at full draw. Then twice as many swordsmen stream in and array behind them. When the cadre is in position, Aslam strolls through the gaping wound in all black, no weapon visible. He sneers as he faces Samuel.

"I have come for another look, Jew."

Samuel tenses. "You will refer to me by my proper title, either royal librarian or vizier of books. Your choice."

Aslam sneers. "I have come for another look, Jew." He twists the word to torture it.

Samuel gives up, opens his arms. "You are always welcome in the Royal Library, Aslam." There is an unmistakable condescension to his tone. He looks at his shattered door. "There was no need to force the door ... I would have gladly permitted you entry."

Aslam's gaze tracks to the Slavic guardsmen. "Tell them to stand down now or I will kill them all."

"I would be happy to, except that the grand vizier insists that their presence is required. I am afraid you must first take the matter up with him."

Aslam flashes a sinister sneer. "My master has taken the matter up with the grand vizier. Jafar has been arrested as a traitor; his edicts are void."

"I see. I suppose you have that in writing."

Aslam reaches into his robe. "Signed by the caliph's regent himself."

"Yes, well ... I will accept you at your word." He turns. "Nasr. You and your men may leave. I am sure Aslam will respect the contents of the caliph's Rare Books Library. Surely defenseless books pose no threat to such men."

The red-robed knight does not move. "We are prepared to die, my lord, in the service of the caliph."

"Nasr, please take your men and leave. There will be no bloodshed in my library. Please go. You have done your duty. Please."

The commander nods, turns, and motions to his men, who file out one by one.

"I will see every corner of every room within this building." He hisses, "And when I find them, you and your family will pay, Jew."

Samuel remains a picture of calm. "You are my guest, Aslam, and I would be delighted to show you about. However, as I have told you previously, they are not here." He opens his hands. "Come, the Rare Books Library awaits. I should warn you, however, from harming the caliph's codices. All are priceless and well beyond your wages should the caliph insist you replace them."

"Books are not what I am after."

"Very well. Shall we?"

"Not just yet." He points. "First, that door. Open it."

"That is my private bedchamber."

"I said open it."

Samuel sighs. "As you wish. I am afraid my wife and daughters were not expecting company." He knocks lightly then opens the door and lifts his palm, inviting Aslam to look.

As Aslam peers inside he sees Rebekah standing beside the wall, shielding their cowering daughters. He surveys the space. The bedchamber is small, two floor mattresses side by side, a small table with a lamp, a bookshelf. Beyond, a private latrine, the door propped open. His eyes come to rest on Rebekah. He bares his bad teeth and hisses, "It is good to see you again, Jewess." His gaze tracks indiscreetly from her head to her toes as he licks his lips. "I trust your girls are well?"

Sara begins to whimper. Rebekah hides her fear well. She meets his eyes but says nothing. She clasps her hands to steady their tremble.

Samuel impatiently says, "Satisfied?"

Aslam turns. "Escort me into the library."

"With pleasure." Samuel exchanges an entire conversation with his quick glance at his wife. He turns to leave.

Aslam motions to two of his guards, who take up station beside the broken door. "No one in or out."

Aslam has been here before, of course, though in fairness it was by moonlight and nearly two years back. They begin to methodically comb the vast maze of the Rare Books Library, room by room. At each major junction of hallways Aslam deposits a guard.

The others were awakened by the battering ram and Levi soon joins Samuel and the entourage. Both men walk just behind Aslam as he intently studies each room, memorizing its layout and contents. From time to time he removes a book from the shelf, opens it, replaces it.

Before long they arrive at Levi's suite. The four are waiting patiently outside, arms folded. He looks at Zaheid, whom he knows. Iuliana stands beside her husband, eyes lowered. "Stand aside, Christian."

He studies Imam Abd al-Gafur. "You, I do not know."

"Hasan is my name. Hasan al-Kamil." His voice is shaky. "I am the new assistant to the royal librarian. This is my wife, Jalida." Salma bows.

Aslam studies them both.

Samuel explains, "With Zafir gone, I needed the services of a new royal translator. Hasan just arrived from the city."

To break the tension, Levi steps forward and opens the door to his suite and motions Aslam forward. Levi exclaims, "Empty. Amazing!"

Aslam silences him. "Quiet, Jew." He walks through the living area and into the room where Iuliana and Salma are staying, then the latrine, then the men's room.

Samuel says, "Iuliana, you and Jalida go and join Rebekah and the girls. Zaheid and Hasan will come with us."

"Certainly."

"I can smell her. This was her reading room?"

"Yes, it was."

"What kinds of books?"

"This room is part of the Library of the Ancient Greeks. One of six rooms in all devoted to such works. In this room, volumes of poetry, literature, mathematics, things that would interest you, no doubt. Perhaps you would like to take a break to read?"

Aslam sneers at the man's sarcasm.

"Show me more."

"This was Zafir's room. Hasan and Jalida will live here once their things arrive from the city."

"Open it."

Samuel turns the lock with his key and pushes the door back. Aslam begins to rudely sift through the boy's shelves; he opens drawers, lifts then drops papers. He leans back and looks up at the skylight above. He looks down and begins to stare at the floor mattress in the corner of the room. He throws back the covers and begins a careful examination of the sheets. He leans down and delicately sniffs.

He turns to Samuel, his smile ugly and wide. "She has been here, I can smell her."

Tense silence.

Samuel shrugs. "That I would not know. As you are aware, she had permission to frequent the library. For a great many months. It is certainly possible she was in his room, though I have no knowledge of it. If she was here, I certainly would not have approved."

Aslam reaches into his robe, withdraws his dagger, leans down and stabs the bedding, ripping it end to end like a butcher might gut a cow. He searches with his hands but finds nothing. He rises. "She was here. Show me more."

An hour later, the entourage reaches the room at the far back of the building where Aslam rested his ear to the wood during the midnight meeting of the confederates of the camera obscura. The night when the books came to Samuel's rescue. Aslam has not forgotten.

There is nothing out of the ordinary.

They walk on to the end of the hallway. Aslam stops and turns the knob on the closed door. Locked. "Open it."

Samuel removes his keys, unlocks it, and pulls it open. Stairs lead downward into the darkness.

"Where does this go?"

"To the library crypt. Where we store books that do not merit display above in the public rooms."

Aslam turns and motions to one of the three remaining guards to remain above. "Show me."

Samuel sighs. "Very well. I am afraid it is cold and dark, quite untidy. Levi, get a taper, we will need light."

A few moments later the group begins their descent.

More of the same, crammed rooms stuffed floor to ceiling with books of all manner and kind. No easy place to hide, that much is sure. Unlike those above, these rooms have no need of privacy doors, and open horseshoe arches connect each to a long central hallway. As they move room by room through the crypt, they light lamps to quell the darkness. The air is chilled and uninviting.

The deeper they move into the crypt, the more Aslam's expression tightens with growing anxiety. Not a trace of his quarry. He was so confident they were here. What will his master think? An edge of desperation begins to seep from his pores.

They enter the next-to-last room on the long hallway and light the lamps. Aslam's gaze first circles the room for clues, as usual. Circular table, pillows, lamps, two braziers, floor to ceiling books.

"This room is much smaller than the others."

Samuel shrugs. "I am afraid they did not consult me when they built the library."

Aslam walks to one of the braziers, opens it, and leans close to smell. He touches the spent coals. "These have been used recently."

Samuel replies. "Yes. We come to this room quite often, you see. We are working on an experiment." He turns and points.

Aslam's eyes come to rest upon the contraption in the center of the table. He frowns. "What is it?"

Levi pipes up, "It is called a camera obscura. Greek for darkened chamber."

Aslam's frown remains fixed.

Levi explains, "We found a notebook by Aristotle. He had drawings of a scientific instrument he used to test his theories. From ancient times."

Samuel adds, "We decided to construct a model of it. So that we might experiment with it."

Aslam studies the object, suspicious. "What does it do?"

Zaheid answers, "Aristotle used it to test the mathematical principles of optics. He wished to understand the origins of human vision."

Aslam meets his eyes with an uncomprehending scowl.

A hard swallow. "How our eyes work."

"Why is it here?"

Samuel answers, "We felt it best not to distract the attention of the visitors to the library. This room is out of the way. We dabble on the camera in our spare time. It is not yet complete."

Aslam circles the table as he studies it. He stops in front of the screen. He touches his finger to the thin sheet of polished paper. "What is inside?"

Zaheid replies, "Nothing. The air we breathe."

Aslam slips his hand into his robe and withdraws his dagger.

Just as Samuel says, "No, Aslam!" the wraith slices a neat, large X from corner to corner. He holds back the paper flap and peers inside.

Zaheid's hurt colors his tone. "You have ruined it. I told you there was nothing inside."

Aslam sheathes his blade and continues to study the room. Something tickles his sixth sense but he cannot decide what. He tilts his head back and delicately sniffs the air. Again. He walks to the book case, extracts a volume, and opens it. The script is unusual. "What are these?"

"Volumes of love poetry from the east. Untranslated, I am afraid." A dramatic sigh. "Someday."

Aslam closes the book and reshelves it. "Come." As he passes back through the horseshoe arch he stops and backs up. He touches a finger to the pair of neat cuts in the frame of the arch. He turns to his right and sees a matching set of marks.

Breaths are held.

"Show me the next room."

They move on.

"Rest assured, I will be posting guards outside. Everyone that comes or goes will be searched."

"Certainly. That will be much safer considering that you shattered my door locks. By the way, Aslam, you might consider apologizing for the trouble you have caused. I told you that they were not here. I am a man of my word."

The man's ebony eyes burn. He says nothing, just turns and leaves, entourage in tow.

The four men move back to Samuel's desk and gather in a tight circle. They stand silently, looking at each other. Samuel grins first, then the others follow. "Just as planned. Well done, my friends."

Zaheid laments, "They broke our camera obscura."

Samuel assures him, "Easily fixed, Zaheid, easily fixed."

The women emerge. The air grows lighter now as Rebekah joins the men with her satisfied smile. "See! Just as we envisioned."

"He did see the marks on the archway," Levi says. "I should have thought to repair those."

Samuel replies, "Yes, he saw them. Still, he made no connection. Who could have?"

Samuel turns playful and says to Rebekah, "Hasan and Jalida make a very believable couple, Rebekah. We better keep an eye on those two."

Salma grins as Imam Abd al-Gafur blushes.

Samuel looks back to their demolished door. "Levi, we must repair the door and find a way to get it to lock. It needs to be secure before we dare check on those three. Any ideas?"

Levi smiles. "Several. Zaheid and I will find a way, rest assured."

"Good. I will signal them that all is well."

Rebekah's tone turns sober. "We must hear from Abu al-Qasim soon, Samuel. We cannot delay triggering our plan. The longer we wait after Aslam's search the more dangerous it will be."

"Agreed."

"Not one thing. Not a single trace. Nothing." His look is incredulous.

Aslam's eyes are stuck fast to the floor by his shame. He offers only a muted, "No, Master."

"I must tell you, Aslam, that I am beginning to question your abilities. You continue to disappoint me." He sighs heavily. "Perhaps it is time for me to consider a Berber to replace you. Al-Andalusi thinks I am a fool to rely on your services still."

"I will not fail you again, Master."

Ibn Abi Amir's gaze grows steely. "No, Aslam, you will not. Do not show your face here again without my daughter. Understood?"

"Yes, Master."

"Now go."

The man hesitates.

"GO!"

Aslam turns and slinks out.

As night settles in, the black wraith sits sulking in his dingy room huddled over a steaming cup of hot mint tea, pondering his misfortune.

All these years doing my master's dirty work, now this. And all because of a stupid girl.

He shakes his head with disgust. 'Do not show your face here again without my daughter.' He grimaces at the unfairness of his Master's words.

His weary frown has not left his face. He begins to chew his cheek.

They must be in the library, everything points to it. I have missed something, but what? What?

He sighs heavily as he reviews the facts.

The girl clearly was with him in his room. I could smell her perfume on his soiled sheets, the same scent as in her reading room. Saqaliba scum.

His eyes narrow.

And that odd hint of her in the small room in the crypt. Why there? Faint, yes, but unmistakable. Orange blossom. She was in that room at least once, I am sure of it. Impossible to know how recently, of course. Still ...

His cheek is bleeding now.

Table, pillows, braziers, the Jew's odd contraption, and books, nothing more. There were those odd marks on the door arch ... but those could have been made by almost anything.

He strokes his beard as he struggles to tease out some hint but gives up and moves on, frowning once more in frustration.

A short while later he circles back to the marks for a reason he could not articulate if he tried.

Two deep cuts. And fresh. And only on the arches of the two small rooms. Perhaps a book crate that a porter mishandled when making a delivery? Still ... the odd thing is that the marks were symmetrical; two neat cuts on both sides of the door arch. And at the exact same height. Almost as if something had recently been attached there, braced into the arch somehow. But why?

He continues to stroke his beard as he noisily slurps his tea and stares into space, engines whirring.

His heart begins to race. He tilts his head to the side with a puzzled look as he sifts this information then he narrows his eyes and begins to nod as the answer breaks free of the clutter and surrenders. He flashes just a hint of a grin, then a full smile of

453

those rotten teeth. His voice finally emerges, a whispered hiss. "Of course ... how could I be so stupid? Clever Jew. Oh, we are not finished yet, you and I, not just yet." He leaps up, grabs his cloak, and disappears into the darkness.

———— ⬓ ————

They are gathered in the crypt to rehearse one final time. The hour grows late; the door repair took much longer than anticipated, and even now the locks are tenuous at best.

Iuliana has put the girls to bed, and Salma and Imam Abd-al-Gafur have been left above manning the alarm cords. These two talk of Algeciras and the sweet briny breeze blowing off the cobalt sea, their cherished gardens, the homes they miss, their mutual friends. It is an easy conversation of two people who have known each other for most of their lives, who having been thrown together by such unusual circumstances have found great delight in the other's company. At unexpected moments she will well up and cry with some sweet memory of her husband, his friend. He holds her tenderly, whispers words of comfort; there are times when their eyes seem to linger on each other.

Below, the braziers and lamps are lit and the room is again cozy and bright. They rest on pillows around the table. Zaheid tenderly attends to the camera, working the ripped frame off the contraption with a blade so he can replace the screen. Rayhana lends her hands, two peas in a pod.

"We have what we need now. Instructions from Abu al-Qasim, and, most importantly, the antidote." Samuel lifts the amber vial, drawing their eyes.

Zafir asks, "How did he get it past the guards?"

Levi smiles. "Abu al-Qasim is a clever one. He suggested it a week back. A special glass container, a bottle within a bottle. He had it blown to his design. The vial of antidote was slipped into the inside bottle and packed with cotton, then the whole container filled with pomegranate juice. No hint of the inner bottle. He had it delivered in the food box with the other stuff. The guards had no clue."

"And his message?"

Levi chuckles. "Scratched into the glass of the vial. Elegant, as always."

Samuel adds, "A simple message. 'Found it! Tested. Exactly one third of one beaker of potion, no more. Double that for antidote. Stinks!'"

Rebekah takes over. "We are set, then. Levi's note and drawings will be discovered by Aslam's spy just after morning salat. The clues should be ample for Aslam to guess how we did it. That should draw him back to us by mid-morning at the very latest. Then events will unfold as planned."

"Should we not wait a day to allow Abu al-Qasim to do more tests?" The edge in Zafir's voice is plain enough to all.

"Zafir, we have been through this." Rebekah's tone is patient but firm. "The longer we delay the more risk we will face, not less. It must be tomorrow."

Rayhana moves to Zafir's side and takes his hand. "I agree. Tomorrow is best. We will be ready at first light."

Samuel nods. "Good, it is settled then. Wait for the signal, then move quickly. And remember your roles." His eyes circle the room.

Rebekah smiles to reassure them. "All will be well. Your new life together is about to begin."

Samuel adds, "You had better get some sleep. Tomorrow will be a long day."

The moon is bloated, an orange-gold sphere hovering massive and haughty above the horizon, too fat to climb into the heavens. The old man's rippled reflection can be seen from the towers of Madinat, marking the slow meander of the Guadalquivir on the plain below. The stars talk conspiracy in the shadows, impatient to enact their plans for a coup to recapture the sky. Soon, very soon.

The air is cold and still, with a sharp, brittle edge. Berber guards dot the walls, no farther apart than a level-voiced call, their cloaks pulled tight against the chill, pulsating bursts of breath-fog dogging their slow steps as they walk the walls scanning the landscape. The city is dark, the flames in the alley lamps turned down to nubs for the night.

A dog unleashes a long run of barks but is cut short by a sharp yelp. A distant neigh rises from the royal paddocks and is answered. A truncated peel of drunken laughter disappears into the night.

Families have long since gone to bed and Madinat now sleeps. All but the courtesans, who ply their trade with skill and grace, gloriously twisting their customers into tight spirals within their beds, teasing out their cries of ecstasy dribble by dribble.

Seen from above, the rooftops of the hundreds of buildings in Madinat al-Zahra are mostly low-sloped gables, tiled to perfection in terracotta. Circular skylights dot the roofs by the hundreds, propped open in summer to offer a cool, pleasing updraft; closed tight and locked in winter. Córdobans are legendary for their love of natural light. Yawning portals of fine brightness by day, dazzling diamonds by night.

The Rare Books Library is no exception, of course. Each room has at least one skylight, and many have more. What finer way to read? The large triangular panes of cut glass high above Zafir's room playfully scatter the brassy moonlight. All but one. One pane refuses its glow, pried loose from its lead caulking and set carefully to the side, helpless to resist.

Lament

With Durr sleeping just on the other side of the thin wall no more than three paces from where they lay, their lovemaking turns slow and deliberate, meticulous, sand dribbling grain by grain through the pinch of an hourglass. And exquisite for it, of course. A lengthy series of exaggerated sighs and muted shivers, of held breaths between clenched jaws, of hands placed over mouths at critical moments, when they push each other close to the precipice, demanding a crying out.

They giggle silently afterwards, proud of themselves for their stealth. She rolls off him, all dimples, then curls up, her head cuddling into the crook of his arm, already her favorite spot in the world. He begins to trace the lovely curve of her hip.

He whispers, "That was amazing. I love you, Rayhana."

She purrs her response, snuggles tighter to him.

These two lie open-eyed in the faint lamp glow of the crypt, their minds drifting against their will to the next day and how it will all play out.

It is almost two hours still before dawn, and the genies scamper about working their mischief. Neither of them has slept more than a few minutes at a stretch. They toss, they turn; covers up, covers down. They flip towards each other, then away, then back towards each other again. A half hour later it all repeats under the fitful haze of insomnia.

He lies wide awake. A heavy, frustrating sigh. He senses that her eyes are open.

He whispers, "Are you awake?"

"Yes."

"We should just get up. We can read. Or play with the camera obscura. Something. Anything."

She answers with her own sigh. "I am exhausted, but my mind refuses to still."

"The same for me."

"We need to be quiet. Durr should sleep." They hear her soft snore through the tunnel leading into the adjacent false room.

A few minutes later they are seated on pillows, lamps and braziers lit, the room bright and warm. He has a volume of poetry open on the table; she tinkers with her precious camera.

They both turn as they hear Durr crawling through the tunnel.

"We wanted you to sleep, Durr. I am sorry we woke you."

"I saw the light and knew you were up. In truth, I have not slept well either. How long before sunrise?"

Zafir answers, "Hard to be sure. At least an hour, perhaps two? We are trying to kill the time."

She nods. "I will go brew us some tea."

Rayhana says, "I hate for you to go to the trouble."

"I do not mind ... a stroll would do me good."

"Zafir will go with you."

She shakes her head. "No. Please. I will be back shortly. I know the way."

Zafir adds, "Would you bring some fruit and cheese as well?"

Durr grins. "Certainly. I am hungry, too." She lifts a candle, lights it on the lamp, and walks through the horseshoe arch, parting the darkness.

A short while later Zafir glances up from his book, the dim glow in the archway announcing her return.

He absently says, "Durr is back," and returns to his poem.

The glow from the hallway brightens as she draws closer with her taper.

Just as Durr frames the horseshoe arch, Rayhana turns to look. She immediately furls her brow and frowns. Something is terribly wrong with Durr's expression. She is pale as cotton, her eyes wide with fear, her face sheer terror. "Durr?"

Zafir's eyes rise from the page as he registers the concern in Rayhana's voice.

They both see Aslam at the same instant standing just behind her. Rayhana yelps her shock and recoils away from the door. Zafir leaps to his feet and pulls Rayhana to his side. The large round table bearing the camera obscura is the only thing between the two of them and Aslam. Zafir mutters, "Dear Allah ..."

Aslam rests one hand lightly on Durr's shoulder and holds his dagger tight up under her chin with the other. He hisses into her ear, "Step inside."

Durr is shaking uncontrollably. She drops the tray with a mighty crash and begins to blubber. "I am sorry, Rayhana, I am so sorry. He was on me before I knew what was happening. I am so sorry ..."

"Shut up!" He pushes Durr into the room. The man's hiss is poisonous. "You two thought you were so clever." He sneers. "Fools. Nothing gets past me, nothing. The Jew will pay for his deception." His face splits to reveal his rotten teeth. "It seems I have caught the saqaliba scum and his missing whore after all. Your father will be pleased to see you, Rayhana. Your betrothed, the giant Berber, pines for your body." He eyes Zafir. "As for you, boy, I told you what I would do to you if our paths ever crossed again. I aim to keep my word. You will never find your way inside a woman again." His crooked smile widens.

The black wraith's eyes track to the tunnel entrance beside the two of them. An escape route that must be sealed. Aslam glances back and does not take his eyes from them as he slowly walks Durr toward the tunnel.

There is a sharp crack as Durr steps on a shard of broken teapot, causing the man's eyes to instinctively flick to the floor. In that instant Durr grabs his dagger arm with both hands and sinks her teeth into him, producing a string of sharp curses. He slaps her ear with his other hand to stun her, and in that second of disoriented hesitation, she slackens her grip on his dagger arm.

Zafir pushes Rayhana behind him and moves around the table to help Durr. Aslam rips his arm free of Durr's grasp, and with an elegant blurred swish, pulls his hand across her throat, a motion so fast they are not even sure what just happened. The point of Aslam's blade ends up directly in Zafir's path. The boy stops and retreats, rejoining Rayhana.

Durr doubles over, sputters, and coughs.

Rayhana cannot breathe.

When Durr stands back up, her expression is one of sad resignation. She stares at Rayhana, silently mouths, "I am so sorry."

The neat line running ear to ear beneath her chin splits open wide and vomits crimson gore.

Rayhana screams.

Aslam smiles.

As her blood gushes from her, a lake with no dam, Durr seems momentarily suspended in time and space, her fear fading now, her expression growing more peaceful with each fleeting second. A crimson pool rapidly widens around her feet. Her eyes grow vacant and her lids begin to flutter. She collapses into the crimson mess.

Rayhana is hysterical.

Aslam laughs his response. "Durr was a fool."

Zafir shakes Rayhana and calls her name. "Rayhana. Rayhana! I need your help." Zafir's voice is remarkably calm. "Please. Rayhana!"

She finds her strength and settles herself. She looks at Aslam, hate filling her eyes. "I am here, Zafir."

"Rayhana, remember our plan."

She nods weakly, sniffs then whispers, "I remember."

"GO!"

Rayhana dives for the tunnel and frantically crawls through. Aslam curses and lunges forward, his blade up and ready. Zafir grabs the camera obscura and lifts it over his head. Aslam stops.

Zafir slings the camera at Aslam.

The black wraith ducks but the camera breaks heavy upon him, causing him to lose his footing. He slips on Durr's blood and falls hard, face forward, his forehead slapping the tile.

Zafir races for the tunnel.

In a blur Rayhana is at the alarm cord. She jerks the cord hard three times. She turns back to the tunnel just as his head pokes through. She screams, "Quickly, Zafir!"

As he wriggles through, Zafir's head is jerked back by his scream, his face a bright flash of agony.

Rayhana runs to him and crouches, grabs his shoulders, and yanks him forward with all her might. His body pulls free of the tunnel, sending her flying back against the wall, smacking the back of her head hard.

He doubles up and grabs at his left leg, writhing, moaning his terrible pain. Dazed, she crawls to him.

Aslam bends down to continue his pursuit, then hesitates. He slowly rises and begins to study the tunnel entrance, calculating, clearly wary of some sort of trap awaiting him on the other side. He realizes that if she has a sword he will lose his head when he pokes through. He stands paralyzed, reluctant to enter the tunnel.

She gasps. The back of Zafir's calf yawns wide from knee to ankle. "Zafir! Dear Allah ..."

He hisses through his clenched teeth, "Run, Rayhana! I will hold him here. GO!"

She just stares at her husband.

"Go, Rayhana! MOVE! There is time! RUN!"

Decision made, her features steady, her body calms.

She takes a take breath, then releases it and whispers, "I will not live without you, Zafir. I will never leave your side, no matter what."

Zafir begins to sob softly, "No, Rayhana, no ..."

He moans between clenched teeth as she drags him into the corner, leaving a messy trail of blood in his wake, and props him against the wall. She stands and makes for the table beside the second tunnel, grabs the flask and measuring beaker. She sits down beside him, carefully measures out the poison into the beaker, and hands it to Zafir. He is woozy from the loss of blood and looks confused.

"Take it with both hands, my love. And do not spill it. Zafir!"

His eyes steady. He nods and cradles the beaker.

She lifts his chin to look deeply into his eyes. "I will always love you, Zafir. Always."

"Our hearts are joined forever, my love."

He can hear the murmur of their voices but cannot make out what they are saying. He smiles. They have moved away from the tunnel exit. "If you think that hurt, scum, just wait until I geld you." He listens. Nothing. Satisfied, he bends down and begins to crawl into the tunnel.

She sets the flask down beside her and begins to tend to his leg. Fortunately, the flow of blood seems to be slowing. Her eyes flit between the tunnel and Zafir's leg. She wraps a cloth tightly around the wound and applies pressure as he grimaces.

They wait.

Rebekah shakes him awake. "Samuel. Samuel!"

He groans.

"Samuel. The bells! The bells, Samuel!"

He sobers. "What?" He looks up at the skylight. "But it is still night."

"I heard the signal bells, Samuel. Three rings. The signal bells."

He is instantly alert, his concern vivid on his face. "What on earth could have happened? Get your clothes on, Rebekah. We will stop by Levi's room on the way. Come, Rebekah, we must hurry!"

Aslam's head tentatively emerges from the tunnel and begins to take in the room. When he sees the two against the wall, his face relaxes and he pulls himself on through and stands, his dagger held loose and ready.

"Quite a place you have here. Fools. It would appear that the end of this silly game is upon us at last." His awful smile settles first on Rayhana. "You, I need alive." His eyes track to Zafir. "You, I do not."

461

As he steps forward, she lifts the flask from the floor and holds it to her lips. Zafir does the same with the beaker. Aslam stops, confusion settling onto his face.

"Poison, Aslam." Her eyes are level, bright, and steady with purpose.

Aslam's eyes widen.

"Yes. Prepared for desperate people caught in desperate situations."

"Poison ..." He sounds dubious.

"Lojana, I believe it is called. Surely you know of it."

He does know this poison, of course, has used it to do his work for him on several occasions. Acts to paralyze the breathing muscles, finally stopping the heart. Quick acting, too, and within hours impossible to detect. Aslam scoffs, "You intend to kill yourself just to avoid marrying the Berber? I do not believe you would do such a thing."

Rayhana's face is a model of feminine will. "Try me, Aslam. Zafir is my husband now. We have been legally married before an imam. We will not live apart, even if it means our deaths. Allah will reward us in the afterlife."

His look of confusion grows. "Married ... how? Who served as your wali?"

Rayhana smiles. "My tetta. Imam Abd al-Gafur presided. From Algeciras. You met them already, Hasan and Jalida."

He considers her words then softly curses.

"Married, Aslam. I would love to see how you explain my dead body to my father. Especially since I was alive when you found me. Turn and leave now or we will drink it. You have sowed enough evil for one night. Now leave!"

The man is not used to indecision weighing so heavily upon him. He teeters in the unfamiliar terrain of uncertainty. The standoff between the dagger and the poison drags out as he mulls over his options. He knows his life is forfeit if he lets her slip through his hands again. Still ...

She sees his decision settle into his ebony eyes just before he makes his move. "Now, Zafir!" She gulps deeply from the flask as Zafir drains the beaker then lets it roll out of his hand onto the floor.

"NO!" Aslam slaps the upturned flask from her hands, shattering it on the tile.

He steps back, frantic now, unsure what to do. He sheathes his dagger and helplessly wrings his hands. There is no known antidote for lojana.

The pale-green syrup dribbles down her chin. Their faces are paling, their lips already fading to light blue. Their foreheads dot with beads of sweat as their breathing first grows quick and labored, then turns shallower and slower as the muscles begin to lose their will.

Her voice is already weakening. "You should have listened to me, Aslam."

He opens his mouth to reply, but closes it.

"Tell my father ..." She swallows hard, fighting for the words. "Tell my father to check the nikah." A weak smile. She curls up against Zafir as if deathly tired. Her husband slides his arm around her and pulls her tight to him. She whispers, "I will always love you."

"And I you."

"I ... believe, Zafir ... I ... believe." She has to gasp it.

It takes everything he has to get his response out. "Yes, my love ... yes."

Their eyes begin a lazy droop, are willed back open, then droop further. They are barely breathing now, their faces pale as a winter's moon. A moment later their torsos convulse once, twice, then their eyes close and they slide into each other, dead.

Aslam stands motionless, open-mouthed and incredulous.

Samuel arrives first and stops in the archway, staring, aghast with horror. When Rebekah arrives she pushes past him. One look is all she needs. She screams her agony. "NO! NOOOOOOOOO!"

The rest arrive. Iuliana begins to wail uncontrollably.

Samuel takes charge. "Levi, you come with me. The rest of you wait here until we know it is safe. Zaheid, find something to cover Durr with. Quick, man!"

Imam Abd al-Gafur leans down beside the dead woman, lays his hand upon her head, and begins to recite prayers of passing over her.

Samuel steps past the mess and crawls through Zafir's blood into the tunnel, Levi right behind him.

Rebekah ignores her husband and follows them. Salma takes her cue and brings up the rear.

As Rebekah emerges in the false room, she sees Aslam leaning against the wall. His dagger is drawn but hangs limply by his side. The man is wide-eyed and dazed, quietly cursing the cruelty of his fate. She pushes between Samuel and Levi to take in the awful scene, and begins to sob. "Dear Yahweh, no. No, please no ... nooooooo ..."

Salma sees the two of them. "Oh dear Allah, what have you done? What have you done to my poor Rayhana?" She turns to Aslam, her hate boiling over. "You killed them, Aslam. They were just married, just ..." She chokes back a sob. "You killed them, Aslam! You!" Her shoulders begin to shake as the dam splits and the tears stream from her.

He mutters, "I thought she was bluffing. How could I know it was really poison? How could I know?" The man is dumbfounded.

"They are gone, Rebekah, gone." Samuel begins to cry.

Rebekah turns on the wraith now, her look withering. "You will pay for this crime, Aslam—you will pay with your life! You will pay, do you hear?!" She shakes her fist. "By Yahweh's might you will pay! And then you will burn in hell for all eternity!"

Aslam is resigned to his plight. His shoulders sag. "I must take her to her father." He steps towards her body.

Salma shouts, "You will NOT touch her! Do you hear me! You are to NEVER touch her ... NEVER!"

Samuel rests a hand on Salma's shoulder, "I will carry her, Salma." He turns to Aslam and states the fact. "Salma and Imam Abd al-Gafur and Rebekah are coming with me."

He nods lamely but does not speak.

Samuel turns to Levi. "Please see to the boy's body. We will need a proper burial shroud."

Levi bites his lower lip to still the tremble. He nods.

Samuel steps forward and scoops her limp body into his arms, her hair waterfalling to his knees. As he looks at her dead face he chokes back a sob. "Levi, first help me get her through the tunnel."

His friend's answer is tender. "Of course, Samuel. Let me go first."

When they are gone, Levi and Zaheid can only shake their heads. Zaheid says, "How could this have gone so wrong?"

"Somehow he figured it out before we wanted him to. Who knows how?"

"But how did he get into the library without us knowing? We worked so hard to prevent that."

"I have no idea." Levi turns to Iuliana, who stands pale and numb with shock. "Iuliana." She stares blankly at Durr's draped body. "Iuliana?" No response.

Her husband softly speaks her name. "Iuliana?" She looks up with full eyes.

Levi says, "Would you go and look after the girls? They may have been awakened by all the noise. Please."

She finds herself and offers a rattling sigh. "Of course."

"Thank you. Zaheid, I will see to Durr. You go and find Abu al-Qasim and bring him. Zafir's wound looks ugly and he has lost much blood. Tell him to bring his instruments."

"What of the guards?"

"They should have gone with Aslam, but be sure first."

Zaheid nods.

"I will administer the antidote. Let us hope that it works as Abu al-Qasim expects."

The two friends exchange helpless looks.

Stone

22 January 977.

As the pale gray leaks onto the horizon, the sharp outline of Madinat al-Zahra slowly emerges from the hazy gauze of early dawn. The dimming stars glance over their shoulders to frown their dismay: another night of reverie cut short, much too short. The bloated orange moon hangs stranded in the air, struggling helplessly, impaled on the crags of the Sierra Morena.

Aslam is known to the Berber guards, of course, but even so, he approaches carefully to state his purpose. He whispers, points to the group, whispers some more.

The black wraith has devolved into a shadow of himself, his will broken by the disastrous events of the night. He knows he comes to collect his master's wrath—probably his own death sentence.

The turbaned guard looks at the group suspiciously, nods soberly, turns, and signals with a coded knock. The door cracks open, words are exchanged, then it swings wide and they are ushered to the center of the courtyard. Six Banu Birzal knights, hands resting easily upon their scimitar hilts, move to strategic points within close reach should the need for action arise.

Suktan and Tahir stand like massive oaks at the edge of the courtyard beneath the peristyle, guarding Ibn Abi Amir's study. The Banu Birzal sentry approaches and speaks with Suktan, who nods once, twice, then looks to the group. He frowns. He nods once more and says, "Tell them to wait there. We will need light—see to it." The man nods.

Suktan knocks gently on the door and is instantly answered.

"Yes?" Ibn Abi Amir is awake and working before sunrise, his normal practice. Ulla is still fast asleep in their bedchamber.

"I need to speak with you, Qadi of the Maghreb." Suktan waits for his master to open the door.

"What is it?"

"You must come to the courtyard, Qadi of the Maghreb. You have … important visitors."

"At this hour? Who?"

"Just come. Please."

He searches the Berber's dark eyes for clues and sees the man's unease. He nods. "Let me fetch my cloak."

Ibn Abi Amir steps out. Aslam stands, head bowed in submission. Beside him are two women and another man. Ibn Abi Amir frowns. He approaches the group and stops. "Mama?" His frown is strangled by confusion, his expression incredulous. "Mama? What are you doing here? Mama?" His gaze tracks right. "Imam Abd al-Gafur? What on earth?" His confusion grows. He recognizes Rebekah. Samuel stands behind her. All four faces are tight and pinched, eyes red and puffy.

He turns to the black wraith. "Aslam, what is going on here?"

Aslam does not lift his eyes. His reply is timid and muted, "I have failed you, Master."

Rebekah and Salma part to allow Samuel to step through, Rayhana cradled in his arms.

Ibn Abi Amir turns from Aslam and gasps. "Rasha ... my Rasha."

Samuel lashes out. "This is what Aslam did, Muhammad. This!" He shakes the girl's dead body. His voice turns accusatory, angry. "This is what the destruction of innocent life looks like, Muhammad. THIS! A needless waste of life. Your daughter is dead. Dead, Muhammad! You are the cause of this. YOU!"

Ibn Abi Amir is speechless. He opens his mouth but nothing comes out. "But ..." His eyes fill and his head sags. "But ... how?"

Salma speaks. "They poisoned themselves, son. Aslam murdered Durr and was about to murder the boy." She chokes back a sob. "They drank poison, son, poison. They said if they could not be together as husband and wife in life, they would be together in death. They loved each other, Muhammad, loved each other more than you can possibly know."

"But ..."

"She is gone now, Muhammad, our beautiful Rasha is gone, robbed of her future. What would Rayya think, son? What would she think about what you did to her beloved daughter? What would she think?!"

At the sound of his wife's name, Ibn Abi Amir's eyes well up. He mutters, "But ... the boy was saqaliba, unworthy of my name, unworthy of Rayhana's love ..."

Salma steps to her son, stares him full in the eyes, as only a mother can, and slaps him hard. He takes the blow and lowers his eyes submissively.

Suktan and Tahir tense as she reprimands their master but hold steady. Matriarchs are held in high esteem in the desert tribes and deserve deference, especially from their sons.

She is incandescent she is so livid. She sneers, "You disgust me! Your father would be so ashamed of you, Muhammad. Ashamed! Where has the Muhammad I birthed and raised gone? What happened to him?!" She sadly shakes her head. "Love has no bounds, you fool. How could you forget the story of you and your Rayya, son? You once knew what true love was. You knew!"

The slap seems to sober him up, but her words wound him deeply, the lingering sting draped upon his cowed features. He mumbles, "But they were not married, Mama. I forbade their marriage. I had plans for her, great plans, plans that would help our family rise to greatness."

Her eyes burn with anger, her stare withering in its fury. "They WERE married, Muhammad! They WERE married. MARRIED!"

His confusion returns. "Impossible. I forbade the marriage ... I refused to act as her wali. No nikah would be valid without my approval."

Imam Abd al-Gafur softly says, "There you would be wrong, Muhammad. Your mother, as Rayhana's tetta, acted as her wali. I found legal precedent for her case in the Sharia Library. The nikah is valid." He widens his eyes for emphasis. "Depend upon it." He reaches into his robe, withdraws the document, and holds it out.

The hands of the knights tighten on their scimitar hilts but do not move farther.

Ibn Abi Amir is recovering, his bile rising quickly. He grabs the nikah, opens it, and quickly scans it. His face hardens as he races down the page. A resigned sigh. "My own mother conspires against me ..." His tone is incredulous. "My own mother. What has the world come to?"

Salma replies, "You were in the wrong, son. How could I not stand up for her? I pray you beg mercy from Allah for the evil you have done. You have killed your innocent daughter and her husband. She was guilty only of finding true love, son. She will never bear your grandsons, you will never be a jiddo to them. Never ..."

An awful stillness settles upon the courtyard.

Ibn Abi Amir continues to stare blankly at his mother.

They all see it happen. In the time it takes to snap a finger something dies within the man, hardening his heart to stone. His face transforms before their eyes.

They brace themselves for the storm they can sense is coming. The air begins to sizzle and spark, raising hairs upon the backs of their necks, just as it does before lightning strikes.

"I refuse burial of Rayhana and her ... saqaliba husband ... in Madinat. The presence of their bones would defile the Shining City." Remarkably, the man's tone is matter of fact, as if he were reciting a shopping list.

Rebekah gasps.

"I care not what happens to them. Bury them in a pauper's grave. Or find a beggar's field somewhere and burn their bones and scatter the ashes."

Salma says defiantly, "They will come with me to Algeciras for proper burial, son."

"I care not." He looks at his mother with dead eyes, his voice level and resigned. "As for you, from this day hence I will never speak your name again. Not once. And if you or Imam Abd al-Gafur ever show your faces in Córdoba or Madinat again, you will be arrested on sight. You will never again lay eyes upon your son, the richest and most powerful man in all of al-Andalus. Put your things in order and be gone by sunset of the third day."

Salma's eyes well up but she stands firm.

Ibn Abi Amir's deadly gaze settles on Samuel. "You defied me, Vizier of Books. You gave the two of them shelter. You played a part in this, a large part." His dead eyes burn into Samuel. "I had Suktan strangle al-Mughira for a lesser crime. In front of his wife and children so that the intended message would be ... properly received."

Rebekah gasps.

Salma's face hardens. "Look at me! Son! Look at me!"

Ibn Abi Amir's eyes slowly track to his mother.

"On your father's grave, you will NOT harm this man, Muhammad. He did nothing but treat Rayhana with kindness. He only wanted the best for the two of them. Just like me."

Ibn Abi Amir sneers. "The man is a Jew, Mama. He defied me."

"He holds no power at court." She shakes her head vigorously. "He is no threat to you, son."

"He deserves no mercy, Mama."

She clenches her jaw, her face flushing with anger. She hisses, "You. Will. NOT. Harm. This. Man. SON." She twists the last word until it snaps. "Promise me! On your father's grave, Muhammad! PROMISE ME!"

Ibn Abi Amir blankly stares as he calculates, his expression unreadable. Almost a minute passes. A heavy sigh is his only response. "Your weakness disgusts me, Mama. I promise. But this is the last request I will ever grant you. Ever."A sinister grin lifts the corners of the man's mouth as he turns back to Samuel. "Your sentence, Jew, will be this." He tortures the word. "One week hence you will bring one thousand volumes from the Rare Books Library to the parade grounds. There they will be put to the torch."

Samuel's mouth falls open in horror. "You cannot be serious. Those books are priceless, Muhammad. And they belong to the caliph, not you."

Rebekah begins to cry.

"Nevertheless, it seems the grand imam has had complaints of lurid volumes in your care." A menacing smile. "Trust me, the caliph will consent to my wishes."

Samuel pleads, "Dear Yahweh ... no. No!"

"The Berber imams believe that Allah desires that we rid ourselves of all temptations. Infidel books are the worst of the lot. I agree."

"I refuse to do any such thing." Samuel stands resolute.

Ibn Abi Amir's grins his amusement. "Either you choose the volumes or I will have the Berber imams do so. I suspect you will find their tastes not so refined as your own. Your choice."

Samuel's eyes burn, but he remains silent.

Ibn Abi Amir flicks his wrist with disgust. "Leave me, all of you." His men usher them out. He motions to Suktan.

The massive Berber draws close.

"Aslam will never see the noon sun. Understood?"

"Perfectly, Qadi of the Maghreb. His will be a slow and painful death." Suktan turns and follows the group out the door.

Ibn Abi Amir stares into space for a full minute before he turns and reenters his study. He lifts his reed pen, dips it in the ink pot, and resumes his work on the document. The caliph's proclamations for the coming day's ceremony.

Prayers

"How much did you give him?"

Levi replies, "Just as you said, two-thirds of the beaker."

"You are sure he swallowed it all?"

"Yes. I massaged his throat like you said. It went down."

Abu al-Qasim nods soberly. "Good. I suppose we cannot know for certain that he had a full dose of the potion, but there it is." He shakes his head sadly. "It is a shame what happened to Durr. She was a good woman."

"Yes."

"Turn him on his stomach and let me look at that leg."

Levi and Zaheid roll him over. Levi has already removed the boy's bloody clothes, cleaned him, and replaced Rayhana's cloth with a fresh dressing. The blood has begun to soak through it already.

Abu al-Qasim leans over the table and removes the bandage. He frowns. "That is no pinprick." He opens his bag to retrieve an implement then begins to prod about the wound. Brother Cleo stands beside him, ready to assist. "The dagger was sharp, that is good. A neat cut, though deep." He studies the foot-long gash. "Thank goodness there is only a nick of the ankle tendon. If that had been severed I am afraid the boy would have never run again." He points with his instrument. "See?"

Cleo nods.

"The bleeding has nearly stopped—a good sign." He continues to probe with his instrument. "Fortunately, he missed the artery." He indicates the vessel. "See, Cleo, by a hair. Lucky boy. He probably would have bled to death if that had been cut."

Cleo nods soberly.

Abu al-Qasim stands. "Yes, well ... this leg will heal nicely, once it is properly disinfected and stitched. He will limp for a few months, then it'll be good as new." He muses. "Still, there is some concern about the amount of blood he lost. It is unclear how that will affect the ratio of antidote to poison. But that is beyond our control, I am afraid." He looks at Cleo and smiles. "Shall we repair the boy's leg, sir?"

Cleo answers with a grin. "We shall, sir."

"Get the blue and gold bottles. We must carefully clean the wound first. That will be key to our success. With a cut this deep, the chance of infection is large." He turns to Levi and Zaheid. "I will need boiling water, Levi, and soap and clean towels. Zaheid, go find some blankets, we must keep the boy very warm. Bring an extra brazier for the room. Two would be better." Zaheid nods. "Oh, and I need more light. Find some lamps."

The two scurry off.

"There, that should do it." He ties off the last catgut suture and Cleo clips it. They stand back, admiring their work like satisfied parents. He chuckles. "The boy will have a nice scar, something to tell his children about. Wrap it in a light bandage, and not too tight. This kind of wound needs to breathe. We will change it twice a day for the next few days. And make sure you disinfect it each time."

The boy's color has returned, his lips once again a healthy pink. His chest rises and falls at a normal pace.

"Why does he not awake?" Levi's anxiety is woven through his words.

"Patience, Levi. His heart rate and breathing are normal, but he is still in a deep sleep. He will awake; give him time."

They have no idea how it goes with the others, of course, good or bad. The long wait is pure torture. Levi stands at the boy's side, wiping his face with a damp cloth. Abu al-Qasim cleans his instruments as Cleo sees to the bandage.

Zaheid begins to pace.

The room erupts with commotion. Abu al-Qasim takes charge. "Lay her on the table beside him, Samuel. Levi, get me some pillows." He lifts her head and places the pillows to keep her head tilted back so that the air passageways remain open. Rebekah gathers her hair and pulls it out of the way. Salma leans down and kisses her forehead. Cold.

Once he is satisfied, Abu al-Qasim says, "Good, good, now move back, all of you." He shoos them away from her. They huddle around, the tension in the room oppressive. He studies her face. Deathly pale, lips deep blue, approaching purple. He feels her hands. "She is freezing. Zaheid, stoke the braziers, please." He sticks his finger in his mouth then holds it under her nose. "Breathing, but just barely." He unbuttons her gown and folds it back, baring her chest. "Forgive me, child." He lays his ear to her and listens. "Slow, but steady. Good." He raises up. "Cleo, bring me a lit candle." He opens her eye with his thumb and forefinger and holds the candle close. Her dilated pupil constricts. He checks the other eye. "Good. Samuel, how long has it been?"

"Almost two hours, I think. Maybe a little less."

Abu al-Qasim frowns. "Much too long. Do we have any idea how much of the potion she actually ingested?"

"No. The beaker was beside Zafir, so she must have drunk directly from the flask."

He sighs, impatiently. "And?"

Levi adds, "The flask lay shattered on the floor when we arrived."

Abu al-Qasim's frown deepens. "The monk's potion was a sophisticated poison, and a lethal one at that." His voice begins to rise with his anger. "I made it clear that it was to be measured very carefully!" He curses his frustration.

Samuel offers a weak reply, "I am afraid things did not unfold as we planned."

Abu al-Qasim nods. "No ... I understand. Forgive me. Levi, bring me the antidote." He lifts the vial and measures out a full beaker. "We must pray for good luck, my friends. And Allah's Grace." He steps to her side, gently lifts her up, tilts her head back, then pries her mouth open with his thumb and finger. He pours a quarter of the amber liquid in, hands the beaker to Cleo, then presses her mouth closed and begins to massage her throat. "Come, my dear, you must swallow this. Come, Rayhana, you must help me. Come, girl, I need your help!"

Ten minutes later the beaker is empty.

He stands and exhales heavily. "All we can do now is wait."

Samuel croaks, "For how long?"

Abu al-Qasim sighs, rests a hand on the man's shoulder. "Hard to say, Samuel. Given the amount of time that has elapsed, and without knowing how much she took, it is impossible to know how this will go."

"I see ..."

He joins eyes with each of them, one by one. "You must prepare yourselves. It is conceivable that her body will live but that she will never wake from this."

Rebekah and Salma gasp simultaneously and begin to cry.

He turns. "We must all pray." He smiles to lighten the burden. "Rebekah, I want you and Salma to bathe her in warm water and clean her up. Get some new clothes on her. She will want to be pretty for her husband when he wakes. And keep her tightly wrapped in blankets. She must be kept very warm."

They both sniff as they nod, pleased to have a task.

"Levi, watch after the boy. He should wake soon. Make sure he drinks lots of water to flush his system. Tell him to speak to her, hold her. He must whisper words of love in her ear, call her back from the grave. It just may help." He turns to Samuel. "I need rest, and a bath. I will check on them in two hours. If anything changes before then, send for me."

Samuel's eyes are full. "Thank you."

"You are most welcome. Cleo?"

"I will stay. And pray."

"Yes. Good. Remember, luck and Grace. We need both." He turns and leaves.

Come, My Love

"Come, my love, you must wake. Your husband needs you. Come, Rayhana, open your eyes. I am here, my love. Please, Rayhana, open your eyes. Please." He kneels before her, whispering words of love into her ear, calling for her, reaching deep into the shadow lands where she lies trapped. He kisses her lips. She is warm, her color returned. Her chest rises and falls at a normal pace. He lays his ear to her chest and listens to the steady beat, then lifts his head and begins again. "Come, my love, you must awake ..."

Rebekah, Salma, and Imam Abd al-Gafur stand vigil with him. Zafir awoke just before noon prayers—just opened his eyes as if from a long nap. He was dizzy and disoriented but otherwise fine. Just as the monks said.

Iuliana has taken the girls back to Samuel's apartment to settle them back into a semblance of normal life. The imam sits on his pillow, absorbed in his Quran. He reads, he prays, he fetches the supplies they need—anything to keep busy. Samuel, Levi and Zaheid come and go. They have cleaned up the mess in the crypt and finished the repairs on the door. Imam Abd al-Gafur helped them properly prepare Durr's body for burial.

Zafir speaks to Rayhana, listens to her heart, strokes her cheeks, takes her hand and kisses her limp fingers one by one, holds them to his face. He buries himself against her neck and cries.

Rebekah and Salma exchange worried looks. It breaks their hearts to watch him.

He refuses to leave her side. They do not press. Instead, they insist he take some food and water, but he will not. The only request he has made of them was to fetch her *Iliad* and his image cast upon silver by the beloved camera. They lie now beside her. He opens the *Iliad*, reads some of her favorite passages, and closes it when his voice breaks.

Abu al-Qasim has made three visits already. He has changed the boy's bandages, the only attention Zafir has permitted thus far. As Abu al-Qasim moves to leave, he exchanges looks with each of them; a worried look, not comforting. He whispers to Salma. "Patience and prayer, that is all we can do. Luck and

Grace, Salma, luck and Grace." Imam Abd-al Gafur pulls her head against him as she begins to sob.

Evening approaches. As the Shining City dims under a brilliant palette of orange and red, the diamonds strut out to dazzle the night.

Zafir is crying once more, his forehead resting against her. "It should have been me. Why did you give me the beaker, Rayhana, why? Why?"

Rebekah lays a hand on his shoulder but can say nothing to console him.

Back in his study, Samuel, Levi, and Zaheid sit huddled together talking about the edict in somber tones. Samuel stops and lowers his gaze as his shoulders begin to shake. He chokes back a sob. The other two offer words to console their friend, then give him space.

Levi holds a paper and reed pen, making notes as they go. Samuel recovers, wipes his eyes, and whispers, "Forgive me," and they begin again. "Are we agreed then upon the untranslated love poetry from the east?" They nod. "If we add those to all the duplicate copies, what does that bring us to?"

Levi stares as his sheet and silently counts. He frowns. "Only two hundred and eleven."

Samuel's sad reply tells it all. "I see ... so few." His voice turns hard. "By Yahweh, I will die before he touches the Greeks, I will die!"

Levi and Zaheid just stare at him. Levi says, "It will break Zafir's heart when he hears of this."

Samuel's reply is firm. "No. I do not want him to know anything about this. He has enough to worry about."

Levi and Zaheid nod their agreement.

The anguish these three confront stands like a fourth presence beside them. The insanity of it all leaves them speechless and numb.

Past midnight, when he can no longer keep his eyes open, he grabs a pillow and climbs up on the table beside her, curls up against her, and pulls her tight to him. They watch him do this but say nothing. When he is asleep, Rebekah gently lays a blanket over him, goes back to her mattress, turns the lamps low, and tries to sleep. She will toss and turn until sunrise.

al-Mansur

Word has spread far and wide of the early afternoon ceremony to be held on the royal parade grounds beneath the grand portico. Rumors race like wildfire through the alleys, carefully cultivated, of course, fueled and fanned or stroked and bent as required by the audience.

It becomes clear that major announcements will be made, news to celebrate. The boy caliph himself will appear and speak. Ibn Abi Amir, the city's savior, will greet the citizens of Madinat and Córdoba for the first time since he has returned from his victorious campaign against White Hands.

Excitement sizzles in the air. Córdobans love their drama, after all. Formal word is dispatched to the city by royal courier to summon various dignitaries. Such people love the attention and formality, relish their newfound sense of importance.

"A personal invitation from the caliph?" Bright smiles. "Why, I would be honored to attend!"

The grand imam and his copious staff, the powerful merchant families, politicians, clerics, diplomats, leading citizens of the city, anyone that matters, really—all are in attendance. Even the Berber clerics are summoned from the camps across the river, to the predictable dismay of Madinat's old guard. The Berbers gather and move about in a cluster of black with their long beards and frowns. The same summons is issued within Madinat, including the caliph's Vizier Council—or what is left of it.

The crowd is ushered onto the parade grounds and settled into positions by importance. As they enter, they are hard pressed to hide their awe. The entire back half of the massive open space is filled with neatly arrayed formations of Berber cavalry in full battle attire, backs straight in their saddles. Imposing. There must be at least three thousand, perhaps four. All can agree that al-Andalus has never seen such a formidable army as this. The anxious buzz of excitement weaves through the throngs.

Ibn Abi Amir approaches the stairway leading up to the viewing stand under the grand portico, Suktan and Tahir behind him, then trailed by al-Andalusi and a dozen of the Berber commanding officers. He begins the climb to his destiny.

The man dons new attire. Gone are the coarse black robes and turban of a Berber sheikh, replaced with the finest clothes available in the city, tailored to perfection. Tan pants and tunic with red ochre silk piping—the colors of the caliph. Over this, an elaborately worked cloak of butter-soft leather.

In the place of his black turban he wears a magnificent silver helmet, a crown almost, with fine gold ornamentation and sculpted leather back-flaps that trail down and rest upon his shoulders. A downward pointing triangle of gold runs from the front lip of the helmet halfway down his forehead. His unkempt desert beard has been trimmed and neatened to fit the current fashion of the city's elite. The man looks positively regal; an Arab statesman-general, a philosopher-king. The new Caesar of Islam, minus the toga.

Hisham is waiting for him at the top of the stairs, also in formal attire, flanked by Banu Birzal escorts. Ibn Abi Amir bows to the caliph, then he and the boy step forward under the giant portico to be seen and heard.

A mighty cheer rises up to embrace them.

For an instant the shadow of a satisfied smile drifts across Ibn Abi Amir's face, then vanishes.

A courtier steps forward and intones to the crowd, "His Royal Highness, Caliph Hisham II, son of al-Hakam II, may Allah bring his soul peace. Grandson of Abd al-Rahman III, the great al-Nasir, third caliph of al-Andalus, sultan of Córdoba, lord of glorious Madinat al-Zahra. Elder of the Umayyad clan, protector of the written word, champion of truth, defender of the faith. May Allah smile upon his reign."

The crowd roars its approval.

The boy raises his arms to quiet them. "Citizens of Córdoba, leaders of the realm, may Allah's peace be upon you. I bring you glad tidings." The voice is remarkably strong for a boy of his age.

Another roar.

"May I present Ibn Abi Amir, my trusted regent, servant of the realm, defender of Allah and the Prophet. Because of him, Córdoba is once again safe, its future preserved for your children and grandchildren. The Christian infidels of Castile have been vanquished, praise Allah." He lifts a hand to Ibn Abi Amir, who bows deeply.

The crowd roars their adoration.

Ibn Abi Amir pauses, surveying, letting the anticipation build. "It is my great honor to dedicate my life in the service of Caliph Hisham and the citizens of al-Andalus. Long live Caliph Hisham!"

"LONG LIVE CALIPH HISHAM!"

He continues, "Citizens of Córdoba. White Hands and the Christians tremble at the sound of the word 'jihad.' I say let them tremble!"

A roar of approval.

He raises a fist. "Allahu Akbar!"

The answering roar. "ALLAHU AKBAR!

"Allahu Akbar!"

"ALLAHU AKBAR!"

"Allahu Akbar!"

"ALLAHU AKBAR!

He bows deferentially to the caliph.

Hisham reaches into his robe and extracts a small scroll, opens it, then reads. "My people. I, Caliph Hisham II, servant of the Prophet, make the following proclamation by Allah's beneficent will. Our trusted servant and protector, Ibn Abi Amir, a man who ably serves me as my regent, will assume the additional roles of grand vizier, military vizier, and protector of the royal treasury. From this day hence, for his great service in defending al-Andalus from the infidels, he will be known to all as al-Mansur Bi-llah—*Victorious by the Grace of Allah*. His name will long be feared by the enemies of al-Andalus. Long live al-Mansur!"

The crowd stumbles in the wake of such an unprecedented decree. Incredulous looks and nervous whispers follow. The awkward delay lasts for exactly four heartbeats, until four thousand Berber knights raise their scimitars and shout, "LONG LIVE AL-MANSUR! LONG LIVE AL-MANSUR! LONG LIVE AL-MANSUR!

The crowd is tentative at first but quickly gathers strength. "Long live al-Mansur. Long live al-Mansur! LONG LIVE AL-MANSUR!"

The satisfied smile does come now, and remains.

Within ten minutes, Hisham is tucked back inside the royal harem for safe keeping.

The second day brings no change. The only difference is that Abu al-Qasim's expression grows heavier, more strained as he comes and goes.

As evening approaches, they gather off to the side to consult. Samuel and Abu al-Qasim relate the events of the ceremony, the new roles Ibn Abi Amir, now al-Mansur, has given himself. No one bothers to respond. It is all too obvious that the struggle for control of al-Andalus is finished. They settle into silence, the only sound in the room the soft whisper of the boy's words into her ear. "Come, my love, you must wake."

Samuel says, "Tomorrow is the third day. Imam Abd al-Gafur and Salma must leave before sunset, at the very latest. Levi has secured a small cart and a donkey for their journey. They will take Durr's body with them to Algeciras. But Levi and I thought that it would be good to have them carry three bodies. As further evidence. He will have spies watching as they depart. But that would mean we would need, uhhh ..."

Abu al-Qasim replies, "Ahhh ... I see. Two more bodies. Yes, of course. We can borrow cadavers that I have used for demonstrations. And I can help prepare Durr's body for travel. I have a preservative I use for such things. Cleo and I will see to it today."

Cleo looks stricken but nods.

"They must be clearly seen by his spies as they leave the city."

Abu al-Qasim replies, "I understand. White burial shrouds. We will just lay them side by side in the cart. Impossible to miss."

"Good. Thank you."

Abu al-Qasim stands looking at them, as if there is more he needs to say but is not quite sure how to begin.

Rebekah touches his arm to encourage him. "Please, say it."

You can see how much it pains him. "If Rayhana has not awoken by this time tomorrow ... I do not think she ever will."

The two women gasp, then nod through their tears.

"She will die within a week without food and water." He hesitates. "The boy needs to know that, Samuel. He must leave the city while there is still time to save himself. Do not underestimate Ibn Abi Amir, Samuel. You duped him, yes, but he is a quick learner, and he has eyes everywhere. Zafir will eventually be seen if he lingers, you can count on it. And we all will suffer for it."

Samuel softly says, "I will tell him."

"Not until tomorrow afternoon. There is still hope. See that he continues to call for her. And try and get the boy to eat. He must keep up his strength. Let us all keep praying, my friends."

They solemnly nod.

His whispers continue to rustle the stillness. "Come, Rayhana, your husband waits for you, come to me, my love ..."

By the time they reach the city, the sun is just breaking over the eastern hills, bathing the landscape in rich streaks of gold.

The air is cool and crisp but not unpleasant. Wisps of mist rise from the deep green river like a simmering cauldron.

They are not alone, of course. Suktan and Tahir ride discreetly behind them, back far enough for privacy, but close enough for protection.

The four of them left Madinat under the cover of night, headed along the Almunya Way back towards the city. Despite her girlish pleas, he laughs and refuses to tell her the purpose of the journey. "You will see, you will see." He points out the various almunyas and who lives where.

They skirt the city walls along the river, pass the entrance to the Puente Romano and the city's main gate, and a short while later bend back right, hugging the water's edge.

He stops his mount, smiles, then pulls a scarf from his pocket and blindfolds her for the last leg. She giggles her excitement. As he ties the knot, he whispers, "I love you, my desert flower. I like surprising you." He gently presses her belly with his hand, feels the pleasing tightness of her quickening. His son and heir.

She smiles, content. "I love you, Muhammad."

"We are almost there, Ulla." He kicks his horse to a slow walk and they move on in silence.

He stops again on a slight rise. "Are you ready?" He reaches up and unties the blindfold.

She is excited. "I am ready, Husband."

"Open your eyes."

Bound by the tight U-turn of the Guadalquivir to the east of the Puente Romano is a massive orchard, nothing more. Thousands of meticulously tended cherry and almond and pomegranate trees stand sleeping, stark in their nakedness.

She says nothing, just stares, confused.

He lifts his hand. "This is a where I will build it, Ulla. The most glorious palace ever known to man. The Shining City will pale in its splendor, my love. We will raise our sons within these walls. This will be our home."

"What will become of the Shining City?"

"Madinat al-Zahra will wither on the vine and rot. The royal treasury and royal mint and all essential government functions will be moved here. The only thing to remain in Madinat will be the caliph. There he will stay in the royal harem until he dies a natural death. He will have no heirs. Hisham is to be the last of the Umayyad dynasty."

"As it should be, Husband. The time of the Maghreb and her peoples has come. We Berbers will rule al-Andalus with a mighty fist. We will vanquish the infidel."

481

"Yes, we will, my love."

"What will you call our palace?"

"It will be known as Az-Zahira." *Dawn* in the desert tongue. "From here I will launch a fiery cascade of jihads that will sweep over the Christian lands in the north and consume them. Soon, my love, they will send wagons of gold to slake the blood lust of Islam's mighty scimitar. Allah will smile upon us, my love, and bless us richly. You will see. You will see."

"I can see it already, Husband."

Al-Mansur smiles and returns his hand to her belly.

Mayhem

24 January 977.

His pleas have grown urgent. He must know in his heart that the hour grows late. His voice is hoarse, his frustration edging close to anger as she continues her stubborn refusal to answer him. He relents mid-morning and has a piece of fruit and some water to pacify Rebekah, then kneels once more at her feet and resumes his pleading. His knees are bruised a mottled purple from their time spent on the stone floor.

In the early afternoon they all gather again, the tones somber and subdued. The time for goodbyes has arrived. They whisper to keep from disturbing him. Salma and Imam Abd al-Gafur are dressed in their travel clothes, the cart loaded and ready. They grow silent under the weight of the matter. Rebekah catches her husband's eye and will not release it.

The burden gathers visibly in heaps upon Samuel's shoulders. He reluctantly nods and moves to the boy's side. When he lays a kind hand on him, Zafir starts. The boy refuses to look up but his whispers become more frantic. "Come, my love, you must wake! Come, my love, you—"

"Zafir." He lovingly squeezes the boy's shoulder. "Zafir."

The whispers cease.

"Zafir. Rayhana is not going to wake." It kills him to say it.

Zafir jerks from under his hand, renews his call. "Rayhana, you must come to me, my love ..."

The women begin to cry.

More firmly now, "Zafir. Rayhana is gone. She is gone."

His whispers continue to race through his lips.

Samuel squeezes the boy once more. "Zafir. It is time to let her go. You must let Rayhana go."

Zafir's shoulders begin to shake as the dam breaches, unleashing a torrent of agony. He hisses through his tears, "I will not leave her, Samuel. I cannot. I will not!"

The men are crying now.

"You must. She is gone, Zafir. Salma and Imam Abd al-Gafur are leaving the city. As his spies follow their departure you will slip through the medina and beyond the wall, just as we planned. Remember the plan, Zafir."

Zafir turns and looks at Samuel, his face a wet mess. "She is sitting there in the shadow lands, Samuel, waiting for me. I know she is. She is confused, yes, she is not quite sure how to get back, but she hears me, I can feel it, Samuel. I cannot leave her now. She needs me."

The women are hysterical.

"Zafir, look at me." He lifts the boy's chin and they lock eyes. "Rayhana is not going to wake ... she is not coming back. You must leave Madinat while there is still time. Right now, Zafir, right now."

The boy gulps the air and sobs, "My heart is breaking, Samuel. I cannot live without her."

Samuel's tone softens. "I know, I know. You must say goodbye to Rayhana now. Please."

Zafir squeezes his eyes shut. He takes a deep breath, holds it, then exhales his anguish. He slowly nods and turns back to her.

Rayhana's eyes are open, watching him, her amber starbursts swimming in her tears.

He gasps.

A weak whisper is all she has left. "I believe, Zafir, I believe."

He screams then smothers her, burying her face under his kisses and sobs. Within a heartbeat the room erupts in mayhem and they are on her, too. Electric flashes of radiant blue zap the air like lightning bolts as heaving sobs of thanksgiving shower down upon the girl. Hearts swell then burst, then swell tight again, the joy so dense it pushes the air from the room.

Loja

She is still weak and wobbly but strengthening by the minute. Her throat is parched as desert sand. She inhales two glasses of honey-sweetened pomegranate juice and licks her lips as the scarlet juice dribbles down her chin. Those in the room cackle with delight.

When Abu al-Qasim arrives he makes her sit back down to examine her. Zafir is beside her, beaming like a madman. He cannot keep his hands off her. Abu al-Qasim playfully chides him, "Move back young man, you are distracting my patient." She is all dimples, then giggles. He places one end of his glass funnel to her chest and fits the other to his ear, listening to her heart and lungs. "Take a deep breath, my dear. Good. Another. Good. One more. Excellent." He uses a candle to check the responsiveness of her eyes. Satisfied, he smiles and says, "You need food, but otherwise, good as new." He frowns. "You had us worried, you know. This young man refused to give up on you—kept calling day and night. Must be love." He grins.

The smile runs away from her face. She whispers, "I was lost in a dark woods. I could not tell which way to go. I wandered for days but could find no way out." When she falls silent and looks down he takes her hand to steady her. She looks up, eyes brimming. "I was ready to give up ... and then I heard you." A tear slides down each cheek. "I walked towards your voice, repeating the only words I could remember. 'I believe, Zafir, I believe.'"

"I knew you would find me, Rayhana, I knew. I knew."

The room grows quiet, full eyes set over smiles.

Abu al-Qasim claps his hands to lighten the mood and says, "Zafir, you must watch that leg carefully. Stay off it as much as you can." He hands him a small package. "Clean bandages and ointment. Change it once a day and spread the salve across the wound. There is a special tea I want you to drink each evening. It will help fight any infection."

"Thank you, sir."

Samuel says, "We have little time. The sun will set in two hours, and Salma and Imam Abd al-Gafur must be through the Gate of the Statue by then. You two must get your traveling clothes on. Rebekah will get them. Zaheid, you and Iuliana prepare food and water for a week. They must travel light, so something easy to carry. Levi, see to the cart and make sure all is ready there. Feed and water the donkey. Let us all meet in my study in fifteen minutes."

The room springs to life.

Samuel appraises them both as Rebekah continues to fuss with the girl's unruly hair, struggling to cage it with the long headscarf. "Perfect. A poor apprentice and his pretty young wife. Rayhana, keep that headscarf tight to your face, and eyes down like a good wife." He smiles at Rebekah's frown. Rayhana dimples. "Remember, Zafir, through the medina to the Trader's Gate. Do not rush, do nothing to attract attention. His spies will be watching the cart, not you." He looks the boy over. "What do you say if the guard asks about your destination?"

"We are traveling to see my uncle and his family. He has arranged a cobbler's apprenticeship for me."

"Where?"

"In Sevilla."

"Good. Keep to yourselves. Make for the river and hire passage on a dhow bound for Sevilla. Then cross country for the rest of the way. Do not travel alone—there are bandits between Sevilla and Granada."

Zafir nods patiently. He has heard this a dozen times.

"It should be easy to join up with a caravan. You will pass through Loja just before you reach Granada; about ten leagues out. A lovely little village. Quiet."

Rebekah rolls her eyes. "And a good place to raise a family." They all smile.

"My brother will be expecting you. Ask for Rabbi Joshua."

"I know, Samuel. Just off the central plaza."

Samuel has the look of a worried father sending his child off alone for the first time. "And your gold?"

"Sewn into my pants." Zafir grins. "Stop worrying, Samuel."

Rebekah takes her husband's hand. "They will be fine, Husband, just fine."

"Yes ... they will be fine." His worried look remains painted on his face. He sighs. "Good."

Zaheid steps forward and hands a small package to Rayhana. "To remember us by."

She unwraps the gift, a thin sheet of polished silver. As she holds it close the faint image steps forward. She sees Samuel, Levi and Zaheid, seated for a portrait, all sporting sheepish, fatherly smiles. She laughs. "I will treasure this forever, thank you." She kisses Zaheid on the cheek. "You must promise me to construct a new camera obscura."

Levi grins. "Oh, we will, you can depend upon it."

Samuel walks to his desk, lifts a volume, returns, and hands it to Zafir. "This is for you. To start your own library."

Zafir reads the spine. "Aristophanes." He looks confused. "But this is the original Greek, Samuel."

"I know, I want you to have it. For safe keeping."

Zafir hugs Samuel, then draws a crying Rebekah to them. The others take their cues and the tearful goodbyes commence.

Levi hugs Zafir from behind, rests his head on the boy's shoulder. "You will be missed."

Salma hugs Rayhana, setting the girl's lip aquiver. "Tetta, dear Tetta. You have done so much for us. When will I see you again?"

"We must give it time, Rasha. I know where you will be, and I will get word to you when it is safe to do so." She smiles through her tears. "When I do come I intend to hold some babies, you know!"

They all laugh.

Rebekah moves to her, squeezes her tightly, then releases her and holds her shoulders as she stares into those exquisite eyes. She says a thousand things without speaking a single word; eternal words only mothers can say to their daughters. Rayhana silently mouths, "I love you."

Rebekah taps her chest. "You will always be in my heart, dear girl. Always." She bites her lip to still the tremble. She whispers, "Take care of our boy."

Rayhana nods through her tears.

And then they are gone.

Dozens of prying eyes discreetly track the clop and clank of the donkey-drawn cart as it winds its way southward through the maze of alleys. The sun is just beginning to set, unleashing a gush of rich color, casting long shadows across the faces of the marbled buildings.

Al-Mansur receives word before they have made it past the Royal Gardens. He listens to the report, nods, and resumes his writing.

The elderly couple yanks the sullen beast by a rope as they make for the Gate of the Statue. The three white shrouds lying side by side are impossible to miss. Those they pass assume they are on their way to the burial grounds beyond the walls.

They exit the switchback of the gate challenged only by hostile stares from the Berber guards. There stands golden Zahra. Imam Abd-al-Gafur nods politely and they begin their long journey to Algeciras.

A long arrow shot away, a poor young apprentice limps along, arm in arm with his shrouded wife. They approach the Trader's Gate. They are asked about their destination then are waved through. The young couple never once turns to look back.

Two days later, just after noon salat, a small crowd gathers on the parade grounds: Al-Mansur and his bodyguards, al-Andalusi, and the highest ranking Berber commanders. The grand imam and his staff have made the journey from the city for the occasion. The Berber clerics are there in force, of course, satisfied smiles set firmly in place. Samuel, Rebekah, Levi, and Zaheid stand huddled together, silent and grim-faced.

The giant rectangle of priceless books is ten paces on a side and head high. The funeral pyre is neat and ordered, each codex lovingly placed end to end by their caretakers.

Al-Mansur nods to Suktan. The giant Berber walks the perimeter, sloshing oil upon the pyre. When finished, he turns and lights his torch then retraces his steps, touching the flame to the oil as he goes.

The four begin to sob as the black smoke thickens into a dark cloud boiling into the still air. It will be seen for miles around. Within half a minute the monolith of books is engulfed in flame.

Rebekah is the first to hear their cries, then Samuel, and finally Levi and Zaheid. First, warbled whispers of confusion in a dozen strange tongues, then a flurry of frantic shouts as they begin to sense that danger draws near. Next, shocked, incredulous pleas, barks of anxious commands by leaders trapped deep within the stacks, helpless to move. The pyre is enveloped in a convolution of voices crying out for some explanation of this madness, for mercy.

The four witnesses stand sobbing. The others gathered there cannot hear the cries of the books, or perhaps they simply choose not to. Al-Mansur steps back from the pyre as the radiant heat begins to blister his face. The others follow his lead.

When the first sharp scream comes Rebekah begins to sway and wail. Samuel pulls her to him. The four of them tighten into a knot of lamentation. Levi begins to recite a passage from the Hebrew scriptures. Zaheid whispers helplessly, "Dear God. Dear

God. Dear God ..." Samuel stands silent in his shock, staring into the flames, numb in his grief.

The screams intensify into a cacophony of agony, a chorus of anguish. The cry of the innocents as they are murdered.

Al-Mansur watches, his face unreadable. The grand imam stands tall, arms folded, looking smug and satisfied; the Berber clerics, righteous and justified.

The screams begin to wane as the flames grow taller still until the books relent and give up their bodies to the consuming fire. One by one the cries fade, then are gone.

Without saying a word, Samuel, Zaheid, Levi, and Rebekah turn as a single person, eyes forced to the ground by their grief. They slowly walk through the grand portico and up the ramped street into the Shining City. The scars they endure this day will never fully heal.

Al-Mansur turns and departs, his Berbers in tow.

They sit cuddled together in the twilight at the stern of the dhow. The stars stand ready to strut onto their stage. The captain docked for the night a half-hour earlier and most of the crew are below decks eating.

He has wrapped his cloak around them both and pulled her to him to still her shivers. "Are you warm enough?"

She tightens her arms around him. "I am fine now."

"The captain says we should reach Sevilla by noon."

"Good. I am anxious to get to Loja."

"I know. Soon."

They fall silent.

"You know, Rayhana, we must choose a new name for ourselves."

"Yes. Any ideas?"

"Well, how about al-Abbas? Zafir and Rayhana al-Abbas. What do you think?"

She shakes her head. "No."

"Well then, how about Zafir and Rayhana al-Mugra?"

Her dimples flash. "No."

He sighs playfully. "Then what would you suggest, my love?"

Her face turns serious. "Our name came to me, Zafir. When I was lost in the dark woods, searching for you. It came to me ..."

"Tell me."

She pauses, as if afraid to speak. "The name I heard was ... al-Khatib." *Speaker of the truth.*

489

His tone turns playful. "Mmmm … al-Khatib. Sounds very intelligent."

She laughs.

He beams. "I like it. From this day hence, we will be Zafir and Rayhana al-Khatib. Of Loja. A name for the ages, my love, you will see." They lock eyes. "I will always love you, Rayhana. Always."

"I believe, Zafir, I believe."

They kiss.

First Epilogue – Collage of Agony

14 February 977.

Only three weeks after the escape of Zafir and Rayhana. The grand imam's unchallenged formation of the Council of Truth for the Written Word was the beginning of the end. Samuel does not receive an invitation to join, of course, not that that surprises him; he would not have agreed anyway. In fact, not a single one of Samuel's librarians or any recognized scholar is invited to join— only clerics.

But, predictably, that is only the beginning. Soon the death threats begin to arrive. The first magically appears on his desk in the Rare Books Library one morning. "Leave the city, Jew, or die." Later that day, a note is pinned to their villa door with a dagger. "I will enjoy flaying you in front of your family. Leave the city, Jew, or die."

The origin of the threats is hardly a mystery. So much for promises. He and Rebekah talk deep into the night. They decide that it would be foolish to wait for a third note. They know full well what the man is capable of. Samuel resigns his position as vizier of books the following morning. Al-Mansur offers him a curt nod, no more, not a single word of thanks for his twenty-six years of service. Samuel has served three caliphs. Three.

He and Rebekah gather the girls and make haste for Granada, Levi in tow. What they cannot carry is left behind. Samuel has had his eye on the place for some time now. Granada has not yet grown large, though it has a sizable Jewish quarter. Still provincial, really, in comparison with Córdoba. Its future is said to be bright, and Granada's *emir* is an educated man, raised in Córdoba in fact, and a great lover of books. He has begun to assemble a respectable collection of his own. Meager, it is true, but growing and in need of a librarian and a well-connected acquisition agent. They leave no forwarding address.

Zaheid holds out for another year. It is the Council of Truth for the Written Word's burning of the science treatises that shocks him to action. Within a week he and Iuliana are in Sevilla, which is quickly becoming known as the new center for enlightened scientific thought. He continues their experiments with the camera obscura. Of course he does.

Eventually, in 1013, eleven years after Zaheid passes, his notebooks make their way into the hands of a delighted Ali al-Hazen ibn al-Haytham, known as Alhazen to the rest of Europe. Zaheid's notes form the basis for an important chapter on the camera obscura in Ibn al-Haythem's seminal treatise, *Kitab al-Manazir—Book of Optics*.

22 May 977.

An interested crowd has already gathered outside the north entrance arch of the Great Mosque. They move close, but not too close. The courtier spreads paste on the back of the large sheet of paper, holds it up to level it with the others, then carefully presses it to the wooden panel reserved for royal decrees. He steps back to survey his work. Satisfied, he lifts his satchel and moves on to the west side of the Great Mosque. He has three dozen more stops to make this afternoon.

The crowd continues to gather strength, silent and expectant. They hold back until the man departs then exchange wary glances and tentatively edge closer, halting two paces away from the board, still too far to clearly read the precise Arabic calligraphy. This will be the third royal decree issued this month.

One brave soul takes matters into his own hands, boldly approaches the panel, and begins to proclaim its contents so that all may hear.

"By Royal Decree of His Royal Highness, Caliph Hisham II, son of al-Hakam II and grandson of Abd al-Rahman III, the great al-Nasir. Third Caliph of al-Andalus, Sultan of Córdoba, Lord of glorious Madinat al-Zahra, elder of the Umayyad clan, champion of truth, defender of the faith. May Allah smile upon his reign."

A buzz of whispers weaves through the crowd. This sounds ominous.

He clears his throat and continues. "Citizens of Córdoba. Hear and obey Caliph Hisham's Royal Decree, issued on the 22nd day of May, 977.

1) From this day hence, all Muslims must attend Friday worship services.
2) From this day hence, no bells shall be rung to announce Christian Mass.
3) From this day hence, Jews of the city must wear the yellow badge.

4) From this day hence, Christians and Jews will not use public hammams designated for Muslims.
5) From this day hence, wine shall not be served in public places.
6) From this day hence, infidel books will not be bought or sold without the written approval of the Grand Imam's Council of Truth for the Written Word.

Citizens of Córdoba. Hear and obey Caliph Hisham's Royal Decree, issued on the 22nd day of May, 977. May Allah bless his reign."

Stunned silence settles upon the crowd.

14 November 977, just outside the town of Atienza in the Upper Marches.

The man coolly appraises his prisoner. "You were a fool to solicit help from White Hands." He shakes his head. "A Córdoban knight begging an infidel for help. What has the world come to?"

General Ghalib stands silently, shoulders bowed, hands tied behind his back. Suktan and Tahir flank the man. Al-Andalusi, bloodied but victorious, stands with al-Mansur. Ghalib has been beaten about the face. He is already an ancient fossil, a discarded relic, clearly spent from these futile two months of civil war against al-Mansur and his Berber army.

His troops fought well, but in the end, outmanned and out-supplied, his ragtag army has been vanquished at Atienza. At the eleventh hour, he traveled to Burgos to solicit an alliance with White Hands. The Christian scoffed and sent him away. It seems he learned his lesson about challenging al-Mansur.

Atienza was his final, desperate stand. And now it is done.

"You, sir, shall be beheaded at sunrise tomorrow. Think on that through the night."

That gruff voice, still defiant in defeat, retorts, "You think I fear death, Muhammad. I do not. I have lived a good life, a life of honor in the service of three caliphs. My beloved Córdoba has much to fear from you. It was for her that I fought you."

Al-Mansur studies his valiant opponent. "You were always a brave one, Ghalib, if misguided." He considers. "Yours will be a clean death." He exchanges a quick glance with al-Andalusi, who nods. The Berber has grown to respect his enemy.

"What is to become of my daughter?"

"Ah yes, the lovely al-Asma. Beautiful girl."

"She is a virgin. Take her as your second wife, Muhammad. She will bear you many sons."

Al-Mansur grimaces. "She is saqaliba, Ghalib. Like you." He spits. "I will be the first to pluck your daughter's sweet fruit, of that you can depend. And then I will pass her on to my officers to enjoy. They deserve to share in the finer spoils of war."

Ghalib's tired, wrinkled eyes begin to leak.

"When they are finished with her, she will join Durri the Small's daughter in the corsair brothel. In Tunis. They say the corsairs have a fine eye for Andalusi women. I am confident she will garner much favor there." He smiles.

Ghalib lowers his gaze as his shoulders begin to shake.

Al-Mansur flicks his wrist. "Remove this piece of rotten flesh from my sight."

3 February 978.

The Barbary corsairs surprise the dromon within sight of Tarragona's city walls. The sleek, flagless vessel slips from the fog bank hugging the coastal inlet and pulls alongside within an hour. They salivate at the sight of the standard: double-headed black eagle set upon gold, the colors of the Holy Roman Empire. This is a bold move to be sure, but nothing new. The sentries on the city walls watch the hunt unfold. When the outcome is certain, then simply shrug and curse the corsairs, return to their posts. What's another vessel lost?

The pirates are disappointed to discover their quarry to be a diplomatic vessel with a paltry cargo. Ambassador Strobel is indignant, of course, at the interruption, and spews his venom. This was to be his triumphant return to Córdoba, after all, bearing lucrative new treaties from Emperor Otto II for expanded trade. He berates the corsairs for interfering with his important mission. He is answered by amused grins.

They slit his secretary's throat to make their point, stopping Strobel's rant mid-sentence, then set about their business of shackling the crew. By the time they get to Strobel he realizes his peril and vigorously demands ransom, waving his safe passage document frantically in front of them. Alas, these corsairs speak only Arabic, and they certainly do not read Latin.

Their catch is destined for the infamous salt mines of Bilma, five hundred leagues to the south. The mines are said to chew through a hundred slaves a month. Those who survive the arduous trip will fetch a handsome price.

Remarkably, Strobel survives the journey and lasts for nearly two months in the mines before succumbing to the elements. Just past noon on a Sunday, he is tossed into a mass grave with a dozen others, his scorched, blistered skin soon to be devoured by the demons of the dark.

4 May 987.

Time passes. Two Greek gods once again inhabit the royal harem. Hisham's wing. Tanned and sculpted Persian twins only a few years his senior, purchased at great expense. The twins appeared miraculously, late one night, years back, just as young Hisham was entering the fevered tortures of puberty. Sent by an anonymous benefactor to instruct the young man on the finer points of lovemaking. Never once has a woman joined them.

He remains a voracious reader with a strong preference for geography and history, even Greek literature and philosophy and science. Codices are selected from the Rare Books Library and brought to him by the armful to devour. Certainly no one can argue with the young caliph's devotion to his faith. He can recite the entire Quran from memory, has done so many times. He knows the Hadith backwards and forwards. He is a student of chess, and is quite capable, in fact, though never the equal of his father. He plays daily with the twins. Cards, too. Hisham is not unhappy.

Al-Mansur visits the caliph once per month, to inform him of events, reassure him of his undying fealty, and, of course, to present documents for his signature. There is a real fondness between the two, you can tell.

And what of Subh? Well, she has not laid eyes upon a man since his last visit ten years back; not even her son. In desperation she made subtle advances on her ladies-in-waiting, but Berbers have no taste for such things. She does what one does in such dire straits. He taught her well, after all. Oddly enough, or perhaps not oddly at all, she still conjures his face and pants his name.

She drinks too much wine and has developed a real fondness for food. Not surprisingly, her voluptuous curves have broadened, and her lovely breasts have begun to sag just a bit, though no man in his right mind would dispute that she is still a desirable woman. Just this year her golden tresses have begun to require ointments and special washes to forestall the slow but inevitable invasion of gray.

She reads, but it does not satisfy her. For whole hours at a stretch she stares into space and daydreams of what could have been, what should have been. Not an especially healthy diversion. Early on she tried to hang herself but was discovered just a moment too soon. Not a rope or a piece of cloth or a sharp implement remains in her suite. It is an odd life she leads in this prison of hers; a sad and lonely life for a woman of her skills.

The Shining City has become a virtual ghost land over the past decade under Az-Zahira's steady rise. It stands now as an exquisitely carved empty shell, a shadow of its former glory. The Rare Books Library remains the Shining City's most valuable asset, and only because the caliph insisted it stay when al-Mansur tried to move it to the city for safe keeping. Madinat's primary role has been relegated to serving and protecting the caliph, though it seems remarkable that a garrison of a thousand Berber troops is required to secure one young man, his mother, and his precious books.

Az-Zahira sparkles like a finely cut jewel, much smaller than Madinat, but majestic and glorious nonetheless. The royal mint spits out gold dinars by the wagon load, day and night. Stamped with the caliph's image, of course, as mandated by law. The coffers of the royal treasury swell with the booty surrendered by Christian cities under siege in the Upper Marches. There is even preemptive tribute laid at the feet of al-Mansur as he relentlessly attacks and subdues under the banner of jihad. He has not lost a single encounter against Christian forces, not one. The paying of tribute to Moors sticks in the throats of the Christian kings, and news of it races across Europe, predictably reaching the ears of the emperor and the pope, where it begins to fester like an annoying splinter.

There was gold aplenty to finish al-Mansur's promised expansion of the Great Mosque. Alas, the grand imam passed before it was completed, but his chosen successor is cut from an identical mold. To say he approves of the addition would be a crass understatement. The massive structure is the largest and finest mosque in the world, universally envied by all who have ever beheld its magical forest of red ochre and white arches.

Not surprisingly, the merchant families have prospered, wildly in fact, under Caliph Hisham's rule. They learned long ago that the only path to the caliph's ear passes through al-Mansur. For a hefty price, of course.

The Berbers? Well, the outcome is obvious, is it not? They continue to stream into Iberia by the thousands, by the tens of thousands. It seems the caliph has issued a royal decree inviting all who make the journey from the Maghreb to become full-fledged citizens of al-Andalus. The Banu Birzal, though powerful still, has become only one of hundreds of such clans. Berber towns begin to spring up and prosper, and Berber knights make up larger and larger fractions of the Andalusi armies. The color black and the donning of turbans become far more common than fashion-conscious Córdobans could ever have imagined.

9 June 997.

Twenty years the man has been at it, these jihads against the Christian north, but all agree that this is the pinnacle, his most daring raid, his signature victory. Al-Mansur makes a surprise dash into the heart of Galicia in the extreme northwest to capture Santiago de Campostela, the famed burial site of Saint James the Apostle. One of the holiest shrines in Christendom, the apostle's remains nestle within the cathedral there. Santiago de Campostela is the culmination of Christian Europe's most famous pilgrimage, *El Camino de Santiago*—the Way of St. James—a journey made by thousands of believers each year since the early ninth century.

Al-Mansur's bold move is a complete surprise. He descends upon the city like a lightning bolt, dispatches its garrison with ease, then burns much of the city. While he spares the cathedral and instructs his officers not to desecrate the shrine, he decides on a whim to steal the cathedral's massive bronze bells as a token of his victory. He forces a hundred of the monks and priests to carry his booty back to Córdoba, where the Santiago bells are installed in the Great Mosque as giant lanterns to stand beside the mihrab.

Europe shakes its fists, outraged. Al-Mansur's shocking action fans the flames of Christian *reconquista* of Moorish al-Andalus. Santiago's bells will remain in the Great Mosque until 29 June 1236, when King Fernando III of Castile lays siege and captures Córdoba, ending Muslim rule there forever. The bells are promptly returned to the cathedral of Santiago de Campostela, where they remain to this day.

Sunset, **24 January 1009.**

Forty-two years to the day that Zafir and Rayhana left the Shining City. Al-Mansur has been dead for seven years, his son Sanchuelo now in command. The son is weak and cruel. He pilfers the royal treasury to suit his every whim. Despised by his people, he is quickly losing his grip on al-Andalus. Such a poor steward of his father's hard-earned legacy.

Córdoba's City Watch is the first to see the orange glow to the west, and within minutes the bells of the city are sounding the alarm. Windows are shuttered and families gather and huddle into their homes. Armories are opened to dispense swords and pikes to all who can wield them. Fires are lit under pots of pitch and oil.

The city's elite, who are already tucked into their fine almunyas beyond the walls for a relaxing weekend, stream frantically back into the city with only their clothes on their backs. The gates of the city swing shut and are bolted, and the city walls, standing massive and toothed, sprout thousands of helmeted heads as Córdoba braces for attack.

Ironically, these invaders are not Christians—they are Muslims. It seems the Berbers have finally turned on their masters.

The dreaded attack does not come. Instead, the marauders, a renegade Berber army twelve thousand strong, descend like locusts upon Madinat al-Zahra. The garrison is overwhelmed within an hour.

Unlike during the attack of 976, the night of the deadly fog, this time the Shining City is not just raped. No, she is crushed to the earth with a single mighty blow, taken forcefully while she screams, then pulled limb from limb and razed to the ground. These Berbers are here to send a message to all of al-Andalus, one that cannot possibly be misinterpreted: "We are ready to claim our due."

Miraculously, Caliph Hisham, now approaching old age, escapes to the city with the aid of the twins.

The Córdobans watch in horror as hundred-foot orange tongues lick at the night sky. The fires burn bright for two full days. Within a week, not a single structure in Madinat al-Zahra stands. Everything of value is pillaged. What cannot be easily carried is shattered or defaced where it sits. Not a single block of marble is left resting upon another. It is a decimation to rival what the Romans did to Jerusalem nearly a thousand years prior.

And what of the Rare Books Library so lovingly assembled by Caliph al-Hakam II? Sadly, it does not survive the massacre. After all, the Berbers have no use for books; most can barely read. The gut-wrenching screams of the codex cinders begin to mercifully trail off by the genie's hour. Come daybreak, breathy, warbled whispers of Greek and Latin still drift with the ashes in the blue, smoky haze that settles thick upon the Guadalquivir valley like the Angel of Death marking the first Passover. A holocaust of enlightenment, the death of culture and learning.

Second Epilogue – Collage of Joy

Algeciras, **11 November 977.**

It has become their habit, something they both look forward to. He greets her each morning at the mosque with a kiss of each cheek, and after leading sunrise prayers, he changes and follows her back to her home, where she prepares breakfast for the two of them. They chatter away, about everything, about nothing. He stops her an hour later when he suddenly remembers that his students are waiting for him at the madrasa. He gathers his things in a fluster, thanks her profusely, then bids her farewell.

She watches him go but does not move, a faint smile clinging to her lips. A full minute passes as she stares into space, then she rises and begins to clear the table.

This morning is no different from the others. He is seated at the table telling her about a troublesome student. She delivers their plates and sits, nods as he goes on and on, her smile set bright upon her face. He suddenly stops, realizing he has been doing all the talking.

"Forgive me. I must be boring you."

Her smile widens. "Not at all."

They fall into a comfortable silence.

She reaches for her tea, but as she does his hand stretches forward to intercept hers. She does not resist. His other hand slides forward. She meets him halfway.

They sit frozen for a moment, both sets of eyes resting on the surprise of their joined hands as if responding to some unseen cue; they raise their gazes in unison.

"Salma ..."

She waits for more, but when it does not come, she whispers a breathless, "Yes?"

Their eyes have not left each other. He swallows hard. He whispers, "Salma. Ana behibek." *I love you.*

Her eyes fill. "Ana behibak."

Granada, in the Jewish Quarter, **24 January 980.**

Rebekah sits on a stool in their bedroom brushing her luxurious dark tresses by candlelight, her left hand lifting her thick hair off the back of her neck while she methodically works it with the brush.

Samuel silently eases in behind her, leans down and gently breathes into her ear as he reaches around her and cups her full breast.

She smiles. "Yes, Husband?"

It is a drama that has played out exactly the same way for many years now. Satisfying and rich. Their lines never change, not one letter of one word. They would have it no other way.

He ignores her and slides her nightgown down off her shoulder to kiss the nape of her neck. She shivers but remains silent.

He whispers, "Shabbat is a time for rejoicing, Rebekah, for enjoying the gifts we have been given."

She tilts her head, amused, then coyly smiles. "And what gifts would those be, Husband?"

"Why, the gifts of your beautiful body, Wife." He works his way across her bare shoulder, her eyelids drooping a bit more with each press of his lips.

A half-hour later, they luxuriate in silence. She is curled tightly to him as he traces the lovely curve of her hip.

"Today is the day, Husband."

He cranes his head to catch her eyes. "And what day would that be, Wife?"

"Three years to the day that Zafir and Rayhana left us. I miss them, Samuel."

"Yes."

"Surely it is safe now."

He sighs. "With al-Mansur, I doubt we will ever be able to say that with much confidence. I have heard rumors of his spies poking around in Granada. It certainly would not surprise me."

She repeats, "I miss them, Samuel."

The silence stretches.

"Did I tell you?"

She cranes now to catch his eyes. "Tell me what?"

"I received a letter from Joshua."

She grins. "Oh? And what did Loja's famous rabbi have to say?"

"Quite interesting, really. It seems he has received a gift from some anonymous benefactor. A book, actually. Ancient Greek, he thinks, but he is not sure. Poor man only reads Hebrew and Arabic, you see." He scoffs. "Can you imagine?"

Her grin widens.

"He wondered if I might come and examine it, tell him whether it was valuable. He said there was no rush. When the weather warms."

Her grin has been traded for a bright smile. "I see. And what did you tell him?"

"Well, I told him I would be happy to visit, of course, it is the least I can do. Just for a few days. I do not see why you should not join me."

She snuggles tighter to him. "I love you, Husband."

"And I love you, Wife."

———— 🔳 ————

Loja, **11 December 982**.

Their home is modest but comfortable: what one would expect of a book binder, but nothing more; certainly nothing that would attract undue attention. His workshop is attached to the back of their house. He has planted orange trees everywhere there is empty space, and they are almost shoulder high now, wonderfully aromatic in the spring.

The young book binder and his beautiful wife, the al-Khatibs, have fit in well in Loja. They have made friends, joined the community. It is always surprising when people learn that he reads ancient Greek, a skill he says he learned in Sevilla as a young boy but has little use for now.

Their one piece of fine furniture is a massive oak bookcase. They keep it in their bedchamber to avoid attracting attention. On the top row rests a beautifully bound codex containing the plays of Aristophanes. Right beside it is the *Ambrosian Iliad*. Their friends have no clue as to the real value of these volumes.

Almost three years back they began to receive codices to add to their collection. Priceless stuff. Always translated Greek; plays and poetry mostly, some philosophy, some science and medicine. Each book arrives on the first day of each month in an unmarked container. Some anonymous benefactor. They exchange knowing smiles as they unpack the box together. Their eyes well up as they reverently lift the codex and whisper its title. They spend the month taking turns reading the book aloud until late in the evenings. At the end of the month they shelve it in their cherished library, already excited by the surprise of what will arrive next.

Late one evening, by the light of a single taper, these two lie wound tight together, the flush of lovemaking still hot upon their cheeks, the faint hue of light blue lingering in the air. He tilts his head and whispers, "Shhh ... listen."

"What?"

"Listen."

They hear the breathy, warbled whisper of ancient Greek wafting from the bookcase. They exchange satisfied smiles.

"Samuel always said that books were alive."

Rayhana is all dimples. "Yes. They are alive. They are."

She reclines by the open fire on a plain divan. She cradles her infant son, who suckle-sighs contentedly at her breast. Her eyes are fixed on the crimson coals as she softly strokes his wispy hair. As compelling a portrait of feminine beauty and grace as ever conceived.

Five years of the kind of love these two have known have honed her beauty into something truly extraordinary, something the greatest poets of antiquity would swoon to write about.

"And how is little Samuel today, my love?"

Her eyes leave the fire to follow his approach. He wears his work apron. "He clings to me with a purpose, that much is sure." She dimples. "Like his baba."

Zafir laughs, then kisses her. His eyes circle the room. "Where is she?"

Rayhana smiles. "In her room playing."

He kneels and opens his arms. "Rayya! Come, my love, your Baba needs a hug. Come to me, Rayya!"

They both watch the door crack then fly wide. She races into her father's embrace. He smothers her with kisses as she giggles, then he lifts her high in the air, unleashing delighted squeals. She is a spitting image of her Mama, all but the eyes. And those curls! Already down to her shoulders, unruly as her mama's. Dark, but with a lovely hint of burnt umber, pushing the dense jumble towards chestnut. He stares into her massive liquid emeralds. "And how is my best girl today?"

He is answered by deep dimples. "Read me a book, Baba! Read me a book!"

Zafir and Rayhana both laugh loudly. He sets her down. "Go get it, my love." She races back to her room.

Zafir turns and locks eyes with his wife. "I will always love you, Rayhana. Always."

"I believe, Zafir, I believe."

They kiss.

The End

Glossary

Adhan - The Muslim call to prayer.

al-Andalus - The lands of Iberia under Muslim rule.

Alcazar - The royal palace.

Alhamdulillah - Arabic for 'Praise to Allah.'

Almunya - The lavish second homes of Cordoba's elite.

Al-Jannah - The Islamic walled garden, an image of paradise having its origins in the Quran.

Arabesque - A form of Islamic artistic decoration based on rhythmic patterns of scrolling and interlacing foliage and tendrils. Often used as interior wall ornamentation in Islamic palaces.

Arpent - A unit of land area roughly equal to an acre.

Ashlar - A large block of limestone cut into a rectangular parallelepiped and used in construction.

Baba - Arabic for 'daddy.'

Battle of Simancas - The decisive 939 C.E. clash between the Christian armies of León, Castile, and Pamplona with the Umayyad army of Caliph Abd al-Rahman III of Córdoba. The Christians routed the Moors and won control of the Duero territory of northern Iberia, the Upper Marches.

Bayah - An oath of allegiance.

Bayt - A Bedouin family tent.

Bishop - An ordained member of the Christian clergy.

Bitumen - A flammable black viscous mixture of hydrocarbons occurring naturally and used as a weapon of war in the medieval period.

Breviary - A breviary is a book of Christian liturgical rites containing the public (canonical) prayers, hymns, the Psalms, readings, and notations for everyday use.

Burqa - An enveloping, face-veiled outer garment (often black) worn by women in certain Islamic traditions to obscure their faces and bodies when in public.

Calendar of Cordoba - The book written by the famous mozarab Reccimund (Rabi ibn Zyad) in the late tenth century. The book contains elements of astronomy and weather, health advice, agricultural calendars, and an interesting picture of normal life in Córdoba during this period.

Caliph - The Islamic supreme leader.

Canon - A part of the medieval Christian Mass.

Chador - An open cloak consisting of a body-length circle of fabric (often black) worn by women in certain Islamic traditions.

Codex - A book made up of a number of sheets of paper containing hand-written text that are then stacked and bound.

Dhimmi - Literally, "protected." The so-called "People of the Book" of al-Andalus are Christians and Jews, each of whom share the same biblical roots as Muslims.

Dhuhr - Noon Muslim prayer.

Dhow - An Arabic sailing vessel.

Dinar - A minted gold coin, by law bearing the face and name of the caliph.

Dirham - A minted silver coin, often cut into square chits for exchange.

Divine Office - The recitation of certain Christian prayers at fixed hours (Liturgy of the Hours).

Dromon - An oared galley.

Eid al-Fitr - The Sugar Feast, a Muslim festival marking the end of Ramadan.

El Camino de Santiago - The Way of St. James, a pilgrimage from the Pyrenees Mountains to Galicia (500 miles) walked by devout Christians since the ninth century. It remains very popular to this day.

Emir - A Muslim title of high office, often the ruler of a sovereign principality.

Genie - Jinn (or genies) are spiritual creatures. They are mentioned in the Quran and inhabit the unseen world beyond the bounds of the universe visible to humans.

Ghazal - An Arabic love poem.

Ghusl - Ritual washing in Islam before formal prayer.

Hadith - Literally, "tradition" in Islam. The collection of the deeds and sayings of the Prophet Muhammad.

Hajj - The pilgrimage to Mecca obligatory to Muslims.

Hammam - Muslim baths.

Hijab - A veil worn by females in certain Islamic traditions to cover their head and chest.

Imam - In Islam, imams lead worship services at the mosque, serve as community leaders, and offer spiritual guidance.

Inshallah - Arabic for 'Allah willing.'

Ird - The Bedouin honor code for females.

Jiddo - Arabic for 'grandpa.'

Jihad - Literally, to "struggle." There are two commonly accepted meanings of jihad: 1) an inner spiritual struggle and 2) an outer physical struggle (with the aim of armed conquest) against those who do not believe in the Abrahamic God (Allah).

Jizya - The tax on dhimmi.

Katib al-Tasrif - Literally, *The Method of Medicine*. An Arabic encyclopedia on medicine and surgery written by Abu al-Qasim (Abulcasis). *Katib al-Tasrif* was highly influential in the development of European medical practices.

Khutbah - A speech given by the presiding imam before a wedding ceremony.

League - About three miles in ancient times. Traditionally, a league is the distance a person can comfortably walk in one hour. By contrast, the Roman league was about one and a half miles.

Madrasa - In Islam, any type of educational institution, religious or secular.

Medina - Literally, "town" in Arabic. A dense array of shops, stalls and living quarters. Alleys in the medina are typically walled and maze-like.

Maghreb - Western North Africa. Literally, "Berber world," known to Europeans as "Barbary" (as in pirates of the Barbary coast). The traditional definition includes the Atlas Mountains and the coastal plains of modern Morocco, Algeria, Tunisia, and Libya.

Maghrib - Sunset prayer in Islam.

Mahr - The wedding gift presented to the bride by the husband.

Mihrab - A semicircular niche in the wall of a mosque that indicates the qibla, the direction to Mecca.

Minaret - A distinctive architectural feature of all mosques. Generally constructed as a tall spire to be used by the muezzin to announce the call to prayer.

Mozarab - A Christian living under Islamic rule in al-Andalus.

Muezzin - The man who announces the call to prayer.

Mullah - A Muslim man or woman educated in Islamic theology and sacred law.

Nikah - An Islamic marriage contract.

Preface - A part of the medieval Christian Mass immediately after the Offertory.

Prime - A fixed time of prayer in the Divine Office in the first hour of daylight.

Qadi - A judge appointed by a sultan or caliph. A qadi possesses the legal power to rule on all cases involving Sharia Law.

Qibla - The direction towards Mecca that a Muslim prays during salat.

Quran - Literally, "the recitation" (of God to the Prophet Muhammad). The Quran is the sacred text of Islam, which Muslims believe to be the revelation of God.

Rakah - A completed sequence of Muslim prayers.

Ramadan - The ninth month of the Islamic calendar. Ramadan's annual observance is one of the Five Pillars of Islam and requires Muslims to fast from dawn until sunset.

Red ochre - A deep, burnt red made from ground hematite (anhydrous iron oxide).

Reconquista - Reconquest of Moorish Spain by the Christians.

Salat - Ritual Muslim prayer, conducted five times each day: pre-dawn, noon, afternoon, sunset, and night.

Salatul Fajr - Dawn prayer on the day of Eid al-Fitr, marking the end of Ramadan.

Sanctus - Literally, "Holy." A part of the Christian Mass leading up to Communion.

Scimitar - A sabre with a curved blade.

Shabbat - The Jewish day of rest. Shabbat (*Sabbath*) is observed from a few minutes before sunset on Friday evening until the appearance of three stars in the sky on Saturday evening. Shabbat observance entails refraining from work of any kind.

Shalandi - A bireme galley ship configured as a horse transport.

Sharaf - The Bedouin honor code for males.

Sharia Law - The moral code and religious law of Islam. Sharia Law deals with many topics addressed by secular law, including: crime, politics, economics, and personal matters such as sexual intercourse, hygiene, diet, prayer, everyday etiquette, and fasting. Though interpretation of Sharia Law varies between cultures, in its strictest definition it is considered the infallible law of God.

Saqaliba - Eastern Europeans, usually Slavic in origin, captured or kidnapped, then sold into slavery to Muslim kingdoms. It was customary in al-Andalus to free slaves after a defined period of service.

Tetta - Arabic for 'grandma.'

Umayyad - The Umayyad caliphate was the second of the four major Islamic caliphates established after the death of Muhammad. The Umayyad regime was founded by Muawiya ibn Abi Sufyan, governor of Syria, with Damascus as its capital. The Umayyads were massacred by the Abbasids in 750 C.E. The lone survivor, young Abd al-Rahman, fled to Córdoba with a dream to resurrect the glory of the Umayyad caliphate.

Vicar General - The principal deputy of the Christian bishop of a diocese.

Vizier - A high-ranking advisor to the caliph.

Wali - The guardian of a Muslim female who legally represents the bride at her wedding.

Walimah - A Muslim wedding feast.

Yarmulke - A kippah, or yarmulke, is a hemispherical shaped cap, usually made of cloth, worn to fulfill the requirement held by orthodox Jews that a man's head be covered at all times.

Zakat al-Fitr - Alms given to the poor at the end of the Islamic holy month of Ramadan.

Reflections

Remarkable as it may strike you, *Shadows* is a true story. At least in its broad brush strokes. Al-Mansur's epic rise to power is archetypal in its treachery, and his cunning leverage of the Berber tribes of the Maghreb to facilitate his conquest of impregnable Madinat al-Zahra and Córdoba is legendary.

Al-Mansur almost single-handedly orchestrated the end of the largely beneficent Umayyad dynasty in al-Andalus while it was still in its youth. Alas, his weak and ineffective progeny end up empowering the Berbers to flex their muscles, setting the stage not only for the destruction of Madinat al-Zahra in 1009 C.E., but also the later Almoravid (1086 C.E.) and Almohad (1146 C.E.) Berber incursions of al-Andalus. Rich irony. These new Berbers, increasingly fanatical and extreme in their practice of Islam, will continually stoke the fires of *reconquista* with their own brand of jihad, setting the stage for Isabel and Fernando, the Catholic Monarchs, to finally capture the Alhambra in 1492 C.E., ending the glory of al-Andalus forever.

Subtract al-Mansur's Berbers, and the story of al-Andalus may well have ended differently. Who knows, *convivencia*, that remarkable period of coexistence between the three Abrahamic faith traditions, might have survived. We will never know, of course. But how different our world might be if it had!

There is no question that the zenith of convivencia in tenth century Córdoba was something quite extraordinary. Certainly it was unique in the ancient world. And even a casual glance at our planet today paints a stark contrast: just consider modern Egypt, Syria, Lebanon, Sudan, Israel ... the list is almost endless. It seems as if any country with a religiously diverse population is in strife of one form or another. Even in democracies like the United States—a largely Christian nation, where one might claim that Muslims and Jews are welcomed and embraced—an event like 9/11 quickly brings those ugly tensions to the forefront. To my mind, tenth century Córdoba offers a lesson for our modern world that continues to wrestle so mightily in finding peace among the three Abrahamic faith traditions.

To be clear, Córdoba's convivencia was not perfect. Christians and Jews, as dhimmi, paid the jizya tax. Depending on the time period examined, there were flare-ups, discrimination, and radicalized Christians (mozarabs) rose up in defiance of the Muslim rulers on several occasions. But at least for a couple of centuries it worked quite well. Harmony was the rule of the day. At its best, the social mobility of Jews and Christians within Muslim society was striking. As depicted in *Shadows*, both Jews and Christians rose to the highest echelons of society, all the way to the caliph's Vizier Council. That fact alone is instructive.

I find it useful to think of tenth century Córdoba not so much as a Muslim society that permitted the presence of Jews and Christians, but rather as a single, diverse population that happened to speak three languages and practice three religions.

When presenting on *Emeralds* I have often been asked what was unique about al-Andalus that enabled convivencia to "work"? And is it possible for our twenty-first-century world to follow that lead and resurrect it? Excellent questions. To my mind, three things made convivencia possible: 1) There was a religious basis for convivencia (in the Quran); 2) The leadership (the Syrian Umayyads) had the vision and the power to insist that this Quranic mandate become the law of the land; and 3) The incredible fruits of convivencia became readily apparent to the whole of Córdoban society, lowest to highest. The benefits of religious and cultural tolerance were self-evident to all, and society as a whole was seen to be better off with a diverse population at its core. There is a message for us in this.

Is it possible to regenerate convivencia? Certainly, point 1, above, remains unchanged, and I think the idea would find a kind ear among many contemporary Christian and Jewish leaders (Pope Francis comes to mind). Point 2 is more problematic, to be sure, since the Umayyads were essentially benign dictators, but leadership can and should be exercised in bold and creative ways. To my mind, Point 3 might be the easiest, and would follow naturally if convivencia were the de facto law of the land.

The linchpin in all of this, it seems to me, lies with education and conversation, the breaking down of the barriers of ignorance among our three faith traditions. How little we Christians know of Muslims, and vice versa. Yes, education is the key. And talking. That was true then; it remains true today. It is my own view that we must begin with the young people. They alone possess the open minds and the willingness, even daring, to imagine a different world, a world blessed with tolerance and peace. A world of convivencia.

Salaam
Shalom
Peace

Language and Dates

To make the book more accessible to readers, diacritics and other accent marks, which abound in both Arabic and Hebrew, have for the most part been omitted. For instance, I use *Quran* instead of *Qur'ān*.

I have chosen to have my Muslim characters use the Arabic word *Allah* for 'God' when they speak, but it is important to emphasize that a Muslim uses 'Allah' in a manner identical to how a Christian uses 'God' and a Jew uses 'Yahweh' (YHWH). That is, the words God, Allah, and Yahweh are simply the English, Arabic, and Hebrew words for the Supreme Being shared by the three Abrahamic faith traditions.

Muslim and Jewish words with no conventional English equivalents, as well as Christian or Jewish words that may be unfamiliar to readers, appear in italics the first time they are used, but not afterwards. They are included with explanation in the glossary.

There are times when my characters are speaking Arabic and Hebrew that I use a Romanized phonetic pronunciation to lend dramatic effect. Such phonetic choices are obviously subject to interpretational latitude. It goes without saying that the languages spoken in tenth century al-Andalus clearly had some significant differences from their modern counterparts, and no attempt has been made to account for these nuances.

Some preferred pronunciations of names, places, and characters:

Abu al-Qasim (ah-boo ahl-kuh-seem)
Al-Andalus (ahl-on-duh-luze)
Al-Jannah (ahl-yanna)
Almunya (ahl-moon-yuh)
Banu Birzal (bah-noo-beer-zahl)
Caliph al-Hakam (kay-leef ahl-hah-kamm)
Córdoba (CORE-doe-bah) – accent on the first syllable
Eid al-Fitr (eh-eed ahl-fit-urr)
Faiq (fake)
Ghalib (gah-leeb)
Gormaz (gore-maz)
Hajar an-Nasar (haj-are ahn-nuh-sarr)

Hisham (hish–amm)
Ibn Abi Amir (ib-en ah-bee ah-meer)
Jafar (yah-farr)
Jawdhar (yawed-harr)
Levi (lev-ee)
Madinat al-Zahra (mah-dee-not ahl-zah-rah)
Rayhana (ray-ah-nah)
Saqaliba (sah-qua-lee-bah)
Subh (soobh)
Umayyad (oou-mah-yadd)
Zafir (zah-fear)
Zaheid (zah-heed)

For convenience, the dates used in the book conform to a Western (Gregorian) calendar (i.e., 2014 C.E., for "the year 2014 of the Common Era," and equivalent to, 2014 A.D., where A.D. stands for *Anno Domini*, "the year of our Lord").

Clearly, however, the Islamic calendar would have been used in medieval al-Andalus. Unlike the Gregorian calendar, the Islamic calendar (Hijri) is based on lunar cycles, and was first introduced in 638 C.E. by the Caliph Umar ibn al-Khattab (592-644 C.E.) using the Hijra as a reference point. The Hijra marks the journey of the Prophet Muhammad and his followers from Mecca to Medina, a journey that began on 21 June 622 C.E.

The actual starting date for the Hijri was chosen to be the first day of the first month (1 Muharram) of the year of the Hijra (622 C.E.). The Hijri date is abbreviated A.H. in Western languages, from the Latinized *Anno Hegirae,* "the year of the Hijra."

All important dates throughout the year within the Muslim world, in the tenth century as well as today, are tied to the lunar cycles of the Hijri, and they "move" each year with respect to the (solar-pegged) Gregorian dates.

Our story begins on 8 April 975 C.E., which in the Hijri would be the 23rd day of the month of Rajab, 364 A.H.

The Great Mosque of Córdoba (La Mezquita)

The Great Mosque of Córdoba is considered by many to be the pinnacle of medieval Islamic architecture. Begun in 785 C.E. by the Umayyad Emir of Córdoba, Abd al-Rahman I, the mosque was built upon the ruins of a Visigothic Christian church. Each successive Umayyad ruler added to the edifice, including Abd al-Rahman II (833 C.E.), and Abd al-Rahman III (the self-anointed caliph, 945 C.E.). Caliph al-Hakam II, his son, increased the mosque's capacity by nearly one-third and added the glorious mihrab in 961 C.E. using gold and mosaics sent as a gift by the Byzantine emperor. Al-Mansur completed the final addition to the mosque in 987 C.E., 1,027 years ago.

The Great Mosque of Córdoba remained in use until the city fell to Fernando III of Castile in 1236 C.E. Various Christian rulers made modifications after that, the most significant of which was the construction of a Renaissance cathedral nave inside the middle of the mosque in 1523 C.E. The addition was made with the permission of Spanish King Charles V, but he was so displeased with the result that he famously complained, "They have taken something unique in all the world and destroyed it to build something you can find in any city." Ironically, to the present day, one can attend Mass in the Great Mosque of Córdoba. I, myself, have.

The Great Mosque of Córdoba is notable for the immense size of its arcaded hall and remains one of the largest mosques in the world. The double-arched design was a unique architectural innovation, permitting higher ceilings than would otherwise be possible with the relatively short columns used in its construction. The double arches consist of a characteristically Umayyad lower horseshoe arch and an upper semicircular arch. The iconic alternating red ochre and white striped color scheme of the arches (the colors of the caliph), atop the "forest" of columns, produce a remarkable visual effect, said then and now to be evocative of palm trees surrounding an oasis in the Syrian desert, the ancestral home of the Umayyads.

The Great Mosque of Córdoba is the kind of place that must be seen in person to be fully appreciated. It is quite unforgettable.

Photographs 1 and 2 were taken of the scaled model of the Great Mosque of Córdoba found in the Calahorra Tower across Puente Romano spanning the Guadalquivir River. This is how the edifice would have appeared after al-Mansur made his final addition in 987 C.E. The other photographs were made by the author in October of 2013.

Photograph 1. The Great Mosque as it would have appeared in 987 C.E. when it was completed. This is a photograph of a scaled model.

Photograph 2. Interior view of the Great Mosque as it would have appeared in the tenth century. This is a photograph of a scaled model.

Photograph 3. Minaret of the Great Mosque from within the Courtyard of the Oranges.

Photograph 4. One of the original entry doors of the Great Mosque.

Photograph 5. Interior view of the double-arched construction of the Great Mosque. The Great Mosque contained 1,200 columns when completed in 987 C.E (it has 856 today).

Photograph 6. The mihrab of the Great Mosque, constructed by Caliph al-Hakam II in 961 C.E. using fifteen tons of mosaics and gold sent as a gift by the Byzantine emperor.

Photograph 7. The gold and mosaic ceiling over the mihrab within the Great Mosque.

Photographs

Included below are photographs taken on my visit to Córdoba and Madinat al-Zahra in October of 2013.

Photograph 8. Aerial view of Madinat al-Zahra as it looks today. The excavated remains of the Alcazar, the Royal Palace, can be seen in the center. Most of Madinat al-Zahra remains unexcavated pastureland (courtesy of Conjunto Arqueológico Madinat al-Zahra).

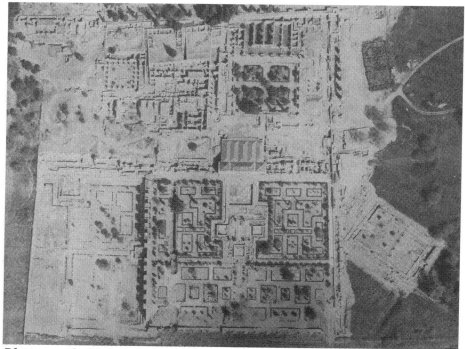

Photograph 9. Aerial view of the excavated portions of the Royal Palace within Madinat al-Zahra. The Hall of Abd al-Rahman III is in the center, the Upper Royal Gardens are in the foreground, the caliph's suites in the extreme upper left, and the Aljama Mosque to the lower right (courtesy of Conjunto Arqueológico Madinat al-Zahra).

Photograph 10. The view towards Córdoba looking east across the Upper Royal Gardens. The Hall of Abd al-Rahman III is at center left (courtesy of Conjunto Arqueológico Madinat al-Zahra).

523

Photograph 11. The Aquaduct of the Valdepuentes. This is the only surviving example of the vast infrastructure supplying water to Madinat al-Zahra (courtesy of Conjunto Arqueológico Madinat al-Zahra).

Photograph 12. View to the southeast across the Upper Royal Gardens and towards the Guadalquivir River. Visiting dignitaries would have approached Madinat al-Zahra from this direction along the Almunya Way.

Photograph 13. The inner defensive wall of the Royal Palace,
separating the Upper and Lower Royal Gardens.

Photograph 14. Courtyard of the Pillars within the Royal Palace, located just below the caliph's suites (courtesy of Conjunto Arqueológico Madinat al-Zahra).

Photograph 15. The Grand Portico, triumphal arches, marking the dividing line between the Royal Palace complex and the formal parade ground for reviewing the caliph's army. The caliph's viewing stand is believed to have been located above the central arch.

Photograph 16. Entrance arches and façade leading into the House of the Pool, one of the most luxurious villas found within Madinat al-Zahra (courtesy of Conjunto Arqueológico Madinat al-Zahra).

Photograph 17. Carved marble pilaster found on a door jamb leading into a villa within Madinat al-Zahra.

Photograph 18. Inside the Hall of Abd al-Rahman III. The caliph's throne would have been to the left in this view, with the building entrance from the Upper Royal Gardens to the right (courtesy of Conjunto Arqueológico Madinat al-Zahra).

Photograph 19. The author standing within the entrance arches of the Upper Basilical Building within the Royal Palace at Madinat al-Zahra.

Photograph 20. Façade with carved decoration in the caliph's residence within Madinat al-Zahra (courtesy of Conjunto Arqueológico Madinat al-Zahra).

Photograph 21. White marble flooring used extensively within Madinat al-Zahra.

Photograph 22. A water-fed latrine within the Royal Palace of Madinat al-Zahra.

Photograph 23. View of Córdoba looking north across the Puente Romano spanning the Guadalquivir River. The Great Mosque is just to the right of the bridge.

Photograph 24. A portion of the outer defensive walls of medieval Córdoba.

Photograph 25. View of the Great Mosque looking east from the top of the Alcazar within Córdoba.

Photograph 26. The Rif Mountains in northern Morocco (courtesy of Sabahat Adil).

Photograph 27. Panoramic view within the Rif Mountains in northern Morocco (courtesy of Sabahat Adil).

Photograph 28. View from the castle mount of the approach to Hajar an-Nasar, Eagle's Rock, within the Rif Mountains (courtesy of Professor Patrice Cressier).

Photograph 29. View of original location of Hajar an-Nasar on the edge of the cliffs overlooking the valley. The building shown is a contemporary mosque (courtesy of Professor Patrice Cressier).

Photograph 30. Some of the scarce remains of the fortress at Hajar an-Nasar (courtesy of Professor Patrice Cressier).

Photograph 31. Remains of the fortress at Gormaz in the Upper Marches.

Photograph 32. Examples of seventh-century Visigothic horseshoe arches that so inspired the architecture of the Umayyad caliphs (courtesy of Museo Arqueológico de Córdoba).

Photograph 33. The base of a column from the Hall of Abd al-Rahman III in Madinat al-Zahra. The carved inscription records the beginning of the building's construction in 953 C.E. (courtesy of Conjunto Arqueológico Madinat al-Zahra).

Photograph 34. Corinthian capital from a column in the Hall of Abd al-Rahman III in Madinat al-Zahra, with the typical Umayyad trephine-carved "wasp's nest" decoration (courtesy of Museo Arqueológico de Córdoba).

Photograph 35. Carved marble water basin from Madinat al-Zahra. Water was fed into such basins from gold nozzles cast in the shape of animals (courtesy of Museo Arqueológico de Córdoba).

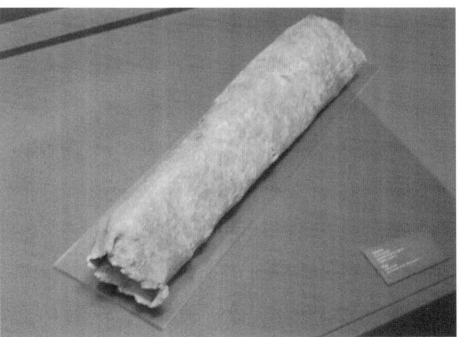

Photograph 36. Lead pipe from the vast water distribution infrastructure buried beneath Madinat al-Zahra (courtesy of Conjunto Arqueológico de Madinat al-Zahra).

Photograph 37. Carved marble tomb inscription from Madinat al-Zahra (courtesy of Museo Arqueológico de Córdoba).

Photograph 38. Tenth century tableware from Madinat al-Zahra. Various green, white, and black motifs were favored by the Umayyads (courtesy of Conjunto Arqueológico de Madinat al-Zahra).

Photograph 39. Carved crystal drinking goblet from tenth century Madinat al-Zahra (courtesy of Conjunto Arqueológico de Madinat al-Zahra).

Photograph 40. Carved ivory box (the size of a hand) belonging to Caliph al-Hakam II (courtesy of Conjunto Arqueológico de Madinat al-Zahra).

Photograph 41. Silver casket showing the intricate metal craftsmanship found in Madinat al-Zahra. The inscription indicates that this box was given as a gift by Caliph al-Hakam II to his son, Hisham, in 975 C.E. (courtesy of Conjunto Arqueológico de Madinat al-Zahra).

554

Photograph 42. Carved marble chess pieces from tenth century Madinat al-Zahra (courtesy of Museo Arqueológico de Córdoba).

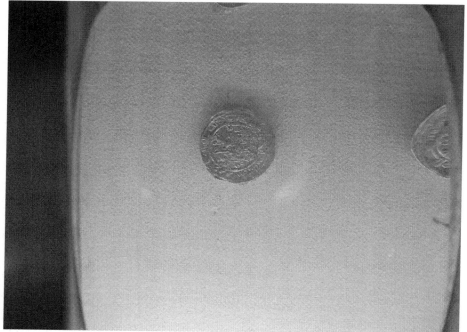

Photograph 43. A gold dinar minted in Madinat al-Zahra during the reign of Caliph al-Hakam II (courtesy of Museo Arqueológico de Córdoba).

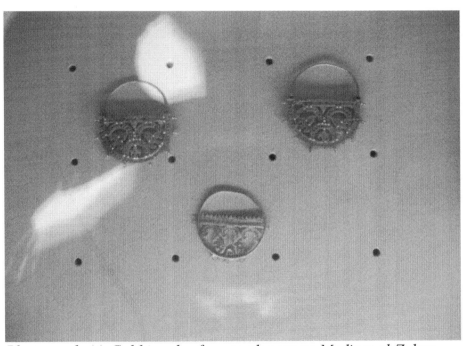

Photograph 44. Gold jewelry from tenth century Madinat al-Zahra (courtesy of Museo Arqueológico de Córdoba).

Photograph 45. A page from a medieval Quran (courtesy of the Rare Books Collection of the Emory University Library).

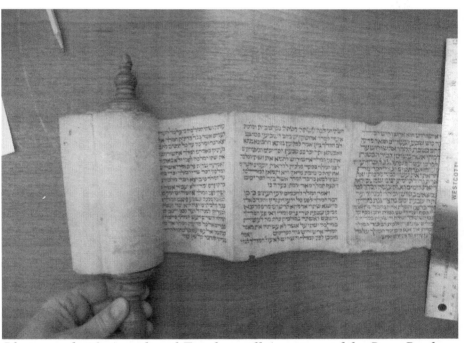

Photograph 46. A medieval Torah scroll (courtesy of the Rare Books Collection of the Emory University Library).

Photograph 47. A page from a medieval Christian Psalter (courtesy of the Rare Books Collection of the Emory University Library).

Photograph 48. The bindings of a medieval codex (courtesy of the Rare Books Collection of the Emory University Library).

Historical Primer

In the Islamic world, the death of the Prophet Muhammad in 632 C.E. without a chosen successor led to several decades of bloody internal power struggle, the remnants of which linger to this day in Shiite vs. Sunni tensions. By 661, however, the Sunni Arab Umayyad clan prevailed, and to solidify their power moved the Islamic capital from Medina (Saudi Arabia) to Damascus (Syria). A rapid swelling of Islamic culture, wealth, and power ensued, launching a conquest of conversion reaching from the western end of the Mediterranean basin to the Near East.

By 711, the Maghreb was breached (land including the rugged Atlas mountains of extreme northwest Africa and the coastal plains of modern Morocco, Algeria, Tunisia, and Libya). An Islamic army, led by an Arab Syrian general named Tariq ibn Ziyad and comprised of a freshly-converted, capable warrior clan of local Berber tribesmen, invaded Iberia at Gibraltar. They rapidly conquered the Iberian peninsula under the banner of jihad, effortlessly absorbing the nominally-Christian Visigoths and post-Roman-era towns and peoples. The incursion of the Muslims was largely welcomed—and in some cases even assisted by—the Iberian Jews, who had long been persecuted by the local Christians. Al-Andalus, the Arabic name for the lands of Iberia under Muslim rule, was born in 711. Al-Andalus would endure for 791 years.

Several pivotal events in the history of al-Andalus are important to *Shadows in the Shining City*. In 750 C.E., the Umayyads in Damascus were slaughtered by the rival Abbasids, and the sole surviving Umayyad heir, Abd al-Rahman, a boy in his late teens, set out on the 2,500-mile journey to al-Andalus to boldly reclaim his own slice of history in a forgotten corner of the Islamic empire, Córdoba, located on the banks of the Guadalquivir River in southern central Spain. The Umayyad regime reemerged like a phoenix from the ashes with the crowning of Abd al-Rahman Emir of Córdoba in 756. He set about unifying al-Andalus, and one of his first mandates, remarkably enough, was to welcome both Jews and Christians into his kingdom.

Al-Andalus blossomed under Umayyad rule. Abd al-Rahman's grandson (the III) declared himself the rival caliph (from the Arabic *khalifa*, "successor" [to the Prophet Muhammad]—supreme ruler of Islam) to the Abbasid caliph in January 929. Unified and under capable and enlightened Syrian-Arab leadership, al-Andalus rose to its full glory.

Córdoba became the crown jewel of Western Islam and a magnet of learning and intellectual fervor that rivaled Baghdad. Late tenth-century Córdoba was the largest city in Europe, with a population of over 300,000. The city was rich beyond belief, with a revenue estimated to be 40,000,000 gold dinars per annum. Public works abounded. The citizens enjoyed baths, sewers, hospitals, running water, indoor toilets, and lighted streets. Córdoba had the largest library in Europe, with over 400,000 volumes in the Royal Library alone. Convivencia reigned.

In 936, Caliph Abd al-Rahman III, following Islamic tradition, broke ground on Madinat al-Zahra, the Shining City, a massive royal palace complex located several miles to the west of Córdoba at the edge of the Sierra Morena mountains. His intent? To create the most lavish Islamic palace in the world, an edifice fitting for a caliph.

Legend has it that 10,000 workers labored four years to complete the first phase of construction. The massive, 112-hectare walled complex of Madinat al-Zahra was built on three enormous terraces cut from the side of the mountain. It contained ceremonial reception halls, mosques, administrative and government offices, the royal treasury, libraries, Islamic gardens, the royal mint, a zoo of exotic animals, artisans' workshops of all manners, a garrison for several thousand troops, parade grounds, orchards, lavish residences for the royal court, and of course, heated baths by the dozen. Madinat was a city of flowing water and elaborate fountains, supplied to the entire complex through aqueducts from the mountain streams of the Sierra Morena. No expense was spared to create the most ostentatious palace in the world.

Our story begins in Madinat al-Zahra on 8 April 975. This period, the late tenth century, is considered the economic, cultural, and intellectual zenith of the 791-year history of al-Andalus.

Primer on the Camera Obscura

A *camera obscura* (literally, "darkened chamber") consists of a closed box with a small hole (a "pinhole," hence, the name 'pinhole camera') on one side and a screen on the other (Figure 1). Light from the exterior surroundings passes through the pinhole into the body of the camera. An upside down image is reproduced on the screen, but, importantly, with color and perspective preserved. As the pinhole is made smaller in diameter, the projected image gets sharper, but also dimmer. A small lens can be used to enhance the tradeoff between sharpness and brightness of the image.

The first known discussion of the camera obscura traces to the Chinese philosopher Mozi (470-390 B.C.E.), who referred to the camera obscura as a "locked treasure room." Aristotle (384-322 B.C.E.) experimented with and wrote about the camera obscura.

The Arab Ibn al-Haytham (Alhazen, 965-1040 C.E.), however, can be considered the father of the camera obscura. He was born in Basra (Iraq) but lived and worked mostly in Cairo (Egypt). Ibn al-Haytham was the first to successfully project an entire image of an outdoor scene onto an indoor screen using a camera obscura, and explain the optical principles involved. His seven volume

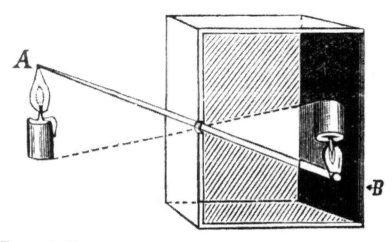

Figure 1. Illustration of the principles of a camera obscura.

Figure 2. A room-sized camera obscura used to capture an image of New York City (photograph by Abelardo Morell).

Kitab al-Mananzir—Book of Optics—is considered the foundation of modern optics.

The camera obscura played an important role in European art (e.g., Vermeer), and contemporary artists still employ its magic (e.g., Abelardo Morell – Figure 2).

Primer on the Ancient Greeks

The ancient Greeks celebrated reason and inquiry above all things. Their accomplishments had a profound influence on the development of philosophy, medicine, architecture, the arts, literature, mathematics, and the sciences; influences that persist to this day. A clear and unbroken chain can be traced from the ancient Greek and Hellenistic philosophers to medieval Muslim philosophers and scientists, to the spawning of the European Renaissance and the Enlightenment and the eventual rise to preeminence of science and technology that so pervades our modern world.

Medieval Córdoba figured prominently in that chain. Sadly, much of this remarkable knowledge generated by the ancient Greeks was lost with the collapse and decimation of the Roman Empire. The Umayyad caliphs of Córdoba methodically sought out, found, purchased, and then translated the myriad of lost treatises of the ancient Greeks, a true resurrection of knowledge and wisdom. Our world would be quite different today if that rediscovery had not occurred.

Aristotle:

Standing tall among the ancient Greeks was Plato's student, the polymath Aristotle (384-322 B.C.E.). Samuel's beloved Aristotle. He single-handedly made important contributions to a plethora of subjects, including: physics, metaphysics, poetry, theater, music, logic, rhetoric, linguistics, politics, government, ethics, biology, and zoology. He was the first to create a comprehensive system of Western philosophy, encompassing ethics, aesthetics, logic, science, politics, and metaphysics; and yes, he did experiment with the camera obscura. Fortunately, he was a prolific writer. A genius for the ages, he was greatly admired by medieval scholars, Muslim, Jew, and Christian alike.

Medicine:

Ancient Greek medicine was a vast compilation of theories that were constantly expanding through new ideologies and trials. A towering figure was the physician Hippocrates of Kos (460-370 B.C.E.), who is considered the "Father of Modern Medicine." The *Hippocratic Corpus* is a collection of about seventy early medical works from ancient Greece that are associated with Hippocrates and his students. The existence of the "Hippocratic Oath" implies that medicine was practiced by a group of professional physicians bound by a strict ethical code.

Literature:

The ancient Greeks placed great value on literature, beginning with Homer's epic poem the *Iliad*, Rayhana's great love. The playwright Aeschylus changed Western literature forever with his introduction of dialogue and interacting characters to his plays, essentially inventing the concept of literary "drama," of which *Shadows* is a descendent. Sophocles developed irony as a literary tool, while Euripides used in his plays to challenge societal mores. Aristophanes, Zafir's favorite, defined and shaped the concept of literary comedy.

In case it has been some time since you visited some of the classics of the ancient Greek literature found in *Shadows*, I have briefly summarized them here.

Homer's *Iliad* is an ancient Greek epic poem set during the Trojan War, the ten-year siege of the city of Troy (Ilium) by a coalition of Greek states. The *Iliad* recounts the events during the weeks of a quarrel between King Agamemnon and the warrior Achilles. The *Iliad* is among the oldest works of Western literature, the written version dating to the eighth century B.C.E.

Sophocles' *Antigone* is a classic Greek tragedy. Antigone, the daughter of the unwittingly incestuous marriage between King Oedipus of Thebes and his mother Jocasta, defies King Creon's edict and attempts to bury her brother Polyneices, who has been declared a traitor to Thebes. The play ends disastrously. Antigone hangs herself and Creon's son, Haimo, her betrothed, kills himself after finding her body.

Aristophanes' *The Wasps* is a classic Greek comedy set during a one-year truce in the Peloponnesian War between Athens and Sparta. Aristophanes' intent is to use satire to ridicule King Cleon of Athens and attack the Athenian law courts.

Euripides' *Trojan Women* is a Greek tragedy with a pointed message. Produced in 415 B.C.E. during the Peloponnesian War, it was intended as a scathing commentary on the Athenian capture of the island of Melos and the wholesale slaughter of its men, women, and children. Euripides's play follows the fates of four women of Troy after their city has been sacked, their husbands killed, and their families sold into slavery.

Fact and Fiction

My litmus test while writing historical fiction is always this: Given what we do know today from the historical record, is this person's actions, or that sequence of events, or this plot twist plausible? There are times, as a novelist, when I deliberately choose to bend history in service of the story. That said, I do believe strongly in full disclosure, and I attempt here to differentiate between what is historical and what is fictional in *Shadows in the Shining City*.

- My main deviation from history lies in the amount of time that elapses during the story. *Shadows* begins in April of 975 and ends in January of 977, a little less than two years. In actuality, al-Mansur's rise to power took almost ten years (971-981). I opted to compress my timeline to enhance the pacing and the dramatic weight of events, especially given the urgency of the parallel love story of Zafir and Rayhana. That said, the key events depicted in al-Mansur's rise and eventual triumph are historical.

- A number of characters in the book are historical, including: Caliph al-Hakam II, Hisham, Ibn Abi Amir, Subh, Jafar, General Ghalib, al-Andalusi, White Hands, Jawdhar, Faiq, Abu al-Qasim, and Reccimund. Some we know quite a bit about, others, only snippets.

- Rayhana is fictional, but interestingly enough, we do know that Ibn Abi Amir had a daughter. That we know this is unusual, in that females generally were not a part of the recorded history of al-Andalus. We do not know her name, but she is recorded as having knitted her father a prayer shawl for his first jihad, as depicted.

- If you are skeptical about the possibility of midnight trysts in the gardens of the caliph, I would suggest that you read some of the love poetry from al-Andalus (Muslim and Jewish). Much of it is charged with eroticism and a palpable sense of longing and desire; always entertaining and often very beautiful.

- Zafir is fictional, though the prominent role of saqaliba (slaves) in Córdoba is historical. Saqaliba had roots originating in Eastern Europe. The mountains of Caratania, Zafir's homeland and the source of a large number of Córdoba's saqaliba, are historical. Saqaliba were primarily of Slavic origin and were enslaved by the armies of the Holy Roman Empire during their suppression of rebellions and territorial conquests, who then sold them to Jewish traders who transported them to al-Andalus (and other locales). The purchase of saqaliba in Córdoba was a very common practice in all facets and ranks of society, particularly within the military. While slavery is never defensible, it should be noted that, by tradition, slaves in al-Andalus were generally freed after a defined period of service and could then become citizens of the realm, at liberty to rise in society according to their abilities. General Ghalib is a famous historical example.

- Tenth century Madinat al-Zahra was teeming with saqaliba, including the caliph's own Slavic Guard, as depicted. As can be imagined, the tensions between the elite of Córdoban society with Arab ancestry (very much a minority) and freed saqaliba was real, as portrayed. Ibn Abi Amir's prejudice against them would certainly have been plausible.

- It is well known that the Umayyad princes fancied blond women, and many a blue-eyed, golden-haired princess was brought from northern Iberia to Córdoba to join the royal harem. They often began their stays as concubines, later transitioning to wives of the ruling elite. Subh is a prominent historical example. She was famous for her beauty (and cunning). Even with their dark-featured Syrian Arab lineage, the Umayyad line slowly but surely became fair-skinned, fair-haired, and blue-eyed. Ironic, given their pride in their Arab roots.

- It is well accepted that Ibn Abi Amir and Subh were lovers, as depicted, and that she had great influence at court, even though she led her life sequestered in the royal harem. He managed her accounts and had access to Hisham. Whether she actually fell in love with Ibn Abi Amir is unknown, but to my mind this is clearly plausible, perhaps even likely. She was too cunning a woman to be duped the way she was. Something had to have clouded her judgment. Her voracious sexual appetite is my invention, but this seemed to fit her personality and the circumstances.

- It is well accepted that Caliph al-Hakam II was gay, or at the very least bisexual. He is known to have kept a male harem. By any reckoning he was a brilliant man, intensely driven by his love of books and knowledge. Al-Hakam was a great patron of the arts and literature, and was loved for this by the people of Córdoba. He was insistent on inclusiveness, tolerance, and convivencia as the correct model for a prosperous society. It was a remarkably enlightened view for the medieval period. Córdoba thrived wildly under his leadership.

- Not surprisingly, Caliph al-Hakam II was not always on the best of terms with the religious elite of Córdoba. On more than one occasion during the final construction phase of Madinat al-Zahra, he missed Friday worship services and was publicly chastised by the grand imam. The grand imam also took offense to his lavish use of gold on the roof of the Hall of Abd al-Rahman III. His additions to the Great Mosque, especially the mihrab, are considered the artistic pinnacle of the edifice.

- It remains unclear exactly why Caliph al-Hakam II neglected to see that his son, Hisham, was properly trained to rule as his successor. As described, the opportunistic Ibn Abi Amir made good use of that oversight.

- We do not know what actually killed Caliph al-Hakam II. He suddenly fell ill and died. I have portrayed that as a deliberate act of poisoning, which to my mind is certainly plausible—and definitely dramatic! But we do not know. If he did die of natural causes, his timing was impeccable and fit perfectly into Ibn Abi Amir's plans.

- The introduction of Berber cavalry changed the balance of power in al-Andalus dramatically. The Berbers were known and feared throughout Europe as highly capable and ruthless warriors, expert horsemen, and especially skilled with bow and arrow. As testament to this fact, it is worth noting that al-Mansur and his Berber army were triumphant in every single battle they fought against Christian armies (57 all told!).

- The foods I had served in both Madinat al-Zahra and the Maghreb are historical. The Córdobans, in particular, ate very well—far better than the rest of Europe.

- Hajar an-Nasar is historical. Interestingly enough, its location was lost to history until very recently, when Professor Patrice Cressier led an expedition to rediscover the ruins about 40 km east of Larache, Morocco, in the Rif Mountains. My use of the maze of canyons in the approach to the fortress is fictional.

- I have tried throughout the book to be respectful of all three of the religious traditions represented. Several things are worth noting. The Christian Mass was different during the medieval period than it is today, and Christians within al-Andalus felt empowered to make their own modifications to the liturgy, as required, especially with respect to language. Arabic Bibles were in fact used in Córdoba. Both changes were resented by the Papacy. In the case of Islam, there were differences between modern Muslim practices and those of medieval al-Andalus. For example, the wearing of turbans by men and hijab by women was not ubiquitous in tenth-century Córdoba. Alcohol, primarily in the form of wine, was widely available (and consumed), even though expressly forbidden by the Quran. Finally, there is ample evidence of educated and influential Muslim women with exceptional social mobility and freedoms in medieval Córdoba. The Jews played an important role in Córdoban society, and they were free to hold political and civic office. They originally welcomed the Muslims as liberators and even assisted them at times during the original conquest of Iberia in the eighth century.

- Some may be skeptical that a festival like Eid al-Fitr could take place as represented in *Shadows*. However, Eid celebrations, even today, differ widely around the world and tend to be culturally specific. Córdoba held the unrivaled seat of power in western Islam and was always ready and willing to trumpet this unique position with a clear preference for the flamboyant. To my mind, it is plausible to have expected the caliph to put on a show for Eid as I have depicted.

- I have seen no direct evidence suggesting that the caliph's Rare Books Library was located in Madinat al-Zahra. That said, we do know there were seven major buildings housing the Royal Library in Córdoba, and that it contained at least 400,000 volumes—probably more. Given his great love of books, it seems quite plausible to me that the caliph would have wanted his most prized books close to him, within his palace, not miles away. Thus, my Rare Books Library was born. My hope is that one day new excavations of Madinat al–Zahra will provide evidence of this assertion. The rest of the structures and locations within Madinat and Córdoba in *Shadows* are accurately depicted.

- Samuel is fictional, but it should be appreciated that Jews were held in high esteem at court during this period, particularly in the professions of medicine and the cultural arts. It certainly is plausible that a Jewish royal librarian oversaw the caliph's holdings.

- Most Córdobans would have been trilingual, speaking Arabic, Hebrew, and Latinia, a hybrid of Latin and early Castilian (Spanish). The well educated might also have known Latin, Persian, Greek, and various Arabic dialects.

- Abu al-Qasim is historical and was highly influential in the development of medicine in the west. The various aspects of Andalusi medicine discussed in the book are historically accurate, including Abu al-Qasim's fascination with creating new surgical instruments (you can see examples in the museum inside the Calahorra Tower in Córdoba), his use of catgut sutures, and his honing of surgical technique using cadavers. He was celebrated as an extraordinary teacher.

- The battle scenes in *Shadows* are accurately represented. Corsairs (Barbary pirates) indeed terrorized the Mediterranean, both Christian and Muslim commerce alike. The battle of Gormaz did occur, though my use of Caesar's famous double-ring siege at Alesia is fictional. It is, however, certainly plausible that Caesar's *Gallic Wars* would have been known. The setting for the ambush of White Hands in the mountains is fictional.

- Ibn Abi Amir, al-Mansur (Almanzor to the west), remains to this day a controversial figure in the history of al-Andalus. He was by all accounts deeply religious, though how he came to that is opaque. Córdoba continued to prosper under his reign, but his willful destruction of the Umayyad dynasty using the Berbers as a lever also set the stage for the eventual collapse of Muslim Spain. There are two tidbits worth knowing about him that are not mentioned in the book: 1) One of his son's by his first marriage (Rayya in the book) eventually joins a coup attempt against him, and when the plot is discovered, the son is promptly executed. 2) In the end, after Ghalib is defeated in

981, al-Mansur has al-Andalusi (and another of his trusted Berber generals) murdered in order to assume absolute power over Córdoba's army.

- Tragically, al-Mansur's burning of books is historical. It seems that he had a particular dislike for anything related to astrology, astronomy, and science in general, and of course any literature he deemed blasphemous or religiously suspect.

- Peter Strobel and Brother Cleo are fictional, but a formal visit of the Holy Roman Empire's ambassador (John of Gorze) did occur about this time, very much along the lines depicted in the book. Remarkably, it took him three years to secure an audience with the caliph. The man was absolutely awed by what he saw and experienced, and he did in fact kneel before a saqaliba, thinking he was the caliph. Reccimund did lead a delegation to Saxony for cultural exchange with the court of Otto I, as depicted.

- The use of the dramatic mercury reflecting pool in the Hall of Abd al-Rahman III is historical.

- Sad to say, the caliph's brother, al-Mughira, was in fact strangled in front of his family during the coup attempt. I should note, however, that I have distorted some of the events surrounding the coup. The saqalibas Jawdhar and Faiq were the original instigators of the coup, with Jafar's reluctant blessing, not vice versa. In actuality, Jafar, in this lessor role, though still treasonous, made the fatal mistake of leaking to Ibn Abi Amir what was about to happen. This precipitated the events of that fateful day. The Berber assault of Madinat during the death fog is exaggerated, though the executions of the commanders of the Slavic Guard is historical, as was the forced swearing of allegiance to Caliph Hisham.

- My stories are told from the vantage point of the elite of Andalusian society (the Arab Nasrids in *Emeralds* and the Arab Umayyads in *Shadows*), which clearly looked down upon the Berbers of the Maghreb as lacking in cultural and political sophistication. The Berbers were certainly much more religiously dogmatic and inflexible, and particularly resentful of perceived Andalusi excesses (the arts, alcohol, etc.) and their tolerant attitudes towards both Christians and Jews. These significant tensions between the Berbers and the Andalusi will worsen over the next 500 years with the coming of the Berber

Almoravids and then the Berber Almohads. It goes without saying that a Berber would have told this story differently.

- We have no record of a camera obscura in al-Andalus until the early eleventh century. Nevertheless, we do know that Aristotle experimented with them and did write about them. Aristotle's lost notebook is fictional, though surely plausible. Ibn al-Haytham's (965-1040 C.E.) seven volume *Kitab al-Mananzir* (*Book of Optics*) contains descriptions of early photographic techniques using bitumen and lavender oil for capturing images generated by camera obscuras. This predates the rise of the photography in Europe by 700 years.

- Sophisticated poisons of many types played an important role in the medieval world. While Farfa Abbey is historical (about 25 miles northeast of Rome), the story of the monk's use of a "potion" to outwit Vandal invaders is fictional, though certainly plausible.

Bibliography

I continue to collect and devour a variety of books on al-Andalus. Included below is a selected list of references that I found helpful while writing *Shadows in the Shining City*. The detailed history of this period found in Hugh Kennedy's *Muslim Spain and Portugal* was particularly useful. Additional references on al-Andalus can be found in *Emeralds of the Alhambra*.

[1] T. Burckhardt, *Moorish Culture in Spain*: McGraw-Hill, New York, 1972.

[2] R. Castejon, *Medina Azahara*: Editorial Everest, Madrid, 1985.

[3] A. Christys, *Christians in al-Andalus - 711-1000*: Routledge, New York, 2002.

[4] O.R. Constable (Editor), *Medieval Iberia - Readings from Christian, Muslim, and Jewish Sources*: University of Pennsylvania Press, Philadelphia, 1997.

[5] R. Fletcher, *Moorish Spain*: University of California Press, Berkeley, 1992.

[6] C. Franzen, *Poems of Arab Andalusia*: City Light Books, San Francisco, 1989.

[7] R. Hitchcock, *Mozarabs in Medieval and Early Modern Spain*: Ashgate, Burlington, 2008.

[8] S.K. Jayyusi, *The Legacy of Muslim Spain, Volume 1*: Brill, Leiden, 1992.

[9] S.K. Jayyusi, *The Legacy of Muslim Spain, Volume 2*: Brill, Leiden, 1993.

[10] H. Kennedy, *Muslim Spain and Portugal - A Political History of al-Andalus*: Addison Wesley Longman, Essex, 1996.

[11] R.M. Leopold, *Al-Zahara – Into the Wings of Time*: W.E.S.T. Works, Córdoba, 1997.

[12] C. Lowney, *A Vanished World - Muslims, Christians, and Jews in Medieval Spain*: Oxford University Press, New York, 2006.

[13] M.R. Menocal, *The Ornament of the World - How Muslims, Jews, and Christians Created a Culture of Tolerance in Medieval Spain*: Back Bay Books, New York, 2002.

[14] Museum with No Frontiers, *The Umayyads – the Rise of Islamic Art*: Ministry of Tourism, Amman, Jordan, 2000.

[15] D. Nicolle, *The Moors - the Islamic West, 7th - 15th Centuries AD*: Osprey Publishing, Oxford, 2001.

[16] J. Augustín Núñez (Editor), *Córdoba in Focus*: Edilux S.L., Madrid, 2001. (Translated by J. Trout.)

[17] J. Schacht and C.E. Bosworth (Editors), *The Legacy of Islam* (2nd Edition): Oxford University Press, London, 1974.

[18] A.V. Triano, *Madinat al-Zahra - Official Guide to the Archeological Complex*: Junta de Andalucía, Córdoba, 2001. (Translated by P. Turner.)

Acknowledgment

My heartfelt thanks to Lawrence Knorr of Sunbury Press for opening the door for my fiction. What a wonderful ride it has been! I am grateful for: Jennifer Melendrez, my incredibly word-savvy editor, for helping to improve *Shadows;* Tammi Knorr, for her assistance with all things related to marketing and sales; and Alison Law, my publicist.

Professor Patrice Cressier, the intrepid rediscoverer of Hajar an-Nasar, whose English is as bad as my French (thank goodness for Google Translate!), converted his original glass slides to a digital format for inclusion in the book. Sabahat Adil was kind enough to take photos of the Rif Mountains for me while she was in Morocco in 2013.

Just for kicks, I included in *Shadows* three snippets from my favorite poet, the Jesuit Gerard Manley Hopkins. I also created a new word or two (on my to-do list for some time now!). I will leave it to the reader to locate them.

I am grateful to Cola Franzen and City Light Books for the use of Ibn Hazm's eleventh century Córdoban poem, "My Beloved Comes."

I would like to express my gratitude to the late Professor Maria Rosa Menocal of Yale. Her terrific book, *Ornament of the World* (the title refers to Sister Hroswitha's description of tenth century Córdoba), was the first book I read on al-Andalus. While we never met, when I was working on *Emeralds* I contacted her and received enthusiastic support for breaking open her beloved al-Andalus using fiction. I told her about the setting for *Emeralds* during the Castilian Civil War. She thought that was a great idea and then went on to tell me to make sure that I also wrote about the rise to power of al-Mansur in tenth century Córdoba. I assured her I would tackle that topic in book two.

I am indebted, as always, to the early readers of *Shadows*, my faithful and steadfast test audience who waited so patiently for me to finish: Preston Bennett, Denise Black, John Boyle, Trish Byers, Maria Cressler, Dennis Day, Tom Jablonski, Bruce Maivelett, Roger Meyer, Tom Nadar, Barbara Nalbone, Patty Smith, Bud Treanor, and Bob Wilhelm. Bravo! Trish Byers was the first to finish the draft of "the beast," and Roger Meyer found the most typos (I would blush if I told you how many!). Patty Smith was a close second on typos. Of this list of early readers, several folks deserve special mention because their feedback prompted me to make some important changes to the manuscript.

Roger Meyer read the draft twice! He offered a (large!) number of thoughtful wording changes, and suggested some modifications to Samuel's final confrontation with Ibn Abi Amir, the pivotal Durr-Aslam-Rayhana-Zafir scene, and the "beefing up" of Peter Strobel's character. Roger also re-read and critiqued my revisions. Above and beyond the call of duty, sir!

Tom Jablonski, in his usual careful way with my stories, identified several logical inconsistencies that needed attention.

Tom Nadar did a thorough job of helping me eliminate verbal anachronisms and other word-quirks. ("This word was first used in 1921, John!")

Barbara Nalbone offered some excellent insights into my characters (and some challenges!), and a number of thoughtful semantic suggestions.

And, of course, my Maria, the owner of Rayhana's amazing amber starbursts. She is the inspiration and guiding light behind every worthwhile thing I have ever done in my life. Maria made me promise after *Emeralds* was published that I would create two lovers our own age so they could remind the world how wonderful love can be as it blossoms over a lifetime shared. Thirty-one years of joy, darling! Just keeps getting better and better. I offer Samuel and Rebekah for your enjoyment, my love.

About the Author

John D. Cressler is Schlumberger Chair Professor of Electronics in the School of Electrical and Computer Engineering at Georgia Tech, Atlanta, Georgia, USA. He received his Ph.D. from Columbia University, New York, in 1990. His academic research interests center on the creative use of nanoscale-engineering techniques to enable new approaches to electronic devices, circuits and systems.

Dr. Cressler and his students have published over 600 scientific papers in this field and he has received a number of awards for both his teaching and his research, including the 2010 Class of 1940 W. Howard Ector Outstanding Teacher Award (Georgia Tech's top teaching honor) and the 2013 Class of 1934 Distinguished Professor Award (the highest honor that can be bestowed on a faculty member at Georgia Tech).

His previous books include: *Silicon-Germanium Heterojunction Bipolar Transistors* (2003), *Reinventing Teenagers: the Gentle Art of Instilling Character in Our Young People* (2004), *Silicon Heterostructure Handbook: Materials, Fabrication, Devices, Circuits and Applications of SiGe and Si Strained Layer Epitaxy* (2006), *Silicon Earth: Introduction to the Microelectronics and Nanotechnology Revolution* (2009), *Extreme Environment Electronics* (2012), and *Emeralds of the Alhambra* (2013), his debut historical novel. *Shadows in the Shining City* is the second release in the *Anthems of al-Andalus Series*.

He and his wife, Maria, have been married for 31 years and are the proud parents of three: Matthew (and now Mary Ellen), Christina (and now Michael), and Joanna. They are the doting grandparents of two little angels: Elena Giess Cressler and Owen Michael Gawrys.

His hobbies include hiking, gardening, all things Italian, bonsai, collecting (and drinking!) fine wines, reading, cooking, history, food as art, and carving walking sticks—not necessarily in that order. He strives for an intentional life filled with social justice ministry, interfaith dialogue, and Ignatian silent retreats. He considers the teaching and mentoring of young people to be his primary vocation, with his writing a close second.

Dr. Cressler can be reached at:

School of Electrical and Computer Engineering
777 Atlantic Drive, N.W.
Georgia Tech, Atlanta, GA 30332-0250 USA

E-mail: cressler@ece.gatech.edu
Website (books): http://johndcressler.com
Website (research/teaching):
http://users.ece.gatech.edu/~cressler

Discussion Questions for Book Groups

- Were you aware of the many marvels of tenth century Córdoba, the Royal Library, Madinat al-Zahra, and the role al-Andalus played in the discovery and translation of the lost knowledge of the ancient Greeks?

- Books play a central role in *Shadows*. In our world of ubiquitous *e*Gadgets, how do you feel about "real" (printed) books vs. electronic books? Which do you prefer? Is there a difference between the two formats? If so, what?

- Are books alive? In what sense?

- Did you enjoy the use of elements of magical realism in *Shadows*?

- Were you aware that Christians and Jews lived peacefully in tenth century Muslim Córdoba and enjoyed unprecedented social mobility during this period? What made it work so well?

- How does the fact of *convivencia* (coexistence among religions) in medieval Spain make you feel regarding the tensions between Muslims, Christians, and Jews that are so prevalent in the twenty-first century?

- Is it possible, even in principle, to resurrect convivencia in our modern world? If so, how? If not, why not?

- For Christian readers, what did you learn about Islam and Judaism that you did not know before? What was surprising to you? How do you feel about the use of Arabic Bibles in Christian liturgy?

- For Muslim readers, what differences between medieval Islam and modern Islam struck you as interesting? Were you aware that significant tensions between moderate Islam and fundamentalist Islam (Umayyads vs. Berbers) existed in medieval Spain? What does it say about the origins of these tensions that they still exist today (e.g., Sunni vs. Shiite)?

- For Jewish readers, were you aware that this period of history, when Jews lived under Muslim rule, is considered the Golden Age of Judaism? How does that make you feel? How has Judaism changed since the tenth century?

- For those readers *not* of these three faith traditions, how do you feel about the role religion played in shaping the development of modern Europe?

- How does it make you feel knowing that a substantial fraction of our understanding of science, technology, philosophy, agriculture, and medicine flowed into Europe through the largely forgotten gateway of Muslim al-Andalus? One could fairly argue that this rediscovered and translated knowledge served as the bedrock for the European Renaissance and ultimately the European Enlightenment, which birthed modern science and with it technology and much that we take for granted in our modern world. Is this information new to you? Does it matter? Why don't more people know about it?

- Did you know what a camera obscura was before reading *Shadows*? How does it make you feel knowing that an Arab (Ibn al-Haytham) was the father of this highly influential device? To what extent is the use of such devices permissible in the production of art (both photographic and via painting)? It is understood today that Vermeer, among others, relied heavily on the camera obscura in creating his remarkable paintings. Does this lessen his genius?

- How do you feel about the role of saqaliba (Slavic slaves) in Córdoban society? Were you aware that this practice existed in medieval Spain? Were you aware that medieval slaves were typically of eastern European descent? Compare and contrast slavery in medieval Spain with slavery in America and other parts of the world.

- What do you think of the Muslim concept of al-Jannah, the walled, private garden, as a mirror of paradise? What do you think of the role water plays in Islamic architecture? What debt does modern Western art and architecture owe to medieval Muslim Spain?

- The Umayyads ruled essentially as benign dictators. What were the negative aspects of this system of rule? Positive aspects? What were the caliph's motives for treating his citizens (and people of other faith traditions) humanely?

- Four distinct love relationships are explored in *Shadows*. Which was your favorite and why? Do all contain equally valid expressions of love? Why do some of the relationships survive and others not? What role does sexuality play in each?

Author's Note:

Ten percent of the author's proceeds generated by sales of this book will be donated to organizations committed to opening dialogue and fostering mutual understanding, respect, and tolerance among Christians, Muslims, and Jews.

Made in the USA
Charleston, SC
16 July 2014